For more information about A.E. Rayne
and her upcoming books visit:

www.aerayne.com

f /aerayne

THE FURYCK SAGA

WINTER'S FURY
(Audiobook Available)

THE BURNING SEA
(Audiobook on pre-order)

NIGHT OF THE SHADOW MOON

HALLOW WOOD

THE RAVEN'S WARNING

VALE OF THE GODS

KINGS OF FATE
A Prequel Novella

THE LORDS OF ALEKKA

EYE OF THE WOLF

MARK OF THE HUNTER

BLOOD OF THE RAVEN

Sign up to my newsletter, so you don't miss out
on new release information!

http://www.aerayne.com/sign-up

THE RAVEN'S WARNING

THE FURYCK SAGA: BOOK 5

A.E. RAYNE

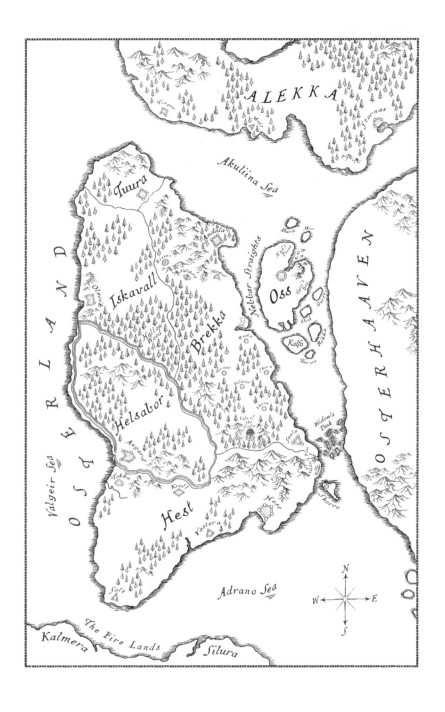

For Cap & Hank

CHARACTERS

In Harstad
Jael Furyck, Queen of Oss
Aleksander Lehr
Thorgils Svanter
Astrid Ranveg
Hedrun Holger, Lord of Harstad

In Andala
Axl Furyck, King of Brekka
Gisila Furyck
Gant Olborn
Edela Saeveld
Eydis Skalleson
Brynna 'Biddy' Halvor
Runa Gallas
Bram Svanter
Amma Furyck
Entorp Bray
Fyn Gallas
Rork Arnesson
Ulf Rutgar
Bayla Dragos
Karsten Dragos
Nicolene Dragos
Berard Dragos
Hanna Boelens
Marcus Volsen
Derwa Fylan
Alaric Fraed
Kormac Byrn

CHARACTERS

Branwyn Byrn
Aedan Byrn
Kayla Byrn
Aron Byrn
Beorn Rignor

In the Kingdom of Hest
Jaeger Dragos, King of Hest
Eadmund Skalleson, King of Oss
Draguta Teros
Morana Gallas
Meena Gallas
Morac Gallas
Evaine Gallas
Else Edelborg
Dragmall Birger
Rollo Barda
Brill Oggun

In the Kingdom of Iskavall
Raymon Vandaal, King of Iskavall
Getta Vandaal, Queen of Iskavall
Ravenna Vandaal
Garren Maas
Aldo Maas

In Rissna
Reinhard Belleg, Lord of Rissna

In the Kingdom of Helsabor
Briggit Halvardar

THE STORY SO FAR

Jael escaped the burning wreckage of Tuura, having kicked
Gerod Gott into a fiery grave, and sailed back to Andala where
she quickly prepared to leave for Oss. Oss, which was under
attack by Borg Arnesson and his brothers who had joined forces
with Ivaar to steal the Island throne.

That is, until Ivaar switched sides, and decided to follow Jael.

Having saved Eadmund, and killed Borg and his brothers,
Jael then convinced his cousins, Erl and Rork Arnesson, to bring
their Alekkans to Andala where she was planning to build a
great army to attack Hest and destroy the Book of Darkness.
Eadmund, concussed, confused, and still spellbound to Evaine,
was reluctant to go anywhere with his wife, but, eventually,
seeing the wisdom in what she was trying to do, he decided to
come along.

Meanwhile, in Hest, the newly-brought-back-to-life
Draguta Teros was not what anyone had imagined. She didn't
want the Darkness at all and had no plans to return Raemus
from the Dolma. In fact, she ripped out the very page that
described the ritual to bring him back. Draguta wanted to rule
as the Queen of Osterland. To be more powerful than the gods
themselves. And, after quickly turning The Following to ash,
she started searching for her sister, Dara, eager to exact her
long-sought-after revenge.

No one was happy about that, especially not Jaeger and

Morana, who were desperate to reclaim the Book of Darkness for themselves. They each set about figuring out how to do just that, with Meena's very reluctant help.

An urgent warning in a dream from Morana had Evaine and Morac escaping Oss' besieged fort, sailing to Hest where Evaine was forced to wait to be reunited with Eadmund and their son. She was impatient and obsessive and oblivious to Jaeger's interest in her until it was too late and he had her trapped, raping her.

The rest of Jaeger's family had escaped Hest in a ship with Hanna, who had tried to steal the Book of Darkness with Berard's help, only to have Jaeger cut off Berard's arm and kill his father. But while at sea they were attacked by Draguta's serpent, their ship was sunk, and Haegen was killed.

After finding their way to Andala with their helmsman Ulf's help, they had the misfortune of having a dragon land on their cottage, killing Haegen's wife, Irenna.

Andala's fort was damaged, the dragon lying across the western wall, leaving them vulnerable, desperate for Jael and Aleksander to return from their journey to Hallow Wood, where they had gone to find the Widow. They had discovered her cottage on fire, but there was no sign of her anywhere. She had left them a note, though, which led them to the Book of Aurea, within which she had hidden a letter to Jael explaining how she wrote both the Book of Aurea and the prophecy. And that her sister, Draguta, was the real Widow, responsible for all those evil acts.

Eager to return to Andala with haste, Jael and Aleksander were attacked by the dragur: dead warriors that Draguta had raised from their leafy graves to kill them and steal the Book of Aurea. But as they were escaping their powerful, blue clutches, Jael heard Ayla's warning that Thorgils was in trouble. Thorgils, who had left Andala on Gant's horse, Gus, chasing after Eadmund who was being called to Hest by Morana. Thorgils, who had crept into Hallow Wood to confront Eadmund, only to be stabbed by his friend and left for dead.

Having tried to direct Jael to Thorgils, Ayla then collapsed, carried into the ship sheds to join Hanna – who had taken ill just before the dragon attack – and many more as the sickness took a firm hold of Andala.

And after being thwarted in her attempts to find her sister, retrieve the Book of Aurea, and kill Jael Furyck, Draguta turned her wrath on Meena, Morac, Evaine, Morana and Jaeger in one big confrontation in the hall. She tried to threaten them into drinking a potion that meant certain death for those who were disloyal to her.

Jaeger had had enough of Draguta and drew his sword, only to be flung into the air and rendered helpless. Sensing that Meena was hiding a powerful knife, Morana demanded she give it to her so she could stop Draguta from killing them all. Meena wasn't sure she should give Morana anything, but knowing it was the knife that killed Draguta in the first place, she realised it was their only hope.

Morana was quickly attacked by Draguta, though, the knife flying away, only to be scooped up by Meena again, who gave it to Jaeger. He threw it at Draguta's head, and Meena finished her off, making sure that she was dead.

But not for long.

Draguta disappeared without a trace, leaving Morana bedridden, unable to speak and Jaeger panicking, anxious for her to return and save him from whatever Draguta planned to do next.

Meanwhile, Jael and Aleksander were struggling towards the nearest town on two horses with an injured Thorgils; Eadmund was riding as hard as he could to be reunited with Evaine, and everyone in Andala was desperately trying to remove the dragon so they could rebuild the wall and make themselves safe again.

Because Edela had seen that the dragur would come.

And soon...

PROLOGUE

'A boy?'

'Yes.'

The woman looked pleased. Pleased but troubled.

'And what will he need to do? What will you require of him?'

The man inhaled sharply, trying to keep his craggy face clear of any emotion. His white eyebrows were up; owl-like. 'I will require nothing of him, lady. It is not I who will ask this of him. It will be his wife. She will come for the shield when it is time.'

'His *wife*?'

'Here, let me show you.' And the man took Eskild's arm, leading her towards the back of the crypt.

Towards the round shield hanging on the stone wall.

'This was made for him. Commissioned by the gods themselves. Stored here, in Esk's house. Waiting for his son. And one day soon, you will become his mother.'

Eskild shivered. The air in the dark crypt was frigid. Or perhaps it was the unsettling words of Conall, the old volka, who had brought her to this sacred place? A wise man she had known since she was a girl. Her father's friend. She had no reason to doubt him. 'But my husband? What shall I tell him?'

'Nothing. You must never reveal this secret, Eskild. They are everywhere. Those who mean us harm. Those who seek the shield. Everywhere.' Conall glanced back at the entrance to the hidden catacombs they'd walked through. The location of the shield had been a closely guarded secret for centuries, passed down from one volka to the next.

He had never revealed its presence to another soul.

Until now.

Pausing in front of the wall, he stopped and stared. The shield was larger than any he'd seen, made with dark wooden slats and edged with a thick iron rim. A silver symbol encircled the shining boss that rose from its centre, with smaller symbols engraved around the rim.

It was breathtaking, and Eskild barely blinked as she wrapped her cloak around her chest, feeling the chill of the crypt seep into her bones. 'But why his wife? Why not my son?' She finally drew her eyes away from the shield and back to Conall. 'If he is to be Esk's son, as you say, why will he not come for it himself?'

Conall coughed, his rheumy eyes sweeping the dirt floor. 'Your son...' he began, then looking up, he smiled kindly. 'The shield is his, made for him, but not until he is ready. Remember what I said now, as there is little time for anything else. Not when your new husband is waiting to whisk you away to Oss.' He patted her arm, stepping away from the shield.

Eskild's soft hazel eyes opened wide as she reached up a hand. 'It's like new,' she breathed, touching the strange symbols. 'It gleams as if it were made today.'

Conall nodded. 'It has never changed in all the years I have cared for it. This shield is powerful. Magical. And our secret alone.'

Eskild turned to him with a frown. 'But how will I know when it is time? Time to give it to this woman?'

'Do not worry, Eskild. When it is time, she will come for you.'

PART ONE

Lost and Found

CHAPTER ONE

'You can't go after him.'

Jael didn't look around, though she knew that Aleksander was right.

He patted her shoulder. 'It will be dark soon. Let's go to the hall, find something to eat. Astrid is with Thorgils. We can stay away a while longer.'

Harstad was a big enough village with a big enough hall that served good enough food, but it wasn't Andala. And they needed to be in Andala. And though they needed to be in Andala, Jael very much wanted to be in Hest.

Because Hest was where Eadmund had gone.

They'd all guessed as much after what he'd done to Thorgils; leaving him for dead in Hallow Wood as he had.

The sky was turning deepening shades of blue, and Jael sighed in resignation, turning to Aleksander. 'Alright, though I'm not really hungry.'

'You have to eat.' He frowned at her. She had barely eaten since they'd arrived.

'Are you Biddy now?' Jael grumbled, turning back for one last glance over the wall. Harstad was ringed by a new wooden fence; tall, with ramparts circling the top and a small tower on either side of its new gates. The ramparts gave a fair view of the pastureland to the north and the Brekkan coast to the east; a clear view of the muddy road that would take them to Hest.

If only they could go that way.

Jael blinked, ready to fall down. Her body hadn't stopped throbbing since the battle with the dragur. Being hit with their filthy blue fists had felt like getting whacked by a sock full of rocks, which she knew to be true, having been whacked by a sock full of rocks once before.

By Gant.

Shaking her head at the memory, Jael followed Aleksander to the stairs, trying to resist placing her hand on her belly.

It was aching again.

'Astrid thinks Thorgils will be well enough to ride in a day or two,' Aleksander said, navigating the wobbling stairs down into the tower room.

'I'm not sure Gus can say the same,' Jael grinned, gripping the railing as she followed him into the dingy room and out onto the street. 'He still looks worn out. Every time I check the horses, he's lying down!'

'Well, at least he'll get a break on the way home. I bought that horse we were looking at this morning.'

'Did you? What's his name?' Jael inhaled the fresh dump of manure a horse was busy depositing onto the street ahead of them, thinking she might vomit.

Aleksander squinted at her as he skipped around the steaming pile. 'Rufus. Are you alright?'

Jael dropped her eyes to her swordbelt, adjusting *Toothpick's* scabbard. 'How many times have you asked me that? I'm fine. It's Thorgils we need to worry about, not me.' She looked up, and her face was troubled. Talking about Thorgils always led Jael straight back to her husband. Eadmund was so lost now. So far away from them, and from himself; heading for Evaine and Draguta, and whatever plans they were making for him.

'I promise not to ask if you're alright again if you promise to eat something. The food isn't that bad.' Aleksander had little appetite himself – the thought of what was happening in Andala had them both distracted and tense – but the rumblings of his stomach reminded him that though his mind wasn't thinking about food, the rest of him certainly was.

Jael smiled wearily. 'I could do with the peace, so alright then, let's go and eat, though don't leave me talking to Hedrun again. He won't stop complaining about his taxes. Apparently, Lothar upped the rate of silver, and now Hedrun's worried Axl will send men for him. Remove him. Or worse. He says his farmers can't afford to pay.' She frowned intensely, not wanting to think about Hedrun's taxes.

'Ha! I do remember Ranuf warning you that being a queen wasn't all battles and ring-giving.' Aleksander stopped, staring at the hall doors, newly carved with an odd pairing of long-tongued wolves and bushels of wheat. The entire village had been rebuilt after a fire had decimated most of it the previous spring. 'Come on. Maybe we can grab something to take back to Thorgils? He didn't look impressed with that broth Astrid was feeding him.'

Jael followed Aleksander into the hall, thinking about Thorgils.

About how they had saved him. And just in time. But then her face fell again, and she wanted to turn away from the hall and head back to the ramparts, desperate to see some sign of Eadmund. Wishing he'd turned around.

Come back.

Escaped the spell that had his soul bound to Evaine's.

She patted the leather satchel that was permanently slung across her body now. The Book of Aurea was still safely tucked in there, and soon they would get it back to Andala, and Edela would find a way to save Eadmund.

***

The fire was struggling, but it gave off welcome heat, and Eadmund leaned into it as the darkness enclosed him. The nights were cold this far south, and he thought longingly of a soft mattress.

A bed.

It had been days since he'd slept in one of those. He'd had one once. A bed better than any other.

A wife in it too.

He thought of the bed, but he didn't think of his wife.

He thought instead of Evaine, and of how soon they would be together.

Closing his eyes, Eadmund could almost smell the meadowsweet scent of her hair, imagining the silky feel of it sliding across his chest. He saw her perfect face and her irresistible lips. The fire popped and he jumped, opening his eyes, disappointed to be alone but for his two horses. He'd stopped at a farmstead, buying another horse, food, two waterskins, a threadbare fur. And then he'd kept going.

Soon he'd be in Hest.

And Evaine would be there, waiting for him.

***

Draguta's thoughts were jumbled, her body weak, but anger throbbed inside her. Pulsing at her temples. Clenching her fists. Anger which needed a resolution. And that resolution was revenge.

As a beginning.

The perfect place to start, though there was nothing perfect about the town she had come to. It was a crumbling wreck of a place, but it was where she would begin again. And who knew where she would end up?

Perhaps back at the start? Perhaps somewhere new...

She certainly felt different than she had before. Lighter. Less present, but somehow more aware. As though she existed in two places at once. As though she could see both darkness and light; slipping between the shadows that hid one world from the other.

The place the gods walked. The hidden place.

Draguta sighed, her eyes wandering the horizon. They were high up here, in a stone town with a stone tower overlooking the Adrano, and as the sun sank towards it, the sea looked like a dark pool of blood swallowing Hest's jagged coastline. It reminded Draguta of her own blood as it had flowed from her dying body, spreading over the flagstones, ruining her dress.

Weakening her. Killing her.

Though, Draguta smiled, not for long.

'My lady?'

Turning, she glared at her red-faced servant, Brill, who had climbed the narrow stone staircase to the top of the old tower. 'What?'

'Your...' Brill sucked in a cold breath, panting, her throat burning, '...supper is ready, my lady.'

Draguta turned back to the view, noticing how much darker everything suddenly appeared. She shuddered but did not retreat, surprised to discover that the darkness was no longer her enemy. 'Well, come along, then, you miserable creature. And after we eat the turgid slop you've prepared, you shall show me what you've collected today, for we have work to do, you and I...'

***

Isaura could barely speak. Edela had tried to be reassuring –

so had Eydis and Biddy – but she remained imprisoned by tall walls of terror and guilt.

It was a warm evening, and they were eating outside in the square. The children had wanted to. They had made friends since arriving in Andala, and their friends were eating outside with their parents, who had been working hard dismembering the dragon all day. Isaura couldn't remember their names, and when they smiled at her, looking as though they wanted to start a conversation, she turned away from their table.

Towards the harbour entrance.

She could see it so clearly.

It was dark now, but torches and braziers were burning around the square, leading towards the open gates where the last bits of the dragon were being carried. Carried in carts and in arms. Dragged by the horses and oxen that had finally been cajoled into going near the corner of the fort where the dragon had fallen. Carried to the harbour where it would join the serpent in its watery grave. Past the ship sheds where the men and women dying of the sickness were being housed. More and more were being taken into the sheds each day.

And now those sheds stunk of death.

And pyres were being built.

Biddy sneezed, and Isaura turned to her. 'Have you seen anything of Entorp today? Or Bruno?' she wondered.

Biddy shook her head, digging up her sleeve for a handkerchief. 'I've seen no sign of Entorp today,' she sniffed. 'Poor man. I hope he's taking care of himself in there.' She was worried, wanting to go and help him, but Edela had insisted that she remain far away from the sheds, which unsettled her further.

Runa sat down beside them with a yawn, wrapping a shawl around her shoulders.

Isaura smiled at her. 'How's Bram?'

'He's better,' she sighed, pouring herself a cup of ale and topping up Biddy's. 'I think he'll be out of bed tomorrow.

Derwa agrees. She wants rid of him. Says she's enough people to be looking after.'

Biddy laughed. 'Sounds about right.' Lifting the cup to her lips, she took a quick drink of the bitter ale, allowing her mind to drift far away from her worries for a moment. But when she looked at Isaura's face, they were quickly back.

There was so much uncertainty at the moment that it was hard to breathe.

'Perhaps Thorgils will return soon?' Runa suggested, seeing how distressed Isaura appeared. 'With Jael? Edela is sure she found him, isn't she?'

'Yes. She saw him with Jael in her dreams. But in what state she couldn't be sure.'

'But he was with Jael, and that's the right place for him to be,' Runa said. 'It sounds to me as though you've nothing to worry about. They'll be home soon.'

Isaura nodded mutely, listening to the chatter around her as the night darkened further, weary bodies relaxing for the first time since the sun's rise. There was laughter interlaced with the whining of tired children, who were long past ready for bed; the crack of the braziers; the smell of smoke and meat and ale, and dead dragon most of all.

More than anything, Isaura hoped that Runa was right.

She wanted Thorgils home, here, beside her. In her cottage. In her bed. In her arms. With her and the children. Together.

And when he was finally home, she would never let him go again.

***

'You're sure you should be eating that?' Jael frowned, glancing at Astrid, Harstad's lone healer, who had been caring for

Thorgils since they'd arrived in the village three days earlier.

Astrid laughed, reaching for her basket as Thorgils gnawed his way through the pork chop Aleksander had brought back from the hall. 'I think it's just what he needs. A man as big as Thorgils requires a lot of feeding to regain his strength.'

Thorgils' eyes shone brighter than they had in days. 'Exactly! I've been saying that for years, and now, finally, a woman who agrees with me. If only my heart didn't belong to another.' He winked at Astrid before biting another chunk out of the pork chop.

Jael was sure that Astrid was blushing as she headed to the cottage door.

The healer was a quiet middle-aged woman, with light brown hair tucked into a faded blue scarf. It matched her blue dress, which was plain and practical, much like Astrid herself. 'I'll return in the morning to check those stitches,' she said, turning back to Thorgils. 'But do take it easy when you get up tomorrow. Use the crutch, and don't go too far at first. Your body is still weak.'

Thorgils was nodding enthusiastically, but Jael could tell that he wasn't listening. She was, though. 'I'll make sure he does. We need him in one piece for the ride home. We have to get back to Andala as soon as possible.' She glanced at Aleksander, who was walking Astrid to the door.

'We do,' Aleksander agreed. 'And thanks to you, we'll be able to take the hungry giant with us.'

Jael could definitely see Astrid blushing now, and she smiled.

It was nice to have something to smile about.

'Thank you for everything,' she added, following them through the door. 'Hopefully, we won't need to bother you too much before we leave.'

'Oh, I don't mind, my lady,' Astrid said. 'It's not often we have a queen visit us here. Not one requiring my help, at least.' And she headed into the darkness, disappearing down the path that led towards the newly built hall.

Jael's shoulders slumped, and her face fell, all good humour suddenly gone. They were in Harstad, a long way from Andala. Days of riding with an injured Thorgils lay ahead of them.

She couldn't remember feeling so tired.

***

'You look as though you could fall down,' Biddy smiled, opening the gate and ushering Edela through it before turning back to grab Eydis' hand.

'I could,' Edela agreed, trekking up the path to the front door. 'And I don't think I'm alone. I can't remember a moment when everything felt as though it was calm. Especially inside my head. It's a jumble of demanding weeds in there, and I stopped being a useful gardener a long time ago!' She dug inside her purse, searching for the key.

Biddy frowned, holding the flaming torch over Edela's purse. 'I wondered why you'd been so quiet. I thought it might be something to do with Jael.'

Edela scooped out the big iron key, feeling around for the lock. 'Oh yes, it's Jael. And Eadmund. Thorgils and Ayla. All of them. Draguta too. A lot of demanding weeds, and I'm not sure which one I need to pull out first!' And opening the door, she stood aside to let Biddy and Eydis pass.

The cottage felt cold, and it was so dark that Edela didn't dare move until Biddy had lit the lamps. Eventually, the room started glowing, and Biddy threw the torch into the charred fire pit, shrugging off her cloak. 'I'll get the fire going, and we can have some hot milk before bed. What do you think, Eydis?'

Eydis didn't answer as she fumbled with her cloak pin.

Biddy bent down to help her. 'Here, that's a bit stiff, isn't it?

I'll get some oil on that tomorrow. Loosen it up for you.' Eydis nodded but didn't say a word as Biddy led her towards her little bed. 'You sit down there. Your nightdress is under the pillow. I'll get that fire going.' Eydis was worried about Eadmund, she knew. And Ayla.

They all were.

There hadn't been any word about Ayla since Ivaar had carried her into the shed. No one had seen Bruno. Nor Entorp. It was a constant, niggling worry.

The sickness was spreading quickly.

Biddy turned in surprise to see Edela with her cloak still on, opening the door. 'Where are you going?' she wondered. 'Edela?'

Edela turned around. 'Don't worry about me. I'm just going to talk to the moon a while. I need answers, and it may have some for me. It often does. Don't worry...' And she disappeared down the path, leaving a very worried looking Biddy to close the door.

***

Eadmund had fallen asleep early. With no one to talk to but his horses, and with nothing to see but the flames of his fire and the shadows hiding creatures he didn't want to imagine, he'd made himself a bed with the almost-big-enough fur and immediately closed his eyes.

And the dreams came.

Vivid, intense dreams, but so different than before.

This time he didn't see Evaine. He didn't hear her voice.

Someone else was there now, calling to him, promising him things.

Holding out an elegant, alabaster hand.

***

Edela walked away from the cottage, following the pale moonbeams, knowing they would lead her to where she needed to go. There were so many answers to find, and her dreams were not big enough for all of her questions.

She had always had a connection to Hymani, the Tuuran Goddess of the Moon. She'd been fascinated by the silvery orb in the night sky since she was a child, soothed by its luminous glow. Whenever she couldn't sleep, whenever she had a knot of a problem she couldn't untangle, she would go and talk to the moon, listening as it whispered back to her.

Edela stopped when she came to the path that led up a rise to a small bench sitting beneath a spreading ash tree. She smiled wistfully, almost seeing Ranuf ordering the carpenter around as he built it for her. A moon-watching bench he'd called it, its back carved to look like a moon surrounded by stars. He'd chosen the perfect spot for it, far away from the bustle of the square and the clamour of those who sought her advice.

A place where Edela could sit and contemplate.

A place to find help, he'd said. And surrounded by ambitious and unstable neighbours, Ranuf Furyck had been a king always in need of her help.

The rise was steeper than Edela's weary legs felt ready for, but that bench was already calling to her, so hitching up her cloak, she panted her way up to its peak, thankful the gods had helped blow the falling dragon far away from both her cottage and her bench.

Sitting down with a loud puff of exhaustion, Edela slumped back, feeling the smooth wood against her spine. Not comfortable but comforting.

Lifting her head, she looked up at the moon, a chill settling over her skin.

She knew then that she hadn't imagined it.

Something was definitely wrong.

***

The cottage was pokey. Unpleasant. Rats scampered in and out through holes in the walls, the wind chasing after them. And though there was a blazing fire in the long pit running down its middle, Draguta still felt cold.

She sat at a wobbling table on a roughly hewn chair, her eyes closed, running a finger around the seeing circle she had painted in her own blood. Inhaling sharply, she opened her eyes and smiled. 'Ahhh, there you are. It has not been long, I know, but oh, how I've missed you.' And frowning, she leaned closer to the circle. 'Dear, oh dear, but you appear to be in quite a bad way. How very sad... for you.' And closing her eyes again, Draguta's red-lipped smile grew wider and wider.

CHAPTER TWO

'Help! Please! Astrid! Somebody get Astrid! Now!'

'Jael? Jael! Jael, what's happening? Jael?'

Aleksander turned back into the cottage, blinking at Thorgils, who looked as terrified as he felt. 'I'm going to take you to her!' he panicked, hurrying to the bed. 'I have to take you to Astrid!'

'No.'

She was so quiet. He barely heard her.

Neither Thorgils nor Aleksander knew what was happening.

'No. Astrid will come. I don't want to move.'

The pain in Jael's body was overwhelming, but the pain in her heart was greater still.

'What's happening?' Thorgils had finally struggled out of bed. It was early. Still dark. He was half asleep, and his injured body was stiff. He blinked at Jael, lying on the bed. She had pulled the furs back, trying to get up. Even in the dim glow of the lamp by the bed, he could see the blood.

Aleksander gripped her hand. 'What is it?' His chest was tight, his heart thudding loudly.

'It's my baby,' Jael whispered, tears rolling down her cheeks. She closed her eyes, gasping as another wave of pain hit, twisting her body, arching her back.

The door swung open, and Astrid hurried inside. Quickly taking in the scene, she inhaled sharply, placing her basket on the nearest table and shooing Thorgils back to bed. 'You stay where you are! That won't help matters any, you pulling out your stitches. And you,' she said, pointing at Aleksander. 'Light the rest of the lamps, and stoke up that fire. I need to see what's going on.'

Jael wasn't listening. She was watching the fear in Aleksander's eyes. She could feel the blood on the mattress, wet against her skin, soaking her tunic. It was everywhere.

Red, like fire. Anger. Love.

Like death.

'Go on, get those lamps burning now,' Astrid said to Aleksander, who hadn't moved. She nudged him away from the bed and bent over Jael with a reassuring smile, placing one hand on her belly. 'I had a feeling, of course, by the look of you, but you weren't saying anything.'

Jael didn't want to say anything.

Thorgils sat down on the edge of his bed, gripping his shoulder, holding his breath. Aleksander was flustered, trying to light the lamps, burning his fingers.

'I'm going to lift up your tunic,' Astrid murmured, seeing that Jael wasn't responding as she writhed around. 'Oh.'

'What? What is it?' Aleksander was quickly by her side, holding a burning lamp. He leaned over, gasping. Jael's stomach was covered in large blue marks. Bruises.

Dragur blue.

'She did this,' Jael said mutely, her eyes closed as Astrid placed her cold hands on her hot belly, feeling around. 'She made them do it. I couldn't stop them... I couldn't stop them.'

'The dragur?' Aleksander was confused.

'Draguta. She knew about the baby when she sent the dragur. I couldn't stop them hitting me. I couldn't protect the baby,' she cried. 'It's my fault. It's all my fault!'

'Ssshhh,' Astrid soothed, watching Jael panic. 'We need to keep you calm. This baby has to come out. It can't stay in you, or it will kill you. You must try and let the pain wash over you

14

like water. Focus your mind on staying calm now.'

Aleksander swallowed. 'What should I do?'

'I need more light. Blankets and towels. I'll go to my cottage, get what I need and return. Perhaps you could come with me?'

Aleksander nodded, squeezing Jael's hand. 'We won't be long.'

'No, we won't,' Astrid promised, turning to Thorgils. 'Watch your queen, but try not to move too much. I don't need to be looking after both of you!'

Jael closed her eyes as Astrid and Aleksander hurried out of the cottage, listening as the door banged after them, neither one bothering to shut it properly.

Thorgils took a deep breath and stood. Grunting at the sharp pain in his stitched thigh, he grabbed his crutch, hobbling across the room to Jael.

'Don't,' she tried.

'Ahhh, well, you seem unable to stop me, lying there as you are,' he said, trying to smile. But he couldn't. And groaning, he collapsed on the edge of Jael's bed, watching her face contort in pain. Reaching for her hand, he held it tightly. 'I'm not going anywhere.'

There was silence.

Neither of them knew what to say.

***

'Edela?' Biddy hurried to open the door, the puppies milling around her legs. 'Where have you been? What have you seen?'

Edela glanced at Biddy as she came into the cottage, fiddling with her cloak pin, her eyes full of tears. She shook her head, not understanding anything.

Not understanding anything at all.

'It's Jael,' she breathed, her voice catching. 'I've seen Jael.'

***

Astrid was back quickly, leaving Aleksander to unpack the contents of her basket onto the table while she hurried to the bed. She had taken most of the lamps from her own cottage, and Aleksander quickly set about lighting them.

Jael was moaning, trying not to give in to the pain and grief that were working to consume her in the darkness. She felt like vomiting or weeping, but she just lay still, gritting her teeth, panting.

Astrid frowned. 'I'll need those towels,' she said to Aleksander. She didn't want to worry him, or Jael, but there was a lot of blood.

'What can I do?' Thorgils wondered. Jael had barely spoken, and he hadn't known what to say, but he wanted to do something to help.

He had to do something.

Astrid stared at him blankly. 'Hold her hand. Stay out of the way. Up there. Hold her hand.'

Thorgils nodded, reaching out to grip Jael's hand again.

She squeezed it suddenly, the pain exploding like a poker stirring a blazing fire. 'Aarrghh!' It was impossible to keep it in.

'So, I was thinking,' Thorgils said, trying to keep his voice steady and calm, 'about how I'm going to make Eadmund suffer when we get that spell of his broken. What do you think?'

Jael swallowed, trying to catch her breath, happy to listen to Thorgils' voice as he nattered in her ear. 'Eadmund,' she breathed. 'Talk to me about Eadmund.'

***

After Edela had explained her vision to Biddy and Eydis, no one had spoken.

There had been surprise about the baby from Eydis, and tears from them all. And then they'd sat quietly with their own thoughts, thinking about Jael.

Hoping she would be alright.

Biddy eventually decided that she couldn't take the silence a moment longer, and she started sweeping. Eydis crawled back into bed, wishing she could fall into a dream. Edela sat in her chair by the fire, feeling too warm for its heat and too worried about Jael to speak at all.

***

Thorgils couldn't feel his arse. He'd been sitting on the stool for hours.

Jael was still in bed, eyes closed, occasionally crying out in pain.

She hadn't spoken in some time.

Astrid had taken Aleksander away to the door. 'Jael has lost a lot of blood, and it's weakened her. We must try to move things along more quickly now. I need the baby out of her, so you must help her focus. I'm going to give her a tincture to see if it will hasten the birth. You try and get her to focus her mind.'

Aleksander's ears were buzzing. He was almost too confused to think.

He nodded anyway.

'Talk to her, guide her, bark at her if you must. Jael is a

warrior, so she needs to know what she's fighting. She needs to know that she's in a battle to save her life now. We have to stop that bleeding.'

Aleksander saw the fear in Astrid's eyes, feeling a hand clench around his heart. He nodded again, thinking of all the times he'd ridden into battle beside Jael. A small part of him had always felt sick with nerves for himself, but most of him had been worried about her.

About losing her.

Jael let out a roar, and Astrid hurried back to the bed. Aleksander took a deep breath, clearing his mind of everything but what he needed to do.

He needed to help Jael save herself.

***

Edela wanted it to be dark. She wanted the day to hurry along. She wanted to feel tired enough to fall asleep and dream, but it was a bright summer's day, and she was alert, twitching, too anxious to sit still, let alone relax enough to sleep.

Darkness would help. Her body would respond to the night, she knew, but the only darkness she could see was in her thoughts.

After Biddy made a meal that no one ate, they went for a walk.

Biddy disappeared into the hall to help Derwa set a broken arm. Eydis stayed with Edela, walking across the square, out through the harbour gates and away from the fort. She could hear water lapping gently around the broken piers, seabirds fighting over the fish they'd caught. She could feel a welcome breeze ruffling her dress, cold on her face, but most of all, Eydis could sense Edela's panic and confusion as she gripped her hand, guiding her down the path.

Their fears mingled together, rendering them both silent; each of them trying to think of something they might do to help.

'Ayla told me once that she could talk to the gods,' Eydis whispered. She couldn't hear anyone nearby, but she spoke quietly just in case. 'If she were here, perhaps... perhaps she could talk to them? They're supposed to protect Jael, aren't they? Isn't the prophecy about that? About how they need her?'

Edela blinked herself out of her trance-like state. 'Yes, the gods need Jael, and they have always protected her, or so I thought.' She shook her head. 'None of this makes any sense.'

'Unless it's Draguta?' Eydis suggested. 'Unless Draguta is more powerful than the gods?'

That was something Edela didn't want to believe possible. She squeezed Eydis' hand, feeling terror pulsing through it, realising that as worried as she felt about Jael – and for the first time in memory, Edela truly did feel worried about Jael – she needed to keep them both calm.

For a dreamer's mind had a habit of wandering away to dark places.

***

Astrid's face was round with dimples, soft lines at the corners of two grey eyes that smiled a lot. She wasn't smiling now as she gripped Jael's hand and spoke in her ear. 'You are tired, I know, but you need to help the baby on its way.' She glanced anxiously at Aleksander, who had been stoking the fire.

Jael's eyes were closed. She couldn't think.

She wanted to think, to make sense of it all, but she couldn't.

Her grandmother had never been wrong. She had seen her daughter. She had been so confident that she would come.

They both had. A winter baby, Edela had said. Jael remembered those cold hands gripping her belly; the smile on her old face. A winter baby like you, she'd said.

'Aarrghh!' Jael grunted, her eyes popping open as she squeezed Astrid's hand.

'Good, that's it,' Astrid said, motioning with her head for Aleksander to take Jael's hand as she slipped hers out of it. 'In a moment, I'm going to get you to push even harder. As hard as you can.'

It was growing dark again now. Jael had been in labour since well before dawn, yet little had happened.

She felt defeated and exhausted, ready to give up. Too tired to push.

Aleksander smiled at her pale face, glistening with sweat. 'You're nearly there. Just another push, then you can rest.'

Jael stared at him, wanting to curl into a tiny ball and hide away from his sympathetic eyes. She tried not to think of Eadmund, though he was all she wanted to think about. She wanted to hold his hand. Cry in his arms.

Their child.

She had lost their child.

It was all her fault.

'Now, push!'

And biting her teeth together, Jael held onto the image of Eadmund's face and screamed.

***

They hadn't spoken since they'd sat down to supper, though each one of them knew they should try and eat something. Biddy had made leek and nettle soup with rye bread, usually one of Edela's favourites, but the smell was turning her stomach.

'Did you hear anything about Ayla?' Eydis asked, trying to distract them.

'I finally saw Entorp. Bruno was with him. Ayla is holding on,' Biddy said, pushing away her bowl. She bent down to pick up Vella, who was whimpering, paws up on her knee. 'Weak but holding on, he said.'

Edela's worries pounded her like a giant wave crashing against the shore. Her heart was racing, her shoulders knotted. She wrung her hands, jumping at a pop from the fire. 'Draguta did this.'

Biddy's eyes were wide. 'To Jael?'

'Yes. She knew about the baby. She saw it. I know she did.' Edela had thought of little else all day, finally coming to the conclusion that Eydis was right.

Biddy shook her head, tears coming again. 'Will Jael live?'

'I...' Suddenly Edela had no confidence in anything she believed to be true. She dropped her eyes to her hands. They looked so withered and old. *She* was so withered and old. But Jael needed her, and she couldn't let her down. 'I don't know,' she whispered, her shoulders curling forward, tears rolling down her sagging cheeks. 'I don't know.'

'Oh, Edela,' Biddy cried, unable to hold herself together any longer; not even for Eydis' sake. She reached for Edela's hand. 'Not Jael. Please, not Jael. Please say she's going to live!'

***

'You need to sleep now. It will help. I must go back to my cottage. Make you another tincture. A broth. A tea. They will help you recover your strength.'

'The baby?' Jael's voice was weak, her hand shaking as she held it out to Astrid. She had no idea if it was day or night.

Everything felt dark. She almost couldn't see. Her ears were ringing so loudly that she couldn't hear much either.

'I've wrapped her up for now. Waiting...'

'Her?' The tears came again. 'Give her to me... please.'

Astrid glanced at Aleksander, who nodded and followed her to the table where the healer had laid the tiny baby, wrapped in a soft woollen blanket. He lifted the small bundle into his arms, shocked by how light she felt. How still. And silently he carried her towards Jael, who had propped herself up in the bed with Thorgils' help.

She looked so weak, he thought. Ghostly. Swollen eyes. Bruised and scratched.

Broken.

But she held out her arms and took her daughter in them.

'I'm so sorry,' Jael sobbed at her first glimpse of that tiny, still face. 'I'm so sorry.' Her tears fell onto the baby's closed eyes, and she gently wiped them away. 'I'm so sorry. So sorry.'

'It's not your fault, Jael,' Aleksander tried, feeling his own tears falling.

But Jael didn't hear him.

She couldn't hear anything but the howl of pleasure as the dragur struck her stomach, over and over again.

Killing her baby.

***

Eydis still had one of Jael's arm rings. She'd tried to return it, but Jael had insisted she keep it. 'Just in case,' she'd grinned before she left for Hallow Wood with Aleksander. 'Just in case you need me, or need to see something for me.'

And now Eydis did. More than anything, Eydis needed to see Jael, to find a way to help her. She rolled onto her side, listening to Biddy's sniffing and Edela's snoring, gripping that arm ring with a desperation she hadn't felt since she'd tried to dream of a way to prevent her father's death.

She didn't want to think about Eadmund or Ayla. She needed to help them too, but for now, there was only Jael.

Squeezing her eyes closed, Eydis brought Jael's face to her mind, watching her wave as she rode away on Tig.

She had promised to come back to her.

She had to come back.

***

'She's hot.'

There was only Thorgils to talk to.

Jael was asleep. Astrid had gone back to her cottage for more supplies.

Thorgils sat in a chair beside Jael's bed while Aleksander paced around, feeling her forehead every few minutes.

And every few minutes, he had the same report.

Thorgils was trying to keep calm. They had been woken early in the morning by Jael's cries of pain, and now, after a long day and night, his eyes were gritty, and his head was muddled.

And his heart was broken.

Eadmund was gone, lost to Evaine.

Jael's daughter was dead, and Jael was...

Thorgils sighed, trying to think. 'Wring out the cloth again,' he muttered. 'We need to keep her cool.'

'I should go and get Astrid.'

'Wait a while longer. Let Jael sleep. It was a long day.' Thorgils glanced at the tiny bundle still lying in Jael's arms, waiting for what would come next. 'A hard day.'

Aleksander nodded. Thorgils sounded calmer than he felt.

He could barely breathe as he took the warm cloth from Jael's head, dipping it into the bucket of water by her bed. 'If only Edela was here,' he mumbled. 'She'd know what to do.' He could feel himself panicking, and he thought of Ranuf's stern face, which instantly calmed him.

Panic was the enemy of survival, Ranuf had drummed into them.

It stopped you thinking and breathing. It made you vulnerable.

Panic wasn't going to help any of them.

Inhaling a slow breath, Aleksander sat down on the bed.

Thorgils could see the worry in his eyes. 'Did you know?' he whispered. 'About the baby?'

Aleksander shook his head, cross that he hadn't even guessed. Jael had been acting strangely for some time, but with so much happening, it was just one more conversation he hadn't found the time to have.

Thorgils needed to move. His thigh had gone numb, and he needed to stretch out his leg.

But he didn't.

He just sat there staring at Jael, hoping she was going to live.

***

'You were supposed to save her, weren't you, Edela?'

The gleeful voice echoed around her head.

Edela tried to ignore it, but it vibrated straight through her, shaking her limbs.

She couldn't escape its triumphant roar.

'And now she will die, just as her baby died. Shall I make you watch? Is that a dream you'd like to have, I wonder, Edela? Would you like to watch your beloved Jael die?'

CHAPTER THREE

Edela's dreams had been of no use. Just a return to the darkness and the crowing voice and little in between.

No Jael anywhere she looked. And how desperately Edela had looked.

But the clouds would not part. They would not let her through.

They were storm clouds, darkening rapidly.

'We should go to the hall. It looks like rain.'

Blinking, Edela turned to Biddy, lifting her boot out of the mud. 'Perhaps you could? I think I'll walk a while longer. I must find where the answers are waiting for me. Wherever that might be.'

Biddy glanced up at the sky, but she didn't argue.

'Keep things to yourself,' Edela warned, staring at Biddy, who was holding Eydis' hand. 'Both of you. We don't need to worry anyone yet.'

Biddy swallowed, disturbed by the tremble in Edela's voice. 'Of course. Look after yourself, though. I don't want you getting sick again.'

'I will,' Edela said listlessly as she turned, heading towards the last of the dismembered dragon. She kept her eyes low, head down, avoiding the drizzle and the enquiring glances of everyone she passed as she headed for the main gates.

There were answers, she knew. And she just had to go and

find them.

***

Thorgils and Aleksander stared at Astrid with weary frowns as she tried to keep them from worrying.

'Willow bark will help. And we'll warm up the cottage, get her sweating a bit. Don't worry,' Astrid smiled encouragingly. 'Perhaps you both need some fresh air? Thorgils, you could stretch your leg, and there's no harm in seeing the sun.'

They shook their heads, neither one inclined to leave the cottage. Jael was getting hotter; barely awake now. She hadn't said a word all day, and they were becoming increasingly worried.

'What about the baby?' Thorgils wondered, glancing towards the basket Astrid had brought to keep her in.

'We must wait on Jael for that,' Astrid murmured. 'Once the fever breaks and she recovers her strength...' She tried to look confident, but the memory of all that blood nagged at her. 'She just needs some time.'

Thorgils could hear the hesitation in Astrid's voice.

'I'll get your crutch,' Aleksander sighed, not wanting to leave at all but realising that the healer was right. They needed to take a breath in order to see things clearly.

Thorgils nodded.

'You can't help her,' Astrid assured them. 'This is Jael's journey now, and it's a path she must walk alone.'

***

'What are you doing?' Jael grumbled, pushing Eadmund's hand away from her stomach.

'Just checking,' he grinned, sitting up.

'Checking what?'

'Well, you've been feeling ill these past few days, so I'm just checking.'

Jael frowned. 'Get away with your checking! I just ate something that didn't agree with me.'

'I'm sure you're right.'

Jael frowned some more. 'Go away, Eadmund Skalleson!'

'You would tell me?'

'If I was pregnant? Oh, they'd hear me sobbing down in Hest, don't worry about that!' Jael grumbled, patting Ido, who was wriggling beside her, ready for breakfast.

Eadmund laughed. 'True, but you'd change your mind. I've no doubt. You'd change your mind.'

'Oh, how little you know me,' Jael yawned. 'There's nothing in the world I want less than a squawking baby.'

Eadmund leaned in to kiss her. 'You're a terrible liar, Jael Furyck.'

***

Edela hadn't been to the tree in months.

She didn't know why. Furia was the Goddess of War – everyone knew that – but she was also the Goddess of Childbirth. Life and death were joined together like day and night. Two parts of a circle. And this was Furia's Tree, where Brekkans from every part of the kingdom would come to seek wisdom, knowledge, answers. An ancient grove, hidden in the forest.

A sacred place of secrets and magic.

Edela sighed. She was sodden and sad, and she wanted to drop to her knees and sob. Her certainty had been shaken. Jael's baby was dead.

And Jael?

The old tree's gnarled trunk was wide. Even Thorgils couldn't have fitted his arms around its massive girth. Its bark crawled with bright-green lichen and moss; its twisted branches hanging ponderously on either side in perfect symmetry. But it was just a tree, and suddenly Edela doubted what answers it could provide.

She stared at the damp ground, covered in a soggy mulch of leaves and twigs. It didn't look inviting for her aching hips, but she eased herself down onto it anyway, deciding that she would close her eyes and let the clouds come and find her.

And though it was raining, and day and not night, she needed answers, and she prayed that the gods would help her find them.

***

Draguta was missing the ample luxuries that Hest had provided. The accommodation Brill had found for them was worse than anything she would have kept a slave in. It would have to do for now, though, Draguta knew. She had more important matters to turn her mind to than the quality of her furnishings.

But when they were resolved?

Well, there would be no need to settle for such poverty then.

Walking down the cobblestoned street, she raised her hand to the tall man on the large brown horse, who rode slowly towards her, leading another horse behind him. Her body tingled with certainty. 'Eadmund!'

Eadmund frowned, pulling on the reins. He didn't know

where he was, but it definitely wasn't Hest. And he didn't recognise the woman, who so clearly recognised him.

Swinging off his horse, he dropped to the ground with a groan, grateful to feel his feet again. 'Who are you?' he asked. 'And where's Evaine?'

Draguta blinked at Eadmund's dirty face and smiled.

***

Evaine was growing sick of the sight of Morac's cramped cottage. She had hidden away from Jaeger since that night in the hall, knowing that although he could find her easily enough, he'd likely not be bothered. Not while he was worrying about Morana and Draguta and his precious book.

Evaine wasn't worrying about Morana or Draguta. She was worrying about Eadmund. Wondering where he was.

Surely he should have arrived in Hest by now?

Morac was no help.

'Morana is the only one to tell you where he is, Evaine, and she has shown no sign of improvement,' he sighed, poking the fire, knowing it was time he made something to eat, though he'd had little appetite since his sister had taken ill.

Since the night Draguta had died. Or so they had thought.

His nightmares were filled with Draguta's beautiful face and her terrifying voice, and what she would do to them if she returned.

Morac had been hiding away from Jaeger, too, only slipping into Morana's chamber once a day to see if there had been any change. Meena was helping Sitha to care for his sister, but the healer appeared to have no clue how to help her, and though Morana was now out of bed, she was as lifeless as ever.

Her eyes were open, but she didn't speak.

She didn't move at all.

Morac lifted his hands to his head, feeling the tension building at his temples, pressing in on either side of him. They were trapped here now, and without Morana to guide him, he couldn't trust himself around Jaeger. Not after what he'd done to Evaine. His daughter's bruises, though mostly faded now, were still obvious enough to make him tremble with rage. He grimaced as the sharp pains in his head intensified.

'*When* will Morana recover? It's been days!' Evaine pushed herself out of the chair, striding towards the door. 'She just sits there dribbling! Useless! And what about Eadmund? Something's happened to him. I know it! I know it! He should have been here by now. I feel as though he's further away than ever!'

'Where are you going?' Morac panicked, though part of him was desperate for a break from Evaine's neverending stream of complaints.

'I can't sit in this prison any longer. I need some air! You needn't worry, Father, there's nothing Jaeger can do to me now. Nothing worse than what he's already done!' And pulling open the door, she disappeared before her father could get off his stool.

Morac gaped after Evaine, wondering whether he should follow her.

Wanting to keep her safe.

Wondering where Eadmund was.

***

Draguta led Eadmund down Flane's cobblestoned main street. A terrible name for a hovel of a place, she thought, rolling her eyes at the shabby peasants staring at her as they passed.

'But when will Evaine come? How will she come?' Eadmund fretted as he walked, leading his weary horses, who blew and snorted impatiently, wanting rest and water, and something to eat most of all.

Draguta was suddenly reminded of what an annoyance Evaine had been with her endless, lovesick drivel. 'First, you need a wash and a change of clothes. Something... fresher.' She wrinkled her nose, flapping a hand at Eadmund's filthy appearance. 'Everyone here works for me now, so we will stop at the tailor's. Though we'll find little there, I'm sure. Nothing worthy of a king, at least. Then we shall eat and talk. Do not worry about Evaine, Eadmund dear. You shall have Evaine. And soon. And then we will all be happy, I promise.'

Eadmund frowned, wanting to know more, but his head was in a fog, and he couldn't make sense of his thoughts. All he could do was follow after Draguta, who was quickly striding away from him, hoping she was right.

***

The castle was pleasant without Draguta. Without his father. Without his brothers.

Jaeger rolled his hands over the smooth armrests of the dragon throne and smiled, sitting up straighter as Meena shuffled into the hall. 'How is Morana? Has she said anything?' he asked eagerly.

Meena shook her head as she edged towards the throne, knowing she was about to disappoint him. 'She is the same.'

Jaeger slumped back with a sigh. 'But how much longer must we wait?' he implored. 'How much longer before Draguta returns? She will return, won't she? Have you seen that? Have you dreamed it?'

Meena blinked, disturbed by his questions. She was grateful to be out of Morana's chamber and away from the smell of her decaying aunt. There was no sign yet that she would recover, and though Jaeger appeared optimistic, Meena had her doubts. 'No, I haven't.'

Growling, Jaeger stood and batted away the offer of a goblet of wine from the very slave he'd ordered to go and bring him a goblet of wine. 'And what are we going to do about that, then? Sit here and wait to be murdered by Draguta? She could be outside for all we know! Plotting! Spellcasting! Up at the stones, even! Preparing to send her creatures to kill us!' He grabbed Meena's hand, yanking her towards him. 'You're a dreamer! But what use are you to me if you don't have any dreams?'

Meena stared into his desperate eyes, unable to look away. 'I, I... I have tried.'

Jaeger pulled her closer. 'Meena,' he breathed, running a hand over her wild red hair. 'We are powerful together, you and I. The gods have seen that. They brought us together. We're here because we're meant to be.' He leaned in, kissing her slowly. 'We are meant to have the book, so you must try to read it. *Now*. You must find a way to protect us from Draguta before it's too late. Before everything we have is destroyed. Before she comes to claim her revenge!'

Meena swallowed, readying a list of reasons why that was a terrible idea, but Jaeger's hands were still in her hair, and he brought her face towards his, kissing her again. And she found herself mumbling, reluctantly nodding.

'Good!' He quickly pushed her away. 'Go. Now. *Dream*! Find me a way to protect the castle. To help Morana. To keep us safe. All of it. Now! *Go*!'

Meena stumbled backwards, terrified that she didn't know how to do any of it. But more terrified by the certainty that Draguta would return and kill them all.

Soon.

***

The Tuuran dreamers were guided by Lydea, the Goddess of Dreams. She was their patron, their mistress, though she did not come to them. Not as she once had. She spoke to the elders. The elderman.

The gods rarely spoke to the dreamers.

But now? Without Tuura? Without the temple and the elders, who'd been consumed by The Following and then the flames? Without the elderman, who was too busy caring for his sick daughter, hoping she wouldn't die.

Who were the gods to speak to now?

'Edela?'

The voice sounded like the softest fur. It felt warm, gentle, comforting.

Edela had fallen asleep against Furia's Tree, hoping to find a dream, but she had found something much better.

She had found a goddess.

'You have questions?' Lydea began, her long white hair flowing down past her waist, curling over her pale-grey gown. Every part of her was the colour of clouds, even her almond-shaped eyes. 'You have questions for me?'

Edela shivered, glancing around, wondering if she was still asleep. She was still in the grove, wet through, covered in leaves. 'I... I wanted to understand what had happened. Why my dreams were wrong.' Her voice broke, tears falling down cold cheeks. 'I saw Jael's daughter in my dreams so clearly. I saw her, and I told Jael. Perhaps if I had seen a different dream, she wouldn't have left? I told her she would be safe. That her child would be safe. It's my fault...' she sobbed. 'It was my job to warn her! To keep her safe!'

Lydea held out a hand, helping Edela to her feet, lifting her chin. 'You must not cry, Edela,' she soothed. 'It is not your fault.

What you saw *was* the truth. It was the fate we were weaving for Jael and Eadmund. It was Jael's destiny to have her daughter. But then...' She looked away, watching a small brown rabbit disappear down a dark hole. 'It seems that Draguta has more power than any of us realised. She has the power to weave destiny itself.'

Edela blinked. 'You couldn't stop her?'

Lydea looked uncomfortable. 'Draguta sent her creatures to kill Jael's child, to take the book, and though we tried to stop her, we couldn't. We tried to save the child, but we couldn't. The dragur were raised by Draguta's magic. With the dark magic of the Book of Darkness. With all the power she has harnessed. It is... greater than we anticipated.'

'Oh.'

Lydea placed her hands on Edela's shoulders. 'You see it, Edela. You see the Darkness coming. You can feel Draguta's strength growing. She is your enemy and ours. Jael needs to fight now. With both hands. With all of herself. She is our weapon. The only one we have now. She must live. She must find a reason to fight.'

Edela didn't know what to say.

'If Jael is to have another child one day, it will only happen because she defeats Draguta. Without that, none of us will exist. Without that, there is no hope.'

'But Draguta doesn't want the Darkness, does she?'

Lydea edged away from Edela, worried that she was revealing too much. Some secrets were for the gods alone to know. The weight of them was too great for mere humans to bear. 'You must wake now, Edela. We will be here, watching you. Doing what we can to help you and Jael. We always will, but for now, it is Jael who must find a way to save herself. If anyone can, she can.'

'But –'

Lydea placed a cool hand on Edela's forehead, and Edela's eyes closed as she slumped into the goddess' arms. Lydea lay the old woman gently down amongst the leaves, then bent over her, smoothing her hair away from her face. It was almost all white now, growing thinner, revealing a pink scalp. Lydea smiled wistfully, remembering the thick chestnut hair of the talented dreamer she had first met as a little girl.

How quickly time had run away from them all. Even the gods.

'Sleep now, Edela Saeveld, and I will send you the dreams you need.'

***

'Perfect!'

Draguta felt elated as she gripped the stone. 'This is just what we need to help Evaine escape Hest.'

Eadmund felt better after a bowl of stew and a cup of ale. Fresher too in clean clothes, but his head was still muddled. 'Why can't I just go and bring her here? Why can't we go to Hest?'

Draguta dismissed him with an impatient shake of her head. 'I have told you that Jaeger will not allow it.' She tightened her grip on the stone, anger rising at the thought of what Jaeger had tried to do to her. Of what Meena had done.

Meena? Meena Gallas?

Of all the people capable of killing her, how had it been that dim-witted girl who had succeeded? Well, she smiled, admiring her very-much-alive self, not really succeeded.

'And why should you care what Jaeger Dragos thinks?' Eadmund grumbled. 'What has Evaine to do with him?'

'Because, as it stands, Jaeger has my castle and my book. He has two dreamers. And he has Evaine. So we must care very much about what he thinks,' she insisted. 'For now. And only for now. But soon...' Draguta glanced around the dump of a cottage. 'Soon we will return to our rightful place, but until then, we must continue our work.

'Our work?'

'Yes, I cannot leave a job half-finished, Eadmund. I may have killed Jael Furyck's baby, but now I must finish her.' She watched him carefully, but Eadmund didn't even twitch. Draguta smiled, running a finger over the symbol on the stone he had given her. It was the symbol stone Morac had given Eadmund when they were sailing for Saala. 'Drink up now, and then we will go foraging. There is so much we need to prepare, for tonight I will go and find Evaine.'

Eadmund lifted the cup to his lips, his weary eyes brightening, his body humming at just the sound of her name.

***

'Edela!' Gant hurried towards the sleeping figure, who lay beneath Furia's Tree, shrouded in the growing darkness.

Biddy's shoulders relaxed away from her ears as she watched Edela rouse herself out of the damp leaves. 'I thought this might be where you'd disappeared to.'

Edela looked puzzled, shivering at how cold it was.

'You're hardly going to be able to help anyone if you lie about in the rain!' Biddy scolded as Gant helped Edela to her feet, brushing the leaves from her cloak.

Edela frowned. 'Well, it's very peaceful out here. No snoring to contend with.'

Biddy smiled, pleased to see that Edela's sense of humour had returned; then she thought of Jael, and her smile fell away.

'Mmmm, but perhaps you should choose a finer day?' Gant suggested. 'Or at least tell someone where you're going. We've been searching for some time, Edela.'

'Well, I'm sorry for that. I'm sure you had better things to do.'

Gant took Edela's arm, walking her down the narrow path that led from the grove into the forest. 'If you consider dismembering a dragon better, then I suppose so. Now, how about we get you back to the fort before it really comes down.' He glanced up at the thick tree canopy, sensing the dark clouds gathering overhead.

Biddy took Edela's other side, surprised to receive no complaints in return.

But Edela was too busy to notice, remembering the feel of Lydea's cold hand on her forehead and her voice whispering in her ear. 'Do not give up, Edela. Do not give up on Jael.'

***

Jaeger was tired of feeling frustrated.

The power he was so desperate to claim was only a fingertip away. He could almost taste it. Closing his eyes, he inhaled the overpowering scent of rotting straw and manure as he passed the stables, heading for the winding gardens.

The day was suffocatingly hot. He needed shade. A breeze. A place to think away from the torturous reminder of the night in the hall and their failure to kill Draguta.

Looking up, he smiled. 'Shall we go into the gardens again?'

Evaine scowled at Jaeger, wanting to turn and run. She'd wandered far away from the castle, along the road, past the ship sheds and the stables, leaving it all behind. She had started walking towards the cliffs where Jaeger had taken her on their ride, hoping to see Eadmund. But there was no sign of him anywhere, and, in the end, she'd returned to the city as the sun started sinking.

She had hoped to make it back to Morac's cottage without bumping into Jaeger.

But now, here they were again.

Jaeger saw a glint of fear in her eyes, and he licked his lips, watching her tremble.

'There's nothing I can do to stop you,' Evaine said mutely. 'Do as you wish.' She swallowed, staring at him, willing him to try and hurt her again. Wanting to shame him. Hoping he could still see her bruises.

Jaeger shrugged. 'How true that is, Evaine. Truer now that I have the Book of Darkness. There's nothing anyone can do to stop me.'

'But you're not a dreamer. Without Morana, what can *you* possibly do?' Evaine's curiosity overrode her fear. 'Without her, the book is useless.'

Jaeger's amber eyes flared. 'I have Meena. And Meena can read the book.'

Evaine snorted, doubting that. 'Well, I wish you luck.' She stepped to one side, but Jaeger grabbed her arm.

'You mustn't be so quick to judge,' he purred. 'Meena is so much more than you'll ever understand. She's my dreamer, and she will help me unleash the power of the book. And with it, I will claim all of Osterland, and destroy every king and queen who stands in my way. Starting with your favourite king,' Jaeger smiled, watching her squirm. 'I must remember to tell Meena to start with Eadmund Skalleson. He's on his way here, isn't he? That should make things so much easier.'

Evaine looked horrified as Jaeger disappeared through the flower-wrapped archway that led into the winding gardens, eager to find somewhere to think.

***

'You're expecting too much of Evaine!'

Draguta raised an eyebrow. 'I don't remember asking your opinion about anything, Eadmund. But in any case, you'd be surprised by how... resilient Evaine can be.'

'Resilient?' Eadmund shook his head, adjusting the drum on his knee. 'You don't know Evaine. There's nothing resilient about her. She's not Jael. She's not a warrior. She can't get out of Hest on her own.'

He was so dispassionate when talking about his wife, Draguta noticed.

It made her happy.

But his droning on about Evaine did not.

'Well, let us give her a chance to prove you wrong,' she smiled. 'Now we are ready. And soon, we will begin. Soon, Evaine will be yours.' Draguta could feel the chill of darkness settling around her shoulders like a cloak.

The pulsing need to be reunited with the book.

And, with Evaine's help, she soon would be.

CHAPTER FOUR

Meena wasn't sure what she wanted.

She stared at the book, too scared to even touch its crisp vellum pages. It was an evil book, and Meena knew that it would try to claim her, and that would help no one except Jaeger. He wanted her to become like Morana and Draguta. Like himself. Lost in the book. A prisoner to its darkness.

But Meena knew that she couldn't let herself falter. She couldn't allow the book to trap her.

'What will you do, then?' Else wondered from behind her. 'Will you try and read it? Help Jaeger?'

She sounded scared, Meena thought as she reached out, tracing the symbols on the page. They were familiar. She'd seen Varna make similar symbols over the years. She had watched Morana draw them.

The words too. They were like Varna's.

But Meena didn't want them to be. She didn't want to let herself think that she could understand them. That she could help Jaeger read them.

But if she didn't?

'I don't know,' she admitted, glancing at the door. 'I don't know what to do. The book hurts people. Everyone wants to hurt people with it. Jaeger. Morana. Draguta.'

Else frowned, wiping her hands on her striped apron as she took a seat beside Meena, glancing at the door herself, wondering if she should lock it. 'But while Morana is ill, and with Draguta gone, no one can use the book. You have a chance.'

Meena swallowed. 'A chance?'

'To take it,' Else whispered. 'Take the book and leave Hest.'

Meena's eyes were round. She shivered. 'I... I don't know how to. I don't know where to go.' That wasn't true. She would go to Andala. To Berard. But Andala was broken, not safe from Draguta. And if Draguta knew she had the book, she would come for her. She would do anything to take it back. 'They would find me. Any of them. *All* of them. They wouldn't let it go.'

'Could you destroy it?' Else wondered. 'Burn it? Throw it into the fire and run away?'

The door swung open, and Jaeger strode in, frowning at Else. 'What are you doing?' he glowered. 'Sitting down like a lady? Why aren't you working? Perhaps you are of no use to me? There are plenty of servants I could choose to be in my chamber. Why should I keep a slovenly old crone like you?'

Meena hurried to her feet. 'I was just asking Else some questions,' she mumbled. 'It was my fault. I was asking if she knew of any way to help Morana.'

'Why?' Jaeger peered at Else. 'Are you a healer?'

'I... well, I have been many things in my time, and yes, I have done some healing work. I used to help my mother when I was young.'

Jaeger didn't care. 'Then go up to Morana's chamber. *Now!* Go and relieve Sitha. See what you can do to bring Morana back to life. And if you can't, I shall get rid of the pair of you!'

Meena blinked rapidly, following Else to the door.

Jaeger grabbed her arm. 'You will stay here. Return to the book. Stay with the book. *Read* the book. Do you understand me, Meena? You need to learn its secrets. You must protect it with your life.'

Trying not to let her disappointment show, Meena gave Else a sympathetic smile and turned back to the table where the

Book of Darkness lay open, waiting to claim her.

***

'Are you alright, Eydis?' Edela wondered, rolling over, watching her little face glow in the last embers of the fire.

'No. I'm worried about Eadmund. And Ayla. And Thorgils. I'm worried about the fort too, and what Draguta will do next. But mostly, I'm sad about Jael,' Eydis sniffed. 'I don't want her to die.'

Biddy closed her eyes, sharing Eydis' fears. Jael had gone off to battle many times, but she'd seen Jael with a sword, and she had confidence in her ability to protect herself. But this was different. It was a test she hadn't faced before, and Biddy didn't know if Jael had the strength to survive it.

'You must try to remember her,' Edela murmured, wanting to reassure them both. 'Try to remember her voice. Try to see her as you do in your dreams, Eydis. You know Jael. She's been broken before, and she fought back. Many times. She won't let this defeat her. She will fight, I promise, so try to sleep now. You might find a dream. You might find a way to see Jael, so sleep now. Just sleep.'

***

It was impossible to think about going to sleep.

'But you must,' Astrid insisted. 'The only thing that will help Jael now is sleep, and you can't help her do that.' She bent down to pick up her basket. 'I will come early tomorrow and see how she is. And remember to give her some of that tincture if she wakes. It will help bring down the fever, and once that's normal, she'll have a better chance of recovering.'

Thorgils couldn't help a wry smile. No one hated a tincture more than Jael, except, perhaps, Eadmund, he thought sadly, still seeing glimpses of his friend's empty eyes in Hallow Wood.

Just before Eadmund had stabbed him.

Aleksander didn't smile. 'Alright, we'll try. But one of us should stay awake. Just in case we need to come for you.'

'Of course,' Astrid said, yawning as she headed for the door. 'The more sleep Jael can get, the more strength her body will have. And her mind. It was a shock.'

Aleksander nodded.

To all of them, he thought.

Thorgils sat in a chair by Jael's bed, thinking about his mother. He shook his head, cross with himself. Jael wasn't Odda. She wouldn't just fade away like an old woman at the end of her life.

Not Jael Furyck.

Aleksander closed the door and came back to the bed, sitting down with a sigh. The bed creaked.

Jael groaned and opened her eyes; opening them wider in surprise at how dark the cottage was. Wondering if it was just her.

'Jael?' Thorgils bent towards her.

Jael closed her eyes again, groaning some more as she tried to move.

'Jael?' Aleksander edged closer.

Jael could hear them both, but she didn't want to speak. She felt odd, so cold and weak. Her eyelids were almost too heavy to lift open again. 'What's wrong with me? What did you do with my baby?' she whispered hoarsely. 'Where is she?'

Thorgils turned to Aleksander, who glanced at the basket on the table. 'We're keeping her safe, don't worry,' Thorgils smiled. 'She's waiting here for you.'

'Waiting?'

Thorgils felt awkward, fumbling for the right words. 'To say... goodbye... before we...' He couldn't find them.

'What?' Jael sounded weak, but her tongue was sharp.

'We were going to make her a small pyre,' Aleksander said softly. 'I thought you'd want that rather than a burial. Unless you'd like to take her back to Andala?'

Jael blinked, forcing her eyes open. She didn't have the energy to move. She couldn't even reach out a hand as the waves of grief surged in her chest, her eyes filling with tears that felt hot against her cold cheeks.

She remembered her baby daughter's face.

As blue as the dragur who'd killed her.

The dragur she had let kill her.

'I want to go home. I need to see Edela,' she whispered, closing her eyes.

'Wait, Jael,' Thorgils said, struggling to his feet. 'We have to give you some more of the tincture.' He grimaced at the stinging pain in his thigh, but he made it to the tincture bottle ably enough. 'Astrid said it will help you, and I know how much you like a tincture.'

Jael didn't smile, but she did open her eyes.

Aleksander grabbed a spoon. 'Here, I'll give it to her,' he offered, watching Thorgils wobble uncomfortably. And lifting Jael up with one hand, he held out the spoon while Thorgils dribbled the tincture onto it.

Jael swallowed it, not caring how vile it tasted. Not caring about anything at all.

She was empty. Lost.

Unsure if she wanted to be found.

***

The smoke was trapped in the back of Eadmund's throat, and he couldn't stop coughing. He could barely see through the thick fug of it. His fingers felt numb, oddly thick, and he was struggling with the drum, unable to maintain a rhythm. He couldn't catch up with the beat echoing inside his head.

The sharp looks Draguta kept giving him told him that she agreed.

'You will need to stay still if I am to find Evaine,' she muttered, her voice a low, hoarse whisper. 'Close your eyes and let the smoke in. Do not fight it, Eadmund. It will take us both to Evaine. Close your eyes now, and let us drift away together.'

***

Morac wasn't usually a snorer, but his breathing was so loud that Evaine was tempted to throw something at him. Between her father's awful noise and the odd smell in his hovel, Evaine knew there was little chance of finding any sleep.

She felt tempted to get up and go for a walk.

But what if Jaeger was out there, roaming the city, searching for a woman to take to his bed, or into those gardens again?

Sighing irritably, she rolled over, trying not to inhale, clamping her hand over her ear, realising that the only chance she had of seeing Eadmund was in her dreams.

She had to do everything she could to try and fall asleep.

***

Jael leaned her head back against the tree, closing her eyes.

'You'll have to do better than that,' Ranuf growled. 'Or perhaps your mother needs to clean out your ears, Jael? How could you not hear me coming?'

'I heard you.'

'Yet, there you are, ready to be pounced on by me. A man twice as big as you. And how do you plan on defending yourself?'

Jael frowned at her father, lifting the flap of her cloak where she'd concealed her sword, her small hand wrapped around its iron hilt.

Ranuf was pleased, though he didn't show it. 'I expected you in the training ring. Aleksander is there, waiting with Gant. No one knew where you were. Not even your grandmother. Though, I suppose, it wasn't hard to find you. Not really.'

'I didn't want to train today.'

Ranuf sat down amongst the leaves. Furia's Tree was wide enough for two, and he rested his back against its broad trunk, sighing. 'Tell me.'

Jael was eleven. Difficult and joyful. Often morose. Always determined.

Her temper was explosive.

'Go on,' he urged. 'Tell me.' His voice was softer now.

'I had a nightmare. I didn't want to train today,' Jael mumbled, trying to shut out the images of Tuura. The nightmares came often. She couldn't stop them.

'What can you do about them?'

Jael shrugged. 'Nothing.'

'Not true.' Ranuf leaned closer, his arm brushing against his daughter's. 'You can fight. You can train. You can defeat your nightmares.'

Jael didn't look convinced.

'We can do no more than the gods allow,' Ranuf continued. 'But we can do that. We can do our best to be strong and brave. To fight and never give in. To never let the darkness win. To protect those we love.' Jael's eyes were on him now, he noticed.

More alert. 'Do you think you can be the Queen of Brekka? Lead our people? When you're so ready to surrender? To nightmares? You would let mere nightmares defeat you? If that's the case, how are you ever going to face down an actual enemy? One standing before you, holding a sword? If you're scared of a nightmare, Jael, what sort of a queen would you be?'

Jael frowned, not convinced that her father really wanted her to be the Queen of Brekka at all.

'What did you tell me when you asked me to make you a warrior? Do you remember? After Tuura?' Ranuf shuddered, the guilt of it still fresh for him as well. 'What did you tell me?'

'I said I wanted to protect the people I loved. That I wanted to learn how to keep them safe.'

'You did. And now? You can't learn to fight by sitting here, hiding. You can't keep anyone safe by giving up.'

Jael closed her eyes, trying to shut out the grunting sounds those men had made as they'd torn off her clothing. Their laughter. Her screams.

The sound of Gant cutting off their heads.

She was tired of those sounds.

Ranuf reached out a hand. 'Come on, now. We have somewhere to be, you and me.'

Jael burst into tears, falling against her father's chest, wanting so much to feel safe. Wanting to feel his arms around her. 'I couldn't save Mother! I couldn't keep her safe from those men. They hurt her. They hurt me! I couldn't stop them!'

Ranuf wrapped his arms around his daughter, closing his eyes. 'I know,' he whispered, his voice breaking. 'I know. Ssshhh. You're safe, Jael. I have you now. You're safe with me.'

***

Everything was perfect. Morac was waiting to take her to the hall, muttering to himself as he ran a hand through his iron-grey beard, sharpening its point.

He looked nervous, Evaine thought distractedly.

She had spent all morning having her hair worked into delicate rows of silver beaded braids, pulled back, away from her face to show off her cheeks. They were flushed pink. It was a warm day, but she was shivering with excitement.

This day had been so long coming.

Her wedding to Eadmund.

'Not yet,' Draguta purred, gliding forward in her silken white dress, her ebony hair shimmering down her back. 'Not yet, Evaine. I have things to do, so many things, and they require your help. So if you wish to be reunited with Eadmund, then you will help me. And quickly.'

Thunder clapped overhead, and suddenly the house was dark, Morac disappearing into the shadows.

'What things?' Evaine whispered, her skin prickling with fear. 'What would you have me do?'

***

One of them should have been asleep, but they both sat by Jael's bed, watching her sleep instead.

Thorgils could barely keep his eyes open. He was distracted, his thoughts rumbling around his head, sometimes tumbling out of his mouth. He placed a hand on Jael's head and frowned. 'She's still feverish. We don't even know if...'

Aleksander glared at him, suppressing a yawn. 'She'll be better soon. We just need to wait. She *will* get better.'

Thorgils dropped his head to his hands, thinking of Isaura. 'Wait till you see Andala. It's not quite how you left it.'

'You mean the dragon?'

'What's left of the dragon,' Thorgils snorted, lifting his head. 'The fort is an open door now. The western wall was crushed. No symbols will keep Draguta out, whatever her plans are. There's nothing to stop her. Just some arrows and sea-fire and a few thousand men. *Men*. Not monsters. Men.'

'But we have the Book of Aurea now, so whatever her plans are, she'll have a much harder time of it. Once we get the book back to Andala. To Edela.'

Thorgils didn't look convinced. 'But Draguta has the Book of Darkness, and surely that's a more powerful book?'

Jael moaned, and they both looked at her, but her eyes didn't open.

Aleksander wondered if he should wet another cloth, trying to imagine what Biddy would do. He was too tired to think clearly, though, and he could feel himself panicking again, realising that he needed to get some sleep before he was no help to anyone. 'All we can do is be here with Jael. She needs us. She'll come back to us soon, and then we'll go home. Leave Draguta and the Book of Darkness for another day. It's Jael we need to focus on now.'

Thorgils yawned, glancing at his bed. 'I'll get some sleep, unless you want to go first? As you say, we need to help Jael, and I can't even think straight.'

Aleksander didn't turn around as he nodded, picking up Jael's ice-cold hand and holding it gently in his.

***

Meena fell out of bed, cracking her hip on the flagstones.

Jaeger jerked awake. 'What? What is it?'

'Nothing,' she gasped, shaking all over as she hauled herself back into the bed. Her heart was pounding, and she was mostly still asleep, but she had enough wits about her to know that she didn't want to encourage Jaeger to wake up.

'You're sure?' he mumbled. 'You didn't have a dream?'

'No,' Meena whispered. 'No.'

She lay still, almost holding her breath, waiting for her heart to slow down. Waiting to hear Jaeger fall asleep.

And, eventually, he did.

Sighing, Meena rolled over, facing the wall. It was a dark night, but she could still make out the indentations in the stones. It reminded her of Varna's chamber, and she thought of her grandmother and her aunt. Both women had been so desperate to get their claw-like hands on the Book of Darkness. And if Morana recovered, the book would be hers. Jaeger would make her use it to cause pain and death. To kill everyone who stood in his way.

Including Berard.

But if she tried to take the book? If she took it and ran, tried to find her way to Andala, what then?

Draguta would see her.

She would watch her, follow her, take it herself, Meena was sure.

And then no one would be safe.

***

Draguta was growing impatient with Evaine, and though it was usually no effort to hold a trance, she felt dizzy, struggling to think. 'You will do it!' she barked irritably, 'for I have Eadmund here, with me. And if you want to be with him again, you will get my book and bring it to me. Eadmund is waiting for you to come, Evaine. But he will not wait long before he turns around and heads straight back to his wife!'

'But, but...' Evaine panicked. 'How? How will I get it to you? I don't even know where you are!'

'Flane,' Draguta said. 'We are in a town called Flane. Take a horse and leave the city. Ride out past the stones. Turn left once you pass them. At the first village you come to, ask where Flane is. Take your father's coins. Pay for someone to help you. Guide you. You are not useless, Evaine, despite what everyone thinks. You're more than capable of completing this journey, as I did. Of bringing me what I need. What will help Eadmund stay safe from Jaeger and far away from his wife. Remember now, Jaeger wants to kill Eadmund and take you for himself. And Jael Furyck...' Draguta couldn't help but smile, almost feeling her life slipping away. 'You don't want Eadmund to give up waiting for you, do you?'

Evaine glanced around. She was standing in her father's house, still wearing her wedding gown, but now she knew that it was all a dream and if she wanted to make it a reality, she was going to have to follow Draguta's orders.

'I must go!' Draguta snapped. 'You will do everything in your power to get that book to me quickly. Take a knife with you, and use it if anyone tries to stop you. You're very experienced with knives, aren't you, Evaine, so I don't think you'll have a problem!'

CHAPTER FIVE

For the first time, Astrid was certain she looked as worried as she felt. 'The fever has a hold on Jael. It will not let her go,' she said quietly to Aleksander. 'Or perhaps...'

'Perhaps what?' Thorgils wondered, creaking anxiously in a chair by the fire.

Astrid glanced at Jael, leading Aleksander over to Thorgils. 'Perhaps she is not fighting it? Perhaps she doesn't want to get well? She lost such a lot of blood. It has weakened her body, and the loss of the baby has weakened her spirit. And she needs both to recover.'

The men frowned.

'That's not Jael,' Aleksander insisted.

Thorgils nodded vigorously. 'Jael knows what she has to do. What danger we're all in. She wouldn't give up. Nothing would stop her coming back. She'll fight. You don't know her as we do.'

Astrid smiled sympathetically at them, seeing both their concern and their affection for Jael Furyck. 'Well, I hope you're right. All I can do is keep giving her the tincture. I will bring a broth too. I left it stewing away overnight. I'll bring that later, and perhaps she will be well enough to try some?' She headed for her basket.

Aleksander wished she wasn't going. 'Should we let her sleep or try to wake her?'

'There's no reason to wake her,' Astrid said softly. 'Jael must find her way back to you on her own.'

***

'Mother?'

Gisila and Branwyn were waiting at the bottom of the path when Edela opened her cottage door.

'Have you been there all night?' Edela muttered, already anticipating the fussing that was about to begin. 'Waiting to pounce?'

'Well, Gant did mention that he'd found you sleeping by Furia's Tree,' Gisila said with a frown. 'And in the rain, no less.'

'And if I am?' Edela countered. 'I'm not some dribbling mess who needs to be tied to a chair as it stands, so if I want to sleep in the rain, I shall!' And opening the gate, she bustled away, ignoring them both.

'Edela!' Biddy came rushing down the path after her, Edela's cloak in her hands. 'Where are you going?'

Gisila and Branwyn stared at their quickly disappearing mother in surprise before hurrying after her.

***

'You will bring Sitha to me,' Jaeger ordered, glaring at Else, who stared back at him, her usual pleasant smile undisturbed by his moody scowl. 'I want to hear her thoughts on Morana. And yours. But not until you return with Sitha. I will make a decision about how to proceed then.'

Meena gulped.

Jaeger noticed. 'Did you have a dream last night?'

Meena stopped herself from lying because she was so terrible at it. 'Yes.'

Jaeger dropped his spoon and picked up his wine. 'About?'

'Draguta.'

Jaeger's eyes widened, the silver rim of the goblet almost touching his lips. 'And?' He spun around, pointing an open-mouthed Else to the door. 'Get on your way, woman! This conversation isn't for your old ears!'

Else blinked, quickly heading for the door.

Meena watched her go, trying to think of something to say. 'Draguta... she was alive in my dream. She looked the same. The same as she did before –'

'And where was she?'

'In a house. A bed. I don't know where she was.'

'And what was she doing?'

'Sleeping.'

Jaeger frowned. 'Dreaming, you mean?'

Meena dropped her head. 'I couldn't say.'

'*You* killed her,' Jaeger reminded her, sipping his wine. 'I may have thrown the knife, but you made sure it killed her. I saw that, Meena. I watched you plunge it into her. You don't want her to return, do you? To take her revenge on you?'

Meena shook her head, hair trembling around her face. 'No.'

'Then we must work together, for if Draguta returns to the castle, the first person she'll kill is me, and then, without me to protect you, she will quickly kill you. And if you want to live, Meena, you're going to have to start telling me the truth. So what did you *really* dream about last night?'

***

Morac was eager to see how Morana was.

Evaine wasn't.

'Are you sure you don't want to come?' Morac asked, holding open the cottage door, disappointed by the intense wall of humidity that greeted him. He wondered if he should go back inside and find something cooler to wear.

'I don't want to run into Jaeger.'

Morac sucked in a breath, immediately irate. 'No, well, nor do I, but I'm keen to see how Morana is. We need her to come back. She can't protect us from Jaeger or Draguta while she sits there, weakening with every passing day.'

'Perhaps Draguta put a spell on her? Perhaps she'll never be the same again? She doesn't look the same. Her face is all droopy. She doesn't even know anyone's there.'

It was what Morac feared most of all.

He didn't know what he'd do without his sister, without The Following, without any purpose and no protection. At the mercy of Jaeger Dragos. Waiting for Draguta to take her revenge upon them all. He looked at his daughter, seeing the fear in her eyes. 'Morana is a strong woman. She will come back to us. She'll find a way to protect us. And Eadmund. He will be here soon, won't he?'

But Evaine just turned away, wanting him to go. She needed to start thinking about how she was going to get out of Hest.

***

It was a chilly morning, but the sky had a glow to it that told Edela it was going to warm up soon, though in her impatience to leave the cottage, she wished she'd remembered to bring her cloak.

Rork Arnesson opened a hall door, holding it as Edela

headed inside, nodding briefly to him. He nodded back, his lips set in a straight line, no smile in his eyes.

'Grandmother!' Axl stood up from his throne and strode towards her, leaving his crutch behind. His leg had healed enough now that walking was almost comfortable, and he was eager to look as competent as he wanted to feel. 'Are you alright? Gant said he'd –'

'I know, I know,' Edela muttered. 'It appears that Gant Olborn has a bigger mouth than I'd realised.' She saw Gant and winked at him.

Gant smiled back, pleased to see that Edela was in such a fiery mood.

It was a good sign.

'We need to talk about what is coming,' Edela said, easing herself down onto the bench beside Amma. She glanced at the hotcake Amma was eating, realising that her cloak wasn't the only thing she'd left the cottage without.

'Have you had a dream?' Amma asked, quickly pushing away her plate.

Edela nodded, listening as the hall quietened around her. 'I have. And I'm afraid that it is not good news.'

Axl was immediately at Edela's side, eager to hear what his grandmother had to say.

As was everyone else.

'Perhaps we should talk in your chamber?' Edela wondered before realising that secret-keeping was a bad habit that wouldn't help them now. 'No, no, let me speak plainly.' She took a deep breath. 'Your sister is very ill.'

'What?' Axl froze.

Gisila and Branwyn had just entered the hall, and they both quickened their pace to the high table.

'What has happened?' Gisila demanded, her chest tightening. 'Where is Jael?'

'She's with Thorgils and Aleksander,' Edela said, smiling briefly at Isaura, who was standing nearby, Mads on her hip. 'I don't know where, but she's in bed. I saw her.'

'What happened to her?' Gant frowned, taking a seat next to Edela, worry etched onto his tired face. 'Is she injured?'

Edela avoided everyone's eyes. 'Well, yes, she looked injured. Bruised. But also... unwell. She can't get out of bed. She's being cared for by a healer.'

Axl rubbed his eyes, struggling to think. 'Does she have the book? The Book of Aurea? Did they get it?'

'Yes, I believe so.'

'But you don't know where she is or what's wrong with her?'

'No.'

The hall was completely silent. No one knew what to say.

Jael was supposed to lead them. Save them. But now?

'That is not all,' Edela said carefully. 'I've seen those creatures again. The dragur. We have to prepare ourselves. They will come here soon, and you, my grandson, are going to have to come up with a way to stop them. It won't be easy to defeat them.'

Axl glanced at Fyn, who had walked in from the bedchambers with Runa. He blinked, realising that Gant was talking to him. 'What did you say?'

'Sea-fire,' Gant repeated. 'We need to make as much sea-fire as we can. It may be the only way to hold them out.'

Edela nodded. 'I agree. They hate fire, so we must make more, and quickly. Every time I think of those creatures, my heart races. I feel as though they're waiting out there, preparing their attack.'

'We need to work the men harder too,' Axl said, thinking out loud. 'We need to prepare as an army.'

'We do,' Gant murmured, nodding to Karsten and Berard Dragos as they entered the hall. 'And we have little time to do it, so we're going to need all the help we can get.'

***

Evaine couldn't think, yet she had an overwhelming need to.

Draguta wanted the book, and Evaine wanted Eadmund, and neither of those things could be achieved if she couldn't find a way out of Hest. She knew where the stables were, of course, and she could take a horse. It wouldn't be easy or pleasant, but she could ride.

But how to do it without being discovered?

Sighing, she hurried towards the markets, wishing that Morana was herself again. She needed advice. Yet, Morana wouldn't want her to take the book, and her father wouldn't want her to leave Hest.

There was no one to turn to now.

No one but Eadmund. And she had to get to him quickly, before he grew tired of waiting for her.

Evaine pushed through the crowd, ignoring the imploring cries of the merchants she bustled past. Coins jingled in her purse, and she would need to spend all of them to prepare for her journey.

Draguta's urgent voice pulsed in her veins, reminding Evaine that she had little time to waste.

***

'How long do you think Evaine will take to get here?' Eadmund wondered as he finished his breakfast. He was well-rested after a deep sleep, but his mind was unsettled. Without Evaine, he felt on edge. He was worried about her too. What Draguta expected her to do seemed too much for someone like Evaine, who had been coddled and pampered all her life.

'Take?' Draguta stretched her arms above her head, yawning. The dire bed in the dire shack was worse than sleeping on the dirt floor, she was sure. Evaine could not come soon enough. 'I have no idea, but we can only hope that the answer is not long.' She stared at Eadmund's perturbed face. 'And in the meantime, I have plans for you. Something to take your mind off Evaine.'

Eadmund frowned, not wanting his mind taken off Evaine at all. 'What sort of plans?'

Smiling, Draguta stood and smoothed down her dress. Not silk. There were no fine fabrics in Flane, but the pale colour of the linen was, at least, flattering, and it would do until she returned to Hest. 'Come along, then, and I will show you what I have in mind.'

***

'Are you sure you should be up?' Aleksander wondered as Thorgils limped into the stables, his crutch tapping the hard dirt floor.

'Astrid kicked me out. For all that they're supposed to help people, healers tend to be quite bossy, I find.'

Aleksander smiled, thinking of Biddy and Edela as he held out a carrot for Tig.

'How are the horses?' Thorgils wondered, glancing around the small stable block. He recognised Aleksander's horse next to Tig, and the big white stallion who'd heroically carried them all the way from Hallow Wood. 'Hello, Gus.'

'They look ready to leave, even Gus, which is good news for us. Though I've another horse here,' he said, pointing to the dark-brown stallion in the next stall. 'He's for you. His name's Rufus.'

Thorgils ran his hand down Rufus' dark muzzle, looking him over, wishing he'd thought to bring a treat. 'He's big enough to deal with me, I suppose.'

'I'm sure Gus will be relieved to hear it,' Aleksander smiled, moving over to give Sky a carrot. 'Gant too. He wouldn't want us bringing back a broken horse.'

Thorgils looked anxious, his mind quickly returning to the night of the dragon and the fire and the fear of losing everyone he loved. He hoped Bram was recovering, and that Isaura wasn't worrying too much. 'You think they're alright there, in the fort?'

Aleksander shrugged. 'I don't know, but I hope so. I hope they can hold on until we get Jael back on her feet. We're all going to need her, and her sword.'

Rufus' breath was warm on Thorgils' hand, and he smiled. 'Mmmm, we're going to need Jael's help, but for now, maybe she needs ours?'

'Maybe,' Aleksander said mutely. 'She's not one for help, though. No matter how bad things get, Jael always prefers to help herself.'

***

Biddy arrived with Eydis and the puppies, and Gant and Axl left them with Edela, deciding that they needed to examine the sea-fire stores. Fyn, who was mending well and using a crutch to get around now, tagged along.

'What do you think happened to Jael?' he asked anxiously, having heard Edela's news from Axl. 'It's not like her to be unwell, is it?'

Gant shook his head. 'No. Never. Not Jael.' He glanced at Axl, keeping his voice low. 'I've a feeling Edela knew more than she was letting on.'

Axl nodded. 'So do I, but we can't do anything about it either way. We have to prepare the fort and the men for when she does return, which will hopefully be before the dragur come.'

'But we also need to start thinking about what we'll do if Jael doesn't come back,' Gant muttered.

Fyn swallowed. 'Jael will come back!'

'I hope so,' Gant said. 'But if she doesn't? Our plan can't be to just sit here and wait for all the creatures to crawl out of the Book of Darkness. We have to decide what we're going to do about it. Until that book is out of Draguta's hands, none of us are safe.'

'We unite our army with Iskavall's and march on Helsabor together,' Axl suggested. 'Wulf Halvardar would listen to us. He'd let us in, wouldn't he?'

'Ha!' Gant snorted. 'Not likely. If that old goat heard about a book that powerful, he'd send his sons to claim it for themselves. Find a way to make more gold. He's never helped anyone in his life that I know of, except himself. The only thing he'll unlock his gates for is treasure, and we don't have nearly enough to tempt him with. Not after the mess Lothar made of things.'

The fort looked and smelled like a charred midden heap, and as they walked past the flattened buildings, now just sticks and ash, it was hard not to feel despondent, especially when they lifted their eyes a little higher and saw the crumbling hole where the last bits of the decomposing dragon were being removed from the wall.

If the dragur were coming, they weren't going to have much trouble getting into the fort at all.

***

'His name is Ollvar, or something like that,' Draguta said,

pointing at the bare-chested, tattooed warrior who stood before them. 'He is going to be training you.'

Eadmund started to protest.

'You think you can beat Ollvar, here? Go ahead, and if you do, I won't insist you train with him. Defeat him, and you shall be my champion, free to pine endlessly for Evaine,' Draguta smiled.

The heavily scarred warrior, whose name was, in fact, Rollo Barda, eyed Eadmund with disdain. He had a wide mouth but such thin lips that it was hard to tell if he was smiling or grimacing. His big head was clean-shaven, shining in the glare of the morning sun, much like his oiled chest, which he was proud to display. His thick arms were powerful, rippled with wounds, old and new, hiding amongst a smattering of roughly-drawn blue tattoos that crept all the way up to his neck, curling around his ears like dragon prows.

He considered Eadmund with a raised eyebrow and a cold sneer.

Eadmund blinked, ignoring the hairless beast as he turned to Draguta. 'Fine. As you say, it will give me something to do while we wait for Evaine.'

'Well, I don't say that,' Draguta cooed. 'Not at all. I require you to train hard, Eadmund. All day, every day. When Evaine is here as well. I have a very particular purpose for you, and you will not be able to fulfill it if you sit around turning back into a useless ball of blubber.'

Eadmund wanted to ask what she meant, but Rollo slapped him on the shoulder, grunting. 'Come on, then. Better to train now before it gets too hot.'

Draguta spun around, lifting the hem of her dress, ready to leave the stench of the training ground behind; eager to return to her seeing circle to watch the painfully slow demise of Jael Furyck.

***

Sitha had healed Jaeger's ankles well enough, but she seemed incapable of helping Morana, which she freely admitted herself. 'What Draguta did to her caused some sort of... apoplexy,' she said in a calm monotone. She was a gaunt, elderly woman with wisps of fine, silvery hair that fell down to a pair of lop-sided shoulders. They drooped even further to the left as she considered the king. Having known his temper since he was a boy, Sitha was well aware of how violent he could become when provoked.

She had seen what he did to his first wife.

Varna.

His father.

Evaine.

'And?' Jaeger looked away from her morbid face towards Else's sunny one. 'What help is there for such a thing?'

'No help that I am aware of, my lord,' Sitha declared, glancing at Else herself, daring her to produce a different opinion.

But Else didn't. 'An apoplexy seems about right to me. One side of her face appears frozen. She seems to have lost the sight in that eye as well. It has a milky film over it. It doesn't respond at all.'

'I've seen her smile. She's responded to me. To what I've said,' Jaeger insisted, displeased with both old women, who obviously had no wits between them anymore. 'There must be something you can do?'

'She has no fever, my lord. No illness. She is out of bed. Recovered. But she is changed. There is nothing to heal,' Sitha said. 'She is not ill.'

'Perhaps it's not healing she needs now, my lord?' Else suggested carefully. 'Perhaps it's magic?'

Meena, who had been stuck at the table, trying to make sense of the book, lifted her head, not sure what Else was up to. Jaeger narrowed his eyes. 'Magic?'

***

Thorgils clenched his teeth and lifted his arm. He was holding his sword, trying to become comfortable with the weight of it again. If only Eadmund had aimed for his other shoulder, he thought with a grin. It faded quickly, though, as he thought of his friend, wondering what would happen to him now.

Wondering how they were ever going to get him back without Jael's help.

Thorgils frowned, annoyed with himself, trying to stop his mind from wandering towards the shadows.

'Don't let Astrid catch you doing that,' Aleksander said, coming through the door. 'You'll have your stitches out for sure.'

'My shoulder's fine,' Thorgils lied. 'Good as new!'

Aleksander looked doubtful as he approached the bed.

Jael opened her eyes, staring at him.

He smiled at her in surprise. 'You're awake.'

Jael blinked, not sure that she was. Maybe it was another dream? She'd been having so many of those. Her mouth felt too dry to speak, her eyes too sore to keep open for long.

'You need to stay still,' Aleksander murmured, trying to keep her calm. He could see the panic in her eyes; the confusion. 'Just rest. You have to get your strength back.'

'I need to get up,' Jael croaked. 'We have to go home.' She frowned. 'The baby. I have to...' Her eyes closed again.

'Just rest, Jael,' Thorgils smiled, hobbling towards the bed. 'We'll go home when you're ready.' He glanced at Aleksander, whose face reflected the worry on his. It was hard to see Jael so lifeless, and though it was encouraging that she had opened her eyes, she appeared too weak to stay awake for long.

'Home,' Jael whispered faintly. 'Need to go home.'

And she fell back into her dreams.

CHAPTER SIX

'There is another type of magic,' Else began, wondering what tangled mess she was weaving for them all, but she saw the interest in Jaeger's eyes, realising that she could hardly back out of it now. Though Meena's rapidly opening and closing mouth gave her pause. 'Magic that doesn't come from your book. Old magic.'

'And who knows that?' Jaeger asked.

'Dragmall,' Else said. 'Your father's volka. He came from Helsabor. A kingdom of wealth and gold, but also a kingdom of many forests. Of thick woodland. Of the creatures that make it their home. He knows a particular type of magic that comes from those places. Similar to that of the Tuurans.'

'And how do you know this?'

Else blushed. 'Long ago we were friends, he and I. Perhaps I could go and see him? Talk to him? He rarely leaves his cave these days, I know, but Dragmall would listen to me. He trusts me.'

Jaeger scowled at her, tempted but suspicious. There was something about the old woman that niggled at him. He was convinced that she was keeping secrets, but he would never find out what they were if he didn't encourage her trust. 'Go then. Go and see Dragmall, but take Meena with you.'

He turned from Else to Meena, not noticing the great relief that washed over Else's face.

'Find out what Dragmall thinks,' Jaeger instructed Meena. 'Take him to Morana if he believes that he can help her. We need to try everything possible to bring her back. Make him realise how important it is. How little time there is.' Ignoring the pain in his aching jaw, which he'd been clenching all day, Jaeger placed his hands on Meena's shoulders, demanding her attention. 'And when you return, you will tell me everything he said. I want to know all of it. There will be no secret-keeping, will there, Meena?'

Meena nodded as Jaeger turned away, her eyes meeting Else's.

Both of them swallowing.

***

Karsten wasn't sure how to feel about the news that Jael Furyck was ill or injured. Stuck somewhere, unable to come back to Andala.

He wasn't sure at all.

He hated the smug, fame-hungry bitch, but she was also their leader, the one with the visions, the one the gods favoured. The woman who would find a way back to Hest so they could take the book and kill Jaeger.

She was a dreamer. A warrior. A woman with answers.

And to lose her now?

Karsten wasn't sure how he felt about that at all.

Berard looked worried. 'But what will we do now?' he wondered as they walked back to the new cottage they'd been assigned after being released from the ship shed. None of them had shown any signs of the sickness, much to their relief, so Nicolene and Bayla had been busy trying to make the most of the smaller, less comfortable cottage while caring for five very miserable children.

'You think we need *her*?' Karsten snarled, though he felt odd himself.

'I think Jael knows what's happening, and we don't,' Berard said. 'She sees what will come. Without her, we're weaker for sure.'

'Don't panic yet, Berard. Knowing her, she'll return. And likely just in time, claiming all the glory for herself.'

Berard frowned. 'Why do you hate Jael so much? You don't even know her.'

Karsten turned to his brother, pointing to his eyepatch.

'Yes, but that was in a battle. She wasn't seeking to cut out your eye, Karsten. You were in a fight! She caught your eye with her sword. It could've been your cheek. It could've been *her* eye. She didn't do it on purpose!'

After navigating their way through the rows of thatch-roofed cottages, they finally arrived at their own, but Karsten wasn't ready to go inside, not wanting to face their mother yet. 'You know that, do you? Sure about that, are you?'

'I'm not sure about anything that happens in someone else's head, but I don't think Jael's that sort of person. From what I've seen, she seems fair. Decent. She is a queen. Ranuf Furyck's daughter. And he was a king with honour.'

It was Karsten's turn to frown, imagining what their father would have made of that statement. Haaron would likely have spat and snarled, though perhaps he would have agreed? Ranuf Furyck had been a sanctimonious king, but strong. Annoyingly strong. In all the years of trying, they'd never defeated him or his equally annoying daughter.

'Perhaps,' Karsten grunted. 'Perhaps we'll never know? If she doesn't come back, that is.' They heard a sudden loud wail that had Karsten closing his eye. 'Although, if Jael doesn't come back, it might take us a lot longer to get to Hest. Her brother hasn't much clue about what he's doing, even with that old man advising him. Maybe it's time you and I thought about what *we* could do? Why do we need to wait on them? Get me into Hest, and I'll have Jaeger on the end of my sword before he's even taken a breath.'

Berard grabbed Karsten's arm. 'Jaeger has that woman with him. You can't think you could make it there on your own? That *we* could? You're not thinking, Karsten. If we even made it that far, Jaeger would kill us both as soon as we stepped into the city, and what good would that do anyone?' Kai's screaming was getting louder, but Berard wasn't letting his brother go just yet. 'If you want to save our family, if you want a chance of claiming the throne for yourself, you can't be reckless. Reckless will get us all killed!'

Karsten shook off Berard's hand.

Berard reminded him of Haegen, and Haegen had always been trying to stop him. Always so cautious. Timid.

And where had that gotten them?

Karsten leaned in, watching as Ulf approached with one of his men. 'We can't sit around and wait to die,' he growled. 'It's Jaeger whose responsible for all of this, so we should be the ones to stop him!' And disappearing into the cottage, he left Berard to wait for Ulf, who was already smoothing down his beard in anticipation of seeing Bayla.

Berard turned to him with a wobbly smile, trying to get Karsten's words out of his head, knowing that if his brother did something stupid to get himself killed, he would be the only Dragos left to stop Jaeger.

***

Draguta was victorious.

Her one true enemy was powerless. Well, she had many enemies, she supposed, but Eadmund was with her now, and

Jaeger was impotent without Morana, who was impotent herself. Draguta couldn't stop smiling as she stared into her seeing circle, watching the pathetic figure of Jael Furyck.

So pale. So ill.

So helpless.

It was the perfect moment to finish her.

Jael blinked, watching over the woman's shoulder, trying to see what she was looking at. Edging closer, she peered into the circle of blood-red symbols, but there was nothing to see, only the dark surface of the wooden table.

But the woman could see something, Jael was certain.

She was watching something. Someone.

Her?

Shivering, Jael glanced around, trying to see where she was. The cottage was no more than a hovel, but the woman? She looked like an elegant lady. A dreamer. Jael frowned, puzzled, turning as the door opened.

As Eadmund walked in.

Jael's mouth fell open, her heart pounding.

He was bright red, dripping with sweat, his tunic wet through, clinging to him.

Draguta jumped, blinking herself out of the trance. 'Why are you back?' she snapped, trying to focus on Eadmund.

'Why?' He looked confused, pouring himself a cup of wine, there being nothing else to drink that he could see. 'I've finished training.'

'Already? Well, let that be the *first* session of the day, then. You must become better than that hulking beast out there. Better than any man here. I want you to defeat every one of them. You must be capable of that and more, Eadmund. Capable of defeating Jaeger Dragos himself.'

'I hardly think that'd take much work. Jael defeated him easily enough.'

Jael shivered, hearing the detachment in Eadmund's voice. He sounded so cold.

Draguta snorted. 'So I've heard, but I don't believe Jaeger was at his best that day. Your wife was lucky to face such a weakened opponent. But now that he is reunited with the book, it will be making him more powerful than before. Much more.' She jammed her teeth together at the thought of Jaeger touching her book; claiming its power for himself. 'That is its gift, you know. Power. And if we allow the book to remain in Jaeger's hands, his power will only grow.' She shuddered, her body jerking violently. 'And after what he did to me? Trying to kill me? He thought that he could *kill* me?' Her voice rose, her pale cheeks turning as red as her lips. 'He made a mistake that night, though. They all did. And when Evaine arrives with what I need, Jaeger will find out just how much of a mistake it was.'

Jael frowned, trying to make sense of everything, but it was hard to keep her focus. She wanted to reach out and touch Eadmund, to turn his head, to make him look into her eyes. To see her. But everything started to fade, and she panicked, wanting to stay in the dream.

There was more she needed to know.

'Find something to eat,' Draguta grumbled, her patience wearing. 'Rest if you must, but then you will go and train again, Eadmund. Again and again. I will need you by my side for what is to come.'

It was Eadmund's turn to feel annoyed. 'But, Draguta –'

Jael gasped, and everything went black.

***

'Eadmund.'

Astrid leaned over the bed, feeling Jael's head, watching her. She appeared to be dreaming. 'Ssshhh,' she murmured, running a hand over Jael's dark hair. 'Ssshhh.'

'How is she?' Thorgils wondered from a chair by the fire.

'Much cooler,' Astrid smiled, pleased by the sudden drop in Jael's temperature.

Thorgils let out a loud sigh, sitting back. 'That's good news.'

'I hope so,' Astrid said, straightening up. 'I'll go and make more of that tincture, but before I do, let me look at those stitches of yours again.'

'They're fine,' Thorgils muttered dismissively. 'Go and make the tincture. It's Jael you need to worry about. Not me.'

'Perhaps, but you're not going to be much use to her if your wounds fester, are you?'

Thorgils relented, standing up, easing his tunic over his head, grimacing at the pain of lifting his arm. He looked down at his shoulder wound, pleased to see that the flesh around the stitches was no longer an angry red.

Astrid frowned. 'Don't be too impatient to go to war. You need to give the wound a chance to heal first. The stitches won't hold if you start swinging a sword before it's healed.'

Thorgils grinned. 'Well, I don't know about that. Seems to me you did a good job. They don't look like they're going anywhere.'

'Perhaps,' Astrid muttered, pointing to his trousers. 'Now, let's see the other one.'

Jael could hear them.

Her eyes were closed, and no matter how hard she tried, she couldn't make them open. Eventually, Astrid's and Thorgils' voices became a buzzing drone in the distance as her mind wandered back to Eadmund.

Eadmund, who was with Draguta, which was surely worse than Eadmund being with Evaine.

She had to find him in her dreams again.

She needed to see where he was.

***

73

Once the old healer and Jaeger's servant had left Morana's chamber, Evaine had locked the door and hurried to a bed, laying out everything she'd bought at the markets, ignoring Morana, who sat in a chair by the flameless fire pit, not appearing to notice her at all.

She had purchased a large leather satchel, into which she'd stuffed a waterskin, a wrapped wedge of hard cheese, slivers of salt fish, a small rye loaf, and a side of pork. There was a tinderbox, a new, bigger knife – which had come with its own whetstone and scabbard – and a pouch full of silver coins she had taken from Morac's cottage. Evaine frowned, realising that she would need to grab a fur to sleep on too; not wanting to imagine the deprivations she would have to endure trying to find her way to Flane.

But none of it would even be possible if she couldn't get the book for Draguta.

The door rattled, and Evaine jerked upright, quickly shoving everything back into the satchel, pushing it under the bed. Standing up, she smoothed down her dress, brushed loose strands of hair out of her eyes and strode to the door. 'Who is it?'

'Who *is* it?'

Evaine shivered, recognising the voice. She turned the key, reluctantly pulling open the door.

'Why did you lock the door?' Jaeger growled, running his eyes over Evaine's breasts, remembering the sweet taste of her. 'What are you up to in here?'

Evaine swallowed as Jaeger stepped into the reeking chamber, trying to meet his eyes. 'Morana needs peace. She needs to recover. Everyone has been in and out all day long. It was too much for her, so I locked the door to give her some privacy.'

'You actually care for someone besides yourself? I find that hard to believe,' Jaeger laughed, walking over to Morana's chair. He could quickly see that nothing had changed, apart from the smell of the place, which had intensified in its foulness. 'And why is that?' Turning sharply, Jaeger rounded on her. 'Why do you care whether Morana lives or dies? Do you think she can keep you safe from me?' And he ran a hand over Evaine's shining blonde hair, bleached lighter by the intense glare of the Hestian sun.

Evaine held his gaze as Jaeger grabbed a handful of her hair, yanking her towards him.

'No one can keep you safe from me,' Jaeger whispered hoarsely, his eyes boring into hers. 'Especially not Eadmund. When he arrives, if he hasn't changed his mind about you and headed back to his wife, I will kill him. And make you watch.' He didn't blink as he released Evaine, pushing her away from him. 'I am the King of Hest, and everything in this kingdom belongs to me. Including you. Including that door, so don't lock it again. Do you understand me?'

Evaine stumbled, nodding, hoping that was the end of it. Her mind was quickly jumping around to what else she needed to gather before she could escape. A horse was surely easy enough. But the book...

How was she going to get the book?

Jaeger cracked his neck as he turned back to Morana, eager to see any sign of a recovery. He bent forward, prodding her shoulder. She twitched but didn't look towards him. He saw drool pooling at one side of her mouth, her lips twisted down unnaturally, matching the drooping right eye above it, which had indeed turned milky white.

There was no doubting that Draguta had done something to Morana, and as much as Jaeger pretended not to care, he knew that he needed her. Meena wasn't ready to read the book – in his heart, he knew that – yet the book was calling to him, desperate to be unleashed again.

He had to find a way to use it before Draguta returned.

***

Meena hurried alongside Else as they left the castle behind. She felt as though she was being watched, which was odd, she knew. Draguta was gone, and Morana was incapable of even moving by herself, but still, Meena felt wary.

And she didn't know what Else was up to.

Luckily enough, though, Else did.

'I almost married Dragmall,' she smiled wistfully, her old eyes seeking out long-forgotten memories in the scenery they passed; remembering a time when she would hurry away from the castle to meet him. 'I was very young. Besotted with him. He was newly arrived from Helsabor, and he knew a great many things. His father was King Wulf's volka, which was partly why he came here, as he knew that there was no chance to further himself while his father lived.'

Meena stumbled on a loose cobblestone, biting her tongue in surprise. 'Why didn't you marry him?' she wondered, grimacing as she tasted blood.

Else sighed. 'My father. He had no love of magic and mystery. Not as I did. I wanted to be a dreamer as a girl. A healer. A witch. Something exciting. I had no real skill, though. No talent at all. My mother let me help her with her healing, but she died when I was quite young, and my father put me into service. I've been a servant in the castle ever since. It kept my father happy and well cared for in his final days, but I often wonder what would have been if I had stayed with Dragmall.'

'He never married, did he?'

'No. He preferred his own company, even when I was with him, so I suppose it worked out best for all of us.'

They'd walked far away from the castle now, past the markets and the cliffs dotted with tiny stone cottages. Past the crowded, narrow roads of the city, across the causeway and up the red-dust path that wound its way into the hills where Dragmall made his home.

Else frowned, thinking of how long it had been since she'd seen him.

Hoping she could trust him.

***

The men in the training ring were loud, grunting and bellowing as they cracked their wooden swords and staffs into one another. Gant barely noticed as he walked past with Ivaar Skalleson and Karsten Dragos.

Not the sort of allies Ranuf would have been happy with.

But then Ranuf hadn't had to face serpents or dragons or a magic book, Gant thought with a wry smile.

'And if we don't have the Iskavallans?' Ivaar was asking. 'If they change their minds? What then?'

'We'll have them,' Gant assured him, scanning the square, wondering where Axl had gone. 'Raymon Vandaal has already indicated that he wants to help us. We only need to work out the terms, and once Jael is back, we'll do just that.'

Karsten frowned. '*If* she comes back.'

Gant glared at him. 'You know something I don't?'

'Only what's been said. It doesn't sound good.'

'You needn't worry about Jael,' Gant snapped. 'You should worry about your men.'

Karsten looked confused. '*My* men?'

'You're a leader, and a leader needs men. Ivaar has his own men, and until Jael comes back, the rest of the Islanders are his.'

Ivaar blinked, surprised by that news; certain that the newly arrived Island lords wouldn't be impressed to hear it.

'I've put together a group of Andalans and Tuurans who'll

be under your command,' Gant said, pointing to the huddle of men, who stood to one side of the new sea-fire shed looking decidedly unimpressed by the idea of being Karsten Dragos' men. 'You'll be responsible for training them. Organising them. They will answer to you, and you will answer to me. And I will answer to Axl.'

'And if Jael comes back?' Ivaar wondered.

'*When* Jael comes back,' Gant said, glowering at them both, 'we'll all answer to her. Every single one of us, including Raymon Vandaal. Anyone who wants to live that is.' He turned to Ivaar. 'The Islanders are busy with the dragon. Once Karsten's done sorting out his men, you can swap over. They need to learn what you expect from them. When the dragur attack, you'll need them organised. Fighting like a unit.'

But Karsten wasn't listening. He was too busy staring at the scowling group of men, who he could tell were not relishing the thought of having a Hestian lead them. Most were Andalans who had fought in Valder's Pass, watching as their friends died, slaughtered by Karsten and his men. And the Tuurans scattered amongst them knew well enough not to trust a Hestian. Aedan and Aron were standing with them. Kormac too.

But every man was going to be needed to fight against the dragur.

Every man, be it Tuuran or Brekkan, needed a leader. And Karsten knew that he was a good one.

He nodded, thinking of his father and Haegen. He'd always wanted to be in charge, convinced that his ideas were better than any of theirs.

And now he had the chance to prove it.

***

Jael opened her eyes, confused. She thought for a moment that she was on Oss. Or in Andala. Then she remembered the baby, and everything fell into place.

And she felt bereft.

'There you are,' Astrid murmured. 'I have some broth, if you feel up to eating something soon?'

Jael blinked, trying to nod, not wanting to eat anything, but knowing that she needed to. She needed to get up. She wanted to get out of bed and find Eadmund. But where was he? In Hest?

'Jael?' Aleksander was by her side, smiling at her. 'Here, have some water. It will help your throat.' He could see her struggling to swallow.

She took the cup in a shaking hand. 'We have to go home,' she rasped.

'You're not strong enough to even sit up yet,' Astrid said from behind Aleksander. 'You'll need more time. More rest.'

Jael frowned.

Aleksander smiled.

'Broth,' Jael croaked, sipping the water. 'Give me the broth.' Her stomach heaved, and she thought she might vomit. Handing Aleksander the cup, her head fell back onto the pillow.

She tried not to think about her daughter, knowing that she was there.

Somewhere.

Waiting.

'Tomorrow,' Jael whispered, closing her eyes. 'I'll be out of bed tomorrow.'

CHAPTER SEVEN

Getta had barely spoken to Raymon since the birth of their son, and Raymon was unable to think clearly because of it. He was caught between wanting a wife who approved of his decisions, and knowing that the decisions he needed to make would not please his wife.

But they would hopefully save his kingdom. If only Getta could see that.

At least he had his mother.

Ravenna smiled at her son as they stood in the doorway of the armourer's hut, watching him bellow at his apprentices, eager to impress the king with both the quality of his product and the workmanship of his men. 'She will come around in time. Motherhood can be daunting. Everything is new. Getta has much to occupy herself with right now.'

'She won't change her mind,' Raymon insisted, turning around with a weary sigh. He was waiting to try on his new mail shirt. It was raining, a light drizzle drifting across Ollsvik's square, and he frowned into it.

Ravenna pulled her hood up over her long golden hair, slipping her arm through Raymon's. 'She will soften eventually. Or, at least, she will come to see that it's more important to protect the kingdom than to pursue vengeance. Surely it can wait? Keeping your son safe is what is important now, no matter what alliances you must make to do so. Alliances aren't forever, as we Iskavallans know,' she smiled wryly. 'They only need to be useful for a time.'

Raymon nodded, watching the head of his army winding his way through the crowded square with a stranger. His shoulders tensed as the men walked towards them. 'Tolbert?'

'My lord,' Tolbert said, motioning for the man to step forward. 'Another messenger from Andala.'

Ravenna tightened her grip on her son's arm.

Raymon glanced around, noticing the many curious Iskavallans looking their way. 'Let us walk, somewhere we can speak freely.' And he indicated for the Andalan and Tolbert to follow him towards the harbour. 'What news do you bring?' he asked once they'd passed through the open gates, heading for the piers.

The lanky young man took a deep breath. 'The King of Brekka wishes to meet with you urgently, my lord. There has been... an attack. A new threat. A danger to both our kingdoms.'

Raymon frowned. The rain was settling in now, and he thought of going back to the hall, but he didn't want to see Getta. And he didn't want Getta to see the messenger. 'What threat?'

The young man dug into his pouch with dirty fingers, retrieving a crumpled scroll. 'Everything is in here, my lord.' He handed the scroll to Raymon, who swallowed, uncertain whether he wanted to know what had happened, but completely certain that whatever it was would only widen the great chasm between him and his wife.

***

'I want to know the truth, Mother,' Gisila demanded, not letting Edela past as she tried to turn down the road towards her cottage. 'Jael is my daughter. You can't keep it from me! Is it the sickness? Does she have the sickness?'

Edela had hoped to avoid her eldest daughter. She knew that Jael hated to be fussed over, and she had promised to keep her pregnancy a secret, but she could see the panic and worry in Gisila's eyes. Glancing around, she tugged her out of the way of a pair of horses pulling a cart of dragon bits towards the harbour gates. 'She has lost a baby.' The words brought tears to Edela's eyes again. The emotion she felt was raw; a confused mix of pain for Jael and anger at herself.

And the gods.

Though, she supposed, that was likely unfair.

Gisila gasped, her eyes round with surprise. '*Baby*? You knew she was pregnant?'

'I did, yes,' Edela murmured. 'And ssshhh, it is not for everyone's ears. That is Jael's secret to tell, not mine. I promised her that no one would know. Not even you. She didn't want her enemies finding out.'

Gisila nodded distractedly. 'But is she alright?'

'I'm not sure,' Edela admitted, worry creeping into her voice. 'She lost a lot of blood. I imagine it would have killed another woman, but Jael is quite stubborn, as we both know.' Edela tried to look more confident than she felt. She was plagued by doubts, and those doubts were growing louder than any other thought in her head.

How could she trust her dreams if even the gods were powerless against Draguta now?

'But do you see her coming home? Do you see her... surviving?'

Edela took a deep breath, feeling as troubled as Gisila looked. 'I... don't know.' It was honest but not reassuring to either of them.

'Oh.'

'But we both know Jael, so that is what we must hold onto now. Jael wouldn't abandon us, would she? She'll cling to life, however hard it is. She will not give in easily.'

***

Thorgils and Aleksander had escaped the cottage for a few cups of ale in the hall. It helped to pass the time, at first, but their minds were soon drawn back to the uncertainty of what was going to happen with Jael; worrying about how long they'd been away from Andala, and what might be happening in their absence.

'I've been thinking that you should go back,' Aleksander said. 'If you're well enough to ride on your own?'

Thorgils looked up from a surprisingly delicious bowl of mutton stew in surprise. 'Go back? To Andala?'

'You could tell them what's happened. Take the book to Edela.' Aleksander finally swallowed a doughy dumpling and reached for his ale. 'I need to stay with Jael. She might think she's getting out of bed tomorrow, but that doesn't look likely. If she keeps improving it will take a few days, at least, and I'm not sure we can wait that long.'

It wasn't a bad idea, Thorgils supposed, and he was eager to get back to Isaura, but he didn't want to leave Jael.

She hadn't left him.

Aleksander could sense his hesitation. 'Jael would want you to go. We both know that. The book needs to get to Edela. Everyone will be safer if she has it.'

Thorgils nodded. 'I will, then.' He didn't like saying it, though. 'In the morning.'

'Good. I think we'll need to get you one more horse. Best you don't break Rufus by pushing him too hard. I'll bring Gus back. Save him the pleasure of your giant arse.'

Thorgils grinned. 'Well, I'm not sure Gus would agree with you there. We have a bond, he and I.'

'Is that right? Gant wouldn't be happy to hear that. He's very protective of him. Gus is a beast in battle.'

'I can imagine.'

'Tomorrow, then,' Aleksander said, taking a long drink of ale, the remnants of the doughy dumpling stuck in his throat now.

'Tomorrow,' Thorgils sighed, feeling his stomach clench.

***

'Hmmm...' Dragmall retreated beneath his long white hair, which hung over his face as he bent forward. He was shy, uncomfortable around people. He liked his cave and his animals, the agreeable silence of solitude.

He frowned, remembering that he had once liked Else too.

'An apoplexy, you say?' Turning back to his shelf, he ran his eye over the various jars and bottles he had carefully balanced on it. Just enough so that it didn't tip one way or the other. 'There may be things I can do. Though, from what you've said, perhaps it is a curse...' He shuddered, having heard all about Draguta Teros. 'I suppose I could take a look and –'

'Good!' Else smiled from near the mouth of the cave. She was still dripping from the walk and not inclined to sit near the fire that was belching fragrant smoke from one end of the cave to the other. 'I shall tell the king to expect you tomorrow. Perhaps noon?'

Dragmall peered at Else in surprise. His cave was long but not especially high, and being a tall man, he'd become so used to bending over that he now had a permanent stoop. Though it didn't stop him brushing his head against the herbs drying in looping rows across the ceiling. 'I will be there. But now you must tell me why you've really come? It's not that long since I could almost read your mind, Else.'

Else blushed, turning to Meena, who hovered behind her. 'I

want you to protect Meena, here. She needs our help. The Book
of Darkness is in her chamber. It will try to claim her, won't it?
All that dark magic? It has surely claimed the king. He wasn't
this way before he found it.'

Dragmall blinked rapidly. He knew who Meena was. He'd
seen the mousey little creature shuffling behind Varna Gallas
since she was a girl. And he'd never liked Varna. She was evil
through and through.

But Meena?

He studied the trembling, twitching woman. 'Have you
ever been tattooed before?' he asked. 'It hurts, you know. Not
sure you look able to take such pain?'

'Tattooed?' Meena's eyes were wide. 'What do you mean?'
She looked at Else, wondering what they were both talking
about.

'Dragmall knows how to protect us from dark magic. He
tattooed me many years ago when he wanted to keep me safe
from your grandmother, who had a habit of doing things to
those she didn't like. And she didn't like Dragmall, and because
he liked me, Varna didn't like me either. So Dragmall tattooed
my arms with symbols of protection. It kept me safe.'

'But, but...' Meena's mind was whirring. 'Jaeger would see.
He would want to know what they were for. He would find
them.' Her cheeks reddened at the thought of it.

'Hmmm, yes, well that is true,' Else muttered, looking at
Dragmall.

'You could say they are for wisdom,' Dragmall suggested.
'The symbols of the old gods are powerful. You could say that
they will help you in your quest to read the book.'

Meena and Else stared at him.

'Well, I do see some things,' Dragmall said shyly. 'Hear
some things too. What Jaeger wants is no secret.' He turned to
Meena. 'You are wrong to think that you can defeat him and
the book and Draguta as well. There are others destined for
that dangerous fate. But you can make yourself safe, and you

should. You have a part to play, I'm sure. Tell Jaeger whatever you need to, but know that if you don't get tattooed, your soul will be consumed by that book as his has been.'

Meena stared at Dragmall for a moment, jumping as a fat white cat wound its way around her legs, miaowing loudly. She nodded. 'I will, then. Get tattooed. Please.'

***

Raymon hadn't even made it through the first line of Axl Furyck's note before Getta was snapping at him. 'You can't help them! If there is some danger, they brought it on themselves. The gods have cursed them for their murderous ways! You must remain here. Protect the fort. Your people. Our family!'

They were in bed, and although Getta was whispering, she was loud enough to wake their newborn son, who started whimpering. Leaning over his basket, Getta stuck her fingertip near Lothar's lips, and he started sucking it. 'You would think of putting our son in danger?'

'Of course not, which is why I'm going to meet with Axl Furyck. I have to find out how we can work together to stop any threat to Iskavall. To you and Lothar.' Raymon rolled over, wanting to be alone with his thoughts. He was beginning to discover how much clearer they became without his wife's voice in his ear.

'But he will just corrupt you!' Getta grumbled. 'Trick you. He wants your men. He wishes to destroy us all!'

Raymon closed his eyes. 'I must hear him out. I won't be a king hiding inside my fort, Getta. A weak king won't survive in this kingdom. I must show strength, and a willingness to fight for our people. I can't cower in my hall, hoping the danger won't find us.' He swallowed. The words came without thinking, but

Raymon felt his reluctance in the wake of them, knowing that the path he was heading down, he was surely heading down alone. He couldn't even hear Getta breathing, but he fought the urge to say any more. He would not keep her safe by being weak. And as much as he was desperate for her to stop being angry at him, he wasn't going to lose her by doing her bidding.

For if the threat Axl Furyck had described in his note was as dire as he suggested, none of them would be safe for long.

***

Jael had found her way back again.

To where, she didn't know, but Eadmund was there, slumped over the table, clearly exhausted. His plate had been only lightly picked at. He looked ready for bed.

Draguta didn't notice as she stared into her circle.

Draguta. It was Draguta. Jael knew that now. She wanted to stab *Toothpick* through her neck, take Eadmund and run, but there was no *Toothpick* in her scabbard, and she was as useless as a breath of wind.

'Perhaps sleep would help?' Draguta suggested, watching Eadmund's eyes close.

Eadmund jerked up, blinking. 'Who are you watching?' he wondered, ignoring her advice. 'Evaine?'

'No. I am watching your wife.'

'Why?'

Jael leaned over the table, again wanting to see something in the circle. Its symbols glowed like burning embers, but there was nothing inside them. Nothing that she could see at least.

'I am watching her die.'

Eadmund frowned. 'What?' He felt odd; a sharp pain in his chest. 'She's dying?'

Draguta kept her eyes on the circle. 'They think she is getting better, but she will die. I have seen it. The gods cannot help her, and she cannot help herself. Soon she will follow her baby onto a pyre. Perhaps they should just wait? Burn them at the same time? Save the wood.'

Eadmund's frown only deepened. 'Baby?' The clouds in his head were parting, and he saw Jael's green eyes blinking at him for the first time in days. He shuddered, his ears buzzing loudly.

'She never told you?' Draguta purred, looking up at last. 'No, I don't suppose she did. She didn't want it, did she? A woman like that? I've done her a great favour there. Perhaps she will thank me with her dying breaths?'

Eadmund stood, feeling disturbed. 'I think I'll get some sleep,' he muttered, turning away from Draguta, whose eyes were already back on her circle.

Draguta didn't answer. 'There was only going to be one winner, wasn't there, Jael?' she whispered. 'Against me?' And she laughed softly, feeling the warmth radiate in her chest like a midday sun. 'You really thought you could win?'

Jael knew that she was crying, but she couldn't feel the tears as they slid down her cheeks. She couldn't see them as they fell to the floor. Turning away from Draguta, she followed Eadmund to his bed. The cottage was small, but there was enough room for four short, narrow beds to hug the walls.

Eadmund groaned as he sat down on one, pulling off his dusty boots, feeling every overworked muscle; wondering why he'd subjected himself to such a hammering from the lipless giant that was Rollo Barda. He unbuckled his swordbelt, hanging it over the end of the bed. Reaching for his pouch, he pulled out the lock of Sigmund's hair. Draguta still had Evaine's stone, but just the feel of his son's hair made him remember what mattered most to him, and as he lay back on the bed, yawning, he closed his eyes, trying to find Evaine; all thoughts of Jael and the baby forgotten.

Jael watched him. She wanted to reach out and grab that

lock of hair, to take it out of his hands. Something about it had the hairs on her arms standing on end.

Eadmund was quickly asleep, though there was nothing new about that, she thought sadly, remembering the feel of his warm feet in their bed, the sound of his muffled snoring in her ear. She kept watching as his chest rose and fell, his breathing becoming rhythmic, and as his hand opened, the strap fell onto the floor.

And Jael could see the symbols etched into the leather.

***

Edela was quiet as Biddy tucked Eydis into bed. She could hear them murmuring to each other, fussing over the puppies, who wouldn't settle.

Just as Eydis wouldn't settle.

Everyone was on edge.

Edela stared into the flames, feeling the cosy warmth of fur beneath her back, thinking about Ayla. She remembered how Ayla had seen nothing but darkness in her dreams. Those words had a terrifying meaning to them now, and Edela felt a great sadness when she remembered how hard they had worked to help Jael and Aleksander find Thorgils. She wished she had known how sick Ayla had been.

She wished she'd sensed it.

Edela closed her eyes, wanting to feel her confidence return. Doubts swirled around her like a whirlpool, though, and she couldn't find anywhere to begin. But she needed to. Without Ayla's help, and without Jael and the Book of Aurea, she had to find the answers to all of their problems. Eydis would help, Edela knew, but it was a lot to ask of a young, untrained girl. She had to take on the responsibility herself. She had to find a way out of this darkness.

And as she finally drifted off to sleep, Edela was suddenly gripped by the very real fear that she couldn't.

***

Evaine closed her eyes, stretching out her legs. The bed was so short that her toes touched the wooden frame. It was uncomfortable, too, with its worn-out mattress, which had lost most of its stuffing. And then, of course, there was her father's constant fussing.

'I will look for somewhere new for us to stay tomorrow,' Morac muttered as he pulled back his fur and crawled into bed. 'We need more space than this. You must have your own privacy, and, as you say, going back to the castle is not advisable for either of us now. Perhaps we need to think about leaving Hest? I'm not sure what's happened to Eadmund, but as soon as he arrives, perhaps we should all go? Find a ship? There are merchant ships in the coves, from what I hear, and now the piers are growing they'll be able to moor in the harbour soon...' Morac's thoughts drifted back to his sister, not sure he could leave without her.

Evaine didn't answer. She was thinking about her plan.

Her plan for tomorrow.

She had been frustrated in her attempts to get into Jaeger's chamber, but tomorrow she had to find a way in, and a way out of the castle too. And as soon as she was out of the city, she would be on her way to Eadmund. The ache in her heart was deep, and she wanted to scream in frustration, but she didn't want her father to keep talking to her, so, rubbing her eyes, Evaine rolled over to face the wall.

'Well, goodnight, then,' she heard Morac murmur.

Evaine didn't answer. She was no longer thinking of her father or Morana or Jaeger. Her mind was fixed on Eadmund and how quickly she could find her way to him.

CHAPTER EIGHT

Thorgils wasn't sure how his body would cope with the long ride back to Andala in the morning, but he knew that Aleksander was better able to help Jael now, and all he had to do was stay on his horse and keep the book safe.

It seemed doable.

'Think you've got enough food?' Aleksander wondered as Thorgils stuffed a wedge of smoked cheese into his saddlebag. He'd managed to sweet talk a basket of food out of the Lord of Harstad's excellent cook, but he was having to work hard to put it into his bag instead of his mouth.

Thorgils looked serious. 'I'm not sure. I'll see what else I can find in the morning.'

Aleksander laughed. 'You've enough for an army! And surely you'll be doing more riding than eating? We need that book in Andala before winter.'

Thorgils looked offended. 'I'm still weak, you know. And as Astrid said, I require healing. Food helps.'

Aleksander glanced at Jael, not wanting to disturb her. Astrid had brought more of the tincture and decided to stay the night to give them a chance to sleep while she tended to Jael, hoping to ply her with as much of the tincture as possible.

She needed her strength back quickly.

Thorgils followed his gaze. 'Sure you don't want me to wait until Jael's ready?'

Aleksander shook his head, turning back to the flames he was drying his boots in front of. 'No. Jael would say to go.'

Thorgils nodded and set about sharpening his knife.

'You'd better look after yourself, though, and not get into trouble, or Jael will be furious with both of us when she's out of bed.'

Thorgils smiled, enjoying the idea of that. 'She will, no doubt. I lost Eadmund, so I can't imagine she's that happy with me anyway. He should be back in Andala, far away from Evaine and Morana.'

Aleksander always felt uncomfortable talking about Eadmund, no matter how hard he tried not to. He shrugged. 'From what he did to you, seems like you had little choice. He wasn't going to be stopped.'

Thorgils sighed, looking up at him. 'You've every reason not to like Eadmund, I know. So do I, come to think of it. But he's like my brother. Has been since my first breath. I'd happily lie down and die for him, no matter what he just did to me.' He bent over his knife, watching the edge come to life. 'Eadmund was never the same after his first wife died. He disappeared from everyone. And himself. But Jael brought him back. I'd never seen him so happy, until Evaine ruined everything with that spell of hers.' Thorgils looked sad. 'Not that you'd care, of course. Not about his happiness. But Jael's no fool. She sees Eadmund for who he really is. You should know that. He's worth fighting for, I promise. Hopefully, one day you'll see for yourself.'

Aleksander didn't look hopeful or keen to find out anything about Eadmund.

He considered himself a fair man when it came to most things, but he'd never seen anything worth saving in Eadmund Skalleson, and nobody was about to convince him otherwise.

***

Eadmund had hoped to find Evaine waiting for him in his dreams, but though he'd found his way to Oss, it was a different time. A time before he'd ever noticed Evaine. He was a boy. Younger than Eydis, he thought, feeling the smoothness of his face, seeing the size of his feet.

'You were so happy,' the woman said. 'Once. Or so I thought.'

Eadmund shivered, spinning around.

Eskild Skalleson was the most beautiful woman he'd ever seen. She looked like a goddess, he thought. Tall, with broad shoulders and a long neck. She carried herself like more than a lady. Like a queen. And he had adored her. As had his father and everyone on the islands. Eskild, with her honey-coloured hair and her warm hazel eyes, was like a mother to them all.

Except one.

'Mother,' Eadmund breathed, running to her, but no matter how fast he ran, she never came any closer. He stopped, eventually, panting in frustration.

'There is little time for me to show you what you need to see, my son. So look and find what you missed the first time. What we all missed...'

Eadmund was confused, glancing around. He was standing in the square. As usual, it was hidden beneath a thick blanket of snow, and the sky was low and grim. Everyone was buried beneath layers of wool and fur, with pink cheeks and red noses; breath smoke streaming from their mouths.

Winter on Oss.

He turned, seeing Thorgils, Klaufi, and Torstan. Boys, just like he was. Boys, who were laughing as they took turns trying to wrestle each other to the slushy ground. Thorgils was the champion, almost twice as big as the rest of them. His red curls bounced around an enormous face as he defeated them one by one, with an almighty roar and a wink at Isaura, who sat nearby with her friends, rolling her eyes.

Eadmund looked down, noticing that he'd already been bested, covered in dripping mud as he was. Then he heard his mother's soft voice again, reminding him. 'Look for what you missed the first time.'

He saw Ivaar skulking nearby, skinny as a rake and miserable as always as he lurked around the edges of everyone else's fun. His brother had always been a lonely boy, struggling for friends, and he eyed Eadmund with a look of anger. But Eadmund saw something new there now: sadness.

Ivaar was standing near Eadmund's dog, Bert.

Nine, Eadmund remembered. He was nine-years-old.

Eadmund watched as Ivaar bent down to pat the black coat of the big, friendly dog. For some reason, Bert had liked Ivaar and often followed him around, as he did now when Ivaar turned and headed down the alley, away from the square and the fun that Eadmund and his friends were having without him.

Eadmund panicked, following them, trying to yell, to call Bert back. But Bert had always been too trusting, too friendly, and he kept on padding after Ivaar.

They wound their way through the maze of cottages and sheds until Ivaar came to a house Eadmund thought he recognised. Turning back to Bert, Ivaar reached into his pouch. Eadmund tried to lunge forward, but his feet were stuck in the snow, and he couldn't move as Ivaar pulled out a sliver of salt fish and bent down to give it to the excited dog.

'There you go, boy,' Ivaar smiled, patting Bert's head before standing up. 'Go home, now. Go on!' And he shooed Bert on his way, turning to the door, resettling his cloak, running a hand through his short blonde hair.

Eadmund frowned as Bert wolfed down the treat and loped away, tail wagging. He could feel his feet moving again as he turned after his dog, following him further into the darkness of the alley, where Bert ran straight into Morana Gallas.

'Hello, dog,' Morana smiled, eyes darting around, checking the shadows. 'Would you like to come for a walk with me?'

Eadmund jerked awake, shivering.

Draguta, sitting at the table, staring into her circle, was so lost in the trance that she didn't notice.

***

It was the smell that woke him.

Aleksander rolled over, mumbling about Thorgils and pork chops. Thorgils was too deeply asleep to hear a thing. Jael was lost in a dream and didn't notice. Astrid sat up, though, disturbed by the groaning, and the strange smell. Wrapping a shawl around her shoulders, she tiptoed over to check on Jael, who hadn't stirred, before looking back to Aleksander, who was sitting up.

A knife in his hand.

She gasped. 'What is it?'

Aleksander scrambled out of bed as fast as his half-asleep limbs would carry him. Quickly dragging on his trousers, he hunted for his boots. 'You need to wake Thorgils up,' he said, glancing at Jael. 'He needs to get ready. Hurry!' And reaching for his mail shirt, he dropped it over his head before grabbing his swordbelt.

'For what?' Astrid wondered, feeling her heart quicken.

But Aleksander was already at the door, pulling it open.

Disappearing into the night.

***

The ravens were everywhere, like a dark, suffocating cloud, and Jael couldn't move. Their screeching calls rang in her ears, their scratching claws raking her arms as she tried to run. There was so much noise. She clamped her hands over her ears, but the sound of the birds was inside her head.

She couldn't move.

Then another noise. A different noise, fighting to be heard. Like wind or voices. Hissing. Waves. Jael couldn't tell. She closed her eyes, trying to hear what they were saying. And when she opened them, the ravens had gone.

Almost all of them.

One sat on the end of her bed.

Jael blinked.

The raven stared at her. One white eye. One black.

Then it opened its beak, cawing loudly.

Gasping, Jael wrenched open her eyes, her chest rising and falling in panic.

The raven was still there.

Jael looked to her right and saw Astrid, frozen to the spot, staring at the raven.

And then Jael smelled it.

Closing her eyes, she gritted her teeth, trying to move her legs.

She could hear the screeching.

'Astrid,' she croaked, trying to move. 'Come... here... now...'

Astrid drew her eyes away from the raven and hurried to Jael, kneeling by the bed. 'Something is happening. Thorgils and Aleksander have gone, and...' She froze, watching the raven as it opened its wings, flapping them loudly.

'Get me Thorgils' crutch,' Jael whispered, trying to swallow. 'Find my swordbelt.' Astrid hesitated. 'Now!'

The door rattled as the healer scrambled to her feet, running for the crutch.

Jael inhaled deeply, shaking all over as she rolled slowly to one side and struggled up to a sitting position.

Her ears started ringing. The door was shaking now. She could hear thunder.

'Put more behind that door!' Jael rasped, though her voice was faint, and the boom of the thunder was loud.

Astrid hurried back with the crutch and swordbelt. 'But you can't get up!'

Jael shoved her head between her knees, breathing deeply as everything started going black. She could hear Astrid pushing more furniture behind the barricade she'd already made. Lifting her head, Jael reached for the crutch and pushed it down onto the earthen floor, pulling herself up with a loud groan.

'My lady!' Astrid exclaimed, hurrying back to help her wobbling queen. 'You can't!'

'Tie the swordbelt around my waist. Scabbard on the right.' Jael kept her head low, trying not to fall down as Astrid fumbled with the belt. 'Another notch,' she panted. 'Tighter.' She could feel the belt sliding down her hips as she swayed. 'Good, now help me to the fire pit.' Astrid grabbed Jael's arm, leading her across the cottage. 'I'll stay here, you break that chair.' She nodded to the chair next to Thorgils' bed. 'Smash it to pieces. You need a leg. Wrap a bedsheet around it. Tightly. Set it on fire. Hurry.' Jael's ears were ringing so loudly that she couldn't hear herself, but Astrid ran to the chair, so at least she could.

Hurrying back to the fire pit with her sheet-wrapped chair leg, Astrid dipped it into the flames, thankful that she had kept a steady fire going all night.

'Come... beside me... close,' Jael whispered, trying to catch her breath. 'You'll need to help me stay upright.' The room was moving, or Jael was. She couldn't tell.

Astrid held the flaming torch in her left hand, grabbing onto Jael with her right.

And then the door burst open, and the raven flew up the smoke hole.

***

'Fuck!' Thorgils was knocked to the ground with an almighty thud. '*These* are the dragur?' Shaking his head, he clamped his teeth together, wishing he had his crutch to help get him back on his feet. He rolled away instead as a blue-faced, hollow-eyed creature threw himself forward. Landing on the ground with a squeal, it scrambled back to its feet, charging after him.

'Fire!' Aleksander yelled, fighting off three dragur with his sword. 'They hate fire!' Shards of lightning struck the square where a row of pyres had been built to burn the bodies of those who had died from the sickness. The stacked wood burst into flames, thunder rolling overhead. 'Torches!' Aleksander cried as he fell to the ground, punched from behind.

'Aleksander!' Thorgils struggled back to his feet, scything his sword into the neck of the nearest creature, pushing another out of the way. The dragur's jerking body swayed precariously but did not fall, so Thorgils ran as hard as he could with only one useful leg, watching as the dragur prepared to launch itself at Aleksander.

But Aleksander rolled onto his back, his short knife in his left hand, stabbing it into the dragur's throat. Quickly pushing the gurgling creature off him, he shook his head, trying to clear his vision as he jumped back to his feet. It felt as though he'd been hit by a boulder. Sword out, he backed into Thorgils, who was hobbling and panting behind him.

Hedrun ran towards them, his mouth flapping open, struggling to tie his swordbelt around his waist. 'What do we do?' he panicked. 'What do we do?'

'Burn them!' Aleksander cried. 'Get your men to light torches! Those with swords and axes should aim for their heads. And stay out of the way of that lightning!'

Thorgils hobbled forward, following Aleksander's advice,

chopping with his sword, hacking into the neck of a charging dragur. He could feel his stitches ripping as the dragur's head jerked back, still attached to its decaying body. Quickly righting itself, it rushed forward again.

Thorgils blinked in surprise. 'I need fire!' he yelled. 'Somebody get me a torch!'

***

Jael didn't know how long she had before she passed out, but the buzzing in her ears and the black patches flashing in front of her eyes told her not long. 'When I say move, run to the left,' she said, watching as three dragur fought their way through the table and chairs barricading the door. 'Wait.' She swallowed, swaying, all of her weight on the crutch, wanting to reach for *Toothpick*. Wanting to feel him in her hand again.

Jael blinked, suddenly realising that she didn't have the book. Where was her saddlebag? And where had Astrid put her daughter's body? Jael clamped her teeth together, forcing herself to focus.

The dragur screeched, their voices rising as they smashed the stacked furniture, clambering awkwardly over the pile towards the women.

'Closer together,' Jael said, her heart like a drum in her chest. 'Wait.'

Astrid edged towards Jael until their bodies were touching. As the dragur cleared the barricade and ran at them.

'Move!' Jael croaked, falling away to the right as Astrid hurried to the left, leaving the dragur unable to stop as they ran headfirst into the fire pit, tumbling over one another into the flames. 'Help me!' Jael urged, limping back to the fire. 'Use your torch! Push them back in!' The dragur were trying to scramble out of the flames. Jael leaned on the crutch, feeling it bite into her armpit, and drew *Toothpick* from his sheepskin-lined scabbard.

Lifting her arm, she was surprised by the weight of her sword, but she brought it up, stabbing *Toothpick* through the stomach of one of the burning dragur as Astrid tried to poke another further into the flames. The dragur kicked out at the healer, knocking her to the ground, the torch rolling out of her hand.

'Astrid!' Jael lifted her arm as high as she could, stabbing the dragur in the chest. It jerked into the flames, hands reaching out. 'We have to go! Pick up your torch! Hurry!' And she stumbled towards the table where the basket of her baby daughter waited, right next to her saddlebag. 'Help me! Get that bag over my head!'

Astrid scrambled to her feet, too scared to think at all as she retrieved her torch and hurried towards Jael, aware that the dragur were still trying to come out of the fire pit as its flames swallowed their writhing bodies; jumping at a boom of thunder that shook the cottage. She slipped the saddlebag over Jael's head with shaking hands.

'You take the basket,' Jael breathed. 'Keep her safe for me. Don't let her go. Please.'

Astrid nodded, grabbing the handles of the small woven basket in one hand, her torch in the other as she followed after Jael, who was wobbling ahead of her, trying to make her way through the smashed barricades.

The stinking dragur now sizzling in the fire behind them.

***

The storm was raging directly above them now, and Aleksander was panting, and Thorgils was bleeding from his opened wounds as he swung a flaming torch into the ruined mouth of a screeching dragur. The dragur screeched some more, stumbling backwards, but it didn't go down.

They were still in the square, fighting off what appeared to be at least one hundred creatures. It was hard to tell. It was a dark night, and the main source of light was coming from the blazing pyres sending towers of flames high into the stormy sky.

'You have to leave! Hurry!'

Aleksander spun around, but no one was there. The noise of the thunder had drowned out the voice, but he thought he recognised it. He waved his torch at the four dragur surrounding him, spinning, watching as the thatch caught in the distance, spreading quickly.

Jael, he thought, panicking. The horses.

Shoving his torch into the face of one dragur, he tried to step away from them. He needed to get to Thorgils, who he could see staggering nearby, bleeding from every limb. 'We have to leave!' he cried. 'Thorgils! Get the horses! I'll get Jael!'

***

'Really? You think you can just leave?' Draguta purred, watching intensely. She was transfixed as she sat at the table, peering into her circle, impatient to see what was going to happen next. 'I want that book, so kill the half-dead bitch, and take it! It can't be that hard, can it? She is almost on her knees. Kill her! *Now!*'

Eadmund woke up, wondering what Draguta was doing. He glanced at Brill, who sat on the corner of a bed, arms around her knees, rocking back and forth.

***

'My lady!' Astrid screamed as a dragur tore at her nightdress. She swung around with her torch, trying to frighten it away.

The dragur jerked backwards, and Jael hobbled up beside Astrid, slashing *Toothpick*, trying to hit it. Exhausted by the effort, she dropped her arm, breathing heavily. The dragur, seeing that Jael had no flaming torch, aimed a punch at her face.

Astrid screamed again as Jael toppled backwards, the dragur throwing itself on top of her, grabbing her saddlebag, trying to yank it off her shoulder.

Jael grunted, crushed by its weight, *Toothpick* still in her hand. But she couldn't lift her sword because the dragur was on her right arm, so she brought up her left arm instead, smashing the crutch onto the dragur's head. 'Give me the torch!' she yelled, trying not to inhale the stench of the creature as it leaned its eyeless face close to hers, untroubled by the blow.

Jael could feel the heat of the fire as she dropped the broken crutch, wrapping her hand around the chair leg, and so could the dragur. It shrieked, backing away from the flames, but it was too late as Jael shoved it into its hollowed-out eye socket. Leaving it there, she staggered to her feet. 'We have to find Thorgils and Aleksander,' she panted, bending over. 'Stay behind me. And don't let go of my baby!'

CHAPTER NINE

Edela couldn't hear for all the screeching. The dragur were everywhere. Blue-tinged, decomposing bodies dressed in rags, lurching forward in odd jerking movements.

But someone was talking to her.

A woman.

She turned and turned, wondering if it was Jael; hoping to see her.

Flames burst up into the night sky as people rushed past her, abandoning their burning homes, heading for the gates. And there she was, walking through them all, her pale nightdress flapping like gull wings behind her.

Ayla.

Her ghostly face was moon-like against the fiery night sky, glistening with sweat. She looked so very ill. Pale. Not like herself at all.

'I am dying, Edela,' she breathed. 'We are all dying. The sickness will kill us. That is her plan. I have seen it. I have dreamed it. Come to me, Edela. Come and find me. Hurry.'

Edela reached out a hand, desperate to know more, but Ayla slid away from her, drifting like smoke, up into the sky.

***

'Jael!' Aleksander ran into the cottage. 'Astrid!' He saw the bodies of the burning dragur in the fire pit; smelled them too. Jael's bed was empty. Her saddlebag and the baby's basket were nowhere to be seen.

Quickly scanning the cottage, Aleksander grabbed Thorgils' overstuffed bag and Jael's armour and ran back out the door.

***

Rufus didn't know Thorgils, and he wouldn't come.

Hot flames were licking the poles holding up the roof of the stables. Thorgils could hear the thatch crackling above him, and thunder and lightning were terrifying the horse too. He had released the other horses, shooing them outside, but he'd kept theirs behind, attaching bridles and saddles as quickly as his swollen hands would allow, wondering how he'd ever thought that punching a dragur was a good idea.

Tig was restless, Thorgils could see; anxious for Jael, no doubt.

He swallowed, hoping that Aleksander would get to Jael and Astrid in time.

'Come on, now,' Thorgils urged, tugging Rufus' bridle. He'd moved Gus and Sky out into the middle of the stables, looping their reins around the only pole that wasn't on fire. Tig was banging against the door of his stall, and Thorgils needed to get him ready too, but Rufus had dug his hooves into the straw, shrinking backwards with every tug. With every boom of thunder above.

And suddenly, Thorgils could smell why.

Releasing Rufus, he unsheathed his sword, spinning around as a group of dragur burst in through the doors.

***

'My lady!' Hedrun ran up to Jael, who was struggling towards the stables, holding onto Astrid, his eyes big with terror. 'They're everywhere! The fire's destroying everything! All of it! All that we've built!'

Jael didn't know Hedrun. He had risen to power after her father's death, but he didn't appear to be a man made for a crisis. 'Leave!' she growled, pointing at the gates. 'The dragur will kill you before the fire does! Get your people out of here. Now! I'll try and lead them away!' And swaying against Astrid, Jael pulled the healer towards the stables, which she could see were on fire. 'We need to get to the horses quickly. They want the book. I have to leave. You need to come with me!'

Astrid nodded, glancing around the burning fort as people and animals milled around in confusion and fear, all of them as panicked as Hedrun. She had no family. Her husband had died years ago, and they'd never had a child live past its first birthday.

Going with Jael Furyck seemed like the best option.

'Quick!' Jael cried as a pack of dragur barrelled towards them, some of them on fire as shards of lightning exploded from the storm clouds. 'We have to go!'

***

Thorgils couldn't hold them off. There were too many, and his injured arm was weak, and their thick blue arms, some wielding giant swords, were not. 'Grrrrr!' he yelled, swinging around with his own sword, hoping some momentum would put more power into his blow.

It did as he finally took off a dragur's head.

But there were eight more with perfectly intact heads swarming around him, knocking him to the ground. Thorgils could smell the smoke. He could feel it clogging his throat as he lay in the straw, fighting off the dragur with his bruised and bleeding forearm, listening to the panic of the whinnying horses and the rolling thunder growing louder above him.

And then a smash as Tig reared up on his hind legs, over and over until he shattered the door of his stall. The dragur were momentarily distracted by the great black beast as he reared up before them, bringing his hooves down, scattering them.

Thorgils scrambled to his feet in surprise, panting, searching for his sword. He couldn't see it in the straw, but as he turned, he could see that one of the dragur had picked it up and was charging for Tig.

'No!' Thorgils cried, running for the blue creature, who lunged at the horse, but as the dragur swung the sword, it suddenly collapsed in a heap, a spear through its skull; the sharp spearhead popping out its empty eye socket. Thorgils spun around, blinking in horror to see Jael standing there. 'Jael!'

Jael's eyes rolled up into the back of her head, and she promptly fell to the ground.

'My lady!' Astrid was quickly beside her, gripping the basket to her chest. 'She's fainted.'

'Jael!' Aleksander ran into the stables, ignoring for a moment the dragur, who were quickly circling them all. 'Astrid, you need to wake her up. Get her on her feet. We'll get the horses ready.' And he ran for Thorgils, but the dragur barely glanced at them. They'd seen the saddlebag over Jael's shoulder, and they could hear the cry of their mistress, loud in their ears.

'Get the book!' she demanded. 'Kill her, and bring me the book!'

Jael could hear Draguta's voice too, and her eyes popped open, her fingers reaching for the saddlebag, pulling it to her chest. 'Get the horses outside,' she croaked, sitting up, blinking at the dragur, who were approaching cautiously. 'Then bring back fire. We have to burn them!'

Thorgils ran to untie Gus, shepherding him outside, sending Sky after him. Rufus was out of his stall now, and after a slap on the rump, he raced out of the stables too. Thorgils turned to Tig, but he wasn't going anywhere. Jael would need him.

Astrid helped Jael to her feet as Aleksander circled them both with his sword.

Jael's head was spinning as she straightened up, but she unsheathed *Toothpick* and planted her feet, gripping her sword with both hands, watching as Tig reared up again, smashing his hooves down into the huddle of dragur.

They scattered, rushing her and Aleksander.

'Jael,' Aleksander muttered, watching her wobble out of the corner of one eye. 'Hold on. We need to get you on Tig. Just hold on.'

But Jael wasn't about to hold on.

She thought of her baby. She saw her daughter, wrapped in the blanket in Astrid's basket, and she remembered what the dragur had done to her.

What Draguta had done to her.

And she knew that Draguta was watching. Listening.

So, sucking in a deep breath, Jael roared, tears stinging her eyes. 'You can't stop me, Draguta! You can kill my child! You can take my husband! But you will never stop *me*! I am coming to kill you! I am coming to rip out your fucking throat!' And after another long breath, she spun, slashing her sword across the face of the nearest dragur, kicking it in the chest as it screeched, curling away from her.

***

Draguta's eyes blazed as she sat there, clenching her fists on either side of the circle, watching as Jael Furyck - half-dead, grief-stricken Jael Furyck - cut her dragur to pieces with the help of her pathetic old lover.

Her beautiful face twisted into a scowl so intense that her head ached. Picking up the wine jug that sat at the head of the table, she threw it at the wall, just missing Eadmund's head. 'Your wife!' she bellowed. 'She will pay! She will pay for this! And you will see to it! Do you hear me, Eadmund? You will kill her! She thinks that she will come and kill me?' Draguta laughed, and it was an ear-piercing shriek. 'But she has no idea what I have planned for her!'

***

Aleksander boosted Jael up onto Tig. 'Hold on tight!' he ordered, waiting while she gripped the reins. 'We'll catch up with you. Lead them out of here. Head for Andala! We'll find you!' And taking Astrid's hand, Aleksander dragged the healer towards Rufus as Thorgils rushed past them with two flaming torches. He threw them into the stables, hurrying to secure the doors before running for the horses, who were tied to the thrashing post in the middle of the square.

Watching as Jael and Tig disappeared through the mass of flames and screaming villagers running for the gates.

***

Eydis was disturbed by the noises in the cottage and the terror of her own dreams. She rolled over, listening to Biddy and Edela, who were huddled by the fire, whispering urgently to one another. 'What's happened?'

Biddy jumped. 'Oh, I'm sorry, Eydis. I was trying not to wake you. I thought you might be having a useful dream over there.'

Eydis swallowed, sitting up, shuddering at the memory of her dream. Blue men had been raging through Andala, killing everyone with their clenched fists and their rusted weapons. The strange noises they made still rang in her ears, and she was struggling to think. 'No, I don't think it was useful,' she mumbled, at last. 'No more than Edela has already seen of the dragur.'

'You've seen them too? I fear they are getting closer, but do not worry, Eydis, we have time.' Edela's voice shook, and she blinked, surprised by her continued lack of certainty. She smiled, trying to hide it, though Eydis would not be comforted by a smile she couldn't see.

Frowning, Eydis pushed away Vella, who was licking her hand, and stood. 'What are you doing?' she wondered, moving towards Edela. 'It's not morning, is it?'

'No, it's not,' Biddy said. 'Edela had a dream. And now she's going to do something she shouldn't.'

Eydis found a stool and sat down, feeling the cold wood beneath her nightdress. The fire was only just coming back to life, she could tell, and the cottage was chilly. 'What are you going to do? What did you see?'

'I saw Ayla,' Edela breathed, tingling with excitement. Nerves too. 'She wants me to come and find her, so I'm going to try another dream walk.'

***

They looked over their shoulders at the burning mess of Harstad in the distance, flames devouring the new ramparts. Lightning shivered down from swirling clouds, keeping the fires blazing.

Aleksander rode in front, Astrid behind him on Rufus, Thorgils bringing up the rear on Gus; all three of them charging after Jael and Tig.

The dragur still standing were escaping, chasing after them, calling to each other like angry ravens. The revolting stench of them was stronger than the smoke belching from the burning fort.

Hearing the horses behind her, Jael slowed down. She gripped Tig's reins with shaking hands, knowing that she couldn't afford to pass out again. They had to lead the dragur far away from Harstad.

All the way to Andala.

They couldn't afford to stop now.

***

Draguta had finally crawled into her bed, and Eadmund wasn't sure if she was sleeping, but she wasn't screaming or throwing things, which was a relief. But despite the silence, he couldn't get back to sleep. The things Draguta had said and the memories of his dreams kept him alert and unsettled.

He remembered his mother's voice, urging him on as he followed his brother. The brother who had killed his beloved dog, or so Eadmund had always believed. He saw Ivaar's scheming eyes so full of sadness, then Thorgils' look of shock as he pushed his sword into his friend's shoulder, leaving him for dead.

Was Thorgils dead?

Eadmund blinked, trying to bring Evaine to his mind, but

he saw Jael instead. His scowling wife. His warrior wife. He saw her defeating Jaeger Dragos in Skorro's charred fort. Smiling. Her sooty teeth. Her green eyes, so alive.

And he remembered what Draguta had said about a baby. Jael's baby.

His baby.

It didn't make sense. None of it made sense. Eadmund couldn't think straight. He couldn't understand what was happening, and then he heard Draguta's voice in his ears, and everything went black.

***

Biddy had tried to convince Edela to delay the dream walk, reminding her that without the herbs she needed, it would be pointless. Edela had suggested that Biddy simply go and find the herbs, and then they could begin.

And blood too.

She needed some of Ayla's blood.

It was well into the morning when a tired-looking Biddy returned with the puppies and a basket full of herbs, stones, and blood. Isaura had come along too when she heard what Edela was planning.

'We shall be glad of the company,' Edela smiled wearily. 'You may drum for me. That will leave Biddy free to care for Eydis.'

Eydis looked put out by the idea that she needed to be taken care of.

Edela glanced at her cross face, then quickly refocused, remembering the urgency in Ayla's voice. 'Let us make a start, then. Bring that basket here, Biddy, and I shall set about making my circle. Isaura, you can help me while Biddy works on the fire. We'll need more flames than that!'

***

They had ridden away from the dragur, far away now, and were finally confident enough to stop and rest. The sun was reaching its peak, and the storm had long since retreated. Slipping her bare feet out of the stirrups, Jael slid down Tig, dropping to the ground with a gasp.

Aleksander was quickly at her side. 'Come and sit down.'

Ignoring him, Jael walked to the nearest tree, eager to rest her back against its generous-looking trunk. She blinked up at Thorgils, who had come to fuss over her too. 'You're bleeding,' she said, noticing all the patches on his tunic and trousers.

'That'll be those stitches of mine,' Thorgils grinned wearily, nodding at Astrid, who looked embarrassed to be wearing her nightdress. 'I'll be needing a few more, I think.'

Jael lifted her knees, resting her head on them, shoulders slumping in a heap. 'We have to keep them following us. We need them to come back to Andala,' she mumbled.

Aleksander gathered the horses' reins, not wanting them to wander too far away. 'And hope they're ready to defend the fort.'

'We're faster than the dragur, but they'll come. Eventually. They want that book. And me.' Jael lifted her head, watching as Astrid tried to convince Thorgils to let her look at his wounds, but he was in no mood for fixing just yet. 'We need some water,' she croaked. 'The horses too.'

They hadn't come across a stream yet.

Giving up on Thorgils, Astrid tried Jael, kneeling down beside her to feel her head.

Jael frowned at her, but she didn't move.

'You're cool,' Astrid smiled. 'Cold even.'

'I know,' Jael yawned, feeling the rough bark digging into her back. 'I really miss my cloak.' She quickly shook away any thoughts of her favourite bear-fur cloak and her spell-bound husband, which wouldn't help her focus at all. 'We shouldn't stay long. We need to find a stream.'

Aleksander nodded. 'We do. We can rest then.'

'Agreed,' Jael said. 'Now, help me back to my feet before I fall asleep!'

***

Ayla had been trapped in the dream – the nightmare – since she'd tried to save Thorgils. She hadn't known that she was ill at the time. She had, in fact, been starting to think and hope that she was pregnant. The odd feelings she'd been having – the tiredness and nausea – all made sense now; if only she hadn't been so blind. Maybe she would have seen it all earlier?

Seen what the woman was doing...

Sighing, Ayla dropped her head to her hands, wanting to hide from the layers of bodies scattered everywhere she walked; those who were dead, those who were dying. All of them abandoned to a miserable fate. She could smell the familiar odour of death. She could hear them crying in pain, twisting in agony.

Gaunt skeletons with big eyes.

And she was trapped here with them, though she had no idea where here was.

'Ayla!'

Ayla looked up, hurrying forward as Edela shuffled towards her. 'You came!' she sobbed. 'You came!' And reaching Edela, she wrapped her arms around the old dreamer, crying in relief.

'Ayla, you poor girl,' Edela soothed, looking around them. 'Where are we? What are you seeing here?'

'It's the sickness,' Ayla whispered. '*Her* sickness. She made it. She made it to destroy her enemies. And it's working. These bodies keep piling up all around me. They're all sick and dying. As am I. I can feel it, Edela. She is pulling me towards her, and I can't stop her!'

Edela gagged at the smell of the place. They were standing in a large field, surrounded on all sides by dark fir trees, tall and coarse, creating an enclosure.

Keeping the dying in.

'Who is this woman?' Edela asked. 'Draguta?'

'No,' Ayla said, shaking her head. 'Her name is Briggit. Briggit Halvardar. She is the new Queen of Helsabor.'

***

The sun was high in the sky by the time they found a stream.

Jael bent her face down to the gently running water and drank eagerly, and when she'd finished, she walked back to the trees where Astrid and Thorgils were going through his saddlebag, portioning out the vast amount of food he had masterfully crammed into it.

Jael was pleased to see that Thorgils' appetite had finally come in handy. There would be plenty to eat on their way back to Andala. Her smile quickly vanished when she caught sight of the basket Astrid had left in front of a tree, well away from the horses, who were at the stream, enjoying a much-needed drink.

Aleksander came up beside Jael, following her gaze.

'I want to make her a pyre,' she murmured. 'Here. I don't want to wait anymore. We don't know what's out there. What Draguta will send next. She needs to go now. To be set free.'

'I can do that,' Aleksander said gently. 'You go and sit with her. I'll make a pyre, and we'll send her to the gods. To Furia.'

Jael nodded, not even noticing as he slipped away into the trees, looking for branches and twigs. She walked slowly to the basket, feeling a heaviness in her body that was nothing to do with her illness but everything to do with her broken heart. The panic of the dragur attack had receded, and Jael felt displaced, her thoughts drifting like the clouds above her.

She missed Eadmund.

More than anything, she missed Eadmund. She wanted him to see his daughter. To hold her in his arms before...

Reaching into the basket, Jael picked up the tiny bundle, tears running down her cheeks. 'I'm so sorry,' she whispered. 'I'm so sorry.' And sitting down on the grass, her back against the tree, she gently held her baby in her arms. 'I was lying,' she cried. 'I was lying when I said I didn't want you. I was lying. I wanted you very much. More than you will ever know.' She wiped her tears from her baby daughter's face. 'I'd thought of a name for you, you see. It was Lyra... Lyra Skalleson.'

And bending forward, Jael sobbed, not wanting to let her baby go.

PART TWO

The Cursed

CHAPTER TEN

'How is poor Hanna?' Edela wondered, so pleased to see Entorp again. He looked terrible, though. Tired and pale, dark circles under his eyes. Even his orange hair was limp, in need of a good wash, she could see.

Entorp inhaled a deep breath of sea air as he walked past the ruined piers with Edela and Biddy, enjoying an escape from the vile odours of the ship sheds. 'She doesn't have long,' he murmured. 'She's held on for so much longer than I would have expected while many around her have died, but she hasn't eaten or drunk in days now. Marcus is preparing himself for the end, though I'm not sure how he'll cope when it comes. He's bereft.'

'Oh.' Edela glanced at Biddy, who looked upset. 'The poor girl. And poor Marcus. It seems that I misjudged the man. He's not who I thought he was at all.'

Entorp wasn't really listening as he suppressed a yawn. 'I can't stay away long, Edela. There is much to do in there.'

'It's the sickness I wanted to speak to you about,' Edela said. 'I have seen Ayla. She came into my dreams, and then I went into hers.' Her body felt weakened by the dream walk, but after what Ayla had told her, Edela knew that there was too much to do to stay in bed. 'Ayla has been dreaming in that shed. Stuck in a world of sickness and death. A world created by a woman.'

Entorp stopped, turning to her. 'What do you mean?' His eyes were suddenly more alert. 'Are you saying the sickness is a spell? A curse?'

Edela smiled, nodding. 'It is. Ayla says it is.'

'Oh, but that's wonderful news,' Entorp sighed. 'A curse!' He glanced at Biddy, who looked surprised by his joy. 'And do you know how to break it? Did Ayla know?'

Edela's smile faded. 'No, no, she didn't. And I don't know either, not yet, but I wanted to tell you about it, to see if you had any ideas. Perhaps you've heard of the woman? Know about her?'

Entorp was confused. 'It's not Draguta, then?'

'No, it's someone called Briggit. Briggit Halvardar. Ayla says that she's the Queen of Helsabor now. She disappeared before I could find out more, but I plan to head straight back to bed and see what my dreams reveal. Eydis is going to help me. She is close to Ayla, so hopefully, she'll be able to help find her.'

'Briggit Halvardar?' Entorp frowned as old memories started to shake off their dust; memories of a time he was always reluctant to revisit. 'I've heard of a woman called Briggit. She came to Tuura. A princess, she was then. A very powerful dreamer. I remember meeting her. She was in The Following.'

Edela glanced at Biddy, a shiver rushing down her spine. 'Oh.'

'Yes, so if Briggit has risen to the throne of Helsabor now, you can be sure The Following is involved in it somehow,' Entorp said. 'And that means we now have two enemies to defeat in the South. Two enemies and no way into Hest.'

Edela blew out a frustrated breath, knowing that everything had just gotten much harder.

* * *

Evaine was desperate. She had been up to Jaeger's chamber

three times now, and each time she crept up to his door, she could hear someone inside. The same someone. Humming and singing to herself.

And she was still in there.

Jaeger would likely return soon, or that ugly girl, and Evaine panicked, knowing that she couldn't leave Hest without the book, but how was she going to steal it if she couldn't even get into his chamber?

Sighing loudly, she spun around, coming face to face with Meena.

Meena eyed her suspiciously.

Evaine almost spat in her face. 'What? What do you want, girl?' she sneered.

Meena's first instinct was to tap her head. She ignored that, instead choosing to stand her ground and stare at Evaine. 'I... live here. In there,' she murmured, pointing to Jaeger's door. 'And I want nothing, except to return to my chamber. What do you want? Why are you here?' She shivered as she spoke, unused to feeling so bold, though part of her still wanted to curl into a ball, watching as Evaine's face reddened with anger.

She looked ready to hit her.

'I, I,' Evaine stumbled in surprise. 'I was looking for my father,' she said, at last, avoiding Meena's eyes.

'He's with Morana. I've just left them. Jaeger was there too.'

Evaine swallowed, glaring at Meena, who wasn't moving. And so, without a word, she turned away, heading back down the corridor.

Meena watched her leave, surprised by the anger coursing through her body; worried that the tattoos had come too late.

Afraid that the book was already changing her.

***

Berard had waited outside the ship sheds, hoping to see Entorp emerge. Or Marcus. He was eager to know how Hanna was. He hadn't heard anything for days – not since they'd been released from their own shed.

Runa stopped beside him with Isaura. They were carrying trays of food. 'Have you seen Entorp?' she wondered. 'I thought he might like something to eat?'

Berard shook his head. 'No one has come out, but a few more have been carried in.'

Isaura frowned, wishing she knew how Ayla was; certain that Ayla was only sick because she had pushed her so hard to help Thorgils.

Runa turned as Ivaar approached.

Ivaar was surprised to see them, and he quickly moved away, not wanting to give the impression that he too, had come hoping to hear news about Ayla.

Runa watched him go before turning back to Isaura. 'Well, let's take the trays inside the shed. Those women helping Entorp will be grateful for something to eat and drink, I'm sure.'

Nodding, Isaura followed Runa into the sheds, leaving Berard to sigh and wonder what he was going to do now.

'There you are!' Karsten called, spying his brother. 'Bayla's decided that you've fallen ill somewhere. That you've got the sickness. I'm surprised you can't hear her wailing and moaning from here!'

'Why does she think that?'

Karsten shrugged. 'Who knows? It's been a hard few weeks. I don't think she's sleeping, and she's definitely not keen to lose any more of us. Who would she have to complain to? Nicolene doesn't care.' He inclined his head away from the ship sheds, but Berard's boots remained firmly stuck in the mud, and he continued to stare at them. 'There's nothing you can do for Hanna by standing here.' Karsten felt odd, remembering the look on Hanna's face before she'd collapsed to the ground in the storm. He hadn't been sleeping much himself, but when he did, that face haunted his dreams.

He couldn't stop thinking about her.

Finally, Berard turned to follow his brother, tired of feeling helpless. His stump was aching, but he'd barely given it much thought until now. 'What of your plans to go to Hest?' he muttered, trying to take his mind off the pain.

'Plans? I don't have any as it stands, but I will,' Karsten assured him. 'I have my own men now. And if I can give them reason enough to follow me, then we may have an opportunity to do something. Keep your ears open, Berard. We're going to find our way to Jaeger soon. One way or another.'

***

'What is it?' Jaeger demanded, trying not to gag. The smell of Morana had his eyes watering. 'What have you seen?'

Dragmall blinked, uncomfortable with Jaeger's closeness. He'd once been taller than the young king, but now Jaeger towered over him. Threateningly. Demanding answers that Dragmall would rather not reveal. 'I believe it is a curse, my lord. Draguta has cursed her for sure. From my understanding of how things went,' he muttered, remembering what Else had told him about that night, 'it sounds as though Draguta was trying to kill you, but what she did to Morana, here? I think she wanted to punish her. It is more torturous to live while a prisoner in your own body, wouldn't you say?'

Jaeger turned to the pathetic, hunched creature perched on the chair before them. She had blinked, sniffed, and dribbled, but nothing more. 'And what can be done about it? This curse. Can you break it? Undo it?' He frowned. 'Is that something the Book of Darkness could help with?'

Dragmall shivered, not wanting to start down that steep

path. 'No, no, my understanding is that the book is about casting spells and throwing curses. Dark rituals. It does not dwell on how to heal or help those it may have hurt.' Bending down, he lifted Morana's chin, peering into her milky eye. 'What we are seeing is the outside only. The prison walls. Morana is not changed. I imagine she's in there, dreaming of a way to get out. And she knows dark magic, curses too, so if someone is to help her, I believe it will be Morana herself.' Dragmall hoped the seriousness with which he spoke would convince Jaeger to leave well enough alone.

He was wrong.

Jaeger snorted, glaring at Morac, who was fascinated by Dragmall and eager to believe what he was saying. 'And how is she going to do *that*? She needs help, can't you see?'

Dragmall sighed, closing his eyes. He didn't want to help Morana Gallas, but it would be useful if the king didn't see him as an impediment to her recovery. Opening his eyes, he tried to smile. 'I propose a bath of spices to stimulate her senses. Cleansing too. Perhaps if we can wake her up enough, Morana may be able to communicate with us? Tell us how to help break the curse? We can cleanse her chamber too. Scrub the floor and walls. Wash it clean of any dark matter.' Dragmall was reaching, he knew, looking for ways to appease his impatient, moody king without actually having to try and break the curse himself.

When he'd looked into Morana's eyes, it was as though she was in there, screaming at him, begging for help. Though for now, Meena, Else, and Dragmall had all agreed that it was better not to let her out.

***

Draguta's mood hadn't improved, Eadmund noticed as she

stopped at the railings with her servant. He could barely breathe as Rollo ran him around the training ring, cracking his wooden staff into Eadmund's aching muscles, over and over again. There was little time to think, but he felt as though something had happened in the night that he should have remembered.

As hard as he tried, though, he couldn't.

Draguta turned away, happy with what she'd seen. Eadmund appeared to be compliant again, which was what he needed to be. She couldn't afford for him to become a problem. Not now. Not when there were so many other problems she had to contend with.

She needed the Book of Darkness. *Her* Book of Darkness.

Draguta's body tensed just thinking about it in Jaeger's clumsy hands.

She needed the book, and Evaine was the key to getting it back. If only she could be certain the stupid girl would be able to escape Hest.

'What are you gaping at?' Draguta growled, nudging Brill, who had just seen Eadmund picked up and thrown to the ground by the enormous, bare-chested man. 'Eadmund will be fine, but I will not. Not unless you find me some more wine. And another dress. This one is filthy!'

Brill turned from the training ring and followed her mistress, who was stalking away, the hem of her dress trailing behind her in the dust, her mind already turning to Jael Furyck and what she would do next.

***

Jaeger glowered at Else as he strode into the chamber. 'You can go,' he grumbled, pointing her to the door. 'I wish to speak to Meena alone.'

Else tried not to look as worried as she felt about that. She bobbed her head and picked up her basket from its place by the door. 'Shall I bring your supper tonight, my lord?'

Jaeger shook his head, his eyes still on Meena. 'No, we'll be eating in the hall, Meena and I.'

Meena looked surprised, staring after Else, who had quickly disappeared through the door.

'Where did you go this morning? Where were you last night?' Jaeger asked, pulling a chair out from the table. And turning it around, he sat down, his eyes never leaving Meena's quickly reddening face.

'I stayed with Morana,' Meena said. 'I told you I would.'

'You did, yes. And as soon as you saw me today, you ran away again. Why is that?' he wondered, searching her big, blinking eyes. 'What aren't you telling me?'

'N-n-nothing,' Meena insisted. 'After I saw Dragmall, I, I thought I would check on Morana. She looked frail. I thought it best if I stayed. She needs someone to stay with her now. She can't do anything for herself, and Sitha can't stay there all the time. Other people need her help, and Morana isn't ill.'

'And you're volunteering to be that someone? *You* want to stay with her?'

Meena started to shake her head but stopped as an idea formed. 'Well, I am used to the chamber. To helping Morana. Perhaps I would be of more use than Morac? He doesn't come often, and I don't imagine he wants to clean out his sister's chamber pot.'

'Why not her daughter, then?' Jaeger asked. 'Surely that sort of help should be provided by a daughter?' He smiled at the idea of Evaine stuck in that stinking stone pit, wiping Morana's arse. 'I don't want to lose you from my chamber, Meena, and Evaine is useless to me, so I couldn't think of a better solution.' He leaned forward, pleased with himself. 'I'll invite her to supper and tell her the good news tonight. Now, let's not talk of Morana or Evaine. I want to know about you.

What did Dragmall say to help you read the book?'

***

Entorp felt shaken after his conversation with Edela and Biddy. Too shaken to eat the meal Runa had left for him. He hurried to check on Ayla, surprised to see that Bruno wasn't there.

Derwa, who had been helping Entorp as his patients started piling up, ran a hand down her white braid. 'I'm afraid Bruno has fallen ill,' she said. 'I had him moved away. Into the first shed.'

Entorp was surprised and saddened, but he nodded, knowing that it was the right decision. Those who were in the initial grip of the sickness were distressed, disoriented, their bowels opening with great regularity. It took some time for their bodies to weaken as much as Hanna's or Ayla's or the men and women who lay on mattresses and blankets around them.

They were quiet. Waiting to die.

They needed peace, so this shed was reserved for them and their loved ones to say their goodbyes.

'I'll check on him,' he mumbled, staring at Derwa suddenly. 'Do you remember a woman called Briggit Halvardar?'

Derwa shook her head. 'No, who is she?'

Entorp stepped closer, lowering his voice. 'She was in The Following, from Helsabor, but she came to Tuura once. Ayla is dreaming about her, according to Edela.'

'Why?'

Entorp retreated, realising that there were too many people in the shed to guarantee discretion. 'I believe Edela is trying to find answers in her dreams. To find out what is causing the sickness. Hopefully, she will soon.'

Derwa didn't look any less puzzled. 'Edela is very

determined, I know. And if there's something to find, you can be sure she'll find it. Now, why don't you come and have a bite to eat? It's cold, but it looks tasty enough, and you don't want to join Bruno in that shed, do you?'

Entorp followed Derwa to the table where his tray of food waited for him, Edela's words echoing in his head. If it was indeed a curse, then perhaps only those who had protection from such things would be safe? 'Thank you,' he smiled. 'But what about you? I think you should take a break. Get some fresh air. I can certainly recommend the benefits of inhaling something new.'

'I think I might,' Derwa said, looking around. 'I can't remember the last time I saw the sun.'

'Yes, yes, you go,' Entorp mumbled, nibbling disinterestedly on a soggy crispbread. 'Stay away as long as you like. I'll be fine here.'

***

Edela was pleased to have the opportunity to lie down. She needed a rest after the dream walk. Never in her life had she imagined doing a single one, let alone the amount she'd completed since that first time with Aleksander.

It was exhausting, though, and her eyes needed little encouragement to close.

Eydis, who lay on her low bed, struggling with a wriggling Ido, who wasn't feeling sleepy, was finding it much harder. But, finally shooing him away and gripping Ayla's wedding ring tightly, she squeezed her eyes shut and tried to focus on Ayla's face, remembering the last time she'd seen her in her dreams.

It had been easy before, and now that she'd given Biddy her symbol stone to take far away from the cottage, she hoped that

Ayla would come and find her again.

They needed to know how to help her.

***

Jaeger ran his hand over the tattoo, watching Meena squirm. The intricate knot of symbols was blue, covered in a thick salve, but he saw how it had bled; how it was bleeding now as he pushed his fingers against it. 'And this will help your dreams? These symbols?'

He sounded suspicious, Meena thought, her eyes watering from the pain he was causing. 'That's what Dragmall said,' she gasped. 'He has them himself.'

'But he's not a dreamer.'

'He said he dreams of things from time to time, but no, he's not a dreamer.'

'Well, we shall see what Dragmall knows of magic, then, for I need you to have dreams. And quickly. We need to find out where Draguta is, and how she will try to hurt us. She didn't need the book to do what she did to Morana, did she? Wherever she is, whatever she is now, she'll be working on ways to hurt us. Know that, Meena. You and I are in this together. She wants us both dead.'

Meena shuddered, certain that Jaeger was right. In her dreams, Draguta was raging, filled with a feverish anger so violent that Meena feared what she would do next. She was convinced that one night she would wake to find Draguta standing over her bed, her hands around her throat. Swallowing, she felt for her scabbard, hanging from her belt, comforted by the presence of the knife, but at the same time worried. The knife had killed Draguta, but not for long.

So what could stop her now?

***

Morac came up behind Evaine at the stables, and when she turned around, he could see that she was in quite a state. 'What is it? What's wrong?' he wondered. 'Is it Jaeger? Has he hurt you again?'

Evaine shook her head, irritated by her father's arrival. She'd been negotiating with a shy stable hand to get a horse, and she wasn't looking to be distracted from her next task, which was to get into Jaeger's chamber. 'No, he hasn't. I just wanted to go for a ride, away from the castle.'

'You?'

'Why not? Jaeger took me riding once,' Evaine said, shivering at the memory; wishing she had seen the warning signs then. 'It was enjoyable. I would like to try again.' She turned to the stable hand, giving him her sweetest smile. His pouch bulged with her father's silver coins, and he nodded at her.

'I shall come with you,' Morac insisted. 'You're not the most confident rider, so it will be good to have me along.'

'I'm not looking for company, Father!' Evaine snapped, her eyebrows sharp. 'I want to ride up to the top of the cliffs and see if there's any sign of Eadmund. I don't want, nor do I require company. I am not a child. I'm about to become a married woman. I have a son. I don't need your fussing!'

Morac couldn't hide his disappointment. 'Of course,' he said, nodding as he turned away. 'You go, then. But,' he added, looking back. 'If you haven't returned by supper, I shall come and find you. Know that.'

'Fine.' Evaine had already forgotten him, her mind humming with urgency. She needed to leave the city. She had her supplies. Her horse was paid for and ready, and she had some of the other items Draguta had requested, but she didn't have what Draguta wanted most of all.

She didn't have the book.

'Oh, I forgot,' Morac said. 'We've been invited to the hall tonight. Jaeger says he wants to talk about Morana. We're to have supper with him.'

Evaine scowled, then her face lightened. 'He'll be eating in the hall? And the girl? Meena?' She tried to keep her voice even, but her nervous energy had her twitching all over.

'She'll be there too, I expect. She seems to be everywhere he is.'

Evaine smiled. 'Well, I shall most certainly be there, Father, but don't wait for me. I may be a little... late after my ride. I want to look my best, after all.'

Morac couldn't read Evaine's face. The stables were poorly lit, and she was standing in the shadows, but something about her voice worried him. 'Don't be too late, though. Not if you can help it. It wouldn't do to irritate Jaeger. While we remain here and Morana is the way she is, there is little we can do but keep on his good side.'

'Of course, Father,' Evaine said, smiling agreeably. 'I promise to be on my best behaviour.'

CHAPTER ELEVEN

Morana agreed with the old man.

It was a curse.

But she'd seen no way to break it. Not yet. Her dreams weren't working.

Perhaps that was part of the curse too?

Deposited in her bed, she stared at the stone wall, struggling to even move her eyes to look somewhere new. Her head was filled with the Book of Darkness, worried that Draguta would return to claim it before she had recovered.

And she would recover. A curse could be broken.

As someone who had thrown hundreds in her time, Morana Gallas knew very well that a curse could be broken, so it was up to her to find an answer.

If only she could see a way back into her dreams.

***

Neither Edela nor Eydis had seen anything of Ayla in their dreams, which worried them both. Biddy had left supper on the table and gone to the ship sheds to find out how Ayla was. All three of them were fearing the worst, and Biddy decided that just hoping and dreaming wouldn't help any of them sleep that night.

The chicken and ale stew was tasty, and Edela was grateful for it; it helped to take her mind off the urgent matter of how to break the curse, if what Ayla believed was true. She bit her tongue, exclaiming in surprise as a memory of one of her dreams drifted back to her.

'Are you alright?' Eydis asked.

'I forgot! In all my worrying about Ayla, I forgot!' Edela smiled. 'I dreamed about Jael. She is coming home!'

Eydis almost bit her own tongue. 'Really? And Thorgils and Aleksander?'

Edela nodded. 'Yes, I saw all of them, on their way home. With the woman who was caring for Jael. They'll be here soon.'

Eydis could feel tears of joy in her eyes. She shivered with happiness, then frowned. 'But is she alright?'

'No, I don't think so. But she's on Tig, riding, so she is well enough on the outside. It's the inside that will need time to heal now. If only she could have a moment to do so, but I fear she will have much to attend to when she arrives back at the fort. I don't think the dragur are going to wait for Jael to recover.'

***

Jael felt better and worse, and everything in between. Half of her was with Eadmund, worrying about Draguta's plans for him, wherever they were. The other half was in Andala, worrying about how they would keep the dragur out.

She was trying not to think of her baby or her body, which felt weak and uncomfortable, and suddenly very empty.

Aleksander watched her face contorting. 'Sun's going down. We should stop soon.'

'Mmmm,' Jael nodded, listening to Thorgils chatting away to Astrid behind them. She could hear the excitement in his voice, knowing that he would soon see Isaura. 'We should. There's a stream up ahead, from memory.' She didn't say any more, but she needed to.

Aleksander could sense it. 'What's wrong?'

'I had a lot of dreams while I was in that cottage,' Jael said slowly, her eyes drifting to the left, watching the clouds darken over the hills in the distance. 'I dreamed about Hanna.'

Aleksander froze, instantly uncomfortable, but Jael didn't sound in any mood for fun. He looked at her, trying to read her face. 'What about her?'

'She's dying.'

'What?' Aleksander hadn't been expecting that. 'What do you mean? Why? How?'

'She has the sickness,' Jael said. 'Ayla too. I saw them in a shed with Entorp. Marcus was there, with Hanna. He was saying goodbye to her.'

Aleksander felt sick.

'I saw pyres. A lot of them. It looks as though it's spreading.' Speaking about pyres reminded Jael of her daughter, and she bit her lip, not wanting to say any more.

But Aleksander had already stopped listening. His body was tense, his hands in fists, gripping the reins, his mind swirling with memories. He kept seeing images of Hanna's horrible little cottage in Tuura; of her in the tavern, sharing a cup of ale with him.

Her smile. Her kindness. Her bed.

He'd been so desperate to run away from her, but somehow, in the back of his mind, he'd always imagined there would be a time when things would be different. When he wouldn't need to run anymore.

But now?

He spurred Sky on, spotting a stream up ahead. 'Come on!' Aleksander called, turning to Thorgils and Astrid, barely able to swallow. 'We camp here for the night!'

***

Evaine had spent two days creeping around the castle, finding the quickest route in and out of Jaeger's chamber, and now she knew that both Jaeger and Meena were out of it, she hurried to Morac's cottage and put on her cloak. It was too warm for a cloak, she knew, but she would be riding through the night, which terrified her. Though she hoped it would make her harder to follow.

Evaine thought about leaving a note for her father, but she quickly decided against it. Once she was reunited with Eadmund and Draguta had her book, they would be able to return to Hest and get rid of Jaeger.

Morac didn't need to know anything until then.

Evaine knew that the stable hand would keep her horse ready and his mouth shut, as he appeared very keen to receive the rest of the coins she had promised him upon her return.

Now she just had to get into Jaeger's chamber and retrieve the book.

Taking a deep breath, Evaine lifted the satchel over her head, adjusting it across her body as she headed for the door.

***

'And where is Evaine?' Jaeger wondered, raising his goblet to Morac, who held up his in return, his eyes struggling to meet Jaeger's.

'She went for a ride,' Morac said, trying to keep the snarl out of his voice. He needed to stay alive to keep both his daughter and his sister safe, and picking a fight with a violent young king wasn't going to help him do that.

Jaeger laughed, running a hand up Meena's thigh, slightly drunk. 'A ride? Evaine?' He smiled at Meena, who was desperate to squirm away from his exploring hand and his hairy lips, which were coming towards hers. Jaeger kissed her, and she closed her eyes, embarrassed.

Morac felt uncomfortable sitting at the table with just the two of them, though not as uncomfortable as Meena looked with Jaeger pawing her.

His eyes kept returning to the entranceway, wanting to see Evaine.

He was starting to become worried about her.

***

Evaine glanced up and down the corridor, checking that no one was around, but just as she reached for the door handle, she heard a noise from inside the chamber.

It was that humming again.

Listening carefully, Evaine couldn't hear anyone else, so taking the risk that Meena was downstairs with Jaeger, she knocked on the door. Her heart was racing, and she could barely catch her breath as the door opened, and an old woman stood there.

Jaeger's servant.

'Yes?' Else asked, surprised to see Evaine, especially after what Jaeger had done to her. 'Can I help you?'

Evaine smiled sweetly, slipping past Else, hurrying into the chamber. She took a quick look around, spying the book on the table. 'I have come to take that.'

Else followed her gaze. 'The book? Why?' The look on Evaine's face, now that she peered closer, was strange. Her eyes were wide and blinking, her chest rising and falling with speed. 'Has the king sent you?'

Evaine nodded quickly. 'He has. He wants it down in the hall. We are to discuss ways to save Morana. He needs the book.' She moved towards the table.

Else hurried after her. 'He wouldn't send you, though,' she insisted. 'Not for the book. That is only for him. Or Meena.'

Evaine spun around, glaring at the old woman, trying to assess how much of a problem she was going to become. 'You are a servant. It is not your place to question a king. Or a lady, for that matter!'

Else blinked, certain now that Evaine was up to no good. 'You will not take that book. I won't allow it.'

Evaine sighed. A big problem, she realised.

And drawing her knife from the folds of her cloak, she stepped towards Else. 'You will shut up and sit down over there!' she ordered, nodding to the nearest chair. 'I have no problem stabbing an old woman, believe me!'

Her eyes were hard and cold, focused now, and Else believed her.

'It's your choice whether you live or die. Try to stop me, and I will gut you and watch you bleed to death before I leave. So think very carefully now.'

Else didn't know what to do, and Evaine could see the indecision in her eyes. She jerked the knife towards her. It was bigger than the one she'd stabbed Edela with and much sharper. She watched the servant shrink away from the glint of the long blade. 'I will take the book, and you will stay quiet,' Evaine growled, edging closer, pressing the tip of the blade against Else's sagging neck, watching beads of blood burst from her skin.

Else flinched, her eyes bulging in terror.

'Good!' Evaine exclaimed, hurrying to the book, slipping it into the satchel. 'Now, you stay there, right where you are, and you'll live long enough to hear your master screaming at you.' Evaine gulped, suddenly panicking that Jaeger would find her with the book.

She had to leave quickly.

Pulling the key from the lock, she opened the door, spinning around with her knife, but Else was stuck to the chair, still shaking, tears in her eyes. Evaine quickly shoved her knife into its scabbard and pulled the door closed, locking it after her and running for the stairs that led to the kitchen.

***

Draguta felt her body relax for the first time all day. 'Good girl,' she smiled, turning away from her seeing circle as Eadmund stumbled into the cottage. She'd started to wonder where he had gotten to, but quickly smelling the ale on him, she frowned. 'Do you think that's the way to become a real warrior? Drinking? Falling and stumbling about like the drunk you used to be? I have no use for *that* Eadmund.'

Eadmund was exhausted after another long day of being battered by Rollo in the scorching heat, and he wasn't looking for conversation or Draguta's opinion about anything. 'You wanted me to train,' he said, heading straight for his bed, 'so I trained. Rollo took me to the tavern after we'd finished. We'll train again tomorrow, so there's nothing for you to concern yourself with. I'm doing what you asked.'

Draguta blinked, surprised to be dismissed so abruptly. She glared at Eadmund as he walked around the table, sitting down on his bed with a loud groan, ignoring both her and Brill, who lurked awkwardly nearby, wondering whether she should offer to help Eadmund with his boots. It was a small cottage, and Brill was struggling to know where to put herself; caught between always being on hand for whatever whim Draguta had, and wanting to disappear so as not to be noticed at all.

'Well, I'm pleased to hear it,' Draguta sniffed, turning back to her circle, deciding that it was best to leave Eadmund alone. He wasn't a problem yet, and she was eager to know if Evaine was clever and resourceful enough to make it to Flane without bursting into tears and turning back to the castle in a pathetic, sobbing heap.

She hoped so.

***

The stable hand boosted Evaine onto the small grey mare he'd chosen for her, happy with the clinking coins in his pouch but worried that the beautiful girl seemed to have no idea what she was doing. 'Sure you want to go riding in the dark, miss?' he murmured shyly.

Evaine flapped him away as he fussed around her boots, making sure they were firmly in the stirrups. 'I am more than sure,' she insisted, swallowing her fears. 'Now, move! Move out of the way!' And sharply kicking her horse, she exploded out of the stables with an urgency to be gone before Jaeger discovered what she'd done.

***

Jael ate all that she could manage before curling up into a ball, eager to find Eadmund in her dreams again. She was trying to take her mind off Lyra, and the dragur, but she was also desperate to know where Eadmund was. She needed to discover what Draguta intended to do with him.

So far, it didn't appear that Draguta had plans to hurt him, but she wanted to know for sure. Or perhaps she didn't? There was such a great distance between them now. It would take weeks, months even, to find her way to him. And it didn't appear that Eadmund wanted to find his way to her.

Listening to Aleksander rustling around in the leaves, Jael reached out and touched his shoulder. 'Are you alright?'

Aleksander jumped; he'd thought she was asleep. 'No, I'm not,' he admitted with a sigh. 'I feel helpless, stuck here.'

'Mmmm,' Jael agreed, yawning. 'But we can't do anything about it except find our way home quickly. And keep ahead of the dragur.' The thought of getting on Tig again so soon was daunting, but Jael knew that each day she would grow a little stronger. A little more able to cope.

Back to herself.

Somehow.

'But what if it's too late?' Aleksander wondered.

'For Hanna, you mean?' It was dark, but the moon poked out from behind a bank of clouds, and Jael could see him nodding. 'Even if you were in Andala, you couldn't help her. Only healers and dreamers can do that. Only Entorp and Edela can save her now. And if they can, you know they will.'

Aleksander was silent, listening to the wind rustling the leaves above their heads; listening to Thorgils moaning and groaning as he tried to get comfortable on the ground. 'I thought there would be time. That I would be able to say...'

'What?'

'Thank you,' he whispered. 'I thought I'd be able to say thank you.'

***

Biddy had returned to report that Ayla was weak but holding on.

Eydis and Edela were relieved, and they both hurried into their beds early, determined to try dreaming again.

And this time, it worked.

***

Jaeger kept rubbing himself against Meena as they walked back to his chamber.

'I have to go and check on Morana,' she insisted, wanting to turn his mind to other thoughts and his body away from hers. 'I should sleep there.'

Jaeger didn't think she had to. 'I told you I'd get Evaine to do that,' he slurred. He'd had far too much wine, though it felt pleasant to let his fears about Draguta retreat for a while. Just far enough so that he didn't have to feel the suffocating panic about what she'd do next.

He didn't want her to come back and use the book against them.

'But you didn't see Evaine, so Morana will be all alone tonight,' Meena reminded him. 'She won't be able to do anything for herself.'

Jaeger sighed, irritated. 'Go, then. But first, come into the chamber, and let me see you naked. In my bed. After I'm finished, you can go.'

Meena nodded, trying not to grimace. Her arms were aching, and she didn't want him touching any part of her. He was never gentle, especially when he'd had too much wine. She reached for the door handle, frowning suddenly at the voice from inside.

'Help! Help!'

Jaeger stared at Meena, grabbing the door handle himself, turning and pushing, but the door was locked.

'Else?' Meena panicked. 'Else?'

'Meena!' Else cried. 'Oh, Meena! It's Evaine! She had a knife! She's locked me in! She's stolen the book!'

Jaeger stared at Meena, his glazed eyes sharpening as he turned and ran down the corridor.

***

Eydis could see Ayla.

She stood before the throne, watching the woman who sat upon it barking orders at the dull-eyed slaves scraping and bowing before her.

She was small, Eydis thought as she crept up to Ayla. Perhaps even Ayla's age. No, older, she decided after taking a closer look at the woman, who had olive skin and perfectly straight dark hair, framing a wide face with sharp eyes.

Golden, like her throne.

Eydis stopped, not wanting to go any further.

'Her name is Briggit,' Ayla murmured, turning around. 'She murdered her grandfather. Stole the throne away from her uncles, who'd spent a lifetime dreaming of claiming it for themselves. From her mother too. She has them all bound. They bend to her will now.'

Eydis blinked as Ayla turned back around, her gaze returning to the golden-eyed queen.

'She's trying to kill us all. She waited in the shadows with her Followers. When they heard that the Book of Darkness had been found, they emerged, and Briggit killed King Wulf, binding the army to her. She controls The Following, and they control Helsabor. The whole kingdom is theirs. And now their queen will weaken the other kingdoms so she can take them for herself,' Ayla said, reaching down for Eydis' hand. 'And if you and Edela don't break the curse, she will.'

***

Jaeger ran until his ankle ached. All the way to the stables.

The stable hand tried to act as though he had no idea what his king was screaming about, just as he'd done when Morac had arrived earlier, but Jaeger threw him against a wall, and the boy quickly confessed that he'd given Evaine a horse. Though he hadn't thought anything of it, he'd insisted.

Hours ago.

Hours.

Jaeger frowned, grabbing the boy's tunic. 'And she didn't say where she was going? You didn't see?'

The freckle-faced boy shook his head, his face reddening as he heard the coins clinking in his pouch. His king was far too wild to notice, though. 'It was dark, my lord. She rode off in a hurry. I don't know where she went.'

He sounded pathetic, Jaeger thought. Clueless.

Shoving the boy away, he turned back to the newly appointed head of his army, a serious, heavily-scarred warrior named Gunter. 'Send men after Evaine Gallas,' he said. 'Follow her. But don't hurt her. And don't approach her. She mustn't see you. I want to know where she goes. I want to know where Draguta is.'

CHAPTER TWELVE

'You look well,' Garren Maas smiled at Getta as she headed away from the hall, eager to take a moment for herself. He hurried to keep up with her, seeing that she didn't appear to be slowing down. 'Motherhood agrees with you. I've never seen you look more radiant.'

'What do you want, Garren?' Getta muttered irritably, trying to ignore the way his voice made her feel.

He was impossibly handsome. Strong. Dangerous.

Not her husband.

Though he'd always wanted to be.

'Want? To see you, of course,' Garren said, pleased that after glancing around to check that her husband wasn't around, Getta had finally slowed down. 'You've been missed.'

'I've hardly been gone,' she snapped, flustered by how intensely his deep-blue eyes were studying her lips. 'I've been with my son.'

'Ahhh, yes, your son. Heir to the throne... as things stand.'

'And what does *that* mean?' His eyes were narrowed, demanding, and she didn't look away.

Garren inclined his head towards the gates, wanting to escape Ollsvik's square, which was busy, being a trading day. Three ships had just arrived from Alekka, and their crews were busy unloading furs, ivory, and soapstone onto carts. Getta was sure she saw a glint of amber too, and she felt impatient, wanting to go and see for herself, but she followed Garren through the gates, far away from the market.

Garren Maas was ten years older than Raymon. An experienced warrior. An ambitious man, with an equally ambitious father; both men driven by an obsessive desire to claim the Iskavallan throne for their family. Once Garren's obsession with defeating the Vandaals had excited Getta, but now he posed a threat to Raymon and their newborn son.

'Your husband appears keen to help the Furycks,' Garren said as they passed the steady flow of foot traffic heading into the fort. He led Getta past Ollsvik's three full piers that stretched out into a narrow harbour, surrounded on both sides by steep mountains, their rocky peaks still covered in snow. 'Formalising that alliance will weaken his position on the throne. And if Raymon falls to the Furyck's ambition, I doubt anyone will have an appetite for your son to follow in his father's failed footsteps. Not when they could find somebody more... suited to the role.'

'You, you mean?' Getta grumbled. 'You're positioning yourself to destroy Raymon? To take his throne? *Now?*'

Garren ran a hand over his blonde beard, shaking his head dismissively. His hair was cropped at the sides but long on top, tied in a knot that was working itself loose. 'Would I do such a thing? No, it isn't me you have to worry about, Getta. It isn't me stoking the flames of rebellion in the darkened corners of your husband's hall. Not at all. I wanted to warn you. To give you a chance to speak to him. If he meets with Axl Furyck, there will be consequences, and Raymon could very well find himself fighting for his life. You know how things go here. We are not a tolerant bunch.'

Getta glared at a man, who stumbled into her as he hurried past with a screaming toddler, feeling her milk leaking. She pulled her shawl around her chest, covering her dress. 'The Furycks haven't been enemies for years. Ranuf and Lothar were welcomed here. Ollsvik is the only home I've ever known!'

'It's not *friendship* they are in fear of, my love, it's ambition,'

Garren breathed in Getta's ear. 'Axl Furyck wants to conquer Iskavall. To take it for Brekka. From what I hear, his ambitions exceed that of his dead father's, and now that he's killed Lothar, he's setting his sights on Ollsvik.'

Getta didn't doubt it, but still, if her husband was killed, what would happen to her? To her son? 'Raymon will not be stopped,' she said carefully. 'He is determined to proceed, encouraged, of course, by Ravenna. He will not be stopped meeting my cousins.'

'Not even by a woman as persuasive as you?' Garren leaned in as close as he dared, though Getta's husband was only a boy and not likely to challenge his best warrior to a fight over his wife. 'Or maybe it's that you realise you chose the wrong man? You and your father both. Maybe you realise what a mistake it was to back the Vandaals over my family? Our claim has always been the strongest, as many will readily admit in private. If you want to save your husband, Getta, you should steer Raymon away from your cousins.' He stepped back, turning towards the fort. 'But then again, if you don't... I might be looking for a queen myself soon. And your place was always destined to be by my side, one way or the other.'

Getta stared after Garren as he strode away, not looking back, so confident with his broad shoulders and his arrogant swagger. She shuddered as the wind picked up her shawl, blowing it away from her, exposing the wet patches of milk on her dress. Hurrying to gather it back in, she turned after him, eager to return to her son.

***

Else was surprised to still be in Jaeger's employment after what Evaine had done, but he didn't appear to blame her, which was a relief. Though he had sent her to care for Morana, which, she supposed, was some form of punishment, if only for having to be subjected to the smell.

But Else wasn't about to be defeated by a little stink.

Dragmall had come to Morana's chamber with her, carrying a bucket of hot water and herbs that he'd picked and steeped, hoping to wash away the smell. Meena had joined them, bringing a new dress for her aunt. They were going to cleanse the entire chamber, and then Morana.

But as for trying to remove the curse?

They weren't going to attempt that. Not directly. Still, the herbs and spices Dragmall had selected were useful for banishing dark magic. Though, Dragmall thought, considering the power of the caster, it was likely to be a stubborn curse.

'At least it will remove the smell,' Else grinned, sticking her cloth into the bucket, inhaling the astringent lemon and witch hazel aroma of Dragmall's concoction.

'Yes,' he agreed. 'And once we bathe Morana, that should improve things further.' He nodded at Meena, who wasn't looking forward to her part in proceedings. She'd been down to the kitchen and organised for the wooden tub in the laundry room to be filled with hot water. The kitchen servants were reluctant to do anything she asked until Jaeger arrived, growling at them to hurry up.

And now the tub was filled with hot water, waiting for her aunt.

Morana's good eye flared as Meena lifted her off the chair, grabbing her arms and leading her towards the door. Morana stumbled, trying to turn away from her niece, wanting to go back to the chair.

She'd heard them talking, and she didn't want to be cleansed by anything. It wouldn't work, of that she was certain, and she couldn't stand the smell.

Dragmall quickly realised that Meena was unable to control Morana on her own. 'I'll help you get her downstairs,' he said, taking one of Morana's arms. 'You'll feel better when you're clean, Morana, I promise.' And gripping her arm firmly, he encouraged her towards the door.

***

Having the very helpful information from Eydis' dream, Edela laid it all out before Axl and Gant in Axl's private chamber. Ayla's knowledge of what was causing the sickness couldn't be proven, and it was better not to panic anyone or provide false hope to those who were worrying about loved ones or themselves.

Ayla may have suspected a curse, but Edela had no idea how to break it.

Not yet.

Axl quickly went from feeling momentarily relieved to being even more disturbed. He sat forward in his chair, leaning his chin on his hand. 'So, even if we break the curse, stop the sickness, join our army with Iskavall's and somehow make it down South without getting burned alive by dragons or killed by dragur, we'll have to face an attack from Helsabor as well now? There's no help to find there? No way to get into their kingdom and slip into Hest to defeat Draguta?'

'None!' Edela insisted. 'And now we know that they're just as eager to kill us as she is. Who knows how many dreamers are scheming behind those walls? How many warriors they've bound to do their bidding?'

'But none of it even matters if we can't stop the sickness,' Gant put in. 'We can't worry about getting to Hest until we do that. And then there's the dragur. They're still coming, I take it?'

'Oh yes, they are,' Edela nodded. 'But so is Jael.'

Axl lifted his head, his eyes bright with hope, his shoulders relaxing. 'She is?'

Edela smiled. 'She is. And Aleksander and Thorgils too. They'll be here soon, leading the dragur to us, I'm afraid.'

'Oh.' Axl's face dropped, his relief once again short-lived.

'So you must get the men repairing the wall to work faster. All through the night. The dragur following Jael won't be alone.'

Gant was puzzled. 'What do you mean?'

'Draguta controls them,' Edela murmured. 'She has power over them. She can raise them at will, it seems, wherever they are. Wherever she needs them to be. And if Jael is coming here, then she will raise every dragur around us to kill her and take the Book of Aurea.' Edela could see that she had worried Gant and Axl, but she'd also worried herself because she had seen the dragur in her dreams. 'You must work on protecting us from those creatures,' she said, trying to focus them all. 'And I will try and break the curse.'

***

Evaine had never been more scared in her life, but the thought of being reunited with Eadmund had driven her on through the terrifying darkness and the unfamiliar landscape, and eventually, she had come to the town Draguta had spoken of, where, with a bag full of Morac's coins, she was able to secure the services of a man to lead her to Flane. He was old, harmless-looking, toothless, and eager to be paid. She had hidden half the coins in her saddlebag, hoping he wasn't simply going to rob her and leave her in the dust.

He didn't look capable of such a thing, nor of raping her, which she also feared. After what Jaeger had done, Evaine now looked at every man as a threat. But Toothless Bergil seemed more interested in getting to Flane for his reward than admiring her figure, which she'd made a point of keeping well covered.

Once Bergil had organised a hearty breakfast for himself and a small bowl of porridge for Evaine, which turned her stomach, they headed off, kicking up the dust as they left Karp at speed, riding quickly towards Flane.

***

Morac had been so surprised by Jaeger's news that he stumbled down onto the nearest bench, his body vibrating with panic. 'I don't understand. Why would she do such a thing?' After a sleepless night of worrying about Evaine, and trying to find her, at least he knew what had happened to her, though it made little sense.

Jaeger eyed Morac coldly, trying to determine whether he was lying. He quickly came to the conclusion that Morac had no idea what his daughter was up to. 'I believe she is taking the book to Draguta.'

'What? Why? Why would she do that? Go to Draguta? After what she did?'

'It's just a guess, but what other motive would she have? Why else would she take it? To use it herself? She's no dreamer, is she?'

Morac's frown dug a deep hole into the narrow space between his wiry grey eyebrows. He shook his head. 'No, but it makes no sense. Eadmund is coming here to be with her. She wouldn't leave. She's bound to Eadmund.'

It was Jaeger's turn to frown; he'd forgotten about that. 'Well, perhaps she's going to find him?'

Morac's shoulders were taut. He felt bereft. Morana had disappeared from him and now Evaine. He was more alone than ever, and, when he looked at Jaeger's angry face, more uncertain of his future.

'I have men tracking her,' Jaeger assured him. 'She will be found, don't worry. We'll soon know where Evaine has gone.'

***

Eadmund cheered, amazed that he'd finally managed to hit Rollo.

Rollo flinched, spitting on the ground. 'Fuck you!' He banged his staff on the dusty surface, bringing it up into both hands as he lunged.

Eadmund jumped back. Rollo Barda was twice as wide as him, with arms like slabs of rock. He knew how it felt to be battered with a staff wielded by those powerful arms. And if he ever forgot, his body was covered in aching reminders.

Draguta smiled as she passed on her way to the tower. She could feel Evaine getting closer, and there was a serenity about her this morning. The sun was bright, and the breeze was light, and her new dress suited her well.

All things felt as though they were coming together again.

Jael Furyck remained a nagging problem, but she would soon see to her, and when she had the Book of Darkness, she would see to everyone else. Both Jael and her precious Andala were vulnerable now. It would be so much easier to destroy them.

Eadmund watched Draguta out of the corner of his eye, his concentration wandering as Rollo grabbed a waterskin, leaving him a moment to catch his breath. Draguta seemed confident that Evaine would find her way to them, but she didn't know Evaine as he did. And despite his overwhelming need to see her, Eadmund was beginning to have his doubts that Evaine was capable of such a journey on her own.

He blinked, jerking around as Rollo whacked him on the arm.

'Come on, my lord! According to your mistress, we've no time to waste!'

***

Now that Edela knew, or, at least, believed that it was a curse, she felt perfectly comfortable about spending time in the ship sheds with Entorp. She had her tattoos of protection, and so did Biddy, who left Eydis in the hall with Amma and came along.

Entorp had stopped to take a quick break. He was becoming weak with exhaustion, but his mind was still alert, and they needed it now more than ever. No one knew more about The Following than him, except perhaps Marcus, who was with Hanna, and Edela didn't want to disturb him.

'If this Briggit is the leader of The Following in Helsabor, then she'll want to bring Raemus back,' she began as they sat around a small table near the door. The breeze was barely noticeable, but it was preferable to being stuck too far inside. They kept their voices low, though nobody appeared to be paying them any mind. 'So she is doing his work already. Defeating Raemus' enemies.'

'And hers,' Entorp added. 'No Follower likes a Brekkan.'

'If Ayla hadn't fallen ill, perhaps we would never have known?' Biddy suggested, fighting the urge to get up and start cleaning the shed. Entorp and his helpers had done their best, she could see, but there was much she could improve upon. Her fingers were itching to be useful, but she blinked, forcing her boots to remain where they were, her attention back on Edela.

'I think you're right,' Edela agreed. 'But we must hurry if we're going to save Ayla. She doesn't deserve to die. Not when she's the one trying to save us all.'

'A curse this potent will not be easy to break, Edela,' Entorp warned. 'Not quickly, at least.'

'No, though perhaps we should try simple things first? I know of some herbs that might work. Some hyssop and coltsfoot, if they survived the snow and the dragon. Maybe some blessed thistle? A little wormwood too. And there are symbols. Perhaps we start with Ayla? Hanna looks far too weak to bother now.'

Entorp didn't look convinced.

'It wouldn't hurt, though, would it?' Biddy wondered. 'While you and Edela keep thinking, and Edela and Eydis keep dreaming, it wouldn't hurt to try.'

'Perhaps the Book of Aurea will have something?' Entorp suggested, stifling a yawn. One of his patients cried out, and he turned away, peering into a dark corner of the shed. 'I should go.'

'It very well may,' Edela nodded. 'I haven't been able to find my way to the book in my dreams, but hopefully, I'll have it in my hands soon. And that might mean a way to help everyone.'

***

'Well, that's much better, isn't it?' Else smiled, looking around the chamber with satisfaction. Dragmall had been up to the winding gardens at dawn, collecting petals from every white rose, adding them to his second herbal concoction. And after the sharp, astringent smell of the first cleansing wash, the chamber now had an overpoweringly floral aroma.

'It does smell better,' Meena admitted, though the chamber was still gloomy with Morana in it. 'And it looks much cleaner.'

'As does your aunt,' Else declared, bringing her brush down through Morana's black-and-white hair for the last time. 'I'm not sure I've ever seen such a bird's nest, but all that brushing has helped, don't you think? Not that I'll be able to use my arm again for some time!' She chuckled and stepped back, admiring her patient, who sat in a chair, dressed in a clean grey dress, with a shining face and a long mane of hair that had been washed for the first time in years. It almost looked silky as it hung down to the floor in great black-and-white stripes.

Meena frowned as she stared at her aunt.

Morana looked ready to kill them both.

Dragmall had left earlier, but Meena was sure she would've wanted to kill him too. She didn't imagine that Morana would thank him for bathing her in all those roses. But Dragmall had insisted that rose had powerful cleansing properties, and who was Meena to argue.

Besides, Jaeger needed to see that they were trying to help her, and Morana herself, if she were ever to return, needed to believe that she had been helped, not harmed by what they were doing.

'Are you sure you don't want me to stay?' Meena asked, sad to be losing Else from Jaeger's chamber. She had come to rely upon her company and advice.

'I'm happy enough to stay here. Though, if I had a choice,' Else said, walking towards Meena, 'I would choose to remain with you. I'm not sure you'll eat a thing without me there.'

Meena smiled shyly as Else took her hands. 'I'll try.'

'I hope so. We don't know how things are going to go now, do we? Now that Evaine has run off with that book to who knows where.'

Else had her back to Morana, but Meena could see her aunt's dark eye pop open in horror, her twisted mouth trying to open. Else turned around, sensing Morana's discomfort. 'Morana? Are you alright?' she wondered, hurrying back to her.

But Morana couldn't move. And though she tried, she couldn't lift her arm to bat away the annoying woman or move her legs to kick her pathetic niece in the shin.

How had they let Evaine escape with the book?

***

The hall was unusually quiet as they ate their midday meal. It kept Getta on edge. She stared into each corner, looking for conspirators, though there were few inside today, and those who'd taken a break to enjoy a cup of ale were loud, not appearing to care if they were overheard.

Garren had unsettled her.

Iskavall was a kingdom divided by deep rivalries, and there had been loud opposition to Raymon's ascension to the throne after his father's death. But Lothar had worked hard to placate and bribe those who were up in arms, negotiating with those who wanted something in return for their support, determined to get his daughter onto the throne.

Lothar had chosen Raymon for Getta, just as he had chosen to support the Vandaals, so he was never going to back away from that fight. But now, without her father to ride across from Andala to smooth the ruffled feathers of his squabbling neighbours, Getta felt vulnerable. Ravenna was useless, except to push Raymon closer to the cliff he appeared determined to throw them all off.

So, if she was going to keep both her husband and her son safe, she would need to nullify any power Ravenna had over Raymon. Getta had to convince him that aligning Iskavall with Brekka was a dangerous move for his whole family.

'Where will you meet them?' Ravenna asked, cutting her sausage in half.

'In Rissna,' Raymon mumbled.

'On the *Brekkan* side?' Getta's eyes flared. 'You'll get yourself killed!'

Raymon blinked at his wife, whose temper had exploded like a bonfire. She had barely said a word as she sat, simmering beside him. But now? 'It makes no difference whether we're in Rissna or Varella. Axl Furyck is requesting that we meet. He chose the location, but you needn't worry. We'll both have our armies. We'll both be protected by our men.' He frowned, noticing how Getta's eyes kept jumping around the hall, as though she was looking for someone. 'What is it? Why are you suddenly so suspicious of the Furycks? You *are* a Furyck!' He tried to smile, but he had no enthusiasm for it, so he was quickly frowning again.

'I *was* a Furyck,' Getta reminded him. 'Now, I'm a Vandaal, and Iskavall is my kingdom.' She lowered her voice. 'And handing it over to my cousins will not endear you to our people.'

'I don't intend to hand anything over to anyone,' Raymon insisted, reaching for his ale. 'But I do intend to keep our people safe. That's why I'm on the throne, after all.'

Ravenna was surprised by how forceful her usually timid son had begun to sound. Like his father, she thought wistfully. It was in him, of course, to be strong. It was in his blood. But she had never seen it emerge before. Not like this. Yet it was when faced with tough decisions that a true king shone. She smiled, feelings of pride fluttering in her chest, but when she looked at the scowling faces of the hard men who sat before them, their furtive eyes turning away from hers with speed, she shuddered, wondering for the first time if Getta was right?

CHAPTER THIRTEEN

'I'll wait for Jael,' Axl decided, smiling as his sister's puppies chased each other around the training ring, annoying his men, who were concentrating. As he was trying to. 'Before we go to Rissna.'

'Makes sense,' Gant panted, coming to a stop. 'Time for something to eat. I can't hear myself think over your growling guts!'

Axl nodded. He'd barely been able to touch Gant with his sword, but it had felt good being up and about, trying to look like a warrior again. His mind kept returning to the battle in Vidar's Pass, wanting to be strong enough to lead his men better than Lothar and Osbert had. And he would need to. A defeat in their next battle would surely see an end to all of Osterland.

Fyn smiled at them as they made their way through the railings.

'Your turn next,' Gant said, taking Axl's sword from him and heading for the training shed.

Fyn looked surprised. 'Me?'

'You think you're just going to watch the dragur from the comfort of your bed, do you? Holding your mother's hand?'

Fyn glanced at Axl, who was grinning at him. 'Well, no, but I was... waiting for Jael and Thorgils. I've never trained with anyone else.' Gant intimidated him. He was economical with his words, often sharp, and he had a look about him that made

Fyn nervous. He didn't feel good enough to fight him. Not after what had happened in the Temple of Tuura. The memory of the spear in his belly was a nightmare he often woke up sweating from.

'Well, I think they're going to need some training when they get back too. I can't imagine either of them are in much shape, from what I've heard. I'll have all three of you in here soon. Axl too. We need our best warriors sharp. It's not going to help any of us if you're hobbling and moaning about the place.'

***

'I have to stop!' Thorgils called to Jael. 'I can't feel any part of my body! We should rest. Eat something!'

'Who knew you were such a baby?' Jael grumbled back. 'We've barely started out!' She almost found herself smiling. Thorgils had a way of making her feel better, especially when he was in a moaning kind of mood. 'Try and last a little longer. We need to keep the dragur far behind us.'

'Do you think they're still following us?' Astrid asked. She was riding next to Jael, uncomfortable in Rufus' saddle, though she hadn't uttered a word of complaint. Not like Thorgils, who had been listing his injuries and ailments since they'd set off again.

'I hope so,' Jael said. 'We don't want them going anywhere else. We need them to come to Andala. All of them. We need to kill them. And Andala is the best place to do it. If we can get there without Thorgils falling to pieces, that is.' She turned to glare at him. 'How Isaura is going to put up with you, I don't know. Not sure she needs another child to look after, and a giant one at that!' There was no smile in her eyes now. She blinked, looking ahead to the next hilly rise in the distance. They were getting closer to where they needed to be. Everything else lay behind them, and for now, that's just where Jael wanted it.

She had said goodbye to her daughter.

And now it was time to focus on the fight ahead.

***

Rollo wiped a hand over his wet mouth before snotting out one side of his nose, then the other. 'Who is she to you, then? This Draguta? Why are you doing her bidding? Letting yourself be humiliated by me every day like you're a little dog she's sent in here for punishment?' He was bright red from the top of his shining head to the waistband of his trousers. 'She's a fine woman, but I wouldn't be caught making a fool of myself for her. No woman's worth that.'

Eadmund frowned, reaching for the waterskin. He didn't have an answer, so he just shrugged. 'No harm in becoming a better warrior, even if I do have to put up with a turd like you training me.'

Rollo bowed, enjoying the insult. 'You were better than this, from what I hear. You had a reputation as a real warrior once. Not this.' He motioned to the panting, filthy, sunburned man before him. 'Whatever this is.'

Eadmund threw away the empty skin, shaking his dripping beard. 'I was. And one day soon, I'll be better than you.'

'Ha!' Rollo's laugh came from deep within his rippling stomach, and it was loud, surprising Eadmund. 'You're a confident bastard... my lord.' He was well aware that Eadmund was a king, but in the training ring there could be only one leader, and that man had to have earned his status. So far Eadmund Skalleson had done little more than run around, taking one whipping after another.

But there was hunger in his eyes.

Rollo could see that.

'Who are you looking to kill, then? What great enemy are you planning to defeat?'

Eadmund could feel Draguta's eyes on him, and he turned to see her watching from the railings, Brill just behind her.

'The greatest enemy of all,' Draguta smiled. 'So I need him ready. You've had enough of a break now, gentlemen. Back to work!'

Rollo frowned, disturbed by the cool intensity in Draguta's eyes and the blank deference in Eadmund's. For a king, he seemed quite happy to be told what to do by this woman.

As most people in Flane appeared to be.

And Rollo Barda had enough wits about him not to make trouble. Nodding, he bent down to pick up his sword. 'Come on, then. Grab your shield. You're going to need it.'

***

It had always amazed Entorp that a body could endure so much, be so near death, so far from life, and yet, still hold on. But as he looked Hanna over, he wondered how much fight her body had left. She was young – that was on her side – but she had neither spoken nor eaten in days.

Marcus looked no better as he sat beside her. 'I will help you,' he said blankly, looking up. His usually clean-shaven face was covered in a scruffy black-and-grey beard. His eyes were tired, dark circles making them look even more pronounced.

Entorp nodded. 'I would like that. I have things to tell you. Things you need to hear.'

Marcus' eyes showed some life as he stood, shocked by how stiff his body felt after sitting for so long. 'What things?' He turned back to check on his daughter before following Entorp to a corner, away from the dying and the grieving.

'Edela thinks the sickness is a curse.'

'She dreamed it?' Marcus' body tensed. 'She's seen it?'

'Ayla has,' Entorp whispered. 'She's likely in the dream now, watching what's happening, what is trying to kill her. She says it's a woman. I thought you might know her. Briggit Halvardar. I believe I met her once. She was in The Following.'

Marcus stumbled, shivering all over.

'I take it you know her, then?' Entorp asked, leaning closer.

'I do,' Marcus breathed. 'I do. She is quite... disturbing. A powerful dreamer, but dark. Very dark.' He shook his head, remembering those cat-like eyes.

'Well, according to Ayla, she's the Queen of Helsabor now. The leader of The Following there too. She sits upon the golden throne, throwing curses at us.'

Marcus didn't know what to say. 'The Following? In Helsabor?' It felt like all the air had been punched out of his chest. He looked at his daughter with new fear. 'Briggit hates me.'

'She does?'

'She... pursued me when I lived in Helsabor, before I left for Tuura. But her father didn't approve of me, and I was intent on becoming an elder. I... I... it was not appropriate. And there was something about her. She was beautiful but angry. I tried to be gentle, but she didn't take it well. As a princess, she wasn't used to being told no.'

'I don't imagine it's about you, though,' Entorp suggested delicately. 'The curse.'

'I'm sure it's not,' Marcus agreed. He was so tired that he could barely form his thoughts into a cohesive stream of words. 'And does Edela know how to break it? *Can* she break it?'

'We're trying,' Entorp said. 'That's why Biddy is here. We're going to start cleansing this shed. Do what we can to remove any evil spirits in here. I'll carve some protective symbols too.

But until we get the Book of Aurea or find out more from Ayla, we're mostly blind. Edela is hoping the book may have the answer we need.'

Marcus looked desperate as he turned back to his daughter. 'Curses are not broken easily, and if Briggit is the leader of The Following, it means she's more powerful than we can imagine. I hope Edela finds what she's looking for and quickly. I don't think Hanna can hold on much longer.'

***

Ayla could see them talking about the curse. She'd been wandering the sheds in her dreams, watching what was happening, horrified to discover that Bruno was sick too. It was like a knife in her heart, and she felt helpless, unable to even touch him.

She'd been all over the fort, too, watching Edela and Eydis try to dream, seeking ways to break the curse. But this was no ordinary curse from one who was trying to injure a rival or destroy a marriage. This curse was dark and insidious, designed to murder thousands; to wipe out the enemies of The Following in Osterland and beyond.

And Ayla was desperate to find her way back to Helsabor. She needed to see how Briggit Halvardar had done it. If she could find out how the curse had been thrown, there would be a way to break it.

The answer, she knew, was waiting in her dreams.

***

'I can't!' Berard insisted loudly, backing away.

Karsten scowled as the men training nearby turned to stare at them. He strode up to his brother, wanting to grab him by the throat. He was tired and irritable.

Worried too.

Nicolene had been taken into the ship sheds in the night.

He couldn't get his thoughts in order, and he knew that, before long, Bayla would be at the railings, demanding he come back to deal with some emergency. Though he supposed it was hard to blame her when her family had been torn apart.

'You can,' Karsten growled. 'And you will, Berard! I'm not asking you to become a great warrior, but you need to know how to defend yourself with that arm. When the dragur come, you'll be with Bayla and the children. If something gets through...' He ran out of breath and sighed. 'With that wall barely mended, something is likely to get through. You'll need to do what you can to defend them. I won't be there, and now with Nicolene...' He swallowed, adjusting his eyepatch. 'I need you to be useful. Helpful.'

Berard could see the fear in his brother's eye. 'Alright,' he said. 'Show me again.' And he firmed up his grip on the sword, glancing at Gant and Axl training nearby; jealous of all those around him with two arms.

Angry at Jaeger for taking his.

Anger helped. Clenching his jaw, Berard thought of Jaeger and what he'd done to Meena, and he swung his sword with force, cracking it against Karsten's.

'Good!' his brother exclaimed. 'I almost felt that!'

Berard nodded and kept going, determined not to be left behind when Karsten went to Hest. Determined to be there, watching, when Karsten took off Jaeger's head.

Hoping that Meena would stay safe until then.

***

'How is Morana?' Jaeger wondered, staring at Meena over his wine goblet. 'Improving?'

Meena didn't want Morana to be improving, though she was starting to realise that her aunt might be a better enemy to have than Draguta. 'Yes, I think so.'

Jaeger's eyes were alert, full of interest. 'You do? And Dragmall? Has he been helping her?'

Meena nodded. 'He came to see her this morning.'

'And Morana seems different?'

'She appears more... awake. Not speaking, but more... alert.'

Jaeger was pleased. 'Good, that's good to hear. Morana was always very useful to me. I shall be glad to have her return.'

Meena couldn't say the same.

'And my useless servant, whatever her name is. Is she still there?'

'Yes, Else is still there. She said she was happy to look after Morana.'

'That woman would be happy about anything,' Jaeger grumbled. 'I imagine she'd even enjoy being ordered about by Draguta.' He swallowed, reminded of what Draguta had done to him in the hall: lifting him off the ground, sucking the air from his lungs. She would have killed him if not for Meena and that knife.

Jaeger smiled, grabbing her hand. Something was different, he realised, staring at her. 'You don't tap your head anymore.'

Meena blinked, surprised that he'd noticed. 'No. I no longer need to,' she lied. She wanted to tap herself nearly every waking moment, but she was desperately fighting the voice in her head, knowing that she needed to become stronger, not weaker. She needed to fight the darkness trying to claim her by moving further and further into the light. She couldn't give in because the light was where Berard was, far away from Jaeger and the Book of Darkness, and that was where she wanted to be.

***

'We should head for the cottage, Eydis,' Edela sighed as they traipsed across the square. She felt defeated by the day. Biddy had cleansed the ship sheds with Runa's help, and then they'd brought in Aedan, Aron, and Kormac, who had worked with Entorp to carve symbols around the walls. But there had been no sign of improvement in any of Entorp's patients, and certainly not Ayla.

It was no surprise to Edela, who felt anxious, sensing that they were quickly running out of time. 'Those puppies are after their supper, I'd say –'

She stopped abruptly.

Eydis reached out for Edela's arm. 'What is it? Are you alright?'

But Edela couldn't speak. Tears flooded her eyes as she stood there in the dusk-laden square, watching Jael ride Tig through the main gates.

'Edela?'

Edela swallowed, gripping Eydis' hand. 'It's Jael,' she said. 'She's home!' And pulling Eydis with her, she hurried them forward.

Jael wasn't sure what she should look at first: the broken wall, the gruesome bits of what must be the dragon, or the old woman and the blind girl charging towards her. She took a deep breath, not wanting to meet her grandmother's eyes as she slipped her feet out of Tig's stirrups, dropping to the ground.

'But where are your boots?' Edela wondered, staring at Jael's bare feet before taking her in her arms. 'My poor girl. I'm so sorry, Jael. Oh, Jael.'

Jael didn't want to cry, but it was hard when she saw a crying Eydis over Edela's shoulder, and when she could feel her grandmother shaking against her. 'I had to leave in a hurry,' she mumbled. 'I've gone through a few boots lately.'

Aleksander smiled as he came up beside her, hugging Edela next. 'We both have.'

'Thorgils!'

Jael looked up to see Isaura running towards them, or, at least, trying to with Mads attached to her hip. He was whining loudly, jiggling up and down, but Isaura didn't appear to notice as she ran to Thorgils, who had just eased himself out of Gus' saddle, ready to moan about how stiff every part of him was, but one look at Isaura and he had no desire to moan at all. She threw herself into his arms, squashing Mads into Thorgils' chest as she sobbed into his filthy tunic.

Thorgils squeezed half of her as hard as he dared, trying not to make Mads cry even more before stepping back, tears in his eyes. He took her face in his swollen hands – that sweet, round face that had kept him going when he felt certain that he was going to die – and he kissed her gently and slowly, not caring who saw.

Now Jael could feel tears coming, and then Eydis was wrapping her arms around her waist. 'Jael!' she cried. 'I was so worried!'

Jael pulled Eydis close, feeling odd; aware that she no longer needed to be worried about her stomach, which felt so different now. Neither the way it had been recently, nor the way it had been before. Just somewhere strange in between.

Much like her.

She quickly shut those thoughts away, stepping back as Aleksander released Edela.

'How's Hanna?' he asked quietly. 'Are we too... late?'

Edela was surprised by his question, but then everything fell into place, and she smiled sadly. 'Hanna,' she murmured.

'Oh yes, Hanna.' Wiping away her tears, she slipped her arm through Aleksander's. 'She's still here. Still hanging on. She's in the ship sheds, so why don't you go and see her, and come back to the cottage when you're done? Biddy will have some food, and there's much we need to talk about.'

'Is there?' Jael looked worried. 'What else has happened?' She gripped Eydis' hand, realising that she might fall down without someone to hold onto.

'I think we need to get you to a chair,' Edela said, noticing how pale her granddaughter looked. 'A chair, a fire, and something warm to drink. Now, come on, I don't think Thorgils will even notice if we leave.'

'I need to see to the horses and help Astrid first,' Jael insisted, nodding to the healer, who stood awkwardly behind them all, conscious that she was still in her nightdress. 'She's from Harstad. A healer. She's been looking after us all. We... we had to leave in the night, and Astrid came along. I need to find her somewhere to stay until she decides what to do.'

'Of course. I'll take you to the hall, Astrid,' Edela smiled kindly, walking towards the shy healer. 'My daughter will know where to put you. And then we can find you something to wear. Eydis, you should go with Jael. She'll be a while with the horses, no doubt.'

'No doubt I will,' Jael agreed. 'By the time I'm finished, I might almost be hungry.'

'But don't do too much,' Astrid suggested. 'You're still very weak.'

Jael frowned, though Astrid wasn't wrong; she was long past ready for bed.

'Come on, then, let's hurry along before it's dark,' Edela said, leading Astrid towards the hall, winking at Thorgils on her way past.

Thorgils barely noticed anyone was there, except Isaura. She had put Mads on the ground now, and he was howling in annoyance, tears streaming down his face as he thumped her leg, but she didn't care.

'I was so worried. Edela saw you covered in blood. I had Edela and Ayla dreamwalking to find you. To help Jael find you.'

'You did?'

'Yes,' Isaura sobbed. 'And now Ayla is ill. Dying. And it's all my fault!'

Thorgils wrapped his arms around her again, enjoying the feel of her, inhaling her smoky hair, which smelled like sage and sausages. He sighed happily, relieved to be back. 'You didn't make Ayla sick. You're not powerful enough to do that. The sickness isn't your doing, so don't blame yourself. But do pick up that son of yours, so everyone stops staring at us,' he grinned, 'and let's head back to your cottage. *Our* cottage. I could really do with sitting in front of the fire. Maybe a cup of ale?' His smile was wide as he stared into Isaura's eyes, mesmerised by how beautiful they were. How familiar.

'I'm sure we could do that,' Isaura smiled, grateful beyond words to have him back. She bent down to pick up her screaming son and leaned into Thorgils as he wrapped his arm around her.

'If we can just stop off at the stables first. I'm sure Gant would appreciate it if I gave his horse a nice rub down after all he's done to help me.' Thorgils dreaded to think how Gant would react to hearing about what he'd subjected poor Gus to, but that was for another day. He had a whole night of being wrapped up in Isaura's arms to look forward to first.

CHAPTER FOURTEEN

Eadmund was beginning to feel like a slave, not a king. Ordered out of bed each morning and sent off to train. Told when to come back. What to eat. Where to sit.

What to think.

And all with the whispered promise that Evaine would arrive soon. But another day had ended with only Draguta and Brill for company, and Eadmund could feel his tension rising.

'Scowling at me will not make Evaine come any faster,' Draguta said, ignoring Eadmund's grumbling and fidgeting as she ate her shellfish broth. It didn't taste of anything, and she was beginning to wonder if she required sustenance at all. She had certainly lost her desire for food, though drinking wine still made her happy. 'I have seen her, and she has done well, so you will be patient. Keep training, and soon everything will change. Once I have the book and Evaine arrives, everything will change.'

Eadmund didn't feel as confident as Draguta looked, but he did sense that Evaine was getting closer. His heart beat faster when he thought of her, hoping she would stay safe.

Hoping she would arrive soon.

***

'Men are following us,' Bergil whispered. He had no teeth, and it was hard to understand his mashed words, but Evaine could see his weasel-like eyes darting around in glimmers of moonlight, and she guessed his meaning.

Jaeger.

'Will they catch us?' She was cold. Shivering. The temperature reminded her of Oss, but she was dressed for Hest, and the cloak she wore was a light one.

'They might,' Bergil mumbled, thinking about the coins he was yet to claim. That prize would feed him and his family for years. If he could make it to Flane and back to Karp in just the one piece. 'If you've got something they want? Or you're someone they want to find?'

Evaine gathered the folds of her cloak around herself. 'It's no concern of yours either way,' she sniffed. 'You are to get me to Flane, and quickly.' The fire spat at her, and Evaine jumped away from the flames.

'Then, that being the case, I think we should get on the horses again. Ride through the night,' Bergil decided, his stiff old bones not looking forward to that. 'We'll be there when the sun comes up if we do. Don't imagine those men will be following us by then.'

Evaine was quickly on her feet, eager to be gone, though the intense darkness of the night worried her. The moonlight, when it came, didn't linger for long, and Evaine was conscious that they were near the cliffs. She swallowed, her need to be with Eadmund bubbling inside her like a cauldron of hot water. 'Well, hurry up, then. We don't want them to catch us, for if they do, there'll be no reward for you!'

Bergil watched as she kicked dust over the flames, pulling himself up on a boulder, thinking about how nice it would be to sit around the fire with his wife, supping his ale. Then he remembered the promise of more coins, and he hurried to ready the horses.

***

Jael felt odd.

Biddy was being so nice. So was Edela. Eydis too. But she just wanted to walk out of the cottage, into the night, avoiding all of their questions and sympathetic words.

Edela was sitting in her fur-lined chair by the fire, flicking through the pages of the Book of Aurea, her eyes wide, the flames flickering on her alert face.

'Do you really think there's an answer to this curse in there?' Jael wondered, running her hand over Vella's back as she lay on her lap. Ido was curled up on her bare feet, keeping them warmer than they had been in days.

'I don't know,' Edela admitted. 'I had thought so, but the curse wasn't from the Book of Darkness, was it? It's one of the Following's, so perhaps not. Still, I'll keep looking. This book will be a great help to us, I'm sure. Once I can understand what it all means!'

Jael smiled, remembering what they'd gone through to keep hold of it. 'The dragur are coming,' she said, reminded of those thumping blue fists. 'I have to go and talk to Gant and Axl. We need to be prepared for an attack.'

Biddy glanced at Eydis, who looked terrified.

'Well, perhaps I can find something in here for them also?' Edela said keenly. 'I may have a very late night, Biddy!'

'I'll have to sit up and keep you company, then. Make you some tea. Keep the fire going.'

'That would be nice,' Edela murmured, only half listening.

Biddy's attention drifted to Jael, who sat there stiffly, looking so pale and sad. She could tell that Jael was uncomfortable. That she didn't want to be noticed; didn't want to talk about what had happened. 'Did you have any dreams while you were gone? Anything to help us?' she wondered, trying to walk around the subject Jael was so desperate to avoid.

Jael nodded, looking at Eydis. 'I did. I dreamed about Eadmund.'

'Is he alright?' Eydis asked desperately. 'Did you see where he was? Where he's gone?'

'Almost. He's with Draguta.'

Edela looked up from the book.

'Draguta?' Eydis' mouth hung open.

'She has plans for him,' Jael said as a way to reassure her, but it didn't sound very reassuring, she supposed. 'But don't worry, she has no plans to kill him that I could see. Which is good. It means that he's safe.'

'Safe?' Biddy was surprised by that. 'With Draguta?'

'If she needs Eadmund, she won't hurt him,' Edela assured her. 'Until we can find a way to rescue him, it's the best we can hope for.'

Biddy didn't look convinced.

'What about Evaine?' Eydis wondered. 'Is she with Eadmund?'

'No. He appeared to be waiting for her to come. I've no idea what that means, but he still looked bound to her,' Jael said, remembering her dream. 'I did see one strange thing. He had a lock of hair. It looked like Sigmund's. A tiny, blonde curl attached to a leather strap. And on the strap, I saw symbols.'

'Symbols?' Edela put down the book. 'Well, that is interesting. It might explain a lot. I shall see what I can find in here for Eadmund, of course, but first, I must find a way to break this curse before it's too late for poor Hanna and Ayla.'

***

Entorp looked Aleksander over with a frown. 'Do you have

the symbols of protection?' he wondered, knowing how much Edela and Biddy cared for this man. Hanna too, it seemed, given how many times she'd called out for him in the beginning.

Aleksander nodded.

'Well, then, come with me, but be warned. It's not a place for anyone with a weak stomach. The smell is quite... overpowering. And Hanna, she is dying, I'm afraid. It might be a shock.'

Aleksander wanted to turn around and leave as much as he wanted to follow Entorp. He didn't know why on either count, but when he saw Marcus sitting on the ground beside Hanna, he felt as though he shouldn't have come.

The shed was dark, just the glow of a few lamps lighting the large, open space. It made for a restful feel, but it was hard to see much, though in this shed, at least, Entorp's patients didn't require much attention. Nor were they disturbed by the light.

Marcus struggled to his feet. 'You've returned,' he said gruffly, his eyes not quite meeting Aleksander's. 'With the Book of Aurea?'

Aleksander nodded. 'Jael will have given it to Edela, I'm sure.'

Marcus looked relieved. 'She says it's a curse, this sickness. The book may have a way to break it.'

Aleksander was surprised by that. 'A curse?'

'But she needs to hurry,' Marcus sighed, standing back so that Aleksander could see Hanna. 'Edela needs to hurry.' Tears burned his aching eyes. He had shed so many now that he was sure no more would fall. It was an endless nightmare, sitting beside his daughter, waiting for her death. Listening as each breath lengthened. Watching as her chest rose and fell. Waking up from a doze in a panic, wondering if she was still there.

He motioned for Aleksander to take his place, walking away to the open door, eager for a breath of sea air. Entorp took one look at Aleksander's face and followed him.

Aleksander turned towards Hanna, shocked by the change in her, as Entorp had predicted. He remembered her round face and her thick brown hair. But she was almost skeletal now, her cheekbones protruding, her hair lank and lifeless as she lay there. So still. He sat down beside the mattress, taking her hand. It was limp and ice-cold, all its weight resting on his own.

Aleksander didn't know her. Not like he knew Jael.

He didn't know her, but part of him wanted to. He could feel that. He had felt that from the beginning. There was something about her.

She couldn't die.

'Hanna.' Bending down, he whispered in her ear. 'Hanna, it's Aleksander. Perhaps I'm the last person you want here with you now.' He shook his head, wanting to say something that mattered. 'I don't know, perhaps I...' He stopped, taking a breath. 'I want you to know that we're going to save you. I'm here now, and we're going to save you. Jael and Edela, your father, Entorp. All of us. You have to hold on, just a little longer. Give us some time, please. Just a little longer.'

Hanna's eyes were closed, but he thought back to the nights in Tuura's tavern when she'd smiled at him, helped him, and, in the end, saved him.

She had the kindest blue eyes.

'Hold on,' he whispered. 'Please. Don't let go.'

***

Gisila kept staring at her, and Jael sighed, knowing what that meant.

No one else did, though, so that was something, but Jael couldn't help being distracted as she sat at the high table, wedged in between Axl and Gant, wishing she'd gone straight to bed.

Axl was full of questions.

Gant wasn't. He could see that Jael wasn't herself, and he was happy to leave her be.

She was grateful.

Gant tried to steer Axl towards the only topic they could do something about. 'How long do you think we've got, then? Before the dragur are here?'

Jael shrugged, realising that she would have to find a bed soon before she embarrassed herself by passing out again. Her ears had started buzzing, and she could barely keep her eyes open. 'We left them behind quickly. But they're dead, so they don't need to stop and rest or eat. I imagine they'll be here before we want them to be. We need scouts out there, looking for them. Fast riders, who can give us some warning.'

'You're certain they're coming here?' Axl wondered, smiling as Amma waved to him before disappearing behind the curtain, heading for bed.

'They're coming for me,' Jael said blankly. 'And the Book of Aurea. The two things Draguta wants. I saw her in my dreams. She was watching, controlling them. She wants the book, and me dead, so yes, they're coming.'

Axl inhaled sharply. 'And how do we kill them?'

'With fire,' Jael said, trying to think, but it was hard when she was so tired. 'They hate fire. Beheading them seems to work, but they're made of stone. Even Thorgils struggled to do that.'

'So we have to find a way to burn them without burning ourselves?' Gant mused. 'That should keep me awake tonight.'

'Me too,' Axl agreed.

'Not me,' Jael yawned. 'I plan to sleep until the sun comes up or the dragur arrive. Whichever comes first.'

'We should double the watch on the walls,' Gant suggested.

'Good idea,' Axl nodded. 'And have the catapults in place. We've been making more sea-fire. We lost some when the dragon came down.'

'I wish I'd seen it,' Jael said. 'Not much left of it now.'

'No,' Gant frowned. 'Though I don't think any of us would

care to see another dragon after the last few days. Or smell one either.'

'Wait till you smell the dragur. You might not mind the dragon so much after that!'

***

Edela's eyes were like heavy weights, and the book's texts and symbols were blurring before them. Biddy had lit every lamp in the cottage, but it made little difference, and eventually, Edela realised that she would need to get some sleep and hope for better luck in the morning.

Closing the book, she thought of the Widow, who she now knew had written the Book of Aurea. Not the Widow, she reminded herself, but Dara Teros.

Edela wondered if Draguta had killed her sister, or if Dara would return to help them? Now would be a good time, Edela thought with a yawn, placing the book on the floor and easing herself out of the chair. Biddy had fallen asleep on her bed, she could see, though she had valiantly tried to stay by her side, keeping her company throughout the night. She'd had a long day with Entorp and Runa, cleansing the ship sheds, though Edela knew that it was only the beginning. They would need more than herbs. More than moon-water and symbols.

Edela knew that what they needed most of all was to discover how Briggit Halvardar had thrown her curse.

***

Ayla watched Edela fall into bed. She could sense her determination to dream, and she needed Edela to dream more than anything. Ayla could feel the threads of her life disappearing, drifting away from her. She tried clinging to them, determined to fight, but the curse was stronger than she was. It was claiming her, pulling her down, away from where she needed to be.

But while she had any will left, she was going to fight for Bruno, and for herself, and for the life that was still waiting for them to start living.

She was going to go and find Briggit Halvardar.

***

Jael was lying in her old bed in her old bedchamber. The one she'd grown up in and lived in with Aleksander until Lothar had thrown them out after moving his own family in. But, despite the familiarity of the room, the welcome comfort of the bed, and the exhaustion of her aching body, Jael was struggling to still her mind.

It was late, she knew.

The hall was quiet. Ido and Vella lay on the end of the bed snuffling in their sleep, and other than the wind whining past the wall and the occasional scurrying mouse, Jael couldn't hear a thing.

But she couldn't make herself fall asleep.

She was haunted by the memory of holding Lyra in her arms, trying to remember every part of her face. Trying not to. Seeing Eadmund in that cottage with Draguta, wanting to know where he was. Knowing that it didn't matter.

Listening for dragur.

Her mind was jumping, and her right hand was flexing,

wanting to feel *Toothpick*. Wanting to run out into the night, grab Tig and ride until she found Draguta and Morana and Jaeger and killed all three of them, before destroying the Book of Darkness.

She felt frustrated. Held hostage. Imprisoned.

And ultimately, she realised, tired. So, closing her eyes, Jael rolled onto her side, arms wrapped around her empty stomach, trying to find a dream.

***

Getta edged towards Raymon.

It was the first time she'd sought his attention in days. He was both surprised and relieved.

'You shouldn't go to Rissna,' she whispered. 'It's not safe.'

Raymon wished Getta wanted to talk about something else. *Do* something else. It had been too long since she'd let him touch her.

'Do you think your cousins plan to kill me too?' He felt irritable, keeping his hands to himself as he lay on his side, watching the shadows on her face dance in the flames from the lamps burning around their chamber.

Getta didn't like to sleep in the dark, and though Raymon found it hard to sleep with so much light, he never complained.

'I think Axl isn't like his father or mine. From what I hear, he's ambitious. Not beholden to any previously held loyalties. Hungry for power. You don't need to be a dreamer to see that. He killed two kings to claim that throne!' Her voice rose sharply, her chest pumping furious breaths, but realising that a different approach was needed to bend Raymon to her will, Getta softened her voice. 'I don't want anything to happen to you, my love. This kingdom has never been kind to its kings.

It's a wonder anyone wants to sit on that cursed throne.'

Hearing the worry in her voice, Raymon reached for her hand. 'Andala has been attacked by a serpent and a dragon. And now, maybe dragur too. If that is true, it's not something we can ignore. We shouldn't ignore it. I have to meet with them, but don't worry, I'll be safe. Tolbert has organised bodyguards to watch over me. To guard my tent. We've already discussed it.'

Getta frowned as he moved closer. 'But what of your men? They don't want an alliance with Brekka, do they?'

Raymon sighed. His body had quickly turned to other thoughts. He didn't want to talk about anything other than how much he'd missed his wife. But Getta stuck out a hand, keeping him back. 'I will think about it,' he said. 'I'll talk to Tolbert. To my mother. I promise.'

Getta wasn't satisfied, but it was something. A start, perhaps. And with some gentle encouragement in the right direction, she was sure she could lead Raymon far away from the danger her cousins posed to them both.

Raymon tried to edge towards her again, but Getta's hand remained firmly in place. 'I've only just given birth,' she murmured before rolling over. 'You must give me some time.'

Raymon felt both embarrassed and disappointed as he stared at the shadow of her back. 'Of course,' he said, almost to himself, trying to remember when he had last felt happy in his marriage.

***

Ayla hoped that Edela was watching. She hoped that she'd managed to lead her here somehow, certain that the answers were in front of them now.

It was like nothing she had ever seen.

The seven women were naked, dancing inside an ancient stone circle, their long hair trailing behind them, sweeping up and down.

The moon was full and bright, its beams painting their twisting bodies with a pale, dappled glow. They were calling. It sounded familiar, Ayla thought. She could make out some Old Tuuran, the language of the gods.

A tall bonfire sparked in the middle of the circle; hungry flames twisting, reaching towards the moon. Ayla looked on as the dancing stopped and one woman approached the fire. For the first time, Ayla noticed that the women weren't alone. The stones were circled by rows of figures in hooded robes. Silent figures standing shoulder to shoulder, watching as the woman bent to the ground and picked up what looked like a bunch of herbs. She threw them onto the flames, calling to Raemus, her eyes flickering like a cat, intense and focused as she ran them over the robed figures.

Enjoying that they were watching.

She crouched again, and Ayla couldn't see what she was doing, so she stepped closer until she was standing just behind her shoulder. The woman stood suddenly and turned around, and Ayla gasped, recognising Briggit Halvardar. She held something small in her hands, and Ayla had to squint to try and make it out. Not vellum, she thought, but some kind of skin. Symbols were marked on it in blood. Fresh. Dripping onto the earth.

Briggit held the skin above her head, chanting, her eyes on the sky; dark clouds suddenly rushing above as her voice rose, filling the circle with a demanding cry. Ayla was suddenly aware of the throbbing roll of drums, and she felt herself stumble, everything blurring around her, worried that she was losing her hold on the dream.

And as Briggit finished her chant, she dropped to her knees again, folding up the tiny skin and placing it into a hole. Ayla bent closer to see what was happening. The small hole in the ground was filled with the bodies of... rats.

Three dead rats.

Briggit covered them over with dirt, picking up her knife and drawing a symbol across it before standing again. The naked women swayed back to her, taking her hands and leading her into a circle, where once again they started dancing.

Ayla stepped back as everything swam around her. The noise was an undulating wave, and she could feel it trying to wash her away, but she held on tightly, digging her toes into the earth, lifting her head to the night sky where the sparks from the fire had made three enormous golden symbols.

And, finally exhausted, Ayla closed her eyes, feeling everything slip away.

CHAPTER FIFTEEN

The banging on the door surprised Eadmund. The sun was barely up, if the faint light coming down the smoke hole was any indication. He most certainly wasn't up as he tried to move his aching limbs towards the edge of the bed in a hurry.

It didn't surprise Draguta, who was dressed and waiting by the door, opening it immediately. 'Well, if it isn't dear Evaine,' she smiled, genuinely happy for the first time in days. 'I had no doubt that you'd make it here. No doubt at all!'

Eadmund scrambled to his feet, not even bothering to find his trousers as he ran to the door. Draguta stood aside to let Evaine past, watching as she threw herself into Eadmund's arms, pleased to see that, although horribly dishevelled, Evaine appeared to have recovered from her bruises. She hoped that Eadmund wouldn't notice anything. It wouldn't do to create problems where there didn't need to be any.

Not until she had everything in place.

Eadmund enclosed Evaine in his arms, squeezing her tightly, relieved that she was safe. 'Are you alright?' He stepped back, looking her over. She was covered in a layer of red dust, though she appeared unharmed by her ordeal.

Evaine nodded happily, rising on her tiptoes, desperate to feel Eadmund's lips on hers, not caring in the slightest that hers were dry and cracked. She kissed him with urgency; with an overwhelming desire to feel all of him, oblivious to Draguta standing behind her.

'I assume you have what I need?' Draguta asked, tapping her foot.

Evaine broke away from Eadmund. 'Yes, yes,' she panted, digging into one of the satchels slung over her shoulders. 'I have it here.' And she pulled out the black leather-bound book, handing it to Draguta.

Draguta smiled, walking to the table where her seeing circle was still drawn. 'And the rest?' And leaving the book on the table, she returned to Evaine, who dug back into the satchel, pulling out a crumpled tunic, a sock, an arm ring and a goblet.

'You were very thorough, I see,' Draguta laughed.

'Well, I wanted to be sure you'd have what you needed,' Evaine mumbled, turning away from her. She didn't care about Draguta anymore. She wanted to be alone with Eadmund. He looked so different. His cheekbones were sharp, his eyes burning with a fire she didn't recognise. His arms felt hard. Strong.

Looking him over, she swallowed, biting her lip.

'Sit down, sit down,' Draguta purred, ignoring the obvious tension in the room. 'There is time for you to be alone. In this rundown heap of a town, there is nothing to do, so there is plenty of time. I have sent Brill out already. She is finding you a cottage. One you can share, far away from me, until we leave.'

Eadmund frowned. 'Leave? For where?'

'Hest!' Draguta smiled. 'Soon, we will be leaving for Hest. Now, let us look at what you worked so very hard to bring me.' She placed the items Evaine had collected beside the book and eagerly opened the black cover, turning the pages, her smile growing. 'Rolled omelette with smoked herring. Eggs in brine. Salted oxtongue with horseradish sauce.' Draguta clapped the book shut. 'It appears that you have brought me the wrong book, Evaine. Did you not check its contents before you took it? Did you not ensure that it was the Book of Darkness and not some ancient recipe book?'

Sitting beside Draguta, Evaine froze. 'I, I...' She blinked

at Eadmund, hoping he could protect her from whatever was about to happen. She remembered the hall. What Draguta had done to Jaeger.

To Morana.

But Draguta burst out laughing. 'You are perfectly safe, Evaine, do not fear. You did exactly as I'd hoped. I didn't imagine you would be clever enough to check the book at all. Now Jaeger and his bug-eyed dreamer think I wanted the book. He sent men after you to find out where I am. Although, I sent men after them, so I imagine they are long dead.'

'But... I don't understand,' Evaine spluttered. 'You didn't *want* the book?'

'No. I wanted Jaeger to think I wanted the book. I wanted his little dreamer to tell him I wanted the book. To hide the real one. To focus on that, and not on what I really wanted, which was Jaeger's things.' She picked up his tunic and inhaled it, wrinkling her nose, smelling the arrogance of the foolish king. Strong and potent, just like he was, but oh so foolish. 'Let Jaeger think he has a way to find me. Let him think he has tricked me. I can assure you it will be the last thing he thinks about for some time.'

***

Aleksander was up on the ramparts, gazing over the valley that stretched from the broken western wall towards Bog's Hill in the distance, searching for any sign of the dragur, when Jael joined him. 'Perhaps Draguta will call them back?' he mused, enjoying the warmth of the sunshine, which was quickly taking the edge off a cool morning.

'I'm not sure she will,' Jael said, nibbling a flatbread. She'd taken a handful from the hall, and they were still warm. She wasn't hungry, but eating would help her lift her sword again without wanting to fall down. She handed two to Aleksander. 'Draguta wants the Book of Aurea, and she wants to kill us. She knows the fort is damaged. An open door.'

Aleksander nodded. 'She could always send more dragons, couldn't she?'

'Mmmm.' Jael was thinking about her conversation with Edela. 'The gods can't stop Draguta's magic. Only the Book of Aurea can. And perhaps Dara Teros. She wrote it after all.'

'If she's alive.' Aleksander bit into the flatbread, pleased that Jael had stuffed cheese inside. It was warm too.

Jael didn't know what had happened to Dara Teros, but they couldn't think about everything at once, so she changed the subject. 'How was Hanna?'

Aleksander stilled. His feelings for Hanna were confusing, but he did know that he felt incredibly sad. 'You were right. She's dying.'

Jael saw the pain in his eyes. 'I'm sorry.'

'She doesn't have long by the look of her,' Aleksander went on. 'Unless Edela found something useful in that book last night?'

'I hope so. I'm on my way to see her now if you want to come along?'

'No, you go. I think I'll stay here, have a moment to myself before the day begins. It's going to be a long one. I'll meet you in the hall when you're done. We can go over the plans for the dragur again.'

'Makes sense.' She turned to leave.

Aleksander stopped her. 'I'm sorry,' he whispered. 'About your baby.'

Jael was quickly uncomfortable.

'I'm so sorry for you.' He saw the look on her face. 'I know you don't want to talk about it, I just wanted you to know. We'll make Draguta pay for what she's done. All of it. We'll make her pay.'

Jael didn't want to be in that place of sadness and tears and grief anymore, so she nodded quickly, heading for the stairs.

***

Despite a heaviness in her limbs from a lack of sleep, Edela was almost dancing around the cottage. 'I could kiss Ayla!' she smiled, handing Eydis her boots. 'The poor woman is on her deathbed but working so hard to save herself and everyone else. Including her husband. And she may just have done it with what she showed me last night!'

Both Eydis and Biddy had been lifted by Edela's good mood since she'd sprung out of bed in a hurry to get going, and they were trying to organise themselves to leave the house with her, not wanting to be left behind.

Biddy kept looking around for the puppies, expecting to see them waiting for their breakfast but then she remembered that Jael had taken them with her. She felt sad, remembering the haunted look on Jael's face; a look masking so much pain, she knew. She had looked that way when Ranuf died. The sudden loss of her father was so devastating that the only way Jael could cope was to retreat into herself. But with so much demanding her attention now, there was likely no chance for her to find a moment alone. Biddy blinked, realising that Eydis was talking to her. 'What did you say, Eydis?'

'I want to come to the sheds. I want to see Ayla.'

Biddy was ready to protest when Edela stopped her. 'You are protected, so yes, you can come. Sit with Ayla and talk to her. Tell her what we're doing. That we've found a way to help her.'

'We have?' Eydis was surprised.

So was Biddy.

'After what I saw in my dreams, I think so,' Edela said carefully. 'I just need to speak with Entorp. Marcus too. See if they can be of any help, and then we'll get to work!'

***

Brill had returned to the cottage with the welcome news that she had acquired a place for Evaine and Eadmund to stay. Draguta was relieved. She could barely stand the vomit-inducing display of affection, and it would only get worse when night fell, she knew. Better to have them out of the way.

And yet...

'You will need to assist me,' she said. 'Both you and Brill. Eadmund, you must leave. I'm sure that naked beast is already waiting in the training ring for you. And Evaine will be far too busy helping me to spend any time kissing you today. You can save that for later. Much later, when you are far away from me!'

Brill looked nonplussed, realising that she was as powerless as a slave to refuse anything Draguta requested. And she had a strong desire to still be alive at the end of it all. Wherever that end might take them.

Evaine, though, looked very bothered. She had waited weeks to be reunited with Eadmund and hadn't envisioned being separated from him immediately.

'Do you want to live? To defeat Jael Furyck? *Kill* her?' Draguta asked, glaring at Evaine. 'Return to Andala to retrieve your son?'

Evaine nodded.

'And how will you do any of that if I cannot get back to Hest and reclaim my book? Hmmm? I am powerful, yes, but that book makes me unstoppable. And to reclaim it, I must defeat Jaeger. So you, my sweet girl, are going to help me.'

Evaine glanced at Eadmund, who kissed her head.

'I have to go,' he told her, realising that he was still without his trousers. 'Draguta is right. We both have work to do, and soon you'll see that too. You must do what you can to help.'

Evaine blinked, feeling an odd shift in things. She stared at Draguta, who smiled back at her, pleased to see how compliant Eadmund was being.

First Eadmund, then Jaeger.

Soon she would have every problem in order.

***

Jael had been surprised to find Edela's cottage empty, and as she walked back into the square, past the training ring, she was just as surprised to find it already full, watching as a limping Fyn was smacked in the face by Gant's battered blue shield. She approached the railings with a smile on her face. 'You've never known pain till you've been trained by Gant Olborn!' she called as Fyn spun around, happy to see her.

Gant shunted him with his shield again, sending Fyn stumbling backwards, struggling to keep his balance. 'Focus seems to be a bit of an issue with this one!' he growled. 'Though I'm working on it.'

Jael was pleased to see Fyn up and about. He didn't look comfortable – his face making all sorts of strange expressions – but it was good to see him out of bed, working hard again. They were going to need everyone they could get their hands on soon. She turned, looking for her brother, and found him fighting Oleg. 'Looks like everyone's working hard this morning,' Jael noted, her eyes widening as she spied Karsten training with Berard, who looked utterly miserable trying to wield a wooden sword in his left hand.

'Everyone but you, it seems,' Ivaar said, coming from her right. 'Aren't you going to join us? Show us how it's done?'

Jael was quickly irritated, but remembering her dreams from Hallow Wood, her face softened. 'No, I've only been out of bed a few days. I'd just be sucking dirt, and I'd rather keep my reputation intact, if you don't mind.'

Ivaar narrowed his eyes, edging closer to her as the training matches carried on around them. 'Have you heard about the sickness? About Ayla? Is she still alive?'

Jael could see the worry in his eyes. 'I don't know. I'm going to the sheds now. Hopefully, there's some good news.'

Ivaar didn't blink.

'I'll tell you what's happening,' Jael promised. 'I'll come and find you.' She didn't know why she felt compelled to be kind to Ivaar. He hadn't treated anyone well, especially Ayla, but perhaps she was beginning to understand why? And besides, Ivaar was an ally, and she wanted him to remain loyal to her.

It wouldn't hurt to let him think that she cared.

Ivaar hadn't been expecting that, but he nodded, turning back into the throng of heavily perspiring men, looking for his training partner.

Karsten Dragos glared at Jael, a sneer curling his hairy lip. 'Look at her, just skipping away,' he grumbled to his brother. 'Not wanting to get her hands dirty. Too important for a training ring now she's queen.'

Berard panted, staring after Jael. Karsten had been chasing him around since the sun was up. His older brother was in a foul mood, and Berard could only guess that it had something to do with Nicolene. He hadn't visited her in the sheds yet, and Berard wasn't sure why. 'What are you talking about, Karsten?' He shook his head, wishing he had another hand to move his sweaty curls off his sweaty face. 'She was sick, you know that.'

'So? You have one arm. That's not stopping you.'

'Jael Furyck isn't our enemy,' Berard hissed, not wanting to be overheard by the Andalans and Islanders surrounding them.

'Not now. When are you going to realise that? We're supposed to be working *with* her, not grumbling about her leadership or her training routine. She is the queen. She is the leader. Stop fighting against an enemy you no longer have!' And with a loud sigh, Berard decided that he would go and check on their mother, who was no doubt in a complete panic without Nicolene.

Karsten blinked after Berard in surprise, quickly shutting out any thoughts of his wife as he searched for a new training partner.

***

Jaeger considered Meena with a frown.

He was growing bored with her excuses; impatient with her delays. And though he was well aware that she had no training as a dreamer, he needed her to become as skilled as Morana, and quickly, because Morana didn't appear to be coming back in a hurry.

Meena picked at her breakfast. There had been a fire in the kitchen, and their meal had been delayed for some time, and despite being hungry, she was anxious, sensing Jaeger's irritation; too anxious to have much of an appetite.

It felt as though she was walking down a narrow path bordered by sharp cliffs. One wrong move in either direction, and she would find herself plunging to her death. She was torn, unable to decide what to do, and nothing she dreamed of or thought about was helping her choose which path to take. As much as she detested Jaeger and feared Draguta, and wanted to escape to be with Berard, Meena could see how much risk there was in venturing down either path.

'Do you think Evaine has found her way to Draguta? That Draguta has discovered the book is not quite what she'd asked for?' Jaeger wondered, running a slice of bread around his plate, soaking up the bloody juice of the lamb sausages, which had been so hastily delivered after the delay that they were badly undercooked.

Meena shuddered. 'Yes. I think so.'

'You do?'

'Draguta is not far away. I can feel her.'

'You can?'

Meena wasn't sure if that was true, or if it was just her fear that she could feel growing, but it was something to entertain Jaeger with, so she carried on. 'She wants to return, to the castle. She wants her revenge upon us all.'

'Well, as soon as my men find out where she's hiding, I'll send an army to kill her.'

'She can't be killed,' Meena reminded him.

'I'm not sure that's true. We could have done a better job last time. Cut off her head... burned her corpse. She *can* be killed,' Jaeger insisted. 'Eventually, Meena, everyone can be killed. We just have to do it right.'

Meena looked at her plate, knowing that he was wrong.

***

Evaine hurried behind Draguta, clutching a heavy basket, trying not to step on Draguta's dress, which wasn't as clean as it had been before they'd started walking around Flane on a seemingly never-ending quest to collect a long list of odd things.

Evaine had quickly grown bored, tired, and hot. She had ridden through the night and not slept at all, and both her body and her mind wanted Eadmund and a bed. Not one part of her wanted to be running after Draguta.

And running she was.

Draguta was a tall woman with a long stride and an impatience that made her move quickly. Brill was much more used to the determination of her mistress and didn't utter a peep as she trotted just behind Draguta's left shoulder, her own basket almost full of herbs. Evaine, she was pleased to see, had the much more unpleasant task of carrying the bodies of the tiny creatures Draguta had caught and made Brill kill.

Tripping over a stone, Evaine fell to the dirt with a yelp, the contents of her basket spilling onto the ground beside her; dead birds and rats tumbling out onto the red dust.

Draguta spun around, already growling. 'Evaine! I require your help. Your assistance.' Her eyes were bright with anger. 'I may need Eadmund, but I am yet to determine whether I need you. You may have noticed that despite still thinking he is in love with you, Eadmund belongs to me now. And I shall decide his fate. And yours. The threads of your life are in my loom, and I shall choose how to weave them.' Draguta glared at Evaine until she was shrinking backwards. 'Or whether it is time to cut them all the way through!'

Dropping her head to the ground, Evaine hurried to retrieve the contents of her basket, shuddering as she touched the still-warm fur.

CHAPTER SIXTEEN

Jael was stunned by how ill Hanna appeared. She looked more like a corpse than a living person, but sensing how distressed Marcus was, she quickly removed the horror from her face and turned to him. 'You've had a difficult time,' she said, hoping to sound sympathetic.

'Well, Hanna has, that's true,' Marcus sighed. He was beginning to wonder if he had finally succumbed to the sickness himself. He had no symbols on his arms, and he'd spent so many days around the ill that he knew there was little chance of him emerging unscathed; certain that it was only his sheer determination to stay by his daughter's side that was keeping him on his feet.

So far.

Jael watched as Entorp and Biddy pulled more stools towards the small table by the door. The shed was home to twenty-four patients now. Four more than yesterday, though two had died in the night. Jael was surprised to see Karsten Dragos' wife among them.

She didn't see Karsten, though.

The shed next door was almost overflowing, filling up quicker than Entorp had thought possible. He was going to have to find somewhere new to keep them all.

'Rats,' Edela said, helping Eydis to a stool as Biddy, Marcus, Entorp and Jael joined them. 'Rats brought the disease from

Helsabor to Saala. And not just Saala. After she cursed the rats, Briggit had the Followers release them into Brekka and Iskavall. Tuura too. She sent rats on ships to Alekka. The Fire Lands. Everywhere.'

'Did she send them to Hest?' Jael wondered.

'I don't know. I didn't hear her say that,' Edela frowned. 'If she knew the Book of Darkness was there, with the Followers, perhaps she didn't see them as an enemy or a threat? Perhaps she imagined they would come together, before Draguta put an end to that?'

'But what does she want? To kill us all?' Jael frowned.

'Well, it's quite an effective way to do it, wouldn't you say?' Edela suggested. 'No armies marching for days. No battles. No wasting time. She can weaken her opposition, wipe out the kingdoms that oppose her, then claim the book for herself, and bring Raemus back.'

'So she wants the Book of Darkness too?' Biddy asked. 'I wonder if she knows how that went for the rest of the Followers?'

'I imagine she does,' Jael smiled, 'being a dreamer. She probably knows what we're doing here too.'

'No, she won't. What we do in here should remain hidden from her,' Entorp said. 'Look around.'

Jael glanced around the shed, noticing for the first time the symbols decorating the walls. 'Good idea. A very good idea.'

'We can no longer protect the fort and ourselves from Draguta. She appears able to see through every symbol we know of, but we thought it worth keeping the rest of them out. Whoever they are. Whatever their plans might be.'

Marcus was suddenly overcome with the need to lie down. He tried to sit up straighter. 'If you know what Briggit did, do you know how to undo it?'

Edela peered at him. 'Are you feeling alright? You look rather pale.'

Marcus shook his head dismissively. 'I'm fine,' he snapped, wanting to get on.

Biddy glanced at Edela, who lifted an eyebrow before continuing. 'Well, yes, I have an idea, thanks to Ayla. I saw the symbols Briggit used. And if there's a symbol used to throw a curse, there's a symbol to break it.'

'But you haven't found them yet?'

For the first time all morning, Edela looked hesitant. 'Not yet. But I will. I brought them here, to see if either of you might know something about them.' And digging into her purse, Edela pulled out a piece of vellum, unfolding it to reveal the symbols she had seen in her dream.

Marcus, who didn't have the knowledge of symbols that Entorp did, quickly shook his head. 'It's not something I recognise.'

'No,' Entorp agreed. 'Although...' And he wrinkled his nose, squinting, wishing his eyesight was as sharp as it used to be. 'That one does look like the symbol for death. Almost.'

Edela held the vellum far away from her eyes, trying to focus. 'I think you're right. I haven't drawn it very well, have I? I'll head back to the cottage and look them up in the book. See what I can find. In the meantime, I've asked Runa to come and help you. I need to keep Biddy with me today. I feel as though we're close. Close to finding exactly what we need.' She smiled at Marcus, but he had turned away, looking at Hanna, who lay on her straw mattress in the corner. Closing her eyes, Edela took a deep breath, trying to calm her building sense of urgency. 'Well, let's head off, then. Jael, why don't you come along? I think there's something you need to talk to me about, isn't there?'

'Is there?' Jael stared at her grandmother in confusion, but Edela was giving nothing away. Turning back to Entorp, she stood. 'You're going to need to start moving everyone into the fort, I'm afraid. And quickly. The dragur will come soon, and we can't have you out here in the sheds. It's not safe. Perhaps go and speak with Axl and Gisila? They'll find somewhere to put everyone. They're already moving the Tuurans inside. Maybe you could make use of some of those tents?'

Entorp nodded, though the thought of transporting all his patients was daunting enough to make him want to fall down.

Biddy saw the panic in his eyes. 'Why don't I come with you before I help Edela? I'm sure we'll be able to sort it out in no time.'

***

Evaine stopped at the training ring, relieved to have been released from Draguta's demanding clutches for a while. She was surprised to see Eadmund with his tunic off, fighting an enormous man, who was also naked from the waist up. She supposed it was a hot place to be training; nothing like Oss where it was either raining or snowing. No one ever took their tunic off on Oss. Not until Vesta, when the games were on, and everyone was full of mead madness, oblivious to the freezing temperatures.

Eadmund turned to her, a smile on his bright red face. He said something to the man and walked towards her. 'I didn't think I'd see you again today,' he panted, wiping the sweat from his brow.

Evaine couldn't stop staring.

'What? What is it?' Eadmund looked around, wanting to find a waterskin. The dust was in his throat, and he couldn't stop coughing.

Evaine shook her head. 'It's just, just that you look so... different.'

'I do?' Eadmund was bemused. 'Is that bad?'

Evaine laughed. 'No, it's not bad. You look like a warrior. A king.'

'Ha! Don't let Rollo hear you, or he'll give me an extra

beating or two!' Eadmund grinned.

'Is that Rollo?' Evaine asked, pointing at the man striding towards them, a waterskin in his hand.

'Here,' he said, throwing it at Eadmund before nodding to Evaine. 'I need a piss, so you've got a few minutes. But only a few.' And smiling, or perhaps scowling, Rollo headed for the nearest latrine.

Eadmund quickly turned back around, peering into Evaine's basket. 'What is Draguta making you do?' He could see the dead birds, reminded of the dream he'd had about his dog and Morana Gallas.

'I don't know,' Evaine admitted. 'Some horrible thing. Something to do with Jaeger.'

Eadmund frowned, reaching a hand up to her cheek. The way the sun was hitting it, he could almost see a bruise. 'Did something happen to your face?'

Evaine gulped. 'Ahhh, just a clumsy accident. Horse riding isn't for me. Not really. I was a little too... aggressive at first. The stupid horse didn't like it.'

Eadmund smiled, imagining how that would have gone. 'Well, you're here now, and if there's any more riding to be done, I'll make sure you get the tamest horse I can find. Maybe a pony?'

Evaine pushed herself onto her tiptoes, excited by the mere smell of him. She kissed him quickly, watching out of the corner of her eye as Rollo returned. 'He's back already,' she whispered. 'But I'll see you soon. And tonight, once we're rid of Draguta, you'll finally be mine again.' And with one last admiring glance at Eadmund's muscular chest, she spun around, almost skipping away.

***

Biddy took Eydis with her to collect the herbs Edela required, leaving an impatient Jael in the cottage with her grandmother.

'Aren't you supposed to be looking through that book?' Jael suggested, pleased to be sitting down but not sure what Edela expected her to say.

'I do, yes, but there is something that happened. Something I don't know.'

'I don't want to talk about what happened,' Jael insisted wearily. 'It's done. I have to focus on what's ahead now. Not what's behind me. I can't change that.'

Edela frowned, watching her squirming granddaughter. 'Nothing is ever behind us. Not really. We just move it out of the way, but it's still there. Especially if we don't face it at the time.'

Jael frowned too, then her face lightened as a memory drifted back to her. 'Something did happen.'

Edela leaned forward.

'I had a dream. I was dreaming about the raven attack in Tuura, but it was different. It was as though they were all talking to me. Yelling at me. One in particular. Then I was in my bed, and a raven was there, and it cried out. But when I woke up, it was still there, on the end of my bed, and then so were the dragur, so I didn't think about it again.'

'You're sure it was real?'

Jael nodded. 'Astrid saw it too. It had one white eye. I've never seen a raven like that before. I think it was warning me about the dragur.'

Edela inhaled sharply. 'One white eye? Oh.'

Now it was Jael's turn to lean forward. 'What?'

'That is Fyr. Daala's raven.'

'Fyr?' Jael looked surprised. 'You told us stories about her when we were children, didn't you?'

Edela was pleased she remembered. 'I did, yes. Fyr is Daala's eyes in the world of humans. Daala sends the raven out to tell her what's happening. To give her warnings. To help her see who needs help and who needs punishing. Fyr is her messenger.'

'Do you think Daala sent her raven to help me?'

'You tell me.' Edela sat back and picked up the Book of Aurea. 'What do you think, dreamer?'

Jael didn't know what she thought. 'I was half dead in that bed. As much as I may have thought I wanted to get up, I wasn't moving. I couldn't. I almost felt trapped there, perhaps by choice? But when the raven came, I left my dreams behind. I came back.'

'Just in time, it seems,' Edela murmured, turning the first page. 'Hopefully, soon, I can say the same.' And looking up, she smiled. 'When the curse is broken, and the dragur are defeated, we will sit with this book, you and I, and find a way to save Eadmund.'

Jael nodded, staring into her grandmother's determined eyes. 'I would like that,' she said quietly. 'I would like that very much.'

***

Meena stared at her aunt. Torn.

Half of her was tempted to pull out her knife and kill her.

Morana glared at her.

Meena swallowed nervously, then stood a little straighter, reminded that she had all the power now. Well, a little power, she supposed. In her dreams, Draguta appeared victorious, which was odd, she thought, knowing that she would have quickly discovered that the book Evaine had stolen wasn't the Book of Darkness. And Meena, for all her trying, couldn't understand why that would make Draguta happy.

She didn't dare tell Jaeger.

Jaeger was elated, thinking he had outwitted her. But did he really imagine he could outwit someone as powerful as Draguta?

Morana appeared to be trying to move, and Meena stared at her again, wondering what she wanted. Her aunt's dark eye was blinking rapidly, and Meena had the sense that she was reading her mind, though there appeared little Morana could do about it, stuck in that chair as she was.

It would be so easy to kill her...

Meena blinked, surprised by her own thoughts; worried again that spending so much time with the book was changing her, or was it just that she hated Morana, who had tortured and teased her and treated her so badly?

But if Draguta returned?

When Draguta returned...

Who would there be to protect them if not for Morana?

Sighing, Meena pulled over a stool and sat down, wishing Else would hurry back. She didn't want to be stuck in the chamber with her aunt glaring at her and her own fears poking at her, and Jaeger no doubt growing irate, charging around the castle looking for her.

She closed her eyes, trying to clear her mind, feeling very far away from ever seeing Berard again.

***

Berard made Karsten stop by the entrance to the harbour. They had eaten quickly and were returning to their men – Karsten's men – for some more training. It hadn't been going well so far. No one seemed inclined to pay any attention to his brother, which didn't surprise Berard. Karsten had been in such an angry, belligerent mood that it wasn't making things easier.

And Berard thought he knew why.

'What are you doing?' Karsten grumbled. 'We have to get back to the ring.'

'You need to go and see Nicolene.'

Karsten froze. 'What do you know about what I need? Who made you the boss of me?' He started walking away.

Berard didn't move.

Eventually, Karsten spun around and stomped back to his brother, his scowl deepening. 'How will it help anyone for me to watch her die?' He leaned in, blinking angrily. 'Because that's what's going to happen. You see that, don't you? One by one, every one of us is going to die. It's all Jaeger's doing. First Father, then your arm. Haegen, Irenna, and now...' And clenching his jaw, Karsten backed away. 'No! Dragur are coming. If they get in, we're all dead.' He flapped his hand at the sheds they could see through the open gates. 'I can't help in there! I can't help Nicolene! But I can help stop the fucking dragur from killing the rest of us. So, stand here all you like. Go see my wife if you need to, but I'm going back to the training ring!' And violently scratching his head, Karsten spun around, stalking away from Berard.

'Hello.'

Berard turned in the opposite direction, a smile quickly erasing his frown. 'Jael.' He was happy to see her, though she didn't look well at all. 'You heard that, I suppose?'

Jael nodded. 'I think Jaeger heard it down in Hest. Your family is having a difficult time of it.'

'We are, but no more than anyone else. Many people were lost beneath the dragon and in the fire. And now the sickness.'

'Not to mention the dragur,' Jael said, inclining her head for Berard to walk with her. She didn't want him exposing himself to the illness. She didn't want anyone in there until Edela had broken the curse.

'Do you really think they're coming?' he asked, looking at Jael's bruised face.

'Yes.'

Berard gulped.

'But they can be defeated, Berard. Everything can be defeated. You don't need to worry, but you do need to train. You need to get that arm stronger. Dragur hate fire. If you can wield a burning torch, you'll be more use than someone cowering in the corner or running away. Come on, I'll take you to the training ring, and we'll see what we can do with you.' She smiled, feeling her right hand twitching.

Ready to fight.

***

Raymon glared at Garren Maas as he passed, watching him whispering to his father before they both turned towards him, smiling.

He didn't like either of them.

Nor did Ravenna. 'Ignore them,' she said, patting her leg for her giant red hound to follow her. He had a love of chasing ducks and had just torn through Ollsvik's square, scattering a flock of them. 'Garren's jealousy is not your concern. He'll grow bored with his games and find himself another wife in time.'

Raymon didn't look as confident as his mother, but he had more problems than Garren Maas to worry about. 'Will I be in danger?' he asked. 'If I make an alliance with Brekka?'

'In danger?' Ravenna was confused. 'We've always had an alliance with Brekka in one way or another. Why would you be in danger for formalising such a thing?'

'Some say Axl Furyck wants to take our kingdom. That killing Lothar and Osbert was his way of announcing his intentions. Murdering two kings to claim a throne. One of many.' They had walked through the rear gates, watching the army being put through its paces by Tolbert and his commanders, who had their warriors strung out across the narrow valley. It was an impressive sight, Raymon thought, satisfied that he would be well protected in Rissna. Garren was one of Tolbert's commander's, and Raymon frowned, wondering why Tolbert didn't appear bothered that Garren wasn't there, leading his men.

'Some people?' Ravenna tried not to snort, though she very much wanted to. 'You should pay less heed to spiteful gossip. Your focus should be on leading your men to meet the Brekkans. Ollsvik is small. Too small sometimes. Everyone sticking their noses into each other's business. And not all they speak is the truth. In fact, I would think that most of it is definitely not the truth. Speak in the hall before you leave. Announce your intentions, explain your reasoning. If our people hear it from your lips, they'll be supportive. They'll want you to go. How could they not? A threat as grave as dragons and serpents? As dragur? How could they not want to act when creatures like that are on our borders? We can't hide from what is coming. They will see that.'

Raymon smiled. His mother was smart and strong, but so was his wife, and his wife saw more trouble brewing than dragons and dragur. And surely only one of them could be right?

***

Jael hadn't lasted long, and she was still trying to catch her breath as she joined her brother on the bench beside the training ring, but she felt better. Lighter. As though by using her sword, she was fighting to reclaim control of herself again. Draguta had hurt her in the most invasive way. She had injured her body and broken her heart, but Jael didn't want to be a part of Draguta's dark plans, whatever they were.

She wasn't going to lie down and give her an easy victory.

'Looks like the dragur will be facing an army of invalids,' Axl grinned, watching Fyn and Thorgils hobble around each other.

Jael nodded. 'Looks like it. Best we hope that lobbing jars of sea-fire at them works. It'll be less painful.'

'They're strong, then?'

'Just a bit.'

Axl looked worried, not feeling very strong himself. 'Well, I hope we have enough of it. Edela mentioned that we were getting low on niter.'

Jael bent over, her ears buzzing again, thinking that she might need to go and find Astrid for more of that tincture. 'We'll have to make do with what we have. Fire arrows are what we need now. I've been at the fletchers, and they seem to be working hard. The blacksmiths too. The fire arrowheads are the best. More accurate. I've got them making more of those.'

Axl nodded. 'I agree.'

'And what about Raymon Vandaal? Gant mentioned that you'd arranged to meet him in Rissna?'

'Mmmm, I thought we should meet to formalise our alliance. He needs to know how serious things are. How essential his men and weapons are to our attack on Hest. To build a big army, we need more men.'

'We do,' Jael agreed, lifting her head slowly. 'And hopefully, he'll give us his.'

'*Give?*'

'Well, he can come along too,' Jael grinned.

Axl was too distracted by the enormity of what was coming to smile. 'How will we do it, though? Take an army all the way to Hest? If the sickness is a curse and the woman on Helsabor's throne is a Follower, we'll be facing a double threat now.'

'We will. But we have our own book, and that book will

help us stay safe. Don't worry. Edela will find a way.'

***

Edela wanted to throw the book through the open door.

It had seemed so simple: finding counter symbols to break the three Briggit had used when she threw the curse.

But it was proving to be more challenging than she'd imagined.

And Edela's sleepless night was starting to catch up with her. She found herself dozing occasionally, the book open on her lap, her grainy eyes unable to focus for long, and eventually, closing altogether.

But within moments, she was jerking awake, panting, grabbing at the book as it slid off her knee, onto the floor.

She'd had another dream.

CHAPTER SEVENTEEN

'You look better,' Thorgils grinned. 'On your feet, even.'

Jael stared at him. 'For now.'

Thorgils was happy to see her. 'Well, don't worry, if you fall down again, I'll pick you up and carry you to bed. I'll even tuck you in!'

'Is there something you wanted?' Jael grumbled, walking away from Thorgils towards the harbour. She wanted to see how Entorp was managing, moving everyone into the fort. 'Shouldn't you be with Isaura? Or training? Something useful. I think we've latrines to dig out.'

'You've many good suggestions there,' Thorgils nodded, looking serious. 'Think I'll take the first one. Sounds like the most pleasant way to spend the afternoon.'

'Perhaps, but it won't help us when the dragur come charging down the hills. We're all going to need somewhere to go and shit then.'

Thorgils burst out laughing, clapping Jael on the shoulder. 'You're back, then. I'm glad, but I'm not going to dig out your latrines. I think my cousin is looking for a job, though. I'll go and find him. Think I saw him with Bram.' Thorgils' eyes twinkled, happy that his uncle was on his feet again.

'I'm sure Fyn would thank you for volunteering him.'

'I'm sure he would!' And with a wink, Thorgils disappeared after Fyn or Isaura... he couldn't make up his mind.

Jael was quickly frowning again, seeing Karsten Dragos lurking outside the ship sheds. He saw her and turned away. 'Karsten!' Jael called, quickening her pace.

He stopped, irritated to have been seen.

By her.

'Are you going in?' Jael wondered as he turned around. 'To see your wife? Perhaps you could carry her out? They're moving everyone into the fort to keep them safe from the dragur.'

Karsten glared so fiercely at Jael that she could almost see inside his soul. She could feel his grief, buried deep inside. He'd lost so many people recently, and she could feel the pain throbbing inside him, desperate for a release, which would be useful if he could keep it inside for the dragur.

Though that appeared unlikely.

'My wife?' Karsten snarled. 'What do you care about my wife? Or my father or my brother? Or his wife?' He stepped towards Jael, peering into her eyes. 'What do you care about any of us?'

Tiredness had a way of quickening Jael's temper, and Karsten had a way of getting under her skin. 'I don't,' she said coldly. 'I don't care about any of you. I care about killing your bastard brother. I care about taking the book from him and Draguta. I care about killing Morana Gallas and her brother, but I don't care about any of you.'

Karsten stepped back, surprised by Jael's anger.

It dampened his own.

'I imagine your wife would like to know that you cared about her, though. She might like someone to hold her hand and make her feel less alone. Someone like her husband, who seems more interested in sticking his knife through my eye to make himself feel better, and less interested in how she feels.' And with that, Jael disappeared into the first shed, leaving Karsten staring after her, mouth hanging open.

***

Usually, it was a simple enough spell, and Draguta wondered if she had overthought it. But Jaeger was powerful, his soul almost entirely consumed by the book now. It wouldn't be easy to command it herself. To bind him to her. To take him away from the Book of Darkness and make him hers.

But that was what she intended to do.

Evaine had brought her everything she needed of Jaeger's, and between the three of them, they'd gathered the herbs, stones, and creatures that she'd require for the ritual. And though Draguta didn't have an ancient stone circle to enhance the power of her spell, she felt confident that, come dawn, Jaeger Dragos would belong to her, just as Eadmund did.

Evaine had been of no use and was more of an irritant than any actual help, so Draguta had sent her back to Eadmund, happy to enjoy the welcome silence with just Brill beside her, dutifully doing as she was bid without complaint.

Brill, it appeared, had no thoughts at all. Certainly none that Draguta could hear, and she was grateful for that as she watched her grinding the tiny henbane seeds in the large copper bowl.

'We will go to the tower tonight,' Draguta murmured. 'It will not be ideal, but we don't have the luxury of waiting for a full moon. Not if we want to return home quickly. I must take Jaeger now before he causes any more problems. Before we are riddled with bed bugs! This is not the place for us, is it, Brill? No, we must return to the castle and see how poor Morana is. And we shall. Soon.'

***

They had disappeared into the winding gardens, hoping to be far enough away from Morana so she couldn't hear their conversation or listen to their thoughts. Meena wasn't convinced that she could really do such a thing, but the way her aunt stared at her sometimes made her feel as though Morana's fingers were in her head, digging around.

Else was trying to be helpful, but she didn't know what to advise. 'It's a choice between two equally terrible things,' she panted, the path rising before them as the late afternoon sun beat down strongly overhead. 'It's like asking yourself, would I prefer to be eaten by a wolf or a mountain cat?'

'Or a bear,' Meena added, thinking of Jaeger.

'The book is the problem,' Else decided. 'Without it, things would be much simpler, wouldn't they?'

'Yes, but to steal it or destroy it would have me killed by one of them. To run and take it would have me followed by all of them. There is no way to get rid of the book without dying that I can see,' Meena insisted, heading for a stone bench, reminded of her grandmother, who'd always needed to sit on it to catch her breath. 'And if I'm dead, I can't help anyone.'

Else sat down beside Meena with a thump. She'd slept poorly since she'd been in Morana's chamber, worrying that the evil dreamer would suddenly come to life in the night and kill her. Her dreams were filled with dark thoughts that had her waking up in a sweat, unable to find her way back to sleep. 'And you really see Draguta returning?'

'I do.'

'Should we try to break Morana out of her cursed state, then? Ask Dragmall to really try?'

Meena nodded reluctantly. 'I think so. I can't keep us safe from Draguta. Perhaps Morana can't either, but she is stronger than me. She can read the book. I can't. I've looked at it every day. Every day! But it still makes no sense to me. I recognise some of the words and symbols, but I don't know what to do with them. The book wasn't meant for me.'

'I'm glad to hear it,' Else smiled, patting Meena's leg. 'But what will Morana do with it? If we manage to bring her back?'

Meena looked worried. 'I'm not sure. But I imagine she'd want to stop Draguta from returning. From trying to kill her.'

'Yes, she would. And surely that's the biggest problem of all? For if Draguta comes back, Morana won't be alive for long. And when she's dead, what will become of the rest of us?'

The clouds drifted across the sun, and suddenly everything felt much darker, and Meena found herself shivering, wondering the very same thing herself.

***

'I will try and break the curse tonight!' Edela announced with some confidence. She'd woken up from her doze with the realisation that she had muddled the order of the symbols. And fixing that mistake had made it much easier to find the answer to breaking the curse in the Book of Aurea.

Entorp looked hopeful.

Biddy was nervous.

Eydis felt excited. 'Can I come?'

'Of course. You are a powerful dreamer, Eydis. I will need you for sure. We will go to Furia's Tree. It is the most sacred place in Andala. The only place I can think of to do it.' She dug into Biddy's basket, pleased with what she'd collected, including the dead rats. 'I will need to ask you to skin one of those poor creatures, I'm afraid,' Edela said, looking at Biddy, who shuddered, not liking rats at all. 'I need to draw the symbols onto it. Just as Briggit did. I must take her curse and renounce it in the same way. Bury it in the ground, as she did. In a sacred place, asking for the gods' help. In magic, I believe, there must be balance. It is the same with healing. Hot and cold. Sweet and sour. And tonight, I will add my weight to the scales, and we will have balance again. And hopefully, no more curse.'

'What can I do?' Entorp asked.

'You must carve symbols as soon as you're able,' Edela said. 'The stonemasons have been building up the hole in the wall. As soon as there's wall enough to join from one side to the other, you must add the symbols onto that new piece of wall. It doesn't matter how tiny you have to carve them. A symbol doesn't need to be large to be powerful. And with the gates closed and the symbols around the walls, we will have a complete enclosure once more. And though it will not protect us from Draguta, it should keep us safe from Briggit and her Followers. They are not as powerful as Draguta is. They won't see past our symbols,' Edela said, smiling confidently, though her insides twisted with doubts.

Karsten looked over at the huddle of whisperers. He wondered what they were talking about.

Jael's grandmother, her servant, the blind girl.

What were they up to?

Sighing, he looked back at Nicolene, realising that he was trying to distract himself.

He didn't want to be here.

Having finally decided to stop avoiding the sheds, he had entered the one he believed Nicolene to be in, only to be told that she'd already been moved into the fort. She had gone downhill rapidly, quicker than anyone they'd seen apparently, and Karsten suspected that Nicolene had been ill for some time but hadn't wanted to say anything. He hoped not. He didn't want to think that any of the children might have caught it.

Other husbands and wives sat around on the floor, kneeling, squatting, sitting. Karsten wanted a stool, but they were all being used by the whispering huddle, and he wouldn't have been able to hold Nicolene's hand if he'd been sitting on one.

He wasn't sure he wanted to hold her hand now.

He couldn't keep still, finally kneeling, swallowing, looking everywhere but at his wife, until, eventually, he reached out and almost snatched at her hand.

It dropped into his.

There was no life in it at all, and that's when his tears came. Karsten couldn't remember when he'd last felt powerful. Untouchable. As though he walked with the gods themselves. It was a feeling that had lived in him as naturally as blood flowing through his veins. Now it felt as though the gods had abandoned him, ripping his family away, one by one.

And Karsten wasn't sure that he wanted to be the last one standing.

***

'Where are they?' Axl felt impatient as he stood alongside his sister on the ramparts. The sun was sinking, and the air was cooling, and there'd been no sign of the dragur yet.

'I don't know,' Jael admitted, worrying for the first time that her instincts were wrong. The dragur had been chasing them, she was sure. Just as they'd tracked them from Hallow Wood. Just as they'd run out of the burning shell of Harstad after them.

But she thought they would've been here by now.

Jael wondered if Draguta had other things on her mind? Though no matter what plans Draguta was making, she would never let them be. She would never let them keep the Book of Aurea. She would send her blue monsters after it one day soon.

Perhaps, Jael realised as a thought took hold, perhaps the book was the only way Draguta could find her sister? If she hadn't already.

'They will come,' she insisted. 'Whether tonight or next month, they're out there somewhere, roaming Osterland. We need to remain alert.'

'I have to leave for Rissna,' Axl said. 'Raymon Vandaal will be there soon, waiting to meet me.'

'*You*? You've decided to take over, then? You don't need me anymore?'

Axl shook his head. 'No. It's just... you weren't here.'

'But now I'm back, so I'll be coming with you,' Jael said. 'Neither you nor Raymon Vandaal is equipped to lead a great army into the fight we're about to head for. We have no idea who we're going to be facing. *What* we're going to be facing.'

Axl couldn't disagree. 'Well, then, I didn't think I'd ever say this, but I hope the dragur come soon. I don't want to leave the fort exposed. If we do, we're likely to come back and find everyone dead.'

Jael frowned, knowing that there was a real possibility of that happening. 'I hope so too,' she said, inhaling the smell of fish as it wafted in from the harbour on a stiffening breeze. The ships had come in that morning with an enormous catch, and the smell of it was everywhere.

Fish, yes, but no dragur.

***

Eadmund opened the door with only a fur wrapped around his waist.

Brill blushed, staring at her boots. 'My mistress wants Evaine to come. She is to help her tonight.'

Eadmund looked back into his new cottage at Evaine, who remained hidden in the shadows beneath the other bed fur. 'Why?'

That stumped Brill. Her long face appeared to lengthen further as her mouth hung open, her brows furrowing anxiously. 'She... requires her to come. There is a spell. Evaine must be there to help.'

Eadmund nodded, finding himself unable to argue against anything Draguta required, as much as he often felt the urge to. 'She'll be there,' he said, closing the door on a flustered Brill, who took a deep breath before turning around and trudging away into the last of the sunshine.

'I don't want to go,' Evaine protested, popping up from beneath the fur, her hair tangled all around her like a snow-covered bush.

And looking at her naked body, Eadmund was ready to agree, but he could almost see Draguta's face, red with displeasure, and he dropped his fur and picked up his tunic, shrugging it over his head. 'You have to go, Evaine. I'm sure you won't be long, then you can come back. Don't worry, we have all night. Besides, maybe I can get some sleep while you're gone? I might need it,' he smiled.

Evaine didn't smile as Eadmund searched the cottage for the clothes he'd ripped off her. They were filthy and needed a wash after her journey, but they were all she had for now, so, sighing dramatically, Evaine shuffled to the edge of the bed and started dressing. 'Why are you so keen to please Draguta?' she asked. 'What has she done to you?'

'She brought me here so you would come. So you would bring her what she needed,' Eadmund said, retrieving Evaine's boots from by the door.

'But you're doing all this training. Trying to please her. Why would you do that? You're a king. She's not even a queen. Not anymore.'

Eadmund was momentarily confused. Part of him could see that it was indeed strange for him to be doing Draguta's bidding, but that thought evaporated before it took hold. 'I may be a king, but I'm not in my kingdom, am I? Neither of us are. Here is where Draguta rules. Hest is her kingdom, queen or not, and we are hers to do with as she wishes. Both of us. We are hers, Evaine. We must help her get what she wants.' And leaning down, Eadmund kissed Evaine's pouting lips. 'Come on, the quicker you help her, the quicker you'll be back in bed with me.'

But Evaine didn't move as she stared after Eadmund, who was already opening the door, wondering what Draguta had done to him.

For this wasn't the Eadmund she knew at all.

***

The King's Hall was packed to the gunwales, ringing with the sound of loud voices, and Jael felt the urge to escape to her bedchamber, not wanting to face the people who were almost lining up to speak to her; none more so than her own mother, who she had so far managed to avoid. But now she found herself trapped between a wall and Gisila, and there appeared no quick exit, not unless she wanted to squeeze past Rork Arnesson, who wasn't inclined to move when he had a cup in his hand.

Jael sighed, rolling her eyes. 'Don't say anything.'

Gisila looked surprised. 'What? What do you mean?'

'I mean there's nothing I want to say about what happened, so don't say anything to me,' Jael grumbled, still looking for an escape. But seeing the hurt in her mother's eyes, she stopped and faced her. 'I don't want to talk about it,' she said, lowering her voice. 'Please, Mother. There's too much I need to do now. Too much I need to think about.'

Gisila knew better than most how it felt to lose a child, and though she had never been especially close to her daughter, she wanted to comfort her in the way her own mother had comforted her during those terrible times. But, she supposed, watching Jael squirm away from her, that was unlikely to work. She nodded, moving out of the way. 'Go on, then. You go.'

Now Jael felt guilty, which annoyed her even more than being pestered about the one thing she didn't want to talk about. She tried to think of something to say to make it better, but she couldn't, so, dropping her head, she turned away, bumping into Bram Svanter. 'Oh.' Reaching out, Jael grabbed him as he stumbled, losing his balance.

Thorgils was quickly behind him. 'You trying to knock my uncle over?' he grinned.

'Doesn't look like it would be hard to do,' Jael smiled, moving a bench closer so Thorgils could deposit Bram onto it.

Bram tried to catch his breath as he eased himself down.

'Are you alright?' Jael wondered as Thorgils disappeared to find him a cup of ale.

'Fine,' Bram assured her. 'Nothing a bit of sea air wouldn't cure.'

'You sound like a man with itchy feet,' Jael said, happy to sit down herself. 'Or a man looking to run away?' She blinked, not sure what that meant.

The look on Bram's face told her that he knew exactly what it meant, and he felt embarrassed. 'No, I'm not. It's just... strange... nearly dying. Waking up to a new family. I...'

Jael saw Fyn talking to Aleksander on the other side of the hall. Axl too. She looked back at Bram, amazed that she'd never noticed the resemblance before. They had the same broad shoulders. Tall. Lots of hair. Like Thorgils, she realised. Fyn glanced shyly towards them. 'Don't run away,' Jael whispered. 'It might feel strange for you, but imagine how Fyn feels? The only man he knew as his father treated him like a turd he stepped in every day. Morac told him he was worthless. He treated him as if he was. That's not something you can undo easily. It's how Fyn feels about himself now. I see it in his eyes. If you reject him too...'

Bram felt foolish. And old. He'd faced death and welcomed it. Prepared himself to go and be with his family. It wouldn't have been a warrior's death. He wasn't going to end up in

Vidar's Hall, supping and fighting with his friends, but he hadn't wanted that. Not really. He'd wanted to see his wife and children again. So desperately. Yet he'd come back. He had wanted to come back when Ayla told him about Fyn and Runa.

And it wasn't that he didn't know how to be a father. He felt almost confident in that. It was the idea of unlocking his heart again and letting them both in.

He wasn't sure if he could do it.

Jael yawned beside Bram as Thorgils returned with his ale.

'Here you go,' Thorgils said, peering at the two weary faces before him. 'Or perhaps it's time for bed?'

Jael stood, shaking her head. 'No, not yet. I want to find Beorn. I haven't spoken to him since we got back.' She glanced around as Fyn approached, looking as though he was dragging his feet, changing his mind with every step. 'Here, you take my seat.'

Fyn gulped, wanting to go with Jael instead.

But Jael stepped behind him, eyeing Thorgils, who took one look at Fyn and Bram and nodded, watching as Jael slipped away. 'Take a seat, Cousin!' he bellowed, 'and let's see if we can decide which one of us has a story worthy of Warunda's time. Me, being stabbed by my best friend, who's bound to an evil girl, and you being speared by a man who wouldn't die. Each very impressive tales in their own right, but Bram might top us both, him almost crushed to death by a dragon!'

Neither Fyn nor Bram spoke, but Bram did lift his cup to his lips, taking a long drink. Thorgils quickly looked around for Isaura, who was better at this sort of thing, but she was talking to Amma Furyck and wasn't looking his way.

Jael found Beorn and turned back to Thorgils, watching him try to coax some conversation out of the awkward statues that were Bram and Fyn. 'You've done a good job with those catapults,' she said to Beorn, shaking her head as a servant offered her a cup of ale. 'Are they going to be able to travel, do you think?'

Beorn nodded. 'They've got wheels, but I don't imagine any horse is going to enjoy pulling them up the hills to get out of this place.'

Jael laughed. 'Don't worry, we can go the long way, towards Iskavall. It's reasonably flat through there, I promise.' She turned as Aleksander approached. He had his cloak on, though it was warm in the hall.

'I'm heading out. I'll check around the catapults. Make sure everyone's wide awake and fully supplied. Better than standing around here, waiting for the dragur.'

Jael could see how worried he was about Hanna. He could barely stand still, which, for someone as calm as Aleksander, said a lot. 'Well, enjoy the night air. I'll head for bed and see you in the morning.' It felt strange to say, and though she wanted to go with Aleksander to check on the men or to see if Edela needed help with her curse-breaking ritual, she could barely keep her eyes open.

The only way she could be of some use, Jael decided, was to see if she could find some answers in her dreams.

PART THREE

The Valley

CHAPTER EIGHTEEN

Kormac and his two sons were on edge as they led Edela, Biddy, and Eydis through the main gates, heading towards the forest. Furia's Tree and its sacred grove were some distance from the fort, and though Edela didn't feel any rain, the clouds were thick overhead, hiding the moon.

During the day, it was a pleasant walk, accompanied by dappled light, birdsong, and the hum of industrious bees from the hives where the Andalans harvested their honey. But in the dark, everything took on a menacing edge.

And then there was the threat of the dragur.

Jael had organised for her uncle and cousins to accompany Edela to the grove, hoping they would keep everyone safe and return them to the fort if there was any sign of danger. The three men carried torches wrapped in pitch-soaked cloth, burning flames to light their way, prepared but hoping not to encounter any dragur.

Edela followed Aedan, muttering to herself, certain she'd forgotten something; convinced that what she had prepared was somehow wrong. Her nerves were plucking like lyre strings as she stumbled, slipping on the wet leaves.

Biddy grabbed her, worried that she, too, would fall.

Aedan turned back to them. 'Are you alright, Grandmother?'

Edela nodded. 'Fine, fine, but maybe you could come a little closer with those flames. It's hard to see where I'm going now.

And the path does become rougher ahead.'

Aedan ensured that both Edela and Biddy were alright before returning to the head of their little group, trying to stay closer to his grandmother.

'We'll be turning to the right at the fork ahead!' Edela called. 'Don't you lead us in the wrong direction, now!'

Aedan smiled as he lifted the burning torch, leading them into the thick forest.

Ears open. Listening for dragur.

***

Eadmund had fallen asleep not long after Evaine left with Brill. There was something about pushing himself so hard that he was almost starting to enjoy. He could feel the change in himself as muscle replaced fat. His strength was growing; a power and resilience forming that he hadn't felt in years.

Rollo was working him harder than anyone he'd ever met.

His mind was less occupied with other thoughts now. He tried to remember what Draguta wanted him to do. He thought about being with Evaine. Sometimes he remembered his son.

He didn't think about anything else.

Until he fell asleep and the dreams came like a flood.

Eskild was worried.

The gods were whispering about the growing power of Draguta Teros and her increasing control over Eadmund. Of how lost he was and how worried they were that he could not be reclaimed now.

But Eskild wouldn't let him go. She would never give up.

Having finally found a way into Eadmund's dreams, she was determined to do everything she could to save him before it was too late.

There was so much he didn't know – so much she hadn't known herself – and it was all to do with Morana Gallas. That witch had destroyed her family from the shadows, piece by tiny piece, so that no one noticed. So that no one thought to add all the pieces together to find the truth.

Until now.

'Eadmund.' He was dreaming of Oss again, and Eskild took a deep breath, seeing which dream he had chosen; knowing what had happened that day. What she now knew had happened. 'Come,' she said. 'There is something you need to watch. Come with me, my son.'

Eadmund could hear his mother's voice. He spun around, but he couldn't see her. He followed her voice anyway, through the square and away from the hall, where he remembered it was his birthday. His thirteenth birthday.

He heard his mother's gentle voice, warm and soothing like a lullaby, and he followed it, down the alley, towards the northwestern corner of the fort; the darkest corner where the oldest cottages were hidden from the sun's warmth.

Where Morana Gallas lived.

Eadmund had walked up to that cottage with Thorgils and their friends many times, daring each other to knock on the door and ask the witch a question.

No one had ever taken up the challenge.

They would get to within footsteps of reaching out to touch her door before running down the alley, their bowels clenching in fear.

Eadmund's feet were urging him on, though he was resisting now. He didn't want to go into the cottage. The door was closed, but someone was inside. He could see smoke rising from the thatch. He could hear bones knocking against each other around her porch.

He didn't want to go inside.

But Eskild's voice was firm. 'Open the door, Eadmund. It is just a dream, but you need to see. You need to see what she did.'

Eadmund lifted a hand to the wooden panels and pushed. The door didn't move, but somehow, he moved straight through it, and suddenly he was standing outside, in a forest, staring at a tiny shack. He remembered it from his time in Rikka with Evaine.

Morana's cottage.

Eadmund froze, not wanting to move forward, but he was quickly at the door, reaching for the handle, and as much as he wanted to turn and run in the opposite direction, he was suddenly inside.

The cottage was as he remembered: dark, smoky, cramped; shelves stuffed full of jars and bottles; herbs strung across cobweb-thick rafters and along the walls. On the floor sat Morana, surrounded by candles and symbols painted in... blood? She wore a fur hood of some sort, and when she lifted her head, Eadmund could see that it was a wolf's head, the animal's top teeth still intact.

Her face was painted; her teeth red.

Eadmund couldn't move. His body held him tightly.

Keeping him where he needed to be.

Morana was chanting as she threw herbs onto the fire, which spat angrily back at her. She picked up something that caught his eye: a necklace of yellow glass and amber beads on a delicate, silver chain. Eadmund had given it to Eskild for Vesta. A sun necklace, he'd told her, having chosen the beads himself. And now Morana held it in her hands as she closed her eyes and started swaying, rocking back and forth on her knees.

More smoke filled the cottage, but Eadmund was untroubled, and so was Morana as she writhed around in her circle now, her voice rising and falling like crashing waves. And then, at the very crescendo of her chanting, Morana tore the necklace apart, scattering the beads all over the ground.

Eadmund turned and ran straight through the door, hearing nothing but the frantic beating of his breaking heart. Everything was silent around him as he ran back into Oss, down the alley, across the square, towards the gates. 'Mother!' he screamed. 'Mother!' There was snow on the ground, ice on the cleared paths, and he slipped as he ran, keeping to his feet as he charged out of the gates and down the hill, bumping into a fur-wrapped old man, who struggled up to him with smoking breath.

'Eadmund!' he panted. 'Your mother! Quick! I'll get the king!'

Eadmund couldn't breathe as he charged past him, running for the ice.

Where his mother was walking, far, far out, towards the stone spires.

'Mother! No!'

***

Jael woke with a start. Eadmund's screaming had been loud in her ears, but now everything was silent.

And then a raven's call.

She tried to catch her breath. Her body shuddered and shook as though she'd been running. Sitting up, she pushed Ido off her feet. She'd fallen asleep so quickly that she'd left a lamp burning, and it was easy to find her trousers, which she hurried on, and then her boots. They were her second pair; full of holes. It was cold, but Jael didn't have a new cloak yet, so she slipped her swordbelt on and stepped out of the chamber.

Into the corridor.

It was late.

Jael realised that she must have slept for some time because there was no noise coming from the hall, just some raucous snoring from the chambers along the corridor. Likely Axl, she thought to herself as she heard it again.

The raven.

Hurrying now, Jael pulled back the thick grey curtain, stepping into the hall. The fires had burned down, and it was darker than she could remember seeing it before. And cold. The men and women sleeping on the benches were perfectly still. Silent. Jael shivered, wondering if she was having a dream.

She could see white puffs of breath smoking before her.

Then the hall's enormous doors started to rattle.

Jael's right hand hovered over *Toothpick*, her brow furrowing as she stepped closer, towards the banging doors. But just before she reached them, they blew open, ushering in an enormous gust of wind, flapping her braids behind her, blowing the remnants of smoke all around the hall.

And sitting there waiting on the steps was Fyr.

The raven with the white eye cawed loudly, turning her head to Jael.

Watching her.

Jael swallowed, walking towards the bird, immediately inhaling the stench of dragon, which still lingered, the smell of fish drifting in from the harbour.

And the dragur.

She could smell the dragur.

***

Edela was anxious because she couldn't see the moon. Thick clouds had trapped it above the tree canopy, refusing to let it out, and she had to rely on the faint glow of Biddy's struggling fire to see what she was doing.

Kormac, Aedan, and Aron had stayed outside the grove, guarding it, watching for dragur, their torches burning.

Edela would have been grateful for the extra light and warmth. She shivered as the wind picked up, thinking of the fur neck warmer Biddy was always threatening her with.

She wasn't sure it was cold, though.

Biddy was trying to encourage more flames in her fire, and Eydis was sitting against Furia's Tree while Edela prepared everything.

Edela wondered if they should have brought Jael along after all. She was potentially the most powerful dreamer of all. Too late now, she reminded herself, jumping at a clap of thunder in the distance.

'We don't need a storm,' Biddy muttered as she straightened up and walked to Eydis, helping her to her feet. 'I'll take you to Edela, and you can sit in the circle. I need to start digging the hole.'

Edela had drawn a circle with her knife in a patch of cleared earth and was now painting symbols onto the three stones she'd placed around its edge, in rat's blood, and her blood. The blood of the dreamer and the blood of her sacrifice.

She hoped it would work.

More thunder.

'Is it the gods?' Biddy asked, helping Eydis down beside Edela, conscious of how still the night was. Apart from the thunder, there was no sign of a storm. 'Are they coming?'

Eydis nodded, making herself comfortable. 'We have to hurry.'

Edela pointed to the middle of the circle. 'If you could dig the hole in the centre, Biddy. As deep as your hand and twice as long. But first, throw the rest of the herbs onto the flames. They look healthy enough now.'

Edela sat facing the fire, using her hand to waft the smoke towards her, suddenly realising what Eydis had said. 'Can you feel the gods?'

'Yes, but they're not coming to help you, Edela.'

Edela's eyes widened as she sensed her meaning. 'No, no, they're not.' Her heart thundered in her chest now. 'Biddy, dig as fast as you can. Once the hole is ready, we must begin!'

***

Evaine kept glancing over her shoulder, wanting to leave.

It made Draguta wistful for Morana Gallas and her twitching niece. They had, at least, been dreamers. Subservient for a time. Aware of the importance of silence of both mind and body, and Evaine's thoughts were so loud that Draguta was struggling to concentrate. 'You do wish to return to Eadmund before dawn, don't you?' she wondered, squeezing Evaine's hand so tightly that Evaine yelped as she nodded. 'Then sit still, and allow me to focus or I shall throw you into my fire and leave you to roast!'

Evaine flinched, certain that Draguta meant it. She swallowed, trying to clear her mind of everything but what was before her, which was little.

They had come to the top of the stone tower. It had been a guard tower centuries before, but when Flane's walls were rebuilt years ago, it was abandoned, left to crumble. Few ventured up here anymore, which made it the perfect place to perform the spell, Draguta thought, trying to ignore all the other things that were not perfect at all; pleased to finally hear Evaine's mind retreat into the background.

She checked on Brill, who was guarding the entrance to the tower before throwing her herbs onto the flames, her fingers dripping with the bloody potion she'd painted the symbols with. She had drunk the rest of it and could now feel its warm iron tang settling in her chest.

Draguta's eyes rolled up as she shot forward, jerking into the darkness with an explosion of flames.

***

The screeching came before the horn.

Thorgils rolled out of Isaura's arms.

The smell in the house was overpowering. Familiar.

Isaura gripped his hand, not wanting him to go.

'Get everyone dressed,' he said, keeping his voice even, grabbing his trousers as his heart started racing. 'Lock the door after me but be ready to leave.' He sat down to quickly put on his boots. 'I'll be back as soon as I can. Have the torches ready to burn and keep the fire going. They hate fire.'

***

'Catapult crews!' Jael screamed across the valley. 'Catapult crews! Light your braziers!' She walked to the other side of the rampart and called the same thing down into the fort. They'd gone over the drill all afternoon, and Jael hoped the men would remember it. Looking up, she saw that the moon was masked by thick clusters of clouds.

Hopefully, that meant the gods were here.

She felt that they were. The hairs on the back of her neck were standing on end. Or perhaps that was the cold?

Jael had no idea how many dragur were out there, but she could hear them edging closer. She could feel them surging forward in rumbling waves.

So could Aleksander as he joined her.

'Them again,' he yawned, slipping a helmet over his head. He tied it under his bearded chin, blinking his eyes open, trying to shake some feeling into his legs.

Jael had run back into her bedchamber and squeezed into her armour, shoving her own helmet on her head. Having had two encounters with the dragur now, she knew that she was going to need all the protection she could get. 'Can you see them?' she asked. 'I can't see a thing.'

'No, but I can smell them,' Aleksander said, squinting at the dark valley, trying to spot anything moving. 'Unless that's Thorgils?'

Thorgils snorted from Jael's left. 'Thought that might have been you. Or Ivaar.'

Ivaar didn't bother to snort. His eyes were trained on the dark shapes in the distance. He could certainly smell something and hear odd noises, but he couldn't see anything either. 'Where are they?' he wondered, trying to wake himself up. 'Perhaps they're afraid of the symbols? Maybe they're working?'

Jael turned as Axl and Fyn edged their way down the suddenly full rampart walk. It was impossible to see much, even with the glow from the braziers they'd set up around the valley, but something was moving out there. She could feel it. 'Let's light it up!' Jael called down the line. 'Gant! Two fire arrows! We need to see!'

'Feels like winter,' Thorgils shivered, jiggling his legs as he tightened his swordbelt. 'Do you think we're about to get snowed on again?'

'I don't think snow would bother them,' Aleksander said, listening to the whistle of arrows shooting over their heads, disappearing into the darkness; his eyes widening as the flames illuminated the valley.

Gant felt his heart stutter.

Ivaar's mouth fell open.

As far as they could see, there was nothing but hollow-eyed dead men jerking down Bog's Hill, filling the valley like a rotting blue flood.

Thousands of them.

'Oh.' Jael turned to Aleksander. 'There's a few more now.' She frowned as everything went dark again. 'Another arrow, Gant!'

And this time they could see the mass of dragur parting to allow one creature through. And that dragur, standing taller than the rest, wielded a long rusting sword, which he held aloft, calling to the army of creatures, who screeched back at him.

And satisfied with their response, he turned back, pointed to the fort and charged.

***

Arriving in Jaeger's chamber, Draguta immediately felt the pull to return to her cottage. Her seeing circle was calling to her, but she couldn't leave her trance.

Not yet.

Jaeger was naked, sprawled across his bed, Meena asleep beside him.

Draguta walked towards them. It felt like wading through water, and she could feel the strain of forcing her body forward, almost dragging herself to the bed. And then she was there, leaning over Jaeger, and Draguta's desire to kill him was suddenly greater than her plan to bind him.

Studying him, she calmed herself, focusing her mind, conscious of the need to leave. So, lifting the ends of the thin, black rope she had tied around her waist, she bent forward and fed one end under Jaeger, digging around to pull it out the other side. He wriggled helpfully, allowing her to grasp it, quickly tying the two ends of the rope into a secure knot.

Binding them together.

And straightening up with a smile, Draguta closed her eyes, throwing back her head as she started to chant.

Meena watched from near the door, not knowing what to do.

Was it a dream?

Was it happening now?

She could see herself lying next to Jaeger, cool moonlight

flooding in through the window, falling across the bed. She could see clearly enough what Draguta was doing. But would Draguta see her?

Panicking, Meena squeezed her eyes shut, trying to find another dream. She didn't want to wake up, or Draguta would see her. And if she saw her, she would surely kill her.

But when Meena opened her eyes, she was still there.

And then Draguta turned around, blinking in surprise.

***

Lightning jagged across the night sky as the dragur ran, surging forward, knocking into each other, following their leader across the valley.

Towards the catapults.

During the afternoon, with Gant and Aleksander's help, Jael had laid them all out, bringing almost every catapult they had into the valley to make themselves a trap.

A dragur catching trap.

And now it was time to spring it.

'Catapult crews!' Jael bellowed, though her voice didn't carry far; the shrill noise of the dragur was too loud, drowning out everything else. 'Release!' The first jars of sea-fire flew into the seething river of creatures, who didn't hesitate as they charged, ignoring the cracking pots oozing black liquid all over them. 'Archers! Nock! Light your arrows!' Jael was straining to see anything. The flickering glow of torches and braziers along the ramparts revealed only shadows. Though those shadows were terrifying enough. 'Aim!' An impossible request. 'Release!' And Jael listened to the pings as the bowstrings snapped back, burning arrows arcing into the night sky, dropping down into the dragur.

And then the first explosion.

Leaving Gant to run the ramparts, Jael headed for the stairs, hurrying out of the main gates to join her Islanders, who were lined up in front of the broken wall between the ditch and a row of catapults. More sea-fire exploded, sparks flying, flames lighting up the rumbling sky. They were going to have to work hard to keep the fire away from the fort, from the catapults, and from themselves.

Jael reached the first catapult, where Fyn was already waiting with his bow in hand. Sending him to the back with the rest of her archers, Jael took over. 'Load!' she cried, her mind jumping to her grandmother, who she knew had left the fort with Eydis and Biddy.

She hoped Kormac and her cousins were keeping them safe.

Her well-trained catapult crew pulled back the hammer, securing the tension, carefully loading another jar into the wooden spoon as the dragur rushed them. 'My archers!' Jael turned to the ten men behind her, standing in two rows on either side of the flaming brazier. 'Light your arrows!'

Some of the dragur were now stumbling in confusion, attacked on all sides, on fire, banging into each other as they forced their way towards the fort, following their leader. Jael could see his sword in the air, its blade curling like those carried by the fearless warriors from the Fire Lands; its tarnished edge winking in the exploding sea-fire.

Untouched by the flames, he crashed forward.

Karsten was bellowing at his men, who were protecting the ditch with the Islanders. They stood behind the catapults, waiting, swords, spears and axes at the ready. 'Hold! Do not move, you fuckers! Hold!' He was pleased to see that they looked angry as they jiggled on the spot, firming up their grips, eyes fixed on what was coming.

He felt angry.

The sound of the dragur had his guts swirling and his blood pumping as he jiggled his axes, finding it just as hard to hold as his men were.

'Fire!' Ivaar called as his crew released the tension on the catapult next to Jael's, jumping away as the hammer snapped back, sending another jar of sea-fire into the dragur.

Thunder was rolling, but the cries of the dragur were growing louder.

There were so many of them.

Surging forward, through the flames.

***

Biddy wanted to say something. She could hear the terrifying sounds of what had to be the dragur attacking the fort in the distance. The explosions came regularly, bursting and banging, and she almost bit her tongue every time, despite the heady fug of smoke dulling her senses. Her body was shaking in fear, but she didn't want to disturb Edela, so she pressed her lips together, waiting.

Edela had entered a trance as she bent towards the tiny rat's skin, painting three symbols onto it with blood, chanting in low, murmuring tones.

Biddy found herself holding her breath.

Hoping those dragur would stay far away.

***

Draguta moved slowly towards Meena. Her breath burned her lungs, though she did not feel weak. Not when she saw Meena's petrified face.

Cornering her at the door, Draguta reached out and grabbed Meena around the throat, knowing that she didn't have time for this. She needed to leave. This was not in her plans. She had other places to be now.

But she couldn't resist.

'You.' She squeezed Meena's throat, watching terror bloom in her eyes. 'Killed me!'

Meena tried to shake her head; she couldn't breathe.

'*Tried* to kill me,' Draguta corrected herself. 'But you couldn't. You can't.' She glanced back at Jaeger, who was still sleeping. The black rope was endless in its length. They were joined now. He belonged to her, and wherever she went, whatever Jaeger did, he would remain bound to her. He would bend to her will, and her will alone. 'Jaeger will live, that is my choice. But you?' She brought her nails around, digging them into Meena's neck, inhaling her fear. 'What should I do with a disloyal little mouse like you?'

***

The sea-fire was burning the dragur, and they were scattering like flaming beetles, running in different directions now, charging for the catapults, past the catapults, into the treeline that edged the eastern side of the valley.

Looking for other ways into the fort.

Lightning shot down from the thunderous sky, exploding the sea-fire, and the dragur panicked further, on fire, clambering on top of each other, pushing and fighting to follow their leader.

A screeching knot of creatures burst forward, aiming straight for the broken wall. Aiming for Jael, Thorgils, Ivaar, Karsten and the Islanders, who stood in front of it by their swinging catapults.

'Nock!' Jael screamed, hurrying behind the archers to join her men. Their swords and axes were out, sweat beading across tense foreheads. Waiting. 'Light your arrows!' She knew they wouldn't be able to keep the dragur out for long. The creatures were too strong, and they weren't able to launch the sea-fire near the walls. They couldn't afford to set themselves on fire, but the burning dragur forcing their way towards the fort had no such worries.

'Spears! Swords! With me!' Jael felt her anger rising, overwhelming any fear that they wouldn't be able to stop them.

That they wouldn't be able to kill them.

The dragur had killed her baby, and she was going to send them all back to their leafy graves for good.

CHAPTER NINETEEN

Biddy could hear the clashing of blades nearby.

Then Kormac's voice.

'Edela!'

Biddy spun around, panicking. The grove was surrounded on all sides by tall hazel trees, packed tightly together, and she couldn't see out, but she could hear that something was out there.

Blades were clanging, grunting and cursing, unfamiliar shrieking noises.

And that smell...

'Edela?' Biddy tried to get her attention, but Edela was swaying on her knees, eyes open, chanting, not there at all.

Edela held up the rat's skin before laying it into the hole where she had already placed the bodies of three rats and the ashes of the one whose skin she'd drawn the symbols onto. It felt as though the darkness was gripping her shoulders, and she tried to imagine the warmth of the sun on her face as she called to the gods, asking for Aurea, Goddess of Light, to help her banish the darkness. Ignoring Biddy's pleading voice and the screeching noises, the booms of thunder, the odd smell, and Kormac's cries, Edela stayed in her trance, struggling to her feet as Aurea came to join her in the battle of dark and light.

Eydis was in a trance, too, watching a woman move into the circle with Edela. Golden-haired and white-robed, she glided into the space before her, her eyes focused on Edela, chanting in a soft, breathy voice. Eydis was transfixed, certain she was in a dream, for how else could she see?

Biddy could only hear Edela. She only saw Edela as she swayed from side to side, her arms extended in front of her, repeating Aurea's calm words.

And then the trees started rustling, and the putrid smell grew stronger, watering Biddy's eyes. And she heard Aedan's desperate cry.

'Grandmother!'

***

'I can help you!'

Draguta blinked. She could hear Meena's pitiful voice in her head, though the girl's lips weren't moving. Those lips were turning black as Draguta continued to squeeze her throat.

'I can help you! Please! You need an assistant to help you! I can help. P-p-please!'

Draguta narrowed her eyes. 'But what of Jaeger?' she wondered. 'How loyal are you to him, girl? Your lover? Your king?'

Meena blinked towards the bed. 'I hate him!' She hoped Draguta could hear her thoughts. 'I hate him! I won't tell him! Never!' She was struggling to see now. Everything was going dark.

And then Meena was falling to the ground, onto her knees.

And Draguta was gone.

***

Aleksander could hear the rhythmic slapping of the catapults. They'd been working steadily since the dragur had charged, and though it was hard to get the full picture of what was happening in the violent bursts of flames and lightning, he could tell that most of the dragur appeared contained in the middle of the valley; pinned in on three sides by the sea-fire attack.

But he could also see that those who weren't on fire were working their way out through the mangle of bodies and flames, finding escape routes. Looking for other ways into the fort. They wouldn't retreat. They would keep trying to get inside, wanting to kill Jael and take the book.

'Hurry!' Aleksander urged, turning to his men, who ran in a ragged line behind him, feeling his shield banging against his back, knowing the beating he was about to get from those stone-fisted creatures. 'We have to cut them off!'

As soon as the horn had blown, he'd taken his men behind the catapults, into the woodland that bordered the eastern edge of the valley, running towards Bog's Hill, hurrying to block the dragur's main escape route.

Hoping to keep them trapped in the valley.

***

The dragur were howling as they sizzled and burned, but Jael could see some of them splintering into smaller groups, unharmed, rushing for the catapults, trying to stop them launching any more of the sea-fire.

Others were running up the hills to who knew where.

Hopefully, not near Edela.

The smoke was dense, stinging her eyes and Jael coughed, spinning as a dragur rushed out of the darkness, its sword aimed at her head. She ducked, sweeping a flaming torch towards its ruined face. The creature jerked away, twisting, looking for an escape, but Thorgils was there, and it didn't have one.

Swinging with all the power his injured shoulder had to give, Thorgils released his axe and took off the dragur's head. His eyes popped open in surprise, but Jael wasn't there to admire his skill; she'd already left, realising that they were in danger of getting outflanked. 'Islanders! Hold your line! Watch your flanks!'

Trying to heave smoky air into her lungs, Jael spun around, looking for where the most danger was coming from as the Islanders dragged themselves into something resembling a line. Ivaar was there too, and his men backed up with her, fanning out across the broken wall, archers forming in the fort behind them near the braziers.

Those dragur weren't getting into the fort.

Not without a fight.

***

'Grandmother!' Aedan ran down the path, up to Furia's Tree, stopping before the three women, who blinked at his flaming torch with glazed eyes. 'We've killed the dragur!' he cried, feeling his right eye closing up, struggling to see. It was as though he'd been hit by a hammer. 'There were only two, but more will come. I can hear them in the forest. We have to go! I need to get you back to the fort!'

Biddy grabbed Eydis' hand, leaving Aedan to take Edela.

Edela was reluctant to leave, hoping she'd finished the spell; wanting to wait and see, to go over what she'd done, but Aurea had gone, and now, she realised, they had to go too.

Aedan froze, gripping Edela's hand. He could hear his father screaming. Quickly scanning the grove, Aedan handed his burning torch to his grandmother, and ran to the nearest tree, ripping off a branch, quickly stripping its leaves. Glancing at Biddy, he stuck it into the fire, urging it to catch. 'You need to take this. Protect Eydis. I've got Edela. Stay close!' And he pulled the burning branch from the fire, handing it to Biddy, kicking dirt over the flames.

'Aron! No! *No!*'

Aedan heard his father's pained cry as he pushed his way down the secluded path, trying not to run. He could feel his grandmother's hand tighten on his, the sharp intake of her breath, but he didn't look around as he hurried her forward.

***

Aleksander's men were lined up across the mouth of the valley now, far enough away from the catapults not to be hit by the sea-fire, but close enough to cut off the dragur's most obvious escape route. They waited, swords, spears and axes ready, choking on the intense clouds of smoke drifting towards them; blinking rapidly, trying to see.

'Hold! Hold the line!' he yelled, knowing that they couldn't afford to let a single dragur through, but he could see at least twenty already running at them now. None of them were on fire. Many of them were carrying some form of weapon. 'Hold!'

He thought of Hanna, praying that Furia would let him see her again. 'Archers!' he bellowed, turning to the men arrayed behind his line. 'Nock!'

***

Jael had one eye on the dragur leader as he battered every Islander who came at him, sending them flying, not caring whether he'd killed them. She could tell that he was only trying to get to her.

And Jael didn't know what to do.

She'd never backed away from a fight, but she was struggling to even lift her sword. She was out of shape, out of practice.

Barely out of bed.

Trying to think, Jael slipped out of her line, running for the nearest catapult. 'I need a jar!' she cried to the loader. 'One jar!'

***

'If you can't kill her, get past her!' Draguta boomed, horrified by the great burning mess in her seeing circle. 'I want that book!'

She had returned to her cottage quickly, feeling the pull of the dragur attack, but her excitement had been swiftly tempered by the fiery scene before her. Thankfully, there were some she could rely on.

Her eyes followed Darius. He had been her son's champion once; a blood-thirsty, giant-sized leader of the highest caliber. And now he would need to lead his creatures to victory.

She would settle for nothing else.

'Get me that book!'

***

'Aron!' Aedan saw his brother sprawled on the ground, Kormac standing over his body, five dragur circling them.

'Go!' Kormac shouted, his eyes quickly finding Aedan, whose terrified face was pale despite the heat from his flaming torch. 'Get them out of here! Now, Aedan! Back to the fort! *Hurry!*'

But Aedan's boots didn't move. He swallowed, ideas jumping around his head, trying to find a way out for all of them.

'Aedan, go!' his father yelled hoarsely, sensing his hesitation, not taking his eyes off the dragur. 'You need to save Edela! You must! Get them all back to the fort now!'

Aedan blinked at his father, who was holding off the dragur with his burning torch as their circle around him grew tighter, glancing at his motionless brother. He felt Edela's cold hand on his, and turning away, he pulled her towards the fort.

***

Jael could see Beorn, Thorgils, Torstan and Klaufi. Even Hassi was there. All of them lined up across the broken wall, fighting to repel those dragur who had escaped the flames unharmed.

Fyn was at the back with his bow. He still wasn't much use, but Jael hoped that she was.

She had to be.

The immense strength of the dragur was pushing the Islanders steadily backwards, towards the ditch. The repairs to the wall were so minimal that a child could have clambered over it without much effort, and though the ditch was deep, it wouldn't stop them for long.

Stepping further away from the fort, back towards the valley of burning dragur and swinging catapults, Jael sought out their leader, trying to draw him away. 'Over here!' she cried, wondering what she was even thinking. 'Over here!'

Darius jerked around, throwing Torstan away, back into the line of Islanders, scattering some as he crashed to the ground.

'Out of shape, out of practice,' Jael reminded herself as the giant dragur barrelled towards her, his rusted sword scything the air. Inhaling slowly, she tried to ignore her taunting thoughts, watching as the giant blue beast jerked closer and closer. She counted in her head, aware that more dragur were swarming on either side of him now, joining their leader's charge.

And then she brought the jar of sea-fire out from behind her back.

***

'No!' Draguta roared, slamming her fists down on either side of the circle. 'No! You fool! No! *Run!*'

***

Jael had no strength in her arms, so she'd left it later than was comfortable, but her aim was still deadly, and when the jar hit Darius, it cracked open on his skull, oozing black sea-fire liquid all over his blue face, dripping down onto his chest.

The dragur on either side of their leader stumbled to a stop, trying to turn and run.

Jael did run. 'Fyn!' she shouted. '*Now!*'

Three heartbeats later, and with Jael running away as fast as her weary legs would carry her, the fire arrow landed in Darius' shoulder. His head snapped to the wall where Fyn stood, bow in hand, relief all over his face.

Grabbing the arrow, Darius ripped it out of his shoulder, promptly bursting into flames.

Jael threw herself to the ground as the explosion rippled through the air, ringing her ears, sending sparks flying, scattering the dragur away from the wall.

Scrambling to her feet, Jael shook her head. She couldn't hear a thing, but she could feel the intense waves of heat from the flames as the burning bits of the dragur leader scattered across the night sky.

***

Edela felt the panic pulsing down Aedan's arm, into the hand that was holding hers. She could feel his burning desire to turn around and go back, but Edela knew that it was too late. There was nothing he could do to help Kormac now.

Aedan was hurrying them around the eastern side of the fort, towards the harbour gates, knowing that somebody would be looking down from the ramparts; hoping that no creatures had crept around to the harbour to cut off their path. But just as he thought it, two dragur ran around the corner. Spotting Aedan and the women, they charged down the muddy track towards them. Aedan quickly handed a crying Edela to a blinking Biddy. 'Stay back! Keep your eyes open!'

The dragur ran at him, one hefting its rusted sword, the other clenching its blue fists. Aedan ran to meet them, shoving his burning torch forward, trying to stick it through the swordless dragur's eye socket.

The dragur may have had no sword, but its arm had the strength of a hammer. It jerked to the side, punching Aedan's ribs, left exposed by his thrust.

Aedan screamed, certain he'd felt something snap. Stumbling, he brought his torch around, keeping both dragur back; watching as they jumped away from the flames.

'Help!' Biddy cried suddenly. 'Help!' She'd seen someone up on the wall. 'Down here! Help!'

Aedan couldn't look around to see what was happening. The dragur were working as a team, circling him now, knowing that one of them could put him down. The one with the sword crept up behind Aedan as he spun, trying to keep them in view, gasping every time he moved the torch, feeling the pain in his ribs, struggling to breathe.

'Down!' came the call from the wall. 'Get down!'

And recognising that voice, Aedan threw himself to the ground with a scream as the archers shot flaming arrows at the dragur.

***

The valley was exploding, showering sparks across the night sky. The thunder and lightning had retreated, leaving the sea-fire to devastate the dragur trapped in the mouth of the catapults. Smoke belched from the fiery carnage like a blacksmith pumping his bellows, clouding everything in a thick, grey, eye-watering shadow, making it hard to see.

Incursions were happening everywhere now.

Jael could hear screams from the walls as Gant and his men on the ramparts fired flaming arrows, sending the dragur running, back into the valley.

The Islanders were still holding the broken wall, though.

No dragur had gotten through.

Jael glanced at Thorgils, hauling air into his barrel-like chest, his face screwed up in pain. She must have looked the same, she thought, stepping out of the line to jab *Toothpick* at the nearest attacker. Fyn was beside her now, stabbing a burning torch at a dragur, who couldn't see a way through. The creature spun around, looking for other options, but Ivaar ran forward and chopped into its neck. And with an ear-piercing shriek, the dragur turned, reaching for Ivaar, its head flopping to one side now, still attached to its rotting neck.

'Not as easy as it looks,' Thorgils panted as the creature lunged for Ivaar's throat. Ivaar stumbled away, and Thorgils strode up behind the dragur, giving the nearly severed head a quick chop; watching as it dropped to the ground, its twitching body collapsing after it.

'Thorgils!' Ivaar yelled as a dragur rushed up behind Thorgils, fists raised.

Thorgils turned just in time, ducking as the dragur flew over him, landing on the ground, Ivaar quickly on top of him, his sword at its neck.

***

Aleksander gagged, fighting his way through a tangled mess of dragur, who were pushing forward, almost crawling over each other to get past his men, lashing out with fists and swords. And from urgent glances to each side, Aleksander could see that their line was starting to break. It hadn't been much of a line, he knew, but in the flashes of flames and lightning, he was beginning to see some real holes emerge. 'Hold the line!' he cried desperately, the pressure from the dragur intensifying as they tried to crash and thump their way through.

More escapees had joined their blue-faced friends now, and they were barging forward, adding their massive bulk to the press to escape.

Aleksander swallowed, wishing he could hear that voice again.

Wondering where Dara Teros was.

***

Having seen Edela, Biddy, and Eydis safely into the fort, Aedan immediately turned to leave before they closed the harbour gates.

Edela placed a shaking hand on his back, tears in her eyes. 'No, no. There's no need, not now. Come with us instead, Aedan. We need to get to my cottage. It's so dark. We need you.'

Aedan's mouth hung open as he let the gates shut before him. His head was a jumble of noise and panic and mostly fog. He couldn't feel anything but the demanding pain in his broken ribs.

'Quickly!' Edela urged, coughing as she turned to Biddy and Eydis. The smoke descending on the fort was like a suffocating blanket now, and she was struggling to breathe. 'Back to my cottage as fast as we can! We have work to do!'

CHAPTER TWENTY

Jael could see that the catapults had stopped firing now. Those men were running back to help defend the wall.

And the gates.

She turned to Karsten as he fell against her, knocked over by the thumping blow of a singed dragur. 'Get your men to the main gates!' she cried, pushing him upright.

Karsten glowered at her. 'You need me!'

'I've got Axl and Rork coming! Look!'

And ducking another right hook from the determined dragur, Karsten spun away. Jael was right; in another exploding ball of fire, he could clearly see the Andalans and Alekkans streaming towards them from the valley. Hacking into the dragur's arm with his right axe, he nodded. 'I'll just finish what I started!' And with one axe still stuck in the dragur's arm, he brought the other one around, cleaving its sharp blade into the creature's neck.

Jael backed away, coughing, trying to see as the bright light from the explosion receded. Along the western wall, it was dark. The crush of bodies was oppressive. The screams and screeches were clanging in her head, and she needed to get a better idea of what was happening.

She needed to be back up on the ramparts.

So spinning away from two lunging dragur, Jael left them to Thorgils and Torstan, crawling up the ditch and over the broken wall, running for the tower stairs.

***

Aedan stood outside Edela's cottage, watching the explosions in the distance. He saw the occasional lightning strike, the enormous cloud of smoke edging closer. It was tickling his throat, and he needed water, but he didn't care. His eyes were full of tears as he stood there, forcing his boots to remain on the porch. Edela's chimes started banging behind him, and he thought of Kayla and his mother, but he couldn't go anywhere. Not until he knew that his grandmother was safe.

Inside the dark cottage, Edela tried not to let her guilt and sadness distract her from what she needed to do. 'More light, Biddy,' she muttered, eyes back on the book that she'd hastily opened across her lap. 'Eydis, you try and focus over there. See if you can find which page I need. If what we know about Dara Teros is true, there must be something to help us in here.' Edela's voice was as shaky as her hands that were busily turning the pages. She'd been so focused on breaking the sickness curse that she'd not spent nearly enough time trying to find a way to stop the dragur.

Something she was quickly regretting.

Eydis tried to calm herself as she listened to Edela mumbling. Edela was upset about Aron and Kormac, who she knew were dead; frightened about what might happen next.

So was Eydis.

The smell of the creatures, even from this far away, was intense and foul, and the noise of the battle had her heart racing. Eydis closed her eyes, hoping it would help her to disappear inside herself. She wanted to hear Dara Teros' voice in her head again, guiding her to the right page.

***

Jael was next to Gant, scanning the valley and the dark hills in the distance. 'Looks as though Aleksander has things under control back there. Some of the catapult crews have joined him.' She turned back to look at the square, worrying about Kormac and Aron. Gant had assured her that Aedan had returned Edela, Biddy, and Eydis to the fort, but he'd been alone.

Turning back around, Jael caught a glimpse of horror on Gant's face. 'What?' And following his gaze and his pointing hand, she saw a fresh wave of dragur surging down Bog's Hill towards Aleksander and his men, who were fighting to keep the escaping creatures in the valley.

Trapping them.

'Stay here!' Jael yelled, running for the stairs. 'You've got the wall! Stay here! Don't let them breach!'

***

Aleksander turned at the noise. It was a victory yell, a high-pitched squeal of triumph that stopped his heart. Everything slowed around him as he took in the sheer number of dragur coursing down the hill towards them in the glow of the flames.

Panic momentarily froze his thoughts, but the smoke tickled his throat, and he gagged, waking up. 'Turn!' he bellowed. 'Turn!' Aleksander knew more men were coming off the catapults to support them, and he could only hope that they'd had seen how urgently they were needed.

'Fire!' he cried hopelessly. 'We need fire!'

And then the lightning came.

***

Draguta felt better. Her smile was back, and it was wide and satisfied.

'Did those fools think a little fire could stop my creatures? A little fire? A little lightning?' She shook her head, feeling her shoulders straighten as she settled into the chair, enjoying the scene of destruction playing out before her.

The tide was shifting.

***

Jael's breathing was ragged as she ran around the eastern edge of the burning valley towards Aleksander and his trapped men, through the trees, where she hoped not to find any dragur lurking. She wished she was on Tig, but Tig was safer in the stables for now. She'd left her Islanders at the broken wall, Rork Arnesson's Alekkans with them, and Karsten's men at the main gates, and taken Axl and his Andalans, who were now running behind her as fast as their smoke-filled, mail covered bodies would allow.

Turning around, Jael bellowed at them, seeing her brother struggling to move just as much as she was. They were hardly the rescuers Aleksander needed, but they were his only hope now.

Lightning exploded across the night sky like golden snakes, and Jael could hear the familiar screeching cries of the dragur as they surged into the valley. 'Hurry!' she panted, stumbling over a rock, wincing. 'Faster! Faster!'

She had a burning torch in one hand, its flame flickering as she ran into the darkness.

***

Eydis felt as though she was walking down a narrow corridor. One side was dark and threatening. She glanced towards it, a shiver streaking down her spine. The other side was light, and she wanted to go that way, but the dark side beckoned, so, taking a deep breath, Eydis turned into the shadows.

***

'Aarrghh!' Aleksander had his hands over his head, certain his forearms would snap as the dragur who had knocked him to the ground in the rush down Bog's Hill clambered over him, smashing their fists into his arms. One of his men cracked a dragur in the back of the head with his axe, knocking it away, and Aleksander rolled, staggering to his feet, his sword in one hand.

His broken sword.

Gasping for air, he spun, trying to find the rest of his men, but he'd rolled away from them, and he had to run, pushing through the dragur to get back to them. 'Come together!' he cried, pulling his boot out of a boggy hole. 'We need to keep them back!' But his voice was lost in a loud roar as more dragur emerged at the top of the hill, thundering down the slope towards them.

'Form a line!' came the familiar voice behind him.

And Aleksander turned to see Jael, Axl, and the Andalans lining up behind him. He didn't have time to feel relieved as he forced his way through to join them. Without a working sword, he wasn't much use at all. But he would do what it took to keep those dragur behind their line.

'Archers! Fire at will!' Jael roared, lowering her arm in a signal to the men at the back, who no longer had any fire arrows but would surely be able to make a few holes in the dragur.

Though, looking at how many more creatures were coming, Aleksander doubted it would be enough.

***

The woman who sat with the books had dark hair. She was a young woman.

Familiar.

Eydis' legs moved with urgency as she hurried towards her.

The woman sat at a table. Moonlight streamed through the window above her, and there was one lamp burning, though it gave off little light. It was enough for the woman to see by, though, as she peered at one book before turning to make notes in the other.

Eydis ran around her, looking over her shoulder, needing to see what she was doing, feeling herself being pulled closer and closer.

The woman stopped writing and closed her eyes. Then, taking a deep breath, she opened them and dipped her quill into a jar of ink, drawing a symbol.

As Eydis looked on.

***

Gant had too many problems to count.

They were out of fire arrows, and while they could tip

burning braziers down onto the dragur, there were too many of their own men packed around the creatures, fighting to keep them away from the vulnerable piece of wall. Too many for the gods also, it seemed. No lightning shot into the tangle of dragur, Islanders, and Alekkans grappling in front of the ditch.

The gates were under assault at both ends of the fort too.

And as for the thickening mass of dragur coming over the hills...

Gant tried to think. Turning, he heard a screech and a scream, and he squinted, not wanting his suspicions confirmed. But then he saw them.

Dragur were inside the fort.

'Oleg!' he yelled down to the square where rows of archers were lined up behind the broken wall. 'Oleg! The dragur are climbing the walls! Look out!'

But it was too late. The dragur were at the archers before they could turn around, one creature stabbing its sword in and out through Oleg's back in a heartbeat.

'*Oleg!*'

***

Jael's torch was long, burning at both ends, and she spun it around, knowing that she had little strength left to use *Toothpick* anymore, but she had to do whatever she could to keep the dragur back. Her men were weakening from fighting against creatures who were twice as strong; who would not go down easily at all.

The lightning was infrequent now, the gods obviously struggling not to hit her men. It made little difference anyway, Jael realised.

They'd run out of sea-fire.

The smell was overpowering, the smoke stinging Jael's eyes as she swung her burning torch, jabbing it into the gaping mouth of the nearest dragur. It gurgled, stumbling backwards, and as it fell, Jael was already turning, looking for her next target.

'Jael!' Aleksander screamed from somewhere in the smoky melee.

But it was too late; Jael was knocked to the ground.

***

Edela kept reading, running her finger down every page, but she was having no luck, and she could feel Biddy panicking beside her, listening with wide eyes as the screeching got ever closer.

Aedan poked his head around the door. 'They're in the fort now. I can hear them running.' His voice was urgent, and Edela knew that he wanted to go and be with his wife and daughter; with Branwyn too.

'Edela!' Eydis shrieked as she burst out of her dream. She was sure it had been a dream; some sort of vision. Whatever it was, Eydis knew what to do. 'Page twenty-seven! Try page twenty-seven!'

***

The wound in Thorgils' head was trickling blood into his right eye, and it wouldn't stop. He rubbed his eye again, trying to see. His ears worked fine, though, as Gant bellowed down to him.

'Thorgils, come inside! The dragur are climbing the walls!

Oleg is down! You need to lead his men!'

That squeezed Thorgils' heart. He thought of Isaura, nodded to Ivaar, and turned to Fyn. 'You're with me,' he growled, turning towards the men defending the broken wall. 'Let me through!' And grabbing a limping Fyn by the shoulder, he dragged him towards the ragged line of Islanders, who were panting and coughing as they desperately fought to keep the dragur out.

Dropping into the ditch.

***

'Climb the walls!' Draguta roared. 'Follow your friends and climb the walls! Get into the fort. I need that book now! *Now!*'

All thoughts of revenge and Jael Furyck were forgotten as Draguta watched her blue creatures pulling away from the fort's defenders, heading for the walls.

They had to get to the book before it was too late.

***

Jael rolled over, teeth slamming together as a dragur smashed her in the face. She'd moved, but not in time, and it had caught the side of her jaw. Everything went black, her ears ringing so loudly that she couldn't hear the creature screeching at her, but she could smell it, and she could see flashes of it as it raised its fist to hit her again.

Something or someone had fallen on her legs.

She couldn't move them.

'Jael!'

She thought she could hear Aleksander again, but it was as though he was speaking underwater. As if she was underwater herself.

The fist came down, and Jael saw her daughter's face, and quickly, blinking the black patches away, she wriggled, dragging her knife out of its scabbard and driving it into the dragur's ear. It screamed and fell onto her, wrapping its hands around her neck.

***

The dragur were running faster now, urged on by Draguta's cry. They could smell the book, and they ran down alleyways, in all different directions, needing to find it for her, their mistress. The one they were bound to serve.

Thorgils was gathering Oleg's men in the square, but the dragur weren't interested in attacking them now; they were running around them.

Towards the hall.

'Fyn!' Thorgils barked, grappling with a dragur as stocky as Rork Arnesson. The creature had both his arms, and Thorgils couldn't move as he tried to turn it around, fighting to escape. 'Stop them!'

***

Aedan couldn't leave his grandmother's porch because she was trying to save them all. He thought only of his mother and his wife. His daughter too. They would be hiding in their cottage, trying to stay safe, just as he needed to stay on the porch, keeping Edela safe.

And then he saw the first dragur appear, running down the dark road towards the cottage. They weren't stopping, and Aedan had the immediate sense that they were looking for Edela and her book.

He slunk back into the shadows of the porch, though his torch was a flaming beacon to those dragur, who quickly broke Edela's gate, ripping it off its hinges as they ran, swaying from side to side, screeching at him.

All eight of them.

***

Aleksander had nothing left. His broken sword was gone. His knife too. Both of them knocked out of his hands, lost in the darkness. There were too many dragur swarming over them, and Aleksander had spent more time on the ground than on his feet. That's where he was now, throwing himself on the back of the dragur who had its hands around Jael's throat, her knife still sticking out of its ear.

Aleksander couldn't move it, but he could see Jael trying to fight it off, her legs kicking like an angry horse.

Suddenly Axl was there with the flaming torch Jael had lost when she'd been punched in the jaw. He jerked it at the creature, who quickly released his sister's throat and backed away, scrambling to its feet.

And then Axl was knocked to the ground by a blow to the side of the head.

'Axl!' Aleksander cried, one arm out to Jael, dragging her to her feet as they pushed their way towards Axl, kneeling beside him.

As the dragur closed in around them.

Jael blinked at Aleksander, panting, drawing *Toothpick* from his scabbard again. Aleksander bent down to pick up the flaming torch, and they stood on either side of Axl as the dragur crept forward.

***

Aedan screamed, but it was quickly cut short as the long-armed creature ducked his torch, punching his injured ribs, knocking the air out of him, the rest of the dragur racing past Aedan to the cottage, smashing open the door.

Biddy shrieked, certain she'd wet herself as she held the burning torch out in front of her shaking body, praying to all the gods, old and new, that Edela would hurry.

Edela was on her knees, Eydis beside her.

The symbol was drawn, the words were spoken, and Edela reached out both hers and Eydis' hands towards the bloody symbol.

'No!' Biddy cried as two dragur jerked towards Edela, another one rushing for the book.

'No!' Aedan grunted, staggering into the cottage, his flaming torch in one hand, pain carved into his face. 'Get away from her!'

Eydis panicked. She couldn't see anything.

But she could smell the dragur; she could hear them too.

She could hear Biddy's and Edela's screams, and Aedan's yelping as he tried to save them.

And then she felt a familiar hand, guiding hers. 'Touch the symbol, Eydis! Here. Put your hand down!' Biddy panted. 'Now! *Aarrghh!*'

And then Biddy was gone, but Eydis slammed her hand onto the floorboards, feeling the blood of the symbol, wet beneath her palm. And remembering the chant, she screamed it out loud as two enormous hands clamped around her neck.

***

'Aarrghh!' Jael yelled, dropping to her knees, bringing *Toothpick* across the waist of a dragur. And then he was down.

They were all down.

And suddenly, the valley was silent.

***

Fyn limped back to Thorgils, who was on the ground, a dragur lying on top of him. Thorgils' eyes were closed, and Fyn panicked. 'Thorgils! Thorgils!' he cried, trying to drag the motionless creature away.

The dragur were all motionless, lying scattered around the dark square, fires burning in the distance. Smoke everywhere.

'Thorgils!'

Thorgils opened his eyes, grimacing. 'You don't need to yell,' he rasped, helping Fyn roll the dragur off him. Looking around, he blinked in surprise at the bodies strewn around the square. 'What happened to them?'

Fyn shrugged as a thought popped into his head. 'I think it was Edela. Eydis or Edela.' A weary smile broke out on his battered face. 'I think they saved us.'

***

Draguta trembled with rage, her hands on either side of her seeing circle, her eyes closed. She didn't want to watch the blazing bonfire consume her dead dragur. She didn't want to see the smug smiles of the victors as they picked through the wreckage of bodies.

Victors of what?

This little battle?

'You may have won. Tonight, you may have won,' she growled, her voice like a roll of thunder. 'But I promise you, it is *I* who will win the war!'

***

Jael didn't want to move. She dropped to the ground, on her knees, panting, her head pounding as it hung. She couldn't breathe. Couldn't hear. Couldn't feel any part of her body.

Axl had moaned and was moving beside her. Aleksander was trying to help him sit up.

'What happened?' Axl wondered, trying to shake himself awake, the stabbing pain in his head immediately demanding. He saw the dragur lying in heaping mounds around them, their men staggering to their feet, shaking their heads too. 'What happened?'

Aleksander smiled wearily, reaching out a hand. 'Once we crawl back to the fort we might find out, though I've a feeling we have a couple of dreamers to thank.'

Jael lay on the ground, staring up at the dark sky, trying not to inhale the stench of the burning dragur and the sea-fire smoke; trying not to think about whether she would ever feel her hands again. 'Perhaps you could send a cart for me? I don't think I can even crawl!'

CHAPTER TWENTY ONE

Jaeger turned as Meena walked to the window where he'd been standing for some time, looking down at the harbour. It was just past dawn, and she was surprised to see him already out of bed. Dressed too.

She frowned.

'What happened to your neck?' Jaeger wondered.

Memories of her dream came rushing back as she blinked at him. 'What's wrong with it?' She felt around with her hand, but nothing hurt.

'You have bruises,' he said, pointing to the discoloured rings around her throat. 'A lot of them. Something you're doing in your sleep? Wrestling wild boar perhaps?' His eyes were almost warm, their usual fiery intensity gone.

Meena shook her head. 'No, it's, I... Morana. She's becoming more herself. Fighting me.'

Jaeger looked almost surprised, but it faded quickly. He turned back to the window, his eyes on the slowly growing piers. 'I think I'll spend the day down at the harbour. See how the fleet is coming along. We're going to need those ships soon, aren't we?'

'Are we?'

Jaeger shook his head, trying to clear the strange haze that was cloaking his thoughts. 'Yes, I think so. Now, get dressed so we can head down to breakfast. I'm starving.' And he carried on staring at the harbour as if in a dream.

***

There were a lot of bruises. A lot of bleeding and broken limbs. A lot of dead bodies too.

Jael felt numb to it all as she walked away from the hall, through the thick cloud of smoke, which had sunk down into the fort now. She'd been with Branwyn, Aedan, and Kayla since they'd returned from the valley, and now it was time to check on her men. Time to check on the fort and retrieve all the arrows, to bring back the catapults, and make more sea-fire. To finish the wall.

But first, Jael wanted to see how Entorp and his patients were.

Edela and Eydis came with her.

Edela was shaken, riddled with guilt over what had happened to Kormac, broken-hearted by Aron's death. She couldn't let herself feel any relief at all. She kept seeing Kormac and Aron before she'd disappeared into the sacred grove, wishing she had seen the danger coming.

'Jael!' Aleksander called as he hurried after them, winding his way through the steadily growing piles of dragur corpses, his throat burning from the smoke. 'Wait!' As much as he felt reluctant to go with her, his boots kept moving him forward, desperate to know the truth.

Edela turned as Aleksander caught up to them, and he took her arm as she stumbled, bringing her close. 'I've got you,' he smiled as they carried on towards the newly erected tent village that Entorp had moved his patients into.

Edela barely noticed he was there as she followed behind Jael and Eydis, every soft thud of her boots echoing in her head.

She worried that she hadn't finished the curse-breaking ritual; that she hadn't done it with the precision required; that Kormac and Aron had given their lives for nothing. Just a mistake.

They shouldn't have been there.

She shouldn't have been there.

But then Entorp emerged from a tent, rubbing his eyes as the morning sun lit up the smoky square.

And he was smiling.

***

Evaine didn't want to leave Eadmund's bed, but Eadmund was already dressed and heading for the door.

'I can't stay,' he smiled, his eyes full of regret. 'Rollo will be banging on the door if I'm not in that training ring early.'

Evaine was tired and annoyed to be losing him so quickly. After all she had done to get to Flane? And now he was just leaving? She huffed and pouted, but it made no difference as Eadmund turned away. 'Eadmund, wait!' Evaine rushed out of bed, naked, wanting to feel him one more time. 'Please, don't go. I don't want to be alone. I don't want to be stuck with Draguta again.'

Eadmund bent down and kissed her, feeling the intense pull of her, but the pull of Draguta was now stronger, and he knew that he needed to be in that training ring. He wanted to keep her happy. 'Come and watch me when you're dressed,' he smiled. 'I'll try not to embarrass myself too much.' And after one more kiss, he disappeared through the door.

Evaine watched him go, feeling oddly unsatisfied. He was hers. They had spent a blissful, sleepless night together, but it wasn't enough.

And after all this time of wanting Eadmund, and having to

share him with his drinking, and his wife, and now... Draguta? Evaine wasn't happy at all.

***

'It was magic,' Karsten explained, leaning over Nicolene. 'Apparently, a woman put a curse on everyone. The new Queen of Helsabor herself. A real bitch, it seems.'

Nicolene didn't look any less confused, but she did suddenly glance around the tent. 'The children?' she croaked, coughing. Karsten smelled of smoke. Of something worse than smoke. The whole tent did. 'Where are the children?'

'With Bayla,' Karsten said. 'The toughest Dragos of all. Not even a curse could touch her!' He tried smiling, but his face ached, and Nicolene was looking at him with such an intense frown that eventually he gave up, glancing over at Berard, who was with Hanna, eager to know how she was.

Berard watched as Marcus brushed Hanna's lank hair away from her face, smoothing his hand over her forehead, hoping to see some life in her. Everyone else was opening their eyes, but not Hanna.

Marcus was starting to panic.

Edela could feel it as she watched him. 'Here,' she said calmly. 'Let me try.' And bending down with a loud crack of her troublesome hip, she placed her hands on either side of Hanna's head. Searching. Hoping to find her.

Breathing deeply, Edela found herself drifting, her mind and spirit weary and distracted. She could sense Aleksander's worry as he stood behind her with Berard. And then Edela saw the most beautiful field of wildflowers, with a babbling stream winding through it. She could hear birdsong and feel the warmth of a golden sun on her shoulders. It filled her heart.

And opening her eyes, Edela inhaled the smoke, blinking at the dull light in the tent. She peered up at the circle of worried faces. Jael was there with Eydis, Entorp too, and he held out a hand to help her up. 'I think Hanna had one foot out the door, ready to leave us, so it will take her some time to return, but she's in there. She's in there, and she's coming back.'

Berard spun around to find Karsten, who had heard the dreamer and was smiling at Berard, just as Berard turned back and smiled at Edela.

Marcus was too shocked to speak, too broken and worn out to feel anything but upset. Tears rolled down his hairy cheeks. 'You're sure? You saw her?'

Edela nodded, noticing the relief on Aleksander's face. 'I felt her, and she felt like life. She's on her way back, don't worry. But perhaps do go and wash,' she said, wrinkling her nose. 'Which is my advice to all of you. The smell in here is making me cry!'

Aleksander wrapped an arm around her shoulder. 'You had a busy night, then, breaking a curse and defeating the dragur. Not bad for a little old dreamer.'

'I'm not that little,' Edela sniffed into his smoky tunic. 'And I'll have you know that I didn't do it alone. If it weren't for Eydis, I'd probably still be peering at that book, trying to find the right symbol. It wasn't written for a woman of my years, I tell you.'

Aleksander turned to thank Eydis, watching her freeze, then spin around as though she'd heard something. And into the tent came Thorgils and Isaura, with Ayla in between them.

'Hello, Eydis,' Ayla murmured, her voice barely a whisper. 'Edela.'

'Ayla!' Eydis sobbed, her hands out in front of her as she hurried to find her. 'Ayla!'

Edela helped her, and soon Eydis had her arms around Ayla, squeezing her gently. She felt weak and limp, but she was standing, and Eydis couldn't stop crying. Ayla looked up, blinking tears out of her own eyes, thinking that soon she would need to lie down again. 'Thank you, Edela,' she breathed, smiling at her over Eydis' head. 'Thank you.'

Eydis stepped back, and Edela took Ayla in her arms. 'No, my dear, thank you. If you hadn't been so busy, we'd never have known the truth. You worked so hard to save everyone. And you did.'

Ayla stumbled, Thorgils grabbing her arm. 'I don't think we've heard the last of that woman, though. Briggit Halvardar. She will find out that you broke the curse. Somehow.'

'Or maybe she won't,' Jael put in, watching Aleksander sit down beside Hanna out of the corner of her eye. 'Maybe we'll be knocking on her gates before she has a chance to find out. The Following won't survive, and nor will she. Not once we get to Helsabor.'

Ayla blinked. 'You're going to Helsabor?' She stumbled again, and Thorgils helped her to the nearest stool.

'We are,' Jael said. 'We have a lot of business down South, it seems. And there's no point in waiting. Winter will be here before we know it.'

'But will you have enough men?' Isaura worried, not wanting Thorgils to disappear again. He was barely hanging together as it was.

'We will,' Jael sighed, wanting a stool herself. 'Once Raymon Vandaal listens to what Axl and I have to say, we will.'

***

'Have you thought about what I said?' Garren murmured, leaning over Getta.

She jumped in surprise, quickly glancing around. 'What are you doing here?'

Getta had taken Lothar for a walk, wanting to enjoy the

beautiful day. Ollsvik was a gloomy place, with persistently grey skies that often led to drizzle, so when a day dawned as blue and cloudless as this one, no one wanted to stay inside, including Getta, who'd been feeling like a prisoner in her chamber since giving birth. She was hoping that it would help Lothar too. He had been miserable, barely sleeping. Getta was barely sleeping either, and she didn't know what to do to help him. She had no inclination to seek advice from Ravenna, though, and she found herself missing her mother for the first time in months. The baby started whimpering, and Getta frowned at Garren, patting Lothar's back, feeling him vibrate against her chest.

Garren smiled. He had followed Getta on her walk, past the harbour and into the forest, where they'd often gone to be alone.

Before Raymon.

There were secluded groves hiding in the forest. Dense knots of yew trees surrounding them. All sorts of private places to get lost.

'You shouldn't be here,' Getta tried again, becoming flustered. 'I want you to leave. So does Lothar.'

'Well, your son might,' Garren laughed, pulling a funny face at the baby, who didn't appear to notice as he sobbed on his mother's shoulder. 'But you? I doubt that's true. You want to know whether you're safe on your throne. Whether your husband is,' he said. 'I know you. You always had an eye on the future. Wanting to rise. And now you have, but what will happen next? Perhaps that's up to you?'

Garren was standing too close, yet Getta was pleased that he was whispering in her ear and not carrying his voice for anyone else to hear. Her eyes darted amongst the trees, her hand still patting Lothar's back. 'And what do you know, then?' she snapped impatiently, trying to hide her desperation for him to reveal everything.

'I know that things in Rissna will not go well if Raymon chooses to offer his support to the Furycks. We're not here to provide men for whatever scheme your cousins are plotting, and Raymon will soon realise that if he does.'

Getta shivered. Garren's voice, at first playful, had quickly taken on an iron-sharp edge. It suddenly felt darker, the sun retreating above the tree canopy. Lothar stopped crying. 'I must go,' she muttered, looking away from Garren's penetrating eyes. 'I will try. Try to talk to him. I have been trying. I'll continue to, but Raymon is a Vandaal. As stubborn as his father and his grandfather.'

'Yes, and look at what happened to those fools,' Garren reminded her, not hiding the contempt in his voice. 'They lost their heads. As your father did at the hands of your cousin. And now the man who took it is coming to claim our kingdom, unless your husband stops him. Unless you stop your husband.' Garren kept his eyes on Getta as he stepped away, sensing someone coming. 'I will see you before we leave for Rissna, and we can talk again. Hopefully, you'll have better news for me then.'

***

Draguta was in a foul mood when she banged on Evaine's door.

Evaine struggled out of bed, covering herself in a fur as she sleepily shuffled towards the door, trying to wake up. She wondered how long she'd been asleep, remembering that Eadmund had wanted her to watch him train.

Draguta's dark eyebrows sharpened with displeasure as Evaine opened the door. 'I do wonder what use you are to me, Evaine Gallas,' she snapped, looking her over. 'But I shall not kill you yet. Not unless you keep giving me reasons to. Now, get dressed and pack your things, for we are leaving!'

Evaine gaped after Draguta as she spun around, heading away from the cottage. 'Leaving? *Now?*'

But Draguta was already well on her way, her fast-moving shoes scuffing up clouds of red dust into Brill's face as she dutifully turned and trailed after her.

***

Else couldn't stop staring at Meena's bruised throat.

Nor could Morana, who sat before them on a chair. There was no fire. It was an unbearably warm day, and even Morana's usually cold chamber was muggy.

Morana didn't notice.

But she did notice Meena's neck.

Dragmall kept trying to clear his throat. He'd brought a basket with him and was busy foraging in it as Else listened to Meena tell the story of her dream.

'A black rope?' Else shivered.

'Jaeger is bound to Draguta now,' Dragmall declared, straightening up. 'She needed to bind him before she could return to claim the book. To render him impotent. Unable to cause her any problems.'

'Then we must get rid of the book quickly!' Else insisted, glancing at Morana, who appeared to be trying to shake her head.

'It is far too late for that, Else. Draguta may already be on her way, and Jaeger will do her bidding in the meantime. If you touch or take that book, you will surely die,' Dragmall warned, glaring sternly at Meena. 'And that won't help us. What we need is someone who can. And,' he said with a sigh, 'it appears that Morana is the only one capable of doing so.'

They all turned to Morana, whose right eye burned with desperation.

Dragmall bent towards her. 'But if we try to break the curse, what will you do to us, I wonder? Those who would help you? Who would be your allies?' It wasn't what he wanted to say, but he didn't want to unlock Morana's prison cell to find his throat cut in the night, and he certainly didn't want anything to happen to Else or Meena. 'Would you stay loyal? Protect us from Draguta?'

Morana closed both eyes, screwing them up tightly, her body shaking with the effort, and eventually, she managed the slightest of nods.

***

Amma knew that she was fussing, but Axl had only just survived the dragur attack, and after seeing to his men, and checking over the fort, he was already preparing for their departure to Rissna. 'But how will you ride?'

Axl ignored her as he limped towards the broken wall. He wanted to talk to the stonemasons, who had quickly been put back to work.

'Perhaps I should go with you?' Amma suggested, trying not to stare at the gruesome dragur corpses being loaded onto carts. Pyres were being built in the valley where the majority of the dragur lay. Those pyres would be burning for weeks, Axl was sure, but the dragur had already risen from their graves once, and he wouldn't take the risk that they could again.

He turned to her. 'I don't think you should come.'

Amma didn't look disappointed, but she did look worried.

'I need you here, running the fort with Gisila, organising the repairs. Turning all the dragur to ash. There's a lot to do. I need you here.'

Amma felt the weight of responsibility drop onto her shoulders, but as terrified as that made her feel, she was also pleased that Axl thought she was capable of such a thing.

'When I kill Jaeger Dragos, you'll be my queen, so you need to learn how to lead and look after our people as much as I do,' Axl said, taking her hand. 'We have to do this together. You coming to Rissna makes no sense. I don't imagine Raymon Vandaal will bring your sister, if that's what you were hoping?'

Amma quickly shook her head. 'Oh no, I wasn't hoping for that.' And she smiled as he wrapped an arm around her, pulling her close. 'Getta is the last person I want to see. I don't envy you if Raymon does bring her along.'

***

'You want to come?' Raymon was stunned. 'To Rissna? But what about Lothar? Surely he's too young?'

Getta was on her knees in their chamber, already packing. 'Are you saying it's not safe for us to come? You're expecting trouble?'

Raymon couldn't keep pace with his wife's moods. 'The army will be with us, but I can't say what's lurking in the forest. The creatures Axl Furyck spoke of could come at us from anywhere. I'd much rather you stayed behind, in the safety of the fort.'

Getta ignored him. She wasn't about to let him out of her sight. Not while she still had a chance to change his mind about the alliance. 'But didn't Axl say their fort was attacked? By a dragon? Surely we'll both be safer with you, my love?' Looking up, she stared into his eyes. 'I want to be with you.'

Raymon was surprised to hear it. 'You do?' It was all he'd been wanting to hear for weeks. She had drifted so far away from him. 'Really?'

Getta nodded quickly, turning back to the chest. 'I do.

Besides, I don't want to be a queen who gets stuffed away, out of sight, like my mother was. My father never once let her have an opinion about anything. Or perhaps, she never tried? But I've no intention of being a silent queen. I don't think you'd have married me if you'd wanted one of those. I want to be by your side, helping you, guiding you. Just as your mother helped your father.' She smiled sweetly, holding Raymon's eyes, until finally satisfied that he had come around to her way of thinking, she looked away, trying to remember where she had left her favourite cloak.

***

'It's good news about Hanna,' Jael said as she walked to the pyres with Aleksander. Gisila was ahead of them with Axl, Branwyn, Aedan and Kayla. Gant and Amma were walking with Edela and Biddy. 'That she'll recover.' She was trying to take her mind off what they were about to do.

Aleksander nodded. He felt too sad to speak.

Fyn was on Jael's other side, limping along with his crutch. He'd only known Aron and Kormac briefly, but they had been kind to him, welcoming him into their family. He felt their loss, and he could hear the painful weeping of Branwyn, who didn't want to be going to the pyre at all.

She didn't want it to be real.

Gisila had her arm around her sister's heaving shoulders, remembering how it had felt to walk to Ranuf's pyre. It had taken many days for his body to be returned from Ollsvik, and by then, he hadn't looked or smelled like her husband anymore. 'Ssshhh,' she soothed. 'It's alright, it's alright.'

But for Branwyn, it was never going to be alright again. She wanted to throw herself to the ground and rage at the gods, begging them to send her son and her husband back to her. 'Aron!' she wailed hopelessly. '*Kormac!*'

Axl moved up to help Gisila, seeing that Branwyn was becoming hysterical.

He didn't blame her.

His mother had fallen apart at his father's funeral, he remembered. The shock of his death had been too much. He couldn't imagine how she would have coped if he'd been lying on the pyre beside his father as Aron was.

Axl tried to shut it all out. His wasn't the only family broken by grief, walking to the pyres lined along the stretch of ground that ran from the harbour gates to the piers; where the piers would have been, he reminded himself, suddenly anxious about how broken the fort was.

The ruined harbour. His devastated people.

And now he would have to leave. Follow Jael. Take the bulk of their army far away from the fort and the people he was responsible for.

Hoping he would return.

Hoping they'd all still be alive when he did.

CHAPTER TWENTY TWO

Dragmall stood next to Morana, flicking through the pages of the Book of Darkness, convinced that Jaeger would burst into her chamber at any moment. And by the look on Meena's face, she did too. She stood by the door, ready to distract Jaeger before he could see what they were doing. Else sat on a chair in front of Morana, looking for any sign that she recognised something.

They had been at it for hours, and Dragmall was ready to conclude that getting Morana to help him break the curse was the wrong approach. But then suddenly, her eyes widened, the dark one blinking with urgency.

Else hurried up from her stool. 'That page!' she exclaimed before Dragmall could turn it. 'She recognised something on that page!'

Meena's eyes were just as wide as she came over to see what Morana had spotted.

'Do you know it? Can you read it?' Dragmall asked.

Meena peered at the page. 'Some of it, I think,' she mumbled without confidence. Leaning over, she touched the symbol, running her fingers around its delicate edge. 'If you are to break a curse, you need to know the symbol that was used,' she said slowly, remembering Varna's words. 'You must discover it's opposite, for every symbol has an opposite...' She stood up, suddenly losing her confidence. 'At least, I remember my grandmother saying that. I didn't see Draguta drawing a symbol that night, but she was chanting. Perhaps she didn't need to use a symbol?' Meena's words petered away to nothing, and she dropped her eyes to the flagstones.

Else could see the interest in Morana's eye, and she turned to Dragmall. 'Can you find the opposite symbol?' she wondered, peering at the volka whose watery eyes were blinking double time.

Meena looked at him too, and she was sure that if Morana could move her head, her eye would be trained on Dragmall as well.

But the old volka didn't say a word.

***

Gant had been quiet. Feelings of guilt, sadness, and relief mingled inside him, leaving him with a permanent frown, which wasn't new, he supposed, though it was getting harder to find a reason to smile.

They'd been preparing to leave on their journey to Rissna for days, and now it was almost time to go, but he wanted to stay and look after the fort, and Gisila, who was distressed, trying to support her grieving sister while worrying about what would happen to those left behind.

Gant felt worried too. Not wanting to return to more broken walls.

Or worse.

Making decisions could be a heavy weight to bear.

His decision to send Oleg down into the fort had kept him from sleeping; that and the choking stink of sea-fire smoke and burning dragur. It was in his lungs, up his nose, in his throat. He couldn't escape it.

Jael had been right about that, he thought as he saw her

approach.

'You went to Ollsvik countless times with Ranuf,' Jael said, flopping down onto the bench beside him with a waterskin. She'd been in the training ring, working with Fyn for a short time and was struggling to catch her breath. 'You must have gotten to know Ravenna Vandaal.' Jael had only been to Ollsvik a few times herself, but she hadn't bothered with making conversation or friends. Now though, she was beginning to realise that conversation was actually a useful tool.

It was hard to rule as a queen when you didn't want to talk to anyone.

Gant bent over, unable to stop coughing, and Jael handed him the waterskin.

He nodded his thanks, taking a long drink and clearing his throat. 'I know Ravenna. Why? Are you thinking you can worm your way around Raymon by talking to his mother?'

'Not really. I just know what people have said about the sort of man Hugo Vandaal was. A spineless, greedy idiot. Much like Lothar. I was hoping Raymon might have one worthwhile parent. That he wasn't just another greedy king looking to line his pockets. Though we can promise him gold if that's what he wants.'

'We can?' Gant had taken another long drink before handing back the skin. 'You'd better fill that again,' he added sheepishly.

'The Southern kingdoms are rich, dripping in gold. If Raymon Vandaal's eyes are on a prize, he can help himself to one when we defeat Draguta. He just needs to give us his army first. A fair trade, wouldn't you say?'

Gant narrowed his grainy eyes. 'You're that persuasive, are you?'

'Me? I doubt it, but I can try. And I will. I'll do whatever it takes to get his army, his archers, his weapons. We've no idea what we'll face in Hest and Helsabor, but I can guarantee you that it won't be as easy as that little dragur attack!'

***

Jaeger felt confused as he made his way upstairs. His dreams had been full of vivid, swirling images of Draguta and the book. And now, instead of being fearful of her return, his body was tingling at the thought of it.

He could feel that she was close.

It was as though her voice was coursing through him like blood.

He could almost feel her inside his head. He could think of nothing else but the urgent need to prepare the castle. His men too. He had to do what he could to ensure that Draguta was pleased with what she saw when she returned.

Jaeger's certainty clouded again, and he blinked, trying to clear the fog as he spied Meena scurrying down the corridor. 'Meena!' he called, but she didn't turn around. She froze, though, right before his chamber door. 'Meena!' he called again, and this time she turned ever so slowly towards him, cradling the Book of Darkness in her arms.

Jaeger's eyes sharpened. 'Where are you going with the book?' He felt suspicious, instantly protective of it, every hair on the back of his neck standing on end.

'I was... I... I was returning it,' Meena mumbled, trying to meet his eyes.

'*Returning* it?' Jaeger frowned. 'Why did you take it out of the chamber? Why, Meena?' He could feel his temper rising as he reached out and grabbed her arm.

'I, I took it to Morana,' Meena hurriedly explained. 'To see if it would help her. Dragmall... he thinks Morana can help break the curse. I thought the book might help.'

Jaeger felt strange. He'd wanted to bring Morana back. To have her read the book. But now? 'And did it?' he wondered. 'Help her?'

Meena realised that she hadn't thought of what to say about that. Knowing that Jaeger was now bound to Draguta made things much more confusing. 'No.'

'Well, I'm not surprised,' Jaeger growled, not caring either way. 'Besides, it would be better if Morana stays like she is. Imagine what Draguta will do if she finds her alive and well when she returns?' He stepped past Meena to open the door, pushing her into the chamber.

Meena almost tripped over her feet. 'Returns?' she wondered lightly. 'You think she's returning?'

Jaeger shut the door, turning around with a smile. 'Yes, she is. Tomorrow.'

***

Evaine had hoped not to sit on a horse again for a long time, but at least she had Eadmund beside her, and they were only riding during the day.

All five of them.

Draguta had informed Rollo that he would be accompanying them to Hest, which was news to Rollo, but Draguta insisted that Eadmund could not be without him now; not after how expertly Rollo had trained him so far. And after suitably burnishing the giant's already enormous ego, she then went on to offer him a substantial reward of Hestian gold, which he could happily take back to Flane once she was satisfied with Eadmund's progress. If, of course, he chose not to stay in the obviously superior surroundings of the city.

Draguta glanced at Eadmund, whose face had turned a deep, golden brown after only a few days of training in Flane's sunshine. He was squinting, rubbing the dusty sweat out of his eyes, hoping to see a cloud coming.

It was so oppressively hot.

Draguta was thrilled. The sun was bright, and her spirits had lifted considerably after the dragur disaster. She was getting closer to home. Closer to her beloved Book of Darkness; to Morana, Meena, and Jaeger.

All of those responsible for her death.

How unnecessary it had all been.

Though, when she dreamed about it now, she was beginning to realise that it was the best thing that had ever happened to her.

***

Edela was unsettled as she looked Jael over, surprised that she was leaving so quickly. 'Again?' she exclaimed. 'The raven came again?'

Jael nodded, sipping the passionflower tea Biddy had made her. The cup warmed her hands, still throbbing from fighting off the dragur.

'The gods are trying to help us,' Edela decided. 'The raven must be Daala trying to help. To warn you of danger.'

'Well, I hope she comes along to Rissna, then,' Jael grinned, trying not to let her gloomy feelings trap her. The smoke from the pyres mingled with the smoke from the sea-fire, and she thought of Eirik for the first time in days, feeling guilty for leaving his island and losing his son.

Not to mention the grandchild he'd wanted so desperately.

'What is it?' Edela wondered, watching Jael's face shifting through many different emotions.

Jael didn't want to say what it was. It was too many things. 'I'm just hoping you'll be alright while we're gone. We won't be away too long. We just need to make our plans with Raymon

Vandaal, assuming, of course, I can convince him that we should be making plans together.'

Edela's eyes drifted to Biddy, who was frowning as she chopped carrots on the table. 'You needn't worry about us. I think Eydis and I have proven that we've got everything under control, with a little help from Ayla, of course. You don't need a sword to save people, you know. Not always.'

'True, but it does come in handy sometimes,' Jael said, remembering the serpent.

'We'll be keeping a close eye on you all, don't worry. And I shall study the book, so I know what I'm doing when the next crisis comes along. You'll be safe, I'm sure, and so will we.' Edela's voice shook, and she felt worried because she didn't know if that was true anymore.

But Jael heard the tremor in her grandmother's voice, and so did Biddy, and nobody spoke for a while after that.

***

Karsten had carried Nicolene back to their cottage, but one look at her face as she scanned the bare walls and the dirt floor and Bayla's unhappy scowl, and he realised that she had probably been enjoying the peace and quiet of Entorp's tent.

But then she saw her two little sons toddling towards her, and she burst into tears.

So did they.

Karsten laid Nicolene on a bed, draping a fur over her, trying to stop Kai and Eron from pulling themselves up onto the bed. 'Wait, wait,' he said, not wanting to get cross, though he had little patience after two sleepless nights. 'Here, Kai, come here.' And picking up his youngest son, Karsten plonked him on his knee. Kai was quickly reaching for Nicolene, who held out her arms as he crawled away from his father into them. Smiling, Karsten bent down to Eron next, but his eldest son just lay his head on his father's knee, waiting his turn.

Turning around, Karsten saw Irenna and Haegen's three children sitting on the opposite bed with something between envy and sadness in their eyes. Neither of their parents were coming back, and the reality of that was growing more painful with each terrifying day.

Bayla looked relieved as she turned to Ulf, who had brought her a basket of fruit. She handed it to her servant and hurried Ulf outside, inclining her head for Berard to join them.

'Do you think, Ulf dear, you could ask about...' she began, searching for the right words, 'whether there are any spare houses? Bigger houses? Not like this miserable shed, which is far too small for our family. With that many children, and Karsten and Nicolene needing their privacy. Berard too. It just won't do.' Bayla smiled sweetly at Ulf, who looked surprised. 'There must be some spare after the dragur attack. Many were killed. Andalans who had homes. Empty homes now, perhaps?'

'Mother!' Berard hissed, glancing around. 'What are you doing? Stealing houses from the dead?'

Bayla looked indignant. 'What I'm doing is my best for this family. As I've always done. Have we not suffered ourselves? We are not blacksmiths or tanners. We are not servants or stable hands! We are the royal family of Hest, and one day soon, we will return to our kingdom, and Karsten will take back the throne from your murderous brother, but until then, I do not see why we should be forced to sleep in a crumbling shack that smells of horseshit!'

Ulf blinked, looking at Amma Furyck, who had stopped to stare as she walked back to the hall with Eydis. He tried to smile, but Amma just looked embarrassed, quickly hurrying Eydis along.

Berard looked even more embarrassed, noticing that more people than just Amma Furyck were staring. Bayla was used to commanding attention everywhere she went, but she wasn't a queen in Andala, and she had no more right to comfort and space than anyone else who was grieving and homeless.

Ulf took a deep breath, braving Bayla's sharp tongue. 'There will be houses, of course, but perhaps it's best if we wait a few days? Let people settle down, find their way. Grieve.' He felt Bayla tense. 'I'll ask around, don't worry, but best give it a few days.'

'But soon you'll be gone,' Bayla panicked, turning to Karsten, who had come out to see what was going on. 'Tomorrow, you'll be gone!'

Karsten nodded, happy about that. The sun was struggling to pierce the hazy veil of smoke, and the afternoon light was faint, but he still found himself squinting into it after the darkness of the windowless cottage. 'We can't go back to Hest if we don't get rid of Jaeger. We can't take back what's ours unless we leave, Mother. We're not going to be able to do it from behind these walls.'

Bayla sighed heavily, knowing that he was right, but terrified that neither of them would return for her. She peered at Ulf. 'And what about you, then? Are you leaving too?'

'No, I'm not. I'll be here, watching the fort. I've been tasked with getting that harbour right, which will take some doing.'

Bayla tried not to smile, but she was pleased. Ulf still looked like an old beggar, but she didn't know what she'd do without him now. He always seemed to be there when she needed him most. And he was so oddly calm, too, no matter what disaster befell them. 'Well, you'd better head off, then, and see what you can do about that new house, even if you have to whisper your enquiries ever so delicately. I'm not going to last long in there!'

Ulf shook his head, smiling as Bayla disappeared back inside the cottage, wondering just what he'd gotten himself into.

***

Dragmall brought Meena and Else back to Morana's chamber that afternoon. He'd spent most of the morning in the quiet of his cave, looking through his books, contemplating what was possible.

He knew magical symbols, though it had always been his choice to stay in the light. He had seen what dark magic did to people. His mother had been a Tuuran dreamer. A Follower. A terrifying woman, who'd eventually left both him and his father to return to Tuura. He was never sure if it was the poisonous ways of The Following that had consumed her soul or whether she had been born that way. His father had been a kind man who had found something to love in her once, though, so Dragmall was convinced that practising dark magic for so many years had corrupted a once loving woman, turning her into an ogre.

After much research, Dragmall believed that he'd found the curse-breaking symbol, but he felt sick at the thought of using it to help Morana, who was surely evil.

But without her...

'We must act quickly,' Dragmall sighed, his frown a jagged canyon between his bushy white eyebrows. 'Draguta will be here soon.'

Meena nodded, worried herself, remembering the certainty in Jaeger's voice. She turned to her aunt, whose good eye was watering. She looked as terrified as Meena felt.

Draguta would surely kill them both.

'I have the symbol we need,' Dragmall announced, retrieving a scrap of vellum from his pouch. 'If you agree, Morana?' And he lifted it towards her, holding it up to her eye.

They all leaned forward, peering at the black-and-white haired dreamer, wanting to see some acknowledgement, but there was little Morana could do. In the end, she managed to blink her eye, hoping that it would be enough.

'I think it's a yes,' Else decided, eager to get on. 'Now, what else do you need?'

'From what you've said, Draguta merely threw the curse in a fit of anger. There was no ceremony or ritual, so I need nothing, except Morana's blood.' Dragmall handed the vellum to Else and turned to Meena, drawing his knife from its scabbard. Spinning it around, he offered Meena the haft. 'I think we'd all prefer it if you collected her blood.'

Meena's eyes rounded, and so did Morana's, as she took the knife and stepped towards her aunt.

***

Jael was pleased to see that preparations for their departure were almost complete, thanks to Gant and Oleg. She felt sad, thinking of those they'd lost fighting the dragur. Men with experience. Trusted men, who had stood by her father's side, and her own; those she felt confident in leaving behind to command the garrison.

There weren't as many left now.

But there was always Bram Svanter.

'Me?' Bram was shocked, glancing at Runa, who stood beside him looking just as surprised. He was sharing his cottage with her now, Runa having decided that she needed to help him until he could get about by himself.

Which would be in no time at all, according to Bram.

Fyn was staying there too. It was a small cottage, and they all felt awkward around each other, but there was an unspoken sense that that was where they needed to be for now. And as strange and new as it felt, it was, at least, a place to begin.

Fyn sat on one of the beds, not knowing where to look.

'You've a calm, wise head, Bram, and we need one of those. And you can't come with us, so we have to put you to good use here,' Jael smiled. 'Gisila will be in charge of the fort. She knows how everything runs. But you will command the garrison, if you think you're up to it? It means getting the sea-fire ready. More arrows. Overseeing the repairs in and out of the fort. Checking on Ulf's rebuilding of the harbour. I know you're a man of the sea, so maybe it's not what you want, but it would put my mind at ease knowing that you're here, with my family. With yours too,' she said, looking around at the three faces, all suddenly frozen.

'I....' Bram inhaled, feeling the strain of breathing; quickly latching onto it as an excuse, though it was getting easier, he knew. And really, he would be of more use walking around the fort, barking orders and thinking of how to keep them all safe than trekking to Rissna, sleeping on whatever piece of dirt he could find. 'And what about your brother?' he wondered, staring up at Jael. 'Does he want to leave his fort in my hands?'

'He does. I've recommended you highly.'

Bram blinked, trying not to show the burst of pride he suddenly felt or the unfamiliar lack of confidence that quickly followed it. He glanced at Fyn, who appeared to be growing taller by the day. 'And what about Fyn? He's no better than me. Are you leaving him behind too?'

Fyn's eyes bulged as he turned to Jael.

She shook her head. 'No, Fyn's with me. He's my man. He goes where I go, even if he's limping. And a few days on horseback will sort him out. Plus a few days of sitting around while we're negotiating.' Jael tried not to roll her eyes at the thought of what lay ahead, hoping that Raymon Vandaal wouldn't bring his wife to Rissna. 'By the time we depart for Hest, he'll be battle-ready again.'

Fyn looked relieved.

Bram frowned, not wanting to lose the son he'd only just found. He could feel Runa tense beside him, knowing that she felt the same.

'But...' Runa began.

'Mother, I need to go. I want to go. I'll be ready, don't worry.'

'Speaking of going, I have to go and check on the sea-fire. We need wagon loads of it to take down to Hest, so we have to double our production now. Hopefully, we won't blow ourselves up before we get there!'

Runa looked horrified.

Fyn grinned. 'Don't worry, Mother. We sailed all the way to Skorro without blowing ourselves up. We'll be fine.'

Jael stopped at the door, peering back into the cottage. 'So, that was a yes, then? You'll do it?'

Bram looked at Runa, who was already nodding as he joined her. 'It was. A yes. I'll do it. I'll look after your fort.'

***

Meena jumped, surprised by a knock on the door. Else looked at Dragmall, who stopped carving the symbol into the flagstone by Morana's feet.

They all stared at the door, which was locked and being banged on again.

'Throw that bed fur over the symbol,' Dragmall hissed, creaking upright.

Else rushed to the bed as Meena approached the door.

'Who is it?'

There was a pause. 'Morac. What's happening? Why is the door locked?'

Meena glanced at Else, who shrugged.

They'd forgotten about Morac.

Turning the key, Meena opened the door, quickly ushering Morac inside before promptly locking it again.

'What are you doing?' Morac wondered, sensing the tension in the chamber. All three looked as though they'd been caught stealing the silver. Then he saw Morana's arm, which Else had bandaged with a strip of cloth after Meena had taken her blood. 'What happened to Morana?' He was irritable, barely sleeping, worried about Evaine, and suddenly suspicious.

'She, ahhhh,' Meena began before realising that keeping secrets from Morac was pointless as he knew his sister better than any of them. He would be able to tell that something was different about her, and if they didn't let him in on their secret, he might inadvertently blurt it out to Jaeger, which wouldn't help any of them. 'We're trying to break the curse.'

Morac blinked in surprise. 'You are?' He stared at Dragmall, who hurried to pull back the fur, struggling down onto the floor again. 'You know it's a curse?'

'It appears so. Morana has been helping us in her own way. Leading us. We think we can break it,' Dragmall said, chipping into the stone with his chisel and mallet. 'But we must act quickly because Draguta will return soon. She can't know what we're doing.'

'But Draguta will know,' Morac insisted. 'She will know! What happened in the hall was because she'd been inside everyone's heads. Seen what we were all thinking. She was going to exact her revenge before you killed her,' he said, staring at Meena.

Meena swallowed, meeting her uncle's eyes. 'Morana can read the book. We need her to stop Draguta. There's no one else who can use it.' She didn't know what she was saying. She didn't know why she believed that Morana would care to keep any of them safe, even if they risked their lives to save hers. 'Draguta has Evaine. She has bound Jaeger to her now. She has Eadmund Skalleson too. All we can do is try. Whatever happens, we need to find a way to stop her before it's too late.'

CHAPTER TWENTY THREE

'You need to rest,' Biddy insisted, grabbing Jael's elbow before she could rush away to check on something else. She had been roaming the fort all day with Axl, with Fyn, with Gant. Thinking about everything, and everyone.

Except herself.

'I'm fine,' Jael grumped, removing her elbow from Biddy's determined grip.

'No, you are the opposite of fine. I've never seen you so pale. You look ready to fall down.'

Jael felt ready to fall down.

She glanced at Astrid, who had been taken under Biddy's wing, working in the tents, helping to care for Entorp's patients, who were improving, though a few were still too weak to go back to their homes.

Astrid's face told her that she agreed. 'I can make you some more of my broth?' she suggested. 'It's good for those who have lost a lot of blood. It's iron-rich. Full of what you need.'

Jael had a strong memory of Astrid's broth, and she wrinkled her nose. 'Alright, you do that and I'll go and sit down,' she lied. 'Soon. I promise. I only need to check a few more things.' And ignoring Biddy's frown, she turned towards Ayla, who was on her knees beside Bruno. She hadn't left his side since she'd left her own sick bed, eager to take him back to their new cottage.

'Ayla,' Jael whispered, drawing a stool towards her. 'I

wanted to talk to you about Briggit Halvardar. About everything you saw in your dreams. We have to defeat her too. A woman like that can't remain upon a throne, not when she wants to kill us all.'

Ayla turned to look at Jael, seeing a vision of the cottage in Harstad. Of the blood. Of Jael crying, holding her dead baby. Her mouth gaped open, and she didn't know what to say.

'Are you alright?'

Ayla shook her head, trying to focus. 'Yes, I... I dreamed about Briggit many times. I walked through her castle with her. It is vast and luxurious, and she commands it from a golden throne, but it's a terrifying place. Those around her are dazed, bound to her. All of them. The Followers, the army, her family. Those she hasn't already killed. She's in complete control of Helsabor, but she's hungry for more.'

Jael frowned, leaning closer. 'Let me guess, she wants to bring back the Darkness?'

Ayla nodded. 'She is a Follower, so yes, the Darkness is her greatest desire. She's filled with dark ambition. Briggit believes that she will be the one to bring Raemus back. That she'll become his wife.'

'His *wife*? But doesn't he want Daala? His own wife?'

'Briggit thinks that Raemus will be looking for a new wife after what Daala did to him. Some Followers, mostly the female ones, imagine that Raemus will kill Daala when he returns.'

'And Briggit said that?'

'Oh yes,' Ayla said. 'I heard her talking about it with a woman. About how one day she would be Raemus' bride. How they would rule the dark world together. You can be sure that nothing will turn her away from that path. It is carved in stone in her mind. The sickness curse was her way of laying the foundations for that. A way to wipe Osterland clean. To remove any threat.'

'So she wants the Book of Darkness too?'

Ayla nodded.

'And what will Draguta say about that, do you think?' Jael wondered. 'Draguta, who apparently doesn't want to bring back the Darkness at all?'

'I don't know,' Ayla admitted. 'But there can only be one mistress of that book.'

Jael was thoughtful. 'Then perhaps it will be up to the book to decide? A book that powerful? I imagine it will have a say in things.'

***

Nothing had changed.

The sky was darkening, Meena could see as she peered up at the tiny window.

It had been hours now since Dragmall had carved the symbol into the flagstone, following the contours of the shape with Morana's blood. But nothing had changed, and Meena could tell that her aunt was panicking. She kept trying to move, but she couldn't, and Meena could feel the frustration almost leaking out of her.

They sat on the beds and stools, waiting to see what would happen.

But nothing did.

'What do you think we should do?' Else wondered, looking at Dragmall, who was slumped on a stool opposite Morana. He was confused, certain the curse should have broken immediately. 'I'm not sure,' he admitted, pulling on his long, white beard. 'But perhaps we should leave you now, Else? You can feed Morana. Put her to bed. There is nothing more we can do for her now.'

Morana's dark eye flared in anger, but it did her no good; she still couldn't move.

Morac looked disappointed as he rose to his feet, hoping to get to his cottage before running into Jaeger. 'You should cover that symbol,' he muttered despondently, pointing to the floor. 'Best no one finds it.'

Else nodded, hurrying to grab the bed fur, dragging it back over the symbol. 'I'll grab some rawhide in the morning. It will look more like a floor covering than a mistake,' she said.

'Well, then,' Dragmall sighed, pointing Meena to the door. 'We shall return in the morning and hope for some improvement.' Perhaps that was the problem, he realised? He didn't really hope for an improvement at all.

But to catch a witch, Dragmall knew, it was likely they needed a witch.

If only they could find a way to free her.

***

They were leaving in the morning, though that would still make them late for their arranged meeting with the Vandaals.

'I sent a messenger,' Axl told his sister. 'To let them know. So they don't think we've changed our minds.' His ale was warm, and he felt disappointed, dreaming of an ice-cold cup to numb his fingers; an ice-cold dip in an almost frozen lake too. His body hurt too much to move. And yet, in the morning, he would have to.

He felt nervous leaving everyone behind.

Meeting their neighbours. Trying to act like a king.

Looking around the hall from his seat at the high table, Axl saw his father's warriors with their countless arm rings and scars. He knew those grizzled, leathery faces, flecks of grey in their beards. Battered and bruised men – burned too – yet ready for more.

He didn't feel worthy of leading them.

Turning to his sister, who was rubbing her sunken eyes, he felt relieved that she was there. 'What do you think Raymon will say?' Axl whispered.

Jael finished her cup of ale and stretched out her back. 'Well, he's already said yes, hasn't he? But who knows what trouble Getta has been stirring up since he sent that note.' She studied the hall. It was packed; full of energy. Nervous warriors were enjoying their last night in the fort. There was some excitement too, she could tell; a sense of anticipation that they were finally doing something. That they were finally going to emerge from behind the walls. Her eyes met Ivaar's before his quickly hurried back to his cup. 'It will be good to talk to Raymon directly, but in the end, he'll have no choice. Our army could crush his, so we can ask nicely, but ultimately, we've more men. Anyone who stands in our way will quickly regret it, as Raymon Vandaal will find out.'

Axl peered at his sister, surprised by the fiery look in her eye. Or perhaps he wasn't. He'd never met anyone more determined than Jael; more single-minded and stubborn.

Except, perhaps, their father.

Jael smiled. 'Of course, it needn't come to that. I can be very persuasive when I want to be.' She swallowed, her ears suddenly buzzing again, thoughts of Eadmund washing over her like a waterfall.

'What is it?'

Jael blinked away the vision, and picking up her empty cup, she buried her face in it. 'Just tired. After three dragur attacks, you would be too.'

'But now they're gone,' Axl said, gripping Amma's hand under the table. Resting it on her knee.

'Well, they're gone for now.'

Amma leaned forward in surprise. 'What do you mean?'

'I don't imagine it's the last we've seen of them,' Jael mused. 'I don't believe that was every dragur in Osterland. If Draguta has a mind to, I'm sure she could raise others. But this time, we'll know just how to stop her.'

***

Eadmund yawned, pulling Evaine closer, trying to get comfortable in the uncomfortable dirt. The air was frigid, and the furs barely took the edge off the plummeting temperature, but her body felt warm, if not twitchy. Evaine was irritable after spending two days on horseback, but they would arrive at the castle in the morning, and Eadmund knew that she would be back to herself again quickly.

He stroked her hair, listening to the incessant chirping from an army of crickets nearby, and the thunderous snoring of Rollo, who was a great shadow in the distance, his mind wandering to his mother. He started to relax, his tension unravelling, at last, his eyelids drooping as a cool breeze ruffled his hair.

His mother, he thought to himself.

Eskild.

And closing his eyes, Eadmund heard her calling to him.

***

Running her hand down Tig's warm muzzle, Jael watched his eyes close. He was rarely still or quiet, much like her, she supposed with a smile. And turning to leave the stables, she yawned, relieved to finally have finished all her checks, confident that they were ready for Rissna. Or as ready as they could be with an army of bruised and broken men, and a hole-ridden fort under constant threat from Draguta and her book.

Jael was surprised to see Ivaar watching her, and she frowned, annoyed that she hadn't heard him. 'What do you want?'

'Nothing,' he mumbled, avoiding her eyes. 'Just making sure everything's ready for the morning.'

Jael walked towards him, closer to the light, seeing the cuts on his face, the tiredness in his eyes. She suspected they all looked much the same. 'And are you? Ready?'

Ivaar nodded. He felt uncomfortable. Not sure how to be around Jael at all.

Once, he'd wanted to touch her. Then he'd wanted to kill her.

And now...

Jael smiled, reading his thoughts. She didn't know how she felt about him either. Ivaar had a complicated story, though much of it wasn't his own doing, as she'd recently begun to discover. 'I've been meaning to tell you, I found out who killed Melaena,' she said, watching the shock jar his face. She could almost see the tension grip his body.

'What? Who?'

'Morac and Morana. The same two who conspired to kill your father.'

Ivaar's mouth opened and closed, memories shuddering into view. He shook his head, seeing Melaena's smiling face as he held it to his. 'Why? *Why*? What did she do to them?'

'It wasn't Melaena they wanted to hurt,' Jael tried to explain. 'It was Eadmund. Everything they've done has been to hurt Eadmund. To drive a wedge between you and your brother. To break him. Render him useless.'

Ivaar was confused. '*Because*?'

'Because a broken Eadmund can't fulfill his role in the prophecy. Because they could get to Eadmund, but they couldn't get to me. I was here, safe with my family, behind these walls. For the most part, it seems.' Jael stopped, taking a deep breath.

'But Eadmund? Morana has been playing games with him since the beginning. Twisting and pulling the threads of his life far away from anywhere that could make him a threat to their plans. So now they only have one problem left to deal with. Me.'

Ivaar was still shell-shocked. 'Those things they said I did? All of them? All the things I was accused of over the years... I didn't do any of them. Not one. Not one!' He felt the oddest sensation, as though he was a boy again. Tears were coming, and he was growing more and more agitated. 'But no one would believe me!'

Jael didn't know what to say. Ivaar had done things that were unforgivable no matter what games Morana and Morac had played with him. She couldn't absolve him of the pain he'd caused or the people he'd hurt.

'I became who they thought I was. Who they made me out to be,' Ivaar murmured. 'I couldn't be who I wanted, so I tried something else. I tried being someone else.'

'And now here you are.'

Ivaar stared at Jael, his thoughts crystallising. 'I'm going to kill Morana Gallas.'

Jael yawned. 'You're going to have to get in line. Wait till Eadmund wakes up and finds out what she's done!'

***

Morana couldn't sleep. Her head was clanging with urgency.

She could feel Draguta getting closer. Evaine too.

And stuck in a chair or trapped in a bed was no place to be. Not if she was going to save herself.

The curse-breaking symbol should have worked. The old man had done everything right. He'd chosen the right symbol, used her blood, carved it into her floor. But she was still trapped.

Helpless.

And quickly running out of time.

Morana closed her eyes, desperate to find a dream.

***

The dream was Oss again.

Eadmund felt happy to see it. His father was there in the distance, talking to Thorgils, who was leaning over the railings, watching Jael fight Fyn in the Pit.

Eadmund felt a sudden jolt, confused, as though two different worlds had collided inside his head. He didn't know what to think.

And then his mother was beside him, her voice soft in his ear, her hand on his arm.

'This is a good dream to have,' Eskild smiled as Biddy walked along with Eydis, the puppies charging past them, getting a stern telling off from Thorgils as they tried to enter the ring. 'This is your home. Your family. This is what is inside your heart, Eadmund. All of it. This is what you love. Who you love. The rest is all dark magic, keeping you away from here. Keeping you from being happy.'

Eadmund felt trapped. His feet wanted to head in opposite directions.

He could feel the battle inside his heart.

Two sides, both trying to claim victory.

He panicked, wanting to see Evaine and Sigmund. Everything would make sense then, he tried to tell himself, feeling his body shiver in protest.

And then his mother's hand, warm on his. 'Come on,' she breathed. 'I want to be over there, don't you? Jael is about to send Fyn flying. You remember that? You have to be there. She will come to the railings. Let you kiss her.'

She was smiling. He could hear it in her voice.

Eadmund frowned, but he was moving now, and though he tried to dig his boots into the dirt, he was still moving. And his mother's hand was gripping his, and suddenly he was leaning over the railings, and Fyn was flying through the air, and Thorgils was roaring with laughter, slapping Eirik on the back, tears in his eyes. And Jael was smiling, triumphant as she walked towards him.

Eadmund wanted to move. He tried to turn around, but she was getting closer, and his mother was still there, and Eirik was laughing, and Jael was coming, and Eadmund didn't move.

'Your turn?' Jael wondered with a grin, staring into his eyes.

Eadmund opened his mouth, but he didn't say anything as Jael leaned forward. Her eyes sparkled in the sunlight. It was cold, and her face was flushed.

Happy.

He wasn't holding his mother's hand anymore.

Jael's eyes were so green, he thought; like a deep ocean, but not cold.

Not now.

And he leaned towards her, not even blinking as he stared into her eyes and kissed her, feeling how cold her lips were.

How familiar.

And closing his eyes, he felt himself disappear.

PART FOUR

Rissna

CHAPTER TWENTY FOUR

'Are you feeling alright?' Axl wondered, holding Amma in his arms. 'You're not sick, are you?'

Amma felt sick. 'No, I'm fine. Just worried. I want to come with you.'

'I know. But I need you here. It's safer.'

'Only if Draguta doesn't send more creatures.' Amma swallowed, feeling guilty for worrying him. 'Though Edela has the book now, and Ayla is getting better. I'm sure we'll be fine.'

Axl didn't look convinced, but he could hear his sister barking orders behind him, and he knew that they didn't have long. 'We'll be back after we speak to the Vandaals. To get the sea-fire, and prepare for Hest. It won't take long. I'll see you soon.'

Amma nodded, not wanting to worry Axl further. 'I hope... I hope Getta hasn't caused problems for you. I doubt she'll be happy to see you. And I do remember how Raymon was around her. Like a loyal dog, so eager to please.'

'Well, he'll have Jael to contend with, and she's more like a charging boar, so I imagine we'll be fine,' Axl grinned, sensing his sister's eyes on him. 'Come on, walk me over to say goodbye to Edela.' And he wrapped an arm around Amma's shoulder, still worried that something was wrong.

Hoping that he was wrong.

'Your best chance is with Ravenna,' Gisila said quietly to

Jael. 'She's an influential woman. There was much noise about a revolt when her husband was murdered. About the Maas' taking the throne. I heard that Ravenna is the one who ensured Raymon followed his father as king.' Gisila frowned, wishing she'd been able to do the same for her own son.

But then she smiled as Axl approached with Amma.

He was the king now. And a man. And one day soon, he would grow as confident as his father had been. If there was time.

Jael looked from her mother to Axl and smiled. 'Ready for a nice long ride?'

Axl nodded. He was, though in the back of his mind, he kept thinking about the dragon, the serpent, and the dragur. And whatever creature Draguta planned to send next.

He prayed to Furia that she would wait until they returned.

***

Rollo was impressed. 'Well, I can see why you've been moaning about your cottage in Flane. That's a fine palace you have there.'

Draguta ignored him as she stared at the castle. She felt at peace, as though every sinew in her body had suddenly sighed.

Home.

Evaine's horse was scuffing the dirt beside Draguta, eager to get moving again. They had stopped to admire the view, high up on the peak, the Adrano to the west, the castle looming ahead of them, and Evaine suddenly wanted to turn to Eadmund and run in the opposite direction, far away from Jaeger Dragos and the memories of what he'd done to her.

She blinked, feeling Draguta's hand on her arm.

'This is a new beginning,' Draguta purred, staring at her. 'For all of us. For you and Jaeger too. You will not recognise him, I promise. No longer will he be that fearsome bear. Think of him now as a little lamb. Completely harmless and so eager to please me. You wait. You have nothing to worry about at all.' And nudging her horse forward, Draguta watched the dark clouds in the distance gathering above the castle, promising a downpour soon. 'Come along!' she called, not bothering to turn around. 'We're nearly there!'

Evaine waited for Eadmund, and he smiled at her as he eased his horse ahead of hers. 'I could do with a bath. And a bed!'

She smiled back, thinking of seeing her father and Morana; fearing suddenly what Draguta would do to them.

Wondering at the wisdom of helping her return to Hest.

***

Jaeger felt a sense of anticipation building as he sat upon the throne. His head was a blur of half-finished ideas and words, and he found himself unable to carry his thoughts to a conclusion. He could feel a growing sense of purpose, though. As though he finally knew which path to take. And at the end of the path, he could see Draguta waiting for him. The book called to him too, but when he thought of it now, he was reminded of how it belonged to Draguta.

Jaeger shook his head, wanting to argue against himself, but that singular thought always returned to defeat any he might have entertained of owning the book himself.

Draguta was its mistress.

Those words rolled around his mind like a cart clattering across the cobblestones.

Draguta was his mistress too.

'Meena!' He sat up, pleased to see her rushing past the

entrance to the hall. 'Where are you going?'

Meena froze, not wanting to stop. 'I'm going to see Dragmall. I thought he might come and see Morana again.'

Jaeger frowned, motioning her into the hall. 'Why? Why do you care about that miserable old bitch? After the way she treated you? Why do you care whether she lives or dies?'

It was a good question.

'I... she's my family,' Meena tried, dragging her feet into the hall, wondering if that was an excuse he would believe; certain she didn't believe it herself. 'Without Varna, I feel... alone.'

Jaeger blinked, trying to keep his train of thought going. 'What about me?'

Meena scratched her head, wanting to extract herself from his company quickly. 'You're not my family. Soon you'll find someone new. Perhaps your wife? I don't imagine you'll keep me around for long.'

Jaeger shook his head. 'My wife?' He hadn't thought about Amma in some time. 'When I find her, I won't be keeping her, I promise. Just long enough for her to watch me kill Axl Furyck. You don't need to be jealous of her.'

He reached out, gripping Meena's hands so tightly that she squeaked.

'We're together for a reason, and that reason is better than any blood ties you may have to a woman who treated you like a slave. Just like Varna did. They never cared for you, so why care about them? Why worry about Morana now? Draguta will be here soon. We don't need Morana anymore.' And he let go of Meena's hands, returning his to the armrests.

How smooth they were. Like skin. Polished by the kings before him, who had rubbed their palms over them. Over and over again. Scheming and plotting. Worrying and grieving. Planning. Always planning to make Hest the largest, richest, most powerful kingdom in Osterland. It was all he could see when he looked at Meena.

The hope of things to come.

And the unshakeable certainty he now felt that Draguta would help him with all of it.

***

Aleksander sat by Hanna's bed. Marcus had stepped outside the tent to talk to Entorp, though Aleksander had the sense that he was trying to give them some privacy.

But Hanna still hadn't opened her eyes.

They all spoke as if she would recover.

But Hanna wouldn't open her eyes.

'I'm leaving,' Aleksander mumbled, looking to see any sign of life. Her face was gaunt and sallow. Her eyes were closed, and her mouth was open, occasionally sucking in a ragged breath. 'We're leaving for Rissna. It's a village on the border with Iskavall. We're meeting the Vandaals there. Apparently, Jael is going to convince them to fight with us.' He smiled. 'She's a determined woman, but still, I've a feeling it won't be as easy as all that.' He paused, listening to some shouting outside, the loud whinnying of an impatient horse too, but it quickly died down.

He didn't have long, though.

'I'll be back soon,' Aleksander said, his voice just a whisper. He didn't want to disturb Hanna, though he doubted she was listening. 'I... we're going to get the Book of Darkness. When we have enough men. We're going to get it. Destroy it. Somehow...'

He stopped, hearing Jael bellow his name.

'I have to go.' Aleksander placed his hand on Hanna's, lightly, not wanting to hurt her. 'Your father will be back shortly. He's just outside.' And lifting his hand, he stood, readjusting his scabbard, resetting his mail shirt, still staring at her face. 'I'll come and see you when I return,' he said sadly, and turning, he headed out of the tent, not looking back.

Hanna drew in a long breath, her lungs straining.

And opened her eyes.

***

'No more kissing,' Jael grumbled. 'We have to go, though who knows where Aleksander is. It's like trying to round up sheep!' And spinning around, she came face to face with Karsten's piercing blue eye.

'What are we waiting for?' he snapped impatiently, motioning towards the columns of jiggling men; the skittering, impatient horses skipping out of line. 'It's only getting warmer!' They were in full armour, sweat already beading along furrowed, smoky brows.

'We're waiting for Thorgils to finish kissing,' Jael snapped back. 'So why don't you go and wait on your horse so he can get on with it.'

Karsten glared at Jael, readjusting his eyepatch, but he shut his mouth and turned back to his men, passing Berard, who was standing with Bayla, feeling guilty that he wasn't going with his brother. But two days on horseback would be too much, they'd decided. Berard needed some time to master riding with one arm. And he would. Nothing was going to stop him going back to Hest to see Karsten kill Jaeger. To get Meena back.

He blinked, aware that his mother was talking to him; aware that Eron was trying to run after his father. Berard hurried after the little boy, who was sobbing, not wanting Karsten to go.

Jael watched the Dragos', sighing in relief at the welcome appearance of Aleksander. '*Finally*! Now we can leave!'

'I could have caught you up,' he grinned, all thoughts of Hanna shut away now. Or so he told himself. 'You needn't wait on me.'

'You think I'd leave without you? I'd happily leave without Thorgils, but you? I need you.' And listening to Thorgils puffing and snorting beside her as he finally dragged himself out of Isaura's arms and away from her lips, Jael turned and walked towards the horses, where she could see Edela and Eydis waiting to say goodbye. 'I hope you'll be busy while we're gone, reading that book, day and night,' Jael said to her grandmother, giving her a quick hug. 'No sleep for you.'

'I think you may be right, but I've always got Eydis to rely on if I miss something. She's turning into a very good dreamer, aren't you?'

Eydis' cheeks flushed, surprised by the compliment; surprised too when Jael hugged her next. 'You won't be long, will you?' she asked.

'No, we won't be long. You'll both be too busy reading that book and organising the sea-fire to even notice I've gone!'

Edela smiled, taking Eydis' hand. 'We'll try, but do be careful. Those Iskavallans are a murderous bunch. And who knows what Getta's been whispering in their ears. Nothing that will help you and Axl, I'm sure.'

Jael stuck her boot into Tig's stirrup, trying to decide if she would rather fall down on the dirt or head for bed. Instead, she hoisted herself into the saddle, adjusting her scabbard before leaning over to give Tig a quick pat. 'Well, off we go again,' she said, smiling at Edela, and at Biddy, who had come to join her. Amma too. 'Take care of yourselves!' And motioning for Gant to blow his horn, she eased Tig towards the main gates, listening to the clanking of helmets and shields hanging from saddles, and on mail-clad backs; the exuberant whinnying of horses excited to finally get moving.

The sound of her heart thudding in her ears, wondering what was coming next.

***

Raymon was pleased that Getta had come along.

Ravenna was not.

She could see her daughter-in-law up ahead, her eyes wide with interest as she rode alongside Raymon, constantly turning to smile and laugh at her husband. He looked more besotted than ever, barely able to keep his eyes on the road. And though Ravenna didn't wish to have an unhappy son trapped in an unhappy marriage, she knew that what Getta was trying to do would put them all in danger.

If she succeeded.

Aldo Maas rode beside Ravenna. He was a lord, an old man now but with a roaming eye that always made her feel uncomfortable. He'd never had any respect for her or her husband, and even now, she could feel him looking her over as though he was inspecting a broodmare. 'You don't look happy, my lady. Are you not enjoying the journey?' Handsome in his youth, Aldo been disfigured by a bear he'd been hunting. Two thick scars ran down from his forehead, through his right eye, trailing down to his lips. For some reason, he chose not to wear an eyepatch, so they were all forced to look at the puckered pink hole that had once been his right eye.

Perhaps he thought it made him look intimidating?

Ravenna wasn't intimidated, but she was wary of the man. When Hugo had been killed, she'd fought hard against Aldo and his ambitious only son, Garren. And not one day had passed since without her worrying about how safe Raymon was on the throne.

'I don't mind the riding,' Ravenna said coldly, her eyes on Raymon, who rode ahead of her. She could sense that the road was narrowing, and she gathered in her reins, hoping to move ahead of Aldo. 'But I'm not enjoying the rain.'

It hadn't stopped raining since they'd left Ollsvik, a constant, cold drizzle. Never getting worse, but never showing any signs of relenting either. They were all sodden and quiet, weighed down by damp clothes and dripping mail. Ravenna could hear the squelching of boots as the army traipsed behind them in columns; the constant groan and clatter of the carts following further back.

'I don't suppose any of us are, but hot fires await us in Rissna. And the Brekkans. Unless, of course, it's all a trap? The Furycks may be preparing to murder their next king!'

Ravenna turned to Aldo with a scowl. 'I'm not sure why you'd say such a thing? You never appeared to have a problem with Ranuf Furyck. You never thought he was trying to conquer Iskavall, did you? So why are you suddenly so suspicious of his children?'

Aldo dismissed her with a loud snort. 'Ranuf's long dead! Irrelevant to what is occurring now, my dear Ravenna. And his children are reckless. Not like their father at all. He was a sober man, respectful of our borders, but those children of his?' Aldo shook his dripping grey curls at her. 'Your boy is walking into a dragon's lair, so he shouldn't be surprised if he's swallowed alive!' And bobbing his head, he motioned for Ravenna to move her horse ahead of his.

Ravenna nudged her horse forward, eager to get away from Aldo Maas and the disturbing look in his roaming eye.

***

Else could tell that Morana hated her company, for though she couldn't speak, her dark eye was alert and pulsing with anger as it followed her around the chamber.

Morac was there. He'd arrived early in the hope of seeing

his sister returned to herself, but there was still no change, and he looked as miserable as Morana appeared angry. 'But what are we going to do now?' Morac sighed. 'If Draguta is coming, what should I do?' He scratched his hair, dropping his head to his hands, worrying about Evaine.

Worrying about himself.

He thought of Runa often, regretting that he'd allowed his sister to unravel the life he'd worked so hard to achieve. It had always been the plan, of course, even when they were children. Their mother would come to them in their dreams and tell them how to manipulate Eirik Skalleson. Morac smiled wistfully, almost missing that time, when it had felt for a moment as though he'd had a mother. As soon as Morana had been able to dream herself, Varna had stopped coming into his dreams. He'd never seen her again, though he supposed it made no sense to feel sad about that. Their purpose, Varna had drummed into them, was greater than family. Greater than love. Their purpose was the greatest of all: to help Raemus return. To help him bring back the Darkness that would set them all free.

Morac felt far away from that now. Far away from wanting it anymore. When he closed his eyes, he saw his fine house on Oss. He saw Runa in her chair by the fire. He saw Respa laying the table and Evaine shaking snow from her white cloak. He remembered going to the hall, Eirik smiling at him as he approached the throne, offering him a cup of ale.

He saw the home and family he'd once had. And when he opened his eyes, he saw his ruined sister and the dank, dark chamber that was now her prison, and he felt lost.

Else tried to reassure him. 'Dragmall will come. He said that he'd come this morning. Perhaps he had some thoughts overnight? Something new we can try?' She handed Morac a cup of peppermint tea. The smell of it was invigorating, she thought, hoping it would lift his mood. 'This might help.'

Morac took it, nodding, not noticing the fresh aroma or the warmth of the cup in his hands. 'I fear it is all too late now.

Meena thinks that Draguta will be here soon. Perhaps we should try to leave? We could take horses?'

Morana's eye flared in panic.

Morac wasn't sure what that meant, but his attention was suddenly diverted to the door as Meena burst into the chamber, panting, her face almost as red as her hair.

'Draguta...' she gasped, trying to catch her breath. 'Draguta is here!'

***

Binding a hapless soul was easy enough.

It felt like a sausage. Malleable. She could twist and turn it with ease. Even a child could bind a hapless soul, but a savage beast like Jaeger? One who'd been exposed to the book for so long? A Dragos king?

Draguta stared at Jaeger intently, eager to know if it had worked. And as she watched him walking down the castle steps, she smiled.

'Draguta.' Jaeger came towards her with confidence, all thoughts of the night in the hall forgotten. He felt elated to see her again, his body humming with the need to please her. Striding to her side, he held out a hand, helping her down from her horse.

The stable hands had rushed into the square, and there was a little step waiting for her to dismount onto. Draguta nodded her approval, sighing contentedly as she stared up at the castle. 'You will find my champion somewhere to sleep,' she said, flicking a hand at Rollo, who dropped to the cobblestones with a thump. 'I'm sure there are rooms for rent near the brothels.' And stepping down, she glided towards the castle as Brill struggled down from her own horse, stumbling after her mistress.

Rollo was relieved to be standing, not liking horses at all. He yawned, stretching out a stiff neck, lifting his tattooed arms above his head.

Ready for some ale.

Eadmund helped Evaine down from her horse, noting how uncomfortable she suddenly appeared as Jaeger approached.

Reaching the top of the steps, Draguta stopped and turned around, holding her breath, a smile teasing the corners of her red lips.

'Your father has been worried about you, Evaine,' Jaeger said, watching her closely. Pleased by how terrified she looked as her eyes darted from him to Eadmund and back again. 'So very worried. We were all surprised that you tried to steal the book. It isn't what I expected. And after all we've been through together, you and I.'

Evaine swallowed, not wanting him to say any more. She felt Eadmund come close, wrapping an arm around her.

'And here's Eadmund Skalleson,' Jaeger smiled slyly. 'At long last. Evaine was starting to think that you weren't coming, my lord.'

Eadmund's body tensed, unsettled by Jaeger's snake-like words and Evaine's discomfort, but noticing Draguta staring at them, he blinked, ushering Evaine forward, ignoring Jaeger entirely.

Rollo followed after them, nodding briefly at Jaeger, not sure how to act at all.

Jaeger watched them go, his mind busy with thoughts of Evaine in the winding gardens. Her screams. The feel of her delightful squirming body. He remembered Draguta warning him away, Jael Furyck stabbing his ankles. He felt the pain and pleasure meld together in a most arousing way, and turning, he snapped at the stable hands, who hadn't moved. 'What are you gaping at? Get these horses to the stables now!'

***

The rain started as soon as they left the fort behind, but it stayed warm, so the great army of Brekka steamed in their armour as they marched towards Rissna. It would take two days to get there. Two days of solid rain by the look of the sky, Jael thought miserably, feeling the water dripping down from her hair into her eyes. She didn't usually mind the rain. Rain was a gift from the gods. Rain meant a good harvest and water to drink. But rain when you were lying in your comfortable bed, buried beneath layers of furs, your cold feet warming on your husband's, was always preferable.

The rain had stopped conversation as most hunched over, trying to keep the water out of their eyes and mouths, so Jael's mind kept wandering in the silence. There were the things she needed to think about, like Raymon Vandaal and Briggit Halvardar. There was Draguta and Morana and Evaine too. Sometimes, her mind drifted towards Eadmund, and she wondered where he was.

But mostly, the rain made her think of her daughter.

It cascaded down her cheeks like tears, and she remembered the pain of giving birth; the even greater pain of losing her baby.

The guilt.

The burning anger and bleak sadness.

And Jael knew that not one part of her would feel right again until she made Draguta pay for all of it.

CHAPTER TWENTY FIVE

It was awkward.

Everyone could feel the tension in the hall, except, perhaps, Draguta, who was so pleased to be sitting on the dragon throne again that she didn't want to think about anything else. She was determined to look forward, not back to that night when she had been killed by those disloyal to her.

But, of course, they had all been disloyal, she reminded herself, except Evaine, who was too self-involved to care about anything other than Eadmund.

'And how is the wine?' Draguta asked, joining the small gathering. 'Better than anything you had in Flane, I imagine?'

Rollo wondered if he should be polite. 'I prefer ale,' he said, deciding against it. 'If you've got some of that?' And he looked down at his fancy goblet with a grimace, his throat burning.

Draguta laughed, enjoying his frankness. 'Girl!' she snapped at a slave. 'Bring Rollo, here, some ale.'

Rollo glanced at Eadmund, who smiled, though he didn't really feel like smiling. His dreams of Oss were rushing around his head, and he clenched his jaw, trying to remind himself of where he was. But when he looked around the hall, he saw Jael, and he remembered his time in Hest with her.

Draguta didn't notice how disturbed Eadmund was becoming. Her mind was skipping ahead, wanting to get to her chamber, eager to feel silk against her skin again. She would need to speak to the tailor to organise more dresses. Her days of looking like a peasant were over.

It was time to reclaim her rightful place.

And then more.

'Shall we go?' she purred, taking Jaeger's arm.

He looked pleased but confused. 'Go?'

'To see my book, of course,' she sighed happily. 'I have work to do, and there is no time to waste!'

***

'Is Evaine here?' Morac asked, panicking as much as everyone else.

Meena nodded. 'In the hall, with Eadmund Skalleson.'

Morac wondered what would happen when Eadmund found out what Jaeger had done to Evaine, but in the meantime, the more pressing problem was what Draguta would do to all of them. He turned to Morana, who sat helplessly on her chair, unable to help them or herself.

'There's nothing you can do now,' Else said, attempting to sound calm while feeling her heart thumping in terror. 'Except, perhaps, think of how to be useful.'

Meena swallowed, trying to stop herself from tapping her head.

'Draguta is a lady. A queen. A grand witch. Surely she doesn't want to do her own scraping about? Digging out plants and grinding potions?' Else muttered, thinking quickly. 'She needs people to help her, doesn't she? Like you told her in that dream. To do all those things she doesn't want to do herself. Skinning animals? Cutting up the poor creatures? All that blood...' Else's imagination was running away with her.

The thought of helping Draguta again made Meena shake

all over. She glanced at Morana, who she could almost feel trying to burst out of her prison. She looked so pathetic that it was easy to feel sorry for her, but Meena forced herself to remember how evil Morana was as well.

Yet, with Draguta back, she would soon be dead.

Morana blinked in desperation, pleading with one eye.

Pleading to be set free.

Else squeezed Meena's hand. 'You're a dreamer. Draguta will see the wisdom in keeping you alive, don't worry.'

Morac glanced at his blinking sister before turning to the door. 'Meena, why don't you come with me? We can face her together, and I need to ensure that Evaine is alright.'

Meena nodded reluctantly, shivers rippling through her body like ice-cold waves.

***

Karsten rode along with no one to talk to.

His men didn't like him, though they'd fought the dragur bravely beside him, following his commands. Berard was back in Andala with Bayla, Nicolene and the five children, which, Karsten decided, was worse than suffering through a two-day march in what appeared to be a never-ending rain shower. And every other person he knew was in Hest with his traitorous brother, where he should've been instead of riding to Rissna begging a boy king for some men. They had enough men, Karsten thought, turning around and running his eye over the winding worm of warriors, who looked as miserable and wet as he felt.

More than enough.

'Enjoying the weather?' Thorgils grinned, riding up to join him. He'd been further back with Torstan, and was making his way up to Jael to see how she was.

'Well, it's not Hest,' Karsten grumbled. 'And it's not warm.'

Thorgils laughed. 'Come to Oss sometime. This is a heatwave!'

He didn't move forward, and Karsten peered at him. 'Why are you so happy, then? Going to this pointless meeting? Leaving the fort vulnerable? If we're leaving it behind, it should be to go to Hest. We've enough men.'

Thorgils looked surprised. 'You think so? After our visitors the other night? We could barely contain them, even with all that sea-fire helping us!'

Karsten snorted. 'And you think a few hundred men will make a difference? We don't need an army of warriors. We need an army of dragur!'

'We do,' Thorgils agreed, squeezing the rain from his beard. 'But now they're ash, so we'll just have to try our luck with humans. Unless Jael can find a way to get us a dragon or two?' Thorgils eyed Karsten, listening to his barely concealed mutterings. 'Why do you hate Jael so much? She gave your family a home. Took you in. Brought you into her army.'

Karsten squeezed the rain from his own long beard, hanging down his chest like a hairy wet towel. 'Best I keep my thoughts about Jael Furyck to myself, you being so friendly with her.'

'Your brother likes her,' Thorgils said. 'And he seems like a wise man to me. It's going to be a long few days. Maybe you'll get a chance to think about it. We're not enemies anymore, and if we keep thinking we are, it's going to make victory harder to come by, I'd say.' And Thorgils nudged Rufus ahead of Karsten's horse, spotting Jael and Aleksander through the rain, which had suddenly started teeming down.

***

Before Jaeger could open the door to his chamber, Meena appeared in the corridor, Morac trailing after her.

Meena saw Draguta and Jaeger and froze, her boots stuck to the floor, her legs wobbling with the sheer terror of what was about to happen. She wanted to turn around and run in the opposite direction, but she could feel Morac's hand on her back, pushing her forward.

Draguta cocked her head to the side and smiled. 'Ahhh, if it isn't the little mouse who tried to kill me. How well you look, girl. Positively glowing with life!'

Jaeger turned to Meena, feeling his chest tighten. He didn't want Draguta to hurt her. Surely he was just as responsible for what had happened in the hall?

Meena shuddered, edging closer, Morac's hand moving away now.

Reaching Draguta, she dropped her eyes, bobbing her head. 'I... I am sorry,' she mumbled. 'I... I...' She was too scared to speak. Her words were in knots, and she was shaking too much to try and untangle them. Eventually, she forced herself to look up, meeting Draguta's eyes.

Draguta threw back her head and laughed. 'You are sorry? Ha!' She glanced at Morac, whose narrow face had blanched; he didn't know what was about to happen. 'You are *sorry* you killed me? Well, that is the funniest thing I've heard, girl! It is not something one often hears, is it? I am so sorry I killed you?'

Meena knew that Draguta's laughter wouldn't last.

Her eyes were so cold.

Draguta did stop laughing as she reached out a long arm, wrapping her hand around Meena's throat and yanking her forward with a surprising show of strength. Meena was quickly off her feet, feeling nothing beneath her boots. 'And how will you show me that you're sorry, girl? What will you *do* for me? How will you convince me that I need you?'

Meena blinked at Jaeger, seeing the terror in his eyes; her own eyes bursting as she tried to breathe.

Eventually, Draguta lowered her to the flagstones, realising that she could hardly expect answers from the girl when she was unable to talk. She loosened her hold on Meena's throat ever so slightly. 'Tell me. Tell me now before I stop your heart beating. Tell me before I twist the air from your lungs. Before I drop you like a stone, straight into the Dolma! Would you like it?' She inhaled Meena's fear, closing her eyes. 'The darkness? The cold?' Her eyes burst open, watching Meena jerk in terror. 'No! I've seen how that would go for you. You wouldn't like it at all!'

'I can help your...' Meena spluttered, choking. 'Spells. I can help with your spells. Your lists. I can... gather what you need. Make your potions. Be your... assistant.'

Draguta smiled suddenly, her face changing like a stormy sky revealing a golden sun. 'Of course you can! And you will! I will be needing an assistant, and without poor Morana, who do I have to rely upon but you and Brill?' She leaned forward, peering at Meena, who now looked like a fish out of water: all bulging eyes and gulping mouth. 'You have learned your lesson, then? About what a mistake it would be to try and deceive me? To betray me?' Draguta was peering into Meena's very soul, looking for answers, watching as she nodded and trembled, twitching all over. 'How pointless it would be to try and kill me again? How futile?'

Meena's nodding was vigorous.

'Good,' Draguta said. 'Then come along into Jaeger's chamber, and we shall see how well you have been looking after my beloved book.' And releasing Meena, she inclined her head towards the door, following after Jaeger, who was already hurrying towards it.

Morac stood watching them go, frozen to the spot.

***

'You needn't be afraid, Eydis,' Edela smiled as they walked to the tents to check on Ayla and Bruno. She wanted to see how Hanna was and speak to Entorp too. His patients were decreasing steadily, but he would not rest until they were all back in their own beds, though Edela hoped she could convince him to stop for a while. 'The Book of Aurea is a powerful weapon, and once we learn how to wield it, we will be a match for Draguta and whatever ghoulish creatures she sends our way.'

But Eydis wasn't frightened of the creatures as much as she was about what Draguta would do to her brother. 'I want to dream about Eadmund. To see how he is,' she said. 'When I think of him, it's as though he's lost in a storm. A blizzard. And the snow is powerful and loud, blowing around me so much that I can't find him anywhere. Sometimes, I see him or hear his voice, but then he's swept away.'

Edela looked sad, then her face lightened. 'There is hope for Eadmund in the Book of Aurea, isn't there? A way to break the spell? So perhaps instead of dreaming about Eadmund, you could dream of finding the answer in the book? A way to save him? You're connected to that book, Eydis, through Dara Teros. She is your ancestor, I'm sure. You can find your way to the right page through your dreams, just as you did when the dragur came. But you must clear your mind of panic. Panic is a dreamer's enemy. Panic tightens our bodies and our minds. It stops us breathing. It stops us dreaming. It creates walls around our thoughts, so the only things that enter our mind are our fears. You must let go of your panic, and the dreams will come. The way to help Eadmund will reveal itself if you can stay calm and believe. Believe that we will find the answer.'

Eydis could feel the tension across her shoulders and the ache behind her eyes; the heaviness in her legs too. She tried to let it all drift away as she walked, determined to open up her mind.

Determined to find a way to help her brother.

***

Evaine sobbed in Morac's arms.

She couldn't help it, and though she felt like a child, she didn't care. It had been a terrifying time, and she longed to feel safe again, though Morac appeared to be shaking so much that when she stepped away from him and looked at his face, she only felt more worried. 'Perhaps we should go?' she whispered, glancing towards the stairs. 'Leave Hest? Go back to Oss?' Rollo had left with a servant, who had been tasked with finding him a bed for the night.

Eadmund had disappeared to find a latrine.

Morac looked keen, but then his face fell. 'We wouldn't be welcomed back on Oss. On any of the islands. Not now.'

'Then we take a ship,' Evaine suggested. 'Go to the Fire Lands. Disappear. Somewhere Draguta can't find us.'

'And what of your son?'

Evaine sighed. 'How do you expect me to get him back? He's in Andala. I can't go there.'

'And Eadmund?'

Evaine looked around, though there were only a few slaves preparing the tables. 'Eadmund is... different,' she murmured, unsettled when she saw his face in her mind now. 'He is mine, but Draguta's also.'

Morac was confused. 'Draguta's?'

'She's done something to Eadmund and Jaeger. Made them loyal to her in some way. Eadmund is different than he was before.' Evaine lowered her voice even further. 'She put a spell on Jaeger. I saw her do it. I think she did the same to Eadmund. He won't leave her, I'm sure. She wants him for something. That's why Rollo's here.'

Morac looked confused, not knowing who Rollo was. 'But what about Morana?' he wondered. 'What will she do to Morana?'

'I don't know. But whatever it is, I don't imagine it will be pleasant.'

***

Morana kept staring at the door.

It hurt her head to move her eye too much, so she tried to keep it still, fixed straight ahead. Waiting. Knowing that at any moment, Draguta could open the door and kill her. And she wouldn't make it fast. Or painless. She would want to savour her revenge; to taste every last drop of it.

It wouldn't be fast.

Morana wanted to close her eyes. She wanted to scream. Else kept humming to herself as she stirred the cauldron over the fire. It smelled disgusting, and soon she would be spoon-fed whatever slop the woman had made.

Like a baby.

There was nothing Morana could do to help herself. Not a single thing.

Except think, she realised. And fight to reclaim her dreams.

If there was time.

Morana tried to sigh, but her body wouldn't even give her that relief. Finally, she managed to close her eyes, eager to disappear inside herself; listening to the beating of her heart thudding in her ears like a horse running.

Running away.

***

Draguta ran her hands over the Book of Darkness, her eyes closed, feeling completely alone, though Jaeger and Meena were there, she knew.

They meant nothing, though. They were useful tools, but ultimately dispensable.

Jaeger would run her kingdom, build her ships, grow her army.

Meena would slave over her potions, dig in the gardens, do her bidding.

But there would come a point when neither of them would be needed.

'Your wife is pregnant,' she said suddenly, looking up, her eyes snapping to Jaeger's. 'It is your child. A Dragos heir. A son. You will need to go to Andala and retrieve her when the time is right, wouldn't you say? Return her to your bed? Surely you cannot abide the shame of it much longer? Having your wife stolen from you by a boy as weak as Axl Furyck? And such a pretty thing she is too, if not a little dull and pathetic. But she will give birth to a strong son. I see that. Your heir.'

Jaeger was too shocked to reply. He glanced at Meena, who was trying not to react at all. 'I... that is good news,' he supposed, though his thoughts about that were clouded. He didn't really feel anything.

'An heir,' Draguta repeated, her face shining. 'And by the time he is ready to rule, he will rule over the whole of Osterland. That is the gift we will give him, you and I.' She frowned suddenly, unsettled, feeling as though someone had touched her with an ice-cold hand.

Draguta turned around, confused.

She was sitting at the table, Meena and Jaeger standing before her.

There was no one else in the room.

Swallowing, Draguta pressed her hands against the cool cover of the book again and closed her eyes, taking a deep breath. And there it was, back again, that certainty. That singular belief

that soon she would conquer Osterland, kingdom by kingdom.
Piece by bloody piece.

***

Amma had come to the tents to see if Entorp needed anything,
and she'd ended up helping Astrid feed some of the remaining
patients.

Edela smiled, pleased to see her. She had a strong suspicion
that Amma was pregnant, but her confidence had been shaken
by what had happened to Jael, and she didn't want to reveal
things that could turn out to be wrong. Not when it came to
something as precious as a child.

She frowned, remembering how sad Jael had looked.

'Are you alright, Edela?' Ayla asked as she came to sit beside
her. She felt ready to crawl into bed, but she had no intention of
leaving without Bruno. Entorp was looking him over, deciding
whether he would let him go, and Ayla was hopeful that tonight
they would be in their own cottage, in a bed. Together.

Edela shook her head, pleased to have an experienced
dreamer to talk to. 'No, I'm not. I feel unsettled, unsure of
myself. While you were ill, something happened.'

'Oh?'

'Jael was pregnant, and while she was away, she lost her
baby. It died.' She gulped in a big breath, feeling tears coming.
'A little girl. I saw her, though. Before Jael left, I saw her alive. I
didn't see any danger.' Her voice was low; it kept catching.

Ayla placed a hand on Edela's arm. 'I am sorry,' she
murmured. 'I saw it myself, but I didn't want to say anything to
Jael. It didn't seem like the right time.'

'Lydea came to me in my dreams. She said that Draguta
can weave the threads now. Change destiny itself. Her power is

growing, and I no longer trust what I see. How can I? How can any of us?'

'Oh.' Ayla felt light-headed. Anxious. Her relief at having survived the sickness and being reunited with Bruno was tempered by the reminder that Draguta loomed above them all like a terrifying storm. 'I think you're right. We can't. We can only try to forge a path ahead. Not get involved in predicting the future.' She looked towards Amma, following Edela's gaze. 'For ourselves, or anyone else.'

***

Draguta felt energised after touching the book; renewed, eager to begin, but also filthy, and impatient to return to her chamber. But she wouldn't be able to enjoy the relief of undressing in her beautiful room if she didn't complete one more task. So, clasping the book to her chest, she sent Jaeger and Meena to the hall to check on Evaine and Eadmund as she turned down the corridor.

***

It tasted disgusting.

Morana gagged as Else pushed the spoon through her lips. She couldn't keep them closed. She could barely even swallow on her own. Not that she wanted to. The stew tasted worse than it smelled; sweet and full of some revolting spice she didn't recognise.

The humming old bitch couldn't cook.

No wonder Jaeger had gotten rid of her.

The door suddenly swung open with such force that it banged against the wall.

Morana spat a mouthful of stew all over Else.

'Oh, Morana, my poor Morana,' Draguta purred, striding into the chamber, surprised by the fragrant aromas. She saw how utterly helpless Morana was, and her smile grew.

Else shook, too terrified to move.

'You will leave,' Draguta ordered, not looking at her. 'Find something to clean. I am going to have a little talk with Morana, here. Just the two of us.'

Else nodded, not even stopping to put the bowl of stew down. She carried it through the open door as fast as her shaking legs would take her.

Draguta glanced around the bare chamber, her nose in the air, before turning back to Morana. She bent down, peering at her milky eye. 'Oh, but doesn't that make you look even uglier,' she grinned. 'Though now that poor Yorik Elstad is ash, there's no one to care, is there?'

Morana was vibrating, desperate to disappear.

Wanting it to be over.

'Shall we begin, then?' Draguta cooed. 'I won't be able to enjoy the rest of my day until I've dealt with you.'

CHAPTER TWENTY SIX

Jaeger stared at Eadmund.

Eadmund glared back at him.

Evaine stood between them, keeping her mouth shut. It would do no good to cause more problems, though the temptation to see Eadmund beat Jaeger to a bloody pulp was hard to resist. Eadmund was becoming stronger and more powerful, and though he wasn't quite as big as Jaeger, Evaine was starting to believe that soon Eadmund might have a chance of defeating him.

Morac fretted beside her, wondering what was happening with his sister. He glanced at Meena. 'I'm not sure why Draguta blames Morana,' he muttered. 'She didn't stab her. She didn't throw the knife.' He looked at Jaeger, his beady eyes quickly scurrying away as Jaeger turned towards him.

'She would have,' Jaeger growled. 'You know that. It's only that she wasn't strong enough. She wanted to, and that's all that matters to Draguta now. She will make Morana pay for her disloyalty.'

Morac stepped forward, anger overwhelming good sense. 'But she'll reward yours?'

Jaeger scowled at the old man. 'I'm the king. Draguta's heir. I made mistakes, but I am part of Hest's future, as is Meena. As for you and your daughter, I have no idea why she'd have any use for either of you. Once she gets rid of Morana, I imagine you'll be next. Perhaps you should run away now before it's too late?'

Eadmund ignored Evaine's sudden grip of his arm, shaking her off as he turned to Jaeger. 'Perhaps you should shut your mouth?' he suggested coldly. 'You not being Draguta and knowing anything about what plans she might have for anyone.'

Jaeger looked surprised. 'You do realise that you're standing in my castle? Insulting me? The king?'

Rollo lumbered into the hall, looking for Eadmund, eager to loosen his stiff limbs with some training. Quickly noticing the tension between Eadmund and Jaeger Dragos, he rolled his eyes, knowing how that fight would work out for Draguta's little pet. 'Eadmund, we should go. I found a training ring. After all that riding, we're overdue some practice.'

Eadmund didn't move. His eyes were still on Jaeger.

Rollo patted his shoulder. 'Come on, we'd better get on with it before you end up making a mistake. You're not ready to take on the king, here. Not yet.'

'He's not as tough as he looks,' Eadmund growled. 'My wife defeated him easily enough. Had him on his back in no time.' He blinked, reminded of his dream again; seeing himself bending towards Jael's lips, drawn in by the smile in her eyes.

Rollo stepped in. 'Well, I'd like to see the size of your wife,' he grinned, dragging Eadmund away before Jaeger could lunge at him. 'Let's go train. You want to make Draguta happy, don't you?'

'Yes, hurry away, Eadmund. I'll stay here and look after Evaine,' Jaeger smiled. 'She'll be perfectly safe with me, don't worry.'

Eadmund froze, glancing at Evaine, whose big blue eyes were blinking rapidly. She nodded at Eadmund, urging him to go with Rollo.

Morac put his hands on his daughter's shoulders. 'You go, Eadmund,' he insisted. 'I'll stay with Evaine.'

Eadmund frowned, suddenly noticing Morac.

Jael's words about Morac killing his father echoed in his head. He clenched his fists as they rolled over him and away, dissolving like mist, and then his mind was clear of everything except the thought that training would please Draguta. 'Evaine, stay with Morac,' he said, glaring at Jaeger before turning to follow a relieved Rollo out of the hall.

Evaine took one look at Jaeger and grabbed her father's arm, hurrying after them.

***

The stool looked like an unstable bunch of old sticks, but Draguta sat on it anyway, the book on her lap.

Morana was desperate to look at it. Desperate to look away from Draguta.

But she couldn't do either.

'You said a lot of things, I remember,' Draguta began. 'That night. You do remember that night, don't you, Morana? The last night you were truly yourself? The night I locked you in this cage?' She laughed, looking at the mess before her. 'And only I have the key.' Lifting the piece of rawhide with her shoe, Draguta uncovered the symbol Dragmall had carved into the flagstone. 'A nice try, but my curses are not broken that easily.'

Morana couldn't breathe. She could feel sweat coursing down her back, pooling between her breasts. Her backside was numb. Her head was pounding. She wanted to move.

She had to move!

'You were not loyal, Morana. Not to me, at least,' Draguta murmured. 'You would not give up Raemus, would you? I saved you when I killed his pathetic Followers. You and the idiot girl. I gave you a chance. Rescued you from a well-deserved death, and how did you repay me? Skulking around, trying to find ways to kill me? Still hoping to bring Raemus back!' Draguta blinked, feeling the momentary panic of being trapped in the Dolma again, and it distracted her.

Morana couldn't do anything but watch.

And wait.

'I have thought long and hard about what to do with you,' Draguta carried on, her hands on the book, feeling its power vibrating up her arms, soothing her. Focusing her. 'And, in the end, I decided to do... nothing.' She stood up and smiled, leaning over, letting Morana see the book she so wanted to command herself. 'I am going to do nothing at all. I have been in the Dolma,' Draguta said. 'And it was torture. Endless days of darkness and cold, but I could move and feel and touch. Compared to your prison, it was pure luxury. So, I realised that killing you would be a gift, Morana. A gift you do not deserve. Not for what you tried to do to me.' She straightened up, inhaling, surprised to smell roses. 'I shall leave you in this prison instead. And you shall have your cheerful servant remain by your side, feeding you like a baby bird, filling your chamber with scented flowers. She will brush your hair and wash you. All those things you hate so much. And she will make sure that you live. I would hate to think that you would simply fade away and die, Morana. What fun would there be in that?'

Standing, Draguta glided to the door, eager to head for her chamber. 'You are mine, my prisoner, and I will keep you for all time. I have your niece, and though she is mostly useless, she will be easier to control than you.' And opening the door, she turned to smile at Morana before closing it behind her.

Morana didn't know whether she wanted to scream or cry.

But she couldn't do either.

***

Morac's mouth gaped open, watching Eadmund train with Rollo. 'Eirik wouldn't believe his eyes,' he said, shaking his head. 'How did Eadmund...'

'Draguta,' Evaine sighed, not caring how Eadmund looked or how well he was fighting. 'She makes him practice all day. That's why she brought Rollo along.'

The training ring Rollo had chosen had no railings, so they had to jump out of the way as the two red-faced, sweaty men came barreling towards them, tumbling into the dust.

Morac coughed, moving Evaine into the shade, under a yellow-and-white striped awning. 'Why does Draguta care about Eadmund?' he wondered. 'What does she want him to do?'

'I don't know,' Evaine admitted. 'But I'm glad she's making him train. Jaeger is going to cause problems, isn't he? The way he was talking in the hall? I'm sure he's going to tell Eadmund what happened to me. What he did to me.' She swallowed, uncomfortable mentioning it. Uncomfortable thinking about it. Turning back to the training ring, she watched as Eadmund and Rollo bent over, hands on knees, drained by the intense heat of the sun.

Eadmund looked up and smiled at her, slapping Rollo on the shoulder before heading over. 'We have to keep Eadmund away from Jaeger. He can't know.' Evaine shook all over, panicking in hoarse whispers. 'He can't know!' She blinked quickly as Eadmund bent under the awning and kissed her.

'Let's go and find something to drink,' he panted, wiping sweat out of his eyes. 'Rollo heard about a good tavern down the street.'

Evaine looked mortified. 'Eadmund, you're a king! You can't go and drink in a tavern.'

Eadmund burst out laughing. 'Would you rather go back to the castle and run into Jaeger? Surely you'd choose a tavern over him?'

Evaine glanced at her father, then at Rollo, who approached, running a hand over his shining head.

'Ready?' Rollo asked.

Morac nodded, taking Evaine's arm. 'Yes, let's go. It will be nice to get away from the castle for a while.' He couldn't stop thinking about Morana, but he wasn't in any hurry to return to her chamber, afraid of what he would find.

***

Dragmall blinked in surprise.

So did Meena.

'She wants you to keep her alive?'

Else shook all over, nodding at the same time. 'Oh yes, if Morana dies, Draguta said she would hold me responsible. That she would... kill me.'

Meena gulped, looking from Else to Morana. 'She wants to punish Morana.'

'Well, that would do it,' Dragmall said. 'It would be different if Morana had lost her mind, but she appears aware of everything. Draguta has her trapped as if she'd locked her in an actual dungeon.'

Else didn't know what to do with herself. She kept peering at Morana to make sure that she was still breathing. 'I think she saw the symbol too,' she whispered, pointing to the piece of rawhide that was no longer covering the symbol. 'Morana couldn't do that.'

Dragmall swallowed, his eyes darting about nervously. 'So, she knows that we tried to help her?' It was unsettling, and he wanted to head straight back to his cave, yet he was worried about Else. Meena too. And confused as to why the curse hadn't broken.

'She knows everything,' Meena said blankly. 'She hears and

sees everything too. We must leave Morana like this, as Draguta wants. You should go, Dragmall.' She spoke boldly, certain that somehow Draguta was listening. 'Go back to your cave. There is nothing for you to do now. Else needs to stay here, and I must go and find Jaeger. Or Draguta. She may need my help.'

Dragmall nodded, knowing that Meena was right. It was better to fade into the background, at least until Draguta had grown bored with the idea of torturing Morana and turned her mind to other pleasures, which she was sure to find in the Book of Darkness. 'I'll walk with you. Good day to you, Else,' he said quickly, bobbing his head. 'And don't forget to come by and pick up those herbs to help you sleep. Hopefully, you can find someone to watch Morana.' And after staring into Else's eyes for a moment, he turned after Meena, hurrying out of the chamber.

***

Draguta lay her head back on the little pillow, enjoying the steaming heat of the water as it lapped over her shoulders. Her body loosened, unwinding with every slow breath, her mind meandering down a winding path, leading to...

She didn't know.

Her urgency to act was dulled by the slumberous warmth of the hot pool; by the relief of being away from the stone hovel that was Flane. Returned to her rightful place. Reunited with the book. In command of a pliable Jaeger and an imprisoned Morana. And she had blunted the potency of Jael Furyck too. Taking her husband, killing her baby.

Draguta couldn't stop smiling.

There were problems – of course, there were problems – but for now, she felt comfortable letting the solutions come to her. She felt no panic. No urgency. Just an overwhelmingly sublime peace.

Let everyone panic around her.

She was in complete control.

***

It was still raining.

'My trousers are so wet, I can't tell if I've pissed myself!' Thorgils laughed.

Jael was too cold to laugh. For all the things she could have and should have been thinking about, what was at the forefront of her mind was how quickly she could get to a fire.

Her teeth were chattering.

'It's not that cold!' Thorgils insisted with a grin, looking at her miserable, wet face.

Jael glowered at him. 'Why do you feel the need to talk to me? Go find another friend. Your queen wishes to be alone.'

'Well, Jael, I don't think that's true,' Thorgils insisted. 'For I've a bit of salt fish in my pouch. Likely it's wet now, but I'm sure you'd enjoy chewing on something while you ride?'

'You think you can bribe me?' Jael grumbled, watching as he pulled a limp strip of fish out of his pouch and wiggled it at her. 'With salt fish?' And finally, she did laugh. 'I hardly think I want to eat that! You can take your soggy fish and stuff it in that big mouth of yours.' Once, she had craved salt fish endlessly, she remembered. Not so long ago.

She had little appetite now.

Thorgils shrugged, taking a bite. 'Suit yourself,' he mumbled, letting Rufus slip back to walk with Fyn, who would surely be better company.

Gant had been off with the scouts, checking the road ahead, and now he made his way back to her. 'All clear that I can see,' he reported, shaking his dripping hair out of his eyes. 'No one and nothing is lurking out there.'

'Good. And hopefully, it stays that way. We need to get to Rissna before our neighbours start getting nervous. If we're not there tomorrow, they might pack up and head home.'

'If your cousin has anything to do with it, I'm sure they will. Getta won't be happy, and she won't be quiet about it.'

'You think she'll be there?'

Gant nodded. 'I do. I know your cousin far better than I'd choose to, and she's not going to let Raymon have his way about anything. Not if there's something she can do to stop him. Like I keep saying, you're going to have your work cut out for you.'

Jael grinned, not caring one bit about Getta. Her mind had already floated away to thoughts of being reunited with Eadmund. She needed the Iskavallan army to attack Hest. And she needed to attack Hest to save Eadmund, and what Getta thought about anything was completely irrelevant, as her cousin would soon find out.

***

The Vandaals were surprised to find that they were the first to arrive in the small settlement of Rissna. A messenger turned up just after they did, with a note to say that the Brekkans had encountered a delay.

Getta flew into a rage, furious with the insult. 'We should leave!' she demanded, clutching her son to her chest. 'My cousins do not even have the decency to be here on time! They have humiliated you! What will everyone think?'

Raymon couldn't get a word in to tell her that he didn't care what anyone thought.

Getta lowered her voice, conscious of the silence; convinced that people were outside their large, luxuriously furnished tent, listening. She hadn't wanted to stay in the hall. It looked no better than the charred shell of an old ship – not big or comfortable enough for the needs of the King and Queen of Iskavall – so she'd waited in the drizzle while her servants hastily erected the tent they had slept in on their journey. 'They will think you're a fool, is what they'll think. A toy! Something to play with. Until they've had their fun, that is, and then they will simply kill you!' Getta felt sick, sharp pains shooting through her chest as her baby son whimpered against it. 'I don't want anything to happen to you, Raymon. What will become of us if you're murdered? Be it by my cousins or one of your own men, who think you too weak to be their king.'

Raymon was caught between wanting to yell at his wife and needing to comfort her. She was changing her mood faster than he could blink, and he didn't know what to respond to first. 'Getta,' he sighed. 'You must try to calm down. Lothar doesn't like it when you're upset.'

Getta was too angry to care.

'I'm not a toy or a child. We have come to meet with your cousins, so I will hear them out when they arrive and make my decision then,' Raymon said, trying to sound more in control than he felt when he looked at his wife's irate face. 'But it will be *my* decision. They will not make me do anything that isn't in the interests of Iskavall. Iskavall will come first. I will not sacrifice our kingdom for anyone's ambition.'

Getta took a deep breath, pleased to hear it. 'What you choose to do will speak volumes to your men about your strength. You may give them arm rings and praise their feats of bravery, but that is just ceremony. Just words. It doesn't inspire true loyalty. They only care about what they see their king do. How their king acts. And you must act as a true king. One who will not be pushed around by Brekka. A king they want to follow. Not one they just want to kill.'

Raymon nodded slowly, realising that for all her wild fury,

Getta might actually be right.

***

Neither of them wanted to return to the castle, but Evaine was more inclined to face Jaeger than she was a night in her father's shack, squeezed into that tiny bed with Eadmund. She wanted to be alone with him, so, leaving Rollo in the tavern, blissfully happy in the company of three, half-naked, equally drunk women, and dropping Morac off at his cottage, Eadmund and Evaine returned to the castle.

Eadmund wasn't happy about it.

'We can find somewhere tomorrow,' Evaine insisted, listening to his grumbles as they walked towards the stairs. 'But for tonight, let's forget about Jaeger. I just want to be with you.' She rested her head against Eadmund's chest, feeling the strength of his arm wrapped around her as they walked. It felt like a shield, protecting her against all those who meant her harm.

'Eadmund!'

Evaine sighed, not wanting to turn around, but Eadmund was already moving towards the hall, pulling her with him.

'Where have you been all evening?' Draguta called from the high table before they could slip up the stairs. 'I had thought that we would be eating together. Celebrating our return.' She inhaled, wrinkling her nose. 'You smell as though you've crawled out of a barrel of ale. Hardly what I would expect from a king. You are not one of the common folk like that great beast, Rollo. Let him go where he belongs. You belong in the castle, with me. Where I can keep an eye on you. Where I can ensure that you are doing everything I require.'

Jaeger, who was sitting next to Draguta at the high table,

frowned.

So did Evaine.

'Now, come, come. Come and sit down, and we shall toast to our new beginning. All of us! All of us have a second chance, don't we, now that I have forgiven you all.' Draguta smiled, looking from Evaine to Jaeger to Eadmund, ignoring the snarl curling Jaeger's lips and the cold fury in Eadmund's bleary eyes. 'We all have a chance to make our dreams come true. I'm sure I'm not the only one with dreams, am I? Evaine? Jaeger? And we shall only realise them if we decide what we are fighting for. *Who* we are fighting. And let me be very clear. It is *not* each other. We will only defeat our enemies by using our strengths, not by undermining each other. We must be united, for the threat coming our way will be great. Greater than you can imagine.'

Three faces turned to her in confusion, but Draguta ignored them, lifting her goblet. 'To new beginnings!'

***

Jael woke up with a mouthful of water. She spluttered, rolling to the side as Aleksander loomed over her, dripping.

'Come on, we've got the tents up!' he called over the thunderous downpour, offering her a hand. 'Let's go!'

Jael was surprised that she'd fallen asleep. She remembered sitting down, her back against the tree, just wanting to rest for a moment before helping with the tents. But now it was so dark, and the rain was thundering down, and she was wet through and shaking. So, blinking to try and see, she followed Aleksander towards the nearest tent.

Bending her head, Jael hurried inside, sitting down next to Karsten and Axl, who looked just as wet as she felt. The rain fell in sheets across the front of the tent as more men hurried inside. Yawning, she watched as Aleksander joined them, followed by Gant and Torstan.

Thorgils shook his hair all over them and sat down with a thump. 'Got anything to eat?' he asked with a grin.

Jael squinted at him with one eye, the other one deciding to stay asleep. She looked around the tent, but there was no bed. There was barely any room to lie down, but there was Aleksander's shoulder, and, with another yawn, she leaned towards him, pleased when he edged closer so she could rest her head on him.

And closing her eyes, she tried to find Eadmund and Oss. It felt so long since they'd been there, together and happy, that Jael was beginning to wonder if it had all been a dream...

CHAPTER TWENTY SEVEN

Biddy ran to grab Ido as he charged out of the cottage, down the path, barking at a cat that was languidly walking down the road. Edela had fallen asleep in her chair and looked to be having a good dream, and Biddy hadn't wanted to wake her.

But Ido had.

When she returned with the guilty-looking culprit under her arm, Edela was yawning herself awake.

'Sorry about that,' Biddy said. 'I thought it would be nice with the door open for a while. Good to air out the place a bit. If only Ido didn't think that every cat or chicken was coming to attack us.'

Edela laughed hoarsely as Biddy hurried to check on the water she'd left boiling in the cauldron, preparing to make a tea. 'Well, who knows, perhaps Draguta will turn all the animals against us? The way Morana Gallas did with those ravens?' Speaking of ravens reminded her of Jael, and Edela was suddenly overcome with sadness, wondering once again what to do about Amma, who she knew was most certainly pregnant.

'Well, that's a thought that will keep me awake tonight,' Biddy snorted. 'And not a pleasant one, thank you. I shall no doubt dream about being pecked to death by chickens!'

'No more than you deserve, Biddy Halvor, having wrung a good many of their poor necks in your lifetime,' Edela grinned.

Biddy ignored her, looking through her bottles of herbs.

'How about lemon balm? I have a bit of lavender I can throw in there too. Might help us both calm down a bit.'

'I think I need to,' Edela said, 'after the dream I've just had.'

Biddy was curious. 'What did you dream about, then?'

'I think we might need Marcus to help make sense of it. Let's have our tea first, then we can go and find him. I'll tell you all about it then.'

Biddy didn't appear impressed by having to wait so long, but Edela felt so unsettled by what she'd seen that she needed a moment to digest it all.

For she had seen Draguta Teros stabbed to death, then get up and walk away.

***

It would have been rude to simply rush into the hall and stick her hands near the flames, but Jael felt tempted as she stood next to her brother, jiggling her legs as Reinhard Belleg, the Lord of Rissna, greeted them formally, eager for the king and queen to meet his entire family, which had expanded since their last visit.

He had a lot of children – three girls and five boys – and none of them appeared to be enjoying standing out in the rain either. Eventually, Jael sneezed, and Reinhard quickly realised that the king and queen were wet through, and his grizzled face reddened like an apple. 'Come inside! Come inside! Your guests are in there, waiting. Or, at least, some of them are. My old hall's not large enough to fit you all, I'm afraid. The Vandaals have chosen to stay in their own tents. You could do the same, of course, but if not, I have accommodation ready for you. Fresh linens and furs. Servants too.'

Jael wished that Reinhard would move his feet as he talked. It was still raining, and she'd been wet and cold for two, long, arse-numbing days. Finally, Jael gave up waiting and marched past him towards the open doors of the hall.

Axl looked after his sister, then turned to Reinhard. 'After you,' he said, just as eager to get out of the rain.

'You certainly chose the wrong time to travel, my lord,' Reinhard smiled as he walked alongside his king. He was a big man, who looked awkward in his new green tunic, which was ill-fitting. A thick nest of curly grey hair jiggled on top of his head, and a bushy grey-and-white beard covered much of his face. He tugged on it nervously as he headed into the hall. 'We were beginning to wonder where the next rain would come from. The crops were looking thirsty indeed. Now, after two days of this, they're swimming!' He stammered to a stop seeing Jael and Ravenna Vandaal standing awkwardly before one another in front of the fire. Neither of them had a drink, nor a seat, and glancing at his weary-looking wife, Reinhard inclined his head towards the two women, his eyes bulging in panic.

'Jael,' Ravenna smiled, unaware of the fuss. 'It's been many years since I last saw you. You are quite different, I think.'

'It hasn't been that long, has it?' Jael wondered, one eye on the fire Ravenna was blocking. 'I don't think I've changed much over the years, have I, Axl?' she asked her brother as he joined them. Aleksander and Gant were outside sorting out the horses and accommodation with Thorgils.

In the rain.

Axl was quickly uncomfortable. He didn't feel much like a king yet, but he didn't want to sound like Jael's little brother either. It was a winding path he was navigating in his mind. Eventually, he just smiled. 'I think you are. A little. Being a queen would do that, wouldn't you agree, my lady?' He bowed to Ravenna, who simply stared at him, amazed by how much he looked like his father.

'I would, and please, call me Ravenna,' she said. 'I do think that becoming a queen or a king changes you. It makes you more aware of yourself. And others. Though that is sadly not true of everyone who ascends to a throne.'

They all knew who she was talking about, though none of them mentioned Lothar by name.

The hall was bright. Reinhard had brought out his expensive beeswax candles, seeing how dull the day was, and their flames danced in sconces around the walls, flooding them with a golden warmth; infusing the smoky corners of the hall with a sweet aroma. Jael eased herself around Ravenna, held her hands to the flames and sighed, not caring for a moment that her trousers were stuck to her legs, or that her hair was trailing down her face, dripping over her mail. She thought of Tig, hoping Fyn was giving him a good rub down and a carrot.

Ravenna tensed suddenly, and Jael and Axl turned to see the tiny figure of their cousin Getta enter the hall, followed by her tall husband, who appeared as nervous as his wife looked angry. Jael glanced back at Ravenna, noting the displeasure on her face as she studied her daughter-in-law. Turning back, Jael could see the fire bloom in Getta's eyes as she strode towards them, her blue dress swishing angrily around her legs.

Raymon hurried to get in front of her, and he was the first to reach Axl. 'My lord,' he said quickly, attempting a smile.

Axl smiled back, nodding at Getta. 'Cousin. I hear congratulations are in order on the birth of your son.'

Jael could sense Reinhard hovering behind them all, wondering when it would be the right moment to usher them to the tables. Meat was roasting – she could smell it – and for the first time in days, Jael was in agreement with her growling stomach. She was actually hungry.

'*Congratulations?*' Getta spat. 'And should I offer you congratulations on your ascension to the throne, *Cousin*? You who murdered my father? My brother?' Her voice was shrill, and the hall hushed quickly.

Raymon swallowed. Getta had certainly not been shy about her feelings, but he'd thought that she might have allowed herself a breath or two before unleashing her long-planned tirade.

Jael eyed the tray of perch and mussels that passed her, followed by an enormous platter of what looked like roast boar. For some reason, it reminded her of Eirik and Oss, and she felt an overwhelming need to go home.

Her attention snapped back to her cousin, who had sucked all the air out of the hall, and any words from Axl's mouth, it seemed, as he opened and closed it without saying anything in response. 'Your father was a loathsome rapist, and your brother was a useless weed. They stole the throne from Axl, who was the rightful heir, and then proceeded to destroy our kingdom. And now they're both dead, so what do you plan to do about that, Getta?' Jael leaned over her tiny cousin, wet braids dripping on the floor reeds.

It was Getta's turn to be lost for words. Her eyes flared as she gripped Raymon's arm, squeezing it tightly, demanding he act.

Raymon opened his mouth, but Jael held up a hand. 'We've had a long, wet ride. We need to see to our men and our horses before we can sit down and enjoy a pleasant meal with all of you, so why not hold that thought until we return.' She eyed her spluttering cousin. 'That should give you enough time to think up something else to say, Getta. Perhaps you could find a reason why Lothar and Osbert should have lived? Though I imagine you'd still be hard-pressed to answer that come tomorrow.' And smiling at Ravenna, and nodding at an openmouthed Reinhard, she grabbed Axl's arm and almost dragged him out of the hall.

Ravenna bit her lip, trying not to laugh.

Her eyes were full of humour, though, and it didn't go unnoticed by a furious Getta. 'You see?' she hissed at Raymon as the Furycks headed for the doors. 'You see how they mock me? How casually they speak of murder? Who will they decide to kill next, I wonder? *You?*' She was seething, trembling with rage.

Raymon blinked at his mother, who had finally gotten her face under control.

'Let us sit down,' Ravenna said calmly. 'I'm very much looking forward to trying your mead, Reinhard,' she smiled. 'It smells delicious.'

Reinhard was relieved to change the subject, and he rushed to show the Vandaals to the high table as some of the Iskavallan lords made their way inside, shaking the rain from their cloaks.

Getta's boots remained stuck to the floorboards, though, as Raymon put an arm around her back, trying to move her gently towards the table, not knowing what was going to happen next.

***

Bram was gripped by an unfamiliar sense of panic as he sat at the high table finishing a cup of ale. He was a calm man, but his body had been jolted by the dragon and his head was reeling from the news about Fyn.

And now he was in charge of a sprawling fort. Or, at least, its garrison.

He wondered what Jael had been thinking.

Scratching his beard, he tried to think as Gisila muttered next to him. 'The hole in the wall needs to be filled in quickly. Can you have more men working on it?'

Bram looked up. 'I could, but more men will get in each other's way. We want a solid, well-built wall, and from what I understand, the stonemasons have it in hand. They don't require more help, just more time.'

Gisila was fretting, her mind overflowing with worries. 'And what about the other walls? The dragur climbed them! So what are you doing about that?' Leaning forward, she cut a slice of smoked cheese, glancing at her sister, who had walked into the hall with Aedan and Kayla.

She looked terrible.

'I have men in the forest, cutting trees. They've been in there since yesterday. We'll be making more stakes. Knocking them into the ground all around the walls. Digging the ditch deeper and wider. I've sent more braziers up to the ramparts too. Burning day and night. We'll keep the fires going.'

'And the fletchers?' Amma asked shyly, remembering that she was supposed to be helping Gisila. 'We'll need more arrows, won't we?' Gisila offered her the tray of cheese, but she quickly shook her head.

Bram nodded. 'The fletchers are busy. The sea-fire shed is filling up again. I have the armourers working on spearheads, arrowheads, helmets. We're constructing more catapults too. They'll take most of them to Hest, but we must have enough here. And the carpenters and shipbuilders are down at the harbour, where they've been since dawn. Everything is in hand, I promise.'

Gisila was pleased to hear it, though she couldn't settle. Without Jael and Axl in the fort, she couldn't settle at all. She stood, smiling at her sister. 'Come, have some supper,' she urged, but Branwyn shook her head and looked away. Gisila was worried, noticing how Branwyn's usually round cheeks appeared sunken and dull. She wasn't sure she'd eaten since Kormac and Aron's deaths.

And then there was Amma, who was looking oddly pale; worried about Axl, no doubt. Gisila was worried about Axl too. The Iskavallans were not to be trusted. Ranuf had told her that enough times. What came out of their mouths was usually masking the plots they were brewing in the shadows.

She hoped that Jael and Axl would be able to see through their lies.

***

Axl hurried outside after Jael, not knowing what to say. He didn't imagine his sister's mood was going to help them convince Raymon Vandaal of anything except to pack up his family and leave.

Jael saw a sodden Gant heading towards them as she turned around to her brother. 'Say it.'

Axl looked surprised. 'What?'

'You think I was wrong. Talking to Getta like that. It's what Gisila would have said, no doubt.' It was still raining, and Jael was already missing the warmth of the fire. 'But Getta is going to cause us problems, so I'm not going to sit around in there pretending otherwise. We need to let her know that we're not here to wring our hands and apologise. Not for killing Lothar and Osbert. They came into our kingdom and stole your throne. They got what they deserved for that, and for what Lothar did to Gisila. They got what they deserved.' Jael glanced at Gant, who looked guilty, him being the one who'd murdered Osbert.

Axl blinked, feeling the rain running into his boots. It didn't appear to be dampening his sister's fiery mood. He looked up as Aleksander, Fyn, and Thorgils approached, having seen to the horses.

'Not the best weather for tents!' Aleksander grinned before seeing the scowl on Jael's face. 'What happened?' He noticed Axl's deepening frown, and he turned back to Jael. 'What did you do?'

'Me?' Jael tried to look innocent, but she felt bad. Tiredness had loosened her hungry tongue, and it wasn't the best start, which was why she'd hurried Axl outside, hoping to take a moment before trying again. She thought of Ranuf, who would no doubt have been just as mortified as Gisila.

She needed to start again.

Taking a deep breath, Jael turned to her brother. 'Let's make sure everyone has a dry bed for the night, then we'll bring some of the men back to the hall with us. Ivaar and Karsten. Rork and the Island lords. Beorn and Torstan. Maybe even Thorgils,' she grinned, happy to see Thorgils' smiling face. 'And I promise to try and behave.' Axl looked relieved, Jael thought as he nodded, disappearing with Gant.

'Are you alright?' Aleksander wondered, wanting to smooth away her intense frown. He had always done it, much to her irritation. It had been a good way to remind Jael to stop. To calm down.

Now, he couldn't touch her at all, and it still felt odd.

'No,' Jael admitted, looking from Aleksander to Thorgils, seeing that both of them knew what she meant, but not wanting to say anything more in front of Fyn. 'Not really. But here we are, so I'd better start being alright. When we were in Hest, I just left Eadmund to do all the king and queen things. But now he's not here, so I suppose I should try and get better at it.' Jael ducked her head, looking to leave. 'I'll just go and see Tig, then I'll head back to the hall. It should give Getta a chance to cool down. Though, after what I said, I'm not sure that's possible.' And remembering her cousin's puckered face, she laughed as she pulled up her hood, heading for the stables.

***

Having decided that Marcus needed a good meal and a chance to breathe some fresh air, Biddy brought him to Edela's cottage, leaving Astrid to stay with Hanna.

But Edela saw that Marcus was barely breathing now as he chewed over what she'd just revealed about her dream.

'Are you sure Draguta was dead? That the knife had killed

her? That she wasn't just injured?' Marcus leaned forward on the stool, rubbing a hand over his new beard.

'Oh yes, the girl who stabbed her pulled the knife out and stuck it back in a few times. Her blood pooled on the floor. She was very dead. They left her there for a time, and Draguta didn't move. Not once. Her eyes were fixed open, glazed even. And then they took her away. Left her body in a bedchamber while they discussed a pyre. The king had demanded a pyre, they said. But when the servants left, Draguta got up and walked out of the castle.'

Biddy had barely blinked. 'Was it an ordinary knife?'

'No.'

Marcus peered at Edela. 'Why do you say that?'

'I don't know, but it felt like a special knife.' Closing her eyes, Edela inhaled slowly, squinting into the darkness. 'It had symbols on it. The same symbols as Jael's sword.' She opened her eyes, staring at Marcus.

Marcus froze.

'What is it?' Edela wriggled forward to the edge of her chair. 'What do you know?'

Marcus took a big gulp of his tea. 'There was a rumour that Wulfsig, the swordmaker, had saved the materials from Jael's sword and made himself a knife. But when he died, none was found. Some thought it was just a story. A myth.'

'Well, I hope it was just a story,' Edela said slowly. 'If the knife and the sword were made of the same materials, and that was the knife that killed Draguta, it didn't work. Not in my dream.'

'But what happened to her next?' Biddy frowned. 'Where did she go?'

'I don't know,' Edela admitted. 'I didn't see that part. I saw her on a horse, riding away with a girl. But I've no idea where they went. They looked to be escaping. It was dark.'

'And she was very much alive? Not some sort of spirit?' Marcus wondered.

'No, not a spirit. She survived being killed. She was alive!' No one spoke.

The fire sizzled, under assault from a steady downpour.

'This is a worry,' Marcus said, at last. 'But we need to know more. We need some certainty about this knife. If it was in any way the same as Jael's sword, then it changes everything. If it couldn't kill Draguta, then how will Jael stop her?'

Edela tried to calm her own rising panic. 'I'll try to dream about it. See if I can discover any more.'

Biddy felt cold all over. 'Who is to say the prophecy is still right? You've seen it yourself, Edela. With Jael. A dreamer's vision can be wrong. Isn't that what Lydea told you?'

Marcus' eyebrows were up. 'You spoke with Lydea? A *goddess* spoke to you?'

Edela nodded distractedly. 'Yes, she said that Draguta is more powerful than they realised. That she can weave the threads.'

Marcus hadn't moved, but it was as though everything inside his body was shifting. Shades of dark and light were moving and changing, and when he blinked, it felt as though he was falling backwards into a great abyss. 'If that is true, then I don't know what hope we have of stopping Draguta. If that is true, she will become more powerful than the gods themselves.'

'How?' Edela wondered.

'The Book of Darkness made her a threat before, but now?' Marcus sighed, tiredness hindering his ability to focus. 'If Draguta can weave the threads, if she can survive being killed by a magical knife designed to kill her, then she is truly capable of anything.'

CHAPTER TWENTY EIGHT

The arrival of Garren and Aldo Maas was the only thing that calmed Getta down. She allowed herself to be shown to the high table, taking a seat beside her husband, her temper bubbling at a frothing boil, her eyes occasionally darting to where Garren sat, whispering to his father, a sly look on his face.

Raymon placed a hand on Getta's knee. She quickly pushed it away.

He'd said nothing. Nothing to defend her or her family. Nothing!

She was livid.

But the Maas' did not need to know that, so Getta clenched her fists and smiled at Reinhard, who was far more comfortable commanding men on a battlefield than he was navigating the tricky waters of social discourse. He kept glancing at his wife, who had a calmer air about her as she walked around the tables with the mead bucket, smiling at her guests as she lifted the ladle and filled their cups, occasionally nodding at her husband so that he might calm down and enjoy himself.

Raymon looked up as Axl and Jael walked back into the hall, followed by a straggling train of wet men whose eyes were quickly on the fire and the mead bucket. Jael didn't look to have improved her mood, he thought, staring at her stern face. Her brother seemed conscious of that as he made an attempt to smile, but Raymon felt his insides churn at the thought of trying to keep his wife and Jael from killing each other. Though, when he looked at the Queen of Oss, he doubted it would be much of a fight. Her face was covered in bruises and cuts, and, still dressed in her armour, she looked ready for battle.

Reinhard was quickly on his feet, showing Jael and Axl to the high table while their men found their way to the few remaining seats. His eyes scoured the hall, checking the tables, suddenly worried that they wouldn't have enough food.

Jael didn't notice as she took a seat next to Raymon, leaving Axl to sit between Getta and Ravenna. She reached for her cup, already full of mead, taking a long drink, and though it was too sweet, it was a welcome balm for her ratty mood and sharp tongue. 'I apologise for keeping you waiting. We've had a busy time in Andala. Another attack. This time the dragur.'

Raymon could see her closely now, and the cuts on her face appeared fresh.

'They attacked Andala?' He was speechless. 'Your fort?'

'Mmmm,' Jael nodded. 'After the dragon and the serpent, we weren't at our best, but we managed to put them down in the end.'

Raymon was wide-eyed. 'How?'

Jael frowned, realising that they hadn't decided what to say about the Book of Aurea. It was never advisable to reveal your strengths or your weaknesses to your enemy, or to your neighbour, who might one day become your enemy. She peered over the rim of her cup, noting the steely-eyed interest of some of the Iskavallans looking their way.

'We trapped them, burned them, cut off their heads. Everything we could think of,' Jael said casually. 'I've no idea how many more are out there, but the ones who attacked us are ash.'

Raymon looked disturbed. 'Do you think they'll come to Iskavall?'

'They'll come everywhere. Eventually. We have more enemies in the South than we ever imagined.' Jael stopped herself, realising that no one wanted Briggit Halvardar to find out that they'd broken her curse, and though Andala was surrounded by dreamer protections, Rissna wasn't. None of them had brought their symbol stones, wanting Edela and Eydis to be able to watch over them.

Getta was furious as she listened to Axl trying to make polite conversation on one side of her, while her husband appeared eager to talk to Jael on her other side. She didn't want him to do anything other than demand an apology for her cousin's appalling treatment of his wife. Pressing her hand on his knee, she squeezed hard.

Raymon knew what Getta wanted, but he couldn't interrupt Jael now.

'That's why we need to combine our armies. To attack Hest. Take the Book of Darkness and destroy it. It's the only chance we have of saving Osterland.'

'And how do you know that?' Getta sneered, leaning around Raymon. 'Are you a dreamer now?'

Jael ignored her cousin while a servant delivered her plate. 'Yes. I am.'

Getta sat back as her own plate was placed in front of her.

'You are?' Raymon was surprised.

Jael grabbed a chicken leg and took a bite, nodding.

But Getta wasn't about to be batted aside so quickly. 'Well, dreamer or not, why should we follow you? Why should we risk our army in *your* fight?'

Axl stepped into the conversation with a fair amount of trepidation. 'Because the prophecy says that Jael is the one to kill the woman who has the Book of Darkness. The one who sent the dragur, and the dragon, and the serpent. The prophecy tells of how Furia's daughter will defeat her.'

Getta snorted so loudly that most eyes in the hall turned towards her. 'Furia's daughter? And why do you think that *you're* Furia's daughter? I'm just as much a daughter of Furia as you are. So is Amma. You've assumed that mantle as though it is yours alone, never giving either of us a thought.'

Jael held her tongue.

'I don't imagine that either you or Amma would be capable of defeating this woman with her magic book, would you, Getta dear?' Ravenna asked gently. 'It sounds as though it's something that only Jael is trained to do.'

Getta glowered at her mother-in-law, though she didn't disagree.

Thorgils winked at Jael, who tried not to roll her eyes. He nudged Aleksander, who looked just as amused by the sour faces at the high table. It was always entertaining watching Jael squirm as she tried to fight her temper and her innate dislike of behaving appropriately.

'You are welcome to lead the Iskavallan army, of course,' Jael said to her cousin. 'No one is stopping you. Though I have my reasons for believing that the Furia's daughter referred to in the prophecy is me. Perhaps I'll tell you what they are later. In private. I'm sure you'll thank me for not revealing them here.'

Getta frowned, not knowing what that meant.

The pressure of her hand on Raymon's knee was only growing, and eventually, Raymon realised that he had to bring up the matter of the murders. 'It doesn't sit well with my wife or my people that you and your brother were so eager to murder your kings. Two of them,' he almost whispered. 'Our kingdoms have always been close, but there are rumours... fears... that your ambition extends far beyond Brekka's borders. That you wish to claim Iskavall for yourselves. That your push into the South is not about safety but power.'

Jael sighed, turning to Raymon, who, she was disappointed to discover, looked far less of a man than he needed to be. He was afraid of his wife. And looking into his blinking eyes, she could tell that he was afraid of her too.

But his men looked hard, she thought. Conniving, but tough. Tougher than their king, who almost shook alongside her. He appeared to have little muscle on him, and despite a pair of broad shoulders, he almost curled forward, not wanting to be seen. But, given some time, perhaps he would grow into his role?

If he lived that long.

'Your wife saw her father with only one eye. Her brother too. That's love, I suppose. And love can be blind.' Jael could hear Getta hissing beside her husband. 'We saw differently, as did the people of Brekka. We saw what Lothar did when he stole the throne, and the night Axl took off his head, he saw what Lothar had done to our mother. He saw the lashings across her back as she was thrown on a bed, Lothar beating her after he'd forced her to marry him.'

Raymon gulped, feeling Getta's hand ease away from his thigh.

Neither of them spoke.

'If the same thing had happened to your mother, what would you have done?' Jael wondered. She leaned forward, seeing the confusion in Getta's eyes and the interest in Ravenna's. 'The Brekkan throne was stolen. It was never meant to be Lothar's, nor Osbert's. We reclaimed it. And that is all. Brekka is Axl's kingdom now. The Slave Islands is my kingdom. All we want to do is protect our people. And to do that, we need your help.'

***

Edela was alone. Puzzled. Staring into the flames. Thinking about her talk with Marcus. Worrying about that knife. Defeating Draguta had been a terrifying prospect when Jael had a sword capable of killing her, but now?

Edela couldn't let anyone go to Hest without knowing the truth about that knife. So, closing her eyes and gripping Jael's arm ring, Edela blew out all her tension and fear in a stuttering breath, shaking her shoulders loose as she sunk back into the soft fur of her chair, trying to remember the dreamer she was.

Old, but not done yet.

***

Raymon worried that Getta was about to lose control of her tongue again. She had held onto it during the meal, and now, as Reinhard's guests stood and started to mingle, a few cups of mead louder, he kept glancing at his wife, who was eyeing Jael and Axl with a look he knew well. She was standing with Ravenna and Reinhard's wife and daughters, but he could tell that she wasn't listening to anything the women were discussing. Her eyes were fixed on her cousins.

It appeared that nothing Jael or Axl had said had changed Getta's mind.

But had it changed his?

As he studied Garren and the warriors who gathered around him and his father, Raymon wasn't sure. He wasn't sure who he had to please. Who he *wanted* to please. If anyone. Perhaps all he needed to do was think about what was right for his people? How to keep them safe and protect his kingdom? Worrying about the ambitions of his men was surely secondary to that.

'He doesn't look like he has a clue,' Aleksander murmured, turning to Gant.

Gant smiled. 'I think Axl knows how that feels.'

Axl tried to look indignant, but Gant was right. 'I think it's easier to become a king when you're older. When you've got arm rings and a reputation. Not just the son of someone.'

'Perhaps. But some people aren't meant to rule, whatever their age. Raymon seems too concerned with what everyone thinks,' Jael muttered. 'You can't be a good king if you're afraid of upsetting people. You need to form your own opinions. Be decisive. He's wobbling like a stool over there. Look at his eyes, darting about, from his men to his wife, and back again.'

'He's a boy, Jael,' Gant tried. 'Of course he's going to look for opinions elsewhere. Axl's right. It's easier to become a king when you've got experience. He barely knows how to make a decision for himself at this age, let alone for an entire kingdom. And Getta isn't making it easy.'

Jael didn't feel inclined to be as tolerant as Gant, and she turned away, her attention drawn to one warrior in particular: Garren Maas. A man with a formidable reputation. 'I've a feeling you're more understanding than his men. They don't have any respect for him. You can see it in their eyes. We're going to have problems.'

All three men turned to her.

'Is that your dreamer's instinct talking?' Aleksander wondered.

Jael shrugged. 'No idea. But I'm watching. Listening. Remembering how tolerant the Iskavallans are of their kings. Likely Raymon's in trouble whatever he chooses to do.' And she turned away, looking for Fyn and Thorgils.

Gant didn't take his eyes off Raymon, worried that she was right.

***

Dara knew the man well. He was a dreamer but not a Follower, and she trusted him implicitly. He was her kin after all. A man she had known since he was a boy.

A man she could rely on.

She smiled. 'You have done well, Aemon. Very well.'

He had long dark hair and blue eyes that twinkled. 'It was not a secret, this knife,' Aemon said, staring at the ivory-handled weapon that he had placed on the table between them, watching the way the flames revealed the symbols etched along its blade. 'Others know of its existence.'

'They do,' Dara agreed. 'But not many. And those who do can be trusted, I believe. They will be dead before long, those old men, and they will take the secret to their pyres.'

Aemon nodded. 'Yes, you're right. They didn't want to even tell me.'

Dara stood. 'And you will never tell another soul, I know. This knife will stay with me now. I shall keep it safe. Away from those who would use it for their own ends. Wulfsig made a mistake,' she said, walking Aemon to the door. 'Though that mistake may be the best thing he ever did.'

***

The conversation in the hall had gone on too long for Getta, and she left to feed Lothar in her tent, but once he was sound asleep in his basket, she was still too angry to go back to the hall. It wasn't dark, but she crawled into bed, wanting to put everything out of her mind. Unable to sleep, she tossed and turned, growing even more irritable, so by the time Raymon stumbled into the tent some hours later, she was ready to burst.

Raymon had been anticipating an attack, but he still wasn't prepared for her fury.

'You can see what they thought!' Getta hissed, conscious of how thin the walls of the tent were as they flapped in a strong wind. 'Aldo and Garren. Your men. You can see the way they looked at the Brekkans. They do not support this alliance!'

'I shall speak with them. Convince them.'

Getta wasn't listening. 'You will be killed. They will *kill* you!'

Raymon had barely taken off his boots. His head was spinning after too many cups of mead and too much conversation. He blinked. 'What?'

'Garren warned me. He said that there were rumours. Talk. About the Furycks. About how they will try to conquer Iskavall after killing you!'

Raymon's shoulders slumped as he pulled off his wet socks and then his trousers. 'You would listen to him?' He wriggled towards Getta, who wriggled away. 'Garren wants the throne for himself, and he wants to twist everything around so that he'll get it. Your cousins made sense tonight. I didn't see ambition in their eyes. Didn't you look at them? At their men? They've just been in a battle. They've come for our help, Getta, as we would if we were under attack. And if we don't unite our armies, soon it will be us. There's no doubt about it.'

'According to Jael.'

'Who is a dreamer.'

Getta sighed, so tired that she couldn't see a way to make Raymon listen.

But she would. She would. She wouldn't let him ruin her future or that of her son's. Raymon may have been tricked into believing Jael and Axl's ridiculous tale, but she wasn't gullible like her husband.

As he would soon find out.

***

Eydis and Biddy returned with the puppies, though Edela didn't say much to them. Her dream about Dara Teros and the knife stayed with her, and she wanted to keep it that way, hoping to find out more. So, after barely eating a perfectly nice stew, she hurried into her bed without a word.

Biddy was surprised but didn't show it. She knew Edela well enough to feel confident that she would come back to them in her own time. She talked to Eydis and the puppies instead, leaving Edela to roll over and close her eyes, gripping Dara Teros' note to Jael in her hand, eager to slip back into her dream.

Hoping to find out what Dara had done with that knife.

***

'Missing your cousin?' Aleksander grinned as he stopped by Jael, whose eyes were on the door. 'Looking for another chance to unleash that tongue of yours?'

Jael frowned at him. 'No. On both counts.'

'Ha!' Aleksander had never been bothered by Jael's temper. In fact, he found it impossible not to enjoy it when she got cross.

Jael dropped a hazelnut into her mouth. 'I wish Getta hadn't come. She has Raymon wrapped around her finger like a piece of yarn.'

'Well, I'm sure if anyone can figure out how to cut that yarn, it's you,' Aleksander said, helping himself to the bowl of nuts. 'You and that sharp tongue of yours.'

Jael frowned at him some more.

'Though I've a feeling you're in for a fight with Getta. You mightn't think you have anything in common, but you seem to share the Furyck temper. And Getta looks ready for a battle of words, if you ask me.'

Jael lifted an eyebrow as a thought popped into her head. 'Perhaps. Or perhaps I've got a weapon that will render her completely silent.' And she leaned forward, kissing his cheek. 'You're a very clever man indeed, Aleksander Lehr. Don't let anyone tell you otherwise!' And turning away to look for the mead bucket, Jael couldn't stop smiling.

***

Dara stared at the knife, her hands by her sides.

It wasn't made for her. It wasn't meant to exist at all. But it did. And if there was a chance she could stop Draguta before her sister became everything she had dreamed of... shouldn't she take it?

She shivered, turning away from the knife, looking around the cottage she'd hidden in for years, protected by the gods. Protected by the symbols she had carved around her walls. Across her floor. Safe and hidden.

For what?

Would it really matter if she died now?

The prophecy was written, protected from The Following. The Elderman of Tuura had enough knowledge to go forward. He would pass that on to those who would follow her.

Did it really matter if it didn't work?

If she died trying to remove the threat her sister posed?

Dara's shoulders were tight as she adjusted her satchel and blew out the lamp before turning back for the knife. And gripping that cool ivory handle, she slipped it into its scabbard, heading for the door.

CHAPTER TWENTY NINE

The day dawned gloomy but dry, and Jael felt relieved, if not slightly irritable as she walked towards the stables to check on Tig. The wind had flapped the walls of her tent all night long, blowing them in and out like a sail in a storm, and she'd tossed and turned in a constant state of disturbance.

She saw Getta walking up ahead of her with her servant, who was carrying a baby. Jael wanted to turn and walk away, her mind quickly rushing back to Harstad, but she ploughed on, realising that she couldn't run away from babies or her sniping cousin.

It was better to face things head-on.

'Good morning,' Jael said as she caught up to Getta, ignoring the gurgling baby. 'Did you sleep well?'

'What do *you* care?' Getta spat, quickly rounding on her cousin. 'You may have blinded my husband to your true intentions, but you will never pull the wool over my eyes. I see your ambition glowing like gold. I know what you truly want, what you and your brother have come here to claim, and it isn't support to defeat a made-up enemy! It's a way to defeat my husband. You think that because he's young, you'll be able to confuse him! Trick him! But you forget that you're facing a Furyck. You're not the only one who knows how to fight, Jael!' Getta had to look up a long way to see Jael's face, but nothing about her appeared intimidated when she took in all those cuts and bruises.

Jael glanced around, but apart from Getta's servant and a red-faced woman chasing a runaway goat, there was no one nearby. Bending down, she lowered her voice anyway. 'You're not a Furyck,' she whispered, her eyes on her cousin.

Getta stepped back, her pinched face suddenly blank. 'What?'

'Your father wasn't a Furyck. Our grandmother, it seems, had a lover. A merchant from Tingor. He was Lothar's real father. You're not a Furyck at all, so your father had no claim to our throne. Nor did your brother.'

It was impossible not to enjoy the horror in Getta's eyes as she blinked, twitching all over.

'What are you talking about? How would you know such a thing?' Getta's voice was barely a breath. It felt as though everything was spinning around her. She felt sick. 'You're making it up! Another game. Another story. You're making it up!'

'The Elderman of Tuura told me when he explained why I was Furia's daughter. Your father wasn't a Furyck. The dreamers knew it, and your grandmother knew it, as did her lover. But no one else.' Jael lifted her eyes and saw Ivaar and Karsten heading for the hall.

She felt impatient to leave.

Getta spluttered, sending her servant on her way with a distracted flap of a hand. 'You have no proof!'

'I don't.'

Getta narrowed her eyes. 'So there is no proof!'

'I'm not sure that's true. I could send some men to Tingor if you like? Make some enquiries? Hunt down your real grandfather, if he still lives? Perhaps he had other children? You may have other cousins. A whole family you don't know about.'

Getta started panicking, heat rushing to her cheeks. 'There's no need for that!' She was suddenly conscious of her wide-eyed servant, still staring at them as she slowly walked away.

Jael tried not to smile.

'And what will you do now? Humiliate me in front of my husband and his men?' Getta clenched her jaw, scanning Jael's face for any sign of her true intentions.

'It isn't a weapon, Getta, so I don't intend to wield it. I just thought it was time you knew that you're not a Furyck. That it's not a weapon *you* can wield. Not anymore. Not when I know the truth. And as for your husband, you will do well to support him. He is young, looking for guidance. I would hate you to guide him in the wrong direction. There are a lot of dangerous people about these days.' And with one last look at her slightly dazed cousin, Jael strode away, already looking forward to drying her boots in front of Reinhard's fire.

***

'Did you have any dreams?' Eydis wondered from her stool, pushing away the wet noses of Ido and Vella, who were impatient to go outside.

Edela froze, her hands on the sock she was about to put on her cold foot. 'I did. Yes. A scrambled mess of things I don't understand,' she mumbled, noting how keenly Biddy was looking at her. Edela didn't know what to tell her yet. She hadn't understood her dreams about Dara Teros and the knife, and she was reluctant to reveal anything until she had more information. Her eyes brightened suddenly as a memory returned. 'I did have a dream about Eadmund, though!'

'You did?' Eydis sat up straighter.

Closing her eyes, Edela took a deep breath as Biddy left the tray of hotcakes on the table and came to sit by the fire. 'He was in Hest.' She opened her eyes, surprised.

'I thought Jael said that he was somewhere else,' Biddy

said. 'Not Hest.'

'Mmmm, she did. But he is there now. He was with a man. Fighting a man.'

'Fighting?' Eydis was worried.

'Well, training, I suppose you'd call it,' Edela hurried to explain. 'They were laughing. Using wooden sticks or something. Naked.'

Biddy blinked. 'They were fighting naked?'

'I meant bare-chested,' Edela laughed. 'Eadmund looked... different.'

'How?' Eydis wondered.

'Well, he didn't look like the Eadmund I remember,' Edela said, not sure how to explain things. 'He was sharp-edged. Lean. Hungry.' She shrugged, realising that she had walked into a dark alley and couldn't find a way out. 'He looked like a champion warrior. One you wouldn't want to fight.'

Biddy frowned at Eydis, not knowing what to make of that.

Edela peered at their worried faces. 'He was safe, though. So whatever else is going on, that's good news, isn't it?'

'She's turning him into a weapon,' Eydis breathed. 'Isn't she? Draguta?'

Edela's smile vanished, knowing that Eydis was right. 'Yes, she is.'

'Then we must hurry, Edela. We must find a way to break the spell before it's too late. Before she unleashes Eadmund upon Jael!'

***

'I don't want you to go,' Evaine moaned, kissing Eadmund again. 'Please stay.'

'Would you rather Draguta was at the door, barking at us

both?' Eadmund grinned, getting off the bed. Evaine's naked body was a temptation he would usually find hard to resist, but he could almost feel Draguta urging him to the training ring where Rollo would no doubt already be waiting.

'But what will I do without you?' Evaine grumbled, following him to the door, too warm to put on any clothes.

'You can look for a house for us,' Eadmund smiled, wrapping his swordbelt around his waist. 'Unless you'd like to stay in the castle, near Jaeger? Spending every night in the hall with him?'

Evaine snorted. 'I would not!'

'Good.' Eadmund kissed her nose, noticing how freckled it was becoming. 'Then get dressed and find Morac. He'll keep you company and out of Jaeger's way.' Frowning, Eadmund realised that he would have to find out what had happened to his father, and whether Morac had killed him as Jael suspected.

And then he would have to decide what he was going to do about it.

***

Morac was incredulous. He had avoided the castle, not wanting to see Draguta. Not wanting to face the truth of what she'd surely done to his sister, so it was a shock to see that Morana was still in her chamber, sitting on her chair without a scratch on her. 'She's letting her live?'

Else nodded. 'She is. In fact, Draguta insists upon it.'

'And will she? Live?' Morac peered at his sister, who looked even more morose than usual as she stared past him to the door.

'She will. According to Dragmall, she will. There is no illness. Just the curse.' Else felt as though she was being watched. She kept turning around, worried that Draguta was outside the door, spying, listening. Somehow, she'd ended up with the task of keeping Morana alive, and Else knew very well what would happen to her if she failed to do so.

Morac felt sorry for his sister, trapped in her prison. He didn't know how to help her anymore. With Draguta back in the castle, it wasn't wise to entertain thoughts contrary to hers. And his most important job now was to keep Evaine safe. Eadmund was here, he knew, but Morac didn't trust him to protect his daughter.

For though Eadmund appeared to have made many changes recently, in a fight with Jaeger Dragos, Morac was certain that Eadmund would lose.

***

Bending over, Jaeger sucked in a breath. It had been days since he'd trained properly, and his lungs burned with the reminder. He looked to a slave, who stood just outside the ring with a towel and a tray. Holding his hand up to his opponent, Jaeger strode towards him, desperate for water.

His body was dripping from the heat of the morning sun, and his mind was swimming with thoughts of Draguta. He wanted to please her. The desire to make her happy pounded inside him like a drum, and she would be pleased by him getting stronger and sharper, he knew.

He didn't want Eadmund here. He didn't need him, and nor did Draguta, despite what she might have said.

If she was to have a champion, it was never going to be Eadmund Skalleson.

'I am impressed,' Draguta purred, stopping by the training ring. She was going to the tailor's with Brill, eager to replenish her dwindling supply of new dresses. 'You almost look like a king.'

'Almost?' Jaeger scowled, rolling back his shoulders.

Draguta frowned, sensing what was behind his performance. 'You will not interfere with Eadmund and Evaine. Eadmund is mine and Evaine is his little toy. Without her, he'll become morose, which is a headache I do not need. I want both of them here, do you understand me, Jaeger? Together. They are nothing to do with you, and you are nothing to do with them. Understood?'

Jaeger clenched his jaw, but the displeasure in her eyes soon relaxed it. 'Of course.'

'Good!' Draguta said, clapping her hands. 'Now, get back to your fighting. On my return, I shall inspect our ships. I am eager to see what progress you're making. We will require a large fleet to repel our invaders.'

'Invaders?' Jaeger was confused.

Draguta ignored him, turning to Brill, who was fanning herself nearby. 'Well, hurry up, you miserable creature, and let us get to the tailor's before he's drunk on wine and no use to us at all!'

***

Jael had sent Axl after Raymon as soon as breakfast was over. She wanted Raymon to feel more at ease around them; to hear from someone other than her. And Axl, she decided, was the perfect person for the job.

Axl wasn't so sure.

He walked Raymon Vandaal through the small fort which sat on the banks of a wide river, surrounded by pastureland. After all the rain that had fallen in the past few days, the river was flooding its banks, soaking the earth, turning everything into a bog. The two men kept to the wooden boards and stones that paved the way to the paddocks where the Iskavallan horses were being corralled.

'You're not married, then?' Raymon asked.

Axl froze, wondering how to explain his situation. 'Well... I'm hoping to be soon. I just have to kill my woman's husband first.'

'*Kill* him?' Raymon was glad that Getta wasn't within earshot.

Axl laughed. 'She was forced into the marriage by Lothar, so he could line his pockets and plot himself an escape from Hest. He didn't care at all that he was marrying his daughter to a monster.'

'You mean Amma?' Raymon was surprised by that. Getta obviously didn't know.

'Yes. We saved her from Jaeger Dragos and brought her back to Andala, but she's still married to the man, so I have to find a way to end him.'

'And what about him? Does he want her back?' Raymon was starting to relax. He felt less intimidated by Axl and not worried about Getta for the first time in days.

Axl shrugged. 'I don't know, and I don't care. He can't have her. She loves me. And he won't be alive for long anyway. His brothers are with us. You met Karsten last night. His other brother is back in Andala. Jaeger took off his arm, so he's learning how to ride and fight with the one he has left. And then he'll come with us. He wants to kill Jaeger too. Jaeger killed their father.'

Raymon stopped, turning to Axl. 'And Jaeger Dragos is with this woman now? Draguta? The one who has the book?'

Axl nodded. 'Together, they're powerful, so we have to come up with a way to stop them. All of them. To destroy the book. If we don't, we'll always be waiting for the next attack. And, I promise you, having had a dragon land on your fort, there's little you can do to protect yourself. Not even the gods can really help us now.'

Raymon ran a hand over his dark chin fluff, trying to think. 'The idea of joining this fight doesn't sit well with some of my men. Those who support the Maas' claim to the throne, at least. I don't think they ever liked your father. Or mine.'

'Well, now they're both dead, so it's up to us to decide what to do, isn't it? Jael isn't Brekka's queen any more than she's Iskavall's, but she's been chosen to lead us by the gods themselves. That's what the prophecy says. And I, for one, would choose to follow her anywhere. She knows how to fight. How to out-think the enemy. How to lead. She's a dreamer too, and if you want to give your son a future and keep your wife by your side, you'll need to risk upsetting a few ambitious men. Leave them to their whispering and choose to join us, because we will be fighting for all of Osterland.'

***

'You should rest,' Runa insisted as she caught up with Bram, who was walking faster than a man newly out of bed should be walking. 'It won't help anyone if you keel over!'

Bram turned, readying a grumble, but he saw the concern in her eyes, and he stopped himself, wheezing in a breath. 'I could do with something to drink,' he admitted. 'It's a warm day. I suppose I could sit down while I drank it.'

Runa blinked in surprise; she'd certainly been expecting a fight. 'Well, come on, you sit here, then. I'll go and find some ale.'

Now Bram did put up a fight. 'I don't need you waiting on me, Runa,' he insisted. 'You're not my servant.'

'No, I'm not,' Runa agreed with a wink before hurrying away to the hall.

Bram didn't have the energy to argue or follow her, so he took a seat at the nearest table, sighing in relief at the pleasure of taking the weight off his aching legs. He felt older than old. He felt half dead.

Ayla smiled as she joined him. 'You look as bad as I feel.'

Bram was happy to see her up and about, though she was right, he thought, she was very pale. 'The people of Andala should feel in safe hands with us to look after them, then!' Bram laughed, gasping at a sudden pain in his chest.

'Well, I hope it doesn't come to that. I don't think your crutch is going to be much use to fight off the next creature Draguta sends.'

'Unless it's elves,' Bram grinned. 'I can probably tackle a wee elf or two!' His smile fell away, his mind quickly turning to how vulnerable they were, waiting for Draguta to decide what to do next.

'You've obviously never met an elf, Bram!' Ayla laughed as Runa came back with a jug of ale and two cups. 'They can be vicious.' She saw the worry in his eyes, and her own smile faltered.

Draguta would come again, she knew. Or, if not her, then Briggit Halvardar and her Followers. And Ayla was suddenly worried that the Book of Aurea wouldn't be enough to stop any of them.

CHAPTER THIRTY

Reinhard had organised entertainment, and though Jael had no patience to stand around listening to Warunda, the poet, tell his well-loved tales of battles and glory, many of her men crowded around the small stage in the muddy square, while the old man strode from one side to the other, accompanied by two young women, one on a lyre, one on a drum, each adding a dramatic flair to his gravelly voice.

Jael was barely listening, still going over what Axl had said about his talk with Raymon. Her brother had felt confident that Raymon would help them, assuring her that the nervous young king had listened carefully and asked a lot of questions. It was a good sign, Jael supposed, or not, depending on how the winds blew and how manipulative Getta truly was.

Jael was agitated as she watched the performance, eager to go for a ride, feeling the need to be alone.

'Got a flea in your trousers?' Thorgils grinned, walking towards her with Karsten, who looked as bored as Jael.

'Thought you'd be listening to Warunda,' Jael said. 'Hoping to hear how Thorgils the Mighty and his famous iron balls slayed the giant serpent single-handedly.'

'Ha!' Thorgils' hair jiggled as he laughed. 'Well, I'll put that idea in his head over a cup of ale later. I'm just keeping Karsten company as he looked so lonely, not having any friends to hold hands with.'

Karsten ignored Thorgils and glared at Jael. 'How long are we going to wait for the boy king to make up his mind? Every moment we stand here scratching our arses is one more moment for Draguta to plan an attack. If she hasn't already. Andala's not safe without us, and we're not safe without proper walls, not like these toothpicks Reinhard has.'

'I doubt we're safe *with* walls,' Jael said. 'I'm sure Draguta has more dragons to send our way.'

Karsten couldn't help but think of Irenna, hoping the rest of his family would still be there when he returned.

'Raymon sounds as though he's made his decision, but I'll confirm it tonight,' Jael said, just as impatient as Karsten, though not about to admit it to him. 'Then we'll head back to Andala and prepare.'

'If there's anything left of it by the time we arrive,' Karsten grumbled.

That managed to dampen even Thorgils' good mood.

Jael didn't know what to say.

Draguta wanted her. And Draguta wanted the Book of Aurea too. But now they were in different places, so which one would she go after first?

Thorgils had turned away to talk to Torstan, who'd arrived with Hassi and Torborn.

Karsten stepped closer to Jael. 'They don't like their king.'

Jael frowned.

'Don't like him. Don't trust him. Maybe won't listen to him either.'

'I know,' Jael murmured, her eyes darting about. 'It could become a problem, so stay alert, and keep your men ready. If there's trouble, we need to be well ahead of it.'

Karsten was pleased to see that Jael agreed with him.

He didn't show it.

***

Draguta didn't turn around when Brill ushered Meena into the chamber.

She was sitting in front of her newly-drawn seeing circle, looking for problems and opportunities. 'And how is Morana?' she wondered. 'Still enjoying the comfort of her prison?' It was impossible not to feel cheered by the thought of Morana stuck in that chair, staring at the door, day after day, with that chirping woman fussing over her. Draguta was sure she'd never come up with a more torturous punishment.

Meena shrugged. 'I haven't seen her.'

'No?' Draguta spun around. 'You seemed very concerned with her the other day. Has something changed your mind?'

'I... no... I... Jaeger wanted me to help her, but then he changed. And now you're here.' Meena's eyes were everywhere but near Draguta's face. 'He is different. He doesn't want Morana's help anymore.'

Draguta stood, smoothing down her white silk dress, enjoying the luxurious feel of the fabric against her legs. It made her happy. Watching Meena squirm made her happy too. 'Yes, he is different, isn't he? And what will you do about that?' She looked Meena over, peering inside her thoughts. 'Nothing. Isn't that right? You will do nothing?'

Meena nodded eagerly. 'I won't say a thing.'

'No, you won't, or I shall find you a seat next to Morana, and you can keep each other company, though perhaps that would be far too kind to either of you? Perhaps I shall put you in a chair in Jaeger's chamber? You can watch when he brings his pregnant wife back to his bed.' Closing her eyes, Draguta inhaled the ripe smell of the frightened woman. 'Though I suppose you have no feelings for him anymore, if you ever truly did? It's not *that* Dragos your heart pounds for, is it?' She stopped, cocking her head to one side. 'Ahhh, I see. What a peculiar choice. To choose a pathetic cripple over a handsome king?' She laughed. 'Ahhh, the things people feel. Does Berard know it, I wonder? Care for you in return?' Draguta watched Meena's hand vibrating against her leg, sensing how hard she was working to keep it by her side. 'Hmmm... perhaps we shall find out one day soon? He wants to come here and kill Jaeger. They both do. The one-eyed and one-armed Dragos brothers! Ha! Do you think Jaeger is quaking in his boots? Waking up in a cold sweat every night, fearing their return?'

Meena tried not to think of anything. Her eyes were on the flagstone just before her boots, and she kept her mind focused on it, trying to think of nothing but stone. A wall of stone, guarding her thoughts.

Draguta frowned, seeing nothing more. 'But enough of that. I want you to bring me some herbs and spices. The list is on the table by the door. Find them and hurry back, but do not be long, girl. You will assist me until I find your assistance unhelpful. And if that unfortunate day were to come, I would likely remember how many times it was that you plunged that knife into me.' She stopped, looking at Meena's belt, from which her scabbard hung. 'Ahhh, the very weapon itself. My sister's knife. And how did you come across that?' She was curious, suddenly cold all over.

The night Dara had stabbed her, centuries ago, she had died.

Draguta had foreseen her own death then, but the circumstances around it had been shrouded in a hazy fog that she'd been unable to penetrate, no matter how hard she tried. Perhaps Dara had had something to do with that too?

And she had been buried in a tomb; brought back to life hundreds of years later by Jaeger's blood and Morana's skill.

But when Meena had stabbed her?

Brill said that she'd woken quickly, though it had felt as though she'd slept for years. But she had stood with little effort. Walked away unharmed. Not a wound on her. No scars to indicate that anything had happened.

It was a puzzle; one that made her itch with curiosity.

Meena could hear Draguta's voice inside her head, and she pulled the knife from its scabbard, trying not to think as she turned it around, offering it to Draguta. 'It was in a room, under a chest. I... I found it.'

Gripping the ivory haft, Draguta immediately stabbed it towards Meena's stomach. Meena gasped, jerking back in horror as Draguta narrowed her eyes. 'I can hear you breathe,' she whispered, leaning closer, the knife's sharp tip barely a fingernail from Meena's stomach. 'I can hear your heart beating, pumping blood all around your shaking body. Do not betray me, girl, or I will show you what it feels like to be killed with this knife. I will show you what it feels like to take your last breath as your blood drains from you. As the shadows come to devour you whole.'

Meena swallowed, slowly nodding her head, too terrified to blink.

***

Morac showed Evaine around the house, confident that she would grow to like it over time. It was almost a house fit for a king. Not the King of Hest, who preferred to live in a grand castle, but the King of Oss, who appeared content to live in anything that had a bed.

It was a spacious house, with a comfortable main room, leading to a separate bedchamber. There was a large kitchen area with a table and a meal fire; another table near a long fire pit with six chairs. The furnishings were old, fusty smelling, draped in cobwebs and layered with dust, but there was a sense of grandeur about the place that Morac thought would appeal to Evaine.

If only she would look beneath the surface.

'I will need servants! More than one. I can't cook or clean. I'm going to be a queen. Did you think of that, Father? Of how I would manage this place on my own?' Evaine grumbled, peering around. The windows were too small for such a large house, and being tucked down an alley, it was hidden in the shadows. Evaine could barely see, but what she did see looked old and unkempt.

She thought of the castle with some wistfulness.

But the castle had Jaeger and Draguta in it, so this dingy house would have to do for now.

Evaine sighed, suddenly filled with impatience. 'But what are we going to do about Oss and Sigmund? I want to go home, where I can be a queen. Married to Eadmund. When is *that* going to happen? Surely you don't plan on staying here now that Morana is Draguta's prisoner?'

Morac studied his daughter. He very much wanted to leave Hest, but as he had tried to explain, they would not be welcomed back on Oss; not once his part in Eirik's death was revealed. And Evaine wouldn't leave without Eadmund, who wouldn't leave without Draguta, who didn't appear to be going anywhere now that she'd returned.

And Morana couldn't go anywhere.

Even Meena was trapped by Jaeger and Draguta.

But there was one person who could find their way out of Hest.

And as that person, Morac knew that it was time for him to make a decision.

***

Edela frowned, running a finger under the faint line of text. Dara Teros had such a delicate hand, she thought sadly, wishing she knew the woman. Wishing she knew what had happened to her.

And whether she was still alive...

Biddy fussed around behind her, seasoning the stew, making the beds, sweeping the floor. 'I can't stop thinking about that knife,' she said suddenly. 'If it truly was a magical knife, made to kill Draguta, then what is Jael going to do?' Leaning the broom against the bed, she dragged a stool towards Edela, her mind whirring. 'Wouldn't this Dara woman know? She saw what would happen. Shouldn't she have mentioned it in the prophecy?'

'I don't know,' Edela murmured, remembering her dreams. 'Though I have seen some things lately...'

Biddy leaned forward with a keen look in her eye.

'I'm not sure what it all means, but I think Dara Teros used that knife herself. That she killed Draguta with it. I saw her with the knife in my dreams. I heard her thoughts. She was going to use that knife on her sister.'

'*She* killed Draguta?' Biddy was confused.

'No, not this time. It wasn't now. It felt like long ago. I've always wondered how Draguta was killed back then. And perhaps now we know? Perhaps it was Dara with that knife?'

'And she died the first time, didn't she?'

'She did, yes. She was brought back to life by Morana Gallas and the Book of Darkness.' Edela felt more troubled by the moment. 'But now? Draguta didn't remain dead this time, and no spell or dreamer was required to bring her back to life. It is quite obvious that the knife isn't working now.'

Biddy felt her shoulders creeping up to her ears.

'Therefore, I think it is safe to assume that *Toothpick* isn't going to work against Draguta either.' Edela stared into Biddy's eyes, seeing her own fears reflected.

How was she going to tell Jael?

***

Before Jael could reach Ravenna, who was busy talking with Gant at the high table, Garren Maas stepped in front of her. The rain had come down again, and those who could had squeezed into the hall, though the roof was leaking and Reinhard was running around with buckets, moving his guests away from the dripping thatch.

Jael frowned. She'd met Garren and his father before. Neither man was likeable, but Garren did, at least, try to be charming, which could be entertaining.

'My lady,' he smiled with a brief nod. 'Last time we met, I believe you were in quite different circumstances.'

Jael heard a familiar bellow, and her eyes darted away from Garren to where a red-faced Thorgils was arm-wrestling an Iskavallan. Torstan, Aleksander, and Fyn were behind him, cheering him on. 'Circumstances change,' Jael said without looking back at Garren. 'As I'm sure you know.' Her eyes snapped back to his. 'As I'm sure you hope. Your ambition is hardly a secret. Not when you're running around whispering it to everyone you meet.'

Garren swallowed, surprised by her frankness. He knew her reputation as a warrior but as a queen? 'My ambition is for Iskavall,' he tried. 'I have the well-being of my kingdom in my heart, as I know you did for your own when you murdered your uncle.'

Jael lifted her cup to Reinhard's wife, Britta, as she approached with the mead bucket. 'Thank you,' she smiled as Britta topped it up with her enormous ladle. 'Of course. Though my uncle stole the throne from Brekka's rightful king, so we were only restoring order.'

'Well, the path to Brekka's throne was always a clear one. Clearer than Iskavall's, at least, though we had all thought that you were your father's heir. He intimated that to us many times when he was in Ollsvik. I heard it from his own lips, so it was a surprise when he passed you over.'

Jael took a gulp of mead, grimacing; it tasted even sweeter than before. 'Perhaps, but I'm perfectly happy with the kingdom I have now. It suits me better, and my brother will make a strong king. Brekka is in good hands.'

Garren nodded, sensing her impatience to leave. 'I suspect so. But Iskavall?' He turned to look at Raymon, who had been cornered by a sour-faced Getta. 'I'm sure you can see our concern. And it's not just my family who worries about the direction of our kingdom. There is a growing sense of unease.'

Jael narrowed her eyes as a big cheer went up, Thorgils clambering onto a table, pounding his victorious chest, oblivious to the blood leaking through his tunic. 'The direction of your kingdom will be onto a midden heap if you don't support our attack on Hest. You may want a crown and riches and power, but what will you have to be king of if everything you desire is just ash? Ambition is worthwhile. Blind ambition is not. Now, if you'll excuse me, I must go and rescue that table.' And taking another drink, Jael left Garren to chew that over while she headed to congratulate Thorgils, disappointed to see that Ravenna had disappeared.

Garren watched her go.

Jael Furyck was an intriguing woman, but ultimately, just a woman, so her mutterings did little to dissuade him. He met his father's eyes and raised his cup, smiling.

***

Evaine wasn't smiling as Eadmund changed his tunic, running a hand through his sandy hair, which had lightened considerably since he'd arrived in the South. Draguta had sent a chest of Haegen Dragos' clothes to their new house, and Eadmund appreciated being able to wear something that wasn't covered in dust and sweat, though it was tinged with the strange sensation of knowing what had happened to Haegen.

'I thought we'd spend the first night here, together,' Evaine grumbled, glancing at her new servant, Elfwyn, who crouched over the meal fire, checking the cauldron. Evaine had ordered the woman to cook a selection of Eadmund's favourite foods.

But now he was leaving.

'I promised Draguta that we'd eat in the hall,' Eadmund said with a weary smile. His nose was bright red. His cheeks too. He wiped a hand across his forehead, surprised by how much he was sweating. Hest had only gotten hotter since he'd last been here.

With Jael.

He blinked quickly, not wanting to think about her.

Evaine huffed, flopping into a chair, running her eyes over the house. Elfwyn had had a busy afternoon, rushing around the markets, buying candles, lamps, and food. And as well as cooking, she'd made a start on cleaning the place, and though it would take days to get things in order, she'd removed most of the dust and lit an array of candles so that the main room sparkled with golden light.

Eadmund didn't notice.

He did notice Evaine's miserable face, though. 'Come on,' he grinned, grabbing her hand and pulling her out of the chair. 'It's just supper. I imagine Draguta wants to hear about my training. That's all. Then we can come back here.' He held her close, feeling her squirm in annoyance. 'And when we do, I won't be thinking about Draguta, I promise.'

Evaine couldn't help but smile then, but her nagging thoughts quickly turned it into a frown. 'Don't you wonder what you're doing here, Eadmund? Running after Draguta? Haven't you asked yourself where it will all lead? What she wants with you? *Why* she's making you train so hard?' She peered into his eyes, looking for signs that he wasn't as lost as she feared. 'Don't you want to go back to Andala for our son? Go home to Oss?'

Eadmund stared at Evaine, listening to her words, but they quickly blurred into clouds as they entered his head. He saw her face, and it was beautiful, then he heard Draguta's voice, and it was demanding.

And nothing else.

He was lost in the clouds.

Then he smiled as they cleared, leaving nothing but the clarity of what he needed to do. 'We should hurry, Evaine. Put on your boots. We don't want to keep Draguta waiting.'

***

'How's your shoulder?' Jael asked Thorgils, who was sitting with Rork and Karsten, having secured a bench in one of the few corners of the hall that was leak-free. All three of them were red-faced and bleary-eyed.

Thorgils laughed. 'Are you suggesting that arm-wrestling wasn't the best thing for a man in my condition to do?' He leaned towards Rork, who, being as wide as a cart, took up most of the bench. 'I could hardly say no to that tit, could I? Boasting that he'd never been beaten. With that puny arm? Ha! They don't grow them very big up here!'

Rork laughed with him, and even Karsten looked like he was enjoying himself.

With nothing to do but sit and wait until Raymon Vandaal made his decision, drinking was the only entertainment anyone appeared interested in.

And fighting, it seemed.

Jael noticed that the tables had been pushed back to the

walls as two bare-chested challengers emerged, chins jutting, eyes rolling, staggering towards each other. Jael was surprised to see that one of them was Aleksander. 'What are you doing?' she mouthed to him, standing as their bench was moved, her trio of companions wobbling to their feet.

Aleksander smiled drunkenly back at her before turning to Gant, who patted him on the shoulder, whispering in his ear as they considered his hulking opponent.

'What's that about?' Jael wondered as Fyn and Axl approached with Raymon.

Axl laughed. 'Aleksander insulted the man's wife apparently, though Aleksander denies it. He thought she was his mother.'

'And they're fighting over that?'

'Gives them something to do, and us something to watch,' Raymon supposed. 'Though, perhaps I could talk to you instead? Unless you want to watch your man fight?'

Jael shook her head, laughing. 'No, I've seen enough of him fight, I promise you. That poor bastard doesn't know what he's in for. Why don't we walk to the stables? Check on the horses?'

Raymon nodded, happy to escape Getta's intense scowl, which had been following him around the hall all night.

They pushed through the cheering crowd, past Thorgils, Rork, and Karsten, who'd quickly realised that it was the perfect opportunity to make a few coins, and were now busy holding out a plate, looking for something to write names down on.

Jael reached the door, turning back just in time to hear a loud cheer go up as Aleksander was thrown to the ground.

***

'Where's Aleksander?' Hanna asked, then quickly added. 'And

Jael?'

Her father sat beside her, his weary face relaxed for the first time in days. 'They've gone to Rissna, to make an arrangement about their armies. Hopefully, they'll return soon and head for Hest to get the Book of Darkness.' He sat back as Astrid came over with a bowl of broth.

She offered it to him. 'It's hot, so you'll need to blow on it.'

Hanna turned up her nose at the smell.

So did Marcus, but he took the bowl. 'Thank you.'

Hanna knew that she needed to eat to regain her strength, but the thought of doing it made her head hurt. She tried to distract her father, who looked so different with his scruffy beard. So tired too. 'How can they? They won't be safe.' She kept seeing Aleksander in her dreams, and the thought that he would put himself in danger worried her.

'No, they won't,' Marcus agreed, blowing on the broth, steam circling his face. 'But we're not safe here either. Wait till you hear what's happened since you took ill.'

Hanna's eyes widened. So far, her father hadn't said much, dismissing her questions, waiting for her to have more energy; waiting until she was able to comprehend things with a clear mind. But she didn't want to wait. She felt weak and weary, but more than anything, she felt impatient. 'Tell me.' Hanna wanted to sit up higher, to get out of bed, but she could barely lift a finger.

Marcus smiled, turning the spoon towards her mouth. 'I'll tell you everything, but first, you need to have some of this.'

Hanna scowled at him, but eventually, eager to hear the whole story, she sighed and opened her mouth.

***

'Enemies, enemies, everywhere I turn,' Draguta hummed, leaning out and peering down the table.

Meena shrunk backwards, reminded of what had happened the last time she sat at the high table with Draguta. She could almost feel sharp claws digging into her back, gripping her with terror.

Jaeger looked oblivious as he devoured his fourth roasted apple. He'd trained for much of the day, spurred on by the sight of Eadmund fighting Rollo, and he'd eaten like a man who hadn't seen food in weeks.

Evaine didn't care about Draguta's mutterings either. She just wanted to get Eadmund back to their house. Reaching under the table, she ran a hand up his leg, pleased to see him turn away from Draguta, smiling at her, his eyes on her lips.

'But which enemy should we defeat first?' Draguta mused. 'There are so many now, I can barely keep them in order.' Lifting her goblet, she stared at Meena. 'Come to my chamber in the morning, girl, and I shall have made my decision. I will dream on it tonight. And in the morning, we'll begin!'

Meena could feel the urgent need to tap her head, but she nodded it quickly instead, slipping her hands underneath her legs, trying to still her shaking body.

CHAPTER THIRTY ONE

Rissna's stables were leaking too. Jael wasn't pleased, but she knew that most of the horses didn't have the luxury of being in the stables anyway, so she wasn't going to complain about Tig being dripped on. Though, perhaps she needed to have a word with Reinhard about repairing his entire fort?

'You have a fine horse,' Raymon said, watching Jael run her hand down Tig's black muzzle.

Jael smiled, pleased that Tig was being so well behaved. 'I do. A gift from my father, many years ago now.' She glanced at Raymon, whose eyes revealed both envy and sadness.

'Ranuf was a good man. He visited my father often. I think he tried to guide him, offer advice, but my father preferred to listen to Lothar. To his detriment.'

Jael turned to him. 'You're right about that. Lothar only saw the future through his own greedy eyes. Whatever benefited him was the right decision to make, no matter who it hurt.'

'Do you regret killing him?' Raymon asked. 'You and Axl? Do you think it was the right thing to do?'

'It was, for many reasons. Lothar wanted to enrich himself, and he was happy to destroy Brekka to do so. He hurt our mother, and he stole Axl's throne, but mostly, Lothar would have ruined our kingdom. He had to go.'

'And Osbert?'

'He would've been an even worse king than his father. He

was smart. Lothar wasn't. Our people deserved better than either of them. And now they have Axl, and he has me, and we won't let anyone take Brekka from us again.'

Raymon nodded, looking around, though they were entirely alone. 'I want to come with you. I want to go to Hest. I'll command my army, but you will lead us.'

'You're sure?'

'I am. My wife is not. My men... I don't know. I'll speak to them. But I believe in what you're trying to do. I want to keep my people safe. Hiding and caring only for ourselves won't keep us safe for long.' Raymon frowned, imagining how Getta would take the news. 'We must fight to make ourselves safe.'

Jael smiled, thinking that sounded like something she would say. 'Good. Then announce it tomorrow, when your men have sobered up and can remember what you've said. Give them your reasons, and let them hear your voice. They'll see the truth if you lay it out before them.'

Raymon wasn't so sure. 'I hope you're right.'

'So do I.' Jael stared at him, wanting to see something more than the gangly boy shaking in his boots.

But she couldn't.

***

'What do you think Draguta is going to do?' Jaeger grunted, shunting Meena against the pillow. He was barely concentrating. His mind was fluttering about like a moth, unable to hold a single thought for longer than a heartbeat.

Meena's head banged against the wooden headboard, and she yelped.

Jaeger grabbed her, pulling her further down the bed, closing his eyes, trying to focus as he gripped her shoulders, pushing himself deep inside her.

Meena grimaced, not knowing if he still wanted her to speak. It was all she'd thought about since supper. Now that Draguta was settled in the castle again, and she had made her decisions about her and Morana – Jaeger too – it appeared that she could turn her attention to her other enemies. And Meena was desperately worried about what that would mean for Berard.

Part of her wanted to dream of him, to see if he was alright.

The other part knew that Draguta would be watching, and she didn't want to draw any attention to him or his family, making them a target for Draguta's wrath.

In the end, she whispered. 'I don't know what she's going to do, but I imagine whatever it is will be terrifying.'

***

Draguta had three tables in her chamber now.

Three seeing circles.

One for Jael Furyck, one for Edela Saeveld – who now had the Book of Aurea – and one that remained empty as she searched for her sister. And Draguta weighed everything like silver as she moved from one circle to the next, letting her mind wander to the possibilities; the probabilities.

She had been thwarted too many times now.

Yes, there had been some success, but her ambitions for Osterland remained stalled, so she was conscious of choosing the path that would guarantee a successful outcome.

But which one was it to be?

Turning away from her circles, Draguta moved to the chair by the fire. It was another muggy night, but she was enjoying the glowing warmth of the flames, unlike Brill, who had crawled into her little bed with nothing but a sheet, struggling to breathe in the oppressive chamber.

Picking up the Book of Darkness, Draguta decided that she would let it tell her the answer. It was the book, after all, that had guided her to this very place.

And it was the book, therefore, that would lead her to where she needed to go next.

***

It was late, and Edela was ready for bed, but she was still in the hall, having spent the afternoon with Branwyn. Her daughter wouldn't eat, and, in the end, Edela had put her to bed in one of the chambers and sat with her while she cried and talked, and cried some more.

Edela had cried with her before disappearing to pick some hops and valerian for a tea that had finally relaxed Branwyn, who had fallen asleep hugging a pillow, tears drying on her cheeks.

Leaving the chamber, Edela made her way to the end of the corridor to where Amma had emerged from the kitchen, looking at her in surprise.

'I didn't expect to see you here, Edela,' Amma blinked. She was in her nightdress, carrying a bowl of raspberries. 'Have you been with Branwyn?'

Edela nodded, noticing the tiredness and worry on Amma's face. 'I have. She is quite broken by Kormac's and Aron's deaths. One would have been bad enough, but two?' Edela sighed, feeling weary herself. 'She has fallen asleep in Gisila's chamber. And what about you?' Though she knew she shouldn't, Edela tried to tiptoe towards the subject of Amma's pregnancy. 'How are you feeling?'

Amma quickly hid her eyes. 'I'm a little tired. Missing Axl. I'm worried about what Getta will do too.' She looked up, trying to smile, but Edela's keen eyes had her blinking. It was as though the old dreamer was fingering her way through her secrets, and she didn't know how to stop her.

'Well, that's a lot to be thinking about,' Edela chuckled. 'Just know that my cottage is not too far away if you need help with any of it. I am very discreet, you know. Dreamers take an oath never to reveal anyone's secrets.'

'They do?'

'Of course! We can't go walking around in someone's head, blurting out whatever we find like an old gossip. No one would ever confide in us then, would they?'

'I suppose not,' Amma said thoughtfully. 'Well, I should go to bed. It's getting late.'

Edela nodded. 'It is. Sleep is what we all need, I think. And a few useful dreams.' She winked at Amma, turning towards the curtain.

Amma watched Edela leave, tempted to go after her, but she didn't want to reveal her fears. Not to anyone.

She didn't want to think it possible that she was carrying Jaeger Dragos' baby.

***

Little Lothar had finally sobbed himself to sleep, and as Getta lay back down in their bed, Raymon edged towards his uptight wife. The feasting had gone on well into the night, and after a rainy day, stuck in the hall, talking and drinking, even he was drunk.

Getta wasn't impressed.

Nor was she impressed by what he'd promised Jael. But

she kept her mouth shut. Jael knew more about her than Getta wanted anyone to know. And she didn't plan on giving her cousin a reason to open her mouth.

'I'll tell the men in the morning,' Raymon mumbled, reaching a hand towards Getta's face.

She batted it away.

He frowned and rolled onto his back. Frustrated.

'What will they do? The Maas' and their allies?' he wondered, all his fears rushing to the forefront of his mind. 'Kill me?' He swallowed, turning to Getta. 'Is that what you really think?'

Getta heard the panic in his voice, but she didn't move.

She didn't love Raymon. He'd provided her with security and status. With riches and power. With a son. He was a means to an end. But if being his wife was about to become a liability, well, Getta was going to have to reassess things and decide exactly which side she wanted to be on. 'Go to sleep,' she murmured. 'Tomorrow, you will discover what your men think. Best you rest now to ensure that your tongue works when you're standing before them. You want to sound like a powerful king, not just the son of a dead one.'

Raymon heard the coldness in her voice, and he closed his eyes, letting sleep wash away everything but the supportive smile on his mother's face as she urged him on.

***

As they emerged from their tents the next morning, the great army of Brekka was relieved to see that it wasn't raining. Everything they owned was damp and stinking, and they looked to the cornflower-blue sky – cloudless as far as the eye could see – hoping it would last.

Thorgils, Karsten, and Rork were sitting outside their tent on tree stumps, sharing out their winnings. Most Iskavallans and a few Islanders had bet against Aleksander, him being only half as wide as his challenger, and the hungover trio had collected a helmet full of coins.

Jael laughed at the state of them. Not one of them appeared able to open both eyes at once. 'You did well, then? Thanks to Aleksander.'

Thorgils grinned, but it hurt his head, and he quickly put both hands to it, trying to make the pounding stop. 'Well, I do remember watching him fight you, so I wasn't going to bet against him.'

Karsten lifted an eyebrow, wishing he'd seen that.

'I did beat him.'

'You did. I still remember that kick.'

Jael smiled as Aleksander approached. He looked even worse than Thorgils, who suddenly put his head between his knees. 'Had a good night, did we?' Aleksander had a black eye and a fat lip. His nose was swollen, and there was an enormous purple bruise on his forehead where he'd been head-butted. 'Everything still working, is it?'

He squinted at her, wishing back the gloomy sky and cold rain. The sun was burning his eyes, and it felt as though someone was squeezing his head. 'Don't know.'

Jael laughed. 'Well, while you were all drinking and fighting, I was doing something useful, like securing Raymon Vandaal's promise to go to Hest with us.'

They all looked at her.

'So, it's done?' Karsten stood up, regretting it instantly as he sat back down, stars dancing in front of his eyes. 'We have a deal?'

'We have a deal. But now he has to sell that deal to his men,' Jael murmured, watching Raymon walk into Rissna's muck hole of a square with his mother and his wife, eyeing the stage Warunda had commanded the day before. 'Though

I can't imagine it will go well. Might be best if I go and help him out.' She saw Axl talking to Fyn and Beorn and, nodding at Aleksander, who was being slapped on the back by a smiling Rork, she headed towards him.

'You look better than everyone else,' Jael grinned at her brother.

Axl shrugged, eyeing Fyn, who was wondering how quickly he could hobble to the latrines. 'I figured that being a king, I should have a little more self-control. Especially here. Around them.' He eyed the Iskavallans, who were gathering around the stage their king had just mounted. 'Is he going to tell them now?'

Jael nodded. 'He is. And then we can start planning our attack.' She felt a lift, just thinking about leaving for Hest and finding Draguta, Jaeger, and the book. Morana Gallas too. But as Jael's mind jumped from Morana to Evaine, and then to Eadmund, she felt a growing sense of dread about what state her husband would be in when she found him.

***

Eadmund watched Evaine walk away, unable to keep the smile off his face.

'That's a fine woman you have there,' Rollo said between gulps of water. They were taking breaks every few minutes. It was a hot morning, and though they'd been up training early, the heat was sapping their energy quickly. 'But what happened to your wife?'

Eadmund turned to him, his smile gone. 'My father arranged the marriage. When he died, I was free to be with Evaine. Jael didn't want to be my wife any more than I wanted to be her husband.'

Rollo laughed. 'Ha! I imagine she didn't. A woman like that? I've heard what she can do with a sword, but perhaps that's all she's good at? Though, I'd thought she'd be like a wild cat in bed.' He inclined his head, hoping to tease out more information. 'She obviously knows how to handle a weapon...'

Eadmund stared at him, trying not to remember anything about Jael in bed. He walked back to the middle of the training ring. 'Come on. Stop thinking about my wife.'

But Rollo didn't turn around. His eyes were on Draguta as she approached, her dutiful Brill trailing behind her with a basket; Meena hanging further back, dripping with sweat, red hair hanging limply around her red face.

'There you are!' Draguta exclaimed happily. 'Exactly where I'd hoped.'

Eadmund strode back to Rollo, ready to hear what Draguta needed, but she ignored him, smiling at Rollo instead. 'You, Rollo Barda. I have a little job for you.'

***

Raymon squirmed as the silence continued.

None of his men cheered. None spoke up.

Jael felt sorry for him. And worried for them. She glanced at Axl, inclining her head for him to follow her up onto the stage. They needed the Iskavallans, and it would be much easier if they believed in the cause. If they could see that there was something in it for them. Obviously saving their kingdom and their families as well as themselves wasn't enough.

'Your king has made the right choice!' Jael called. 'He will lead you to victory over Hest! Over those who wish us all harm! Over those who want to destroy our kingdoms and kill our families! We must fight to set ourselves free. Together! And when our victory is still ringing in our ears, and our enemy's blood has turned Hest red, we shall take their gold and come back to our kingdoms and celebrate! Our victory will be the greatest victory Osterland has ever known! A victory for the gods themselves to admire! A victory to make you rich beyond your wildest dreams!'

There were a few cheers then, mainly from her men, but Jael saw more interest in the Iskavallans' eyes now, and she was encouraged when a few of them clapped their hands, nodding to each other, joining in.

Karsten wasn't. He fiddled with his eyepatch, ignoring his clanging headache, glowering at Jael, who had just offered up Hest's riches.

Jael stared at him, reading his look, realising that he had a point, but still, Karsten wasn't going to have a kingdom if they didn't get enough men to try and reclaim it. And once they defeated Briggit Halvardar, she would see to it that Karsten's coffers were topped up with Helsabor's gold.

Raymon looked relieved as he turned to her and Axl. Getta had disappeared, but his mother was still there, and he could see her weaving her way through the crowd, encouraging the cheers of their men. 'We should go and plan, then. I want to know how you think we can get to Hest without being attacked by dragons and serpents.'

He looked nervous, Jael thought, but excited too, and she smiled, eager to begin.

***

Edela hadn't had any more dreams about Dara Teros or the knife, but she had woken up with a clear image of how to help Eadmund. And looking through the Book of Aurea, she'd quickly discovered the ritual she needed.

It was surprisingly complicated, so Edela brought Biddy, Eydis, the Book of Aurea and the puppies to the square, where Ayla was sitting at a table, enjoying the sunshine. The puppies soon grew bored with waiting by the table. No treats were on offer, and no crumbs had fallen their way, so they raced off towards the wall, hoping there would be a bit of dragon left to chew on.

Ayla ran her eyes over the page, squinting in the bright sunlight. 'Yes, I think it could work.' She glanced at Eydis, who looked as though she was holding her breath. 'It sounds terrifying, but it could definitely work, Edela. If you think you're strong enough to try such a thing?'

Edela was pleased to hear it, but she agreed with Ayla. Breaking the soul spell would require her to do things she had never imagined possible. 'Well, I do hope so. With Eydis' help, I think I should be able to do it. If it will work. Draguta didn't cast the spell on Eadmund. It was Evaine, with Morana's help, but this is certainly worth a try.'

'It is,' Ayla agreed. 'But there is a lot to do. A lot of things we'll need to find and prepare before tonight.'

'Mmmm, releasing a soul appears to be harder than it was to trap it in the first place. But if we manage it, then Eadmund will be free from Evaine. Free to return to Andala.' Edela could see Eydis sit up straighter, her face glowing as Runa walked towards them with Sigmund. Edela smiled at her as she stood, reaching for Eydis' hand. 'Why don't we make a start, then? The sooner we get to work, the sooner we can bring Eadmund home. We need him here with us, don't we, Eydis? And we need to get him far, far away from Draguta as quickly as possible!'

***

'But what about Eadmund?' Rollo wondered, not pleased but realising that he had little say in the matter. And then, of course, there was the prize on offer.

It was a lot of gold, he thought, staring at the chest Draguta had opened.

'You needn't worry about Eadmund,' Draguta murmured, watching his greedy eyes widen. 'I have a feeling Eadmund will be very busy while you're gone. In fact, I shall see to it. He'll be ready and waiting for your return. And you will return quickly, won't you, Rollo dear? I would hate to think of what would happen to all this gold if you were to delay.'

Rollo's eyes were transfixed by the gleaming contents of the chest. 'I'll come back as soon as it's done.'

'Good!' Draguta smiled, barely able to contain herself. 'Then go. Your ship is waiting. I have paid the merchant well. He has an experienced crew, and they are already in the cove. It has all been arranged, so hurry along, Rollo Barda, and I shall find you in your dreams.'

CHAPTER THIRTY TWO

Eadmund hadn't known what to do with himself when Rollo left with Draguta. He didn't imagine he'd take long, so he found another training partner: a Hestian, about half Rollo's size. The man was so quick on his feet and adept at wielding his sword that Eadmund found himself chasing him around the ring, his newly found confidence eroding with every stumble. Panting, he held up a hand. 'Think I need a drink,' he croaked, turning for the ale jug, only to come face to face with Jaeger.

'If you can't beat Edlan there, you don't stand much chance of beating your wife. Or me.' And with the wave of a hand, Jaeger sent Edlan on his way and entered the ring.

'And what makes you think I want to fight either you or Jael?'

Jaeger laughed, cracking his neck, hungry for a fight. 'What makes you think you have a choice?' he wondered. 'Draguta will decide who you fight, not you.'

Eadmund knew he was right. He could feel it.

So could Jaeger.

They were both bound to her in some way. She needed them, and they wanted to please her. It was a desperation so profound that they could almost taste it.

'Draguta will decide who you fight and who you fuck.'

Eadmund stepped towards Jaeger, all thoughts of water gone. '*What?*'

'Do you think you're with Evaine because you want her?' Jaeger's eyes were sharp; amber slits glinting in the sun. 'Because you *love* her?'

Eadmund stopped a hand's breadth from him, jutting out his chin. 'What do you know about me? About what I want?' he growled.

'About you? More than you do,' Jaeger growled back. 'I know Evaine put a spell on you and forced you to love her. I know she took you away from your wife.'

Eadmund frowned. That was something he'd heard before, and it irritated him just as much coming from Jaeger Dragos' flapping mouth. 'You're making a mistake talking to me about Evaine. Or Jael. Neither of them are anything to do with you.'

Jaeger smiled. 'Well, Evaine and I are... friends. I'm concerned. Worried that you'll break her heart when you wake up from your dream and realise what you've been doing. Likely you'll run back to your wife, and leave her here, all alone... with me.'

Eadmund felt a rush of emotion, hot and demanding, as it swarmed his body, building towards his fists. Then he heard Draguta's voice like ice in his veins, and he took a deep breath. 'It must be hard to feel so empty inside? So lonely that you feel the need to try and take what other people have? I knew someone like that once, and he's alone now too. So why not go and find your own life, Jaeger? And a new wife? One who wants you, though that might take some time. I'm sure most people can see what a fucking bastard you are.' And with one final look of disgust, Eadmund turned for the ale jug.

Jaeger lashed out, aiming a punch at the back of his head.

He missed.

Eadmund had felt him coming, and he'd spun at the last moment, dropping his head to the side, holding one fist up to protect his face, smacking the other into Jaeger's jaw.

Jaeger felt the crack, and then the crack in his ribs as Eadmund punched him there too. Before he could get his fists in front of his face, Eadmund smacked him in the eye. Jaeger's head snapped back, fire sparking in amber eyes. Staggering away, he shook his head, sweat and blood flying as he straightened up and charged.

***

Rissna's hall was beginning to stink like a barrel full of wet socks. The leaking roof had dampened the walls, the floor, and the furs, and despite the sunshine, the mix of damp, ale, smoke, and whatever the cooks were stirring in their cauldrons was overpowering. They all decided to take a break in the fresh air before returning to finalise their plans.

'We'll leave first thing tomorrow,' Jael said, turning to Gant as they wandered away from the hall towards the small training ring, where a few Iskavallans were working up a sweat. 'I want to get back to Andala.'

'Have you had a dream?' Gant looked worried, eager to head back himself.

'No, but the sooner we return, the sooner we can prepare for Hest. I have a feeling Draguta won't sit on her hands much longer. Not after we destroyed her dragur. She'll come up with something new soon.'

'Mmmm, well, I think we've made a good start on how things could go. And Raymon seems like he's got a clever head on his shoulders, young though it may be. I see a king in there.'

Jael wasn't so sure, but she didn't say so. 'Well, I only hope he can hold that head when he gets on the battlefield. His men will be watching. They're barely with him now. Let's just hope he's not as cowardly as his father was.'

Gant raised an eyebrow. 'I'm not sure Hugo was cowardly as much as stupid. He had little sense of how to plan a battle.

He was always more focused on the glory than the actual act of fighting. Lucky for him, he had a neighbour like Ranuf to get him out of trouble. Which he did, countless times. He really was a wet fart of a king. No wonder he was murdered.'

'I don't envy Raymon. He's sitting in a pit of snakes, waiting for one to lash out and bite him. And if he's not careful, they will.' Jael saw Ravenna cradling her grandson, and she headed away from Gant.

'I'll see you back at the hall,' he called, hand in the air.

Jael nodded but didn't turn around. She'd been looking to speak to Ravenna Vandaal since they'd arrived, but she wasn't sure why.

'Jael.' Ravenna smiled at her, handing the baby to Getta's servant. 'I never thought you'd emerge from the hall. Is it going well?'

Jael opened her mouth to speak, but images burst into view, and then she couldn't speak at all as they whirled around her head, confusing her, upsetting her.

She stared at Ravenna, grabbing her arm. 'We need to talk. Now.'

***

Jaeger couldn't breathe. His lungs were burning as he spun, blocking Eadmund's clenched fist. Eadmund was a different man than the one who'd been at Hest in the spring. He had a punch on him that would've felled a weaker man, Jaeger was sure. But Jaeger wasn't a weak man, and he shifted his feet, jabbing with his right hand, slipping through Eadmund's guard, catching him on the chin.

Eadmund stumbled backwards, grunting, scuffing up the dust, which tickled his throat and irritated his eyes. Shaking his head, he threw himself forward, hammering blows into Jaeger's stomach; ducking, swaying, punching him again. Harder. Feeling the power in his arm, the ease with which he could move, block, strike, defend.

Jaeger fell back, winded, teeth gritted, slipping out of Eadmund's path. He ducked one fist, trying to use his longer reach to hit Eadmund in the face again. But Eadmund came at him quickly, visions of Jael flashing before his eyes, remembering how she fought. And grabbing Jaeger's arms, he curled his leg around the back of Jaeger's, working to bring him down. Jaeger fought back, trying to free his arms and keep on his feet, but Eadmund had unbalanced him, and he fell to the dirt with a thud.

Eadmund was quickly over him, smashing his bleeding fist into Jaeger's face.

'Eadmund! What are you *doing*?' Draguta barked, Evaine at her side. She glared at him as he backed away, fist in the air, staring up at Draguta in surprise. 'How will it help any of us if you kill each other? How will it help *me*?'

Jaeger rolled away, coughing.

Eadmund tried to open his one closed eye as he made his way towards Evaine, who blinked at him with a mixture of worry and irritation.

Draguta tapped her foot as Jaeger approached, trying to catch his breath. 'Surely you have things to do that don't involve beating each other to a pulp?' she growled. 'I require *both* of you! And I would prefer it if you had all your parts working, including your brains!' And spinning on her heels, she left Eadmund and Jaeger glaring at each other, and headed towards the winding gardens to see how Meena was coming along.

***

Getta had let Ravenna take her son so she could go for a walk, wanting a moment to think. But even in the quiet of her own company, she couldn't think at all.

Raymon was going to get them all killed, and she didn't know what to do.

'Getta!'

Getta frowned, recognising that voice, walking faster. Talking to Garren wouldn't help. He would just smile and tease, tangling her up in knots for his own amusement, as though her life was a game.

She didn't turn around.

But Garren wasn't to be deterred as he reached her, guiding her away from the road, towards the tents.

And with a sigh, Getta let him.

'What do you want?' she demanded when they'd walked down between two rows of tents, away from any prying eyes. 'Here is no place to talk. I must find Lothar. Ravenna took him somewhere. Raymon will be looking for me too.'

Garren smiled, watching her squirm, enjoying how flustered he made her. 'I only need a moment of your time,' he promised, his voice low and husky. 'I wanted you to know that I don't blame you. I won't let anything happen to you.'

Getta felt her heart thud. 'What do you mean?'

Garren drew her further into the narrowing gap between two tents. He couldn't hear anyone moving about inside either of them. 'Your husband has made a mistake placing our kingdom into the Furycks' hands. He has made a grave mistake, Getta, but I'm not about to sit back and let him destroy Iskavall.'

'You're *threatening* him?'

Garren bent forward until his breath was warm on Getta's face, and his nose was almost touching hers.

Getta felt a familiar twinge in her stomach, and she didn't back away.

'As I've said before, there are those who are unhappy. Those who care about who sits upon our throne. Who believe that a true king is needed to steer Iskavall in the right direction. I can't deny that I am one of those people, but I'm not threatening your husband, merely guaranteeing that nothing will happen to you. Whatever transpires in the future, you and your son will be safe. Protected by me.' Garren leaned in even closer, kissing Getta, feeling her respond. 'I won't let anything happen to you,' he breathed.

Getta couldn't stop herself. She was desperate to feel safe. Being married to Raymon had felt like having a grown-up child. She was tired of thinking for him, sick of needing to push and cajole and help him. Garren was everything Raymon wasn't, and she felt herself clinging to him with more than just desire.

Suddenly, Garren pulled away, pressing a finger to Getta's lips, turning his head to the right, listening to the voices coming from within the nearest tent.

***

Ravenna swallowed, feeling a sudden heat on her cheeks. 'I don't know what you're talking about,' she tried, fiddling nervously with her rings.

Jael stared at her, glancing back to the tent flap, but she couldn't hear anyone around. 'My father,' she said again. 'Tell me why my father was holding your son... when he was a baby.' Every part of her felt as though it was slowly slipping down a steep hill. She could barely breathe, not wanting Ravenna to answer her just as much as she did. 'I saw you. I saw him.'

'*Saw?*' Ravenna didn't understand.

'Just now, when you gave your grandson to the servant, I saw you and my father.'

Ravenna blinked.

'I know you're lying, Ravenna. About everything. Tell me

the truth. Surely I deserve to know if it's to do with my father?'

Jael didn't want to know.

She kept seeing her father's face.

Ravenna took a seat on the bed. 'I...' She felt sick. 'I promised your father I would never say. He wanted Raymon to stay safe. It was the last thing he said to me.'

Jael closed her eyes.

'I loved Ranuf,' Ravenna sighed. 'I did. We loved each other.' She saw the pain in Jael's eyes as she opened them. 'Hugo was a ridiculous man. Not the husband I wanted, but I was forced to marry him. Your father came to Ollsvik many times when Hugo was new to the throne. Iskavall had been unstable for years. He'd known Hugo's father, and he wanted to help secure his position, thinking that the stability would, in turn, help Brekka. We became close. Hugo and Lothar would drink. Ranuf and I would talk.'

Jael took a seat opposite Ravenna, her body stiff, her thoughts muddled.

'Eventually, he started coming to visit me, using Hugo as an excuse.' She paused, tears in her eyes. 'We fell in love. I didn't mean for it to happen, but I couldn't help it either.'

'And Raymon?'

'He is your father's son. Your brother.'

Jael put her head in her hands. 'Does he know?'

'No. No one knows. Just Ranuf and now you. Hugo is dead, but I fear what would happen if anyone were to find out that Raymon was a Furyck.'

Jael lifted her head, wanting to scream. The shock was too much. She could hear her father's voice in her head, trying to calm her down.

She ignored it.

'That's why he was always going to Ollsvik? To visit you and your son?' Her anger was burning. 'That's why he couldn't come to Tuura with us, because he was with you and your son?' She stood, ignoring the confused look on Ravenna's face.

Jael paced the tent, her thoughts jumping between childhood memories; thinking about her father, hearing his words which now took on such different meanings.

Ravenna panicked, seeing Jael's reaction. She stood, trying to get her attention. 'You can't tell anyone,' she whispered, grabbing Jael's arm. 'Please. Not Raymon, not Axl. Not anyone.'

Jael glared at her, shaking her head. 'Why would I want to tell anyone? Why would I? You think Raymon would be the only one hurt by this? What about my mother? Do you know what she went through when my father was in Ollsvik with you? What we both did?'

Ravenna finally understood what she meant, and her face paled. 'Ranuf never got over what happened in Tuura. He felt so guilty for not being there to protect you both.'

Jael shook her off, too angry to look at her. It wasn't Ravenna's fault, she knew, but old memories had a way of distorting reality, and when she remembered Tuura, it was always as a ten-year-old girl, not a twenty-eight-year-old woman. 'I won't tell anyone,' she mumbled, her voice sounding distant in her ears as she walked out of the tent without looking back.

Ravenna stood, open-mouthed, watching her go, tears streaming down her cheeks.

***

Getta grabbed Garren's arm, her eyes big and blinking. Everything she'd believed about hers and Raymon's parentage had been turned upside down, and she didn't know where things stood.

Where she stood.

But Garren did.

His smile was wide as he brought Getta into his arms and

kissed her.

***

Amma had been eager to go for a walk, wanting to escape the hall and leave behind everyone who had a question for her. She needed a moment free from all the noise, so heading through the harbour gates, she turned to the left, leaving the builders and their hammering behind.

Amma had tried not to show her annoyance when Eydis had asked to come along, but she felt it. She felt as though her head was being squeezed like a ripe plum, ready to burst. Her body was changing. She wanted to vomit sometimes, and other times she was so ravenous that she could have gotten up in the middle of the night and eaten another supper.

Her back ached, and her mind was never at ease.

And she didn't know what to do about any of it.

Eydis reached out, searching for her hand. Amma gave it to her, and Eydis smiled. 'I'm sorry you're sad,' she said softly. 'You should be happy.'

Amma frowned, wondering what she could see. 'Why do you say that?' she asked hesitantly as they came to the small rise which led around to the cove. 'Why do you think I should be happy?'

'Because of the baby, of course.'

Amma stopped, turning to her with blinking eyes. 'You can *see* it?'

Eydis nodded. 'I can. I think Edela can too, but she doesn't want to say anything. I can hear it in her voice when she talks to you.'

Amma could barely breathe as she continued walking. The path to the cove was private and colourful, bordered by thickly entwined rowan trees, infused with the scent of flowering raspberry and blackcurrant bushes. It smelled sweet as the wind blew in from the sea, adding a hint of salt to the air.

Amma didn't notice.

'You are worried? About not being married to Axl?' Eydis guessed, not sure that she was the right person to be talking to Amma, but she wanted to do something to help her friend. 'About what people will think?'

'No.' Amma shook her head. 'No, it's not people I'm worried about. Not yet at least.'

'Then what?' Eydis could hear men walking towards them, and she closed her mouth, feeling Amma's grip tighten on her hand.

Amma smiled at Bram and Ulf as they walked past, turning around to make sure they were far enough away before bending down to Eydis. 'I'm worried about whose baby it is.'

Eydis blinked in surprise. 'Oh.' And the realisation of what Amma meant sunk in. 'You mean Jaeger Dragos?'

Amma nodded, which she quickly realised wasn't helpful for Eydis. 'Yes. What if it's not Axl's? I don't know whose it is.' She peered at Eydis. 'Do you think you could tell? You or Edela? Or Ayla? Is that something a dreamer could find out?'

Eydis shrugged. 'I don't know. But perhaps it's time you told Edela? It's not something you can keep a secret. Not for long.' She thought of Jael and felt sad, suddenly realising why Edela hadn't said anything.

Suddenly worried that she had.

'Axl will be home soon,' Amma muttered, almost to herself. 'And then he will leave. For Hest. I don't want to upset him. Worry him. It would only make him confused or angry or both. I need Axl to focus on the battle that's coming, not on a baby he doesn't need to know about yet. Anything could happen. I don't want anyone to know, Eydis. Promise me. Promise you won't say anything.' She turned to Eydis, gripping her hands, staring into her milky eyes.

Eydis could feel Amma's terror, and she didn't know what to do, except nod. 'I promise.'

***

Jael stormed away from the tent, looking for something to hit. The first person she came across was Ivaar, walking with a woman whose breasts were bulging over the top of her dress, jiggling as she walked. Ivaar's eyes were all over them, a sly look on his handsome face.

Jael glared at him, and he turned to her. 'Are you alright?'

'You should be doing something useful,' she snapped.

'Such as?'

'We're making plans in the hall. Why aren't you in the hall?' And deciding that she'd get little satisfaction from hitting Ivaar, Jael strode off in search of Gant.

***

Gant had returned to the hall with Axl and Aleksander, and he now stood around the high table, scribbling on sheets of vellum, sketching out how they would approach the South.

Karsten and Thorgils were there too.

No one mentioned Helsabor, except Raymon Vandaal. 'But wouldn't Wulf Halvardar help us? Give us men? Join with us?'

Gant looked at Aleksander, then shook his head. 'Helsabor has kept to themselves since I was a boy. Nothing will bring them out from behind their walls. They're happy where they are, so we can't consider them. Old King Wulf has made it very plain what he thinks about the rest of us.' Gant didn't want to lie to the young king, not when they needed him to trust them, but nor did they want to be overheard by the dreamers in Helsabor.

Not until they had a chance to do something about them.

There would be time to reveal more, he knew, but until it was safe, it was better for all of them if the Iskavallans remained in the dark.

Raymon smiled as Jael entered the hall, but the look on her face quickly had him frowning.

'Gant,' Jael said, ignoring everyone else. 'Could I have a word?' Her lips barely moved, and her eyes were cold as Gant stepped away from the table, following Jael outside.

She didn't talk as they walked, leaving Gant busy trying to figure out what had happened. Jael had been acting strangely all day. For longer than that, he realised as he thought about it.

They walked out of the fort, past the horses, towards the forest, and when they were inside the cover of trees, hidden from the road, Jael turned on him. 'Did you know? About Raymon?'

Gant quickly dropped his eyes, avoiding hers.

Jael's anger only burned brighter. 'Does anyone else know?'

'No.' Gant was quiet, but he lifted his head now, his eyes darting around, checking the trees. 'No one knew but your father until he told me. He needed someone to talk to, but I'd already guessed. I saw them together. I guessed about Raymon.'

Jael rubbed her chin. She felt sick.

'Your father loved Gisila, but...'

'But what? They drifted apart?'

'I...' Gant shrugged. 'I can't answer for Ranuf. He loved you all, but he fell in love with Ravenna, it's true.'

'And he kept it all a secret? A secret life! He had a secret life?'

Gant wanted to reach out to try and calm Jael down. She was too loud.

Jael saw it in his eyes, and she took a breath. 'He didn't

come to Tuura because of her. If he'd been there...' Tears stung her eyes, and irritated, she blinked them away. 'If he had been there, it wouldn't have happened. It wouldn't have happened!'

'He never forgave himself, Jael. Know that.'

'It's too late! I... I thought...' She shook her head. 'He was like a god to me! But he had a secret life. Another family!'

Gant reached for her hand, but Jael moved away.

'I thought I knew him.'

'He didn't love you any less because of it.'

'Well, he didn't love me enough to tell me the truth!' Jael wanted to cry and scream. Everything was crumbling inside her. She was losing everyone. Her baby. Eadmund. Her father.

'It was dangerous for anyone to know the truth. Dangerous for Raymon. You can see that. It's dangerous now.' Gant was worried; Jael was losing control. 'You'll undo all our plans if you reveal this now.'

'You think I'd *say* something?' she spat. 'I'm not stupid, Gant! Gullible, obviously, but not stupid!'

Gant watched her eyes jumping around like fleas. 'Jael, what is it? What's wrong? It's not just this, is it?'

She glared at him.

'When you came back from Hallow Wood, you were different. Something's wrong. I know you.'

'Do you?' Nothing about her was making it easy, Jael knew. She didn't want to tell him anything.

'I'm mad at Ranuf. That's all.'

He gave her a look she knew well. Gant Olborn wasn't a dreamer, but he'd known her all her life. She had few secrets from him.

Jael hung her head, staring at the mud and soggy leaves of the forest floor. 'I had a baby,' she whispered. 'In Harstad. I lost a baby. She died. I almost died too.'

Gant couldn't even shake his head. The shock rendered every part of him still.

'I've lost Eadmund, and my baby, and now my father... I...'

She looked up, rubbing her eyes. 'We have to go back. Make plans. They're leaving this afternoon. We don't have long.' Sniffing, she tried to move past Gant, but he grabbed her arms and pulled her into his.

And he held on tight.

'I'm so sorry, Jael. I'm so sorry for you.'

And Jael felt the strength and warmth of those arms around her.

And she cried.

CHAPTER THIRTY THREE

Else left Morana with Meena and quickly escaped the castle, wanting to get some air. To see the sun. To hear something other than Morana's rasping breathing. It sounded almost as though she was working hard, trying to escape.

Else didn't like Morana, but she'd come to feel sorry for her; unhappy that she'd ended up a prison guard, knowing that she was in the prison as much as Morana.

Leaving the castle far behind, Else headed straight for Dragmall's cave, pleased to have rekindled their friendship after years of little contact. He'd always been enjoyable to talk to, and though they could say little to each other now about anything they actually wanted to talk about, she was looking forward to some company.

Dragmall popped his head around the mouth of the cave as Else panted up the steep path towards him, a smile on her face. 'This is a surprise!'

'I thought you might see me coming,' Else wheezed, hands on her hips as she tried to catch her breath.

'Ahhh, but that would make me a dreamer,' Dragmall said, leading her into the cave, which smelled strongly of damp, but also of fish oil from the lamps stuffed into little holes in the walls. 'Which I most certainly am not, as you well know.'

'Oh, I always wanted to be a dreamer,' Else said wistfully, pleased by how cool the cave was. The brief walk from the castle had left her dripping, and she looked around for the source of the breeze she could feel on her face, wanting to stand near it. 'Knowing the future. Knowing other people's futures. Casting spells.'

Dragmall laughed. 'I think you'd have made a terrible dreamer, Else. You could never keep a secret. You would have blurted out everything you saw in your dreams.'

'That's true,' Else admitted, taking the tree stump Dragmall offered her. 'I would have been unable to stop myself!' Looking up, she noticed the rows of drying herbs strung across the ceiling. 'You mentioned something about herbs the other day, I remember.' Her eyes met Dragmall's as he turned around with a cup of small ale, handing it to her. Else took a sip, her eyes never leaving his. 'Something to help me sleep? Morana blows like a storm all night long. I'm not sure I've slept since I moved into her chamber!'

'I did, didn't I?' Dragmall muttered casually, walking towards his shelf where he took down a small glass bottle stuffed with dried herbs. 'You could try this. I've used it before to help me sleep.'

'And did it?' Else wondered just as casually. 'Help you?'

Dragmall nodded. 'It did, yes.'

He placed the bottle in Else's hand, and she smiled.

***

Brill was washing Draguta's hair as she sat in the large wooden tub, which had been carried into the hall. Despite being an unbearably warm day, a fire was blazing in the stone hearth, and Brill was dripping with sweat as she leaned forward, sleeves rolled up, trying not to fall into the tub.

'Girl!' Draguta called as Meena scuttled down the stairs.

She smiled, listening to Meena's boots as they stuttered to a stop before shuffling ever so slowly into the hall.

Meena was surprised to see the tub. She quickly looked away from Draguta's luminous body; her small breasts on full display above the steaming water.

'And where have you been today?' Draguta murmured. The water was hot, and the fire was hotter, and she almost felt ready for bed. 'I have another list ready. More errands to send you on.'

Meena kept her mind clear, not wanting to reveal her thoughts about that. 'I was looking after Morana.'

Draguta frowned. 'Why?' She sat up straight, away from Brill, who, still holding onto her hair, was almost pulled into the tub. 'What has happened to that old woman? She's supposed to be with Morana. You are not Morana's assistant anymore.'

Meena felt protective of Else. She didn't want to get her in trouble. 'Else needed a break. Some fresh air.'

Draguta frowned at Meena, curling a finger in her direction. 'Come closer. I cannot see your lies from over there.'

Meena gulped, creeping towards the tub, stopping a few steps from its edge as Draguta leaned over it, almost inhaling her.

'Well, I suppose we can't have the old woman dying on us, or we would need to find someone new, and I don't imagine anyone could irritate Morana as much as she does. But...' Draguta added, her eyes no longer sleepy, 'you will ask my permission in future, for I require your assistance at all times. No matter who you are with or what you are doing. You are to be exactly where I need you to be, waiting for me to call on you. Do you understand?'

Meena nodded emphatically.

'Good!' Draguta exclaimed, easing backwards so that Brill could finish soaping her hair. The gentle aroma of lavender was gradually undoing her knots of tension, and her thoughts were starting to drift. 'Now, get along, up to my chamber. The list is waiting for you. And don't be long. I shall be ready for you after my nap. Ready to get to work!'

***

Eadmund tried to sit still, but his body was humming. Something had happened to Rollo, and he didn't know what. He hadn't come back to the training ring, and he hadn't gone to his room above the brothel. Morac had offered to see what he could find out, so Eadmund had walked back to the house with Evaine, waiting for Morac to return while she fussed over him.

He tapped the arm of the chair as Evaine cleaned his face, washing the dust out of his eyes, but his body was as tense as his mind, his thoughts becoming so turbulent that eventually, he shook her off and stood.

'I haven't finished,' Evaine complained. 'Elfwyn will need to stitch the cut on your cheek.'

'No, she won't,' Eadmund insisted. 'It's fine.'

'You can't see it,' Evaine insisted just as firmly. 'It's deep.'

Eadmund didn't care. 'It's stopped bleeding for now, so let's just see what happens.' He looked around for his swordbelt. 'I need to find Rollo.'

'You won't find him in Hest,' Morac said, pushing open the door, eager to escape the boil of the midday sun. His damp tunic was stuck to his back, and he pulled it away, wishing that Evaine's new house had more windows. It felt even hotter than outside and smelled strongly of onions.

Eadmund turned in surprise, pulling his own tunic away from his back. 'Why? Where is he?'

'I don't know, but he left on a ship. I couldn't find out anything more than that. He went up to one of the coves and bordered a merchant ship, but no one could tell me where it was going.'

'A ship?' Eadmund felt an odd sense of loss. He had started to enjoy Rollo's company, and he'd come to rely on his skill and direction in the training ring. 'Is that Draguta's doing?'

'I've no idea,' Morac sighed, taking a seat, peering at Eadmund's face. 'You should let Elfwyn stitch that cut. It looks bad.'

Evaine grinned triumphantly at Eadmund, who sat back on the chair, feeling the blood pouring down his cheek again. 'Alright. But then I have to go and talk to Draguta. I need to know what's happened to Rollo.'

***

Jael felt oddly better after her talk with Gant. Everything she'd believed about her father had been turned upside down, and she wasn't sure how she felt, but some of her tension had gone, and she'd almost been able to think clearly as she outlined her plans for the attack on Hest.

Just the thought of taking action had lifted her mood.

The thought of getting closer to Eadmund. And Draguta.

It was the middle of the afternoon when she walked Raymon back to his tent. 'You're leaving now?'

He nodded. 'We have a lot to prepare when we return to Ollsvik. I want to make a start.'

'Makes sense. We'll head off in the morning,' Jael said, watching Getta approach with Ravenna. She felt the urge to turn and run in the other direction, but she kept walking. It felt strange to be around Raymon now. Jael tried not to stare at him, but she found herself wanting to see any resemblance to her father, though she wasn't sure if it would help or just make everything feel worse.

'We are packed and waiting,' Getta said shortly, taking her baby back from Ravenna. He was starting to fuss, and Getta was convinced that Lothar didn't like being held by his grandmother. 'Will you be much longer?' Her eyes were cold. Ignoring Jael. Questioning her husband.

'No,' Jael said. 'We're done. Our initial plans are made, but there is no point in going any further until we meet at Vallsborg.' She avoided Ravenna's eyes, watching Getta frown. 'You'll be safer once we defeat Draguta and destroy the Book of Darkness,' she tried, feeling Raymon squirm with embarrassment beside her, seeing that his wife was so obvious in her disapproval. 'And your husband will show his men what a good king he's going to be by leading them to victory and protecting your kingdom.' Jael's smile was forced. Her eyes were as lifeless as Getta's. And nodding to her cousin, she turned to Raymon. 'I wish you a dry journey home. And we'll see you soon.'

Raymon smiled, reaching for his son. 'We'll see you soon.'

Getta looked irritated, but she handed Lothar to his father, and with one final scowl at Jael, she spun around, following her husband.

Ravenna remained behind. 'Thank you,' she whispered.

Jael was confused. 'Thank you?'

'You're trying to help him. I know it was a shock, but I'm grateful that you're still trying to help him.' She shook her head, tears leaking into the creases around her warm brown eyes. 'I've been so worried about what would happen to Raymon. He has many enemies, but he's just a boy. He's not ready, and Getta is...' Ravenna stopped herself. 'I wish you a safe journey, Jael.' And dropping her eyes, she turned away after her son.

Jael watched her go, thoughts whistling through her head like the wind through Eadmund's old cottage.

She sighed, trying not to see her father's face.

***

'I could sleep till Vesta,' Entorp yawned, flopping into Edela's chair. There was only Hanna left in his tent now. Everyone that had survived the sickness had been carried back to their own homes. Most only needed the minimal care of being slowly nourished back to health. They had no symptoms any longer, just overwhelming weakness. Some hadn't eaten or drunk for days as their bodies shut down, preparing for death, and there was little Entorp could do to help with that. Astrid and Derwa were going to check on them regularly, and Marcus was staying with Hanna, who wasn't ready to be moved yet, so there was nothing for Entorp to do.

Except help Edela and Biddy solve all their problems.

They had missed his company, and now, finally having him back again, there were a lot of things to catch him up on.

Entorp had been surprised to learn that the Widow was not, in fact, the Widow, but Draguta's sister, who had apparently killed Draguta with a knife made from the same materials as Jael's sword, which now appeared useless. He kept shaking his head, not sure he'd taken it all in. 'Well, the only one who knows the truth of it all is Dara Teros herself,' he said, at last. 'You must work on trying to find her, Edela. She must be able to tell you more about the knife and the prophecy. The shield too.' He frowned, feeling as though he'd stepped into a blizzard of problems.

'Do you think she's still alive?' Biddy wondered, working the pestle in the large bowl Edela was adding herbs to. They were preparing everything they needed to break the soul spell, and though Biddy was trying to concentrate, Edela was feeling tense, welcoming the chance to talk about something else.

'I don't know,' Entorp admitted. 'She spent most of her life waiting for the prophecy to be realised by the sound of it. It would seem unlikely that she put herself in harm's way just as it was all starting to fall into place. She must have known that Draguta would return one day?'

'I hope so. I hope she's still alive. There's so much I would like to ask her.' Edela picked up a bunch of sweet basil, adding three leaves to the bowl. 'Especially about Jael's sword.'

Biddy stopped grinding, staring at Entorp. 'If Jael's sword won't kill Draguta... if she's unstoppable, what can we do?'

Entorp smiled. 'I don't think anyone is unstoppable, Biddy. Even Raemus was killed in the end, wasn't he? There will be a way to end Draguta once and for all. And if it's not going to be Jael's sword, we'll find something else, don't worry.' He turned from Biddy's worried face to Edela's equally worried face. 'Perhaps you will, Edela? In your dreams?'

'Ahhh, my dreams,' Edela sighed. 'They are a web of mysteries and secrets that confound me most nights, but I will try. And in the meantime, I must focus on tonight. According to the book, we're supposed to pick the juniper berries at dusk. So drink up, Entorp, and you can come with me, as I don't think I have the legs to climb up that juniper tree anymore!'

***

Meena had spent far too long chasing after a toad, and now the sun was going down, and Draguta would soon start getting annoyed.

Why did every spell call for a creature that was impossible to catch, she wondered, her mind wandering as she traipsed back through the winding gardens with a heavy heart. Her thoughts didn't belong to her, and it would do her no good to let them escape the prison she was trying to hide them in. Eventually, Draguta would see everything, she knew; tug out every weed growing in her head.

Closing her eyes, Meena inhaled the strong scent of jasmine, reminded of her childhood spent trailing after Varna, who only ever spoke to her in barking orders. And then Morana, and now Draguta.

Meena saw a turtle-dove watching her from the sagging bough of an old elm tree, and she felt envious as it flew away, wishing she could follow it up through the trees, their bright-green leaves rustling in the breeze. Up over the walls of the gardens and far away from Hest.

Sighing, Meena looked away from the empty bough, back down to the list.

Belladonna was next.

The sky was turning pink.

And Draguta's sharp voice was ringing in her head.

***

'No fighting tonight,' Jael grumbled to Thorgils as they walked to the hall with Ivaar, who'd reluctantly tagged along, not knowing what to do with himself. 'I'd like you to be able to use both eyes when we go to Hest. Your arms might come in useful too!'

Thorgils looked indignant. '*Me*? I only organise the entertainment. I couldn't possibly take part with all of my injuries. You've no need to worry there.'

Jael snorted as he opened the door and ushered her inside, following quickly behind her, letting it close in Ivaar's face.

Ivaar stared at the door, his shoulders sagging.

Karsten came up behind him, slapping him on the back. 'Come on! One more night of fleecing these stupid bastards before we go.' He lowered his voice and winked at Ivaar. 'You look like just the man we need.' And pulling open the door, he pushed Ivaar into the hall, relieved that the sunshine appeared to have improved the smell. He saw the bushy raised eyebrows of Rork Arnesson, who was quickly motioning him over to a corner, and he pushed Ivaar some more. 'Let's go.'

Jael turned to watch Karsten leading Ivaar over to Rork, shaking her head. 'I'd like to see that,' she mumbled to Thorgils, whose beard was already dripping with ale. 'Ivaar Skalleson grappling one of Reinhard's men.'

'Ha!' Thorgils laughed. 'So would I, but that pig's arse isn't going to make a fool of himself. Damage that pretty face of his? I'd eat my own turd if he did that!'

Jael shook her head. 'That's not something I ever want to think about!' And she left Thorgils to find his way to Karsten and Rork.

'Drumming up more business?' Gant asked, inclining his head towards Thorgils.

'Looks like it. They're trying to find another sucker,' Jael said, smiling at Aleksander, who couldn't smile back because his face hurt too much. 'Having finished with you.'

'I won, didn't I?' he muttered.

'Yes, and with all your teeth too,' Jael grinned, taking the cup of ale Gant offered her, feeling her body start to unwind. She didn't feel right, but now that the Vandaals had left, she felt better.

There would be time to think before they met again. And, until then, Jael was going to focus on getting her men back to Andala and preparing her army.

Noticing Aleksander's raised eyebrows, she turned as Ivaar stripped to the waist, facing up to Reinhard's champion, a thick-necked wall of a man with arms like trees. Jael saw Thorgils' wide-eyed surprise and burst out laughing.

'This should be good,' Gant said, moving ahead of her to get a better view.

Aleksander put his arm around Jael's shoulder, pushing her

after Gant. 'Come on, there's room over there.'

Jael kept her eyes on Ivaar, whose growling opponent struck the first blow – a sharp jab to Ivaar's throat – thinking how much Eadmund would have enjoyed this.

***

Draguta wasn't inclined to care what Eadmund thought, though she was surprised by his insolence. It was a constant puzzle. He was bound to her as tightly as Jaeger, but she had to keep going back into the spell to tighten the knot that bound Eadmund to her.

It kept loosening, and she didn't know why.

'Who knew you would become so fond of that hairless beast?' she muttered, eyes fixed on him, frozen and unimpressed. 'But what Rollo is doing is none of your concern. He will return when he has completed his task, and only then, so we will speak no more about it. Do you understand me, Eadmund?'

The knock on the door came at the perfect time, and as Brill opened it to reveal a red-faced Meena, Draguta stood, sending Eadmund on his way. He was still frowning and not moving with any great speed, so she pressed her hand against his sweaty back to help him along.

'And what about training?' he asked, turning at the door.

'You will have to find someone new,' Draguta said brightly. 'Rollo will not be gone long, and after your little wrestle with Jaeger, you appear to be well on your way now. A few more weeks, and you'll be capable of killing anyone I choose.'

Eadmund scowled as Draguta shut the door in his face, reminding herself that she would have to sort him out later. She glided towards Meena with an eagerness to begin. 'Now, what do you have for me here?' And running her eyes over the bunches of herbs, mushrooms, and spices, she clapped her hands together, inhaling the fusion of earthy aromas. 'For all your very obvious flaws, you are a good gatherer of things, Meena Gallas. This all looks perfectly in order.' And handing Meena a piece of vellum, she turned to the door. 'The instructions are all there, so you may start preparing everything now. Brill will assist you.' Draguta lifted her eyebrows at Brill, who nodded. 'Wonderful! Enjoy your evening, ladies, as I shall enjoy mine!'

Meena didn't turn around as Draguta slipped through the door, humming to herself. She glanced at Brill, who looked even more miserable than she felt, and sighed.

***

Ivaar was sitting shoulder to shoulder with Thorgils, who'd drunk so much ale that he could almost cope with the experience of congratulating their new champion.

'How is that possible?' Jael wondered, shaking her head as Torstan sat down beside her. 'That Thorgils is talking to Ivaar as if they're long lost brothers over there?'

Torstan was drunk too, and he only grinned in response. A yellow-haired woman pushed herself in between them, and Jael moved away, leaving them to it.

'Looking for somewhere to sit?' Aleksander called.

'You're not drunk, are you?' Jael wondered.

'Depends on why you're asking,' Aleksander decided with a wink.

'Ha! I guess I'm looking for conversation, but so far, I haven't found anyone who isn't spitting or dribbling ale all over themselves or me.'

'There's always Axl,' Aleksander said, nodding to her brother, who was sitting with Reinhard, now a good weight of coins lighter after betting on his champion. 'Seems to be holding himself together over there. And there's me. But I can't even hear myself think in here. Let's go outside.' And not giving Jael a chance to argue, he grabbed her hand, leading her out into the night.

'I need a new cloak,' Jael grumbled, struck by how cold it was as they walked away from the hall.

'You can have mine,' Aleksander offered.

Jael shook her head, wrapping her arms around her chest. 'You keep it.'

They walked in silence, watching the fires burning around the tents where groups of men and women gathered for more drinking and storytelling. Without the Iskavallans, everything suddenly felt a lot less tense.

'Do you think they're alright in Andala?' Aleksander frowned. 'You haven't had any dreams, have you?'

His eyes were so dark, they looked almost hollow, and Jael was reminded of the dragur. 'No. Not about that.'

'What about...' he almost whispered, 'Hanna? Do you know if she's alive?'

'I don't, no, but I hope so.'

Aleksander didn't say anything as they walked past the latrines, getting a whiff of what it smells like when a thousand men descend upon a small fort. They hurried past, heading out of the gates, along the muddy road. 'And how are you?'

'Impatient.'

He laughed. 'Sounds about right.'

'I'm just ready to begin. I'm tired of waiting for the next attack. *I* want to be the next attack. I want to rip out Draguta's heart and burn it to ash. I want to destroy her and her book so they can never hurt anyone again. And I want to get my husband back and go home to my kingdom.' She turned to Aleksander, grabbing his arms. 'I'm done with waiting. It's time to make ourselves safe again!'

PART FIVE

My Father's Son

CHAPTER THIRTY FOUR

The Iskavallans made their camp in the forest, stopping not long after dusk, erecting their tents quickly and setting fires. Some chose to hunt for their supper, others making do with what they'd brought from Ollsvik and found in Rissna.

Ravenna had eaten with Raymon and Getta, though no one had spoken much as they sat around their fire, keeping to themselves, tired after the day's journey.

Getta had ignored Garren and his conniving eyes, sensing them on her whenever he was near. She'd barely been able to think since hearing about Raymon's real father. Since hearing about her own. She shivered, remembering the taste of Garren's lips, the feel of his body against hers. Finally, unable to ignore the intensely arousing feelings, Getta grabbed Raymon's hand and led him into their tent.

Raymon was surprised but pleased. She hadn't spoken to him since they'd left Rissna, and not much before that. 'It was a long day,' he murmured, not feeling tired as he turned to her.

Getta let him pull her towards him, though he wasn't Garren, and she desperately wanted to feel Garren's hands on her. Raymon was kissing her, but she was barely there, her mind wandering to her father, murdered by her cousins, and to her husband, who was now their brother.

And what was Garren going to do about that?

'Come to bed,' Raymon smiled.

It was dark in the tent, and despite her body throbbing with need, Getta was more tired than anything, but she sighed and followed him, not wanting to think at all.

***

Else had waited all day to give Morana the herbs. She had understood what Dragmall meant immediately when he'd mentioned them. He used to brew himself a dreaming tea when they were together. To help free his mind, he would say. To see those things the gods hid from humans.

Else suspected that Dragmall was a dreamer, but he would always deny it.

Still, he did say that the tea worked wonders.

And now she would see if it worked for Morana, though it would be impossible to know. But perhaps, if it helped Morana dream, she could find her own answers and a way out of Draguta's prison for them all.

Else tried to stop her mind from racing towards the things she was trying to conceal. Instead, she smiled and held the sweet-smelling tea up to Morana's lips.

Morana frowned. She didn't want the stinking tea.

She tried not to inhale, blinking at Else, who ignored her and lifted the cup higher so Morana could smell the tea, and suddenly, Morana stopped blinking and tried to open her mouth.

***

Edela felt nervous as she focused on the page. It was dark in the cottage, despite Biddy bringing in three extra lamps. Dara's writing was faint, or perhaps it was that time had faded it? And Edela knew that time had certainly faded her old eyes, so she squinted and re-read everything, wanting to get it right.

She thought of Jael as she sat there, listening to Biddy fussing over Eydis, and Entorp, who was tapping distractedly on the drum. More than anything, Edela wanted to free Eadmund and bring him back to Jael and Eydis.

She placed the Book of Aurea on the ground and picked up Eadmund's wedding band, which she positioned on her knee, reaching forward to grab her knife.

A candle burned before her. She'd carved symbols into it, and in the floorboards, making a circle inside which she sat.

Uncomfortable, unconfident, but impatient to begin.

Ayla was there too, and she smiled at Edela, sensing her tension, wishing she was strong enough to help.

'Are you ready?' Biddy wondered, peering at her face. Edela had gone very quiet.

'I am,' Edela breathed, taking one last look at Eydis, who Biddy had positioned beside her, inside the circle. 'Put your hand on my knee, Eydis, and make sure you inhale the smoke slowly. It will be very strong, I should say, with those herbs. Short, slow breaths to begin, and then we'll drink the potion.'

Edela's voice drifted away, and Eydis felt panic flutter in her chest, worried that she wouldn't be able to help her.

Worried that they wouldn't be able to save Eadmund.

***

'You are so beautiful,' Eadmund smiled, all thoughts of Rollo gone as he ran his finger over Evaine's lips before bending to kiss them. 'So very beautiful.'

Evaine sighed with happiness, hearing the desire in his voice. It was dark in the bedchamber. Dark and muggy. Her body was slick with sweat as she lay beneath him, feeling him sliding against her.

Arching her back, Evaine closed her eyes, every niggle and irritation drifting away like fireflies into the night.

**

Jael's dreams tortured her with pictures she didn't want to see. They'd started the moment she closed her eyes, and no matter how desperately she twisted and turned in her creaking cot bed, she couldn't wake herself up.

She saw Eadmund in bed with Evaine. On top of Evaine.

She saw her dead daughter.

And then she saw her father with Ravenna. They were in a bedchamber, sitting on a fur in front of a fire, watching their baby son.

'He needs to go to sleep,' Ravenna smiled.

She looked so young. There wasn't a line on her face.

Ranuf held out a hand to stop her taking the baby. 'Just a little longer,' he tried. 'Please. I have to leave in the morning. Just a little longer.'

Jael could see the sadness in his eyes. The torture.

She didn't care. She wanted to look away.

Ranuf bent down and lifted up his son, beaming as Raymon gurgled at him, smiling toothlessly, kicking his legs. Ranuf brought him into the crook of his arm. 'My son,' he murmured as Jael turned away, looking for another dream. 'My son.'

Jael closed her eyes, squeezing them tight.

'Jael!' Ranuf's voice was urgent now. '*My son!*'

***

Edela felt that Eydis was with her. She couldn't see her, but she didn't feel alone in the darkness.

She was in a house. It looked like a grand house. Not Andalan, she was sure, for the walls were made of stone. Edging cautiously towards the light, Edela found a door, and she slipped through it, entering a bedchamber, candles burning on either side of a large double bed where Eadmund and Evaine were sleeping.

Edela heard a sharp intake of breath.

It wasn't her.

She couldn't swallow. Her head was pounding, and she felt uncomfortably warm as she crept towards the bed, trying to see what she hoped was there: a rope, connecting Eadmund to Evaine.

It was dark, shadows shifting over the sleeping bodies from the flickering lamps, and she was struggling to see. Evaine stirred, and Edela froze, realising that she had to hurry. She felt the strain of holding the trance, and Edela knew that it wouldn't be long before she was on her knees, back in the cottage.

Leaning forward, she reached around Eadmund's chest, searching, and finally feeling the smooth, slender rope, she grabbed it. Evaine rolled over, groaning, and Edela could see that the rope was draped over her, like a black snake coiled around her body. She ran her hand down the rope, feeling it shake as she found where it entered Eadmund. It wasn't tied around him at all. And pushing gently, trying to keep her breathing steady, Edela eased her hand all the way down... into Eadmund's soul.

***

Jael gasped, sitting upright. Her heart was banging in her chest, and she couldn't catch her breath. It was raining, she thought, but she quickly realised that the noise was inside her head.

Rubbing her eyes, she swung her legs over the side of the bed, trying to breathe. Her father's voice came back to her, and she frowned, dropping her head to her hands, not wanting to think about him at all. Not wanting to remember her dream of Ranuf with his baby son. It felt too strange.

How had he had another family?

Jael shivered, suddenly cold. The tent was dark, the sides flapping, and she looked around for her fur, which had fallen onto the ground. And when she sat back up with it in her hands, she came face to face with Fyr.

***

Edela pushed her hand down until she felt a knot, and grasping it, she froze. Everything had suddenly gone black. She tried blinking, but her vision did not clear. 'Eydis?' she panicked, trying to blow small breaths out through her mouth to calm herself down. Her hand was in Eadmund's soul. She couldn't stop now. 'Eydis, help me.'

And suddenly, there was light, and Edela swallowed, still gripping the knot, working hard to pull it back out. But it wouldn't budge. 'Eydis, make the symbol,' Edela panted, hearing a buzzing in her ears like a swarm of bees. 'Make the symbol now.'

And then Edela saw her, as Eydis leaned over her brother,

painting a symbol on his naked chest. It represented an ending. A breaking of what had been. A time to start anew. And Edela felt the knot slip away, all resistance gone, and she pulled it straight through Eadmund's stomach as though she was lifting a feather.

Eydis blinked at Edela, too terrified to speak, watching as she cut through the rope.

Holding both ends in her left hand, Edela started chanting the words she'd memorised from the Book of Aurea. And when she was done, she dropped the pieces of rope, turning to look at Eydis, who had gone.

And when Edela turned back around, so had the rope.

Or, at least, one of them had.

As her eyes adjusted to the darkness, Edela could see another rope. It wrapped around Eadmund's waist, thinner than the other one, and as Edela grabbed it, she felt an explosion shoot up her arm, and then everything went dark.

***

'Wake! Up!' Jael screamed, running out of her tent, buckling her swordbelt around her mail shirt, pushing her feet deeper into her boots. 'Wake up! We ride now!'

Rissna was suddenly alive with noise, bodies staggering out of tents, stumbling out of the hall. Jael ran to the stables to ready Tig, almost smacking into a wobbling Ivaar, who grabbed her arms, struggling to focus on her; Thorgils and Karsten right behind him.

'What's happened?'

Jael didn't have time to explain. 'It's Raymon! I need everyone who has a horse! We have to ride now!'

The moon was just a sliver and not much to see by, but as

she turned around, Jael saw the shimmer of wings as Fyr flew away to the east.

Where they would need to go, and quickly.

***

Biddy hurried to Edela's side as she tipped forward, perilously close to the flames.

Entorp dropped his drum, rushing to check on Eydis, who had opened her eyes but looked as though she too was about to fall over. The cottage was filled with smoke, and none of them could breathe easily.

After helping Edela into her chair, Biddy opened the door, taking a quick breath before pouring cups of water for everyone. 'Here,' she said, handing one to Eydis, another to Edela. 'Have a good drink of that.' And she bent over, coughing before returning for the other two cups.

'Eydis?' Entorp was worried. She seemed to be trapped in the trance. 'Are you there?'

Eydis heard Entorp's voice as though it was drifting somewhere in the clouds above her head, but she nodded slowly, trying to pull herself back into the cottage.

Ayla was beside her as well now. 'Can you dip a cloth in some water?' she asked Biddy. 'She's very hot. We need to wake her up a little more.'

Edela couldn't stop coughing. The water didn't help, and her mind was tumbling as if she were rolling down a grassy bank. She saw the rope in her mind, and looking down at her shaking hands, she saw that she was still holding the knife.

Ayla held the wet cloth to Eydis' neck, then draped it over her face, and eventually, Eydis blinked, panicking. 'Edela!' she croaked, her throat so dry that she had to swallow to find some saliva. 'Edela! What are we going to do about the other rope?'

***

Jael's men weren't ready fast enough for her liking. Many of them were drunk but sobering quickly in the cold night air as she waited on Tig, urging them on with impatient eyes.

Eventually, Aleksander was beside her; Gant, Axl, Thorgils and Fyn lined up behind them. 'We ride fast!' she yelled to her men. 'And we don't stop! Take care of your horse! Keep your eyes open! And if you're still drunk, you're at the back!' And nodding for Gant to blow his horn, she tapped her boots against Tig's flanks. It hadn't taken him long to wake up, and he shivered with excitement as he galloped away from the fort, down the muddy track that led into the forest.

Jael blinked her eyes open wide, hoping she'd be able to find her way in the dark. Then she heard the raven, just ahead of her, and she dropped her head down, closer to Tig's, pushing him on, into the forest.

After Fyr.

***

It was strange not to feel any elation. Edela knew that she had cut the rope that bound Eadmund to Evaine. She had felt it shrivel and die.

But the other one?

What was that?

'What happened when you touched it?' Ayla asked.

'It felt like a spark ignited. Like lightning. Everything went dark, and I woke up here,' Edela said. She wanted to lie in her bed, but there was too much to discuss. Her body hadn't stopped shaking, and her breathing was rapid, but she ignored all of it as she tried to focus her thoughts.

'It must be Draguta,' Ayla decided. 'She has bound Eadmund too. Or Morana Gallas?'

'I couldn't even touch it, so how are we going to cut that rope?'

'I don't know,' Ayla admitted, the smoke still addling her own mind. 'We need to look in the Book of Aurea again, but not tonight, Edela. You must sleep now. Eydis too. That took a lot out of you both.'

Eydis could only nod sleepily as Biddy helped her to her feet, guiding her to her little bed before going back for Edela.

Entorp frowned at Ayla, watching as she stood. 'If Draguta has bound Eadmund to her, he will do whatever she wants, to whomever she wants. He is most certainly not free now.'

***

Eskild studied her son as he walked towards Morana's tiny cottage. Made from wisened bark logs, topped with a grass roof, it was hidden in the trees, as though it were part of the forest itself. But there was a door, and smoke wound its way out of the roof, and Eskild could smell the rich flavours of meat cooking as she followed Eadmund inside.

Morana bent over her cauldron, stirring with a long wooden spoon. Lifting the spoon to her lips, she blew, then tasted the stew, quickly looking around for the salt. 'It worked last time,' she grumbled. 'Why are you so worried now?'

Eskild turned to see Morac sitting across from his sister.

As usual, he looked as though he was sucking a lemon: his thin lips pursed, his face twisted into a scowl. Miserable man, she thought to herself as Eadmund walked away from her to the other side of the cottage, watching with interest.

'Eirik's a man, bigger than the girl. What if there's not enough? What if it just makes him sick? Doesn't kill him? He might suspect me,' Morac panicked, his eyes on the bottle he held in his hands.

Morana snorted as she sprinkled salt over the stew, stirring it again. 'Do you think I'm stupid, Brother? *Me?* After all these years, Eirik Skalleson is finally going to get what he deserves. Don't you think I'd ensure there was more than enough to kill him? I'd happily have him suffer a slow death, but we can't take the risk that he'll reveal something.' She glared at her brother. 'You had no trouble killing Eadmund's wife, that stupid little bitch. Now you just have to kill his father, and Eadmund will be one step closer to us. One step closer to being ours.' And she turned away to look for some bowls.

Eskild felt as though time itself had stopped. She could feel the flutter of her lashes as her eyes opened and closed ever so slowly, watching as Eadmund lifted his head and stared at her, his eyes full of pain.

And anger.

***

They rode through the forest, thundering down narrow paths, around tall birch trees, following Jael, who didn't stop, nor look around. She rode with intense concentration, trying not to drive them straight into a tree trunk. The night was a cloak over both her and Tig, and only by remaining alert was she going to get them through the forest in one piece.

Aleksander rode just behind her, Sky following Tig closely, the bite of the wind keeping them wide awake. Eventually, he could see dawn coming. The sky was lightening, and as the path widened, he rode up next to Jael, whose tired eyes remained fixed ahead.

'What's happened?' he called.

But Jael only glanced at him before refocusing, pushing Tig harder, knowing that they were getting close.

Not knowing if they would be in time.

CHAPTER THIRTY FIVE

Eadmund was woken by the clatter of the iron poker hitting the cauldron. He jerked upright, rubbing his eyes, wondering if it was still night, then he saw some streaks of light creeping under the door. He grimaced, feeling a dull ache in his stomach, looking down at Evaine, who was moaning, not wanting to wake up yet.

'Go back to sleep, Eadmund,' she mumbled, curling towards him, flapping a hand in his direction. 'Sleep, my love.'

Yawning, Eadmund turned to the bedside table and took a sip of water. Evaine appeared to have fallen back to sleep, so he lay down again, pulling the sheet away from his chest, pressing a palm against his stomach. The room was hot, and he felt sweaty, but when he touched his stomach, it felt like ice.

He stared at Evaine, watching as she fell back to sleep, trying to make sense of the whirlwind of memories rushing around his head.

***

Getta rolled over, her eyes wide, ready to scream before a smoky hand clamped over her mouth. She panicked, wanting to look around. There were men in her tent. She could hear noises outside.

Shouting. People running.

Getta knew that Raymon had been dragged out of bed. She was conscious of being naked. It was barely dawn, and she squinted, trying to make out the face of the man who leaned over her, then her attention shifted as she saw another man approach, bending down.

'Ssshhh,' Garren smiled, indicating for the man to remove his hand. 'You're safe.' And he helped Getta sit up, retrieving her dress from the ground and handing it to her. 'Get dressed.' And turning, Garren nodded for his men to leave.

Getta's heart was thudding so loudly that she couldn't breathe. 'Where's my son?' she panicked, trying to swallow. 'Where's Raymon?'

Garren sat on the bed, watching as she pulled on her dress.

Getta didn't want to see his eyes, but she could feel them all over her. She shook, in shock, not really believing what was happening. All the things she'd thought about and considered; all that she'd wished for and imagined. It had just been in her head. Frustrations and annoyances. Fantasies and dreams. She was terrified to think that it was actually happening. 'What have you done?' she whispered, hearing more screams; the whinnying of horses. 'Where is my son?'

Garren smoothed hair away from her rumpled face. 'Remember what I said? You're safe, Getta. I won't let anything happen to you. Now put on your boots, and we can talk about your son.'

***

Jael watched Fyr flying up ahead, her sleek, black feathers

glistening in the early light. The sky was brightening quickly now, and Jael could feel her throat tightening. She didn't think Raymon would have led his army too far off the main road, though they could hardly camp in a tangle of trees. He would've needed to find a clearing large enough to accommodate all his men and horses.

But where?

Jael could feel them getting closer. Fyn's bow was strung across her back, banging with every crash of Tig's hooves onto the ground, the quiver of arrows banging with it.

'My son!'

She heard her father's urgent voice again, her heartbeat quickening.

Fyr disappeared into the trees, and Jael yanked Tig's reins, pulling him after her.

***

Getta's eyes bulged as Garren took her out of the tent, into the clearing where they'd camped for the night. The sky was a greyish, light blue. Smoke was drifting from blazing fires. Men stood around them, their eyes turning to Garren as he brought Getta forward.

'Getta!'

She quickly spotted Raymon on his knees, a man behind him with a knife.

Ravenna was beside him; Aldo Maas with a handful of her hair as he stood behind her, pressing himself against her back.

'Garren,' Getta tried, afraid that she might vomit. 'Garren, it shouldn't be like this!' She gripped his arm, pleading with him. 'This isn't the way to do it.'

'Getta!' Raymon called again. 'Where's Lothar?'

Getta spun around as more and more of those loyal to Raymon were brought towards the fires, kicking and fighting, knocked down to the forest floor.

Surrounded.

'What are you doing, Garren?' Ravenna begged. 'Let my son go! Please! He's just a boy! If you want to be king, be king! But let him live!' She was crying so much she could barely get the words out. '*Please!*' She felt no fear for herself. Only her son. 'Aldo!' She could feel the old man behind her. She could see the glint of his knife out of the corner of her eye. 'Please! Not my son!'

Aldo bent low to her ear. 'Pray to your gods, bitch,' he growled as his son came forward.

'Raymon Vandaal must die!' Garren bellowed. 'He is no Iskavallan! He is not our rightful king! His father stole the throne! His grandfather stole the throne! But at least they were Iskavallans!' He spun around, watching the puzzled faces of the men who gathered around him. 'This nothing pup is a Brekkan! Ranuf Furyck's bastard! Put on our throne to help the Furycks claim Iskavall for themselves!'

The shock on his men's faces was pronounced, but the shock on Raymon's was greater still.

'No!' Raymon cried. 'No! It's not true!' He looked at his mother, seeking her support, but Ravenna closed her eyes, tears streaming down her face, and he knew. '*No!*'

Garren turned to Getta, his voice a whisper in her ear. 'You will watch. And when we're done, you will have your son back. But not until we're done. I need your loyalty, Getta. I cannot have a wife who isn't loyal.'

The shock was a clattering sound in his head, and Raymon couldn't breathe.

He saw Getta nod at Garren, and he screamed.

***

Jael's head was up. 'Get ready!' she turned and cried to Aleksander, who passed the call down the pounding train of horses streaming behind them. They were riding single file. At pace. The path was too narrow for more.

Jael gripped Tig with her knees and dropped the reins, pulling the bow over her head, nocking an arrow.

***

They thought it was thunder, looking up at the sky, which made no sense as the morning had dawned clear, and then they saw Jael Furyck thundering towards them on her giant black horse, her mail shirt and battered helmet gleaming in the sunlight.

'Kill them!' Garren yelled to his father, pushing Getta into the nearest tent and unsheathing one of his swords.

'My son!'

Ranuf's words rang in Jael's ears until she couldn't hear anything but his desperate plea, and drawing the bowstring past her ear, feeling Tig charging forward, straight for the Iskavallan camp, she looked at Ravenna, who had a knife at her throat, and she aimed for the man standing behind Raymon.

'No!' Raymon screamed as his captor flew backwards, an arrow through his forehead, his mother slumping to the ground beside him, her throat sliced open. Jael quickly nocked another arrow as the path widened and her men filled the clearing on either side of her. Releasing her bowstring, she shot Aldo Maas in the back of the neck as he ran away from Ravenna.

Slipping the bow back over her shoulder, Jael unsheathed

Toothpick and kicked Tig towards the scattering men.

'*Mother!*' Raymon threw himself over Ravenna's body, but her neck was gushing blood over her nightdress, and her eyes remained fixed open in shock. Hauling himself to his feet, Raymon turned away from her, running to find his sword and his wife.

'Don't kill them all!' Jael bellowed. 'We need them! Get the ones running!'

And her men urged their horses on, fanning out into the clearing, weapons raised, sharpened blades catching the morning light.

Jael brought *Toothpick* down into the scalp of a stumbling Iskavallan, who'd been charging after Garren Maas. The man tumbled to the ground as she drew out her blade, nudging Tig with her boots. She saw Raymon out of the corner of her eye, running, a man she recognised chasing him with an axe. 'Raymon!' she yelled. 'Get a fucking sword!'

And Raymon turned, shocked to see who was trying to kill him, quickly ducking the axe swinging for his head. He'd been dragged out of bed half-naked and didn't have a weapon. In the confusion of the attack, he didn't even know where his tent was. Throwing himself at Tolbert's waist, Raymon knocked him to the ground, punching him in the nose as Tolbert worked to free his blade, aiming it at Raymon's head. Raymon staggered, tipping to the side, righting himself as he ducked the blade, swinging another punch at Tolbert's nose. Breaking it. Now Tolbert's eyes were watering, and everything had blurred as he struggled onto his knees. He only saw shadows, and he didn't notice the big one looming over him until it was too late and Jael had stabbed *Toothpick* through the back of his neck.

'Here,' she said, handing Raymon a sword she'd picked up. 'Come with me!'

'But Getta!' Raymon tried. 'What about Getta?'

'We have work to do if you want to see Getta again, now come on!' And Jael ran towards Thorgils, who she could see, off his horse, fighting a man almost as big as him. She quickly scanned the clearing, looking for Garren, but he had disappeared when she'd stopped to help Raymon.

Thorgils dispatched the look-alike tree with a swift butt of his head before dropping to the ground to slice his knife across the man's throat.

'Thorgils!' Jael called as she ran past him. 'Look after Raymon! Don't let anything happen to him! I have to go!' Because she had just seen Garren Maas jump on a horse and kick it through the trees. Running for Tig, Jael sheathed *Toothpick*, and mounting quickly, she urged him after the grey horse, straight past Gant.

Who watched her go, turning to assess the situation. They'd released Raymon's men and put down the main thrust of the uprising, but small clusters of fights were splintering. 'Let's finish this! Round up the rebels, and let's finish this now!' he bellowed, taking charge.

Jael heard him as she slipped through the trees, confident that Gant and her men could snuff out the rebels quickly, but she would need to get their leader.

A man like Garren Maas would never stop trying to steal the throne.

She had to put him down.

***

Garren's horse skidded around the trees, struggling with her footing on the rain-soaked forest floor. His head was low, ducking branches, avoiding the thick bough his horse had just slipped under, his heart pounding in time to her hooves; a rhythmic, steady beat. And then another sound.

Turning, he saw Jael Furyck thundering after him.

Jael saw the panic in Garren's eyes, but also the determination to escape. The forest was a maze of entangled trees; narrow, snake-like paths curling around gnarled trunks. There was no clear stretch that she could see as she worked the reins, guiding Tig with her knees, but she didn't need to. He could see well enough where he needed to go. The tree cover was light, and the sun was getting brighter, and they could both see where Garren Maas was.

Jael knew that she had to stop him escaping, though she wasn't convinced she was strong enough to fight him yet. Not with a sword. But she couldn't see a way to use her bow in the maze of trees. She needed Garren to find his way to a clearing.

Until then, she had to keep up with his very fast horse. 'Come on, Tig!' she growled, dipping lower as a branch slapped her in the face. 'Come on!'

***

Thorgils kept one eye on Raymon, who appeared well-equipped to handle his sword, but he had the sense that the young king was looking to bolt and find his wife. His eyes were skittish, skipping around the tents, not paying as much attention as he needed to the man trying to kill him.

Thorgils kicked an Iskavallan in the balls, his shoulder aching and his head pounding. Astrid wouldn't be pleased with him, he thought, feeling blood pool in his shoulder wound, which had no doubt ripped open again. 'Finish him!' he barked at Raymon, who was shuffling from side to side, parrying and thrusting but getting nowhere. 'Like this!' And Thorgils chopped his sword into the man's neck, knocking him sideways, stumbling as Karsten shoved him out of the way of the axe that was swinging for his own neck.

Thorgils shook his head, scrambling back to his feet, one eye on Raymon, who appeared to be concentrating now, the other on Karsten, who finished off Thorgils' attacker with two quick blows across the man's middle. Spinning around, he heard Rork bellow as he dropped to his knees, a spear in his shoulder.

'Rork!' Karsten yelled, running for him.

Thorgils suddenly had two men on him, and he couldn't help Karsten or Rork, but Aleksander was there, severing the head of Rork's attacker; Karsten quickly dragging Rork to his feet, away from danger.

'Aarrghh!' Thorgils screamed as someone sliced across the back of his thigh. Turning with a growl, he raised his sword, but Raymon was there, his blade through the Iskavallan's back. He nodded at Thorgils and spun away, trying to find his way to Getta. He needed to know that she was safe.

Running, head swivelling, looking for his wife, he slipped on the bloody pine needles of the forest floor, crashing to his knees, one of Garren's men looming over him.

'Raymon!' Axl had just cut down one Iskavallan, and he saw the young king fall, but he had no way through to him. Swapping his sword into his left hand, he drew out his knife with the other, planting his feet and flicking his wrist, watching the blade snap through the air, landing in the neck of the man, who'd just drawn blood from Raymon's forearm.

The man fell, and Ivaar was there, hand out, pulling Raymon to his feet. 'Come on!' he yelled. 'You're with me!'

Thorgils joined them, remembering Jael's words. 'You don't leave!' he grumbled at Raymon. 'Not till we're done! And we're not done till I say we're done!'

Ivaar nodded at Thorgils, and they stood on either side of Raymon as the Iskavallans charged.

***

Garren could hear rushing water. He knew that he was close to a stream, and he spurred his horse on, checking quickly behind him to see how far away Jael Furyck was.

Her horse was bigger, more powerful, but he'd had enough of a head start to keep just ahead of her. Turning around unbalanced his horse, though, and as he turned back, she stumbled, her legs tangling, tripping and falling in the wet leaves just before the stream. Jael yanked the reins, skidding Tig to a halt, too close to use her bow and arrow. Sliding out of the saddle, she unsheathed *Toothpick*, running towards Garren as he staggered to his feet. He hauled two swords from the scabbards strapped across his back, ignoring the pitiful cries of his injured horse, who roared in agony, her front shins snapped, unable to stand.

Jael thought quickly, assessing the situation, her father's voice calmly walking her through it as if they were in the training ring.

'Two swords. Slippery surface. Stream. No help.'

And she remembered the look in Ravenna's eyes as Garren's father had slit her throat, and her father's face in her dream as he'd held their son.

How happy he had been. How in love.

And the clarity of that thought wiped away everything else.

'Kill him.'

She could almost feel Ranuf's breath on her neck, his hand on her shoulder.

'Kill him, Jael. For me.'

***

Garren's men were overwhelmed. Their leaders were dead or gone, and the Brekkan army was crushing them, smothering them.

Killing them.

Aleksander spat out a mouthful of blood, one eye on Raymon Vandaal, still on his feet, flanked by Thorgils and Ivaar, who were working hard, fighting off his attackers.

But there were not many now, and no more were rushing to join them.

Aleksander spun as Axl jerked an Iskavallan towards him, his arm around the man's throat. He had no sword. He was sobbing, begging for his life.

'We take prisoners,' Axl said, pleased that Aleksander was quickly nodding. 'Raymon should decide their fate, not us.'

'Throw down your weapons!' Aleksander called. 'You're outnumbered! Throw down your weapons!'

'We surrender!' one man yelled. He was older, blood dripping from a gash in his forehead, his sword in the air. '*Please!* We surrender!'

Gant lifted his own blood-red sword, panting. 'Hold!' he cried, scanning the clearing, watching more Iskavallans – those who had followed Garren and Aldo Maas – raising their weapons and their hands. They were surrounded. Abandoned.

At the mercy of their king.

Thorgils brought Raymon towards Gant.

'Your men, your problem,' Gant said shortly, looking around at the mounds of bodies, hoping not to find many of their own men lying amongst the slaughtered Iskavallan rebels. The smell of smoke and blood and bowels was intense. 'What do you want to do?'

Raymon couldn't think. 'I want to know where my wife and son are. That they're safe. Please, gather these men together and guard them.' He kept turning around. 'I need to find my wife.' He wanted to find his mother too, but he knew that it was a futile wish.

He couldn't help her anymore.

Gant nodded, turning to Thorgils and Aleksander, Ivaar

and Karsten. 'Bring them in!' he called. 'To the fires! On their knees! They will wait for their king's judgement!'

***

'You will die!' Garren yelled.

'I will,' Jael said calmly, trying to keep her breathing steady, though she was desperate to fill her lungs with air. 'But not today.' She firmed up her grip on *Toothpick*, waiting to see what he would do.

Garren had two swords. Likely he thought that was an advantage.

Jael scuffed her boots deep into the slippery leaves, searching for solid earth, her eyes never leaving his.

Garren lunged, swords twirling, his long blond hair floating behind him like Eidur, God of the Hunt. Jael dipped to the left, leaving him to stumble to a stop before spinning around. Every part of her felt slow and heavy, and she knew then that he would defeat her with his swords.

But she didn't plan to defeat him with hers.

Turning to face him as he came at her again, Jael stepped back, just out of reach as Garren slashed his right sword towards her throat. She jumped back again, making him come after her, watching the frustration spark in his eyes. Garren swung his left sword, quickly following with his right, and Jael stepped back, swaying out of reach, listening to Garren's horse moaning in agony.

She blinked away the distraction, bringing *Toothpick* up to block a blow, drawing him quickly away as she edged back again, feeling the ground sloping towards the stream now, trying not to lose her balance.

The stream was rushing, its water high after the deluge of

rain.

'What were you going to do?' she panted. 'Kill Raymon? Kill Getta? And then what? Take the throne and hide behind your walls? Try to defeat Brekka?' She wanted to distract him now, her feet in constant motion, her eyes watching his swords.

'Getta?' Garren's face changed. 'You think I'd kill Getta? It was our plan, together! She doesn't love that *boy*! She never wanted *him!*'

That surprised Jael, though she didn't doubt his words, and she didn't stop looking at his swords as he twirled them impatiently now, lunging for her.

Skirting the tips of the blades, Jael turned him around.

Now she was facing the stream, lashing out with *Toothpick*, four quick slashes from side to side. Garren was downhill, working to keep from sliding as he bellowed, swinging powerfully with both swords.

The soggy carpet of leaves covering the bank of the stream was slippery.

Taking a quick breath, Jael jumped back, dropping her weight onto her left leg and slamming her right boot into his chest. Garren's arms flailed uselessly as the ground gave way, and he tumbled backwards, into the rushing water.

Jael waded in after him, *Toothpick* in both hands as he struggled back to his feet. The blow to Garren's chest had winded him, and the fall into the stream had knocked his swords out of his hands. Quickly realising that, he threw himself at Jael, but she jumped back, out of reach, and he fell into the water again. Jael was over him in a heartbeat, her boot on his back, pushing him under the water, stabbing *Toothpick* straight through his neck.

***

'Getta!' Raymon ran for his wife as she emerged from a tent, clutching their son to her chest. Her eyes were wide with terror, and now confusion. She didn't know what would happen next, but while she was the mother of Raymon's son, she wasn't going to let anything happen to herself.

Raymon checked them over before pulling them both into his arms. Lothar was screaming, red-faced, hungry and frightened. 'Are you alright?' he breathed, feeling Getta tremble against him.

She could only nod, not knowing what he knew.

'What did he do to you? Garren? What did he do?' Raymon stood back, looking her over again. His eyes were sharp, searching hers.

'Nothing,' Getta insisted. 'I am unharmed. Nothing.' She shook her head, tears flooding her eyes. 'I want to go home, Raymon. Please!'

Raymon looked up to see Getta's equally terrified servant standing by the entrance to the tent. 'Hilda, take my wife. Keep her safe until I return.' And turning away, he headed for the rebel prisoners, waiting to hear his judgement.

He didn't want to walk towards them at all; he wanted to run to his mother because she was dead, and he didn't want her to be. He wanted to cry and throw himself on her body and never let her go. But instead, gritting his teeth, Raymon strode towards Gant, not knowing what to do. His mother was dead. Some of his men were dead and dying. He could hear them.

He couldn't think.

Gant could tell. He drew Raymon away from the eyes that were all fixed on him.

'Where's Garren?' Raymon asked blankly. 'He did this.'

'Jael went after him. I'd say he won't be coming back.'

Raymon thought he might vomit. Or sob. 'My mother,' he began, his tears coming quickly now. He knew that Gant was a man to trust. He'd come to Ollsvik with Ranuf Furyck many times.

Ranuf Furyck. He couldn't even begin to understand that.

Trying to see through his tears, Raymon turned to Gant. 'If I kill them all, what message does that send?'

'Well, some maybe went along with Garren out of fear. Small-minded people tend to flock to men like him. Men who feed into their fears, burnish their egos, gild their dreams of gold and glory,' Gant muttered. 'You kill them, you send the message that you won't tolerate disloyalty. But perhaps you set yourself up for another rebellion? If you come down too hard, you'll crush any respect they may have for you.' He looked at the men on their knees before the fire. 'You may as well hand their sons a sword. One day they'll find a way to come for you again.'

Raymon frowned, and he looked just like Ranuf.

Gant blinked to see it.

They looked up as Jael and Tig entered the clearing. Alone.

Gant nodded, his shoulders easing away from his ears. 'Ask your sister over there,' he said, smiling at the horror on Raymon's face. 'She's the one who saved your life.'

CHAPTER THIRTY SIX

Edela stayed in bed while Biddy rushed in and out of the cottage. Breaking the soul spell had taken a lot out of her. She felt slightly displaced, as though not all of her had returned. And she couldn't stop looking at her hand; the one she had pushed inside Eadmund's soul.

It felt so cold, tingling when she touched it.

It had been an unsettling experience. Edela had felt so much pain and sadness inside Eadmund, and it was still affecting her as she struggled to find her way out of the darkness.

Ayla came to visit her. Entorp too. Eydis brought Amma, who brought a big slice of apple cake. And then Marcus came with news of Hanna, which made Edela smile as she ate the cake and explained what they'd done the night before.

'Another rope?' Marcus was stunned by that; amazed by what Edela had managed to do. 'A binding rope?'

Edela nodded. 'It was different, but I fear it is the same. And it must be Draguta's or Morana's, which means that poor Eadmund must be Draguta's or Morana's to control.'

'But perhaps no longer Evaine's?' Marcus suggested.

'Well, I hope not. I wouldn't like to go through that again!' Edela gave her plate to Biddy, who handed her a cup of chamomile tea. 'Though we will have to do something to cut that rope.'

Marcus frowned. 'I don't imagine that stopping Draguta

will be as straightforward, though. Not if she has changed.'

'What do you mean?'

'Well, I thought about it last night. I kept trying to imagine what Dara Teros saw as a girl. What she recorded as the prophecy. She saw her sister turning into a monster. She saw the threat of Raemus and the Darkness. But what if she missed something? She was a young girl, not a trained dreamer. What if she missed something important? If she didn't understand what she was seeing?'

'But she would have revisited it over the years, wouldn't she?' Edela murmured. 'Seen it through more experienced eyes?'

'I'm sure she did. But if she did miss something, or if something has changed, we need to be prepared, Edela. You and Eydis and Ayla are important. The only dreamers we have here, so we need to get Ayla tattooed. I've had Entorp work on me, and he will tattoo Hanna as soon as she is well enough,' Marcus said, his arms still aching with the reminder of Entorp's tapping. 'You three and the Book of Aurea are our only insight into what will come next. Your dreams are the only way we have of helping Jael and Eadmund. Of getting them to where they need to be. In Hest, ready to defeat Draguta. Ready to take her book.'

***

Eadmund had barely spoken since he'd crawled out of bed.

Ignoring his breakfast, he'd wrapped his swordbelt around his shrinking waist before heading out to the training ring, knowing that he needed to find someone new to practice with. He still felt disappointed that Rollo was gone but less curious about where he was now.

He was completely lost in his dreams.

Morana's cottage kept rushing towards him as though he was being thrown in through the door, the trees blowing violently around it. And inside were Morana and her brother.

His father's best friend.

'Eadmund!' Draguta's smile widened as she saw him walking towards her. 'Off to train?' She quickly frowned, seeing that he was wearing his old tunic again, which made him look less like a king and more like a man who worked for the king. 'Perhaps we should take you to the tailor's when you're done? Find you something new to wear? Something befitting a man of your status. There's no need to wear that old rag or Haegen's hand-me-downs.'

Eadmund nodded. 'Yes, of course.'

He looked odd, Draguta thought. Distracted. Compliant, yes, but something was off. Her attention was immediately diverted to Jaeger, who walked towards them with his master shipbuilder. Just the men she wanted to see. 'You have come with good news?' she wondered.

'We have!' Jaeger grinned, pleased to see her. Not at all pleased to see Eadmund, who squared his shoulders, enjoying the sight of Jaeger's battered face; barely feeling the discomfort of his own. 'More carpenters have arrived, so we have a good chance of seeing a harbour full of ships come winter.'

'*Winter?*' Draguta was horrified. 'You're telling me that I need to wait until *winter?*' She glared at Jaeger, whose triumphant smile retreated. Winter was an ambitious time frame for replacing an entire fleet of warships. He had imagined that she'd be pleased. 'And in the meantime?'

Jaeger took a deep breath. 'It takes months to build a ship, especially here. Timber must be brought in from Tuura and Alekka. Some comes down from Kroll, but mostly we need to import the materials.'

Draguta didn't care. She wanted ships.

Her vision of a mighty fleet and a formidable army wasn't

a new one. She'd been dreaming of it since her son, Valder, had ruled the dragon throne all those years ago. Once power was claimed, it needed to be protected. Kingdoms that were conquered needed to be ruled. Draguta had never subscribed to the ravings of The Following, whose salivating lunatics wished to scorch the earth and block the sun.

She wanted to rule. To be the only ruler in the land.

'We need men, as much as we need ships,' Jaeger added. 'We lost many in the battle with the Islanders. Ships need crews.'

Draguta narrowed her eyes, looking from Eadmund to Jaeger. 'And I know just where to find them. Ships too.' And biting her lip, she turned away from them both, heading for the castle.

There was one more seeing circle she needed to draw.

***

Jael kept eyeing Getta. She could almost see the guilt etched onto her face.

Her cousin barely spoke, keeping her eyes low, focusing on caring for her baby; fussing over him when he appeared perfectly settled and content.

Raymon didn't notice. He'd ordered Garren's accomplices killed. Beheaded. The rest were pardoned after taking an oath of loyalty to support him as king but not before he'd been forced to address his parentage; revealing his lack of knowledge of it before that moment when Garren had announced it. He looked so shell-shocked that most appeared to believe him. They believed him too when he said that he was no more Brekkan than Hugo Vandaal had been. That he wanted to protect Iskavall from what was coming; to lead them to a great victory in Hest. Raymon's voice shook, and he had to stop himself from looking to where his mother's body lay, covered in a cloak. In the end, his voice had broken as he proclaimed his own oath to protect Iskavall and its people, and his men, who he asked to fight with him and for him.

Jael thought it had gone well. He was a boy, untested, and now a bastard, and that didn't inspire confidence, but he was what they had, and she got the sense that with the support of his senior men, Raymon had enough to see him through their attack on Hest.

She hoped so. They couldn't afford to lose men now.

Raymon found her as she stood by Tig, adjusting his bridle. There was nothing more they could do except head back to Rissna and prepare to leave for Andala.

'How did you know?' Raymon asked quietly. 'What Garren would do?'

Jael stared at him. She didn't want him to look like Ranuf, but sometimes, she realised, the way he frowned reminded her of her father. *Their* father. 'I had a dream about you. I heard Ranuf's voice, then my raven led me here.'

Raymon looked surprised. 'You have a raven?'

'Seems that I do,' Jael smiled, though she didn't feel happy. 'I'm sorry I couldn't save your mother. I wanted to. My father would have wanted me to.'

'I didn't know,' Raymon tried, tears in his eyes as he felt the sharp pain of loss again. It was like a wave that would crest, then draw itself out to sea before crashing over him again with renewed force. He felt sick. 'I didn't know about Ranuf.'

'No, nor did I,' Jael said quietly, still not ready to feel alright about any of it. 'But now you do, which will make things both harder and easier for you, I suppose. But at least you know the truth.'

'I'm not sure how Getta will take it,' Raymon admitted, turning to look at his wife, relieved that she was unharmed; both her and Lothar.

Jael peered at Getta, who stood by her servant, hiding her

face from them. She held her tongue, not wanting to touch that thorny subject; not when she looked in Raymon's eyes and saw the pain and confusion lurking there. He needed to put his feet on solid ground, even if it was with a traitorous bitch like Getta. 'Just focus on getting back to Ollsvik and preparing your men. Listen to your advisors. They will help you. Now that the Maas' are dead, you have a better chance of holding the throne.'

Raymon nodded as Jael mounted Tig.

She was suddenly starving, thinking that it was a long way back to Rissna; hoping Reinhard would have a hot fire and a plate of food waiting. 'Up on your horses!' she bellowed, turning Tig around, feeling his impatience to leave. They'd lost two men, not had any sleep, and no one looked happy, but Jael felt relieved knowing that they'd saved a king. And his men.

Not as happy about saving his scheming wife, Jael thought, glaring at Getta before kicking Tig off down the path back to Rissna.

***

Runa smiled, watching Tanja walk away with the young man she'd taken a shine to since arriving in Andala. She'd asked Runa to watch Sigmund while she took a break. Runa hadn't wanted to ask what that break would entail, but it wasn't so long since she'd been young, she thought, remembering what taking a walk with Morac had meant. Smiling, she turned around, popping Sigmund over her shoulder, quickly frowning. 'Bram!' And she hurried towards him as he bent over, hammering nails into the arm of a new catapult. 'Should you be doing that?'

Bram turned around, surprised to be asked. He felt the eyes of his men on him, and he looked embarrassed as he straightened up, trying not to grimace. 'Doing what?'

'Building,' Runa said with an exasperated sigh. Bram appeared so eager to look in charge that she kept finding him doing all sorts of strenuous tasks. 'You're supposed to rest. Your chest is fragile.'

Bram frowned, leading Runa away from the catapult, annoyed by her nagging but not wanting to say anything to hurt her feelings. She had moved into his cottage and was treating him like an old man who'd lost control of his senses. It was the last thing he wanted to feel like, though he didn't doubt that he looked and sounded the part. 'It's not too much work to bang in a few nails, Runa. I was just lending a hand. The more catapults we get finished, the more they can take to Hest. You needn't worry about me. If a dragon didn't kill me, I doubt a little building will!' And breathing out a raspy groan, Bram stomped away towards the harbour, deciding to check on Ulf.

Runa looked after him in surprise, her cheeks warm with embarrassment. She turned away, almost bumping into Ayla, who was walking with Eydis and Amma. 'Oh! I'm sorry!'

Ayla held out her arms to stop Runa knocking her over, then smiled at the gurgling baby. 'He's grown so much. Either that or I was ill for longer than I realised!'

Amma's eyes were on the blonde baby too. Sigmund appeared to be enjoying all the attention as he wriggled in Runa's arms, his head wobbling about.

Runa was happy for the distraction, letting her worries about Bram drift away. 'Oh no, I think he's going to be a big boy. As big as his father, maybe? He'd drink all day if we let him.'

'Well, that does sound like Eadmund,' Eydis joked. 'The old Eadmund, at least.' She remembered seeing her brother lying in that bed next to Evaine, watching Edela cut the rope. She wondered if it had worked.

If they had truly broken the soul spell.

***

Eadmund trained all morning. And then kept going.

The sun rose to its highest point, and he'd run out of water, and he could feel his skin burning and dust scratching his eyes, and his stomach rumbling, but he kept going.

He saw Morana, Morac, his mother.

Ivaar. Evaine.

All the pieces of the puzzle slotting together like a horrifying nightmare, and he couldn't look away. And his anger heated to a boil, and he slammed his opponent to the ground, jumping on top of him, his forearm pressing down on his throat, his weight on the man's chest. Eadmund's eyes were cold, unrelenting, as he increased the pressure of his arm, watching the man's eyes pop and panic, and though he heard him tap the ground, yielding, Eadmund was reluctant to stop. He maintained the pressure, watching for a moment longer as the panic turned to terror, the hand tapping the ground more urgently now, and finally, waking himself up, Eadmund eased away from the man, who scrambled across the red dirt, grabbing his throat, glaring at him.

'You're in a fierce mood today,' Morac grinned.

Eadmund spun around, suddenly cold all over.

Morac waited at the edge of the training ring with Evaine, who was smiling, having not seen Eadmund since he'd hurried out of the house without eating his breakfast.

Taking a deep breath, Eadmund walked slowly towards them.

'You're bright red, Eadmund!' Evaine laughed. 'Surely that's enough for the day? It's too hot for anything but swimming!'

'Good idea,' Eadmund said, ignoring Morac as he grabbed Evaine's hand and led her down the road, towards the square, eager to get as far away from her father as possible.

Morac looked after them in surprise, feeling an odd

sensation tighten his throat.

***

Morana wanted a visitor.

She was sick of the sight and sound of Else. She wondered where Morac was. She wasn't sure when she'd last seen Evaine. Even Meena or Dragmall would have been preferable company to the chirping, humming servant, who kept peering at her with that annoyingly cheerful face, checking to see if she was still breathing.

Morana almost wanted to die just so Draguta would kill the old bitch.

Though, she realised, more generously, the old bitch had taken a risk getting the herbs for her. Giving her that dreamer's tea had undoubtedly done something because Morana had dreamed for the first night since the curse. The herbs had definitely helped, and Morana wanted more. She needed to find a way to let Else know that they were working.

A way that Draguta wouldn't notice.

Though, she considered, that appeared unlikely if what had happened in the hall was any indication. Draguta appeared acutely aware of what each one of them had been thinking. She obviously spent her days digging into their minds, and Morana knew that she risked being killed, or worse.

But what else was she to do?

Else bent forward again, her face close to Morana's and Morana wanted to cringe away, but then she stopped and forced herself to focus. She had to listen and try to communicate.

'What about some tea?' Else asked slowly, watching Morana's eyes. The milky one was still unresponsive, so she focused on the other one. 'Did you enjoy that tea I made for you yesterday? Would you like some more?'

Morana squeezed with every bit of strength she had, closing her good eye. She quickly opened it again.

Else acted as though she hadn't seen a thing. 'Well, I think I'll make some for myself, so I may as well give you some. I'm sure it won't hurt.'

Morana felt her muscles relax, the tension in her body easing as she listened to Else bustling around the cauldron, preparing to boil the water, humming to herself again.

And this time, Morana didn't mind.

***

Meena felt as lost as Brill, who hovered on one side of Draguta's chamber, while she hovered on the other. The curtains flapped as the breeze from the harbour picked up, and Meena lifted her face to it, enjoying the feel of the air on her skin.

If only it were cool.

Draguta appeared oblivious to everything but the new circle she sat in front of, studying it eagerly. She hadn't spoken in some time as she considered things, but taking a deep breath, she finally pulled herself out of the trance and turned away from the table, pointing at Brill. 'You will find Eadmund and bring him to me. And you,' she said to Meena. 'You will find Jaeger. I want them both here. Now.'

***

There were coves dotted along Hest's eastern coast, down steep paths that led to private, white-sand beaches. Eadmund led Evaine to one that he'd been told was good for swimming. And when he saw the sea rushing up onto the sparkling foreshore, he felt the knots of tension in his shoulders release, then he turned to Evaine and frowned.

She was too busy admiring the cove to notice. 'This is perfect!' she cried, looking back at the steep rise of the pale cliffs behind them. 'And nobody here but us!' Rushing towards him, Evaine was surprised to see Eadmund back away, and when she looked up at him, there was no smile in his eyes. Or on his lips. 'What's wrong?' Her stomach clenched in fear. 'Eadmund?' She gripped his hands as he stared at her. 'Eadmund?'

Taking a deep breath, Eadmund forced a smile. 'We don't have long. I have to get back to training.' He leaned forward, kissing her on the cheek. 'Let's hurry.' And kicking off his boots, he unbuckled his swordbelt.

Evaine watched him for a moment, trying to see if he was alright before hurrying to slip off her own boots, just as eager to get into the water.

***

No one had wanted further delays for their return to Andala, but after a sleepless night and two long rides, Jael decided that they needed to stay in Rissna for one more night. Reinhard didn't look happy, anxious about how much more food and ale he was going to have to supply.

But Thorgils did.

'You're still bleeding,' Jael reminded him. 'Someone should sear that wound. Stitches don't appear to work on you!'

Thorgils was too busy eating to care. 'I've wrapped some cloth around it. It'll stop soon.' He raised his cup to Karsten, who sat opposite them, already planning what entertainment they could drum up before they left.

Jael rolled her eyes, turning to Axl, who'd barely spoken since they'd sat down. He didn't look as though he'd eaten much either. 'The sausages are good,' she tried. 'And we've another long ride in the morning. Best fill up now.'

Axl blinked, staring at his sister as if for the first time. 'I'm not hungry.'

'You're thinking about Raymon?' Jael wondered, lowering her voice beneath Thorgils' great bellow as he started calling out for challengers. 'About Ranuf?'

Axl nodded. He had a temper almost as fiery as his sister's, but he didn't feel any anger about Raymon; about the secret family their father had had. He felt sad. Riding up on Jael's shoulder as the path had widened, he'd watched as Ravenna's throat was cut, listening to Raymon's screams.

He couldn't stop thinking about his own mother. He thought about Amma too; impatient to get back to the fort.

'I don't understand what Ranuf did at all, but at the same time, I understand it perfectly,' Axl whispered to his sister. 'He didn't want to hurt us, and he didn't want to hurt them. He tried to protect everyone. Think about everyone. And in the end, it didn't even matter because he was dead, and he couldn't help any of them.' Axl heard Ravenna's screams again, cut short so violently, and he shuddered. 'He couldn't keep them safe.'

'No,' Jael supposed. 'He couldn't. But he taught us how to keep ourselves safe.'

'Well, he taught you.'

Jael grinned. 'He taught you too, idiot. You were just impossible. You wouldn't listen.'

'And you did?'

Axl was smiling, and so was Jael as they both thought about their father.

'We'll have to tell Gisila,' Axl said, catching Gant's eye. He was looking their way, no doubt guessing what they were talking about.

Jael sighed, following his gaze. 'We do, though I'm not sure she needs to know about it just yet. What with Kormac and Aron, the fort being so vulnerable, and us heading off to Hest soon. Now isn't the best time.'

'No,' Axl agreed, just as eager to avoid the talk as his sister; suddenly distracted by the sight of a bare-chested Karsten Dragos strutting into the middle of the hall, Thorgils at his side, looking for challengers. 'Oh, this I want to see,' Axl smiled, all thoughts of the day drifting away like a whirl of smoke up through the thatch.

***

Looking from Eadmund to Jaeger, Draguta felt a charge.

Her two kings. Her loyal soldiers.

Bound to her. So eager to do her bidding.

Although, at that moment, they both appeared too confused to do anything.

'Attack Helsabor?' Jaeger frowned, shaking his head. 'We don't have the men. We don't have the ships. We can't get through their walls or into their harbour.'

Eadmund didn't say anything. The thought that Jaeger was standing so close to him was like an itch he wanted to scratch. He fought the urge to turn and thump him.

Draguta laughed, ignoring the tension between them.

'No, you can't get through their walls, but I can,' she smiled. 'With the book. With my creatures, my monsters. I can.'

'But why Helsabor?' Jaeger wondered. 'When you want to kill the Brekkans? When Helsabor isn't a threat to us?'

'You needn't worry about the Brekkans,' Draguta assured him, running a finger around her seeing circle. 'I have the

Brekkans right where I want them. But Helsabor has a fleet larger than any in Osterland. Larger than your Islanders, too, Eadmund. They have warriors of the highest caliber. Weapons. Gold. Everything we need, just sitting there, waiting for somebody to come along and help themselves.'

'Wulf Halvardar –' Eadmund began.

'Is dead!' Draguta finished. 'His granddaughter stuffed a pillow over his face until he pissed himself. Poor old, pathetic Wulf is no more. She sits upon that golden throne now, plotting and dreaming with all her little friends.'

'Dreaming? Is she a dreamer?' Jaeger wondered.

'Briggit? Oh yes,' Draguta mused. 'An ugly name for a surprisingly attractive woman. And not just any dreamer either, but a Follower.' She shuddered. 'My least favourite kind. It will be a pleasure to kill her and all those frothing lunatics who follow her around like dogs after a bone. And we will. Together!'

Eadmund recognised the familiar pull towards Draguta. Her desires were palpable, and his need to please her was too, but now he could feel something pulling him in the other direction. He felt as though he couldn't breathe.

'Eadmund?' Draguta peered at him. 'What is it?'

Blinking quickly, he smiled at her. 'When do we begin?'

CHAPTER THIRTY SEVEN

Edela couldn't wait to get going. After a good night's sleep and an intriguing dream, she had a spring in her step, and she charged ahead of Biddy and Eydis with the puppies, on her way to visit Alaric. She hadn't seen him in days, and she was eager to find out how he was coping with the constant terror and threat of being trapped in the fort, waiting to see what Draguta or Morana would do next.

Edela frowned suddenly, thinking of Morana Gallas. The evil woman hadn't appeared in her dreams for some time. It was as though she'd disappeared, which was odd and unsettling, though perhaps Draguta had decided that there could only be one mistress of the Book of Darkness? And Edela doubted that was a fight Morana would have won.

'You're sure you don't want us to come along?' Biddy wondered as they stopped at a fork in the road. To the left was the hall, where Biddy was going to leave Eydis with Amma before checking on Branwyn. To the right was Alaric's cottage.

'No, no,' Edela insisted. 'It's not far, and I've some life in these old legs today. You go on, and I'll come to the hall when I'm done. I want to see how Branwyn is myself. And Amma.'

'Amma?' Eydis asked. 'Why Amma?'

Edela studied Eydis, seeing a look on her face that made her curious. 'Oh, I imagine she's worried about Axl,' she said lightly. 'And I promised I'd keep an eye on her.'

Eydis didn't appear convinced by that, but Edela turned away without revealing anything more; not looking back as she hurried down the path towards Alaric's cottage, which had only just managed to survive the fall of the dragon.

Alaric opened the door with a happy smile. 'I had thought you were hibernating!' he said, ushering Edela inside. 'Every day I've had my fire going, and my small ale topped up, waiting for you to come.'

'I don't believe you,' Edela grinned, adjusting her eyes to the dim light as she quickly scanned the little room. 'Though your fire does look welcoming,' she admitted, sitting down on the stool he pulled out for her, holding her hands to the flames. Her right hand still felt like ice, and she was eager to get some heat on it. 'But let's see what that small ale tastes like.'

Picking up the jug, Alaric poured two generous cups. Despite the trials of living in the fort, so close to the precipice of death, he had been enjoying the company of Derwa, Edela, and Biddy. Entorp too, though since the sickness, he'd not seen much of him. 'Well, see what you think, then?' And he handed Edela a cup, smoothing down the few strands of white hair left on his head, watching her face with interest.

'Not bad,' Edela decided after a quick sip. 'I can almost taste the ale.'

Alaric sat down, satisfied with that. 'So, what brings you here this morning besides my small ale?' he wondered, recognising the look on her face. Edela's blue eyes had an energy about them that quickly had him on edge, knowing that she no doubt required him to reveal something he'd rather not discuss.

'I've come about the prophecy,' Edela said. 'I need to know more about it.'

Alaric looked surprised. 'But wouldn't Marcus be better to talk to? He knows much more than I do. I never read it!'

Edela smiled. 'Well, Alaric dear, it's not so much what was *in* the prophecy as what happened to it. And I've a feeling that's something you know much more about than Marcus.'

Alaric's eyes widened, then retreated quickly. 'Ahhh, well, I don't know about that.'

'Alaric...'

Closing his eyes, he sighed. 'What is it that you want to know?'

***

Eager to take a break from her seeing circles, which were revealing little, Draguta decided to go to the markets. It was a pleasant day, though her mood was fraying as she turned around to glare at Meena, who trailed behind her with a typically morose face. 'Sad to be losing Jaeger?' she wondered, watching as Meena tripped over in surprise at being spoken to. 'Perhaps you'd like to go with him? Into battle?'

Meena's bulging eyes had her smiling.

Draguta turned back around, ducking beneath a striped awning, eager to see what new trinkets had arrived. Pointing at Brill, who was carrying her basket, she motioned for her to hurry up, leaving Meena to lag behind.

Which Meena quite naturally did.

Her mind was awash with fears that she was working hard to conceal. It was exhausting. She was afraid to fall asleep, worried that Draguta would appear in her dreams. She didn't want her mind to wander to Berard, and she knew that just by thinking about him, she was putting him in danger.

Draguta was planning something, but she didn't know what, and she didn't know when, but it would be soon. She could tell by all the items Draguta had her gathering and by the confident look in her eyes that she would act soon.

'Hurry up, girl!' Draguta barked, and Meena jumped, straightening up as she scurried after her.

***

He looked nervous, Edela thought, studying Alaric over the fire, watching as the flames licked the blackened sides of his tiny cauldron. Water was heating, and though Edela could sense that it was boiling, she didn't say anything. 'Are you sure? Sure you don't know who took it? The prophecy?'

Alaric lifted his hands to his red cheeks, rubbing his white stubble. 'The prophecy was stolen centuries before my time. You know that. It was nothing to do with me. I wasn't even born!'

'But the scroll in the temple? The copy of it?'

'Well, it was not so much of a copy,' Alaric began. 'From what Marcus said, it was more... notes on what the original contained.'

'And that was the one Arbyn Nore was beheaded over?'

'Yes.' Alaric was growing more uncomfortable, unable to sit still. He stared at Edela. 'Why are you asking? Have you seen something in your dreams?'

Edela leaned forward, placing her empty cup on the only table in the room. 'Your cauldron is boiling, Alaric dear,' she said softly.

Alaric sat up, remembering that he was going to make himself a cup of fennel tea, but now he had the small ale, and he felt flustered. 'Let it boil. Unless you'd like some tea?'

Edela shook her head. 'I am on the hunt for answers about the prophecy,' she said. 'It's very important. If Jael is going to face Draguta, we need to know everything. And there is no one to ask. Dara Teros has disappeared, and I haven't seen a sign of her in my dreams. The only way to find out what I need to know is to see the prophecy itself. And if not the prophecy, then that scroll would come in very handy.'

Alaric squirmed. 'It may have been destroyed. It wouldn't

have been stolen by anyone who wanted to protect it. Surely anyone stealing it meant to destroy it, so the knowledge it contained was never revealed?'

'I'm not sure why you'd think that,' Edela said sharply. 'The scroll was already hidden in the temple. It was safe there. Or as safe as it could be with those Followers prowling around. No, I think whoever stole it meant to use it for themselves. The prophecy revealed what would happen and how to stop it. How to stop Raemus returning. And Draguta. And anyone stealing that would have found those answers for themselves.'

Alaric swallowed, suddenly interested in a hole in his trousers. 'Well, I can't say anything either way, for I didn't steal it, Edela!' He stood up suddenly, conscious of the boiling water splashing over the sides of the cauldron, sizzling the flames.

Edela watched him with a frown, convinced that Alaric Fraed knew much more than he was letting on.

***

Jael's eyes were on Karsten and Thorgils up ahead, talking to an injured Rork Arnesson, riding three abreast as they began the journey back to Andala. An unlikely trio, she thought to herself, turning to Fyn with a smile. 'How are you enjoying being a Svanter, then?' It was a warm morning, and she was barely missing her cloak.

Fyn looked surprised by the question, glancing at Thorgils, who had just slapped Karsten on the back. 'Well, I...'

'Don't feel like one yet?'

He shook his head.

'No. I expect Raymon Vandaal feels much the same, having just discovered that he's a Furyck. Consider yourself lucky that you get the chance to know your real father. He never will.' Jael felt odd talking about her father. She could hear the sharp edge to her voice; the sound of resentment.

Fyn stared at her. 'It must feel strange for you too. Discovering a new brother?'

Jael realised that they were going to have to tell Gisila. Everyone knew. It wouldn't be fair for her to find out from someone else. 'It does. I can't say I'm happy.'

'No? I expect Bram feels the same about me.'

'What?' Jael turned to him. 'Is that what you think?'

Fyn shrugged. 'He had another family. I don't expect he wanted to be lumped with me.'

'He said that, did he?'

'Well, no, but...'

'He chose to come back, from what I've heard, *because* of you. If the news had been that upsetting, I imagine he would have sailed off into the sunset, but he came back. It will just take time. For all of you.' Jael went quiet, thinking about her father. 'It hurts to love. And sometimes it hurts so much that you're afraid of loving again. If Eydis hadn't given me Ido and Vella, I wouldn't have had another dog. Imagine how Bram feels losing his entire family as he did.'

Fyn nodded. He felt strange. There was relief that he wasn't Morac's son. Hope that he would have a chance to forge a relationship with his real father. But fear that ultimately Bram wouldn't want him any more than Morac had.

Jael saw that the path was narrowing ahead, realising that she would have to slip ahead of him soon. 'But I love my annoying puppies. I'm glad they were forced on me, and even though you're not small and fluffy, I'm sure Bram will grow to love you too!' And she spurred Tig on, turning back with a wink.

***

Runa watched Bram scurrying away from her, heading through the main gates, surprised by how quickly he was moving. And though it pleased her to see that he was getting stronger, she was disappointed that he didn't appear to want her company. Though she could hardly expect him to. Fyn was his son, but she was... nothing to him at all.

'Amma!' she called, hurrying to pick up the walnuts Amma had dropped as she walked away from the market with Eydis. 'I think you've got a hole in your basket!'

Amma spun around in surprise, taking the walnuts from Runa before gulping suddenly, looking around the square in a panic.

Runa was concerned. 'Are you alright?'

But Amma ran away from her, strawberries and more walnuts dropping from the quickly growing hole in her basket as she slipped down the nearest road, and vomited the contents of her breakfast into the rubbish pile outside someone's cottage.

'Amma?' Eydis turned her head, wondering where she'd gone.

'Come on, Eydis,' Runa smiled. 'You come with me. I don't think Amma was feeling very well. I'll take you back to the hall. We'll just pick up all these things on the way.'

***

Else dribbled honey onto the porridge, handing Dragmall a bowl. He was quite surprised to be offered breakfast this late in the morning, though he didn't tell her that he'd already eaten his own.

'I'm sure there's more than enough to go around,' Else had smiled distractedly.

'I brought you some more herbs,' Dragmall said, blowing

on the hot porridge. 'If they helped you? To sleep?'

Else nodded, taking a seat before Morana, stirring the honey into the oats. 'Thank you. They seem to be working well.' And she blew on the porridge, trying to ease the spoon into Morana's mouth.

Morana blinked at her. She wanted to scream.

No honey. She hated honey!

But she did want more of those herbs of Dragmall's, so she was pleased to see him there. She'd had another dream. More than one.

There might be a way to free her. Something they hadn't thought of.

If only she could find a way to communicate with them. She needed to see Meena. There had to be a way she could find her in her dreams.

'Well, here you are, then,' Dragmall said, placing his bowl on the floor and pulling another tiny jar from his pouch. He'd made this dose stronger, adding the powder of fly mushrooms, confident that a dreamer as experienced as Morana would be able to handle their potency.

Handing the bottle to Else, his eyes caught Morana's as he sat back down, certain he'd almost seen a smile.

***

Having been unable to extract any further information from a very tight-lipped Alaric, Edela left him to his muttering and headed back to the hall, wanting to see how Branwyn was. And Aedan. His broken ribs were causing him a lot of discomfort, she knew, though not as much as his broken heart.

'Hello,' Runa smiled, walking towards Edela with a bowl in her arms. 'Are you off to see Marcus? He's taken Hanna back to his cottage, you know. I'm bringing some of Astrid's broth. It seems to be the cure-all for everyone at the moment.'

'No, I wasn't. I was heading to the hall,' Edela said. 'Enjoying the sunshine. It's so pleasant today. Almost warm!'

'Well, you should go to the market. There are a lot of traders about, and more ships came in today. I saw some lovely furs. I might get something to make a new cloak for Fyn. He still seems to be growing out of everything!'

Edela was pleased to see Runa looking so happy, or perhaps busy, she thought on reflection. She was talking fast, eyes darting around.

Perhaps not happy at all?

They walked together for a while, and when Runa was confident there was no one within earshot, she leaned in. 'I saw Amma earlier.'

'Oh?'

'She didn't look well. She ran away from me and vomited.'

'Oh.'

Runa searched Edela's face for clues, but Edela quickly turned her eyes to the wooden boards of the footpath they were walking down.

'I'll check on her. See how she is,' Edela promised, looking up once she'd managed to get her face under control. 'Gisila's been so busy helping Branwyn that I don't think she would have noticed. Thank you, Runa. I shall let you know how she is.' And dropping her eyes again, Edela turned abruptly, bustling away in the opposite direction.

***

Meena finally emerged from the markets after hours of being trapped in the claustrophobic heat, trailing after Draguta, sheltering beneath the awnings that were supposed to diminish the intensity of the sun but somehow made everything more oppressive.

She was dripping in her new dress.

Draguta had taken her to the tailor's, but instead of getting a dress made, she had found one amongst a pile of seconds. And though it didn't fit Meena properly, it was the first new dress she'd worn in years. The light blue linen felt crisp against her skin, not soft and nearly worn through like her old dress. Draguta had thrown that at the tailor, demanding he burn it so she didn't have to smell it anymore.

If only Draguta had noticed her boots, Meena thought, looking down at their flapping soles and myriad of holes as she hurried up the castle steps. She came to a crashing halt, almost banging into Draguta, who had stopped to talk to Evaine and Morac.

'You look miserable, Evaine,' Draguta smiled, peering at Evaine's face. 'Something I should know? Something about... Eadmund?'

Evaine swallowed, shielding her eyes from the sun. 'No. Nothing. He told me about going to Helsabor. I'm just worried about what will happen.' She could feel Morac twitching beside her, wanting to escape Draguta's interrogating eyes.

Draguta laughed, ignoring Morac entirely. 'What will happen is that my kings will conquer that pathetic place and return to me with a new army and a great fleet that will fill our harbour, and gold enough to buy more. More ships, more warriors from the Fire Lands.' She turned around to look at the harbour, frowning at the state of the piers. 'Those men down there will have to hurry up!' And spinning around, nearly knocking Meena over, she strode back down the steps, leaving everyone gaping after her.

***

'There you are!' Edela smiled triumphantly, stepping into the sail weaver's cottage. 'I didn't expect to find you in here.'

Many houses had their own looms, where Andala's wool was woven into garments and blankets, but when she'd become queen, Gisila had had a cottage built just for sailmaking. The labour-intensive process could take up to a year and required the attention of the most skilled weavers, and with the amount of sails Ranuf went through, Gisila had been determined to keep the women working day and night, always having the next sail well underway before it was needed.

Amma turned to Edela in surprise. 'I promised Axl that I'd keep an eye on the new sails. Make sure everything was going well. Which it is.' She nodded to one of the women, who was using a wooden sword to beat the weft of the nearly finished sail, and headed to the door where Edela looked red-faced and out of breath. 'Are you alright?'

'Me?' Edela chuckled. 'I expect I look ready to fall down, but, yes, I am. It's actually you I came to see.'

Amma looked intrigued as she walked Edela down the steps of the cottage. 'Have you had a dream?'

'No, but I did talk to Runa, who mentioned that you were unwell, so I came to see how you were.' She took Amma's arm, moving her towards the footpath, feeling her tremble.

'Oh.' Amma could barely move one boot after the other. It was no easy thing to fool a dreamer, and she wasn't sure she should even try. 'I...'

Edela didn't look at her. Amma sounded so nervous, and she didn't want to lead her anywhere that she didn't want to go.

Amma glanced around. She saw Ulf in the distance, walking with Bayla Dragos, but they were far away. Just seeing a Dragos made her uncomfortable, though, and she realised that she needed to talk to someone. 'I think maybe... I am with child.'

Edela stopped, turning to her. 'You do?' She tried to look encouraging, but Amma appeared ready to cry. 'You are very young, I know. It must be daunting to think of becoming a mother?'

'I...' Amma leaned closer. 'It could be Jaeger's, couldn't it?'

Edela's eyes widened. She hadn't thought of that, so gripping Amma's hands, she closed her eyes, taking a deep breath as she considered things. And opening them, Edela sighed. 'Yes, I think it could.'

CHAPTER THIRTY EIGHT

Jaeger couldn't stop staring at Meena during supper. They were eating in the hall, Meena sitting on one side of him, Draguta on the other.

'You look different,' he said, draining his goblet. 'Very different.'

'I have been tidying up your little mouse,' Draguta laughed, leaning forward and eyeing Meena, who did look more presentable than usual. 'But she still needs a good scrub. I've never seen such hideous skin! I found that dress, though, and Brill spent some time on her hair.' She frowned. It still looked like a bird's nest, though not as wild as before. 'It's a beginning.'

Jaeger smiled his approval at Meena, who didn't care, she just wanted them both to stop staring at her. Bending her head to her soup, she dunked a piece of bread into it.

'I could hardly stand to look at her. Or smell her,' Draguta continued. 'So you can expect even more improvements soon. It will make it much less embarrassing for you to be seen in her company.'

Jaeger peered at Meena, trying to see her through Draguta's eyes, but he couldn't.

'And how did your preparations go today? For Helsabor? Are you ready to leave?'

Jaeger turned to her in surprise, his knife in mid-air. 'Leave? *Now?*'

Draguta looked just as surprised. 'You are not planning on leaving soon?'

'Well, soon, yes,' Jaeger said. 'But it will take some time. We must plan our attack. It's a well-fortified kingdom. You will break down the walls, I know, but we will need a clear idea of what to do once we get inside. We must gather all the knowledge we can before making our plans. I have called a meeting for tomorrow. My helmsmen, my best warriors, some of the merchants who know Helsabor well. We'll discuss everything then.'

Draguta narrowed her eyes, pursing her lips. 'I see. And what does Eadmund think about that? Your *plan-making*? Is he in agreement with how cautiously you are approaching everything?'

'Eadmund?' Jaeger spat out his name. 'He doesn't know my army. My men. My kingdom. He doesn't know Helsabor either. He'll do as I say.'

Draguta carefully put down her spoon, pushing her bowl away, turning to Jaeger with sharp eyes. 'You are both my kings, Jaeger dear. Eadmund is not your subordinate. You will plan this assault together. And you will hurry up about it too, for I do not want to be sitting here when winter comes, wondering why you are still drawing little maps and having pointless meetings!' Her voice rose, ringing with displeasure. 'A true king acts! He does not dither. And Helsabor is a kingdom run by a dreamer. Briggit is watching. Waiting for us. Making *her* plans. And the longer you suck your thumb and fret, the harder her defenses will be to breach.' She picked up her goblet, inhaling the wine, which smelled sweet, like blackberries, instantly calming her tension. 'Do I make myself clear?' She sighed loudly before taking a drink. 'I'm beginning to see the benefit of having two kings, for if one displeases me, well...' And Draguta smiled over the rim of her goblet before turning away from Jaeger, who sat there digging a frown into his forehead, imagining himself smashing Eadmund Skalleson's face into a bloody mess.

***

Eadmund forced himself to smile.

He forced himself not to say anything.

He forced himself to sit there and listen and nod and be everything he needed to be to get through the meal without incident.

'That was delicious,' Morac sighed, slumping back into the chair, stuffed full. 'I did find you a superb cook, didn't I?'

Evaine nodded distractedly, though she'd not eaten much herself. Eadmund seemed odd – as though he wasn't quite there – and she couldn't stop worrying. His eyes were cold, and his lips were tight, and his body was rigid as he sat beside her.

Eadmund could sense that Evaine was disturbed. 'Your father's right. I've never tasted lobster cooked like that. We'll have to have it again.'

Evaine flashed him a smile, which he tried to return in kind.

Morac reached for his goblet as Elfwyn approached with the wine jug. 'Yes, I agree. And far better than anything I've eaten in the castle,' he added, smiling at Elfwyn, who was a surprisingly attractive woman for a servant, he thought, admiring her full lips and warm brown eyes. 'And certainly far better than anything in my hovel.' And laughing, Morac stared at Evaine, who frowned at him, deciding that her father was drunk.

'Well, you're the one who chooses to live in such poverty, Father. Surely you can see that the alternatives are much more agreeable?'

Eadmund wanted to kill Morac.

He sat there with that bleary-eyed grin on his face, and Eadmund wanted to take his knife and push it into his throat. His dreams taunted him, and every waking moment he saw Morana and Morac conspiring to kill Melaena and his father.

And who else?

What else had they done together?

Eadmund sipped his wine. It was unbearably sweet, and he grimaced, trying to back away from his anger. Trying to smile again. He wanted to keep Evaine calm. Happy. It would make things so much easier.

An opportunity would come, he knew.

And he would take it.

***

Jael went for a walk with Aleksander after a tasty supper of salmon and mushroom stew.

The day's ride had been long and warm, and her thoughts had wandered towards her father regularly, before retreating. She didn't want to think about him or Raymon, and she definitely didn't want to think about Ravenna.

'This raven of yours is becoming useful,' Aleksander grinned, listening to the song of the crickets as they slipped through the trees, heading for the stream.

Jael laughed. 'I'm not sure she's *my* raven, but you're right, Raymon wouldn't be alive without her. If only I could have shot two arrows at once.'

'You've done it before,' Aleksander reminded her.

'Ha! I have. Badly. Both in the same direction.' Jael's smile faded. 'What happened to Ravenna... I can't stop seeing it.'

Aleksander was quiet, thinking about his mother's death; watching her fall over his father's body, her throat slit. He shivered. 'You did the right thing. Ravenna would've thought so too. Maybe she'll come into your dreams and tell you herself?'

'Maybe.'

'Do you think Raymon will last long? With everyone

knowing his true lineage?'

Jael shrugged, then stopped, turning to him. 'Before I killed Garren, he told me that Getta was with him. Part of it. That she was plotting with him to get rid of Raymon.'

'Did you say anything?'

'No. He'd just lost his mother.' Jael frowned as they came to the stream, bending down to fill their empty waterskins. It was nearly dark, and the air was rapidly cooling down. 'I hope it was the right thing to do, but I had the feeling that Getta was regretting it.'

'I imagine she's waiting for you to tell Raymon what you know.'

'Maybe I will. He's just so young, and he's got enough challenges without knowing that his wife betrayed him. But if Getta comes to Vallsborg with him, I'll be sure to let her know what would happen if she tried anything again.'

'Well, that would be enough to scare me!' Aleksander laughed, standing up with a full waterskin, slapping at a midge buzzing around his face. 'We're going to be eaten alive tonight!'

'You certainly are. They don't seem to like me. Not sweet enough, I guess.'

'You? Not sweet? They just have to get to know you, then they'd find out how sweet you truly are!'

Jael laughed, walking away as Aleksander slapped his neck. 'Come on, then, before there's nothing left of you!'

***

It was finally dark, and Edela couldn't wait to hop into bed, but she didn't feel ready for sleeping. Her mind was so full of problems that she felt a sense of panic, unsure what to dream about.

Eydis and Biddy sat opposite her on stools, trying to help her decide.

'Well, the prophecy makes sense to me,' Biddy said. 'It's the key to all that will happen. Having knowledge of that could save Jael's and Eadmund's lives. And many more.'

Eydis frowned. 'But what about Eadmund? Shouldn't you try and dream about him? See what to do about the other rope?'

Edela frowned, pushing away Vella, who was trying to crawl onto her lap. She smelled horrible, and Edela wrinkled her nose.

'I know,' Biddy said. 'I'll wash them in the morning. Not sure where they've been today, but knowing those two, they've been rolling in dragon guts again.'

'What about Amma?' Eydis murmured, wondering if Edela knew about the baby.

'Amma?' Edela glanced at Biddy, who looked on blankly.

'She's pregnant,' Eydis said. 'Isn't she?'

Edela nodded, and Biddy's eyes widened. 'She is. And she's worried. Worried that it's Jaeger Dragos' baby.'

Biddy's eyes widened some more. 'Poor Amma.'

'Mmmm,' Edela agreed. 'I can imagine how upsetting that would be.'

'Will she tell Axl?' Biddy asked.

Edela shrugged. 'I don't know what she'll do, but I'm not sure it's anything we can help her with. I think I'd better stay far away.'

'Well, then,' Biddy decided, 'it has to be the prophecy for you. And Eydis, why don't you try and find Eadmund?'

And having agreed upon that, Biddy proceeded to make some hot milk to relax them all.

***

Eadmund kissed the top of Evaine's head.

She frowned, wondering why. Why was he kissing her head when her body was naked, pressing against his? When he hadn't been able to keep his hands off her since their reunion in Flane.

Why was he kissing her head?

She sat up and leaned over him, bending to kiss his lips, teasing them with her tongue. He didn't respond. The lamps flickered, and she could see the deep crease between his eyes where he was frowning. Sitting back on her heels, she sighed. 'What has happened, Eadmund? Something's wrong. I know it is.'

Eadmund tried to smile, but his frown wouldn't budge.

'Nothing,' he muttered. 'Except being here with Jaeger. Being stuck here with him is what's wrong. And now we have to attack Helsabor together. Side by side. How is that going to work when we want to kill each other?'

Evaine relaxed slightly. It was an explanation that made sense. 'Do you have to go? Does Draguta need you when she has Jaeger?' Saying his name made her feel sick. She couldn't look Eadmund in the eye. 'I don't understand why she needs you. Why we can't just go home now. You have your own kingdom to worry about.'

Eadmund tried to understand it himself, but any desire to rebel against Draguta met the strong resistance that pleasing her was more important than anything else. His thoughts eased, and he rubbed his beard with both hands, trying not to think at all. 'Draguta needs me. I don't think she trusts Jaeger. And who could blame her? After watching how he defended Skorro, he's sure to make a mess of Helsabor.'

'And what's in Helsabor that Draguta cares about?' Evaine wondered. 'When you claim it, what will happen there?'

'I imagine she'll kill Briggit Halvardar. Install her own people to run the kingdom. Bleed it of its assets. Use them for conquering the rest of Osterland.' He felt detached and strange, as though his head and heart were on opposite sides. The words came as easily as breathing, but his body was almost jerking in protest.

He could feel an ache in his heart.

Evaine's mind started whirring. 'And Helsabor is rich, isn't it? Richer than Hest?'

'I don't know. Apparently, they have a golden throne, so perhaps? Richer than Oss, at least.' He thought of his own wooden throne, its well-worn armrests and tall back. His father's chair.

And thinking of his father led Eadmund back to Morac again.

And he scowled.

***

Morac had come to sit with Morana after supper, giving Else the opportunity to escape the chamber for a while. He was still salivating over the lobster, and the perfectly sweet wine, which had made him quite sleepy. He was thinking about Evaine's servant too. She really was a beautiful woman.

Morana tried to glare at him. Her brother's thoughts were droning, and she had grown bored with listening to them. She doubted he noticed. Morac had always been self-involved. Never selfless enough to be a true Follower. Never clever enough to see what was hiding in plain sight.

He'd always had his sister to look after him, to see that which he'd missed himself. She had guided him and rescued him, and helped him navigate the dangerous waters in which he sailed.

But now?

Now, Morana couldn't help him at all.

He was entirely on his own.

Else opened the door, unable to mask her disappointment at being back in the chamber. She had enjoyed roaming the castle and the city as a servant to Irenna Dragos, and even when she'd been working for Jaeger, she could get out and about, but being stuck inside a stone prison with a silent patient was making Else almost as miserable as Morana. 'Thank you,' she said. 'I was able to get a few apples, which I'll stew to add to Morana's porridge and honey in the morning.'

Morac looked at her. 'Morana hates honey.'

'Oh. Draguta insisted I give it to her.' Else put her basket on the bed and started rummaging through it. 'I shall boil some water, make a nice tea to settle our stomachs. Can I get you anything?'

Morac shook his head, yawning, thinking that he should find his way back to his cottage. 'No, thank you. I've drunk quite enough for one night. And at my age, that just means I'll be up all night long!'

Else nodded, thinking how right he was.

***

Edela had gone to bed holding the Book of Aurea – their strongest connection to Dara Teros – hoping that somehow it would lead her to the prophecy. The letter Dara had written to Jael was something, but not enough.

Not when their entire existence was at stake.

Edela's dreams rushed impatiently towards her like a stiff breeze off the ocean, and she felt herself blinking in their force, almost blown backwards, away from the clouds she so desperately sought to enter.

The swirling images whipped around her, rushing by so

fast that she struggled to make out their meaning. She saw a younger, kinder Draguta with her two dark-haired sisters, and a girl she hadn't seen before. And suddenly, the whirlpool stopped, and the little girl remained alone.

Staring at her.

'Do not look for me, Edela,' she said. 'Not here. Draguta is watching.'

And then everything went dark.

***

Sigmund couldn't sleep by the sound of it, and nothing Tanja was doing appeared to be working, so Runa got up to see what was happening, bumping into Amma, who had crept into the kitchen to find something to eat.

They both jumped.

Runa smiled. 'I doubt anyone can sleep with that noise,' she whispered, inclining her head to the door.

'I didn't know you were staying in the hall again,' Amma murmured. 'What about Bram?'

Runa looked embarrassed. 'Oh, he decided that he's well enough not to need any help, so I came back. Better to go where I'm useful.'

Amma nodded, easing past Runa. 'Well, goodnight, then.'

'Amma.' Runa touched her arm. 'I'm only just down the corridor if you need anything. Even if it's just to talk.' She didn't know why she felt compelled to say anything, but she could tell that the girl was pregnant and feeling awkward about it.

She knew how that felt.

Amma's eyes were big as she stopped by a flaming torch. 'Thank you.' She was beginning to think that everyone could tell; that they were all staring and whispering about her. And she knew, worst of all, that Axl would return soon.

And Amma didn't know how she was going to tell him.

Runa watched her go before turning towards Tanja's chamber, thinking that maybe Sigmund was missing his parents. She wondered if Evaine thought about him anymore?

If Eadmund even remembered he had a son?

***

Eskild walked beside Eadmund.

Oss' square looked different than when she had been the queen. It felt smaller somehow. More buildings had encroached upon it over the years, and Ketil and Una's fire pit took up a fair amount of room now. But it was still as muddy as ever, she smiled to herself, her arm through Eadmund's. He turned suddenly, releasing himself from her hold, walking towards the table, where he sat down with a frown.

Aleksander had just arrived, he remembered.

Aleksander Lehr. Jael's lover. Her best friend. Her family.

And his insides had flipped, and every fear of losing her had emerged from the shadows to taunt and panic him. But, he reminded himself, Jael had chosen him. Chosen to stay on Oss as his wife.

He sat there, trying to remember that.

Looking up, he saw Morac approach the table. He watched him sit down, talking to him. And Eadmund must have been talking back because Morac kept nodding, asking questions.

And they sat like that for a while until Morac pulled something from his pouch and handed it to Eadmund.

Eadmund told himself not to take it.

'You have to take it,' his mother said from behind him. 'Take it and look at it.'

Eadmund reached out and reluctantly took the leather strap from Morac, his eyes on that tiny golden curl, and he felt a pain in his heart, remembering his son.

'Look at it,' Eskild breathed. 'Turn it over, Eadmund.'

And as Morac got up to leave, Eadmund turned over the leather strap and saw the symbols.

CHAPTER THIRTY NINE

Jael felt an urge to move, but her body wasn't as keen. She rolled onto her side, pulling out a pebble that must have been wedged into her back all night. Sitting up, she shook off her fur and pushed her cold feet into her boots, staggering out of the tent, only one eye open.

'Thought you were planning on staying in there all morning!' Thorgils grinned as he approached with Fyn. They'd been up early fishing and had three good-sized trout between them. 'You'll miss out on breakfast!'

Jael stared at him. 'Do you ever stop bleeding?'

Thorgils looked over his tunic, now almost entirely red with dried blood, down to his trousers, which he could see were leaking. 'Ha! No, it appears not. We'll be home soon, though. I'll get Astrid to sew me up as tight as a corpse!'

'Well, hopefully, nothing happens on our way back home, or you might well be a corpse!'

Fyn frowned.

Jael patted him on the back. 'Come on, let's eat, then we'll ride. I want to get back to Andala as quickly as possible. We should ride as late as we can tonight. That should see us home in the morning.'

Now they both frowned.

'What have you been dreaming about, then?' Thorgils wondered, following Jael as she headed for the nearest fire.

'Draguta?'

'No, I didn't have any dreams. But she must be plotting her next move. How could she not? And I'd rather be back behind Andala's walls, able to protect everyone before she makes it. Wouldn't you?'

Thorgils nodded, thinking of Isaura and the children; hoping that Draguta would take her time before unleashing her next creature upon them.

***

Draguta peered inside one of her seeing circles, searching the clouds, quickly finding what she was looking for. 'Ahhh, good. We won't have long to wait at all.' She glanced at Meena, who hovered by the door, not knowing where to put herself. Draguta was almost pleased with the look of her now. She'd had Brill brushing Meena's hair again, and it was almost tamed, though it was still that disgusting red colour. 'You may go. Go and enjoy the morning. Perhaps visit your aunt? Tell me how she fares, though I imagine I can already guess the answer to that.' Draguta's smile was satisfied as she nodded for Brill to pour her more wine.

Meena blinked, wondering if she'd heard her correctly.

'And do see how Jaeger's plans are coming along. I shall finish here, then be down to check myself. I do not have time to wait around while Jaeger and Eadmund decide whether they can play nicely together. Jael Furyck is not wasting any time. Her army will be on the march before we know it.'

Meena didn't wait to hear what else Draguta would say. She started backing up towards the door, eager to escape.

But Draguta appeared to have forgotten she was even there. Her attention was immediately drawn back to Briggit

Halvardar.

What an interesting challenge she was going to be.

***

Eadmund had left the house before Evaine had dragged herself out of bed, which worried her further. She fretted as she walked beside Morac, wringing her hands. Her father had arrived early, which annoyed her. Now that she had her own house with Eadmund, she didn't intend to spend every moment in her father's company. Though, she supposed, at least it gave her someone to talk to about Eadmund.

'I don't imagine he wants you checking up on him all the time,' Morac suggested tactfully, watching Evaine twisting her fingers, eyes darting around as they walked towards the piers, where they could see Eadmund and Jaeger arguing. Evaine appeared oblivious to everything but her own internal turmoil, however, which he guessed was something to do with Eadmund. He had seemed a little moody of late, though Morac couldn't blame him, having to contend with Jaeger and Draguta as he was.

'You don't think he knows, do you?' Evaine wondered suddenly, watching the two men intently. 'About what Jaeger did to me? You don't think that's why he's different?'

Morac shook his head. 'I think it's unlikely Jaeger's head would still be on his shoulders if that were the case,' he suggested.

Evaine wasn't so sure. She felt such a terrifying emptiness inside her body. It was as though Eadmund had drifted away, and though she could see him and touch him, he no longer belonged to her.

Jaeger watched Morac and Evaine approach, and then

Meena too. 'It appears that Draguta is sending all her little helpers to find out what progress we're making.'

'Well, she'll be disappointed, then, won't she?' Eadmund grumbled. 'Standing out here arguing isn't going to help us. We should be planning around that map table of yours.'

Jaeger hated everything about Eadmund, but he couldn't deny that he was right. Draguta seemed to think that they could just turn up outside Helsabor's walls and wait for her to break them down. And though Jaeger didn't doubt that she could, he didn't know what would be waiting for them once she did. The Helsaborans had a reputation as cowards, but they were extraordinarily wealthy, with a fleet to rival any kingdom and a well-trained army manning their defenses. But how strong were they really? When it came to a battle, no one had any idea what they were capable of. 'Agreed,' he said as Meena reached him.

Meena looked from Jaeger to Eadmund to Evaine to Morac.

Only Morac looked happy.

Everyone else scowled at her.

'Draguta will come and see how your plans are going,' she mumbled shyly. 'Soon.'

Eadmund nodded, impatient to have some plans for her to see. 'Well, as I said, we can't do much about those piers. It's the last thing we need to worry about. The ships can drop anchor, and the crews can swim to shore if need be. And some ships will fit in the coves. You'll just have to move out the merchants.'

'Who won't be happy.'

'No. Or you could bring them into the sheds. There's still some room in there.'

Evaine smiled at Eadmund, who smiled back before quickly turning to Jaeger. 'Let's get to that map table. We need to talk to your most experienced men. Your brothers' men.'

Jaeger glared at Eadmund. 'What? Why?'

'They led your army behind your father, didn't they? Haegen and Karsten? Their men would've been inside their heads. We need to know what they know. What they suggest.

Your father's men too.'

Jaeger couldn't get a word in as he followed Eadmund across the square, towards the castle.

Evaine watched them go, her face falling.

'He's loyal to Draguta,' Morac whispered as they stayed behind with Meena, watching the two kings stride towards the castle steps. 'You can see that now. They both are. They're clearly hers.'

Meena knew that Morac was right. Part of her was relieved that Jaeger was tied to Draguta. On her leash. But she knew that it also meant he was no longer loyal to her, and without Morana, or even Else, she suddenly felt very alone.

***

Ulf saw Runa walking towards him with Bayla Dragos, and he smiled.

Bram turned in the other direction, looking for an escape, but Ulf grabbed his arm, and Bram turned back with a forced grin.

'I thought you'd be further along than that!' Bayla snorted. 'The amount of time you spend here?' And she looked down her long nose at them both.

Ulf wasn't bothered in the slightest. 'Well, the thing about piers is that most of the work gets done where you don't see it, so we're well along, in fact. You're just seeing the surface. And that's no way to judge anything. Come, come and look beneath the water and you'll see. There's a lot more going on under there.' And without waiting, he took Bayla's hand, leading her closer to the water's edge.

Bayla pushed her boots onto the wooden boards that ran around the harbour, but Ulf was stronger than he looked, and a gentle tug had her quickly following him.

Leaving Bram with Runa.

'I didn't know you were friendly with the queen,' Bram muttered, his eyes on Bayla, who was bending awkwardly to peer at what Ulf was pointing to.

Runa laughed. 'I'm not, but I managed to stop her grandson crying the other day when it seemed that nothing would, so she's decided I'm a wise woman or some such thing. She keeps seeking me out, asking my advice,' she whispered. 'I do feel sorry for her with three orphaned grandchildren on her hands. And losing her son and husband like that? No matter what we might think of the Dragos family, that's a punishment I wouldn't wish on anyone.' She thought of Fyn, her forehead creasing with worry, hoping he'd be back soon.

Bram peered at her. 'No, it's not. Family's important. It's a treasure you try hard to protect. Though, sometimes you can't.' He looked away.

'No, you can't,' Runa agreed with a sigh. She watched as Bayla straightened up, giving Ulf an almost-smile before lifting her nose in the air again. 'Though, sometimes you get a second chance.' And she glanced at Bram before dropping her eyes and turning away. 'I'd best get back to the hall.'

Bram watched her go, feeling strange all over.

***

Karsten wasn't sure how he felt about returning to Andala. He was excited by the prospect of preparing to leave for Hest. Thoughts of killing Jaeger, of how he would do it, and what he would say, were ever-present. Thoughts of claiming the throne and being able to return home too.

But then there was the imminent prospect of seeing Nicolene

again.

Her betrayal was like a thorn bush he couldn't move around. Every time he thought he might see a way clear to forgiving her, he felt another thorn jabbing him. Images of her naked with his brother were never far from his mind. But then thinking of Nicolene would always lead him to Hanna, and he worried that she'd died while they were away.

'I've been thinking,' Thorgils began as he eased Rufus up beside Karsten. 'This arrangement of ours doesn't need to be over.'

'What do you mean?' The light was bright as they rode across a boggy meadow, and Thorgils' blue eyes had a glint in them that intrigued Karsten.

'We made a fair bit of coin, you, me, and Rork.'

'And?'

'Well, you don't know how long it'll be till you're dipping into your father's coffers. Might be useful to have a few coins. I'm sure your mother would appreciate it. Or your wife? My mother was always quieter when my father came back from raiding with a chest full of plunder. He got to enjoy some peace for a few days!' Thorgils smiled, thinking about Odda and her whip of a tongue.

Karsten didn't want to talk about his mother or his wife, but he couldn't deny that he'd enjoyed fleecing the Iskavallans and the men of Rissna. 'We could do that. What does Rork say?' He looked around, but Rork had turned away, talking to Torstan.

'Rork's in,' Thorgils grinned. 'Not sure we can convince Aleksander or Ivaar to fight again, so it might be up to you to get things moving.'

Karsten lifted an eyebrow, but he didn't think that sounded like such a bad idea.

Aleksander watched from a few horses behind. 'I can guess what they're talking about,' he laughed. 'Thorgils has been at me all morning.'

'To do what?' Axl wondered.

'Fight for them when we get back to Andala. He's looking to repeat his success.'

Axl laughed. 'You seemed to enjoy it.'

'Well, I've found that drinking and fighting are the perfect remedies for a broken heart. But I don't think I should make a habit of it. I prefer to see out of both eyes.'

Axl looked behind him to where Jael was riding with Ivaar. 'Is it still hard? With Jael?'

'What do you think?' Aleksander sighed, his eyes fixed straight ahead. 'Do you imagine you'd get over Amma quickly?'

Axl shook his head. 'No. When she was with Jaeger Dragos, I couldn't even breathe. Nothing felt right when I knew he had his hands on her.'

'Mmmm, it gets easier, I suppose, but it doesn't feel right, even now. Even knowing how Jael feels about Eadmund. It doesn't feel like it's supposed to be this way.' He shook his head, trying to banish his gloomy thoughts. 'I'd be happy to wake up one day and feel different. It would be nice to let it all go.'

'Maybe you will, when you meet someone else?'

Aleksander frowned, tightening his grip on the reins, his dark hair blowing across his eyes. He tried not to think about Hanna. 'Someone else? I think we're a little busy for that, don't you? And who knows what will happen with Draguta?' He tried to sound light-hearted, but there'd never really been anything light-hearted about him. Not since Tuura. He'd always struggled to find the light after that night.

Except with Jael.

***

Draguta came to join Eadmund and Jaeger at the map table, eager to hear their plans, but she ended up feeling as though she was stuck between two children squabbling over a toy. 'The point is to conquer Helsabor,' she muttered, trying to find some common ground. 'Surely that is doable for two men as powerful as you? As big and strong and clever as you?'

Eadmund glared at Jaeger. 'I don't know the terrain here,' he said, pointing to what appeared to be a pass through the mountains, heading for the western coast of Helsabor, 'but it seems as though this is the obvious place to go.'

'Which will make it the most defended part of their wall,' Jaeger said, as if bored.

'And if we attack there, they will expect it,' Eadmund went on, ignoring the roll of Jaeger's eyes. 'And they'll put their men there. The bulk of their men. So we should divide our forces and send half of them around to the south. Here.' He pointed to another pass. 'We can attack them on two fronts at the same time.'

'And?' Draguta wanted more. 'What about their fleet?'

'We can't attack them by sea,' Jaeger insisted. 'We don't have the ships to launch from here, but once we breach the walls and get into the city, we can send our crews to the harbour. Secure their ships, and sail them back to Hest.'

'And Briggit Halvardar and her dreamers? Her Followers?' Draguta mused. 'They will cause problems.'

Jaeger and Eadmund looked at her.

'But I will keep them busy. At least until you get to her. In her castle. I imagine she'll be waiting for you.' Draguta turned to Jaeger. 'It will be your job to bring her to me.'

'*Bring* her?' Jaeger frowned. 'Why not kill her?'

Draguta laughed. 'But what fun would there be for me in *you* killing her? No, you will bring Briggit and her pack of rabid dogs to me. All of them. I want to dispose of them myself. When it comes to dreamers, I've discovered, it is better to take things into my own hands. You just need to ensure that you deliver her into them.'

And she stared at Jaeger until he felt his stomach twist

painfully, unable to keep a smile on his face.

***

Eydis was eager to tell Amma that she'd had a dream about Jael and Axl returning to the fort soon. But when she found Amma in her chamber, she could hear that she'd been crying. Eydis felt uncomfortable, unsure if she should stay, or whether Amma would prefer to be alone.

'I'm sorry, Eydis,' Amma sniffed, wiping her eyes. 'You have such good news. I don't mean to be silly.'

Eydis felt her way to the bed and sat down next to her. 'It's not silly to be worried about your baby.'

Amma cringed, not wanting it to be real. She was missing her mother. She had thought of telling Gisila, but Gisila had been so busy looking after Branwyn that she didn't want to bother her. 'It's not the baby I'm worried about. It's Axl,' she sighed. 'I can't promise him that the baby is his. And I don't know how that will make him feel.'

Eydis didn't know what to advise. Amma was barely three years older than her, but she lived in another world, and Eydis had no experience of such things. She tried anyway. 'I don't imagine you would hate Axl if it happened to him? You would want to stay with him and face it together, wouldn't you?' Her dark eyebrows were up, hoping that Amma could see beyond her clumsy attempt at understanding the situation.

Amma did. 'I would. Of course.' She felt a little brighter. 'It wouldn't matter to me. Not really. I'd just want to be with him.'

Eydis smiled, hearing the lift in Amma's voice. 'I think if you love someone, you must be able to weather the storms with them,' she said. 'Because there will always be storms, won't there?'

Amma nodded, daring to place a hand on her stomach. 'I hope you're right, Eydis,' she said tentatively. 'I hope you're right.'

***

Jael tried not to think. Her mind was full of angry ravens, all calling to her, and she didn't want to pay attention to any of them. They just needed to get home. Home meant a chance to think and plan.

Ivaar was the perfect company.

He barely spoke, though he was riding beside her, and she wasn't sure why. Eventually, Jael decided that the best way to ignore the ravens was to turn her mind to someone else's problems. 'What's wrong?'

Ivaar blinked in surprise. 'Wrong?'

'You're riding beside me. You hate me. You don't want my company, so I imagine there's something wrong. Something you want to talk to me about?'

Ivaar frowned. Jael was a frustrating woman. Always piercing straight to the heart of things with that viper tongue and those penetrating eyes. There was no pretence. No gentleness. It was like being hit with an axe. 'I suppose so.'

Jael stared straight ahead, not making it any easier.

Ivaar could see Thorgils' red curls bouncing up and down as he slapped Karsten on the back; the two of them as thick as thieves now. 'It's Isaura,' he muttered irritably. 'I want the divorce. I want it official.'

Jael raised an eyebrow.

'It's humiliating. She's my wife. With another man. At least make it end. I need a new life. A new wife.'

'Got someone in mind, have you?'

Ivaar scowled. 'No.'

Jael didn't want to feel sorry for him, so she looked away, her eyes darting through the trees. 'Well, I don't imagine I need Eadmund to do it, do I?'

'I don't imagine so.'

'Then we'll do it when we get back. Come and find me, and bring Isaura. I'll write something down. We'll discuss a settlement. It will be done.'

Ivaar nodded, pleased with that. He stared at Jael, who still hadn't looked his way. 'And what about you? What will you do about your husband?'

'There's not a lot I can do about Eadmund,' Jael muttered. 'Evaine has Eadmund, and I have an army, and one day soon, I'll take my army and get Eadmund back.' She turned to Ivaar, sharpening her eyebrows. 'And then we'll go home to Oss, so get your mind off the throne because it won't be yours, Ivaar Skalleson. It will never be yours.'

Ivaar scowled at her some more.

'You just need to find yourself a queen with a kingdom,' Jael grinned. 'I'm sure there's a lonely queen floating about somewhere looking for a man as well presented as you.'

'I'm not sure what I ever saw in you, Jael Furyck. You really are the most irritating woman I've ever met,' Ivaar grumbled, trying his best not to smile, his mind wandering to the very appealing thought of marrying a wealthy queen. 'Ake Bluefinn has two daughters. I'd just have to give it a few years until they're of marrying age.'

Jael laughed. 'Well, there you go. As long as you promise to stay in Alekka and not come anywhere near my islands.' She glared at him.

And he glared back at her. 'I might. Depends on how persuasive my new wife is.'

***

Set free from Draguta, Meena had enjoyed her afternoon.

Jaeger had been occupied with planning the invasion of Helsabor, not seeking her company, so she had wandered away from the city, choosing Fool's Cove to take a swim, surprised that she felt bold enough for such an indulgence. But despite the pleasure of feeling cool for the first time in weeks, Meena couldn't relax. She kept looking over her shoulder, staring up at the path, imagining someone coming down, seeing her naked. Eventually, she spotted a ship entering the cove, and she scrambled out of the water, hurrying to put on her clothes.

And then she walked all the way to Dragmall's cave.

She didn't know what she was doing, but she could almost hear a voice in her head, urging her on.

And when she arrived, she discovered why.

CHAPTER FORTY

Edela had debated going to see Alaric again, but, in the end, decided against it. He didn't appear inclined to reveal what he knew, and despite a good sleep, Edela didn't have enough energy to try and pry anything more out of him. She was eager to get to the hall and see how Branwyn was. So were the puppies, it seemed, as they ran ahead of her, almost urging her on. Likely, they'd run out of dragon to nibble on and were searching for treats elsewhere.

She smiled, thinking of Jael, looking forward to her return.

'Edela!'

Edela turned, surprised to see Alaric shuffling towards her, his face red with the effort of chasing her down. He stopped before her, unable to speak, trying to catch his breath.

'You're the last person I expected to see running after me today,' Edela frowned, peering at him with sharp eyes. 'After how we left things.'

Alaric dropped his head. 'Well, yes,' he muttered into his chest, 'I don't blame you.'

Edela stared at him until he looked up at her with flushed cheeks, though his eyes remained steady as they considered hers. 'I am sorry,' he sighed. 'Sorry that I... did not tell you the truth.'

'About?'

'Well, I didn't steal the prophecy... but I... do know who did.'

'You do?'

'It was... Arbyn Nore. I... I wasn't allowed near the room where the most sacred scrolls were kept. That was only for the elderman and his scribe. No one even knew of its existence, but Arbyn told me about it. He had no one else to talk to, and, I suppose, neither did I. It was lonely, being in the temple from dawn till dusk every day. The elders wouldn't talk to us. The dreamers only told us their dreams, but otherwise, they kept to themselves. We confided in each other.'

Edela watched him, not wanting to interrupt.

'He was a good man, Arbyn. My friend. He lost his head, I know, but I didn't want him to lose his reputation as well. He had been so loyal once, to the temple, to the elderman. When he told me what he'd done, I couldn't believe it, but he was much changed by then. Something was wrong with him. I see that now. Perhaps it was The Following?'

'Alaric...'

'I should have told you, I know,' Alaric sighed. 'And I'm sorry for that. But I know no more than that. He sold the scroll. To a merchant, he said. I don't know who bought it or where it is now. I promise, Edela. I promise!'

Edela patted his arm. 'I believe you, and I'm grateful that you finally told me the truth. It will help to have this knowledge, I'm sure. Now I just need to work on finding that scroll in my dreams!'

***

Dragmall wasn't surprised to see Meena.

He had, in fact, been waiting for her. 'I've made some tea, if you'd like a cup?' he asked, pushing Meena towards one of his tree stumps. He had only the two, never having had much company in his cave before.

Meena nodded. 'Yes, please.'

Dragmall picked up the cups, offering her one. 'It's still warm,' he smiled, sitting down with his own. 'And how is your aunt?'

Meena looked down at her cup. 'She is the same.' And feeling Dragmall staring at her, Meena lifted her eyes, intrigued by the intensity in his.

'Well, Morana was never kind to you, was she? Not from what I saw. Much like your grandmother before her, so I expect it is no more than she deserves.'

Meena wasn't listening, she was busy watching Dragmall's eyes, and suddenly his thoughts were louder than his words. Bending forward, she focused on sipping the tea, which tasted bitter. She could see tiny, curled-up flowers floating inside the cup; little bits of mushrooms too. Inhaling the earthy smell, she tried to focus on Dragmall's thoughts.

He stopped talking, but his thoughts carried on, and they sat in silence for some time, drinking their tea.

Eventually, Meena finished and lifted her head. 'That was very nice,' she mumbled. 'My grandmother sometimes made me a tea when I had nightmares. She wanted to keep me quiet, she said. Not disturbing her sleep.'

Dragmall laughed. 'Sounds like Varna.'

'I've always had nightmares, I suppose, but her tea did help. It made me sleep without waking.'

Dragmall's bushy eyebrows were up, and so was he, placing his cup on the dirt floor of the cave as he headed to his shelf. 'I can give you something to help with that,' he muttered. 'Now, let me see what I have here. There's nothing worse than being terrorised by nightmares, I know.' And turning around with a small glass bottle, he smiled.

***

Draguta stood on her balcony, watching the sun sink into the sea. Its golden light glittered across the water, pink streaks painting the sky above it. Quite beautiful, she thought, feeling a sense of peace soften her body.

The Dolma had been an endless nightmare she could never wake from, and her eagerness to see and feel the sun had been an ever-present need when she'd first returned.

But now?

Now when she saw that the day was ending, welcoming back the darkness again, Draguta didn't feel fear at all. She was changing, she realised. Even her body felt different. It was no longer cold, and she could feel a steady warmth pulsing in her veins.

She felt more like herself, and yet, somehow, utterly different.

Turning around, Draguta walked back to the book. It was calling to her, and she pressed her palm against the page. 'Soon,' she smiled. 'Just a little longer, and everything will be in place, and then we shall begin again, my friend. Just a little longer...'

***

Eventually, it became too dark to see much, so Jael made everyone stop for the night. She felt tense, worrying about what was happening in the fort. It had been days since the dragur attack, and she kept trying to imagine what Draguta would do next.

She thought of Fyr too, wondering if the raven would come

again, her eyes scanning the thick tree canopy above their heads, listening to the birds settling down for the night.

'Expecting something?' Gant asked, chewing a toothpick as he leaned back against a tree. 'Or someone?'

Jael turned to him. 'I'm always expecting something, aren't you?'

Gant nodded. 'Having seen that serpent and the dragon? Always. Not to mention the dragur. Never thought I'd see my nightmares come to life.'

Fires crackled in the distance, crickets chirping loudly. It was getting cooler, and Jael edged closer to the fire. 'Well, maybe tonight's entertainment should be trying to guess which creature Draguta will pull out of our nightmares next?'

Axl was sitting on the other side of Jael, sharpening his sword, and he frowned, not wanting to think about any creatures until they were inside the fort again. 'I expect she needs to send them as she doesn't have any men,' he yawned.

'Well, she has men,' Jael reminded him, 'but most of them are dead.'

Axl laughed, looking at Gant. 'Do you really think there's more of them? The dragur?'

'I imagine so, but I don't think she'll keep sending dragur, will she? She wants to be more effective.'

'It depends on what Draguta hopes to achieve,' Jael mused. 'Killing me? Taking the Book of Aurea? That seemed to be what she was after before, but now, I don't know. I think she wants to defeat us and rule Osterland, but how will she achieve it?' Her mind drifted to Eadmund, and she remembered her dreams of him with Draguta. 'I'm sure she's making plans. And I know they involve Eadmund.'

Gant could hear the odd detachment in Jael's voice. 'To kill you, you mean?'

'I expect so.'

'But Eadmund couldn't. He wouldn't,' Axl insisted. He didn't know Eadmund well enough to predict such a thing, but he didn't believe that a man who loved his wife could kill her, no matter how tightly bound in magic he was. 'Would he?'

'Defeat me?' Jael laughed, remembering her husband. 'No, but perhaps he'll try to. You only have to look at what he did to Thorgils.' She turned to Axl, and her eyes were dark. 'Don't underestimate the power of magic, Brother. It's a weapon like any other, and you can make people bend to your will and do your bidding without them ever being aware of it. So Eadmund had better hope that he doesn't find himself facing me in a fight.'

Axl blinked.

So did Jael. Anger had burst from the pit of her stomach. Anger about her father and her baby, Evaine and Draguta.

Eadmund too.

She turned to Gant with a frown. 'When we get back to Andala, I'm going to need to do some training. The shape I'm in, I think even Axl could beat me.'

Gant laughed, and Jael winked at her brother, pushing all thoughts of Eadmund far from her mind.

***

Eadmund barely made eye contact with Evaine during supper. There was little conversation, so they mainly listened to shouting from outside their house, which wasn't far from the tavern Rollo had taken them to.

Eadmund wondered again what had happened to Rollo.

He was still training, in between planning with Jaeger, but it wasn't the same. Rollo had pushed him hard. He'd knocked him down and battered him relentlessly, never giving him a chance to even catch his breath or think that he was improving. It was just what Eadmund had needed, and he almost missed the bruises and cuts; the marks of how hard he was working.

He hoped that wherever he was, Rollo would be back soon. 'The wine tastes sour,' Evaine muttered. 'Don't you think?' Eadmund blinked at her, returning his attention to the room. 'I hadn't noticed.' He'd finished his cup quickly, not wanting any more. 'I think I'll head for bed.'

Evaine hurried to join him. Her limbs were tense, a state they'd been in for years, watching Eadmund's every movement, every look. Wanting to see the certainty in his eyes that he loved her. That he belonged to her.

Evaine had spent so long looking for it, but mostly she'd seen a bleary-eyed haze and a drunken smile. For a brief period, there had been raw desire and need in his eyes, but now there was nothing but polite coldness. It was as though he was looking straight through her. Evaine was convinced that Eadmund was no longer hers, and she didn't know why. But as desperate as she was to go to Draguta and demand to know what she had done to Eadmund, she was just as afraid that Draguta would take him away from her altogether. Maybe she wanted Eadmund for herself? She certainly looked at him in a way that she hadn't before.

Her thoughts chased each other in faster and faster circles, and eventually, Evaine turned back to the table for her wine, swallowing a big gulp.

'Is something wrong?' Eadmund asked as she wandered into the bedchamber.

Evaine shook her head. 'I was thinking about Sigmund,' she lied, pleased to see Eadmund's eyes come back to her. 'I miss him.'

'You do? You've hardly mentioned him.'

'Well, I've done nothing but think about him,' Evaine promised indignantly. 'You've been busy training or with Jaeger. You've hardly seen me. I speak to my father about him all the time. There's no one else to talk to.'

Eadmund didn't believe her. 'He's safe with Tanja and Runa.'

'And your wife?'

Eadmund frowned. 'I doubt she'll have anything to do with him. Jael's not fond of babies.'

Evaine peered at him, though she only saw annoyance. 'I imagine so, but Sigmund is *our* son,' she reminded him. 'And he needs to be with us.'

Eadmund nodded. 'I'll speak to Draguta. See what plans she has for Andala. Make sure that Sigmund will be safe.' He felt a sudden fear for his son, knowing that Draguta wouldn't sit by while the Brekkans rebuffed her efforts to defeat them.

She wouldn't sit by for much longer.

***

Amma tried to distract herself as she listened to Branwyn sobbing through the wall. Gisila was trying to encourage her sister to eat and sleep, and it appeared that she was having a hard time doing either.

It was a cruel thing to have both a son and husband taken away, Amma thought, realising that she could find herself in the same position one day. Her hands were resting on the rounded bump of her belly as she lay on the bed. It was barely noticeable, she knew, but she could feel it. She knew a child was in there.

But whose?

And what would Axl think about it either way? She wasn't even his wife. She was still married to Jaeger. A man who would undoubtedly try to kill her and Axl as soon as he found a way.

Sighing, Amma closed her eyes, wishing she could see into the future.

Wishing she could see what was coming.

***

Else tucked Morana into bed with a smile. She kept staring at Morana's good eye, convinced that the dreamer was trying to communicate with her. But what was she trying to say? It was impossible to know, Else realised. Morana was locked in her body, just as Draguta wanted her to be. And Else knew that it was safer if she just left her alone.

Eventually, she padded back to her own bed, which had been Meena's, and before that, Varna's. The mattress was thin, with a strong odour of urine, and she kicked herself for not going to the stables to ask for some fresh straw. She would go tomorrow, as soon as she could find someone to sit with Morana. She needed to find some lavender too, and wash out the mattress cover before she carried out her errands.

Pulling the threadbare fur up to her shoulder, Else rolled over, wistful for her old bedchamber behind the kitchen. It had been tiny and cramped, tucked inside a rabbit warren of nooks and crannies where the servants slept, six to a room. And though there was little privacy, it had somehow felt more like home than this miserable stone box. There was friendship and conversation amongst the servants. A chance to share gripes and gossip. To not feel as alone as they actually were.

Sitting up suddenly, Else headed back to the other side of the chamber, certain she'd heard something, but when she peered at Morana in the dull moonbeams shining down from the tiny window high above, she could see that her eyes were closed.

She hadn't moved.

Shaking her head, Else crept back to her bed, unable to stop yawning.

Morana heard her go. She wanted to scream. She needed something of hers or Meena's. She needed something tucked in beside her to help her find a way into Meena's dreams.

For she had seen a way to break out of her prison.

But she was going to need help to do it.

***

Jaeger had been oddly calm since Draguta's return. He had still been attentive, eager for her company, but Meena noticed that his anger ebbed and flowed now, and when he was with her he seemed less agitated. He never spoke about the book or Morana. And when he wasn't talking about his plans for Helsabor, he talked about Draguta.

Endlessly.

Meena felt relieved, eager to disappear inside herself when she was with him, hoping he would fall asleep quickly. It helped when he drank a lot of wine as he had tonight. And now he was snoring beside her, and she was trying to fall asleep herself, but her mind skipped from one worry to the next, and her legs jumped about, and every time she thought she was ready to drift away, her eyes popped open, and she was wide awake again.

In the end, Meena decided to focus her mind on swimming, wondering if she could find another opportunity to go to Fool's Cove again. The night was muggy and still, and she closed her eyes, remembering the chill of the water on her hot skin, washing away the sweat and heat. She imagined the bright sun overhead as she lay on her back, hearing nothing but the gentle lapping of water around her face.

Totally alone.

And finally, Meena slipped away into a dream, where she found herself standing in water. In a dark, airless cave.

The sound of dripping, loud in her ears.

***

When the rain came down, thumping onto the cottage roof, the puppies took fright. Ido, who'd been on Biddy's feet, hurried up to her pillow, almost sitting on her ear. Vella, who'd been lying against Eydis' stomach, jumped off the bed and hid in the corner of the kitchen.

Disturbed by both of them, and surprised to see that Edela and Eydis were still sound asleep, Biddy shepherded the puppies into her bed, trying to get them to stop shaking. 'What big babies you are,' she smiled sleepily, pulling the fur over them all. 'Come on, lie down. Lie down, now.' But Vella wouldn't, and Ido started panting, and, eventually, Biddy began to wake up. 'It's like having children,' she grumbled, hoping that Eydis and Edela were having some useful dreams.

***

Edela's eyes were on the woman in the red dress. She didn't look like the rest of the people in the tavern. Perhaps it was the red dress, Edela thought, which stood out amongst the greys and beiges. It was a cheerful colour.

But she was not a cheerful looking woman.

'And how do I know it's the real one?' she hissed sharply. 'That it is not some trap? Some trick?'

The man frowned. He had an eyepatch and greasy dark hair that fell over his other eye. 'Well, I want my coins, so it's not a trap, nor a trick, but as for it being the real one, you'd have to tell me. I'm no elder or dreamer. How the fuck would I know?'

He was a coarse man, the woman thought with a sneer, but

if he had what she'd been hunting all these years, he could be as coarse as he liked. 'And where is it, then? When can I see it?' She tried to take the edge of desperation out of her voice, but she'd been after this prize for some time, and the thought that she had finally come to within a fingertip of it had her barely able to sit still.

'We'll need to trade. Upstairs.'

'*Upstairs*?' The woman shook her head, painfully aware of what was going on upstairs. 'That is not the sort of transaction I had in mind.'

The man laughed, looking her over.

She wasn't young, but her figure was still desirable, and her face was more than pleasing. He was sure she'd have no problem working upstairs. 'My master has a room. He's waiting in it with your prize. If it's what you're after, you can take us to the chests of gold. All five of them.'

The woman nodded and stood, not wanting to delay.

Noting the impatience in her keen, golden eyes, the man hurried through the heaving tavern, climbing the narrow stairs up to the noisy second floor, down the dark corridor. And opening the door of the last chamber, he ushered her inside, leading her towards the bed where Bruno Adea sat with a smile upon his face.

'Do you have what I came for?' the woman asked as soon as the door closed behind her. 'Do you have the prophecy?'

***

Meena flinched, spinning around, convinced that something had touched her. The cave was so dark, and she couldn't see anyone, but it felt as though something was out there. Swallowing, she tried to quell her rising panic. If she could just stay calm, maybe she could slip away? Wake herself up? Find another dream?

Her breathing quickened, though, and soon Meena abandoned all thoughts of trying to stay calm as she spun and spun, feeling the sharp, wet rocks cutting into her hole-ridden boots. Dragging herself out of the shallow water, which appeared to be some sort of stream, Meena stood on the slippery cave floor, looking around.

She didn't know where she was.

Gulping, she turned slowly to the right, trying to see a way out. But there was no source of light. It was dense and dark and dank, and her panic was now starting to consume her, and then she felt it again.

It felt like a hand.

And spinning around, she was hoping to see nothing.

But this time, she came face to face with Morana.

CHAPTER FORTY ONE

Morana almost threw herself into Meena's arms.

She could barely see her niece, but she would recognise that twitching body anywhere.

'Where are we?' Meena wondered. 'Why are you here?'

'It's the Dolma,' Morana guessed. 'Looks like the Dolma to me.'

Meena shook all over.

'We have to take the risk that Draguta can't see inside here,' Morana said quickly. 'You need to help me.'

Meena frowned, not wanting to take any risks at all when it came to Draguta.

Morana pinched her arm. 'I can't help any of us if you don't help *me*. You can't read the book, can you? Can't get rid of Draguta? But you want to, just as much as I do. I can smell it!'

Meena didn't speak.

Despite the darkness, Morana sensed that Meena had clamped her lips together. 'Don't speak, then,' she grumbled, 'but do listen. I am dreaming. The tea is helping my dreams. Those herbs are powerful. I'm guessing you've had it too, otherwise, we wouldn't be here together. So keep drinking it, and go to Dragmall. He's close to the answer. The symbol was right. What he did was right, but how he did it was wrong. This curse must be broken with Draguta's blood, not mine. It's the only way.'

Meena's eyes bulged, but she kept her mouth closed.

'You will take some of Draguta's blood and try the symbol again. In a different part of the chamber. Anywhere. Look in the book. There is a chant. Words. You must say them over the symbol as you trace it in her blood.'

Meena shook her head, determined not to find herself in trouble with Draguta.

Morana grabbed her, watching the jerking shadow before her with both eyes. Both eyes, and two working arms and legs. She felt so relieved that she didn't want to wake up. 'I can free us all.'

It was a lie, and Meena knew it as she peered into Morana's black eyes. It felt as though she was looking straight back into the cave, and she turned away from her aunt, desperate to find a way out of the dream.

***

Edela was too disturbed to eat any apple hotcakes. 'I'm going to see how Ayla and Bruno are.'

'In *this* weather?' Biddy wondered, listening as the rain continued to pelt down. 'Shouldn't you wait a while?'

But after her dream, Edela wasn't inclined to wait another moment.

Eydis stood, smoothing down her dress, adjusting her belt. 'I'll come. I want to see how they are too.'

Edela frowned.

'What is it?' Eydis asked, sensing her hesitation.

'It?' Edela played coy as she wrapped her cloak around her shoulders. 'Oh, nothing, apart from being half-asleep,' she smiled, glancing at Biddy, who was eyeing her with suspicion. 'That rain kept me awake for most of the night, I'm sure.'

That only heightened Biddy's suspicions. She knew very well, being wide awake herself with those two annoying puppies, that Edela has slept soundly for most of the night. 'I'll come too,' she said, helping Eydis on with her cloak. 'May as well see how everyone is in the hall. See if there's anything I can do.'

Edela nodded distractedly, her mind already focused on what she was going to say to Ayla. She couldn't talk to Bruno yet.

She didn't know if she could trust him.

***

Morac was at the door early, much to Eadmund's annoyance. He appeared to have an eye on his servant, which irritated Eadmund further, remembering how poorly he'd treated Runa.

Not to mention Fyn.

'Jaeger has his men out, stretched from one end of the square to the other,' Morac announced, helping himself to a slice of bread, which, though cold, was still soft and better than the day-old flatbreads he'd eaten for his own breakfast. He grabbed a slice of cheese and rolled it up, stuffing it into his mouth.

Evaine came out of the bedchamber, frowning at him. 'Why are you here?' she grumbled. 'What's happened?'

'Happened?' Morac looked from her moody face to Eadmund's scowling one and wondered what he'd walked in on. 'Nothing, I just thought Eadmund would like to know that Jaeger's not waiting around out there. He's sent someone for Draguta, apparently. She's asked to inspect his men. I thought you'd want to be there,' he said, wolfing down the bread and looking around for something to drink.

Eadmund nodded. 'I do, thank you.' And he turned back to

the bedchamber for his swordbelt.

Morac smiled as Elfwyn came towards him with a jug of milk and a cup. She really was a most agreeable woman, he thought. 'Will you come with me to see Morana?' he asked Evaine, taking the cup with a nod to the shy servant, who bobbed her head and quickly disappeared back to the kitchen.

'Why?'

'*Why*? Because she's your mother, of course. Why wouldn't you want to see her?'

'What's the point of visiting her?' Evaine grumped. She had woken up so many times in the night that her temper was fraying like an old rug. 'We may as well just stare at the wall instead. She can't say anything, and she can't do anything about what we say, so why bother?'

Eadmund came back into the main room, and Evaine's attention was drawn to him. 'Will you be long?' she wondered.

'I'll be all day, I imagine,' Eadmund said quickly, heading for the door. 'There's a lot to do. And I still need to find time to train.'

He was looking even leaner, Evaine thought. And though it wasn't unattractive, she missed the way he used to look. And the way he used to look at her. 'I shall come and find you later. Bring you something to eat.'

Eadmund wasn't listening as he pulled open the door, nodding briefly to Morac. 'I'll see you later, then.' And he quickly shut the door.

Morac grabbed another slice of bread and cheese. 'Shall we go?

Evaine realised that she faced a day alone if she didn't go with him. 'I'll come,' she said irritably, 'but only if we don't stay long. I can't stand the smell of her!'

***

Thorgils was brimming with excitement at the sight of the fort in the distance. Not having paid much attention during their journey to Rissna, he'd been surprised by how close they were to Andala.

And he couldn't have been happier.

But then he frowned, looking at Karsten, whose wary eye was fixed straight ahead. 'Looks like it's still standing.'

'Looks like it,' Karsten agreed cautiously. 'But it would've been hard to take down all of the walls. Unless she sent an army of dragons. We just have to hope that what's inside is still standing too.'

'Mmmm,' Thorgils mumbled into his wet cloak. Despite the rain, it was a warm day, and he could feel himself starting to steam. 'Hopefully, they've made that wall a little higher too. It's not going to be long before we're off again. And who knows when we'll return from Hest.'

'*If* we do,' Karsten said, his thoughts drifting to Jaeger.

Thorgils turned to stare at him. 'You think your brother will defeat us?'

'Jaeger?' Karsten spat. 'He won't. No, I'm saying that once I defeat him, I won't be returning to Andala. I'll be home, where I belong. I'll sit on the dragon throne, send for my family, and stick Jaeger's head on a pike outside the castle so I can smile at it each day as I walk past.'

'Ahhh, brotherly love, it's a beautiful thing. I always wanted a brother or two, but maybe they're more trouble than they're worth? I only had a best friend, and look at what he did to me.'

'At least you're not Berard,' Karsten said. 'Your arm's still attached to your shoulder.'

'True.'

'So you've got a chance to take your revenge. Berard has to sit back and watch me do it for him.'

'You're a bit confident,' Thorgils snorted, thinking of Skorro. 'I remember your brother, and he's going to take some beating. If we even get that far. If the monsters don't kill us all first.'

Karsten peered at Thorgils, troubled by the very same thought. They had men now. More men than Jaeger did, he knew. But they were only men. And who knew if those men were capable of defeating monsters...

***

When the rain eased, Ulf took Bram to the harbour to look over the sheds.

Most were kindling.

'Not sure there'll be any forest left by the time we're done here,' Ulf laughed, stretching out his back. 'It took years to get this harbour built to Ranuf Furyck's satisfaction. He wanted to bring more trade into Andala. A market to rival Hest's.'

'I don't suppose he was allowing for serpents or dragons,' Bram grinned as a crew of strangers wandered down the path from the cove. He watched as the men on the gates lifted their spears and went out to meet them.

Bram walked over to join them.

'Your harbour's not quite what I'd imagined,' the big man said. He was taller than Thorgils, with a shining bald head. Tattoos everywhere. 'We've moored up the coast. In a cove.'

'And you're from?'

'Helsabor. Rollo Barda's the name. We've a shipload of skins. Some salt and spices. A bit of tin and soapstone too. Been round the Fire Lands. Thought we'd try our luck here.'

Bram narrowed his eyes. Having spent much of his life at sea, he was suspicious of this man, who didn't look like any sort of trader he'd met before. Not with arms like those. Not with all those scars. 'And you didn't go to Hest?'

Rollo laughed, shaking his head. 'We were warned away. Their harbour's as bad as yours. But mainly we heard that things had changed. Thought we'd try Andala instead before heading up North.'

'Well, I'm Bram Svanter. If there's anything you need while you're here, I'm the man to find. You can head into the fort, grab a cart. Bring your goods in. I'll look them over and get you a table. We can go over how things work here.'

Rollo nodded, sensing that Bram Svanter wasn't a man to try his luck with. The old man's eyes were sharp, taking in everything about him and his men. He just needed to get into the fort and not cause any trouble. Draguta would be watching, he knew. And he had work to do.

Rollo reached out an arm, clasping Bram's. 'Maybe you could point me to where I could get my men a drink of ale and a bench first? It's been a long and wet few days.'

His smile was wide, though Bram wasn't sure he was really smiling at all. 'Head to the hall. You'll find someone there,' he said before turning back to Ulf, who was studying Rollo as closely as he was.

They both stood back, watching as the straggly crew followed their bald-headed leader in through the gates.

'Looks like the offspring of a giant and a god,' Ulf murmured, shaking his head. 'Wouldn't like to come up against him in a dark alley.'

Bram nodded, thinking how right he was.

***

Leaving Bruno to sleep, Ayla headed for the hall to see what she could do to help, running into the three wet figures of Eydis, Edela, and Biddy on the way. 'Bruno is much better today, but I've left him in bed. He needs some sleep,' Ayla smiled, looking much better herself. Her brown eyes were bright again as she took Edela's hand and helped her up the hall steps, frowning at the train of big men following behind them.

Edela didn't notice as she tried to think of how to steer the conversation towards the prickly subject she needed to discuss, and wanting to get rid of Biddy and Eydis before she did. She was barely listening to Ayla chatting away beside her as they headed into the hall.

'When did you and Bruno meet?' Edela wondered as Biddy excused herself and headed for Gisila and Branwyn.

Eydis stopped by Amma, who led her towards the fire, where Selene and Leya were playing with a giggling Mads.

Ayla was surprised by the question. 'Oh, it must be seven years ago now. Time has gone so quickly, and yet it feels as though we're still newly married. I expect that was the life of a merchant. Never putting down roots. Never feeling as though you have a home, or the chance to make one.'

She sounded sad, Edela thought, though she didn't look Ayla's way. She was too busy trying to decide how to begin, but, in the end, she simply blurted it out. 'I had a dream about Bruno.'

Ayla stopped, hearing the tension in the dreamer's voice. 'What about?' Her voice was a whisper, searching Edela's eyes, which were struggling to meet her own.

Edela glanced around. She could see Alaric and Derwa talking in the distance, looking their way, but there was no one in earshot. 'He was in a tavern. I don't know where, and I don't know when, but he looked much younger. His hair was black. He was clean-shaven. Thinner too.'

Ayla waited to hear more, her shoulders tightening.

'There was a woman.' She saw Ayla's lips twitch. 'She wanted to trade something with him. Five chests of gold for the...'

Ayla leaned closer, watching as Edela glanced around again.

'Prophecy.'

'What? *The* prophecy?'

'I'm not sure it was the actual prophecy. It could have been the scroll stolen from the temple years ago. Alaric mentioned that a merchant bought it.'

'And you think Bruno took it?'

Edela shrugged. 'I don't know. A woman wanted to buy it. It seems that Bruno had it, though I don't know if he gave it to this woman. I woke up before I found out much more, unfortunately. I wanted to tell you. To see what you thought about it?'

Ayla didn't know what she thought about it, but her arms had started shaking.

'Do you think Bruno is well enough for us to ask him?' Edela wondered delicately. She could see that she had unsettled Ayla, and after what Ayla had just been through, she felt guilty.

'Yes, we can talk to him.' Ayla felt odd. Hesitant. Bruno had never spoken about his life before her in great detail, and she had never pried, but she'd always had the impression that he'd been happy to leave it all behind.

And now she was about to find out why.

***

Jael felt uneasy as they approached the main gates down the narrow path that wound its way between two sloping mountains. She couldn't see anything unusual, and she hadn't seen the raven again, but every wet hair on the back of her wet neck was standing on end.

She kept seeing visions of Eadmund; fleeting glimpses of him with Evaine. But he looked so different that she wondered if she was just imagining things. He didn't look like the Eadmund she remembered. He was all sharp edges and cold eyes. He had a jaw, cheekbones, and a hardness about him that wasn't familiar at all.

'Are you alright?' Gant asked, riding up beside Jael. She hadn't spoken much to anyone since they'd set off, and he couldn't help but worry about her, especially after what she'd told him about her baby.

'Just wondering how things are in there,' she said, nodding towards the fort.

'Mmmm,' Gant agreed, feeling the tension in his shoulders tighten further. They had no idea what they were about to ride into. 'Hopefully, Draguta found something else to do while we were gone.'

Jael's mind wandered straight back to Eadmund.

'Are you... going to talk to Gisila?' Gant mumbled, looking straight ahead. Gus and Tig walked side by side, their ears swivelling, already picking up the familiar sounds of home. 'About Raymon?'

Jael sighed. 'I suppose I am.' She didn't want to think about how that would go.

'It will be a shock for her.'

'You don't think she suspected?'

Gant shrugged. 'I honestly don't know. Things were difficult with them at times. As stubborn as Ranuf was, your mother could be just as bad.' He frowned. 'I don't think things were ever right after your brothers died. They went their separate ways to deal with the pain, from what I understand. And then, of course, Tuura happened...'

Jael kept her mouth closed. She didn't want to imagine what her father was doing when he wasn't in Tuura protecting his family.

Gant knew what her silence meant. 'When we all came back, and Ranuf learned what had happened, he fell to pieces,' he said quietly. 'No one saw it, of course, but he wasn't good for a long time. What happened to you and Gisila... losing Harald. The three of us had been friends since we were crawling.' Gant dropped his eyes, reaching out to pat Gus. 'Fianna too. He blamed himself for all of it. It never left him, Jael.'

Jael was almost glad to hear it.

'Perhaps it's better coming from you?' she suggested craftily. 'Telling Gisila? You know more about it than I do. You'd be able to explain it better than I could.'

Gant wanted to argue with that, but he couldn't. 'I think you're right,' he admitted. 'Your father didn't carry all that guilt on his own. I was there too.' His voice grew reed-thin; Jael almost couldn't hear him over the loud clopping of the horses down the path. 'I let you all down that night.'

Jael squeezed his arm. 'No.' She shook her head. 'No, you didn't. You saved us from being killed. Those men would have killed us, but you killed all of them. You saved our lives.'

Gant kept seeing the image of Aleksander running for his mother, watching as she cut her own throat. 'I didn't save everyone.'

'No, but you never can. Which we're about to find out when we head for Hest. You always have to make choices about who will live and who will die. They're never easy.'

She thought about Ravenna.

'And what about Eadmund?' Gant wondered. 'Will you have to make a choice about him? If you can't save him? If he stands in your way?'

Jael dropped her eyes to her hands, watching her wedding band glinting in the returning sun. 'I don't know,' she admitted. 'I have to believe that we can save him. That there's time. But if we can't...' She looked up at Gant, swallowing. 'I honestly don't know.'

***

Eadmund had bitten his tongue throughout Jaeger's performance, watching as he puffed out his chest and showed off his Hestian warriors to Draguta, explaining their strategy for attacking Helsabor. He'd walked alongside them, trying not to groan as he listened to Jaeger's self-important drivel. Draguta was listening eagerly, it seemed, occasionally glancing at Eadmund for confirmation of what Jaeger was saying. Mainly he just nodded. His mind was far away, thinking of Oss.

'Eadmund?' Draguta snapped. 'You've barely said a word. Why don't we leave Jaeger to sort out the men, and you can walk me back to my chamber?'

Jaeger looked annoyed.

Eadmund was pleased that it was over. He smiled at Draguta and turned towards the castle, eager to get out of the sun. He had a permanent burn on the back of his neck, and he felt wistful for the cold gloom of home.

'Tell me,' Draguta murmured as he followed her up the steps. 'When did you stop feeling anything for Evaine?'

Eadmund blinked in surprise as she waited for him to catch up to her.

Draguta laughed, slipping her arm through his. 'You do realise that I can read your thoughts, don't you? I can see inside your soul, Eadmund, and I know for certain that it no longer belongs to Evaine.' She looked around quickly, not wanting to deal with the scene a wailing Evaine would certainly cause if she found out.

'I...' Eadmund shrugged. 'I'm not sure. A day or so.'

'Hmmm, and what does that mean? Remember now, I see and hear everything. Lying to me would be pointless, and it would displease me greatly to think that we couldn't trust one another.'

Eadmund heard the disappointment in Draguta's voice, and his body responded with panic. 'I don't know what it means. I just don't feel the same. I don't feel anything.'

'I'm not sure that's true,' Draguta mused. 'Not really. I

imagine you love Jael Furyck again, don't you? You loved your wife before Evaine bound you, so it makes sense that you would love her again now that her spell is broken. Am I right?'

Eadmund tried to clear his mind and his heart, but he could feel Draguta squeezing his arm, and he felt torn, confused, and eventually, desperate to please her by telling her the truth.

'Yes. I do.'

CHAPTER FORTY TWO

Axl smiled at Jael over Amma's head, feeling his body sink against her in relief that she was alright. That everyone was alright.

Jael smiled back, squeezing Eydis tightly.

'We've had so many dreams, Jael!' Eydis exclaimed, turning towards where she knew Biddy and Edela were standing. 'Well, Edela has had more than me, but we've been busy. Well, Edela has.'

Jael laughed. 'So what have you actually done, Eydis? Looked after the puppies, I hope?' she said, bending down to pat Ido and Vella, who weren't puppies any longer, she realised. They wriggled themselves into a frenzy, jumping up at her, pink tongues flapping. As badly behaved as ever.

'You're back, then?' Bram grinned, looking from Thorgils, who was buried in Isaura, to Jael. 'No problems?'

Jael glanced at Thorgils. 'One or two. How about you?'

Bram was intrigued, suddenly shy as Fyn approached with Runa. 'We haven't stopped. Been working on the piers and getting that wall higher. More catapults too.'

'So I see,' Jael said, smiling at Runa, who didn't appear any closer to teasing Bram out of his awkwardness. 'Still, it needs to be higher than that. We don't want to leave here with half a wall.' Her eyes drifted to Gisila, who was hugging Axl; Gant standing behind them. Jael inclined her head towards her mother, and he frowned at her. 'And the sea-fire?'

'Hopefully, you'll have enough. We've got vats of liquid, but we need more jars, so I've had the potters at work on those.'

Jael was nodding, only half listening. She needed a drink and something to eat, and she wanted to hear about Edela's dreams. 'Let's get the horses sorted, then head to the hall!' she called to those men who stood around her, stretching out stiff limbs and aching backs.

There were grunts and nods of approval at that.

'Still standing?' Karsten grinned at Berard after extracting himself from Bayla, who had quickly complained about all the things that were wrong with the cottage they were still stuck in. Thankfully, Ulf had come along and turned her attention to something else. Nicolene was still in bed apparently, which had only added to Bayla's irritation.

'Still standing,' Berard smiled, relieved to have Karsten back. He was feeling stronger, riding and training every day, when he could escape Bayla's clutches. He didn't feel useful with a sword yet, but he was confident that he'd be able to ride to Hest without causing himself or his brother too much embarrassment.

Karsten leaned towards Berard as they made their way to the stables. 'And what about Hanna?' He hadn't seen Marcus, which concerned him. 'Is she... still alive?'

'She is. She's with her father. I saw her this morning. She's sitting up. Eating. She asked about you.'

'She did?'

Berard was surprised by the interest in his brother's voice. 'Mmmm, she wanted to know how everyone was.'

Karsten adjusted his eyepatch as they walked towards the stables, past Aleksander, who had been caught by Edela.

'Where have *you* been hiding?' Edela smiled, peering at his bruised face. 'I wondered if you'd had an accident, though I hadn't seen anything bad happening to you in my dreams. Though something does appear to have happened to your face.'

Aleksander put an arm around her shoulder, giving her a squeeze. 'It was an interesting journey, to say the least.'

Edela frowned. 'And?'

Aleksander saw Gant walking away with Gisila, knowing what that would be about. 'I'll tell you everything over a bowl of stew, after I see to Sky. But tell me something before I go... how is... Hanna?' He lifted his voice, trying to sound casual, but he could see Edela's keen eyes sharpen, twinkling in the sunshine.

'Hanna is well.'

Aleksander blinked in surprise. He'd been steeling himself for bad news the whole ride home. 'Well?'

'Go and see for yourself. She is recovering now. Doing very well.'

Aleksander found himself nodding, though every part of him had just tensed uncomfortably.

Edela didn't notice. She was watching Ayla hurrying away from the hall, hopefully going to see if Bruno was awake. Soon it would be time to talk to him about the prophecy, she knew, and though she desperately needed answers, Edela wasn't sure if Ayla was going to like what Bruno had to say.

***

Draguta stared into Eadmund's troubled eyes, smiling as she came to a decision. 'Stay with Evaine. It will keep her quiet until I decide what to do with her. I have enough people to think about for now.' And leaving Eadmund on the steps, she headed for the heated baths, eager to feel the steaming water on her skin. Sensing that Eadmund wasn't moving, she turned around. 'You are free now, Eadmund. Free from Evaine, but not from me. You will never be free from me, and one day soon, Jael

Furyck and her dreamer friends will discover the truth about that.' And sweeping her white dress around, she disappeared through the doors.

Eadmund watched her go, unable to move.

His heart was throbbing with the need to go back to Andala and find Jael. He could feel the ache in it; the emptiness and pain finally revealed now that he'd been released from Evaine's spell.

But as he watched Draguta disappear into the castle, he knew that she was right.

He could never leave her.

She needed him.

***

Gant wanted to do it quickly, though it didn't feel like the right time, and he didn't think Gisila would respond well to what he had to say.

He *knew* Gisila wouldn't respond well.

He couldn't decide where to do it either, but having handed Gus off to Thorgils, who was happy to take him to the stables for a rub down, he took Gisila's arm and led her across the square, towards the harbour. It was a nice walk, through the trees, listening to the birds, busy above their heads, the waves crashing in the distance. But he was distracted, tense, knowing that he was about to hurt her.

Gisila felt just as tense as she walked beside him. 'What happened?' she asked, eventually. 'Something happened, didn't it? I saw the way everyone was looking at me. Just tell me, Gant. I want to know.' She felt a sharp pain in her chest, almost afraid of what he was going to say.

Gant nodded. He was tired after a mostly sleepless night,

and his thoughts were scattered like birds across a meadow as he struggled to begin.

Gisila tried to help him. 'Is it something about Axl? Or Jael?'

Gant shook his head, then stopped himself. 'No, and yes. It's about... Ranuf.' They walked over a little mound, muddy after the rain. Gant grabbed Gisila as she slid.

'Ranuf?' Gisila hadn't been expecting that, though the ghost of Ranuf Furyck still loomed large over Andala three years after his death. 'What about him?'

'He...' Gant saw how desperate her eyes were, and he took a deep breath. 'Raymon Vandaal is his son.'

Gisila shuddered in horror. 'What?' It didn't sound real, but she knew Gant. He almost looked in pain having to tell her. '*What*? I... what do you mean? Ravenna? He was with Ravenna?' Her thoughts jumped quickly, trying to make sense of things. 'When? For how long?'

Gant knew that he couldn't hide anything from her. It had all been hidden for too long. Gisila couldn't be the one person kept in the dark. Not now. 'Since just after Hugo took the throne. Up until his death.'

Gisila's mouth fell open.

She closed it and promptly spun away from Gant, hitching up her dress and walking back over the slippery mound, hurrying all the way back to the fort.

***

Axl sunk into his throne, relieved to be home. Relieved that his home was still in one piece, or, at least, in the pieces he'd left it in. There was so much to do, he knew, but for one moment, he wanted to enjoy being with Amma again. He pulled her onto his knee, watching her squirm. 'You look as though you haven't slept since we left. Are you sure you're alright?'

At that moment, Amma was wondering if she needed to vomit, but she nodded, trying to smile. 'It was worrying, not knowing what would happen every night. Listening for creatures. It was hard to sleep. Every noise woke me up.'

Axl inhaled the sweet honeysuckle scent of her, watching as Gisila strode into the hall, past Branwyn, heading for the bedchambers. He frowned, guessing what that was about; not sure what he could do to make it any better, though. It felt more than strange knowing that his father had had a secret life, though now Ranuf seemed more of a man; not the god they'd all made him out to be.

Amma scrambled off his knee. 'I have to go and see about something in the kitchen,' she mumbled, scurrying away.

Axl looked after her in surprise, his attention quickly moving to his cousin, Aedan, who'd come to see his mother. He looked as lost as Branwyn. Axl had left him in charge of replenishing their sea-fire stores, hoping it would give him something to keep him occupied, but he appeared just as broken as when they'd left.

Standing up, Axl filled two cups with ale, turning after Aedan, almost knocking over his grandmother. 'Sorry!'

Ayla grabbed Edela as she stumbled.

'Are you getting so tall that you can't see me down here?' Edela chuckled, not stopping to talk to Axl as she followed Ayla towards the doors, her nerves rattling.

It was time to go and ask Bruno what he knew about the prophecy.

***

Brill had been sent to find Meena.

'We have work to do,' Draguta declared when Meena arrived, her eyes on one of the seeing circles before looking up in surprise. 'Why are you all wet?'

Meena had only just walked back into the city after disappearing for another swim. She had planned to walk to Dragmall's, but Brill had stopped her, insisting that she hurry back to Draguta. 'I had a swim.'

'Where?'

'In the sea.'

Draguta frowned. 'Obviously, I am not giving you enough to do! Swanning about like a lady? You need to know your place, my girl, and it is not as the Queen of Hest. You may be Jaeger's little toy, but that is all you are and something you won't be for much longer if you carry on like this!'

Meena dropped her eyes, feeling her wet hair soaking through her new dress, dripping on the floor.

'Where are the things the Furycks left behind?' Draguta mused. 'Whatever happened to them?'

Meena blinked in surprise. 'Morana took them. I think she put them in a chest in her chamber.'

'You will bring them to me. All of them. And find a towel, so that you don't leave more puddles on my floor!'

Nodding quickly, Meena turned for the door, trying not to imagine what Draguta was up to now.

***

Eadmund had walked far away from the castle, Draguta's words ringing in his ears.

Jael's too.

Jael.

He remembered everything about her. Every scowl and

smile.

Every scar.

The taste of her lips. The look in her eye.

Those eyes...

People passed him, going into the city, following after each other, down the dusty, red path in a long line. Not many were going his way, and Eadmund was jostled as he walked. He barely noticed as he tried to picture Oss. His house. Biddy standing by the cauldron, telling him off for his muddy boots. The puppies crawling up his legs, wanting to go outside and play. Askel rubbing Leada down in the stables. Fyn and Thorgils coming to get Jael for training.

His father.

Eirik wasn't there anymore. He wouldn't be on Oss when he returned.

If he returned.

Eadmund's shoulders slumped as the path narrowed, leading towards a sharp rise. He stopped, turning back to look at the city, seeing the castle gleaming in the afternoon sun. He wanted to keep going, to keep walking until he left it all behind. Until he was far away from Hest. Until he was on his way home.

Home.

He wanted to go home.

Closing his eyes, Eadmund heard Draguta's demanding voice, and he swallowed, knowing that he had to head back to the city. He hadn't trained enough. Not nearly enough to please Draguta.

He had to hurry back.

***

It took a while for Bruno to find any words.

Edela's question stunned him so much that his thoughts froze, though memories were quickly swirling of a past he had buried long ago. He glanced at Ayla, seeing the fear in her eyes. She sat on the edge of the bed, keeping her distance.

'There was a time when I was in debt. I owed a great debt. I needed coins,' he began hesitantly, stopping to clear his throat. 'A lot of them. Chests full of them. I owed a man, a lord in Silura. Keld of Sundara was his name. I'd been his man since I was a boy. Rose up the ranks until I was commanding his fleet. He'd trusted me with his ships and his crew, and I was responsible for losing them. They were burned in a raid that went wrong. My raid.' Bruno paused, watching Ayla, but she just stared at him, her mouth slightly open, her eyebrows knotted together. 'We raided a lot... I wasn't a merchant then.' He looked embarrassed. 'After the ships burned and his men died, Keld took my sister. Said he'd keep her hostage until I brought him new ships and the crews to sail them. Compensation too.'

Ayla blinked in surprise. She hadn't known that Bruno even had a sister.

'Leesa was young, only eleven.' Bruno's voice caught. 'I'd raised her when our parents died. She was my only family, and Keld wasn't the sort of man to leave your family with. So I did what I could, as quickly as I could. Took what men I had and stole a ship. Headed for Helsabor, raided the coastline. It wasn't enough, but I developed a reputation quickly, and one day when we were in Angard, I was approached. Promised five chests of gold if I could retrieve a scroll for this woman. It was kept in the Temple of Tuura.'

'And who was she?' Edela wondered, edging forward. 'The woman who wanted the scroll?'

'Her name was Neera. She was Wulf Halvardar's daughter.'

'You knew this for certain?'

Bruno nodded. 'When I returned to Angard, she came herself. She wanted to see it. I think she was a dreamer.'

'You do?'

'It's what I remember thinking at the time. The way she talked. The things she knew.'

'And you gave it to her?' Ayla asked. 'The scroll?'

'Yes, I traded it for the gold. She paid for it, kept her side of the bargain, but Keld didn't. My sister was long dead by the time I returned with his ships.' He looked down, still haunted by the shock of the day he'd discovered that. 'It was my fault. When my mother was dying, she'd begged me to take care of Leesa. And instead, I got her killed.' He looked up, tears in his eyes. 'She was just a child.'

Ayla felt chilled to the bone.

Edela was still on the hunt for answers, though, wanting to confirm that Bruno's story was truthful, thinking about what Alaric had told her. 'And how did you get the prophecy?'

Bruno sighed. 'I went to Tuura, putting myself out there as a successful merchant. I came with spices and glass. Silver and silks. High-quality items that drew the attention of those who knew people at the temple. Then I started asking around, letting it be known that I had a lot of gold to pay for a particular item I needed. Eventually, a meeting was arranged with a man who worked in the temple. He told me he didn't know what I was looking for, but when I showed him the gold, he was suddenly eager to help.'

'Who was the man?' Edela wondered.

Bruno shrugged. 'I can't remember his name. He was a scribe, I think.'

'And how do you know he gave you the right scroll? That it wasn't just a ruse?'

'Well, I don't. I couldn't read it. But Neera Halvardar could. She looked it over, rolled it back up and handed over the chests. And that was the last I heard of her.'

Edela was intrigued.

Ayla was speechless. She felt as though she didn't even know the man sitting opposite her.

Noticing the tension between them, Edela stood. 'I should

leave. You will have things to discuss, I know,' she said awkwardly, heading for the door. She stopped, looking back at Bruno, who was looking at Ayla, who wasn't looking at him at all. 'I am sorry,' she added. 'About your sister.'

Bruno nodded distractedly. 'Thank you.'

Edela quickly pulled open the door, already knowing where she needed to head to next.

***

Else was pleased to see Meena. So was Morana, though there was nothing she could do to communicate with her, so she worked hard on clearing her mind, not wanting any thoughts about her dreams to enter it. She was intrigued, though, as she watched her niece, wondering what Draguta was up to now.

Meena was quickly on her hands and knees, dragging an old chest out from under Morana's bed.

Else frowned. 'Why are you all wet?'

Meena sat back on her heels, brushing dripping hair out of her eyes. 'I had a swim, though I wish I hadn't now. Draguta was cross.'

Else ignored that and smiled. 'Oh, I'm glad to hear it. Where did you go? I would like to take a dip myself one day. It's becoming so hot in here.' She looked at Morana, who appeared to be glaring at her, although she looked like that most of the time, Else realised.

'Just to one of the coves,' Meena said, relaxing for a moment. 'It's called Fool's Cove. The water was so cold.'

Else's dress was sticking to her, and she looked wistful, longing to feel cold.

'I'll ask Morac to watch Morana,' Meena suggested. 'Then you can go for a swim.'

'Well, I wouldn't say no to that! And I might visit Dragmall while I'm out. See if he's got any more herbs for me.'

Morana was pleased to hear it, hoping that Morac would come. And quickly.

She needed to get back into her dreams.

***

Evaine had tried to cheer herself up by dragging Morac to the markets before they went to visit Morana. She wanted to buy more furniture for the house, hoping to make it look and smell more enticing for Eadmund, though she knew that the house wasn't the problem. And no new bed fur or lavender added to the floor reeds would help with that.

Morac spent most of the time chatting with Elfwyn, who didn't know what to make of the attention she was getting, and who tried to drift further back to encourage Morac to walk with his daughter instead.

'Will you go to Helsabor?' Evaine wondered, elbowing a woman in the ribs as she passed, not bothered by the foul look she received in return. 'With Eadmund?'

Morac shook his head. 'No, I don't expect so. It was different, fighting with the Islanders. They were my people. Eirik was my king. But this is not my fight, and I'm an old man now.' He stopped, turning to smile at Elfwyn. 'Well, not that old. But unless I'm required, I shall remain here. I want to keep an eye on you and Morana.'

'Why?' Evaine snapped. 'Morana is done for. There's nothing for her to do now but sit in that chamber and wait for death to come.'

Morac didn't want to think that was true, but likely it was. 'She is still your mother,' he tried. 'Are you saying you feel nothing for her? That you don't care?'

'That's exactly what I'm saying! I care about Eadmund and our son. I care about getting away from here. Going home and becoming the Queen of Oss. I care about all the things you've been promising me since I could walk!' She quickly bit her tongue, realising that she was almost yelling. Leaning closer, she lowered her voice. 'All the things you and Morana promised. *Promised* would happen!'

Morac didn't understand. 'But you have Eadmund. He's here, with you. You don't have your son yet, but you will soon. Eadmund will see to it. And once Draguta has finished with him, he'll make you his queen. Of course he will.'

Evaine stared at her father, shaking her head. 'Do you even *see* what is happening with Eadmund? He is gone, and nothing we do will bring him back to me.' She blinked, surprised by the certainty she felt and by the idea that had just sparked. 'Unless...'

'Unless?'

'Unless Morana could help?'

They both turned as Meena rushed up to them, red-faced and panting.

'What do you want?' Evaine grumbled.

Meena ignored her, her eyes on Morac. 'Else wondered if you would watch Morana while she takes a break?'

Morac looked at Evaine, who smiled, and they both turned to Meena. 'Of course. We'll come right away.'

CHAPTER FORTY THREE

Edela was distracted, hurrying across the busy square on her way to see Marcus when she spied Jael talking to Aleksander, and she realised that she needed to talk to her granddaughter most urgently of all.

Jael smiled as Edela approached.

'Will you walk me to Marcus' cottage?' Edela asked, noting the interest in Aleksander's eyes, which quickly turned away from hers.

Jael left her cup on the table and nodded, intrigued. She was keen to know about the dreams Eydis had mentioned, but Edela didn't speak until they were well away from the square.

'It's Eadmund,' Edela said with a smile. 'We broke the spell.'

Jael stopped as though she'd run into a stone wall. She spun around, grabbing Edela's arms. 'What?' Her body shook. '*What?*'

Edela hurried to calm the happiness blooming in Jael's weary eyes. 'We broke the soul spell, Evaine's spell. But there is another.'

Jael cursed herself for believing it could all be that simple. 'Of course there is,' she sighed as they started walking again.

'I went to Eadmund and dug into his soul. I cut the binding rope that joined him to Evaine,' Edela whispered, sensing Jael still beside her. 'But there was another rope tied around him, and when I touched it, I disappeared, out of the trance, so I'm not sure how we can possibly undo it.'

'So Draguta has him, then?'

'I would say so.'

Jael's body suddenly felt heavy with the dread of what was to come. 'Keep dreaming,' she urged her grandmother. 'And find a way to cut that rope. I can't fight Eadmund. It can't come down to that, can it?'

'There's more, I'm afraid,' Edela warned her, and she told Jael about her dream of Draguta being killed with the knife; her dreams of Dara Teros too.

'And you're sure the knife is like my sword?'

'Yes, I am.'

Jael scratched her head. 'So Draguta is more powerful than Dara imagined when she wrote the prophecy? More powerful than the sword or the knife?'

Edela nodded. 'Yes, it appears so. That's not to say that you won't be able to use your sword, but I think it's time to try and find this shield of Eadmund's.'

'But Eadmund isn't ready. He's not even on the right side of what's coming,' Jael insisted.

'No, he's not. And the prophecy might all be wrong. Who knows?' Edela said with an ever-deepening frown. 'But that shield was made for a reason, and if it's not Eadmund who is going to wield it, then it will have to be someone else. We must find it, Jael. We have the Book of Aurea. We have your sword, whether it works or not. And now we need to find that shield. It may be the one thing that will keep you safe.'

Jael wasn't so sure. 'I may as well walk towards Draguta with a white banner flying by the sound of it. Give her everything she wants! She took my baby. She has my husband. And now she's taken away the power of my sword.' She shook her head, wanting to scream. 'I don't see how we can stop her. I don't. I just don't!'

'We'll find a way,' Edela assured her granddaughter, trying to sound more confident than she felt. 'Don't you worry, now.

We'll find a way.'

***

Draguta sat on the bed, looking through the chest Meena had brought back from Morana's chamber. It was a small, musty box stuffed with nothing she wanted to touch, but there were items in it that would be useful, she knew.

Lifting up a pale-yellow dress, she glanced at Brill, who stood before her, waiting to be of assistance. 'Come here, you miserable creature. Come and tell me who these clothes belonged to.' She could almost feel it herself, but she wanted to be certain.

Brill didn't want to be responsible for getting anything wrong, but she nodded and sat down beside Draguta, blinking at the yellow dress. 'I would guess Amma Furyck,' she mumbled into her own dress. 'Jael Furyck wore trousers, and her mother would not wear such a thing. It's a girl's dress.'

'I am pleased to hear how observant you were, Brill,' Draguta said with satisfaction. 'That will make all of this much easier indeed.' And she turned back to the chest and pulled out a wristguard.

***

Morac and Evaine sat with Morana, pleased to be rid of Else, but neither knew what to say to the depressed-looking woman, who sat lifelessly before them, staring at the door.

Eventually, Morana closed her eyes.

Evaine started to speak, but Morac grabbed her arm, his eyes insistent as she glared at him. It would do neither of them any good to say what they wanted out loud. He knew his sister had a way of reading his thoughts, and he hoped she was doing it right now.

It was still a risk, but it was all he could think of to do.

If Draguta had bound Eadmund to her, Morac knew that they could quickly become irrelevant. And though he'd made subtle enquiries about merchant ships heading to Silura, he knew that it was going to be hard to convince Evaine to come with him.

He let everything float into his mind.

Everything that was happening in the castle with Draguta: her plans for Eadmund and Jaeger, her invasion of Helsabor, Briggit Halvardar's rise to power.

He wanted his sister to know all of it.

Morana watched them both, intrigued. Evaine looked miserable, and she quickly began to understand why. Without Eadmund, there was no point to her life, she knew. No point to anything.

Morana didn't care, but she was curious about what Draguta was planning next. Once she found her way out of her prison, she needed to destroy the vengeful bitch quickly, so she was eager to know everything that had been going on.

Squeezing her right eye, Morana blinked at Morac, and he smiled.

***

Gant wondered if he should go and check on Gisila. Eventually, he convinced himself that she would need time to let it all sink in; that seeing him would only make everything worse.

'How did it go?' Jael asked as she wandered towards him with Aleksander and Aedan. They had come to check on the sea-fire production.

Gant squirmed. 'As you'd expect, I think.' He glanced at Aedan, wondering if he knew what they were talking about, but he realised that it didn't matter. Soon everyone would. 'She walked off before I could say much.'

'I don't blame her,' Jael said. 'Imagine how she feels? Oh wait, I don't need to, my husband had a son with another woman too!'

No one knew if Jael was trying to be funny, but she had a grin on her weary face, and they all relaxed a little.

'Maybe you should go and talk to her?' Aleksander suggested.

'*Me?*'

Gant was quickly nodding in agreement. 'You should. She probably wants someone to talk to. Someone who understands what it feels like.'

Now it was Jael's turn to squirm. 'Maybe, but let's check on the sea-fire first, then I'll think about it.' The wind whipped her braids across her face, and she looked up, seeing that the sun had well and truly disappeared for the day. 'Might be a storm tonight.'

Their eyes followed Jael's, no one looking pleased by the thought of that.

***

The wind rattled Marcus' door, but Edela didn't notice as she stared at him, waiting for him to speak. He was sitting on Hanna's bed, feeding her some broth, his brow furrowed as he took in the full weight of her story.

Edela smiled at Hanna, pleased to see how well she looked. Not well enough, but better than the near-death skeleton of a few days ago.

Marcus turned to her. 'It does sound as though it was the scroll stolen from the temple. And it's been in Angard all this time?'

'I imagine so. In the hands of The Following, by the sound of it.'

'In the hands of Briggit Halvardar's mother,' Marcus murmured.

'Really? Neera is Briggit's mother?'

'She is. Whether she still lives, I don't know,' he admitted as Hanna shook her head, not wanting any more broth. Marcus put the bowl on the table and turned back to Edela. 'I wouldn't call what Bruno took the prophecy, though. It was a scroll of notes. Memories. I don't know how accurate they were, or whether the person who wrote them had even read the prophecy, but it's all we've ever had to go on. The only one who truly knows what is going to happen is Dara Teros.'

'I think you're right,' Edela agreed. 'But I am worried that Briggit and her mother know more than we want them to know. They know the danger Jael and Eadmund pose. They know about the sword and the shield. They know about Draguta. All of that was in the scroll, wasn't it?'

Marcus nodded. 'It was, but they've done nothing. In all the years since Neera bought that prophecy, they've done nothing that we know of.'

'But they're starting to now, with her daughter murdering her grandfather and taking the throne. With her trying to murder all of us with that sickness curse. They're starting to now.'

Marcus looked worried. 'Jael can't go to Hest while The Following rules in Helsabor,' he warned. 'She needs to destroy them first. They are a threat to her and us. They will want the Book of Darkness as much as Draguta.'

'I agree, but now that it appears Jael's sword won't help her, what of the shield? Do you have any idea where it is?'

Marcus shook his head. 'Its location wasn't written in the scroll, and the gods have never revealed anything about it to me. It was always meant for Eadmund. His to find when it was time.'

'But now he's the last person who should have it,' Edela murmured. 'So we're going to have to find it ourselves. Before anyone else does.'

***

Meena had been called back into Draguta's chamber and given another list.

'For tonight,' Draguta had said. 'These are the last items I require for our return to the stones.'

Meena's heart had skipped a beat.

'Tonight,' Draguta had repeated, sending her on her way. 'And do not take all day, girl. You will have much to prepare when you return.'

And now Meena walked towards the winding gardens, already wistful for the feeling of cold water washing over her skin. The sun had slunk behind a bank of dense clouds, enhancing the humidity of the afternoon.

Jaeger smiled as he approached the twitching figure. Somehow, Meena always made him feel better. 'Where have you been all day?' he called, leaving the stables. He'd ridden up to the cliffs with Gunter, the head of his army, talking over their proposed route to Helsabor, and now he was dripping with sweat, and eager for some wine and shade.

Meena stumbled to a stop just as she was about to turn under the archway into the gardens. 'I've been doing things for Draguta.'

'What things?' Jaeger wondered. 'What's she planning now?' He'd been intrigued by Draguta's lack of urgency since her return. She had kept her plans for the Brekkans very close to her chest.

Perhaps the truth was that she didn't have any?

Perhaps her mind was solely on conquering Helsabor now?

'I don't know,' Meena admitted, wanting to leave. 'I have to go into the gardens,' she insisted as Jaeger came even closer, bringing her into his arms. He felt more sweaty than she did.

It wasn't pleasant.

'Why don't I come with you?' Jaeger suggested slyly, remembering his time in there with Evaine.

Meena panicked. 'Draguta is doing something t-t-tonight!' she stammered, trying to ease away from him. 'At the stones. I have to hurry. There'll be a lot to prepare once I get back.'

'Oh?' Jaeger stepped back. 'Tonight? And who will she be taking to the stones, then?'

Meena shrugged, wishing the answer wasn't her.

***

Draguta stood on her balcony, watching the sun retreat for another day. The clouds appeared to be thickening, though she didn't feel worried. The gods might think they could play games with her, but she felt no fear at all now.

Knowing that the knife was powerless had set her free.

Nothing could stop her now. Nothing, and no one.

She thought of Taegus, her love, and Valder, her son, and her contentment suddenly vanished. All that she planned to build would be empty without them. But she would find a way to bring them both back. There would be a way...

It was everything to her: claiming Osterland, destroying her enemies.

Defeating her sister.

And she would.

One by one, she would.

'You wished to see me?' Eadmund asked, walking out onto the balcony. His face was bright red, having just finished his second training session of the day. He could barely lift his arms, but it had felt good defeating his opponent, imagining what Rollo would have said. Probably not much, he realised with a tired grin.

Draguta spun around, her red lips lifting into a broad smile. 'I did. And here you are! Come,' she said, motioning to the small table, where two goblets and a jug of wine were waiting. 'I thought you might need something to drink after your long day.'

Eadmund could smell the wine, and he didn't want it. 'Thank you,' he said, taking a seat.

'I was pleased with what I heard today,' Draguta purred. 'You and Jaeger might make a good team after all.' She laughed at Eadmund's scowling face. 'Or perhaps not. But do remember that Jaeger is my heir, and I require him to sit on the throne of Hest, so you will always do your best to protect him. And you will not kill him. One day, I'm sure, I will no longer have any need for him, but until then, he is mine.'

Eadmund nodded, deciding that he was too thirsty to ignore the wine, and he took a sip, trying not to grimace as it burned his throat. His mind wandered to Oss, and Ketil's and sitting outside with Thorgils in the snow, listening to his stupid jokes. And he remembered what he'd done to him.

Draguta was talking. 'We will be going to the stones tonight. And I want you there, Eadmund. I want you to watch.'

'Stones?'

Draguta smiled. 'Everything will become clearer once we get there, don't worry. You will enjoy what I have planned... or, at least, I will!'

***

Jael felt uncomfortable approaching Gisila's door, hoping her mother wasn't in her chamber.

She knocked quietly.

There was no reply, and Jael was quickly edging back into the corridor when she heard Gisila's voice.

'Come in.'

Taking a deep breath and feeling her shoulders sag in resignation, Jael pushed open the door, hoping she wasn't about to make everything worse.

Talking to her mother never tended to go well.

Gisila was sitting on her bed, staring at the wall. At the tapestry on the wall. It had been Ranuf's favourite. A gold and red embroidered scene of the Oster and Tuuran gods locked in a ferocious battle: mighty warriors with flowing hair, dragons and serpents, arrows flying, bursting flames and bloody death. It had been his grandfather's, and Ranuf had loved it since he was a child. He would sit there even as a man and just stare at it, transfixed, always finding some detail he'd never noticed before.

'Did Gant send you?'

'He did,' Jael said, sitting on the bed.

'I don't see what you can say to make it any different.'

Jael could hear that her mother had been crying. 'I don't suppose I can. But he was worried. He didn't mean to upset you.'

Gisila rounded on her. 'But he knew, didn't he? All those years, he knew. He betrayed me as much as your father did!'

'Ranuf was his best friend. His king. How could he go and tell you what was going on without being disloyal? He wasn't in an easy position.'

'You're going to defend *both* of them? That's why you came?'

Gisila shook her head. 'You may as well leave. I don't want to hear it!' She was agitated, wanting to rip the damn tapestry off the wall and feed it to the fire.

It wasn't going well.

'I don't want to defend anyone,' Jael said quietly. 'I'm still mad myself. Still in shock. I didn't come here to defend what Ranuf did because I can't. But I can understand more about why he did it now that I've had some time to think. He wanted to protect Raymon. If anyone had found out, Raymon would've been in danger. Perhaps from Hugo Vandaal himself? Perhaps from the very men who tried to kill him the other day? I imagine Ranuf thought it was the only choice he had.'

Gisila bit her tongue.

'Though he could have told you.'

'Well, he was obviously not as brave as he led us all to believe, was he?' Gisila spat. 'But he was a better liar than I ever imagined. Pretending that we were all a family? That we were *his* to care for? That he was fighting to keep *us* safe?' Pain broke her voice.

They sat in silence, seeing both sides. Seeing their own.

Not understanding and understanding at the same time.

Feeling betrayed.

'I'm sorry,' Gisila said finally.

Jael blinked in surprise. '*You're* sorry?'

'About your baby. I'm very sorry, Jael.'

Jael didn't want to go back to that place, though it was impossible. Her body ached and throbbed with the reminder that she'd had a child. As did her heart. She shook her head quickly, trying not to bring the images to mind. 'Draguta will pay for it. Soon. I'll make her pay for everything.'

It was Gisila's turn to look surprised. 'Do you think it was her fault?'

'I know it was, and when I run my sword through her throat, I'll remind her of what she took from me. Of how she killed my daughter before she'd even taken her first breath. And then I'll watch her life bleed out of her while she takes her last.'

Gisila could hear the pain and anger in her daughter's voice, and it stopped her thinking about Ranuf for a moment. She reached out a hand, gripping Jael's. 'I hope you do, Jael. I hope you do.'

***

Axl was surprised by how much fuller the fort seemed.

'It's that time of year,' Bram reminded him as they walked around the market stalls, brimming with traders and customers alike. 'And word hasn't gotten around yet that the harbour is nothing but toothpicks, so they've come as usual.'

'I'm glad to see it,' Axl smiled. 'We need them.' He ran his eye over the gaggle of men crowding around the stalls; some he knew, others strangers. 'I was thinking that when we rebuild the sheds, we should build a tavern. What do you think?'

Ulf was walking on his other side, and his eyes sprang open. 'Well, you'd be a popular king if you did that. They'd forget all about Ranuf for sure,' he joked.

Bram nodded eagerly. 'It's a good idea. You can put a few sheds out here that aren't just for ships. The traders and their crews could pay for ale, a bed for the night. Entertainment...'

Axl laughed. 'Sounds as though you two have experience with that sort of thing. Perhaps I should put you in charge of it?'

Ulf looked at Bram, and they both turned to Axl, nodding.

'Ha! Well, when I get back from Hest, we can talk again, but feel free to come up with ideas in the meantime.' Axl suddenly felt odd, not at all confident that he would actually return from Hest. It felt like the sort of battle many wouldn't come back from.

His mind wandered to Amma, wanting to spend as much

time as possible with her before they left again. 'Come on,' he said to Bram, trying not to let his worries consume him. 'Come and show me what's been happening with that wall.'

***

There had been so many things to gather, and it had taken such a long time to hunt down some of the more obscure items that Meena was panicking as she ran up the castle steps, worrying that she'd not left herself enough time to prepare for...

... whatever Draguta was planning.

Scurrying in through the castle doors, Meena had her head down, running through the excuses of why she'd taken so long, when she bumped into Evaine, who staggered back with an angry scowl.

'Watch where you're going, you stupid girl!' she spat.

Morac, who was behind Evaine, didn't intervene to defend his niece. In fact, he glowered at Meena himself as he walked past, eager to get back to the house to see what Elfwyn was cooking for supper.

Evaine quickly left all thoughts of Meena behind as she spied Eadmund in the hall with Jaeger, arguing around the map table. 'Eadmund!' she called out, hurrying towards him, ignoring Jaeger. 'I haven't seen you all day.'

Eadmund didn't appear bothered by that. 'We've had a lot to do. We'll be leaving in a few days. I doubt you'll be seeing much of me before then.'

Evaine wasn't pleased to hear it. 'Well, we were just going back to the house to see about supper. You can walk with us.'

'I'm going to have supper here, Evaine. Draguta's invited me to go to the stones tonight, so I need to be here. And so do you, Morac. She wants you to come and drum for her.'

Evaine and Jaeger frowned at Eadmund.

Morac looked on in surprise. 'She does?' He swallowed, feeling his heart thump in his chest, remembering what had happened the last time he went to the stones with Draguta. 'Why? What is she planning?'

CHAPTER FORTY FOUR

Rollo had spent the day familiarising himself and his men with the fort. They'd set up a stall in Andala's packed market, leaving a few men to haggle with customers over their goods while they slipped through the crowds, assessing the walls and the doors, the guards, the harbour, the hall.

Their eyes had been everywhere, though the returning king appeared too busy to notice. When he looked at Axl Furyck over his cup of very good ale, Rollo could see how distracted he was. How his eyes always sought out the pretty girl with the long brown hair, who was usually only an arm's length from him.

They appeared very close. In love.

Rollo blinked, looking away to the other Furyck.

Jael. Eadmund's wife.

She was in the middle of a huddle of men, though she was tall enough not to be dwarfed by them. She stood talking to them as equals. He wondered if Eadmund thought about her? If she thought about him? She seemed happy enough when she was talking, but every now and then, he would see her eyes drift away, and there was sadness in them.

Her reputation made her formidable, but her size did not. There didn't appear to be much meat on her bones. She might have skill, he supposed, but a man like him could snap her in two before she'd even drawn her sword.

Jael could sense someone staring at her. 'Who's that?' she

asked Bram, her eyes on Rollo. 'The giant over there?'

Bram frowned. 'I can't remember his name. From Helsabor,' he said. 'They've had a successful day by the look of it.'

Thorgils turned to follow Jael's gaze. 'He's even bigger than Tarak,' he grinned, his arm around Isaura, who cringed at the reminder of that gruesome day. 'He'd better not mess with you!' And Thorgils lifted his cup to Jael.

Jael snorted. 'I think he could blow me over right now. I need to train. *We* need to train,' she said, looking from Fyn to Thorgils. 'We're hardly going to be a formidable sight standing before Draguta and whatever army she assembles. Limping, hobbling, ready to pass out.'

'I like your confidence, Jael,' Thorgils smiled. 'Thinking we'll get that far!'

Aleksander laughed. He'd felt distracted since they'd returned, wondering if he should go and see Hanna. He didn't know what he would say to her, so he'd worked hard to keep himself too busy to face the question. But now the day was over, and it was staring him in the face. 'We can only hope that sea-fire and symbols will help us. Jael and her sword too.'

Jael looked worn out by the thought of it. She remembered her talk with Edela and suddenly felt less confident about *Toothpick*.

'What?' Thorgils nudged her. 'You're not losing your edge, are you? Scared of facing those monsters all of a sudden?'

'No, but your breath is terrifying me right now,' Jael said, 'so I'll just step over here, if you don't mind.'

Bram laughed, catching Runa's eye as she walked past with Sigmund in her arms. He looked away, but not before Thorgils had noticed. Fyn too. They exchanged a glance, both a little wobbly on their feet after celebrating their return.

Fyn felt odd but in a good way. He wondered what would happen if his mother and his real father were to... he shook his head, quickly realising that he didn't actually want to think about that at all.

But Thorgils was happy to. 'Why don't you go and see Runa?' he suggested, unable to stop grinning at Bram. 'She's looking a little bored with just a squawking baby for company. And nobody's a bigger squawker than that Sigmund Skalleson. Just like his father before him. I remember Odda complaining about what a pain Eadmund was as a child. And an adult. Ha!' He laughed, banging cups with Fyn, who'd enjoyed the joke.

Bram hadn't. He felt hot all over, uncomfortable in his tunic. He could feel a sharp pain in his aching chest; a discomfort that made him want to leave.

But he didn't.

And taking a deep breath, he looked up with a smile. 'Time for a refill. Who's with me?'

Fyn and Aleksander nodded, leaving with Bram. Isaura was called away by one of her servants, who had Selene and Mads, both in tears, wanting their mother.

Leaving Thorgils and Jael.

'You and me tomorrow, in the ring,' Thorgils said, leaning in. 'But we'll need shields. I need something to protect this prick of a shoulder. It breaks open at just the look of a sword.'

'Or a dragur.'

'That too, though I'm thinking we've seen the back of them now.'

'Did you just say that out loud?'

'You're suspicious?' Thorgils laughed, draining his cup and wiping a hand over his dripping beard. '*You*?'

'Suspicious? Not really. I just think the gods like to have fun with big-mouthed idiots like you, so I'd sleep with one eye open tonight and a long stick beside your bed, ready to set on fire. Just in case those gods decide to make you pay.'

Thorgils was happy to see a twinkle in her eye. 'I shall. But as you're my queen, I'll be looking for you to come and save me.'

'Me?' Jael shrugged. 'No, I'll be tucked up in my bed, dreaming of Oss. You're on your own tonight!' And she headed off for a refill.

***

Draguta felt a hypnotic sense of calm as she sat in front of her seeing circles. She'd been in a trance for much of the evening, watching how things stood, eager to know if everything was in place.

Checking on her enemies.

She felt confident. At ease. Convinced that her plan would succeed.

Running a finger around the bloody symbol she was drawing, Draguta looked up at Meena, who had stopped what she was doing to stare. 'What are you thinking, I wonder?' she mused, surprised by how utterly blank Meena's thoughts often were. Surely the girl wasn't clever enough to keep them at bay? That took discipline that only a true dreamer could master after years of practice.

Meena pushed the pestle back into the bowl, adding in a sprinkle of anise seeds, trying not to gag at the putrid smell of the paste she was making. They would be drinking the mixture at the stones, and knowing what she'd cut up and ground into it, Meena was already doubting that she could keep it down. 'I'm thinking about Morana,' she mumbled. 'Thinking that I don't want to end up like her.'

Draguta smiled. 'What a good answer that was, girl. A very clever answer indeed. Though I'm sure Morana would enjoy the company!' She licked her bloody finger, shivering with pleasure at the thought of Morana trapped inside her prison.

Meena noticed traces of blood on Draguta's lips, quickly shutting away any thoughts of Morana, but not before Draguta had spun around and glared at her again.

***

Runa put a sleeping Sigmund down in Tanja's chamber. She was going to stay with him while Tanja disappeared with her young man again. As happy as she was to look after the baby, she couldn't help but feel a twinge of envy at the thought of young love. She remembered how it had felt with Morac all those years ago, and even with Bram. That nervous excitement. Being in a constant state of need and anticipation.

It was almost too long ago now to remember.

Wandering back into the hall, she found a seat beside Biddy, sitting down with a loud sigh.

'Long day?' Biddy's eyes were on Eydis, wondering if she was ready to go back to the cottage, but her face was still shining, happy to be talking to Jael and Thorgils. Fyn too, Biddy noticed with a grin. She felt long past ready for bed herself. Some days passed in a blur, and though Biddy couldn't exactly list what she'd been doing, it felt as though she could close her eyes and fall asleep right there.

Runa smiled. 'I can't remember, but probably not as busy as tomorrow will be or the day after that. Everyone will be rushing around, getting in each other's way. There's just so much to do.'

Biddy could see the worry in Runa's eyes when she glanced at Fyn. 'It's an unsettling time,' she said. 'But better to be doing something than just sitting here waiting. I don't know how we'll say goodbye, though.' She swallowed, thinking about Jael. Wondering what was going to happen with Eadmund.

Worrying about that knife.

Her mind quickly skipped over all the people she was worried about, and she was surprised to realise how long the list was.

'I agree,' Runa said quietly. 'It will be hard.'

'At least you'll still have Bram.'

Runa frowned. 'I think he's trying to get away from me. Every time I go near him, he runs in the other direction. We haven't spoken about things at all. Not Fyn. Not anything.'

'Oh.' They were sitting near the fire, and with all the bodies squashed into the hall, and the summer evening being a surprisingly warm one, Biddy could feel herself needing a breath of fresh air. She stared at Runa, who looked miserable. 'I think the only answer is time. Time for you all to get used to each other. To let things unfold as they're meant to. I imagine Bram is still trying to find his way after the dragon. Discovering he had a grown son must have been a shock too.' Her eyes wandered to where Gisila stood, looking in shock herself. She saw Gant heading towards her, wondering if that was the wisest move. Turning back to Runa, Biddy squeezed her arm. 'It will all shake out soon enough. Just try not to force it. Give Bram a little more time.'

Gant had had enough cups of ale to take the edge off his fear about confronting Gisila again. He shook his head. It wasn't fear. He just didn't want to see the disappointment in her eyes when she looked at him anymore.

Gisila glared at him as he approached.

Axl quickly made himself scarce, not wanting to be in the middle of that conversation.

'What do you want now?' Gisila asked shortly. 'I'm ready for my bed, so make it quick.' And she started walking towards the curtain.

Gant hurried alongside her. 'I wanted to explain.'

'*Here*? In front of everyone?' Gisila hissed. 'I can barely stand it. All the eyes on me! Everyone talking about me! If you have something to say, at least say it in private.' And she led Gant through the curtain, into the corridor, before turning on him. 'I don't know what you think there is to say. Ranuf had another family. You helped him cover it up. You lied. For him! You knew where he was when we were in Tuura. He was your friend, and you protected him. Why feel the need to care what I think after all this time?'

Gant didn't know what to say.

Gisila smelled like honey. She'd been drinking mead, and everything about her smelled so sweet, though her scowling face was anything but.

He dropped his eyes. 'I've always cared about what you thought.'

Gisila stopped frowning. She hadn't been expecting that.

'From the moment you arrived here, I always cared about what you thought, Gisila. I've always cared about you,' he said softly, looking up and staring into those deep brown eyes. He'd been staring at those eyes for thirty-five years.

Knowing she was Ranuf's. Always Ranuf's.

Reaching out, Gant touched her cheek, watching her eyes. They stayed on his. Unblinking. 'I never told you because you weren't mine. You were Ranuf's wife. He was my friend, even when I thought he was wrong. And for what he did to you, I think he was very wrong.' And taking a deep breath, Gant leaned in and did what he'd been dreaming of for thirty-five years.

He kissed Gisila.

***

Eadmund couldn't stand Jaeger's company, so after they'd eaten and discussed their plans for Helsabor, he found somewhere to sleep. He didn't imagine he would have long before Draguta sent for him, but after the day's training, his body was exhausted, even if his mind wasn't.

The chamber he chose was the one he'd slept in with Jael.

He remembered stumbling down the hall with Fyn the night of their escape, trying to send Osbert on his way. Trying to get them out of Hest safely.

Burning the harbour.

But more than that, he remembered his time in the chamber with Jael.

Eadmund didn't bother to undress as he lay on the bed. It was too hot for a fur, so he stretched out on the linen sheet, leaning his head back against the pillow, closing his eyes, seeing Jael sitting on top of him, her hands on his shoulders, a smile in her eyes.

Staring at him.

He could almost feel her swaying against him, pushing her hips against his.

And he opened his eyes, enjoying the silence, pleased that Evaine wasn't lying beside him, touching him. He felt overwhelmingly sad, not understanding what had happened, and how it had happened, and most of all, how he'd let it happen.

Eadmund tried not to think of what he'd done or what he was about to do.

Nothing made sense, so he closed his eyes, imagining his wife as she arched her back, almost feeling her shudder against him.

***

Aleksander watched Jael talking to Ivaar. Her brother-in-law was one of her least favourite people, he knew, but she was smiling and relaxed. It was good to see. The hall was packed full of relieved men and women, happy to all be back together again for a short while.

Just a short while.

Aleksander turned towards the doors, thinking that he

wouldn't mind a breath of fresh air, when he saw Marcus approaching. He wanted to move, but he was wedged in between Berard and Ulf, and suddenly, Marcus was there. He was such a tall, awkward man, and Aleksander wasn't sure that he was going to say anything at all, but he did.

'Hanna said your name more than anything else while she was ill,' Marcus said plainly, not completely sure what he was doing. 'Over and over, she called out for you.'

Aleksander's mouth fell open.

He really wanted that fresh air now.

'So I thought you might have come to see her today.'

Closing his mouth, Aleksander swallowed. 'I...' He rubbed a hand over his dark beard. 'I thought she would be too ill for visitors.'

Marcus peered at him. 'Did you now?'

'I wasn't sure I would be welcome,' Aleksander tried.

'Hanna hasn't said anything to me, but I believe she was disappointed not to see you.'

Aleksander struggled to find any words that would stop Marcus glaring at him. 'I'll come in the morning,' he mumbled. 'If you think that would be alright?'

'It would.' And nodding briefly, Marcus turned, looking for Entorp. 'But not too early,' he added over his shoulder. 'She needs her sleep.'

***

Karsten had been stuck in the cottage with Nicolene, who was back to her sniping self, keeping an eye on her while Bayla went to the hall with Berard and Ulf. Eventually, Nicolene had closed her eyes, lulled to sleep by the dulcet moaning of the children.

The servant had them all under control, so Karsten had

slipped away before anyone missed him. He was hoping to talk to Rork and Thorgils again, to see what they could do about setting up another fight. There were a lot of contenders about the place that might be worth a go.

But then he'd seen Marcus striding away from his cottage, and stopping, Karsten turned towards it.

Marcus' servant wasn't about to let him in, though. She was a short, wide woman with a hairy chin, and she almost blocked the door, but Karsten heard a voice from within – a weak voice, to be sure, but a familiar one – and the servant stood aside with a grumble.

Hanna smiled at him as he pulled over a stool.

Karsten was amazed by how well she looked. 'Been eating a lot, have you?' he wondered with a grin.

'Why do you say that?' Hanna asked. She couldn't get out of bed yet, but she was growing impatient, bored with no one to talk to but her father and their servant, who wasn't one for conversation.

She was pleased to see Karsten.

'Well, you almost have cheeks again. Last time I saw you, you looked a little like a dragur.'

Hanna's newly replenished cheeks revealed dimples he hadn't noticed before. 'I'm surprised to hear that, as all I've been eating is thin broth. Nothing but broth. I've been dreaming about roast chicken and dumplings.'

'Well, I could bring you something back from the hall if you like?' Karsten suggested, leaning forward to make sure the beady-eyed servant wasn't listening.

'I'm not sure my father would let you in,' Hanna admitted. 'Perhaps tomorrow? Roast chicken for breakfast would be nice.' She yawned, suddenly exhausted.

'I won't stay long,' Karsten promised. 'I was just on my way to the hall. Everyone's in there tonight, I think. Celebrating that we're all still standing.'

Hanna touched his arm. 'Don't go just yet, Karsten,' she

said. 'I wanted to thank you.' She took a deep breath, trying to find some reserves of energy. 'I remember seeing you, in the storm. That's the last thing I remember. My father said you took me to the hall. That you took care of me when the dragon came down. I can't believe I missed that.'

Karsten adjusted his eyepatch. 'Well, lucky I didn't leave you where I found you, or you wouldn't have missed it at all! It came down with a bang.'

'So I hear. I'm sorry about Irenna. Your family hasn't had an easy time of it, have they? When I'm well enough, I want to come and see the children. Help with them, if you'd like?'

Karsten shook his head. 'You might need to be able to stand first. Five children can be a lot of work, just ask Bayla. With Nicolene being ill, she's had her hands full.'

Hanna smiled, closing her eyes. 'I can imagine,' she yawned.

Karsten didn't reply, and Hanna didn't say another word, and eventually, he realised that she was asleep. So, nodding to the servant, who looked pleased to see the back of him, he took his leave, heading for the hall.

***

Draguta had sent Brill to fetch Eadmund, which had taken some time as no one knew what had happened to him. Eventually, she'd found him, dragging him out of his dreams of Jael, and now he walked away from the castle after Draguta and Meena, who were at the front of their little party. A sleepy-eyed Morac followed them with the drum, leaving Brill far at the back, struggling with two baskets.

Having finally woken himself up, Eadmund waited for her, offering to take one. The smell emanating from the basket was eye-watering, and he gagged, holding it away from himself, inhaling the night air, which wasn't as cool as he would have liked.

Draguta strode on ahead of them, oblivious to everyone.

She had seen how things stood, and now she was disappearing inside herself, connecting with her power, searching for any obstacles.

She felt calm. Focused.

Ready.

***

Morana lay on her side, watching moonbeams flicker across the stone wall. Else wasn't asleep. She was fussing around the fire, banking it for the night after heating up water to make Morana another cup of Dragmall's herbs. The woman was more useful than she'd ever given her credit for, Morana realised.

Those herbs had a chance of saving her.

If only she could trust Meena. If only the twitching idiot wasn't the key to it all. Relying on her to do anything was impossible, she knew, but Meena had to see that there was no way out of this mess without her help.

She was the only one who could use the book to get rid of Draguta.

Meena had to see that.

Else cried out in surprise, not expecting the knock on the door. It was very late, well past time when anyone should have been walking around the castle. She edged towards the door, her heart hammering in her chest. 'Who is it?'

'Dragmall,' came the hoarse whisper.

Else unlocked the door and hurried Dragmall inside. He was dressed in a cloak, a leather satchel slung over his shoulder. 'What are you doing here? At this hour?' she whispered, inclining her head towards the bed where Morana lay, not sleeping at all.

Dragmall was struggling to catch his breath as he pulled the satchel over his head. 'I have come... I have come to rescue Morana!'

PART SIX

Friends & Enemies

CHAPTER FORTY FIVE

Else had quickly helped Morana to sit up, and was now trying to put on her boots. Morana trembled with anticipation as she sat on the edge of the bed, her dark eye alert, willing them both to get on with it.

Dragmall was kneeling on the flagstones, fumbling with a tiny jar, his fingers shaking too much to begin.

'Draguta will see us!' Else panicked. Even saying the woman's name terrified her. 'She will see what we're doing!'

'She has left the castle. Gone to the stones.' Dragmall was telling Morana more than Else. 'This is what time we have, so we must use it and hope that she's too preoccupied to notice us.'

Else closed her mouth, struggling to swallow, not sure what was going to happen. She finished Morana's boots and spun around, searching for her cloak.

Dragmall finally twisted the lid off the jar. 'Water,' he said. 'I need water. Hurry, Else.'

Morana wasn't sure if she was even breathing. She had no idea what Dragmall knew – whether Meena had managed to tell him something or whether he'd discovered the answer on his own – but she was suddenly worried that it wasn't going to work.

Else handed Dragmall the water jug, spilling some on him.

He took it in both hands, pouring just a few dribbles into the jar, handing it back to her before twisting the lid back on and giving it a quick shake. 'We must hurry,' he muttered, almost to himself, worrying that he was far too old for such a terrifying ordeal. Though there was more life behind him now than ahead of him. His time was nearly over.

Better to have died fighting against the evil of Draguta Teros, even if it meant embracing the evil of Morana Gallas to do so.

***

Jael found Aleksander on the ramparts. She grinned at him. 'How did I know you'd be here?'

He shrugged. 'Because you're a dreamer? Now I know how you always found me when I used to hide from you!'

She laughed.

'What are you doing here?'

'Couldn't sleep,' Jael yawned. 'Although, maybe I didn't want to sleep. Sometimes I can't face the dreams.'

It was a dark night, the moon covered in a dirty haze that Jael was sure was from the constant smoking from the dragur pyres. They were all ash now, she was relieved to see, but the stench of their blue corpses lingered.

'And then there's the worry of what's coming next,' Aleksander said, catching her yawn. 'Hopefully, Edela can find some ways to protect us from Draguta.'

Jael nodded, moving her hand to *Toothpick*, feeling the cool moonstone beneath her fingers. Her sword had given her confidence; made her believe that she had a chance of defeating Draguta. But now? 'Mmmm, I don't imagine Draguta will stay quiet for long. Not when she doesn't have the Book of Aurea, or me.'

'She might just wait until we're out in the open. Our army, the Iskavallans...'

Jael didn't want to think about that.

They had no choice but to leave the fort, and though they couldn't risk being attacked at sea, going overland posed more danger than anyone was comfortable with. 'Maybe we don't go into the open at all?' she mused. 'Maybe we head into Hallow Wood? Work our way out through there?'

Aleksander blinked in surprise. 'You're keen for a repeat of that adventure, are you?'

'There won't be any dragur in there now, and maybe the gods will hide us? Keep us safe from Draguta?' It was one thought, but Jael didn't like the idea of going back into that wood again either.

'I like your optimism,' Aleksander laughed. The moon was bright for a moment, shrugging off its hazy cloak, and he stared into her eyes. 'How are you?'

Jael frowned, looking out over the valley. 'I'm... standing. You?'

'I'm confused.'

'About?'

'Too many things to tell you.'

Jael was intrigued, but she didn't push further, though she did feel a sudden urge to tell him something. 'Edela broke the binding spell. Did she tell you?'

'She did?'

Jael nodded. 'Eadmund is free from Evaine. Finally.'

'But?' Aleksander could hear it in her voice.

'He's bound to Draguta too, and that's not something Edela can undo at all. Not yet, at least.'

'Oh.'

'But he isn't Evaine's. After all this time, he isn't Evaine's.'

Aleksander could hear the relief in Jael's voice; her desperation to be with Eadmund again.

Perhaps he wasn't so confused after all...

***

Amma could tell that Axl wasn't asleep.

He usually sounded like a blowing horse, but tonight he was silent and still. He didn't even appear to be breathing. Amma couldn't sleep herself. It was becoming a bad habit she'd fallen into since the dragon attack. She kept waiting for something to land on the hall. She kept sniffing for smoke, which was pointless, she knew, as the entire fort stunk of nothing but smoke.

Reaching out, Amma placed her hand on Axl's chest, edging towards him.

'I thought you were asleep,' he murmured.

She smiled, closing her eyes. 'I'm better at pretending than you are.'

'Is that right? Not sure I wanted to know that,' he grinned, wrapping his arm around her, feeling her snuggle in closer. 'Why can't you sleep?'

Amma sighed. 'I'm just scared. Wondering what will attack us next.'

Axl didn't blame her. Knowing you had an enemy in Hest or on Oss was a different feeling than knowing your enemy had arms that could reach right into your fort while you slept. 'Soon we'll attack them,' Axl tried to reassure her, though he didn't feel confident about how that would go. 'And they will die. All of Draguta's monsters. Just like the dragur did. Draguta too. And when I kill Jaeger Dragos, I'll come home and marry you.'

The thought of that made Amma both happy and sad.

But mostly, she felt scared.

She propped herself up on an elbow. 'Promise that you will. Promise that won't risk your life. I want you to come home, Axl. I don't want to hear songs sung about how brave you were. How you sacrificed yourself. How you were a hero. I want to be sitting next to you while they sing about others. Not you.'

Axl pulled her back down, kissing her, feeling her tears against his cheek. 'I promise,' he said.

And he meant it.

***

Sometimes, Draguta missed Morana Gallas.

Her niece was a dithering idiot, who moved as quickly as a snail. There was no urgency about the girl at all. At this rate, it would be dawn before they began.

'Well, which one is it?' Draguta barked as Meena looked from one bowl to the other. She had placed them both on the ground by the sacrifice stone, where Draguta stood, waiting, one hand on the book, ready to begin.

It was a still night, which surprised her. And despite the thick clouds, Draguta couldn't feel the gods coming. But she could feel a burning impatience that rose up into her throat, ready to explode.

'This one,' Meena decided, at last, bending to pick up the bowl on the left.

Brill was beside her, and Draguta flapped her hands at both of them. 'Well, go on, then. You don't need me to tell you what to do!'

Brill followed Meena, trying not to let her eyes wander to the large stone shadows looming in the darkness, like giant spirits coming to claim them.

Eadmund stood back from the fire, away from the flames that flickered brightly, thanks to the absence of any wind. He took a copper cup from Brill, noticing the symbols etched around its rim. They reminded him of the ones on the leather strap. And lifting the cup to his lips, he was immediately aware that this was what he'd been smelling in the basket. Draguta eyed him as she walked past with the other bowl, and he threw the liquid down his throat, trying not to vomit it straight back up.

Meena worked to keep her mind clear as she held the bowl, watching while Brill gave Morac a cup.

'There's no need for him to have it!' Draguta snapped from where she was drawing her circle with her knife. 'Give Meena a cup and then come and help me!'

Morac looked relieved as he tapped nervously on the drum, making eye contact with Eadmund, who frowned at him before turning back to the fire.

Meena swallowed the foul potion, spluttering and gagging but managing to keep it down. Brill left her to run after Draguta, and Meena found her mind wandering back to the castle.

She quickly tried to focus again, walking towards the basket of herbs.

Soon, she knew, it would be time to begin.

***

'Put on your boots, Else,' Dragmall whispered. 'Take what you can stuff into a bag. Anything you have to eat. Get your cloak and gather your things. If it works, we'll have to run. Draguta won't be gone for long. And she may not need to come back to discover what we've done.'

Morana sat up straighter.

Else's guts were griping, and she needed to use the chamber pot, but she nodded and tried to concentrate on doing the simple tasks Dragmall had given her.

Dragmall looked up at Morana. 'I don't trust you,' he admitted. 'But this is a risk I will take, and I hope, in return, you will protect both Else and myself from whatever is coming.'

Morana couldn't nod, but she wanted to. She could blink, though, and she did.

'Well, then,' Dragmall said, 'I suppose nothing is stopping us now.' And he picked up the jar into which he'd scraped some of Draguta's blood from her seeing circles, using the water to make a bloody paste, and he began to paint the symbol onto Morana's forehead. He would paint it on the flagstones also. But to be sure, he wanted to draw it on Morana herself.

And taking a deep breath, Dragmall started to chant.

He knew Tuuran. His mother had taught it to him – the language of the old gods too – though it had been so long since he'd spoken the words out loud that they sounded unfamiliar, and Dragmall suddenly worried that he had it all wrong.

Morana held her breath, feeling the watery blood run down her forehead, onto her face. She closed her eyes, praying to Raemus that Dragmall would free her.

And quickly.

***

Draguta tried to calm down. Her irritation with Meena had disrupted her thoughts, and her focus had drifted, but everything had to work together, and she needed to be at the centre of it all.

It wouldn't help if her mind was scattered.

Taking a deep breath as she stood before the fire blooming in the middle of her circle, she inhaled the fragrant smoke, shutting a door on every other distraction. Closing her eyes, Draguta felt the darkness still her mind. She could sense the book nearby, its desire to be released coursing in her veins.

Her body started throbbing.

A singular, pulsing sensation that awakened every part of her. And opening her eyes, Draguta dug into the purse hanging from her belt, pulling out a large, yellowish fang. Dipping it into the bowl of bloody potion before her, she listened as the beat of the drum and the humming of her body melded into one harmonious vibration. And leaning towards the earth, she started to draw a symbol.

***

Gant didn't want to leave. Gisila wasn't asleep, he knew, but perhaps she wanted him to go? He turned to face her, smiling. Even after all these years, she still took his breath away. He brushed strands of dark hair out of her eyes. 'Should I leave?' he whispered, leaning so close that he appeared more ready to kiss her than go anywhere.

Gisila looked confused. 'Why would you leave? Do you have things to do?'

He smiled.

So did she as she kissed him. 'I'd rather you didn't leave. This bed has been very empty lately.'

Gant was too busy kissing to answer her for a while, then he stopped and stared at her. 'You've been missing Lothar?' he asked with a grin.

'I have not. Nor Ranuf. I've just been waiting for you.'

'You have?'

'Of course. I'm not blind. And Lothar wasn't either. He knew how things stood. Why do you think he beat me that night?'

'He beat you because of *me*?' Gant was horrified.

'He was suspicious. Jealous. And he had every reason to be,' Gisila said, stroking Gant's serious face, happy to forget all about her dead husbands. 'After he died, I wondered how long it would take you to find your way here. Though I must admit, I wasn't sure you ever would. You do tend to keep things close to your chest.'

'I wish I'd come sooner,' Gant breathed. 'I wish I'd saved you from Lothar too. From what those men did to you in Tuura.'

Gisila put a finger to his lips. 'It's done, all of it, and I am not broken by it. I'm still here. Ranuf might have betrayed me, but I'm still here. And so are you. So don't you dare think about leaving. Not tonight.'

***

Rollo could hear Draguta's voice in his ears, urging him on.

He hadn't slept, but he had been watching from the shadows as the men and women stumbled out of the hall, looking for somewhere to sleep. Most returned to their cottages and tents. The traders and their crews would return to their ships.

But not Rollo.

He'd been waiting all night, watching the clouds as the wind picked up, pushing them across the moon, hiding him as he crept around the walls.

Waiting.

And now he just needed the signal.

***

Jael watched as the woman walked towards her.

Her white hair was straight, long, almost touching the

floor, yet she did not appear old. Her cloak was black, and it shone as she walked, almost glittering like a sea under the sun. Everything but the woman was blurred, and Jael could feel a vibrating hum pulsing in her body as she waited.

'Do you remember me?' the woman asked, stopping, her hands resting by her sides.

Jael frowned, memories stirring. 'I do.'

'I have not visited you for some time, Jael, but I have always been around, watching you. Your happiness and your pain. Your journey to becoming a woman, a warrior, and now, at last, a dreamer. But, of course, you were always a dreamer. I told you that once, do you remember?'

Jael swallowed. 'I don't know who you are.'

The woman grabbed her hands. 'I am Daala, and you must hurry, Jael. Hurry! *Now!*' And spinning around, she transformed into a sleek raven, cawing loudly, her cry echoing through the night as she turned her white eye towards Jael and flew away.

CHAPTER FORTY SIX

The howl lifted the hairs on the back of Eadmund's neck. His senses were dulled by the smoke, twisted and turned by Morac's mesmeric drumming, and Draguta's rolling chants.

But the howl quickly sharpened his focus.

Where was it coming from?

His eyes were open, searching through the stones that surrounded them, but Eadmund couldn't sense any movement.

Draguta was calling, gripping his hand.

He could feel her, but he wanted to pull away. He needed to see what was coming. He had to keep her safe.

Eadmund froze.

There it was again.

And then he saw Jael's face.

***

Jael rolled out of bed, blinking, trying to wake up as she wriggled on her trousers. Grabbing her mail shirt, she shrugged it over her head, feeling the weight of it pushing down her shoulders as she hurried to find her boots.

Gant was in the corridor when she opened the door.

Axl too, dressed for battle.

Jael shoved her helmet over her braids, hurrying to the grey curtain.

'Stay here,' Gant said, turning to Gisila. 'Stay in the hall.' He smiled at her quickly before following Jael and Axl.

Runa came into the corridor, clutching Sigmund, who was crying, woken by the terrifying noise.

There it was again.

'What is it?' Amma asked, shaking in her nightdress, fearing the answer. 'Wolves?'

***

'It's not wolves!' Aleksander called as he joined the race to the ramparts. 'I know wolves better than I'd ever want to, and that's not wolves!'

Rork Arnesson was nodding as he joined them. 'Sounds like a pack of dogs!'

Jael spun around as Ivaar came running. 'Get the Islanders together! I want you all behind that wall! Now!'

Ivaar nodded, turning into the darkness.

Jael spotted Bram hobbling towards her. 'Bram! Get every brazier going. Light up the square! Ulf! Help him! We need to see what we're doing! Archers to the ramparts!' And she quickened her pace, remembering Daala's words.

Thorgils ran to catch up with her, still buckling his swordbelt. 'Sounds like dogs!'

Jael didn't say anything, and though it didn't sound like any dog she'd ever heard, it definitely wasn't wolves. She saw Fyn and Karsten running towards her. 'Up to the ramparts!' she cried. 'Let's see what's going on!'

***

Dragmall sat back on his haunches, watching as Morana sucked in a long, rasping breath before propelling herself off the bed. She tumbled forward onto the old man, who held her up, helping her to stand.

Else bit her tongue in shock, quickly tasting blood.

'Leave!' Morana croaked, glancing at Else. 'We need to leave!'

***

Everyone was hurrying to the western side of the fort.

Rollo could see Jael Furyck with her men and archers up on the ramparts, the rest of her army rushing around the fort, lining up behind the half-built wall that bordered the valley.

The square was loud with noise and panic. Even the livestock were roused to life. Sleepy ducks ran after each other in a quacking flap; goats bleating, looking to escape.

Rollo ran to the harbour gates. 'We need to let more men in!' he cried to the guards. 'The crews are out there! My men are out there! We've weapons. Let them in to help!'

One guard looked at the other before calling up to the men on the ramparts, who gave the signal to open the gates.

'Hurry!' they shouted. 'Let them in!'

Rollo stood back as the guards lifted the wooden beam, dragging open the gates. His men nodded at him as they hurried into the fort, watching as the guards pushed the gates shut, quickly securing them again.

They were in. All of them.

Now they just had to find what they were looking for.

***

Runa tried to soothe a sobbing Sigmund, wondering where Tanja was, knowing that only milk from her would calm him down now. She swallowed, hoping that Fyn and Bram were safe.

Amma hurried back into her chamber to get dressed.

Gisila frowned at the screaming baby, wanting the noise to stop. She couldn't think or hear what was happening outside. 'I'll get him a bit of honey water from the kitchen. You get dressed, Runa. We need to be ready.' She could barely breathe with the panic coursing through her body, but panic wasn't going to help get them through whatever was happening out there.

Swallowing as she hurried into the kitchen, Gisila hoped that her mother had found something in that book of hers.

***

'No!' Edela insisted as Biddy tried the door. 'Keep it locked. I don't want you going out there. We don't know what that noise is!'

She was sitting close to the fire, searching through the Book of Aurea.

'But Edela,' Biddy panicked, turning back to her, pushing the wailing puppies off her legs. 'If we don't know what it is, how can you stop it?'

It was a good question, but Edela knew that leaving the cottage was too dangerous. She felt that strongly. 'We'll find out soon, won't we, Eydis?'

Eydis was kneeling on the floorboards, her hand on Edela's knee, nodding slowly. She was already slipping away. It was as if Dara Teros was taking her to where she needed to go. Closing her eyes, Eydis drifted into the darkness, immediately sensing something behind her.

She could hear strained breathing.

Panting.

And turning around, Eydis saw a pair of red eyes staring at her.

***

Else felt too scared to move, but Dragmall couldn't help both her and Morana, so she picked up her feet and kept ahead of them, leading the way out through the kitchen, away from the castle, worried that they were going to run into Draguta.

Worried that they didn't need to run into Draguta for her to stop them.

But she kept running anyway.

Morana didn't have enough energy to speak; her stiff body would barely move on its own. She just had to hope that Dragmall had been clever enough to think their escape through carefully.

If Draguta were to find them now...

***

'Fyn! Aedan! Fire arrows!' Jael called, wanting to see more. The clouds had swallowed the moon, and the valley was a big black hole. She could feel rain streaking across her face, but it didn't feel like a storm. And Jael had the feeling that no gods were coming to help them tonight.

The flaming arrows lit up the sky as another howl sent shivers racing up and down her spine. And then she saw the red eyes. All across the valley, pairs of glowing red eyes. Jael swallowed, turning to Gant, whose mouth had fallen open. 'The barsk! The barsk!' she called, spinning back to the eyes that suddenly appeared to be moving at pace, heading for the wall. And then a loud rumbling spread across the valley as the barsk roared and charged. 'Archers!' Jael yelled. 'Fire arrows! Nock! Light your arrows! Quickly! Fire at will!' She turned to Gant and Axl. 'You keep them busy up here. I need to be down at the wall. They'll jump it!'

***

Draguta smiled. 'Of course they'll jump it, you useless woman. And more. They will tear your people to pieces, limb by limb.'

Eadmund felt as though he was trapped in a nightmare. His eyes were closed, listening to Draguta's voice echoing in his head. He couldn't see her, but he could see Thorgils, Torstan, Fyn. Ivaar too.

Jael was running towards them.

And the red-eyed dogs, who were charging for the broken wall.

Eadmund shivered. He knew the barsk. They all knew the barsk from their nightmares. Odda would tell stories about those terrifying creatures to him and Thorgils when she wanted to punish them for being nuisances all day. Tales of those flesh-eating dogs were guaranteed to have them waking up in tears.

Eadmund couldn't breathe, he couldn't swallow.

And then he heard Draguta laughing.

***

The banging on the door had Bayla screaming, shaking all over. The children were wailing, and she knew that she needed to be comforting and calming them, but she was frozen with terror.

She couldn't move.

Berard was at the door quickly, one eye on his mother and Nicolene, who blinked back at him with little confidence that he could do anything to protect them.

'It's Ulf!' came the hoarse cry.

Bayla looked as though she was about to fall down as Berard pulled open the door, ushering Ulf inside. He hurried to her, and she fell into his arms. 'What's happening? What is out there? Ulf?'

'It's the barsk,' he panted, feeling Bayla shudder against him. 'We're going to barricade ourselves in here. Lucky I didn't find you a big cottage with lots of windows, so we've only got that one door to worry about.' He pulled her out of his arms. 'Nicolene, you sit over there with the children. All of you on one bed. Bayla, you help me. We're going to move everything else behind that door. Berard, you stand guard.'

Bayla stared at him, not moving.

'Now!' Ulf barked, grabbing her arms. 'Bayla! Help me! *Now!*'

***

Runa didn't know the man.

'Quick!' he called. 'We have to go!'

Another man came through the curtain. He was smaller, with an eyepatch, his face covered in tattoos.

'Who are you?' Runa wondered, feeling her heart quicken.

Amma emerged from her chamber, fully dressed now. 'What's happening?'

'The king sent us,' the first man said, his eyes on the crying baby, who was screaming louder than any child he'd ever heard. 'We're to take you out of here. To safety.'

Amma eyed the men. She didn't move. 'No, he wouldn't do that. He'd send someone we know. We don't know you.'

And she held her ground as the two men edged closer.

***

Draguta blinked in fury.

How was Amma Furyck not bound?

She had worked the spell herself. Used the girl's clothes.

How was she not bound?

'Take her!' she cried. 'There is no time! Take her now!'

***

The dogs were running towards the wall.

Trying to jump over the wall.

Bram had had men digging out the ditches around the fort, and they were deeper and wider than before the dragur attack, but the barsk jumped them effortlessly, slipping through the sharpened stakes, throwing themselves at the broken section of wall.

'Archers!' Jael screamed up to the ramparts, trying to remember everything she knew about the barsk. 'Burn them!' She was with her Islanders, behind the western wall. Axl was there too, his Andalans armed with swords and axes. And then the first one was in. 'Spears!' Jael yelled, searching for Aleksander. 'We need spears!' And she swung *Toothpick* into the neck of a red-eyed dog, that yelped, teeth bared, drool flying, snapping back at her. Jael jabbed *Toothpick* through his throat, hearing his pained cry as he opened his jaw and froze, collapsing to the ground as she pulled out her blade.

'Jael!'

Spinning around, Jael saw Fyn.

He'd been standing with the archers, firing arrows at the barsk, but the one charging him had three arrows sticking out of its body, not troubled in the slightest as he leapt at Fyn.

Thorgils got there before Jael could, shunting Fyn out of the way, letting the barsk come at him instead.

'Thorgils!' Jael sheathed *Toothpick*, drawing out her knife, throwing herself onto the back of the growling black dog that had flown onto Thorgils, sending him to the ground with an almighty thump. She stuck her knife into the barsk's neck, jerking back as his head spun around, fangs out, snarling at her. Pulling out the knife, Jael quickly moved it into her left hand, stabbing it into the dog's red eye.

She fell away, rolling, up on her feet, watching the barsk drop to the ground. 'Aim for their faces, Fyn!' Jael growled as he nocked another arrow. 'Headshots!' And turning, she ran for Axl, who had a barsk's jaw clamped around his leg.

***

Edela couldn't concentrate at all.

She kept asking Eydis the same question. 'Are you sure?'

Biddy was becoming concerned. 'Edela! She's sure!' The puppies were trembling and whimpering, and she was trying to keep everybody calm, but she wasn't feeling very calm herself.

Edela could certainly hear the howling, and it made her hands shake as she held the book on her knee. 'Here!' she said, running her finger down the page. 'This is it!'

All three heads suddenly snapped to the door as the handle creaked, slowly turning. The puppies ran to it, barking loudly.

'Biddy,' Edela whispered. 'I don't think that's a barsk.'

Biddy swallowed, walking nervously towards the door. She stopped some distance before it. 'Who's there?' she called, trying to strengthen her voice, looking around for some sort of weapon.

There was no answer.

And then they heard the first kick.

Biddy ran for the table, pushing it towards the door, but she was too late as the door flew open, coming off one of its newly repaired hinges. And there in the doorway stood an enormous bald-headed man, with the thinnest lips Biddy had ever seen.

***

'No!' Runa was gripping Sigmund as the tattooed man tried to rip him out of her arms. The bigger man had a filthy hand over Amma's mouth, not bothered by her wriggling and kicking.

He was impatient. Irritated by the women and the screaming baby.

They had to leave. Now!

He knew there was an escape through the kitchen, leading away from the square so they wouldn't be seen. They'd left some men inside the hall, seeing to anyone who got in the way.

The tattooed man finally ripped Sigmund out of Runa's arms.

'No! No!' Runa yelled, lunging for him. 'Help! Someone help!'

The man had Sigmund in his left arm, his right hand free to draw his sword, which he stabbed straight through Runa's chest, watching horror bloom in her eyes as she tumbled backwards, choking on her scream. He drew out his bloody blade as the man next to him tightened his hand over Amma's mouth. He could feel her trembling, desperate to escape, but he wasn't letting their prize go.

Turning, they headed down the corridor towards the kitchen, where Gisila stood waiting.

'What are you doing?' she yelled, legs shaking, heart pounding. She held an axe in both hands. It was sharpened daily, used to chop firewood, but what she could do with it, Gisila didn't know.

Ranuf had tried to teach her once, but she'd shown little interest in it.

But now?

She thought of Gant, desperate for him to appear. 'No!' she yelled again, lifting her neck, trying to straighten her shoulders. 'Release them! Let them go!'

'Or what?' The tattooed man holding a wailing Sigmund snarled, running his eyes over her figure. Gisila Furyck was a little scrawny for his taste, but she was still a fine woman. He'd watched her all night in the hall.

A very beautiful lady indeed.

His companion was less inclined to waste time, knowing that the baby's noise would draw people's attention before long. 'Kill the bitch, and let's go! We have to go!'

***

The terror was neverending. The snarling, growling, howling coming closer and closer.

Nicolene and Bayla had their hands over Kai's and Eron's ears as they sat on the only bed that hadn't been shoved against the door. Ulf had Halla on his knee. She curled towards him, hiding her face in his chest as he wrapped his arms around her. He glanced at Valder and Lucina, who were older, but just as terrified as their little sister.

Ulf was terrified too but trying not to show it, though he was sure his voice was shaking as much as his body. 'It won't be long now,' he soothed. 'Not long now. They'll stop those dogs soon. Edela has a book, a magical book. It will have an answer, won't it? A way to send those creatures back to where they came from. Don't worry now.' And he swallowed, looking at Berard, who stood behind the barricades, listening to the Andalans getting slaughtered.

Hoping Karsten would be alright.

***

More and more of the barsk were jumping over the walls. The archers were firing arrows from the ramparts, but there were too many of them. They were as black as night, hard to see, fast and powerful, untroubled by the flames.

Jael spun, horrified by how many were inside the fort. 'Catapult crews!' she yelled. They needed to stop them in the valley. 'Catapult crews! Launch the sea-fire! Karsten!' He ran up to her, Rork with him. 'Get your men onto the catapults. Fire over the wall! Into the valley! We have to stop them there!'

'Jael!' Rork cried.

'Aarrghh!' Jael yelped as a barsk jumped up, clamping its fangs around her left arm. The leather protecting her wrist was strong but not going to stop those sharp teeth for long. She jabbed *Toothpick* through the dog's black belly, listening to it yelp as it released its jaw, dropping to the ground, quickly jumping at her again.

Jael swung *Toothpick* back, ready to finish him off, but Karsten was there, taking off the dog's head. Panting, Jael nodded at him, spinning quickly, listening to the cries of her men as the barsk ripped them to pieces. 'Hurry! Get to those catapults! Now!'

And then a raven's cry.

Over all the growling, barking, screaming panic, Jael heard the raven's warning. And she turned around to see Fyr sitting atop a cart.

Everything stopped.

The noise was gone, and Jael was left with one clear image. The Book of Aurea.

***

'No!'

Biddy ran in front of Edela, the puppies barking around her feet.

'Give it to me, and I'll be on my way,' Rollo said calmly. Draguta was going to pay him handsomely to bring back that book. The woman and the baby too. He wasn't looking to kill anyone. Not an old woman or a blind girl, but he needed that book.

He could feel Draguta urging him on.

She wouldn't let anything get in his way, and nor could he.

Rollo edged forward, his hands out in front of him, his sword in its scabbard. He didn't need it. Not to defeat two women and a girl. 'I don't want to hurt you, but I will have that book.' And he pushed Biddy away, knocking her over, kicking out at the puppies, his heavy boot smacking into Ido, who fell away, yelping. Vella was at the man, yapping angrily, teeth bared.

'Ido!' Biddy scrambled back to her knees. She couldn't help Ido now as she threw her arms around the leg of the man, trying to stop him from touching Edela.

Who was holding the book.

'No!' she screamed.

CHAPTER FORTY SEVEN

Jael heard Biddy's screams as she ran down the alley towards Edela's cottage, but they were in her head, ringing like warning bells as her boots slammed down on the earth, panic throbbing in her chest.

She sheathed *Toothpick*, trying to run faster, listening to the urgent whinnying of horses in the distance, thinking of Tig.

Turning the corner, her eyes were up, scanning the road, and there he was.

That giant man with the shining head.

Bigger than Tarak, and heading down Edela's path towards her broken gate.

Jael didn't want to imagine what that meant about the people inside the cottage. She hauled out *Toothpick* and drew in a breath. 'Who are you?' she yelled. 'Who sent you?'

'Jael!' Biddy cried from the doorstep. 'He's got the book!'

Jael let out a sigh of relief, but she didn't turn to Biddy or Eydis, who she could hear sobbing.

'You're going to have to get past me,' Jael panted, well aware that compared to the hulking beast before her, she didn't appear very threatening. Blood was dripping from a bite on her leg, a bite on her wrist. She couldn't even catch her breath after running.

Ranuf's voice was calm in her ears, and she welcomed it for the first time in days. 'Use your head, Jael. He's big. You know how to play this game. Finish him quickly. Edela needs the book.'

Eydis reached for Biddy's hand. 'What's happening? Biddy? Tell me!'

Biddy's eyes were on the dark road, squinting. 'Jael is here, but she can't defeat that man. She's not herself. You go,' she whispered, bending down to Eydis. 'Go back inside and stay with Edela. Find poor Ido. I'm going for help.'

Eydis squeezed Biddy's shaking hand, then let go, hurrying inside.

***

Draguta felt Eadmund tense beside her.

'Well, now, isn't this interesting,' she mused. 'But we don't want Rollo to have all the fun, do we? Not when I have plans for you.'

Eadmund's body clenched. He'd fought Rollo, and he'd fought Jael, and surely Jael would know that she couldn't beat Rollo. Not the way she looked.

He'd never seen her like that. So pale. Teeth gritted. Panting.

Yet, Draguta needed that book, and he didn't know what to think.

Jael needed to step aside.

Eadmund wanted to call out to her. Let him go!

She just had to step aside and let Rollo go.

'I don't mind if you *hurt* her,' Draguta purred. 'She deserves that for how much trouble she's caused. But leave her alive, Rollo dear.' She smiled, listening to the growls of the barsk and the terror of the Andalans and the horrific wailing of Sigmund Skalleson, but there was one noise Draguta couldn't make out.

In all the carnage and chaos, there was one noise Draguta

couldn't make out at all.

***

Morana's feet wouldn't move. She was so stiff and weak that she couldn't lift them, so her boots scuffed along the dirt road after Else, almost dragging behind her like a thick rope.

It was the only sound they could hear as they hurried towards Fool's Cove.

Else had tucked Morana's hair into her cloak, hoping no one would recognise her, but once they were out of the kitchen, they hadn't seen a soul.

And now Dragmall was left to hope that they could find the ship.

When he'd listened to Meena's thoughts, she'd told him all about Fool's Cove and the ships moored there. Meena had shown him the way out, and Dragmall had organised their passage with a merchant, who had greedily taken his coins.

Meena had shown him the way out, knowing that she would have to stay behind to face Draguta's wrath alone.

Else was sniffling beside Dragmall, and he knew what that was about.

Morana couldn't care less about leaving Meena behind, she just wanted to get onto that ship. She could hear Dragmall going over the plan in his mind.

It was going to work if they could just get onto that ship.

***

Gant screamed, trying to shake off the teeth of the red-eyed dog that were clamped around his arm; razor-like fangs piercing his skin. More and more of them were jumping the wall. The catapults were shooting sea-fire, but too many barsk had already crossed the valley into the fort. He could hear the horses panicking too, and he worried about Gus.

Aleksander hacked an axe into the barsk's neck.

Once. Twice.

And on his third chop, the jaw released, and Gant shook his arm, clenching his teeth against the pain. His mind raced to Gisila, and spinning around, he saw Bram, struggling to help Thorgils fend off a snapping dog. 'Bram! Get to the hall! Make sure they're safe in there! Now!'

'Gant!' Bram pointed behind him as a barsk knocked Aleksander to the ground, paws on his chest, jaw open.

Thorgils brought his sword down across the dog's back, severing its spine. It howled in pain as it staggered, falling onto Aleksander, who quickly pushed it away. He struggled back to his feet, watching as Bram hurried towards the hall, swinging his axe as another black dog leapt out of the shadows.

***

The giant had a giant sword, which made sense, Jael supposed, and she could see very quickly that *Toothpick* wasn't going to help her.

'I don't want to hurt you,' Rollo tried, walking past the broken gate, out onto the deserted, dark road. He thought of Eadmund. He knew that this was Eadmund's wife. And though Eadmund didn't appear to care about her, she was still his wife, and Rollo had no issue with her. 'I'm going past you. With this book. Understand? You're not going to stop me taking it to

Draguta.'

Jael was getting fucking sick of Draguta.

Sheathing *Toothpick* and drawing her bloody knife, she ran at Rollo, sliding across the muddy road before she reached him, slicing her knife across his ankle. He barely stumbled before turning and running away, knowing that his crew would already be heading for the ship.

He wasn't going to waste his time fighting Jael Furyck.

Jael stared after him, surprised. Quickly on her feet.

Running after him.

***

Edela was bleeding as she bent over. She had drawn a symbol, hoping she'd remembered it correctly, though she hadn't been able to remember the chant. 'Eydis,' she breathed, trembling, trying to steady her nerves. The howling of the barsk was only getting louder. 'Eydis, is there any way you can find the words?'

Eydis was crawling on her knees, trying to find Ido, who was whimpering in the distance. She was too scared to think at all. 'I'll try,' she said, swallowing. 'I'll try.'

***

Rollo could hear Jael coming, and he grunted in annoyance, turning as Jael threw herself to the ground again, slashing her knife across the front of his knees, as deep as she could, feeling her blade strike bone. The giant wasn't going to be running anywhere if she could help it. Rolling away, she was pleased to hear the pain in his voice as he roared in anger.

Now he was mad.

Rollo came at her like a mountain, then, and Jael waited, counting until he was almost at her and his sword was high in the air, and her heart had stopped, and then she dropped, skidding across the ground again, backhanding the knife, dragging it across the back of his knees. Rolling, she was on her feet quickly, facing him.

'Fuck!' Rollo bellowed, stumbling as Jael drew in some air.

She needed to be fast.

Faster than a big, lumbering rock, who couldn't move as nimbly as she could; not with shredded knees, leaking all over the ground. Bending down, Jael yanked her other knife out of her sock and ran at him again, armed in both hands now, sliding across the mud, puncturing his ankles, just above the bones.

Knives in. Knives out.

Rollo had the book in one hand, his giant sword in the other and Jael needed to bring him down quickly before he grew bored with her game or she ran out of air or the barsk came to kill them both.

Edela needed that book.

She had to hurry.

***

The doors to the hall pushed open easily, and Bram ran inside with a frown, ready to tell someone off, but he saw the trail of blood and his heart hammered in his chest.

He could smell death.

There were bodies by the door. More bodies as he moved through the hall.

He couldn't hear Sigmund. He couldn't hear anyone at all. 'Runa! Runa!' And he ran to the grey curtain, slipping on blood. Runa's blood.

A torch flickered its flame across the corridor, and Bram could see Runa lying on the ground, her legs bent, her eyes open, her pale nightdress soaked red. 'No!' he screamed, dropping to his knees. 'No! Runa!' he cried, pulling her into his arms. '*No!*' Bram sat there, rocking her gently, ignoring the howling of the barsk and the terrified cries of the dying.

Her body was chilled. Still. He could feel it.

There was no life in it anymore.

Shock and pain flooded every part of him, then a movement caught his eye, and he turned his head towards the kitchen, seeing another body. Lying Runa back on the bloody ground, sobs heaving in his aching chest, Bram struggled back to his feet, hurrying towards the figure. 'Gisila!'

Her eyes were closed, blood leaking from her belly, he thought. He couldn't tell. There was too much of it. Her arms were cut. An axe lay by her side.

'Gisila?'

***

Biddy rushed into the square, screaming at the sight of the terrifying black dogs. They were enormous, vicious, their deep growls rumbling like thunder. One turned at the sound of her cry, lifting its head, fangs bared.

Red eyes locking on her.

Thorgils ran in front of Biddy. 'What are you doing?!' he yelled, a spear in his hand. 'What are you doing here?' Then he frowned. 'What *are* you doing here?'

'Jael,' Biddy panted. 'It's Jael!'

***

Jael was running out of steam, and Rollo was running out of patience.

His men would be waiting. He had to hurry.

But his legs were spilling so much blood that he was having trouble moving them. His knees wouldn't bend, and his ankles felt weak. He realised that if Draguta wanted him to leave with the book, he was going to have to do something to stop Jael Furyck. 'I know your husband!' he called, gnashing his teeth against the building waves of pain.

Jael stilled, hauling in another breath, feeling it burn her lungs, crouching.

'I know Eadmund! I've trained him! Drunk with him. Watched him with Draguta! He's hers now!' He wanted to unsettle her. Distract her. 'And Evaine! He loves her! Couldn't keep his hands off her!'

Jael saw a flash of Eadmund. She saw their daughter's face too. And she blinked it all away, Rollo's words drifting across her like a breeze.

She needed that book back.

Now.

Slipping one knife inside its scabbard, she grasped the other in her right hand and charged. A man like that could snap her in two, she knew.

But only if he could catch her.

Rollo watched her coming. He could hear Draguta, sharply reminding him that he couldn't kill her. But he had to hurt her. He needed to stop her.

Lifting his sword, Rollo kept his feet planted, knowing that he'd have to aim for an arm or a leg.

A stomach wound would likely be the end of her.

He aimed low, and Jael anticipated it, throwing herself up

over his sword and onto his chest, the knife haft in her mouth now, her hands around his thick, tattooed neck.

***

Thorgils had ordered Biddy into the hall, and run to find Jael.

As Biddy pushed open the doors, she clamped her hand over her mouth, knowing that something terrible had happened. She could smell it.

And suddenly, she could hear it.

'Who's there?' she called out nervously, hovering near the door, remembering the man who'd stolen the Book of Aurea.

'Biddy? Biddy? Help me! Quick!'

'Bram?' Biddy raced forward, her eyes widening as she passed the bodies on the ground. 'Bram!' And she ran to the curtain, where she saw Runa. 'Runa! No!' Heart thumping, she spun around, and there was Bram, kneeling by Gisila.

'We need to help her. She's still breathing!' Bram struggled to his feet, Gisila's blood-soaked body limp in his arms. 'I'll take her to a bed.' He walked as fast as he could towards the chambers, moving around Runa's dead body, trying not to look at her.

Biddy couldn't think. Her eyes were full of tears as she turned away from Runa, stumbling after Bram. Then she heard the low growling coming from the hall. 'Bram!'

Bram had heard it too. He hurried out of Gisila's chamber, looking for that axe. 'Go to Gisila! Barricade yourself in! Hurry! Put the chair behind the door!' And picking up the bloody axe, Bram stepped back through the curtain.

***

Jael fought to hold on as Rollo swung her. His hands were full, and though he wanted to toss the book and free one of them, he knew that he couldn't.

Jael wasn't going to wait for him to figure out what to do with her, though. She had to get the book to Edela. So clambering up his chest, she freed a hand, pulling the knife out of her mouth, slamming it into the top of his shining head. Releasing her hold on him, she dropped to the ground, stumbling backwards.

Rollo screamed, crying out, his sword falling out of his hand as he hurried to pull out the knife, his face running red with blood.

***

'No, no, no!' Draguta bellowed, her body as rigid as stone.

Meena felt the grip of Draguta's hand crushing hers.

Eadmund was lost in a wash of noise and confusion.

Watching Rollo. Watching Jael.

Feeling Draguta's anger explode all over him like burning sea-fire.

***

'Jael!'

Thorgils was running down the road towards her, two snarling barsk chasing after him.

Jael quickly unsheathed *Toothpick*, turning from one

problem to the next. Rollo had the knife out of his skull, and he tried to lunge for her, but his legs staggered, going in different directions, wobbling at his sliced knees.

He felt the blood gushing down his back; the searing pain in his head.

Draguta screeching in his ears.

Everything started going dark, and all he could see were two pairs of red eyes. Stumbling, he crashed onto his knees.

'Get his sword!' Jael yelled, brandishing *Toothpick* as Thorgils ran behind her. 'Give it to me!'

Thorgils was ready to protest, but he didn't. It was a heavy sword, and he doubted Jael could do much with it, but he didn't say a word as he handed it to her.

Gripping both swords and feeling herself tip slightly to one side, Jael held them out as the barsk charged. 'Get the book and take it inside to Edela! Quick! We need her to stop this!'

Rollo fell onto his face, the book dropping out of his hand.

Thorgils ran to scoop it up, shutting all thoughts of the red-eyed dogs out of his mind as he ran up Edela's path, into the cottage.

***

There had been two barsk waiting in the hall for Bram.

One went down quickly, his hind legs almost severed by the axe's sharp blade. The other was bigger, angrier. It ran towards Bram, its jaw snapping, spittle flying. The hulking black dog had the taste of blood, and it wanted more. Bram kept the axe close, trying to think. His chest was burning, full of fire.

He couldn't stop seeing Runa's face.

Swinging as the barsk charged, Bram felt the axe's blade nick the dog's skin as it skidded past him, spinning quickly, its growling a threatening rumble now.

Angry. Pawing the floor.

'Bram! Move!'

Bram looked up to see Fyn standing in the doorway.

So did the barsk. It spun, low on its haunches, red eyes trained on Fyn, ready to pounce.

Fyn drew back his arm, trying to keep himself steady as he threw the spear.

The running barsk yelped, collapsing in a heap, the spear straight through one of its red eyes.

Fyn was too shocked to move. He glanced around the hall at the bodies and the blood, then hurried to Bram, seeing the pain on his face as he stumbled, leaning on the axe. 'Are you alright?'

Bram opened his mouth, looking into his son's eyes.

And slowly shook his head.

***

Axl clenched his teeth as he swung his sword, slicing back and forth, trying to fend off the snapping black dogs, feeling his leg weaken, trying not to think about the wolves that had nearly killed him.

The barsk were bigger than any wolves.

And they could almost fly, it seemed, as more and more were scaling the western wall, throwing themselves over the stakes and the ditch and into the fort. Axl heard a shout as Karsten went down, a barsk's fangs piercing his ankle, another jumping on his back, knocking him to the ground.

'Karsten!' And charging towards the man who had tormented him in Hest, Axl hacked into one barsk's neck before turning to face the next one, who released Karsten's ankle and jumped up at him.

Gant threw his knife at the giant dog, but his hand was slippery with blood, and it barely grazed its black fur as it clattered to the ground. 'Shit.' He drew out his sword and ran for it, but Karsten got there first. Limping, he chopped his axe down, straight through the dog's middle, cutting it in two.

Aleksander ran towards them, blood pouring down his arm. He'd been up on the ramparts, checking the valley. 'More are coming!' he cried. 'Where's Jael?'

All three men shrugged.

Aleksander didn't want to panic, but he never felt right when Jael wasn't beside him.

'Watch out!' Axl yelled as two more barsk sailed over the wall.

***

Thorgils was running back down the path from Edela's cottage to Jael, who looked ready to fall down and just as he thought it, she did.

'Jael!' he cried, skittering down the slippery path, trying not to fall over himself.

The two barsk charged for Jael, who straightened out her legs, listening to the thudding paws, wishing her arms felt stronger as she brought both swords up at once, skewering the jumping red-eyed dogs straight through their bellies. 'Aarrghh!' she screamed, feeling the weight of them as she quickly released her hold on the swords, letting them drop to the ground.

The yelping barsk tried to move, but they were impaled on her swords, and it was Jael who quickly wriggled away from them.

'Not sure you really needed my help,' Thorgils panted,

looking at Rollo's bloody corpse and the two skewered barsk.

'Has Edela got the book?'

Thorgils nodded.

Jael drew *Toothpick* out of one dead dog, bending over, trying to breathe. 'Good... stay with them... guard them. I have to go and see what's happening!'

And she ran into the dark night.

Thorgils watched her go, kicked both black dogs to make sure they were dead, then headed back up the path to the cottage.

***

'I have to go,' Fyn insisted as Bram sat him down. He panicked, suddenly thinking about his mother. 'Can't you hear it? I have to go!' He swallowed, not liking the look in Bram's eyes or the blood all over his chest.

Fyn's eyes were drawn away to the bodies lying motionless around the hall.

He stood. 'I have to go!'

Bram grabbed him. 'It's your mother.' Tears were quickly in his eyes, but he was struggling to get out any words. 'She's... dead.'

Fyn jerked away from him. 'No!' Limping towards the doors, he shook his head. His eyes were up, not wanting to recognise a body. 'No!'

Bram was after him, but Fyn already had one hand on the door, pulling it open.

'Fyn!'

His son disappeared, and though Bram knew that he needed to get back to Biddy and Gisila, he couldn't let him go. 'Fyn!' And he pulled open the door, ready to run after him, but

Fyn was still standing on the steps, not moving. He turned back to Bram, tears in his eyes. 'No!' he sobbed, falling into Bram's arms. 'Please! *No!*'

CHAPTER FORTY EIGHT

With the Book of Aurea back in her hands, Edela quickly found her way to the spell, but she could barely see through her tears. She needed to though. She needed to get rid of the barsk quickly.

'Edela?' Eydis could feel her pain, and it worried her.

'I've found the words, Eydis,' Edela said quietly, trying to still her body; wanting to leave the cottage but knowing she couldn't yet.

'Edela?' Thorgils was just as worried as he bent down, a hand on her shoulder.

Edela looked up at him. 'Find Derwa, please. You know where she lives?'

Thorgils nodded.

'Take her to the hall! Hurry, please! We will come as soon as we're finished here.' And taking a deep breath, Edela placed her hand over the symbol and started chanting.

***

Draguta stood.

Vibrating with anger.

She glared at Eadmund, who couldn't focus on her at all. He

was struggling to pull himself out of his own trance, confused as to where he was. He wasn't sure what he had seen. What was real and what he'd hallucinated.

Surely most of it?

'Your wife will die!' Draguta spat. 'Know that. And *you* will kill her!' She turned to glare at Brill, who sat by Morac in a haze of smoke; both of them clueless as to what had just happened. Whatever it was hadn't gone well, and Brill shivered as she struggled to her feet, hurrying after Draguta.

***

The barsk collapsed to the ground like a dark wave as Jael ran back to the western wall. One by one, their bodies dropped, jaws releasing, red eyes fading.

Everything was suddenly quiet.

Jael felt relief loosen her aching body, but as she scanned the scattered piles of gouged bodies and screaming men and women, her shoulders tightened right back up. She saw Gant, Axl, Aleksander. All still standing. Beorn, Karsten, Berard. Ivaar, Torstan. Aedan and Rork.

No Fyn.

'Where's Fyn?' Jael yelled. 'Fyn!'

'He went to the hall,' Axl said, gripping his sister's arm as he stumbled. 'I saw him go to the hall.'

Jael was suddenly cold all over. She stared into Axl's eyes, then turned slowly towards the hall, watching Fyr, who sat on the steps staring at her.

The raven cawed loudly, flying away.

And Jael ran.

Axl had seen the look in his sister's eyes before she turned, and he hobbled after her, Gant and Aleksander behind him.

Jael threw open the doors, running past the bodies, her eyes on the grey curtain. 'Mother!' she called. 'Mother!'

There was blood everywhere.

'*Mother!*'

Axl was behind her. 'Amma?'

Jael saw Fyn and Bram embracing; blood all over the ground.

And then Runa's body, lying on the floor. 'Runa!' Her heart broke, but she couldn't think about that yet. 'Mother!' And Jael threw open Gisila's chamber door.

Gant could hear Jael, and he wanted to stop and not see. Every part of him froze apart from his legs, which kept moving him forward. Images of kissing Gisila rushed to the front of his mind as he ran.

Biddy turned as they all raced in. 'She's alive,' she assured them quickly, holding up her hands, covered in blood. 'I need Derwa, though. Entorp too. More light. I have to stop the bleeding.'

Aleksander nodded. 'I'll get them!'

Axl's mouth was open, and he couldn't think. His mother's eyes were closed. There was blood all over her. He couldn't think.

And where was Amma?

Jael was at Gisila's bedside, holding her hand. 'Mother?'

She heard Axl calling Amma's name, and she frowned, looking up at Gant. 'Sit with her.' And Jael ran after Axl, to where Fyn and Bram had gathered by Runa's body.

Fyn was sobbing, dropping to his knees. 'Mother!'

'Amma!' Axl was panicking. 'Amma!' Panicking and running into the kitchen, then back out into the hall.

Jael checked in Sigmund's chamber. There was no Amma. No baby in the basket. She ran into the corridor, her eyes full of sympathy for Fyn and Bram, spinning around, looking for Axl.

'Where's Amma?' her brother screamed, his eyes full of terror, his chest thumping.

'Sigmund's gone,' Jael said, pushing through the curtain as the pieces of the puzzle came tumbling together. 'That man! He had more men! His crew! They took them!' And she ran through the hall.

'Who?'

'The man who tried to take the book. He broke into Edela's cottage. I killed him. He had a crew with him. That giant! He said he knew Draguta! We have to get to the cove!'

Axl was quickly at the doors, running out into the night after Jael.

***

They were away, to who knew where.

Dragmall hadn't asked a lot of questions when he'd found the helmsman in the tavern that afternoon. The man had let it be known that he was leaving, happy to take on a few passengers for a fist-full of silver coins.

Dragmall wasn't sure it was the best way to spend his savings, but he knew that it was the path he'd decided to walk down, and he wasn't the sort of man to change his mind. And now that he'd decided to help Morana stop Draguta, he needed to make sure they could disappear.

And quickly.

Morana was shivering as she sat next to Else, her mind skipping from one thought to another, trying to find an answer to what she knew was the grave danger they now faced. As soon as Draguta discovered they had gone, she would do anything to stop them.

But now that she was out of her prison, Morana felt confident that she could do something to stop her. She glared at Else, who was sniffing next to her, still moping about leaving

Meena behind in Draguta's clutches.

Meena, who would be blamed for everything.

Morana smiled, feeling no gratitude towards her niece. And closing her eyes, she tried to find a symbol to protect them.

***

Thorgils helped Derwa into the hall, his heart sinking with every step. He saw the dead black dogs, the bodies of some men and women he vaguely recognised. He could smell death, and as he approached the curtain, he could hear sobbing.

Derwa gripped his arm, sensing his reluctance to go any further. 'We can't help anyone from out here,' she said quietly, feeling a sense of trepidation grip her own body.

Thorgils nodded and pulled back the curtain, ushering Derwa ahead of him.

He needed to find Isaura. He needed to know that she was safe.

The doors were open as he passed the chambers, and Derwa left him, moving down the corridor to where she could hear Biddy. Thorgils turned slowly to his right, blood slick under his boots. He saw Fyn and Bram leaning over a body.

Bram looked up, sensing that someone was there.

Fyn turned, sobbing uncontrollably, and Thorgils stepped forward, taking him into his arms. He saw Bram over Fyn's shoulder, holding Runa's hand.

And he saw Runa.

'Ssshhh,' Thorgils murmured, closing his eyes, Fyn's tears dripping onto his shoulder. 'Ssshhh.'

***

Jael and Axl ran out through the open harbour gates, Aleksander just behind them. The guards were dead, throats slit, and Jael could feel her throat tightening. She yelled at men to join them. Islanders followed her. Ivaar and Beorn. Rork too.

The moon was out now, watching them, guiding them.

Jael hoped the men would be in the cove. They were traders, Bram had said.

They must have come in a ship.

Despite the determination of the moon, it grew dark as they ran through the trees, and Jael stumbled into a hole, righting herself quickly, Axl passing her, ignoring his bleeding leg.

They had to get back to the hall, to Gisila.

But he had to save Amma. He had to save Amma!

They came to the cove, out of breath. The long stretch of sand was lined with beached ships; more ships anchored in the calm water.

'Amma!' Axl screamed, running down to the shore, wading into the water. 'Amma!'

There was no movement amongst the ships, nothing out at sea. The moon looked down on the water, shimmering a path, but there were no ships out there.

Axl ran back to Beorn, who had staggered to a stop beside Jael, hands on his thighs, blood dripping from his gouged forearms. 'We have to launch a ship! Now!'

Jael held out a hand. 'No!'

'We have to go after them!'

'They've gone! They're not here, Axl. They've gone!'

Beorn nodded. 'If we took to sea, where would we go?'

'Hest!' Axl yelled, looking at Aleksander, who shook his head.

'We don't know they went there,' Aleksander tried, though

he doubted that was true.

'Draguta would kill us at sea,' Jael warned. 'And you'd never get Amma back then. Stop and think, Axl!'

'How can I *think*?' Axl roared, running back into the water. 'Amma! Amma!'

Aleksander gripped Jael's arm. 'Go back to the hall. Be with Gisila. I'll bring him.'

Jael tried to catch her breath.

More than anything, she hoped they were taking Amma to Hest. She hoped they were taking Sigmund to his father. That Draguta hadn't taken them for some other reason.

Her thoughts raced quickly back to Gisila. To Runa and Fyn and Bram.

And with one last look at her distraught brother, she turned back to the path.

***

Gant held Gisila's hand as Derwa looked her over, turning at the gasp in the doorway.

'Gisila!' Edela sobbed, hurrying to her daughter, all thoughts of trying to remain calm swept away in a flood of tears as Gant stood to let her through.

Biddy put her arm around Eydis' shoulder, quietly explaining what was happening, though she wasn't really sure what was happening herself.

Eydis felt strange, feeling pulled in many different directions. 'I need to see Fyn,' she whispered. 'He's crying. I can hear him. Please, Biddy, take me to him.'

Biddy nodded, watching Gant embrace Edela, who leaned into his chest, sobbing as Derwa worked on Gisila. She had sent Branwyn for thread and a needle.

They needed to sew her up fast.

***

Jael didn't speak as she hurried back to the hall, past the bodies of the barsk, who no longer had red eyes. They were black now; dull like their coats. Reaching the hall steps, she turned. 'Ivaar, see to the Islanders. Rork, take your men. Go through the houses, look for wounded. Beorn, check the stables. See that the horses are safe...' Jael couldn't think as she saw her cousin limping towards them. 'Aedan, we need to burn the dogs quickly.' She thought of her own dogs, hoping they were alright. 'Out in the valley. Organise crews. The sooner we burn them, the sooner they're not a threat.'

They all nodded, but Jael didn't notice as she headed up the steps, hoping she wasn't too late.

Hoping her mother was still alive.

***

Edela and Branwyn were sitting on one side of Gisila while Biddy assisted Derwa, who was bent over, sewing up Gisila's stomach wound.

No one spoke when Jael arrived, but Edela turned to her, holding out a shaking hand, and Jael came to her grandmother, kneeling down beside her.

'Where's Axl?' Edela wondered.

'Aleksander's bringing him. Amma and Sigmund are gone. Axl wants to go after them. Aleksander's trying to calm him down.'

'Draguta won't hurt Amma,' Edela murmured distractedly. 'She won't hurt her.'

Jael stared at her grandmother, wondering why she was so certain.

Edela didn't notice. She was attempting to gather herself into something resembling a dreamer. Closing her eyes, she gripped Jael's hand, trying to release her fears for her daughter. They were unhelpful and wouldn't serve anyone. Instead, she tried to hear the calm voice of Lydea, imagining her dreams flowing towards her like clouds. Trying to see a vision of Gisila where she was healed and happy again. Breathing in and out, shoulders rising and falling, Edela found herself drifting away.

Sensing that her grandmother had disappeared, Jael stood. 'I'll be back soon. I need to see Fyn.'

***

They'd walked back to the castle in silence: Meena, Eadmund, and Morac.

Meena didn't want to go inside, but Jaeger would be waiting for her, she knew, eager to hear what had happened. She trudged up the steps, leaving Morac to walk Eadmund back to his house.

Eadmund didn't speak. He felt as though he was still at the stones, trapped in the smoke, seeing Andala. Watching Jael kill Rollo.

He'd seen Thorgils, too, trying to help Jael.

He felt displaced, drifting, his thoughts swirling around him like a blizzard, and in the centre of it all stood Draguta, her pale face glistening, her blue eyes as frozen as Oss' harbour in winter.

Morac was talking to him, and Eadmund didn't want to answer, so he nodded, realising that he was at his door, and Morac had a hand in the air, walking away with a promise to return tomorrow.

Pushing open the door, he walked inside the house, his mind drifting back to Jael. He didn't want to sleep next to Evaine; didn't want her touching him.

It was so still. So quiet.

So dark, Eadmund realised as he held out his hands, feeling his way to the bedchamber, knowing there were stools and small tables somewhere in the main room that he didn't want to trip over.

A lamp was burning next to the bed, and his eyes adjusted to the light, his head still swimming as he stood there, watching Evaine sleep. Naked. Her long, blonde hair wrapped around her.

And Eadmund's body pulsed with anger, knowing that she had trapped him.

Put a spell on him.

He wanted to kill her.

***

Jael touched the blanket in Sigmund's basket and saw a flash. She heard Runa's cry, and she turned to Fyn, who stood by his mother's bed, staring at her still body, willing her to be alive again.

But she wasn't.

'Runa tried to save Sigmund,' Jael said softly. 'That's how she died. She wouldn't let them take him. She held him in her arms, and she stared those men down.' Jael could see it so clearly; she could feel Runa's terror. 'She was so brave.' Her voice broke, seeing the moment Runa was stabbed.

Fyn turned to Jael, rubbing his eyes. 'Who were they? Who did this?'

'I don't know, but Draguta sent them. They tried to take the Book of Aurea for her. They took Amma too.'

'Amma?' Eydis panicked. 'Where? Where have they taken her?'

'I'm not sure,' Jael said carefully. 'Hest?' She looked at Thorgils, whose eyes kept returning to the open door. 'Why don't you go and check on Isaura?' she suggested.

Thorgils nodded, feeling guilty for wanting to leave. He would return, but he needed to know that Isaura and the children were safe.

'I'll go with you,' Bram mumbled. 'I need to take a breath of air. Fyn?'

Fyn shook his head, his eyes on Runa.

'I'll stay with him,' Eydis promised. 'I won't leave.'

Jael's heart broke for Fyn, sitting with his dead mother, and squeezing his hand, she turned to follow Thorgils and Bram out of the chamber, needing to find out how her own mother was.

***

Entorp arrived with his salves, earning a grateful smile from Derwa, who quickly put him to work. She wiped her hands on her apron and shuffled over to Edela, Biddy, Jael and Gant.

Axl and Aleksander came through the door as she started speaking.

'Gisila is lucky. The wound in her stomach is deep, but it's missed anything important. So now we will wait and let Entorp's salves work their magic.' No one looked encouraged by that, though. 'Gisila has youth on her side,' Derwa tried. 'She will fight. It's in her blood after all.' And she smiled at Edela, who looked on the brink of tears again.

Axl hurried past them all to the bed. 'Mother!' he cried, utterly bereft, on his knees, holding her hand.

Jael turned to Gant, who appeared in shock. His eyes wouldn't focus on her at all, so she grabbed his arm. 'We need to secure the fort.'

He nodded, swallowing. 'I'll see to it. You and Axl take as long as you need here.' And with one last look at Gisila, lying in the bed they'd just been in together, he dropped his head, disappearing through the door.

'Jael,' Biddy said quietly, pulling her away. 'I need to go back to the cottage. I have to see the puppies.'

Jael froze. 'Why? What happened?'

'That big man,' Biddy said. She'd felt frantic ever since she'd arrived in the hall, desperate to go back and see what had happened to poor Ido. 'He kicked Ido. I don't know if he's alright. I didn't go back. I... I need to go.'

Jael shook her head, her heart skipping in fear. 'I'll go. Stay with everyone. Check on Eydis and Fyn. Organise the hall. The bodies...' She looked at Aleksander. 'We need to treat the injured.' Her own arm was still running with blood, but the shock of everything was keeping the pain at bay. 'Astrid and Ayla will help. Perhaps you could organise them?'

Biddy nodded as Jael glanced at her mother before hurrying out of the chamber.

***

Meena crawled into bed, lying on the very edge of the mattress, not wanting to wake Jaeger by reaching for a fur.

She tried not to think, which was hard as the smoke had

a way of teasing out even her most deeply hidden thoughts. All those things she was trying so hard not to think about kept floating into her mind.

Draguta would come for her, she knew.

If Dragmall had saved Morana, Draguta would come for her.

Meena closed her eyes, listening to Jaeger breathing beside her, wishing she still had the knife. But her scabbard was empty, and there was nothing to save her now. Not even Jaeger, who was bound to Draguta.

He would stand aside, she knew. Let Draguta claim her revenge.

Meena's mind wandered to Berard, and she realised that she would never see him again. She couldn't help but wonder how different everything might have been if she'd left with him and his family that night.

For some reason, she'd believed that staying behind was important.

That she would be able to help.

Closing her eyes, Meena lifted her hands to her head, curling herself into a ball.

Whatever Draguta was about to do to her, Meena hoped she would make it quick.

***

Karsten was banging on the door, impatient to get into the cottage, but it was taking Berard and Ulf some time to pull all the furniture away. Bayla had two sobbing grandchildren on her knees, unable to help.

Eventually, Ulf pushed away the last bed and opened the door.

Karsten rushed in, dripping with sweat and blood, scanning the terrified faces of his family as they blinked at him. 'Everyone alright?' he panted as Nicolene burst into tears, hurrying towards him.

Berard nodded as Karsten turned to his wife, pulling her into his arms, squeezing her tightly as his sons chased after their mother, wrapping themselves around their father's legs.

'You're alright,' Nicolene breathed into his neck. 'You're alright!'

Bayla's shoulders dropped in relief as she wrapped her arms around Halla and Valder, pulling them close. 'It will take a lot more than a curse and an evil book to stop the Dragos family, won't it, now?' she said, lifting her head, tears in her eyes as she looked around their revolting little cottage, not caring how dark and miserable it was for just a moment.

***

Jael tried to push everyone out of her mind as she ran to Edela's cottage.

Runa and Fyn, her mother and Amma. Sigmund.

She tried not to think about any of them.

The moon's light was generous as she approached Edela's path, and Jael could clearly see the mountainous corpse of the man who'd tried and failed to steal the book lying amongst the dead barsk. Turning away from him and not caring about them, she ran up the path, pausing at the broken door.

Taking a deep breath, Jael stepped inside.

Vella rushed towards her, whining, paws up on Jael's leg.

There was no Ido.

'Ido!' The fire was almost out, and it was dark in the cottage. Jael couldn't see him anywhere. 'Ido!'

And then she heard a faint whimper as Vella raced back to her brother, licking his face.

Jael made her way to the corner of the cottage, past Edela's bed, dropping to her knees where her little black dog lay on his side. 'Ido,' she breathed, running a hand down his back. 'It's alright.' And realising that he couldn't stand on his own, she scooped him up, feeling him tremble against her as he tried to lick her face. She sat back against the bed, holding him gently, trying to catch her breath. 'It's alright now. You're safe. You're safe with me.'

CHAPTER FORTY NINE

Dawn came like a bandage torn off a wound, and they could all see the devastation the barsk had wrought.

'We have to finish the wall,' Karsten sighed, turning to Aleksander, who stood beside him, rubbing swollen eyes. 'We can't leave for Hest if it's not finished. Who knows what else will get in? I'm not leaving my family until it's finished.'

Aleksander nodded, wanting to get back to the hall to see how Gisila was, but the scene around them was grisly. He couldn't leave. Not yet. The barsk had ripped their men to pieces, and the square was filled with the plaintive sounds of those in pain; dying sounds too. He could hear people calling out for loved ones, hysterical, needing help as Astrid, Derwa, and Biddy hurried around, bending over, seeing who could be carried into the hall, and who wouldn't make it inside. Entorp was there too, with Marcus, tending to the injured, comforting the bereaved.

The fort smelled of death and smoke as the corpses of the barsk were loaded onto carts and taken out into the valley, where they would be piled into the enormous pit Rork and his Alekkans had already started digging.

'Can you find Ulf?' Aleksander asked, noticing Bram sitting at a table outside the hall with Ayla. 'Get him to supervise the stonemasons. We need more fortifications around the ditch, too, though I'm not sure anything could've stopped those dogs. I've never seen anything jump like that.'

Karsten shook his head, certain he was right.

Aleksander clapped him on the shoulder and headed for the hall, realising that he needed to see how Axl was. Between worrying about Gisila and being terrified for Amma, Axl was all over the place. But, at least, for the moment, he'd stopped talking about taking a ship to Hest.

Nodding to Ayla and Bram, Aleksander walked up the steps, into the hall.

Bram hadn't said anything for some time, and Ayla was beginning to wonder if she should go.

'I thought I had time,' Bram mumbled suddenly, dropping his head to his hands. 'I thought there'd be time.' And he lifted his eyes, staring at Ayla. 'I... I wanted to.' He stopped, his shoulders sagging. 'I wanted to. I just...' And the tears rolled down his cheeks.

Ayla put her arm around Bram's shoulder and brought him towards her, feeling his body shudder against hers. 'I'm sorry, Bram,' she whispered. 'I'm so sorry.'

***

Edela felt odd. Lost.

Gisila hadn't woken up. She lay perfectly still. Breathing.

That was something.

Everyone was busy. She could hear the noises from the hall, and though Edela knew that she should be out there, trying to help, she was struggling to tear herself away from her daughter.

She didn't know what was going to happen.

Edela blinked.

She didn't know what was going to happen!

Everyone she loved was in danger, and she didn't know

how to help them. She couldn't keep them safe. Couldn't warn them. Couldn't help them.

What use was she?

Her granddaughter had lost her baby and nearly her life. She'd lost her grandson and her son-in-law. And now her daughter lay before her, unconscious. Maybe dying.

Jael placed her hands on Edela's shoulders. 'You need to come with me.'

Edela spun around. 'What do you mean?' She blinked, confused as Jael pulled her to her feet.

'I can hear you, Grandmother,' Jael said. 'I can hear your thoughts, and you need to come outside. They need your help. Ayla and Astrid. Derwa and Biddy. You can't sit in here blaming yourself.' Her eyes flickered to Gisila, and she swallowed. 'You saved as many people as you could. Don't forget that. You can't falter now. Can't give up when we're nowhere near ending this. I need you.' She gripped Edela's hands. 'I'm going to Hest, and I need you.'

Edela stared into Jael's eyes, feeling tears fill her own. 'I...' She shook her head. 'I didn't see what would happen to your baby. I didn't see what would happen to Gisila or poor Runa. How can I help you anymore?'

Jael smiled, feeling her own tears coming. 'You're a dreamer. You told me that over and over again. You're a dreamer, you said. And it took me a long time to believe it. But I do. Because of you, so you can't give up now. The gods are with us. The Iskavallans are with us. The Islanders. The Alekkans. All of us. We won't let this stand. What she's done. What they want to do. Draguta. Briggit. We won't let this stand. We will fight. All of us. Dreamers and warriors. Me and you.'

Edela felt the strength in Jael's hands as they squeezed hers, and she found herself nodding, trying to block out the taunting voices in her head that told her she wasn't even a dreamer anymore. 'We will fight,' she whispered, staring into Jael's eyes. 'Me and you.'

***

Eadmund stood with his back to Morac and Evaine, pouring wine into ornate silver goblets. It annoyed him that Evaine had bought the ridiculous goblets to replace the cups, which had been perfectly usable.

He didn't like the wine either. It had been an odd day of barely being awake, and he felt like ale, not wine.

Wine reminded him of his father.

They were talking behind him, Eadmund knew, but he wasn't listening. He was thinking of Jael. Of his son. Of Draguta.

Of his mother and Melaena.

'Isn't that right, Eadmund?' Morac wondered.

Eadmund turned around. 'What?'

Evaine was surprised by the coldness in his eyes. It was as though he was looking at strangers.

She shivered.

Morac didn't notice; he was too busy smiling at Elfwyn as she placed a bowl of cherries on the table. 'Evaine was just telling me that you are leaving tomorrow. For Helsabor?'

Eadmund nodded, coming back to the table, handing Evaine and Morac their goblets of wine.

'And by the time you return, your son will be here,' Morac said, looking at his daughter, who didn't register much interest in that news.

Eadmund carried his own goblet to the table, sitting down opposite Morac. He took a sip of wine, lifting the goblet in the air. 'To defeating our enemies,' he said, tasting the sour tang of the wine.

Morac smiled and touched his goblet to Eadmund's. 'To defeating our enemies.' And he sat back, relaxed, drinking his wine.

Eadmund watched him, remembering his dreams.

He could almost feel his mother's hand on his shoulder, imagining that she was there, watching too.

'Though not everyone knows who their enemies are, do they, Morac?' Eadmund murmured. 'Sometimes, we mistake them for friends.' His lips barely moved. His eyes remained fixed on Morac. 'Sometimes, our greatest enemies are hiding right in front of us.'

Morac shuddered. It felt as though Eadmund was peering inside his soul.

Then he shuddered again, feeling hot all over. Swallowing, he felt an urgent need to go outside. To jump into the sea.

Water! He needed water!

Then a pain in his chest, and he dropped the goblet onto the table, wine spilling everywhere.

'Father!' Evaine was on her feet, rushing to him as Morac clutched his chest. 'Eadmund! Help him!'

But Eadmund didn't move.

Eadmund didn't blink.

He wanted to watch every moment of it.

Morac was gagging now, trying to breathe, unable to take any air into his lungs, his eyes bulging in terror. He tried to stand, but his legs had no strength in them, and he collapsed to the floor, rasping, the pain in his chest overwhelming him. He reached a hand towards Evaine, panicking as everything went dark. 'Help...' he gasped.

'*Eadmund*!' Evaine shrieked as Morac's head fell back on the floor, his eyes fixed open, wine dripping from the table onto his legs.

Eadmund stood and walked over to Morac, making sure that he was dead.

And then he walked towards the door.

Evaine was sobbing, hysterical, but she struggled to her feet, stumbling after him, grabbing his sleeve. 'Where are you going? Eadmund? Where are you going?'

'I'm leaving, Evaine, before I kill you too. For what you did to me. To Edela. Taking me away from Jael. Destroying my life.' He shook her away, grasping the door handle. 'Our son is the only reason you're not on the floor with your father.'

And pulling open the door, he strode out of the house.

Evaine screamed, running out onto the porch after him. 'Eadmund! No! No! Come back! Eadmund! *Please!*'

***

'How's Ido?' Aleksander asked as Jael joined him at the table. It had been a long day, and those who could had found a bench in the hall, resting their aching bodies, taking a moment to drink and eat, wanting to feel something that wasn't fear and grief.

Jael poured him a cup of ale, and one for herself, wanting to take the taste of blood out of her mouth. 'His leg is broken. A few ribs too. And he's lost a tooth, but other than that, he seems alright. Biddy is fussing over him. She had Derwa set his leg.'

'And you?'

'I'm ready for things to be different,' Jael said, staring at him over the table. Every part of her vibrated with anger and pain, and exhaustion most of all. 'I'm ready for Draguta to die.'

Thorgils joined them, grabbing the jug of ale, his shoulder leaking blood all over his tunic again. 'So when do we leave?' Isaura was with Fyn and Eydis, helping prepare Runa for her pyre. He'd come to the hall looking for Bram, but he hadn't seen him anywhere.

Ivaar and Karsten sat down beside him.

Axl came limping over with Rork and Ivaar, bringing another jug of ale and more cups.

Jael squeezed over, moving closer to Thorgils, glancing around at the bloody and bruised faces, certain she looked no better; worried she wouldn't be able to keep her eyes open for much longer. But she thought of her daughter and her husband, and she straightened her spine. 'When that wall is finished, we go,' Jael said, looking at each of them. 'It's time. Time to finish this.'

THE END

EPILOGUE

Briggit Halvardar pushed one woman away and turned to the other. She'd never been able to decide who she liked better. Who pleased her more. So they were both in her bed, by her side, day and night.

She licked her finger, watching the woman's eyes narrow.

'That bitch Draguta thinks she can come here and take what's ours,' Briggit murmured. 'But she doesn't realise that we've been ready for this moment. Waiting for it. Preparing for it.' She exhaled slowly, feeling an overwhelming sense of calm still every part of her. 'When we are done here, my love, you will go. Find Teran. Tell him it is time. Our enemies are on the march. We are finally ready to begin.' And bending forward, she pushed her finger into the woman's mouth, biting her lip. 'It's time to return Raemus to his rightful place. Here. By my side.' And sighing with pleasure, she kissed the woman deeply, her golden eyes flickering to the giant shield hanging on the wall above the long stone hearth.

READ NEXT

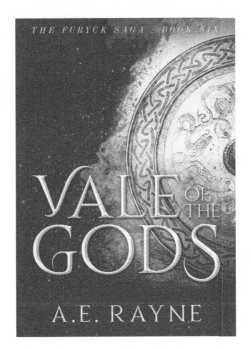

VALE OF THE GODS

ABOUT A.E. RAYNE

I live in Auckland, New Zealand, with my husband, three kids and three dogs. When I'm not writing, you can find me editing, designing my book covers, and trying to fit in some sleep (though mostly I'm dreaming of what's coming next!).

I have a deep love of history and all things Viking. Growing up with a Swedish grandmother, her heritage had a great influence on me, so my fantasy tales lean heavily on Viking lore and culture. And also winter. I love the cold!

I like to immerse myself in my stories, experiencing everything through my characters. I don't write with a plan; I take cues from my characters, and follow where they naturally decide to go. I like different points of view because I see the story visually, with many dimensions, like a tv show or a movie. My job is to stand at the loom and weave the many coloured threads together into an exciting story.

I promise you characters that will quickly feel like friends, and villains that will make you wild, with plots that twist and turn to leave you wondering what's coming around the corner. And, like me, hopefully, you'll always end up a little surprised by how I weave everything together in the end!

To find out more about A.E. Rayne and her writing visit her website: www.aerayne.com

Sign-up & get notified: www.aerayne.com/sign-up

Made in the USA
Monee, IL
06 March 2022

92385183R10402